A PROLOGUE TO LOVE

TAYLOR CALDWELL

A Prologue to Love

Doubleday & Company, Inc.

Garden City, New York

It is not possible for us to know each other except as we manifest ourselves in distorted shadows to the eyes of others. We do not even know ourselves; therefore, why should we judge a neighbor? Who knows what pain is behind virtue and what fear behind vice? No one, in short, knows what makes a man, and only God knows his thoughts, his joys, his bitternesses, his agony, the injustices committed against him and the injustices he commits. . . . God is too inscrutable for our little understanding. After sad meditation it comes to me that all that lives, whether good or in error, mournful or joyous, obscure or of gilded reputation, painful or happy, is only a prologue to love beyond the grave, where all is understood and almost all forgiven.

SENECA

PART ONE

Remember now thy Creator
in the days of thy youth . . .
ECCLESIASTES

CHAPTER ONE

The child sat on a large black boulder and looked at the sea, and she was all alone under a sky the color of smoke and beside waters as angry as an intemperate man and grayer than death.

Gulls cried piercingly as they swirled in the harsh wind and dived to the leaden crests of the waves and threw themselves upward again as if despairing. Though it was only four o'clock in the afternoon of a late September day, the bitter air threatened winter, and there was no sun, only a pale silver blur in the gaseous heavens. There was no sound but the furious thunder of the ocean hurling itself on the dark and gleaming sand, the gulls, and the wind which assaulted the tall and dying clumps of sea grass on the dunes behind the child. Water and sky appeared to mingle together without a horizon; the gusts of wind lifted the child's braids and blew wisps over her poor coat. But the child did not move; she huddled on her stone. It was as if she were waiting mournfully yet eagerly, as a woman waits for the return of her lover who has been long gone from her sight. She was unaware of her cold hands, which were reddened and without gloves, and of her cold feet in shabby buttoned boots, and her icy knees covered meagerly with darned black stockings. Occasionally she absently pulled the shawl about her neck and huddled deeper in her coat, which was too small for her. Nothing lived in that wild scene but the child and the gulls, and only the gulls moved. A long time had passed. The lonely girl, ten years old, waited with a vast patience beyond the patience of children, and her eyes never left the sea and her ears heard nothing but the savage voice of the tumultuous waters.

A considerable distance behind the child stood a very old and wind-scarred wooden house, tall and battered, its fretted woodwork sagging, its narrow windows unlighted except for a feeble lamp in the main room downstairs, its broken steps rough with blown sand, its chimneys without smoke but for one at the east end. The shingles on the roof curled. There were no gardens, no trees about the house, and only the sea grass in sandy clumps. The house stood alone, without neighbors, on a slight rise surrounded by outbuildings as dilapidated as itself, and with a tiny shanty behind it. An atmosphere of desolation and extreme poverty hung over the house like a mist, and an air of abandonment. Each surge of the wind beating on the gray and pock-marked walls threatened to blow the wretched building down, to scatter it on the sandy earth, there to be buried by the veils of sand streaming in the gale.

Two women, one very old, one middle-aged, sat by the only fire in the house, in the parlor. But the fire was of driftwood, thriftily gathered each day, and it smoked and burned fitfully. One single lamp, burning kerosene of a particularly bad odor, lighted the long and narrow room, which was furnished with miserable sticks of furniture as poor as the house itself, and as old. The floor was covered with a straw rug which had long lost its color; the few tables and chairs were splintered and unpolished, for they had been made of rough wood never stained or varnished. The wind entered here through cracks never mended, and the flame in the plain oil lamp flickered. The wood smoldered in the fireplace, which was built of stones gathered from the shore.

The women shivered. The old woman's cheap black dress was covered with a number of afghans, and her thin shoulders by shawls which sent out an odor of peppermint and age and mold. She sat very close to the fire, holding out her hands to the vague heat and muttering under her breath discontentedly. Her face, in the uncertain light, had a kindly yet predatory expression, wise and disillusioned, with a touch of hard humor in the lines of her wrinkled and sunken mouth. The eyes, black and small, had an unusually sharp and youthful glance, which never overlooked anything. Her untidy white hair was heaped over her forehead; her big-knuckled hands were blue from chill. While she warmed them she rocked in the only rocker in the room, and the creaking sound was like a complaint. She chewed red-striped peppermint candies which she kept in a bag on her knees.

The younger woman was dressed more neatly; her gray woolen dress with its tight bodice and full draped skirt was old and carefully mended, but it fitted her fine and buxom figure as if made of the best satin. Her curled hair was ruddy, her manner vivacious as she set a table for a meager supper—the dining room, dark and somber, was too cold to be used today. Her face, round and pink, was both intelligent and good-tempered, and her blue eyes, alert and friendly, occasionally glanced at the old woman. Then her pink mouth would quirk, and one of her reddish eyebrows would raise. She often seemed about to speak; then, as if vexed, she would rattle a cracked plate made of the cheapest ironware, white and without a pattern. A kettle sluggishly began to hiss on the fire.

"I don't care!" said the younger woman with a defiant lift of her plump shoulders. "I'm going to make myself some tea to warm up a little! You can have one cup with me, Kate, and don't grumble about the waste again. I'm tired of all this."

"Well, if you're that tired, why don't you leave, Beth?" asked the older woman, splintering a peppermint deftly with her false teeth.

Beth went to the sand-dusty window and looked at the child at a distance, sitting there motionless on the boulder. The woman grumbled, shaking her head as if exasperated by her own weakness. She said angrily, "Because of Carrie, and you know it."

"That little monster is nothing to you," said old Kate, and rocked as if laughing internally. "If I was in your place I wouldn't stay because of *her*. No sir. Not that I don't like the kid; maybe I don't. But I promised her mother I'd stay, and it's all arranged; was arranged a long time ago." She sighed. "You'd never believe it, looking at Carrie, but her mother was a beauty, pretty as a painting, with yellow hair and big gray eyes and a lovely figure." Kate's voice held a hint of her early girlhood in the Midlands of England. "Best of all, she had a beautiful soul." She cackled. "And better than all else, she had a lot of money. *He* got it, of course. There were some said he married her for her money. Maybe. But I think he cared for her too. Now, now, don't go romantic on me again, Beth!"

Beth came back to the fire, her blue eyes bright with curiosity. "He's still got the money, hasn't he? He isn't the kind to spend anything, God knows. Some say he's rich——"

Kate cackled again and rubbed her hands. "Never listen to strangers and the foolish gab they talk. As for me, I keep my own counsel." She looked at Beth shrewdly. "Living here like this every summer, and then in that house in Lyndon, would you say he was rich? It's bad enough here in Lyme; it's worse in Lyndon in the winter. Colder than death, with hardly any fires, and the snow about like mountains. Would you say a rich gent would live like that, eh, Beth?"

"Not in my book, he wouldn't," said Beth vigorously. She paused, her big plump finger on her plump lips. "Yet he's always in Europe, sailing or steaming away months in the year. Must have business in those foreign places. Poor men don't have business anywhere."

"Hum," said Kate. "Well, I'll have a cup of tea with you; always did like a nice cup of tea, though most times we have to buy it out of our own pockets when the can runs low—which it always does. You buy the tea this time, Beth?"

Beth sat down and looked with a frown at the kettle, which was refusing to come to a boil on the low and smoldering logs. "No. I charged it. Down at the village yesterday. Thirty cents a pound; not very good, but better than usual."

"Mr. Ames did buy us some China tea last time he was in the old country," said Kate. "Now, I'm not defending him, but you have to give a man justice sometimes."

Beth snorted. She glanced at the window; she could just see the blurred and silent figure of little Caroline Ames; now, in this twilight, it seemed to be one with the gray sky and the sea, as if carved from the substance of the boulder itself. "I often wonder," said Beth. "He hates that poor little girl; you can see that with half an eye. But she loves him to death, the poor mite. Worships him. She's looking for the ship that's supposed to bring him tonight or tomorrow. It's a funny thing about love: you don't need to have it returned to love somebody. Loving's enough."

Kate said, "There you are again! Romantic. You and your Charles Dickens and his books you're always reading. Don't be romantic, girl; no romance in real life."

"I don't know about that!" said Beth with spirit. "I was married; I loved Harry with all my heart."

"And he ran off with a trollop, taking your savings, too, five years ago," said Kate cynically. "That's what you told me. Romance!"

"I loved him. That was enough, even if he didn't love me." She sighed, thinking of the house, the very little house, which had been hers in Lyndon, near Boston. She had had to sell it, for she had no money to maintain it. Well, there was no use thinking of the past; she, Beth, was forty-five years old, and women that age were still too young to sink themselves in useless memories. She turned her thoughts determinedly to the mystery which was John Ames and his little daughter Caroline. She had been with the family for five years and knew almost as little now as she had known on the evening of her arrival. She received eight dollars a month as an assistant to old Kate, who no longer could do much as a housekeeper. Beth had a very healthy and human curiosity. As she filled the tin teapot with hot water and took the can of tea from the mantelpiece, she became determined to learn something more from the taciturn Kate. Her blue eyes sharpened, but she was careful to use guile, for Kate was very cunning and any information was taken from her unawares and only when she was in a good temper. Beth made very strong, rich tea, not sparing the leaves this time. She poured it into two big thick cups. She reached to the mantelpiece and brought down a box of plain cookies. "There, we'll have a feast," she said.

Kate held the hot cup greedily in her worn hands and accepted three cookies. She placed them beside the bag of peppermints on her knee. She regarded Beth with kindness and gratitude. "You're a good soul, Beth," she said. "And being a good soul is very good, though stupid."

The wind shrieked against the house; the small fire trembled and fell low. The flame in the lamp bent, almost expired. The women drew closer to the hearth.

"Carrie will take cold out there," said Beth. "I think I'll call her in soon. It's silly for her to sit there, watching. All the ships dock down near Marblehead or in the port of Boston, not here."

"But she can see them come in," said Kate, smacking her lips over the tea. "Leave her be. She don't have much amusement besides watching for her daddy's ship."

Beth sipped her tea delicately, watching the old woman under her red eyelashes. She said casually, "You took care of Carrie until I came four years ago. That's six years you had of her, isn't it? You said you stayed because of her mother."

"True," said Kate, sucking loudly at her cup. "I promised her mother. Ann Esmond, that was."

"When the poor young thing was dying, after the baby's birth?" suggested Beth.

Kate grinned. "Wrong again, you and your romance! You're thinking of *Dombey and Son*. Nothing like that. Caroline was three years old, and healthy as a colt. My Ann caught cold." She stopped grinning, and a dark and vengeful look crept over her face, and she stared at the fire. "I brought Ann up; I was her nanny, fresh from England; she was my own child, in my heart. Ann and her twin sister Cynthia. Pretty as pictures. Both of 'em. Never married, never had a child of my own. They was my children. There's a portrait of them in Cynthia's house now. You should see it sometime. Well. Ann caught lung fever in that damned cold house in Lyndon, and *he* was too near to call a doctor in time, and so she died. I said to myself, said I: 'If that girl dies, I'll leave this house tomorrow, and be damned to him and his brat!' Then Ann asked me, right on her deathbed. Loved that kid, she did. Never had any real feeling for her, myself."

"Ah," murmured Beth pitifully.

" 'Tisn't that I despise her, as her dad does," said Kate. "But she's so ugly, and not like my Ann at all. Not even like *him*. Wonder, sometimes, who she does look like; somebody barmy, no doubt. Maybe that's why he avoids her. Maybe she reminds him of somebody."

"Perhaps," insinuated Beth eagerly, "he doesn't like Caroline because she's a disappointment. He wanted a son?"

Kate grinned all over her wrinkled face. "Wrong again. You better stop reading Dickens. They wanted a daughter, especially *him*. 'Give me a daughter, Ann,' I used to hear him say. 'Not a son. I don't want a son.' "

"Why?"

Kate pulled her afghans tighter on her withered knees. "I don't know. So, he got a daughter, and he hates her. No telling what people are like."

"Perhaps he doesn't like Caroline because she isn't pretty like her mother."

"Never heard him say anything about her looks. I've just got a feeling she reminds him of somebody he hates."

"It's a mystery," said Beth, delighting in it.

"Nothing's a mystery," said Kate crossly. "Everything's got an explanation, if you can find it. How you go on about mysteries! But lonely people love 'em." Her voice was thin and had a tone of crackling to it, tinged with malice.

A heavy gust of wind, massive as an avalanche of stone, fell against the house, and the gloomy light darkened at the windows. The walls trembled, and the ancient floor vibrated. Beth shuddered. "I've had five summers of this," she said. "People who come to Lyme leave September first. But not us, dear me, no! We stay until the first snow flies. The house in Lyndon's worse than this for cold, but at least I can go in on the train to Boston in twenty minutes and look at the shops and see somebody besides us. By the way"—and Beth poured another cup of tea for Kate—"why don't we ever see the neighbors? Nearest one's a mile away, but that isn't too far. People by the name of Sheldon, I heard in the village, and they live here. They've got a boy, Tom, about twelve; could be a playmate for Carrie."

"He don't like neighbors; never did," said Kate cryptically. "He hasn't any friends; never had. How my Ann could put up with him I'll never know. But he doted on her. And kept her locked up like a prisoner. Not that she ever minded; he was enough for her, poor child. Sometimes he'd take her to London and Paris and Berlin; it was a gala occasion for her, as if she'd never seen them places before with her father."

"Well, he's a dandy," said Beth. "And dresses like a prince. Sometimes I could speak my mind to him and tell him about Carrie's old worn clothing! Like a beggar." She brightened. "I suppose he never got over his wife's death. Mourned for her."

"Not he," said Kate. "There's some made for mourning and some not. He's not." She rubbed her papery palms together and meditated. "It's all business with him. Importing or something." She looked slyly at Beth, as if amused at the younger woman's unsatiated curiosity.

"Where did he meet your Ann?" asked Beth. "If you don't mind me," she added, bridling.

"Oh, I don't mind telling," said Kate indulgently. "In her father's house; she had just come out; it was one of the grand parties. No mystery about it. Mr. Esmond had some business with him; don't know what. But Ann looked at him, and he looked at her, as if he was a nob, and he wasn't."

"A nob?"

"Oh, that's English for aristocrat; gentry. And he isn't gentry. But never heard, even from Ann, where he came from, except that once she said Boston. He was an orphan, she said, since he was a little chap. That was all. No family."

"And her father let her marry him!"

"Ann had a mind of her own, for all she looked so soft. And Mr. Esmond didn't seem displeased. I heard him say once that *he* had a future. Anyway, Ann inherited two hundred thousand dollars when Mr. Esmond died, and Cynthia got the same. Two hundred thousand dollars. That's a fortune. She turned it over to *him*."

"So he's rich, in spite of him living like a beggar and making us live like beggars too," said Beth resentfully.

"Um. I didn't say he was rich, now. Investments went down during the war; haven't come back yet. Maybe he lost it all." The old woman smiled under her long nose. "Well, you get eight dollars a month. That's not a fine sum. You could get more elsewhere. With a warm room and a fire of your own, and better money, and a cheerful house around you."

"I know," muttered Beth. "But it's Carrie. Somehow, I can't go away and leave her."

"Never be sorry for anyone to your disadvantage," said Kate. "That's a fool's way, and a weakling's."

"It could also be Christian," replied Beth angrily. "And having some pity!"

Kate lifted her old head abruptly and stared without blinking at Beth. Her mouth grimaced after a few moments. "You mean that," she said flatly, and shook her head. "God help you, girl, you mean that. You're a mystery if there ever was one."

"Not me," said Beth. But she was a little pleased. "I never told you, but I have a little pension. Fifteen dollars a month. A government pension. After Harry—went away—and I never knew it!—he enlisted in the army. He was killed in Virginia, just before the war ended. I didn't even know he was in the army. But he must've loved me after all, for the government notified me of his being killed, and about the pension."

"More likely he used you for an excuse not to marry his strumpet," said Kate. "Now, don't come over all wounded, Beth. So you have fifteen dollars a month. You can afford to stay here and look after Carrie after all."

She lifted her bony finger and shook it at Beth. "Now, let me tell you something. When *he* comes home, you ask him for more money. Two dollars a month more. Tell him you'll leave unless he gives it to you. He'll not get another woman to dance attendance on his brat for eight dollars a month! And he'll not dare put her on me again."

The wind became more violent; the old windows rattled fiercely. The light was crepuscular, and the fire sank even lower. Puffs of icy air blew through the room.

"Oh, you're very independent," said Beth, tossing her head.

"That I am," replied Kate with a satisfied snicker. "And I did it for myself. I'd not have left Ann when she was alive, but after she died I went right up to *him* and said, 'I'm off, sir. I've got a little money saved, and there's my old sister in England, with a sweets shop, and Ann left me two thousand dollars.'"

She paused, smiling with pleasure at the memory.

"Well," resumed Kate. "He was in a quandary. He was paying me twelve dollars a month. No other servants. Where would he get a woman, even an old one, to work for him, in two houses, with a brat, and putting up with everything as I do, for that bit of money? Not that he didn't try! He did. So one night he comes to me and says he'll pay me fourteen dollars a month and looked at me like he was the brother of Queen Victoria, herself. All pleased with himself for being so generous. And I said no. Not Kate Snope. I was off to England. He couldn't buy me with any wages."

She popped another peppermint into her mouth and sucked it voluptuously. "I let him think that over for a bit. And then he comes to me with his stony face. He'd pay me fourteen dollars a month, yes. And he'd make a bargain with me. For every year I'd stay with him, taking care of his houses and his brat, supervising things, he'd put five hundred dollars to my name in the bank! Now, what do you think of that?"

"Five hundred dollars a year!" exclaimed Beth, awed. "Why, you must have thousands from him by now!"

"Yes," said Kate happily. "I made him pay me back from Carrie's birth. That's five thousand dollars. No go, otherwise. 'And moreover,' I says to him, 'I want help.' And so you came."

"So he must be rich, after all," said Beth. "Five thousand dollars, and five hundred extra every year!" She was incredulous. Then her eyes narrowed. "But didn't you tell me that your Ann had asked you to stay with her child and that you'd promised never to leave Carrie? Didn't Mr. Ames remind you of that?"

"He didn't know," said Kate. "And I'm trusting you to say nothing to him. But if you can't hold your tongue and you tell him, that promise or not, I'll leave. I'm that hard."

"I'm not a tattler," said Beth proudly. "But goodness! You must hate him."

"Always did," said Kate, placidly chewing a small cake.

Though it was growing much colder and the light was very dull now, Beth Knowles forgot the child watching the sea outside. She was absorbed in the strange story she had been hearing. She said, "How old was Miss Esmond when she married *him?*"

Kate's face changed, became tight, almost evil. "She was only twenty. And he was thirty-four, almost old enough to be her father. He's forty-five now; he never changes. Those that are wicked never change; the devil's with them, taking care of his own."

A thin long plume of smoke, far out on the ocean, divided the sky and sea like the stroke of a pencil. Caroline sat higher on her boulder. "Oh," she murmured aloud, "let that be Papa's ship! Please, good Jesus." She clasped her small broad hands tightly on her knees and watched the smoke. For a few moments it dwindled, then became larger. But she could not as yet see the ship.

No one but Beth had ever taught her any religion or had taken her to any church. She did not remember her young mother well, nor if that mother had taught her any prayers. The name of God was not spoken in the houses of John Ames, except in a whisper at night, beside Caroline's bed. As Beth's theology was simple and her knowledge little, Caroline knew only that the Christ had died on a cross in some far country which she mingled in her mind with the fairy tales she read hungrily. He, too, was somewhat mythological in the child's thoughts. When she thought of Him, which was seldom except at bedtime and on such occasions as this, she visualized Him as a knight in armor, with a pennanted spear and an iron shield.

"Good Jesus," repeated Caroline again, straining her eyes across the plain of furious water. Then she hugged herself with joy. The dim shadow of a ship could now be seen. Was her father on that ship? He had been gone a long time, ever since she had been brought here in June after school was closed. (Only Kate had heard from him, a single curt letter. "A shame!" Beth had cried to the old woman indignantly. "Never a word about his child, either, you said!" "Don't be sentimental," Kate had chuckled.)

The silent shadow of the ship streamed toward Boston Harbor. Now it disappeared around the side of the great rocks on the beach. If it could be docked that night, John Ames would arrive home in the morning. Still, Caroline sat on her boulder, watching the gulls now. The blur of silver which was the sun moved far down to the west. Suddenly one long colorless ray pierced the gaseous clouds and shot down like a long sword onto the sea. Where it pierced it turned the water to an arctic turquoise, like a brilliant pool in the midst of a gray and turbulent plain. The gulls screamed louder. The wind tore at the girl's shawl, whipped her face savagely, almost blew her from her seat.

"Hello!" said a strange voice at her shoulder. She started violently, then caught at the sides of the boulder to prevent herself from falling. She turned her head, for she abjectly feared strangers. A boy of about twelve was standing beside her, laughing, a big boy with a face bright red from cold and wind, a handsome boy whose bare head was covered with a thick cap of strong black hair.

Caroline did not reply. She stared at him anxiously. He kicked a wet stone. He was poorly dressed, even more poorly than herself; his wrists extended far below his short sleeves, and the trousers he wore were stretched hard to meet his knees, so that he had a long, lithe look, somewhat wild and unkempt. The wind blew his hair from his ears, and they had a faunlike shape, pointed and pale, contrasting with the color on his wide cheekbones and on his full, smiling lips. He had eyes as blue as a winter sky, and his nose was short and virile, his chin deeply dimpled.

"I'm Tom Sheldon," he said. His voice was strong, almost manly, and full of warmth and gaiety. "You're not scared of me, are you? Why, I'm your neighbor. We live only about a mile from you. You're Caroline Ames, aren't you, old Ames' girl? Heard about you in the village."

Caroline did not answer. Old Kate was always warning her not to speak to strangers. "One never knows," she would say wisely with a menacing gleam in her eyes. Caroline had come to believe, in spite of Beth's fitful efforts, that those one did not know were in some way ominous. The little girl began to shift uneasily on the boulder. She glanced at the house; if the boy "did" something, this terrible easy boy, she would scream and Beth would come running.

"You scared?" said Tom, and laughed in her face. He studied her, his head held sideways. "Say, you're not as homely as everybody says. Say, you're almost nice-looking." He peered at her, thrusting out his head. "Why don't you ever come to the village? The old man keep you locked up?"

Caroline, to her immense surprise, heard her voice answering with weak indignation. "He's not an old man! Don't you dare talk like that! I don't know you. I'm going home." She dropped to the shingle, then paused, for Tom was laughing at her. For some reason her anger vanished. He had said she wasn't homely!

She did not know how to talk with strangers, and her lips fumbled. She said proudly, "My papa is coming home. I just saw his ship."

"You mean that old ship that just went by?" asked Tom, waving his hand toward the sea. "Why, that was nothing but an old freighter. I can tell. Your pa on a freighter?"

Caroline was silent a moment. She reflected. "I don't know," she said finally. "It's suppertime. I've got to go in."

Tom put his cold hands in his pockets and eyed her with humor. "They say your pa is as rich as Croesus," he remarked.

"Who's Croesus?" asked Caroline, preparing to run off.

Tom shrugged. "Hell, I don't know," he replied. "But that's what they say."

"You swore," said Caroline reprovingly. She pulled the shawl closer about her broad shoulders. Then she did something she had never done before. She giggled. Tom regarded her with approval. "Hell," he repeated, hoping to evoke another giggle. "You sure aren't so damn homely."

He gazed at the stocky little girl, with her big shoulders and her very short neck, her heavy arms and heavier legs, her bulky body in its wretched dark red coat. She had a clumsy, slow manner. Her square face had a stolid look and was without color in spite of the bitter gale, and her mouth was large and without mobility, her nose almost square, with coarse nostrils and spattered with large brown freckles. Her solid chin would have suited a youth rather than a girl child, and so short was her neck that it forced a fold of pallid flesh under the chin. Her very fine dark hair, wisping out from its thin long braids, did not lighten her unprepossessing appearance. The wind dashed her braids in the air like whips.

Caroline was tall for her age, but she was half a head shorter than Tom. The children stared at each other, face to face. Caroline with reluctance and fear, but also with a desire to learn again that she was not truly ugly. She gave her benefactor a shy smile, and when she did so her eyes lit up and sparkled. They were remarkably beautiful eyes, a golden hazel, large and well set under her broad, bare forehead and sharp black eyebrows, and they possessed lashes incredibly thick, and they were extremely soft and intelligent, limpid in the last light from the sky.

"There!" said Tom. "Why. you're real pretty when you smile. You've got real pretty eyes, and nice white teeth, too, though they're kind of big." He was pleased with himself; he had discovered something unknown to anyone else. He was naturally friendly. In spite of the poverty of his family, he felt no inferiority. He was without fear, for he was strong. He was also gentle in his heart and curious about all things. Caroline's hands stopped clutching at her shawl. She basked in the memory of what this boy had told her. She lifted her head as if she were a beauty, and for the first time in her short life there was a curious lilting and warmth in her chest.

"My mama was very pretty," she said. "Aunt Cynthia's got her picture. It was painted by a great artist. In New York."

"You must look like her," said Tom with large kindness. Caroline shook her head and pulled down her whipping braids. "No, I don't look like Mama at all. She's dead."

"You must look like your old man, then," said Tom.

"Oh no," said Caroline, as if this were an insult. "My papa's very handsome. He's tall and has blue eyes and curly brown hair and dresses very stylish. He buys all his clothes in New York. And he isn't old. You mustn't say that."

"Never saw him," said Tom, eying her shrewdly.

"He's been away all summer, in Europe," said Caroline. "He's on business."

"He sure is rich, they say."

Caroline reflected on that. But it was a matter of indifference to her. She was not quite sure what it meant to be rich, or poor. "I don't know," she said.

"You don't know! Why, that's funny," said Tom. "Now, I know we're poor. Sure know we're poor! My dad does odd jobs around for the folks in the summer colony." He examined the Ames house and the grounds with a critical eye. "Your pa could use my dad, but then the folks in the village say your pa is as tight as his skin. Tighter. Never spends a cent. He don't even have a carriage."

"We don't need one," said Caroline. "Not here, anyway. But we've got a carriage in Lyndon. Old Jim drives it. Papa always says we've got to be careful."

"Bet you never have any fun," said Tom suddenly. "You kind of look that way."

Caroline became confused at all these remarks. What did "fun" mean?

"Bet you never play with any other girls," Tom continued.

"Well, no," said Caroline uncertainly. "Papa doesn't like strangers in the house. He doesn't want me to get diseases, either. I have to come right home from Public School Number 10. That's eight streets from where we live in Lyndon."

"And you don't play with the girls at school?" said Tom.

"They don't like me," said Caroline, as if this were perfectly normal.

"Why not? You look like a nice girl."

"I don't know why. They don't even speak to me. Only the teachers talk to me. I like Miss Crowley the best. She bought me a blue ribbon for Christmas last year. It was awful pretty." Caroline looked at Tom. He was no longer smiling. "Hell," he muttered, and kicked a stone viciously.

Then he turned to Caroline again. "Your pa's rich, and you go to a public school," he said, as if accusing her. "The summer people who come here send their girls to private schools, and I'll bet they don't have half the money your pa has!"

Caroline was confused again.

"And they've got servants, too," went on Tom wrathfully.

"So do we," said Caroline eagerly, wishing to please him. "We've got old Kate, who was my mother's nurse, and she's our housekeeper, and we've got Beth, who's awful nice, and she helps Kate and takes care of me."

"Your clothes are terrible," said Tom. "Like they come off a Salvation Army line, like mine. Why don't your pa buy you some pretty dresses like other girls have, and a fur muff? Bet you look worse than even the girls in your public school."

"I guess we aren't rich after all," said Caroline with distress. Being rich suddenly seemed very desirable to her. "We have to be very, very careful, Papa always tells me."

"Ho!" snorted Tom.

"I've got ten dollars in my tin bank in the house," offered Caroline. She drew a deep breath and added over the bellowing of the wind: "I haven't told her yet, but I'm going to give three of them tomorrow to Beth. It's her birthday."

"That's nice," said Tom, gentle again.

"She gave me a birthday present last April," said Caroline. "A little doll; she made the clothes herself. It was the first doll I ever had."

"Don't you get Christmas presents?" asked Tom disbelievingly.

Caroline shook her large head. "No. Papa doesn't believe in them. He says it's a waste of money and foolish. But he gave me three dollars on my birthday."

"Doesn't he ever bring you anything when he comes home?"

"No," said Caroline, surprised. "Why should he?"

"I'll be damned," said Tom.

Caroline twisted her hands together. She had heard anger in Tom's voice. "My papa loves me very much," she said. "And I love him more than anything. I don't need presents."

Beth came out on the rickety porch, her head wrapped in a shawl. "Carrie!" she shouted, taking a careful step or two toward the treacherous broken steps. "Carrie, you come in now and have your supper! And who're you talking to?" She peered at the children in the sullen half-light.

Tom waved to her. "It's just me, Mrs. Knowles!" he shouted back. "Tom Sheldon. Just talking to Carrie here. Mind?"

"Well, no," she screamed, and smiled. "Come on, Carrie." She returned to the house and shut the battered door. She went to the fire, still smiling. "Well, something's happened I'm glad of. Carrie's talking to the Sheldon boy. Real natural, like a child should."

"She can't talk to him," said Kate. "*He'll* never stand for it. You know what he thinks of the village people. I'll give that girl a talking to." She twitched her shawl. "Why doesn't the brat come in?"

"I'll be right here tomorrow," Tom was promising Caroline. "Same time. I have to help my dad during the day."

"Come back tomorrow," said Caroline. "Be sure and come back!"

Kate never permitted anything to interfere with what she fondly called her "digestion"; she decided not to upbraid Caroline until after supper. But her expression was grim. As the two women and the child sat at the table in the bleak lamplight and firelight, she gave Caroline intimidating glances, of which Caroline was utterly unaware. Caroline was thinking of Tom as she ate. Her beautiful hazel eyes glowed in her plain, nearly ugly face. The thick lashes that sheltered them were like a hedge about golden pools. There was even some color on her square cheeks. She had a dreaming expression, soft and reminiscent. Beth watched her, her sentimental heart yearning and tender. Why, the poor little thing was almost pretty! And all that came from just once being natural and talking to another child!

The dinner was plentiful but poor in quality, for Kate "watched" the bills scrupulously. Beth did the cooking, but there was little she could accomplish in the way of a fine meal under the circumstances of a restricted budget. And what, she would ask herself despairingly, could one do when the purse permitted only tough, boiled meat and boiled turnips and mashed potatoes without butter, and coarse bread and weak tea? She was certain that *he* fed himself well in all those foreign places and in Boston and New York and Washington, for he had a sleek look, and his skin was well tended and polished. But his child could eat like a beggar for all he cared.

Caroline ate absently and with her usual silence. She had never known excellent food in all her life. She was permitted but one cup of milk a day, and never any sweets or cakes except what Beth could bake her, the ingredients of which Beth bought herself from her meager wage. Caroline had never been truly hungry and had never relished any meal. Her palate was so blunted that on the twice-yearly occasions of her visits to her Aunt Cynthia on Beacon Street she could not enjoy the splendid and delicately flavored food. It seemed very odd to her that anyone could eat pheasant with chestnut dressing, wine-flavored sauces, roast meat and peculiar vegetables, such as artichokes under glass, and glacés, and rich fruit cakes, and coffee floating in cream touched with brandy.

In the way of old people, Kate became drowsy after supper and forgot that she must admonish Caroline. So at eight o'clock Beth took Caroline's hand and led her from the room, carrying a half-burned candle in an old brass holder. The narrow hall outside the parlor was as black and cold as death, whistling with the wind that penetrated the thousand cracks in the ancient house. The faint candlelight shifted in these drafts, showing the unpolished floor, on which there was no carpeting, and the shut door of the dining room that reflected back no gleam of burnished wood. The woman and the child hurried up the echoing stairs, which trembled under their tread. They reached a long thin hall with closed doors; a mouse squeaked away from them, and Beth jumped. The little beams of the candle flickered in the musty gloom; the house smelled of mold and mice and bad drains and memories of boiled cabbage. The damp walls were peeling, the timeless wallpaper of roses and leaves dripping slightly with sea dampness. Beth opened a door, and the air that gushed out at her was bitterly arctic.

The room they entered was small, with a high cracked ceiling. The walls had been only plastered more than forty years ago; they were discolored with damp to a soiled gray. Here, also, there were no carpets; the small window was uncurtained, with only shutters to keep out the night and the early sun. A narrow bed with no counterpane stood in the center of the room, its thin cheap blankets smooth, its pillowcases very white from Beth's scrubbing. A chest of drawers, with the varnish warped upon it, lurked against a wall, and there was one single rush chair near the bed. This was Caroline's room, no better and no worse than the other bedrooms, and without heat of any kind.

Beth put the candlestick on the chair, for the room had no table. "Lord," she said, "we'll have to get to bed in a hurry, won't we, dear? Now, let me help you get undressed." Caroline was ten years old, but Beth loved these ministrations, which filled her lonely heart with affection. She stripped off Caroline's wool plaid dress—an ugly plaid of serviceable serge bought two years ago—and then the girl's knitted petticoats and woolen drawers and darned cotton stockings. The child stood before her, hugging her thick body for warmth, while Beth shook out the flannel nightgown which she had folded in the morning under the pillows. The flannel had once been white; it was now yellow from countless washings. "There," said Beth, dropping the too short garment over Caroline's shoulders and smoothing it down with the gentlest hands. "Now we'll be comfortable. Get into bed, sweetheart, and I'll hear your prayers."

But Caroline, who seldom spoke, now wished to talk. "I like Tom," she said shyly. "He's awfully funny, but I like him. He swears. I like to hear him swear."

"Boys shouldn't swear," said Beth, without reproof, however. "Tom's a good boy. He was just bragging to you, the way boys brag to girls. I'm glad you like him." Beth tucked the blankets closely about Caroline's chin. Then she sat in the candlelight and smiled at the child, putting the candle on the floor, repressing her shivers.

"I do like him," said Caroline, and her child's voice, naturally husky and slow, trembled a little. "Not the way I like Papa." Beth smoothed the long thin braids of dark hair. "Beth, do you think Papa will be home tomorrow?"

"I'm sure I don't know," said Beth, and her voice hardened.

"Tom thinks he should bring me presents. Isn't that funny?"

"Very funny," said Beth. "Now, let's pray and go to sleep."

But Caroline was not prepared to pray yet. She studied Beth solemnly. Then she smiled, and those wonderful eyes of hers, so pure, so large, so absolutely beautiful, made the woman catch her breath. "You know what he said, Beth? He said I was pretty. Honest he did."

"You are, you are!" said Beth fervently, as if defying someone. "You have eyes like an angel, and a lovely smile. Oh, my dear, do smile often! Do you know you seldom smile?"

"You mean I'm really pretty?" asked Caroline, her voice trembling again. "Cross your heart?"

Beth immediately crossed her heart, and her comely face shone as if fresh from tears. Caroline at once giggled. The child nestled on her starched cold pillows. She folded her hands and recited:

> "Gentle Jesus, meek and mild,
> Watch the night this sleeping child."

It was too cold for the nightly Bible reading. Beth was already numb; her throat scratched, and she sneezed. She stood up and lifted the candle. Then Caroline put out her broad hand and caught Beth's dress and she colored shyly.

"Beth," she whispered, "you thought I didn't know it was your birthday tomorrow. But I did!" She unclutched her other hand and revealed three dirty one-dollar bills. "They're for you, for your birthday! I got them out of my bank."

Beth took the old and rumpled bills and looked at them by the light of the candle. She could not speak.

Caroline sat up in alarm. "Beth!" she cried. "What's the matter, Beth? Why are you crying? Beth, Beth, why are you crying?"

CHAPTER TWO

Kate received a letter from Boston and clicked her teeth. She said to Beth, "Well, *he* isn't coming out here to take us to Lyndon, after all. We're to pack, call a hack, get on the train ourselves, and open up the other house and close this. Better move, Beth. School's already open in Lyndon, and the brat's got to go."

"He's staying in Boston?" asked Beth.

"For a bit, a few extra days."

Beth's eyes brightened. She said, "Maybe he has a secret love there."

"No secret love," replied Kate with her crone's chuckle. "He's got an office there. How sentimental you are, my girl."

"He's handsome enough," said Beth hopefully. "And not too old. And he dresses well."

"Like a toff," Kate agreed. "Well, you'd best get down the bags from the attic. There's some old blankets there too. Better pack them; we'll need 'em in Lyndon. I've a feeling we're in for a hard winter this time."

"They're just rags," said Beth. She climbed the shaking narrow stairs to the gloomy attic, holding high her brown woolen skirts to keep them from the thick soft dust. Once in the attic, she shut the decrepit door and licked her lips, then tiptoed to one of the tiny windows at the end of the long cold room. She rubbed a spot in the dusty glass and peered out, smiling like a conspirator. Tom and Caroline, far behind the windowless lower back of the house—as Beth had advised—were tossing a ball to each other. Caroline was learning to run quite lightly for one of her bodily form. Beth could see her smile. The child jumped on the low dunes; now Tom was chasing her playfully. The wind blew her braids; there was a rosy color on her cheeks; she pushed Tom and he pretended to be overwhelmed and fell flat on his face. Caroline clapped her hands.

Sighing and smiling secretly to herself, Beth looked for the bags they had brought in June. Long black spiderwebs, like thick nets, hung from the rough wooden ceiling with its pitched roof; the dust on the floor was like a carpet. It was very cold here, and yet airless, and had the musty, almost evil, smell of shut old places. Mice squeaked constantly in hidden corners dark with age and shadows. After gathering the tattered bags and her own straw suitcases, Beth paused. She listened intently. But Kate never came up here on her arthritic and ancient legs. There was no sound but the heaving and incessant pulsing of the sea, like a gigantic and mysterious heart. Beth had bought a naked waxen doll in the village for Caroline's Christmas present; she had spent the three dollars Caroline had given her for her birthday. It was very pretty and large, with blue glass eyes tangled in a thicket of spiky lashes, and it wore a perpetual rosy smile, and its arms and legs could be moved. Moreover, it had a mane of coarse yellow horsehair. It deserved the finest of satin and silk and velvet clothing. Thoughtfully the woman eyed some old trunks in the attic. Old trunks were famous for containing cast-off dresses and laces and ribbons. Beth tiptoed to the trunks and opened one. It held nothing but rusty iron tools and some chains. She closed it; the next one held not a thing but dust. What had become of the dead Ann's dresses and mantles and hats? There was one last trunk, and the lid creaked loudly when Beth opened it.

A flat thin parcel, wrapped in newspaper so old that it was yellow and broken, lay in the bottom of the trunk. Beth curiously picked it up; she knew at once from the weight and the bumpy border of the parcel that it was a picture of some kind. The newspaper crackled and fell apart in her hands. The light in the attic was failing; Beth carried the parcel to the window and, holding it close to her eyes, peered at the newspaper. It had been published, not in Boston, but in a strange place called Genesee, New York, and the date was April 4, 1839. Thirty-one years ago! The paper drifted in crisp fragments from Beth's hands. Then recklessly she tore the rest away.

It was a portrait, about twenty inches by twenty-eight. Beth held it closer to the gray and uncertain light. It was as if the young Caroline were looking up at her from the canvas. The shimmering golden eyes smiled at Beth from the square pale face with its big chin and coarse nose. Big ears flared from the sides of the too large head; that head appeared to be set, as Caroline's was, almost solidly on the wide shoulders, with practically no neck. But the dark fine hair was very thin, appearing hardly more than a glimmering lacquer over the skull.

Then Beth, holding the portrait closer to the indistinct light, saw that this was a portrait, not of a girl or a woman, but of a man of about thirty-eight or a little younger. He was dressed in the fashion she remembered of her own father; he did not wear the modern wide black or crimson or dark blue cravat. He wore a white stock pierced with a simple golden pin. Beth knew nothing of art. She only knew that the face—especially the eyes—was very vivid and alive. She saw that some words had been brushed upon the lower right-hand corner of the canvas, and she had to squint to read them.

"Self-portrait. D.A. 1838."

The canvas had been set in a carved wooden frame; flecks of gold still remained on it; they filtered on Beth's hands. A gust of wind caused the fragments of paper on the floor to move and whisper like old dried leaves, and Beth started. Suddenly there was a harsh pattering on the wooden roof; it had begun to rain, and the large drops were stonelike on the thin shingles. Beth put the portrait back in the trunk. She brushed up the fragments of old paper and tossed them onto the portrait. But even in that dusk the eyes shone up at her, living and vital, and very kind, with a hint of shyness. Shivering, Beth closed the trunk with a feeling that she was shutting away, not a portrait, but a face that lived and understood. It was a kind of horror to her, thinking that those eyes now stared in darkness.

She gathered up the empty bags and lumbered down the stairs with them. Kate was drowsing before the low driftwood fire. She opened her eyes as Beth entered. "You took your time," she grumbled. "I could do with some of your tea; my feet are like death."

"Where is Carrie?" asked Beth.

"In the kitchen. Stuffing herself, as usual, the sly fox. I heard the cupboards opening."

Beth sat down and absently brushed dust from her skirts and hands. "The kettle's hot," suggested Kate impatiently. Beth continued to dust herself. "You never told me," she murmured. "Did *he* have any brothers?"

"*Him?* Nary a one I ever heard of. Why?"

"I just wondered. Didn't you say he was from Boston?"

"That's what I heard, from Ann. Born in Boston. Dear me, are you never going to stop being curious about him? What's he to you?"

"After all!" said Beth, looking up. "It's natural to be curious about people! Am I a dead stick?" She paused while Kate peered at her humorously. "Never mind. Did you ever hear of a place called Genesee, New York State?"

"How you change subjects! No, I never did. Did your husband come from there?"

"I don't know," said Beth vaguely. "It just floated into my mind—Genesee. Did you ever see *his* father, Kate?"

"No, for goodness' sake! Heard his parents died when he was almost a baby."

Beth thought, 1839. She shook her head, baffled, then took the tea can from the mantelpiece. She stood with it in her hands and looked about her at the dreary walls with their peeling wallpaper. There were no pictures in this house. She thought of the portrait in its trunk, immured in the attic, and shivered again.

"Have you got a chill?" asked Kate in her sharp voice.

The man stood in the middle of the beautiful drawing room of the house on Beacon Street. The room was long but narrow, for the house itself was that shape, and of rosy brick with gleaming white shutters and a door of polished wood with a fine old fanlight above it. It was the first of October, but chilly, and a fire burned briskly in a white marble fireplace of Italian origin and excellently carved. The tall windows at each end of the room, framed by French draperies of blue and rose and gold brocade, let in the mellow sunshine of autumn. One window looked out at the brick-paved street with its opposite houses equally as well built and handsome as this; the other window showed a small garden. The golden leaves of an elm tree brushed the grass; each leaf was plated with gilt sunshine.

An Aubusson carpet covered the floor of the room in shades of gray, dim blue, muted yellow, and pale scarlet. These shades were repeated in the French chairs and sofas scattered about the room; little fragile tables with silver or glass lamps stood about, holding exquisite boxes of Florentine origin, or tiny ivory statuettes, or English dancing figures in swirls of porcelain lace, or small vases of flowers. The walls had been painted a soft ivory, and the high ceiling was ivory also, with moldings of gold. A great portrait of two young blond girls, dressed in identical dresses of blue velvet, hung over the mantelpiece.

The smoky eyes, set in faces like blush roses, smiled down at the man. It was impossible to discern any difference in the features of the girls, and it was apparent they were twins. Pearl necklaces curved about their long white throats, and pearls were fastened in their ears. Their lovely hair was parted in the center and then allowed to fall in cascades of curls about their dainty shoulders. One girl sat, the other leaned, standing, behind her.

The room had a rich odor of spice, burning wood, and flowery perfume. An occasional carriage rumbled on the bricks outside; the mellow light, almost tawny, brightened through the polished windows. It sprang back in colored light from the huge crystal chandelier hanging from the ceiling.

The man frowned. A door near the fireplace opened, and a maid in black bombazine and a white frilled apron and cap entered the room, carrying a silver tray on which were a glass decanter filled with sherry and two small glasses of curious shape. She curtsied and then placed the tray on a table by the fire. "The mistress will be down in a moment, sir," she murmured, and retreated from the room. The man lifted one of the glasses; it was as smooth as silk, and carved and heavy. He hesitated, then filled it with sherry. He stood and sipped. It reminded him of the mellow day and the mellow city. Ann had once said, "Boston is an autumn city, even in spring or summer. Like a topaz." Another carriage rumbled past the house. The fire blazed stronger, and the scented air was pleasantly warm. No, thought the man, it isn't like a topaz. It's like this sherry, aged and matured. He opened a box on the table and took out a glacé chestnut and chewed it. Cynthia spared herself nothing. He frowned again.

He began to wander slowly about the room. But he finally came back to the fire. He studied the sherry bottle; it was really a carafe, and he had never seen it before. But Cynthia was extravagant; she was always buying beautiful things, though she could not afford them. This was eighteenth-century, he was certain; it was of the most gleaming crystal with an overlay of silver tracery, vines, bunches of grapes, tendrils, with little faunlike faces peeping mischievously through the broad leaves. What delicacy, what tenderness, what marvelous care to expend on a bottle! Americans spent their time and effort on larger and worthier things. Disdainfully the man turned from the bottle, thinking of blackened and bellowing factories and foundries and turning wheels. These had significance; beauty had not. A steaming ship filled with products of industry had more meaning than statuettes and silken rugs, poetry and paintings, literature and art. Science was the new god, and deservedly so; it was not decadent and perfumed. It was money, and there was nothing in the world but money. There never had been, really, in spite of unmanly and posturing fools who quoted Keats and Shelley and delighted in texture and shape.

He heard a soft gay trilling, and a door opened and a woman of thirty-one tripped gracefully into the room, lifting a pretty white hand in welcome. He never saw Cynthia without a catch in his gloomy heart. She was tall and slender, with a charming and youthful figure, like a girl's; her dress of silvery satin had a tight bodice with little brilliant buttons undulating to her lissome waist; the front was smooth, daringly so, over her rounded hips and thighs, but the back puffed in an exaggerated bustle under which had been caught bunches of artificial violets. Her slippers were silver, pointed and traced with silver beads, and just appeared from under the flowing hem of her gown.

Her face was an older face than the one in the portrait, but it had retained its girlish bloom, dazzling and fair, and her white throat was unlined and the pearls of the portrait glimmered on it. Her blond hair had been cut into wavy bangs on her clear forehead, lifted high on the back of her small head, then permitted to float almost to her shoulders in glossy and gleaming curls. Her lips were a bright pink glow, and her large gray eyes, full and luminous, shone through heavy golden lashes. Unlike her innocent portrait, she now had a saucy but extremely intelligent expression, full of liveliness and very sprightly.

So Ann would look now, thought the man, if she had lived. He had forgotten, however, that Ann had always been more gentle than her sister. Ann, her father often had said, was a dove. But Cynthia was a shining bird.

"Dear John," she said now in a light but firmly pretty voice. She gave him her cool hand and smiled up at him. "How nice to see you again. Really. I was pleased to receive your letter. How well you look! Europe always renews you." There was a tiny malice in her tone, and she tilted her head quizzically.

"I'm not too decrepit, even if I am forty-five," he answered, trying to retain her hand. But she deftly removed it and patted her curls, continuing to look at him. She said thoughtfully, "Forty-five! I must admit you are well preserved." She smiled again. "Do sit down. Have you had sherry? Dreadful thing, sherry, isn't it? I prefer brandy." She sat down with a silvery rustle and clasped her hands in her lap. One of her fingers bore a large diamond set in emeralds, and a bracelet of emeralds circled her slim wrist.

She lifted her beautifully formed arm and pulled at the bell rope, and when the maid entered she ordered brandy. John Ames watched her; he thought how perfect she was. He said, trying to be arch, "Brandy? Is that a lady's drink?"

"Don't be foolish, John. It doesn't become you, with that heavy stiff voice of yours and your stiff manner."

He frowned. "Am I that pompous, Cynthia?"

"Gracious, no. You're never pompous, my dear. That's one of your few charms. There, I am teasing you again."

John Ames was very tall and lean, without gauntness, and though his posture and mannerisms were exceedingly stiff he had a certain grace. His black broadcloth suit had been excellently cut in London, and his brocaded vest of black and gray fitted him exactly. His polished boots had also been made for him in London, of the best of black leather. He had a long, well-shaped face and a strong, somewhat brutal mouth from which deep cleft lines extended downward. Cold blue eyes, very bold and merciless, looked out from under a forehead without wrinkles, and his brown hair, thick and slightly curled, had no gray in it. There was a diamond in his black cravat and another on his right hand.

He is almost a gentleman, thought Cynthia, regarding him pleasantly. But he is a man; there is no doubt of that! He makes me tingle, which is quite naughty of me, I am sure, for he is my brother-in-law. She sipped her brandy and looked up over the brim of the glass at him as he stood near her on the hearthrug. Her gray eyes twinkled with amusement.

"Do sit down," she urged again. He sat down opposite her. The mellow sunlight heightened the colors in the rug and gilded Cynthia's hair. "Tell me all about everything," she said. "How was dull old London and my dear, lovely Paris?"

"You've forgotten that your 'dear, lovely Paris' and France are now engaged in a war. And 'dull old London' is making a pretty profit from it." He smiled at her, and his somber lips parted to show square white teeth.

"I keep forgetting," said Cynthia. Her face changed. She made a restless gesture with both hands. "I never look at the newspapers. I loathe wars. How terrible of Germany to attack France!"

"I believe it was mutual," said John Ames. "But wars are in the nature of men; they spring out of their character. However, the French statesmen were fools; they knew it was inevitable that someday they must fight Germany, since Prussia defeated Austria in 1866. The French are penurious; they waited until it was too late to buy the munitions they needed. But now, when it is too late, they have the chassepot, a breech-loading rifle, far superior to the Prussian needle gun. They also have a machine gun; the mitrailleuse. English patents, sold for a very pretty price. This won't help France, however. The war isn't expected to last more than a year, if that."

Cynthia gazed at the glass in her hand. She said almost abstractedly, "You must have made a lot of money from those armaments, John."

"I always make a lot of money," he said coldly. "But what do you know of these things, Cynthia?"

"My dear John, I may be a woman, but I'm not a fool! Do you know what I heard a friend say once about you? 'John Ames is a bird of disaster. He always appears where there is carrion.'"

He laughed. "Complimentary! A profit is a profit. I dabble in anything profitable. I have a dozen investments and businesses."

"Some legitimate, no doubt," said Cynthia.

"True."

Cynthia said nothing. He waited, but still she did not speak. Then he said, "Why didn't you buy that land and properties in Virginia, as I advised you to? They could have been had for almost nothing; they were sold at a handsome profit just before I left for Europe."

"You bought and sold them yourself?" asked Cynthia quietly.

"I did. But I gave you the first opportunity."

"You don't understand, John. I couldn't have done it. The poor South!"

"Your 'poor South' killed your husband in Georgia," he said with contempt. "Your husband, George Winslow."

"It was stupid of him to apply for a commission and go to war," said Cynthia, and her lovely eyes flashed. "I tried to dissuade him. But it was all bugles and drums and brass buttons and patriotism! Why didn't Congress do as Lincoln first suggested: pay the southern plantation people for their slaves, then free them? Think of the tens of thousands of lives that would have been saved, and the money, and the calamity, and the ruin and destruction! Think of the sorrow that would have been spared, and the bitterness, and the crimes of the Reconstruction, and the undying enmity and hate, and the burned cities, and the widows and the orphaned children!"

John Ames did not speak. Cynthia's eyes were full upon him. "You made a lot of money out of that war, didn't you?"

"I did."

"You never applied for a commission yourself, John."

"No. I was not a fool like your husband."

She put down her glass. "Let us talk of something else," she said in a strained voice. "But first I wish to say this: I was offered a good pension by the government. I refused it. To me it was blood money."

"A silly gesture."

"The world, thank God, is full of what you call 'silly gestures,' John."

"And it can't afford them. It is just an expensive pose."

"I can't afford expensive poses, John, either. I have exactly $23,598.13 left; I received my banker's statement this morning. Aren't you stunned?"

He was. Cynthia, like Ann, had inherited two hundred thousand dollars from her father, wisely invested so that even the War between the States had not depreciated it too radically. After the war her stock had risen in the general prosperity which always seemed to come like a fat beast after all wars, surfeited with dead flesh and blood and dead hearts. Her husband, George Winslow, had been a solid member of a solid law firm, and a Bostonian of a most impeccable if not wealthy family. He had probably left Cynthia at least fifty thousand dollars.

"How did you spend all that money?" exclaimed John Ames, completely aghast. He stared at her as though she were a murderess.

"I spent it—living. Something you would not understand," she answered. She waved her hand about the room. "I buy precious things; I adorn life. I have four servants, and I pay them well. I spend a fortune on my clothing and jewels. I give expensive parties. I travel. Do you see that carafe, for instance? I paid two hundred dollars for it. I have fine pictures, originals. I go to New York and have a suite in the best hotels and enjoy the opera and invite friends to dine with me. I adore champagne, and champagne is expensive. Do you know what this dress cost me? It is actually silver thread and was made in France. My wardrobe is full of such dresses, and sables. My perfume, of which I use considerable, costs fifty dollars a vial." She was becoming excited; she looked at him as if she hated him. "I imported an Italian bedroom set, seventeenth-century, and it cost three thousand dollars, not to mention the charges for shipping, which were enormous. I have lived as I wished to live, John, since the war. This is my house; George and I lived in a very ugly old barn which his parents left him; I loathed it. I paid twenty thousand dollars for this wonderful place."

He could not believe this profligacy, even from Cynthia. He had known she was extravagant. But this was beyond belief. His hands clenched on the arms of his chair. She began to laugh at him, full of delight and gaiety.

"You resemble a waxwork of yourself!" she cried with genuine mirth. "Now you won't be tormenting me all the time to marry you, dear John! A penniless woman!"

"And how long do you think what you have left will last you, Cynthia?" She made a light gesture. "A year, at the most."

"You have a son. Timothy. He is ten years old."

"And what will become of him? I do not worry. For before the last of my fortune has run out I will marry. It may surprise you, John, but I have many suitors, and I'll marry the richest and live as I like to live."

"Marry me, Cynthia," he said, and leaned toward her.

Her face became very strange, and she looked at him in silence for a long time. When she spoke her voice was quiet. "John, I did you an injustice. I thought that at least part of the reason for your marrying Ann was her money."

"It was. I am not a liar except when it will serve my purpose. But I loved Ann too. Not as I am now afraid I love you, but still I loved her."

His cold blue eyes had lost their mercilessness. He even stretched out a hand to her pleadingly. "Cynthia, I want you. Why? I don't know. But, seeing you now, I understand that what I felt for Ann was as nothing to what I feel for you. You—you are a lightness in my life; I can't put you out of my mind. You are reckless and frivolous; you are also intelligent, which Ann was not. Do you know what my life has been?" His voice suddenly took on icy violence. "I tell you, it has been unbearable——"

"Even with Ann?" she asked gently. "Oh, even with Ann?"

"I had Ann for four years. Only four years. Before that, and since, there has been nothing for me."

He pressed his lips together. "I never told anyone; I never told Ann. I shall not tell you. I need you to make me forget."

She pitied him for the first time and was astonished at her pity. Who could feel compassion for John Ames? She laced her fingers together and looked down at them reflectively.

"You're very mysterious, John. You always were. I think that's part of your fascination."

"Then I'll continue to be fascinating; I'll never tell you. Well, Cynthia?"

She shook her head slowly. "John, I've told you a thousand times. Your way of life is abhorrent to me. I have no objection to your money; I suppose some of the gentlemen who want to marry me have smears on their cash, too, one way or another.

"Our individual ways of life, John, are incompatible. I love my life and detest yours. Ann and I were brought up in a gracious and comfortable household, with every warm luxury possible, and laughter and dancing and many affectionate friends. Then you and Ann were married. She went to live in those appalling houses of yours, and her life became stringent and arduous, in spite of old Kate's efforts to relieve the physical misery. I asked Ann one time how she could endure it. And she said, poor darling, that it was the kind of life you wished and that it made you happy, and so it was her wish and her happiness. I'm not like that, John. Perhaps I'm more selfish than Ann, but I shudder at the thought of living as Ann lived. It is possible I don't—love—you as Ann loved you. But I love you enough not to make you miserable. And you'd be miserable with me, with my house, my friends, my way of life, and my appetites. Isn't this house beautiful? But you never thought it was. You were frank enough to tell me it was meaningless, decadent, and expensive. To me, money is to be spent to make existence joyous and charming, to lift us above the level of animals, to surround us with beauty, which is the most precious thing in the world. To you, money is desirable for its own sake and should not be spent except in investments to make more money. I don't understand that at all! It sounds like gibberish, and dangerous gibberish, to me. Yes, yes, I know you've tried to explain, but the more you explain, the more baffled I become. We could never understand each other, and that would be tragic, and we'd finally come to hatred. I don't want that to happen."

Her eyes filled with tears. "John, you dress very fine; you've told me that you do this only to make an impression on those who can assist you in adding to your fortune. You've even told me that if I marry you, you will be content to live here, in my house. But I know what would happen; over the years the servants, one by one, would be dismissed and not replaced. The house would never be repaired, never added to, and would decay. Slowly I would be squeezed and smothered to death. No, no. I don't love money for the reasons you do. John, it's your fear, translated into investments and businesses and bank accounts."

"Don't talk like a fool, Cynthia!"

"I don't know what you're afraid of, John," she continued, as if he had not spoken. "You were very, very poor once, so Ann told me. You were almost penniless until ten years before you married her. But I know many men who were as poor as you were and who are now rich, and it is a joy to them to spend their hard-earned money. In fact, they're more extravagant than those who inherited money. It's as if they can't get enough of what they had been deprived of in their youth." She paused. "And they don't hate people, as you hate them."

He stood up and began to pace the room, his hands thrust in his pockets. "You are talking gibberish, Cynthia," he said.

She threw out her hands hopelessly. "You see? We can never understand each other. Again, you find your meaning in life, and your pleasure, in having money. I find the meaning and pleasure in spending it. And when I marry, which I will after all my fortune is gone, I'll marry a very, very rich man whose fortune I cannot exhaust and who loves life and beauty as I love them and will deny me nothing."

"You'd sell yourself," John Ames said. "Like a strumpet."

She was not offended; she even smiled. "Oh no. I have three gentlemen in mind; I like them all. I'll be a good wife, I will produce more children, I'll be a charming hostess; I'll embellish life for the man I marry; I'll be devoted to him. We'll be happy together."

Her face became meditative. "Yes, I'll want more children. Timothy is a disappointment to me. He has a generous allowance; he saves almost all of it, though he's only ten years old and should have a child's eager appetites. I want more normal children, John."

He stopped before her. "You are thinking of Carrie, Cynthia," he said accusingly. "You aren't fond of her, though she's your sister's child."

She replied candidly, "How could one be fond of Carrie? It is not her appearance at all, though you have tried to say it was. It's something else; she is very queer, for a child. She makes me uncomfortable; she is wretched when she visits me. But imagine Caroline in this house! One has to think of children too. She would be absolutely miserable. What have you done to Caroline, John? Why do you hate her so, the poor thing?"

"Don't be absurd. Cynthia, you'll never have to see Caroline. I won't bring her here."

Now she stood up in one swift and rustling movement, and her eyes blazed at him. "How can you say that, when she adores you so? Have you no natural feelings for your own child, the only child you have? You are a cruel and terrible man, John!"

They faced each other like hating antagonists. John said, deliberately and coldly, "I don't consider myself cruel and terrible. I admit I detest Caroline, but you'll never know the reason. When I look at her I——" An expression of complete revulsion stood in his eyes. "I didn't deserve Caroline. But I do my duty by her. I don't want her to be like—— There's a weakness in her, a deadly weakness. I'm doing my best to eradicate it; I must eradicate it!"

"You'll kill her, John, you'll kill her." Cynthia spoke with bitter emphasis. "That's what you really want, isn't it? If you can't change her to what you want, then you'll destroy her."

"I'll change her," he said.

Cynthia shrugged helplessly and half turned away. John looked at her profile, at the gloss and sheen of her hair, at her exquisite figure. He caught her arm and swung her to him. "Cynthia, look at me! I love you. I can't live without you." He pulled her into his arms and rested his cheek on the top of her head. She stood quietly and did not move. Then after a long moment she turned her head and gave him her lips, and there were tears on her cheeks.

"Oh, Cynthia," he murmured.

Finally she gently disengaged herself and sat down as if exhausted. Her shoulders and head drooped, and she shook her head over and over.

"The answer is still no, John."

"Cynthia, you can't marry anyone else." He sat down near her and tried to take her hand, but she drew it away.

She did not answer. She put her hands to her wet cheeks and sighed. Then she dropped her hands and looked at him. "John, I was fond of George. I've not been inconsolable. I am a normal woman, and I delight in everything pleasant in life. Do you understand me?"

He stared at her with anger and outrage. He said slowly, "Yes, I think I do. You're quite shameless, aren't you, Cynthia?"

"Perhaps. I told you I love life. But I could have married those men, John. They ask me, always. You see, I am not a liar."

"I wish you were, Cynthia! I wish I could believe that you've told me this so that I'll go away and never come back."

"Yes, it is the truth. And I don't want you to go away and never come back."

"What in God's name, then, do you want?"

"Don't say 'God,' John. You never believed in Him; you've told me that. I'll tell you what I want, and as usual I'll be frank."

Her great eyes looked at him with much seriousness.

"I can marry tomorrow if I wish. But I prefer to be free for one more year. Then I'll make my choice. Unless——"

"Unless, what?"

"Unless we can come to terms satisfactory to both of us."

"Cynthia!"

"I'll make a bargain with you, John. I love you. I didn't know how much until today. You will settle twenty-five thousand dollars a year on me for life; we'll go to my lawyers and it will be put in writing. For life."

He drew back a little, coloring. "As my wife, Cynthia——"

"I don't intend to marry you, John."

He dropped her hand. "What are you saying?" he exclaimed.

"You understand very well. Take your choice, John. I can't live your life, and you can't live mine. We'll compromise. Do you know the sacrifice I am making? I don't like Timothy's character; I wanted more children. I am willing, with you, not to have them. If I married another man, I'd not only have much more than twenty-five thousand dollars a year for life, but I'd have a congenial existence, respectable and pleasant. I am prepared to give that all up—for you."

He stood up. Cynthia smiled sadly.

"Are you going, John? You refuse?"

He stopped, his back to her. "How can I refuse?"

She laughed softly. "Even though it means twenty-five thousand dollars a year?"

"Even that."

She stood up and went to him and put her arms about his neck and pressed her cheek against his. But he stood stiffly. "I really am a fool," she murmured. "I am giving up a great deal for you."

"And for twenty-five thousand dollars a year," he said dryly.

"Only for twenty-five thousand dollars a year. You see, we look at things differently. We'll go to my lawyers tomorrow. And they'll be astonished, knowing you. For here you are, out of the generosity of your heart, willing to settle all that money on me, as your dead wife's sister, and in view of the fact that I am a lone widow who is almost bankrupt! What wonderful family feeling you really have! To give me a trust fund!"

Now he held her to him and began to kiss her. But she finally pulled herself away, gasping a little. She laughed. "Ah, no. You'll get no free sample of what you're buying, John!"

She smoothed the disheveled silver fabric over her breast and exclaimed with mirth that he had broken two buttons, and she shook back her disordered hair and opened her pink mouth as if to catch a breath. Then she looked at him curiously, and he thought that her expression was calculating and that she was thinking of the trust fund he had agreed to and he was angry.

CHAPTER THREE

Mr. Carlton Bothwell, Cynthia's lawyer, neatly rearranged the papers John Ames and Cynthia had signed. His ruddy face, under its eaves of white hair, was inscrutable. He loved Cynthia and he had been a close friend of her father's. He knew all about John Ames. Extraordinary that such a man could have settled so much money, for life, on dear little Cynthia, who was only his dead wife's sister! Mr. Bothwell was happy for Cynthia; he was also inquisitive. He thought of his son Harper, his partner, who was a widower and doing excellently. The Bothwells of Boston always did excellently; they had the Midas touch, the older Bothwell thought, quite without originality. But it was not the sort of incredible Midas touch which Ames possessed. He looked down at the papers on his large mahogany desk and scratched his chin delicately. Harper, like several other gentlemen in Boston, was in love with Cynthia Winslow. This trust fund would not expire on Cynthia's marriage. Mr. Bothwell smiled genially.

The golden-red sunshine of the October day brought out flecks of dull crimson on the backs of the heavy lawbooks lined against the mahogany paneling of the office. A scarlet fire whispered and rustled on a black marble hearth; the black and green leather chairs looked very comfortable. A large window looked out upon the street, which clattered with traffic. A lamplighter was already beginning his scuttling rounds outside, though the sun still stood like an enormous bloated red moon high in the west. Mr. Bothwell carried the papers to his steel safe in a corner, which was concealed by a pierced Chinese screen of black teakwood inlaid with ivory.

Mr. Bothwell, a short wide man, had never been able to overcome the rolling waddle of his sturdy Irish father. He sat down behind his desk and peered beamingly over his glasses at John Ames, who sat stiffly and coldly, and at Cynthia, so luscious in her sable jacket, her sable hat and her sable muff, and her dark blue woolen frock. Her gleaming curls lay on the rich fur about her throat. But it was at John Ames that Mr. Bothwell looked the closest. Damned if the man didn't look like one of those English aristocrats! Yet everyone knew he was an enormously rich nobody. Mr. Bothwell chuckled.

"This is a very fine thing, John, a very fine thing!" he said in a ripe voice. "There aren't many brothers-in-law who would do so much for a dead wife's sister." He fingered the big black pearl in his cravat; his fat thighs swelled against the broadcloth that covered them as he lay back in his chair unctuously.

"One does one's best," said John coldly.

One could always recognize the plebeian by his addiction to meaningless platitudes, thought Mr. Bothwell.

"John," said Cynthia demurely, though her eye sparkled, "is very punctilious about duty. Isn't he a love?"

"Heh, heh," said Mr. Bothwell amiably. If there was anyone who looked less like a "love" it was John Ames. John's face was paler than usual, and there were grim corners about his mouth. He even gave Cynthia a formidable look. Mr. Bothwell began to wonder why he had voluntarily made this gift to Cynthia. "Shall we have a drop of sherry?" he asked with a fond glance at the young woman.

"No," said Cynthia. "You know very well, Uncle Carlton, that I hate sherry. Now, if you have some of that fine Scotch whiskey——"

"It just happens that I received a new shipment from Pierce's today," said Mr. Bothwell. He had been quite a beau in Boston and New York and appreciated a refined lustiness in women. There were too many sticks among the proper ladies in Boston. He opened a drawer in his desk and brought out a crystal decanter and three shining glasses.

"None for me, thank you," said John with another icily sullen look at Cynthia.

"Sherry, then?"

"No, thank you."

"Then it seems that Cynthia and I will have to toast each other alone," said Mr. Bothwell. He smiled to himself. If that rigid Croesus thought that by his disapproval he would be able to quell Cynthia's spirits, he was mistaken.

The whiskey was delightful. Mr. Bothwell's ruddy Irish color deepened. He relaxed even more in his chair. Cynthia drank expertly, not like a scrubwoman in one gulp, not like a squeamish lady who made a wry face, but with knowing approval. "I must order some of this," she said. "Dear Uncle Carlton. You're looking so well."

"The sea, you know," said the lawyer with a wink. "I'm not the kind who takes his wife, in full dress, out on Bailey's Beach at noon. I prefer a session with my friends in some quiet clubroom at the hotel. I do ride, you know, Cynthia, and I'm fond of a brisk walk all alone at night before retiring. What did you say, John? Excellent! Let me pour you a glass at once. Taste in whiskey, as in wines, is cultivated."

John Ames' mouth tightened. Did the old rascal mean that as an insult?

"I'm sorry you and Aunt Matilda can't come tonight to my birthday party," said Cynthia. "I'm making it quite a gala affair. Harper is coming too; I've always been so fond of Harper. And it's so sad that he lives alone in that huge house, though it's very beautiful, and with such a marvelous view of the river."

Mr. Bothwell smiled blandly at her. "Harper's loneliness can be cured at any time," he suggested. "He is waiting."

John Ames was thinking with dismay: A gala affair! He knew Cynthia's extravagance. She was discreetly gazing at her muff.

"I trust," he said ironically, "that I am also invited, though I expected to leave for Lyndon very early tomorrow. And I know your parties, Cynthia. They usually last to dawn."

He was angry. He had expected, now that the matter of the trust fund had been concluded, that he would spend the night in Cynthia's bed. He had been thinking of little else. He had wondered why he should feel so much emotion, so much terrible desire, so passionate and overwhelming an urge. Nevertheless, he considered her a woman without the proper decencies of women, a light-minded creature without solid values. He did not believe in the least now that wealthy men in Boston wanted to marry her and give her all she wished. That, he believed, was the tormenting goad she had applied to him, and it still stung. She was ungrateful and unscrupulous; she had brought him here under an aura of duty, for which he had nothing but loathing, and after robbing him she was dismissing him. He gripped the arms of his chair.

Cynthia turned to him. Her beautiful eyes were very soft and tender; he did not see that. She said, "But, John dear, you simply can't leave tomorrow! I have so much I want to say to you. Remember, I am alone, and you are all I have left in the world. Except Timothy," she added with haste, thinking of her son.

He stared at her with sudden penetration. He had totally forgotten, in these last few days while painful negotiations had been going on, that she had refused to marry him and that she had said she loved him.

In her turn Cynthia was studying him also, and she could almost hear his thoughts. She smiled sadly to herself. Dear John. She would try to bring some joy to his stony life; in spite of himself, he enjoyed parts of her existence, though he objectively disapproved of them. When he had said to her, "I can't live without you," he had spoken more truth than he knew.

He saw the warm promise in her eyes. He would not be cheated, then. Cynthia might have no morals or honor, but she had a gay way of fulfilling the minor obligations. Why had he been such a fool as to take her word for it that wealthy and distinguished men in Boston wanted her, she a penniless woman with a child? Wealthy men married wealth; they did not marry women with whom they had slept for nothing.

Again he remembered that she had said she loved him. Cynthia was not a liar. He detested himself; she would have come to him without that money, wife or not a wife.

They arrived at Cynthia's house in the amber dusk of the autumn evening. A little sunlight remained; it fell redly on the burdens of crab apples weighting down the trees in the garden; the fiery fruit stood against the deep and polished blue of the October sky. A woman of responsibility would have had her servants garner all that incredibly lush fruit. But not Cynthia! She had said quite seriously that she preferred to leave it for the birds who did not migrate; she could get along very well without glasses upon glasses of crab-apple jelly in her cellars. "Can you imagine me eating such jelly on my hot muffins in the winter while the birds who do not desert us in the autumn are starving?" she had asked of him.

John did not believe that any human being was of any value at all, except in so far as money was concerned. But he hated waste. As Cynthia tripped away to change he looked gloomily at the endless profusion of pink and scarlet fruit on the trees. She had not even picked the apples and pears along the gray stone wall at the rear! Sometimes she would eat a warm fruit in laughing apology to the damned birds. She had birdhouses on every tree and what she called "feeding shelves" for the winter. As he watched the birds eating the fruit he thought of the night—after that damned gala affair. Her birthday! She was Ann's twin; her birthday was really in April.

This was only an excuse for the party. But there would be the night, or rather the dawn, after the party, and he began to feel very hot and his face flushed and became moist, and he wiped it carefully with his fine linen handkerchief. He had loved Ann. But this was something entirely different. It was baffling, infuriating, crushing, and, in its way, intolerable.

He heard a stealthy footstep on the thick rug of the drawing room, almost a sliding footstep. He turned. Cynthia's son Timothy stood on the other side of the fireplace, looking at him silently. Timothy was Caroline's age, and up to the time of the trust fund John had thought of Timothy as a husband for his daughter. But the boy was now penniless, unless his mother saved some of the new money, which was very improbable indeed.

Timothy was tall, and fair like his mother, and had her gray eyes. Considering that Timothy resembled Cynthia, it was surprising to John Ames that he did not like his nephew. He had many traits of which John approved. He was careful, neat, circumspect, quiet; he did not speak easily and laughed very seldom. There was a seriousness about him beyond his age, not the far solemnity of Carrie which infuriated her father, but a concentrated, adult seriousness. John knew that Timothy saved every penny he received as gifts. He had shown John, even at six, his big porcelain pig-bank. Once he had told John that he wanted to be just like his uncle. There had been respect and admiration in his gray eyes as he looked at John.

John remembered that day last spring, as he stood looking at Timothy now. He remembered very acutely his sudden diffused revulsion, and then his sudden shocked awareness of his revulsion. Of course it had vanished almost instantly and had been replaced with approval. The boy had sensible values; he was no fool like his mother. Still, John disliked him.

"How do you do, Timothy?" he asked in a formal voice. He felt restive.

His thoughts did not fit the presence of a child whose mother he had just bought.

Timothy had been well brought up in Boston. But then, his mother had been an Esmond, his father a Winslow. He said with the utmost balanced courtesy, "How do you do, Uncle John? And how is Caroline?" he asked, the question phrased in exquisite politeness; as if he cared a damn about Caroline, John commented to himself.

"She is very well," said John, still formal. Damn the boy. He made even men feel gauche and cumbersome. "How is school?"

"Splendid," said Timothy. His fair cheeks were faintly colored. He was very handsome and moved with grace. He bent and poked the fire, and his blond hair caught the light. There were no smudges on him, no griminess. When he looked up at John with deference, the eyes were almost his mother's.

"I have decided to be a lawyer," said Timothy after he had fastidiously brushed up the hearth. "You remember, Uncle John, that you told me that even a boy should consider his future."

"But I thought you wanted to be a financier, Timothy."

Timothy smiled, a reserved and secret smile. "I think that I'll be a lawyer for financiers," he said.

John thrust his hands into his pockets, a gesture he usually abhorred. But now it gave him a sense of lightness, of combativeness, of ease. He felt free.

"Good," he said, and did not mean it. He wished the boy would go. His presence was like something noxious in the room. His was not a clean ruthlessness. It reminded John of a place where quiet serpents lurked, of a place where discreet men talked in low voices, smoked expensive cigars, tried to outwit men like John Ames, and drank sherry and looked at each other with well-bred and evil glances, and had cuff links they had inherited from great-grandfathers. Oh yes, the Bourse, and the Reichsbank, and London. And of course St. Petersburg. But men like John Ames were not fooled by them and had weapons superior to theirs, forged of brutal iron.

Timothy stood before John Ames, not stiffly or awkwardly as most young boys stand, but with an adult restraint and poise. John, all at once, was uneasily impressed by a kind of potency the boy had, a stillness. Timothy said, "I've been reading some of Uncle Carlton's and Uncle Harper's lawbooks. They brought them to me. *Fundamentals of Law* and *Basic Law*. I am also taking Latin in school."

His young voice had a dry precision in it, and John was reminded of the London, Boston, and New York lawyers he knew who spoke exactly with those intonations. There was a quick itch between John's shoulders. The boy was definitely pernicious.

"Good," said John again. "But don't boys in your school play cricket— and things?" He had not the slightest idea what well-to-do boys did in their exclusive private schools.

"Yes. I am very good at those. Too," said Timothy with a slight smile. "After all, the other boys will be my clients. They like me."

John said, "Well, grow up fast, Timothy. I may need you myself."

Why couldn't the horrible boy smile as a boy smiled? Timothy did smile, but it was chill and accepting. He inclined his head. At that moment Cynthia rustled into the room, smiling. A faint frown wrinkled the smooth skin between her brows at the sight of her son, who bowed to her.

"Dear me, Timothy," she said. "I thought you were having your tea upstairs."

"I was going, Mother," he replied. He looked at Cynthia, and it was as though something like glass moved invisibly over his young and handsome face. Cynthia hesitated, then she kissed him quickly and gave a slight push. This was intended to impress him with the fact that he was still a child; it was also an attempt on the part of Cynthia to hide her aversion and to assert her authority. Timothy ignored the push; he bowed to John, then again to his mother, and walked with a stately grace out of the room.

"Dear me," sighed Cynthia. "Everyone tells me he is a most extraordinary boy, so good, so intelligent. His teachers just worship him. Now George was not in the least like him, nor am I. I just don't know where he came from!"

"He will be a great lawyer," said John gloomily. "The kind men like myself need; we give them retainers."

"They keep you out of trouble," Cynthia laughed. "Never mind. How distinguished you always look, John! If you were a lumberjack you'd still look distinguished."

If Timothy had been cut with dry steel-point, his mother had been cut with a flashing diamond. She literally sparkled from head to foot, from her formally dressed blond hair heaped in puffs and curls upon her small head to her pretty feet. There was a diamond bow in her hair, and her slippers twinkled with brilliants. A diamond chain hung about her neck and a large pear-shaped diamond dangled from it just where her full white breast began. She wore a gown of rose brocade, which twinkled when she moved; the hem, fluted, reminded John of the stola of Grecian women. The rear was gathered into a great and shimmering bustle. She had never appeared so beautiful to him, with her delicately flushed cheeks, her exquisite cheekbones, and her great gray eyes.

I've bought something admirable, thought John, appeased, and his desire came upon him again. He kissed her roughly. "Careful," said Cynthia, satisfied with the kiss. She lay back in the circle of his arms and looked at him with deep and passionate love.

"You know very well it isn't your birthday, Cynthia," John said as Cynthia sat down with a silken rustle.

"Of course I know," she said gaily. "But anything is an excuse for a party, isn't it? I am also having a birthday cake, with candles, for my fictitious birthday. After all, it is a day to celebrate."

His pleasure in her dropped. "In what way?" he asked. "Because I've just signed twenty-five thousand dollars a year over to you?"

She did not answer him for a moment. Her smile went away; she looked at him with intense gravity. Then she said in a low voice, "If that is the way it appears to you, what can I say?"

She made an effort to be lively again. She held out her arm to him, smiled once more, and said in a vivacious tone, "And look what you gave me for my birthday, dear John! Thank you so much. It's delightful."

She was showing him a bracelet he had not seen before, a wide bracelet crowded with diamonds so large and so bright that it was almost blinding. "And think of it," said Cynthia, "it cost only twelve thousand dollars! Isn't it a bargain?" She looked at him with a strange expression and repeated more slowly, "Isn't it a bargain—all of it?"

But he saw nothing but the bracelet and was aghast. He drew back from her; it was twilight now and the only brilliance in the room was Cynthia. "My God!" exclaimed John. "That is about half of what you still have in the bank and in your investments! Cynthia, you are a fool! You must take it back at once; you can't afford it."

She folded her hands in her lap and looked down at them. Now he could not see her face in the dimness. She said, "My bank account and my investments are still intact, what there is of them. I had the bill for this bracelet sent to your office, John, in Boston."

He was enraged. "And when I deduct the cost from the amount 'due' you this year, what will you have left? Twelve thousand dollars for twelve months——"

"Oh no," she said gently. "Don't you remember? You gave me this as my birthday present."

"You must think I'm an idiot!" he said violently, walking far away from her and looking back over his shoulder at her. The old and awful terror was on him again, the old dry sickness in the throat. "I can't afford such things, Cynthia. It's outrageous; it isn't in the contract."

"Contract?" she repeated.

"Yes, contract!" he shouted. "The trust is one thing. But this is outrageous. I won't stand for it, do you hear me? You'll buy what you need thriftily, out of income. And not a penny more!"

She lifted her arm and looked at the bracelet. "It's really beautiful," she said. "I always wanted it." Then she stood up.

John said with more violence, "Are you accustomed to accepting such things—from men? Do you know there is a name for a woman like that?"

"I don't accept 'things—from men,'" said Cynthia quietly. "I've never accepted anything, John, except flowers, or a pair of gloves, or some bibelot, as a gift from any of the gentlemen I know. A woman doesn't accept jewelry or money from men she doesn't love."

"And I suppose the men you—you——" He could not finish; he felt as if he were choking.

But the maid came in then to light the candles and the lamps and Cynthia watched her, as if every movement were important. The maid kept her head down but smirked under her nose; she could smell the violence and anger in the room. She lingered as long as possible. She wanted to hear more, but neither spoke until she had gone and softly closed the door behind her. Then Cynthia removed the bracelet from her arm and put it on the nearest table. "It doesn't belong to me any longer," she said in a low voice. "You didn't give it to me."

Then she added brightly, "Oh, I see some of our guests are coming. A carriage is drawing up outside." She touched the petit-point bell panel that hung near the fire. She rustled to the door, her face gleaming with smiles, and John hastily walked to the table and took the bracelet and put it in his pocket. He would return it tomorrow to the jeweler.

Cynthia's parties were noted for gaiety and charm and glitter. All who came were connoisseurs of fine food and wines, of art, of music, of sophisticated conversation. They bored John Ames to death; he endured them sullenly because at Cynthia's parties he frequently found men who could be profitable to him. It never occurred to him that Cynthia deftly arranged this. On the contrary, he often wondered why men of great affairs should be attracted to such frivolous gatherings.

He looked about him tonight. The room was alive with gems of many colors, Paris gowns of every hue, and a dozen pretty feminine faces. The men moved among these lovely creatures like sleek black seals in shining water. And everyone laughed and talked rapidly. It was very unlike most Boston parties John had attended. It reminded him of Paris, for no one talked of business, no group of men huddled together in the American manner, smoking and drinking privately and unaware of the women, impatient if one intruded. Cynthia's parties were distinguished for a Continental air, where women were cherished, their new gowns admired, and compliments made to them gallantly; where men discussed the newest additions to the Museum or talked easily of friends in London and Budapest and San Francisco and Berlin, and women chatted of Worth, the British royal family whose members were known to them, and also of the things which John Ames contemptuously labeled as "culture."

They had all met John Ames several times before, not only in Cynthia's house, but in their own offices and in his. Many of them disliked, feared, or hated him. They often wondered among themselves why Cynthia could stand him. He was no asset to any conversation; his handsome but gloomy face rarely smiled. He showed no appreciation for a special dish at the table. He never complimented a lady. He did not talk easily to anyone. Outside of his potency and his power to make or break a man, he was a clod, in the opinion of the gentlemen.

Gracious efforts at the table were made to draw him into the conversation for Cynthia's sake. They failed. He ate the splendid meal, so marvelously prepared and served, as if it were bread and cheese. He barely touched the wine. He stared straight ahead of him, in somber silence, opposite Cynthia. Yet it seemed that he did not even see her, and she had never looked so beautiful. She was pale, sometimes a little abstracted. Yet someone had only to speak to her to bring a flash of joy and affection and pleasure to her eyes; she replied always with wit and lightness. Mr. Clark Brittingham, a very eligible bachelor in his late thirties, was more than ever entranced with her. He turned his intelligent eyes on John and bit the corner of his groomed mustache. It was a nuisance, but this fellow stood as a sort of brother to Cynthia, and he must be approached. Tonight.

John, always so acutely perceptive, became aware of Mr. Brittingham's distasteful glances thrown at him along the table. He turned his head abruptly and looked at the other man with his hard blue eyes. Mr. Brittingham smiled at him pleasantly, and John forced himself to smile. Brittingham, he reflected, was the richest man present, with the exception of himself. He had given a vast gift to the Louvre in Paris, and in consequence he wore the red, blue, and white ribbon of the Legion of Honor. A Rembrandt? Yes. It has cost Mr. Brittingham some seventy-six thousand dollars, John remembered. Something tightened in John's throat, and for a moment the great and exquisite dining room was too hot for him, too airless. It reminded him of a fire; the fire hung before his eyes like a conflagration. He moved restlessly in his chair. He made himself think of the business he had done with Mr. Brittingham, one of the most prosperous pieces of business in his life.

Now all at the table rose; the gentlemen were bowing, with the exception of John, for the ladies were preparing to "retire" and leave the gentlemen alone with their brandy for a little while. The room rustled with silk; there was a fairy tinkling of bracelets, earrings, and necklaces. Then the ladies moved from the room like tall and sparkling birds of many colors, and the door closed after them. The gentlemen sat down. John sat among them like a statue. He hated this period. No one would talk business. It was not proper, according to these idiots. They would only eye him out of the corners of their eyes. Be sure they were thinking of business, though they would not mention it! John seethed with contempt. He would be visited by at least three tomorrow; he already had made appointments.

It was very ridiculous. When these men sat in his office the elegance disappeared, the extreme courtesy, the oblique and graceful phrase. Then they were as blunt as stone and as avaricious as tigers, and even their faces were entirely different. It was as if their very flesh became heavier, their expressions grosser. There was no talk of art and "culture" then! It was gold, and gold only, and be damned to know how it was to be acquired. Prentice, there, sitting down with a cultivated smile: he and his father had made most of their money "blackbirding." Cynthia would call him a murderer, and it was quite true. And there was Vaughn: he had made several fortunes smuggling arms to the South in his fleet of fast clippers in the late war. Vaughn was an abolitionist: he had been a colonel in the Union Army and had many decorations, including one from Lincoln himself.

The conversation flowed about and around him, and it was as if he were surrounded by ghosts who did not know he was even there. But he knew very acutely that they were aware of him, and weighing him, and wondering

41

how they could use him, and hating and fearing and furtively admiring him. He was not a "gentleman" to them. He had no proper background; he was a nobody; no one knew from where he came; he had no family. He had sprung from nowhere, powerful, ruthless, even terrible, and they preferred not to think of him when they were not doing business.

The Franco-Prussian War was remarked upon at the table with serious expressions and head-shakings, then dismissed. But tomorrow it would be talked of exclusively—in his office. God damn them, thought John Ames, seeing in his mind now the avid eyes he would see tomorrow, the tight lips, the moisture on foreheads.

The gentlemen prepared to join the ladies. John had not said twenty words. And he had spoken these only to Harper Bothwell, who was content with the family fortune as it was. He had many stories to relate about courtroom episodes, and they had been much enjoyed. Harper and the other gentlemen moved toward the door, and John followed them. Then he felt a discreet plucking at his arm and turned to see Clark Brittingham smiling at him. "A moment, John," he murmured.

John pulled his sleeve away rudely. "I can spare you half an hour at two tomorrow," he said with curtness.

"I'm sorry. But this isn't business, John. It's a private affair."

Mr. Brittingham waited until they were alone. "Dash it," he added with a rueful smile, and repeating a British phrase which he had acquired, "it'll only take a moment. These formalities! They aren't even necessary, but one has to think of Cynthia."

"What has Cynthia got to do with it?"

"Everything. Oh, I suppose I shouldn't be bothering you. These proprieties! But I think Cynthia would prefer it this way, as you are her brother-in-law and she has no other mature relatives."

"Well?" John stood away from him stiffly.

"I've always wanted Cynthia," said Clark Brittingham. "I wanted to marry her before she married that simpering fool of a George Winslow. How a girl of Cynthia's intelligence and discrimination could have married him is one of those mysteries we're always encountering, isn't it? Thankfully, he removed himself in a blaze of glory, if one can use a cliché. I see you're impatient. I'll come to the point. I want to marry Cynthia; I've wanted to marry her since we were children in dancing school. Do you know?"

He smiled reminiscently.

John could only glare at him in absolute astonishment.

"My father," went on Mr. Brittingham, "wanted to arrange the marriage with old Esmond. The Esmonds were just a cut above the Brittinghams, though they did not have as much money. It was a social privilege to be invited to their exclusive affairs. And the girls! What beauties! They could have married anybody——"

Then Mr. Brittingham flushed deeply. He had just remembered that Ann Esmond had married this blackguard, this nobody, this man without family or schools or background. He went on hastily, cursing himself, "When they came out it wasn't only a Boston affair; it concerned a dozen cities, and even Paris and London. They were presented at Court, you know. All fuss and feathers."

Mr. Brittingham drew a deep breath and stood up straighter. Let the bounder say what he willed. Cynthia was no longer a girl; she was a widow and had a son. She could make her own decision. "In short," he said coolly, "I want your permission to marry Cynthia. Oh, I understand your permission isn't necessary. But I think Cynthia would like it."

John averted his face. It was impossible. Brittingham was fabulously rich; he was a close friend of the Belmonts and the Vanderbilts. His fortune was respected even in Europe, where his name was well known. He, John, must enlighten this pretentious imbecile.

"I think you ought to know," he said in a harsh voice, "that Cynthia has no money beyond a mere twenty-six thousand dollars or so. She spent it all," he went on, throwing the words at Mr. Brittingham. "She's very extravagant; she hasn't the slightest idea about money and what it means."

"I know," said Mr. Brittingham with a smile that John considered idiotic. "That's part of her charm. And who's more charming than Cynthia? The Esmonds had a great distaste for money; it was never mentioned in their house. Old Esmond was a gentleman of the old school." In saying this he deliberately excluded John from the company of those who could have understood Cynthia's father.

"I want to give Cynthia everything I have," said Mr. Brittingham. "I can even reconcile myself to Timothy, who is not exactly the most ingratiating boy in the world. I want Cynthia for my wife. I want her to have everything she wishes. She adorns everything she does."

John spoke with an effort. "Have you asked her yourself?"

"Yes. And she always eluded me in that graceful way of hers. She's like sunlight—you know. I see I am getting fatuous. I don't know what I'll do if she won't marry me."

He spoke with quiet intensity, and looking into his small brown eyes, John knew that he spoke the truth. He said, "Don't worry about Cynthia's financial state, which you seem to know. I just settled twenty-five thousand dollars a year on her for life. After all, she is my wife's sister."

Mr. Brittingham raised his eyebrows. "Really. How generous of you. But Cynthia won't need that when she marries me. Very generous. But completely unnecessary when Cynthia marries me. May we consider it concluded, then?"

John was silent.

"I'll speak to Cynthia tomorrow," said Mr. Brittingham with determination. "I don't mean to be offensive, but whether you give your formal consent or not tonight doesn't matter. There are a dozen men like myself who want to marry Cynthia, and I must hurry and be there first, with emphasis. That is why I asked you for your permission."

"And if I don't consent?"

"Then be damned to you," said Mr. Brittingham with cool simplicity. "I'll just keep after Cynthia until she marries me."

He looked John up and down as if he were observing a very low fellow. Then he turned and walked out of the room, leaving John alone near the cluttered table of silver, flowers, damask, and glass, all shining under the enormous crystal chandelier.

Cynthia had not lied after all. She could marry Brittingham; she could marry others. She could be the social leader of leaders, not only in Boston, but in other cities. Yet she had chosen to give herself to him, John Ames, without marriage. She would put herself in a very scandalous position. John shook his head dazedly. All at once he was aware of the weight of the bracelet in his pocket, a single bracelet. Brittingham would be happy to buy her a dozen of these, and more, and give her his name.

CHAPTER FOUR

The ladies were grouped about Cynthia in the drawing room, standing in postures of ecstasy, hands clasped, heads bent, and Cynthia, all triumph, was bending over a large chair on which she had placed a framed canvas. Now the gentlemen merged with the ladies and there were exclamations. Cynthia looked about her, peering over Mr. Brittingham's shoulder. "Oh, John!" she cried. "You must come and see! I've been keeping this a surprise for you, but I could not—I could not hold it hidden until Christmas. I just had to show everyone."

John had been standing in the doorway. Every head turned to him and every face smiled. "Lucky dog," said Harper Bothwell. "Not everybody gets such a gift."

"Oh, I'm keeping it for myself, in a way," said Cynthia, laughing. "Of course it will be John's, but I have just the spot for it, right over there near the south window. You see how greedy I am?"

John approached slowly, seeing no one but Cynthia. Her face was illuminated with pleasure and excitement. Cynthia seized his hand and pulled him playfully to the chair. "Look, isn't it magnificent, and yet isn't it terribly sad and just a little frightful? I was so lucky to get it. There are only twenty unsold, and I'm ashamed to say what I paid for it. It will be worth a fortune in a few years; in fact, it's a fortune even now!"

What did a damned picture matter? Every wall was crowded with pictures. Then he looked down at the picture, and he was sick. He remembered it very well; he thought it had been destroyed with all the others; he had believed that not a single one had remained.

It was not an exceptionally large painting; it could not have been more than three feet square. It was of a new style called "impressionistic," and when a few paintings in this style had first been on display in the Boston Museum there had been some well-bred rioting and many indignant epithets. There had been angry cries of "degenerate art, caricature, unrealistic, mad, crude, illiterate drawing and painting, thick-colored porridge thrown

on with a palette knife, barbaric, an insult to nature and all true artists!"
Newspapers had written stern editorials; art critics had ridiculed; there was
not a tea or dinner where this "outrage" was not discussed in firm voices
and denounced.

Cynthia's acquisition was of this impressionistic style. The artist had
painted a scene that consisted only of a dark range of chaotic purple hills,
blurred as if glimpsed through a curtain of rain. The sky above them loomed
with strange cloud-shapes, apocalyptic and threatening, touched with sharp
fire in the gray hollows, prophetic with vague and enormous faces. The
foreground undulated in a dim yet savage green, a boundless wilderness
without trees or flowers, and scattered only with grotesque boulders thrown
by a giant. A man walked on it, a small figure against all that palpable and
frightening color, all that pressing silence, all that majestic and menacing
sky, all those broken purple hills. It was hard to tell if the figure was a man or
a boy; the artist had managed to suggest both age and youth in the uncertain body in its dull clothes. The face could not be clearly seen; it was partly
turned away, the eyes blindfolded, the strong arms outstretched, groping.

When John Ames had first seen this thing—which had horrified him—
the artist had smiled at him pleadingly and his hazel eyes had been sad.
"Don't be like this, Jack," he had said. "Before God, don't be blind like this.
Look. See. For your soul's sake."

John had stepped back, repelled and full of hate, and he had said nothing.
The hate was with him again. It was monstrous. It was as if some evil he
thought had long been destroyed had resurrected itself and was confronting
him again. But there was not only this, there were nineteen more, unsold.

"I see you're overcome, John," said Harper Bothwell. "And I don't blame
you. Magnificent. Even though it's a gloomy theme and unlike the artist's
usual luminous colors, it's compelling, vital. Not calculated, like Seurat. It's
full of emotion."

"I admit I'm not taken with these impressionistic painters," said Mr.
Prentice. "But you have to agree they've brought a new dimension to art.
Positive color, sensation, brilliance. Not realistic, of course, but——"

"John," said Cynthia, her smile disappearing, "don't you like it?"

"Ames," said Harper with enthusiasm, and he turned to John with a
smile. "Any relative of yours?"

"No," said John. His left hand clenched against his side. "No."

"Don't tease John," said Cynthia, looking at John searchingly. "David
Ames came from Genesee, New York State. And John's from Boston.
Dear John. Don't you like your Christmas present?"

He had attracted the attention of the others; he could see the ring of
faces too closely, too highly colored.

"I—I am afraid I am no judge of art," he said dully.

"This is art at its greatest," said Harper Bothwell with envy. "Cynthia, if
John doesn't like it, I will give you twice as much as you paid for it."

"Then you'll pay me eight thousand dollars," said Cynthia. She was still
studying John with anxiety. "But it's not for sale. I had no sooner bought

it than a man from the New York Metropolitan Museum of Art asked me to sell it to him for ten thousand, and I would not. I love Ames' pictures. They don't speak; they cry out."

"I wonder who that poor clod is pictured there," said Mr. Prentice, pointing to the blind figure.

"All of us, to a certain extent," said Mr. Brittingham.

Ten thousand dollars. Ten thousand dollars—offered. John found himself breathing with difficulty; his bones seemed to be trembling in his flesh. Hatred sickened him. Ten thousand dollars—offered—for this daub, this vicious and stupid thing, this ridiculous crudity. It had first been offered for fifteen dollars, to pay a month's grocery bill. And it had been refused.

He could remember everything so clearly, for he could never forget it. His mother, Cecilia Ames, had been buried only two days. No one knew where her husband was, "that crazy painter who bought that run-down Schmidt place where you couldn't raise an ear of corn. He runs off for weeks at a time. Didn't he go once to Mexico and come back with pictures good enough just for hanging on a barn or in a field to scare the crows? You'd think he'd try to raise chickens or a few hogs so his kid and his wife would have something to eat once in a while instead of running into debt at the general store for a little salt pork and bread."

Cecilia Ames had literally died of starvation in the shaggy old farmhouse in the winter, when there was no fuel except for what her son could obtain by chopping down dead trees for the fire. She had been a gentle, silent woman. She had tried to plant a vegetable garden, but she was city-born and -bred, and so was her son. The resulting vegetables were dwarfed and meager. Frail and uncomplaining, she scrubbed to the last pushing of her strength, but the ancient house sifted dust and grit, and the bare planks of the floor breathed out dust at every step. John could remember that house well. His terror, his unending fear, his unspeakable humiliation, his hopelessness, and his hatred had been born here. But more than all else, his fear, which would never leave him, which was sleepless and lay down with him at night and rose with him in the morning. He had been fourteen years old. He and his mother lived on the little he could earn in the village four miles away, cleaning out stables, mending chimneys, currying horses, shoveling snow, washing windows, and many other chores. Some weeks he could earn nothing at all. He remembered the faces. . . .

He had been alone with his mother when she died. He had held her in his arms. The dying had not been hard, only the living. She had merely drawn one deep breath and then was still. She was so light in his arms, for there was little flesh on her patrician bones. He had laid her down very carefully, as though afraid those bones would break and a broken thing would be lying on that bed with its ragged blankets. Then he had walked through the hip-high snow to the village for the doctor, under a moon of ice, in a silence that enveloped him like death. His mother had been buried near a fence in the "poor corner" of the small graveyard, and there was no marking on her grave, not even now. For she had never lived in that house where she had died; she had only been exiled there. Her son worked in the village for two months to pay for her grave, a matter of twenty dollars, which included her bare wooden coffin. Then he had gone away and never returned.

Yes, he remembered the night of her death very well; he remembered her burial. He had been alone afterward in that forlorn old farmhouse for two days. The old minister who had quavered his prayers at the grave of Mrs. David Ames had taken pity on her son and offered him temporary shelter. But John remained in the house for those two days, a boy of fourteen, wild with hatred. His father had been away two months. He had not even written his wife or sent her any money, possibly for the reason that he never had any money, he who once had been invited to Albany to be on the staff of the state prosecuting attorney.

Alone, John in his agony of mind and his rage of spirit remembered the barn where his father stored his unsold canvases and where he often added finishing touches to them. The barn began to loom before him as a dread thing. He built a fire on the cold hearth of the almost unfurnished living room, and he lit a long thick stick in it. He then went out to the barn and set it on fire. He watched it blaze. He felt that in that barn lived all the evil which had killed his mother, which had brought unsleeping agony and shame and hunger to him. He would kill the thing once and for all.

David Ames had kept all his unsold canvases but one there because his wife, who had been a Hollingshead of Albany, shuddered at the sight of them. A promising young lawyer, he had met her in her father's house; the walls had been weighted with paintings by distinguished and formal artists. They had made him shudder, just as his own paintings had made his wife shudder. But it was in that house that he had known, like one giving instant, large, and spontaneous birth, the desire, the impelling need, to paint, the conviction that there was nothing else of value in the world.

The boy, John Ames, hugging himself in his thin and mended clothing, warmed himself at the conflagration he had created and laughed with hysterical joy. The leaping flames climbed the old gray walls; they caught on rubbish, devouring and chattering; they roared through the opened door. They soared against the black sky, blotting out the moon. They shouted and streamed in the winter wind. The fire stank of rotted wood, of paint, of straw burning, of death.

Almost beside himself, the boy did not at first hear the shouting of a man. But the shouts came nearer. Dazed with his almost voluptuous rapture, he turned his head. His father, carrying his cardboard suitcase, was floundering up the hill toward him, snow spraying in red-tinged clouds about his stocky figure, his panting breath audible even above the sound of the fire. And then he had stood twenty feet away and looked at the barn. He made no outcry now. The snow heaved like marble about him; his square face fluttered with the dancing crimson.

The man and his son stood there in utter silence, watching the barn. The roof fell in, and scarlet sparks blew upward like a fountain of terrible light, like fireworks, like the pyre of a giant. David Ames never spoke again; he never voluntarily moved again. He watched the end of his work, the end of some hundred canvases, the end of his life. Without even a sigh he sank down into the snow and died.

They found one hundred dollars in his purse. No one knew where it had come from, and no one cared. Twenty dollars of it was taken for his grave, a considerable distance from the grave of the wife he had not known had died before him. The rest was given to John, his son. John had paid the grocery bill of twenty dollars; he had paid his mother's doctor. He had bought himself some warm clothing. There was nothing left but the debt of his mother's funeral, and he worked in the village until he could repay that debt. He had not thought of himself as being the cause of his father's death. But when he went away he carried David Ames' self-portrait with him as a reminder, as a warning, as an object to inspire courage, as the source of his strength—for he had resolved never to be poor again.

He never forgot. He had thought that all but what he had of his father's work had been burned in that holocaust. But some had escaped. That was probably the source of the mysterious one hundred dollars which had been found on David Ames' short and stocky body. That money had brought him immortality, for it had saved those canvases.

Ten thousand dollars—offered.

He said to Cynthia now as she linked her arm in his and gazed at him with increasing anxiety, "You should have taken that ten thousand dollars, Cynthia. Yes, you should have taken it."

Cynthia sold it. If John detested it so much, she thought with regret, then it must not be where he would be confronted with it in this house. Harper Bothwell bought it. He hung it over his Adam mantelpiece and he lent it out on exhibition. He was offered twenty thousand dollars for it a few years later and refused. He would often stand below the painting and look up at it and wonder of whom it reminded him.

CHAPTER FIVE

Caroline Ames loved the autumn of the year. She knew that many people preferred the spring and spoke of it as being hopeful. But she was never so hopeful as in the autumn, and she could not explain it to anyone. She had read somewhere: "The seed is the prophecy of the tree." Seeds came only at this time of the year. When Beth Knowles complained that autumn was only "the beginning of those awful winters," Caroline thought of it as the busiest time of all the months. Under the warm brown silence of the days she sometimes believed she could hear the bustlings of seeds settling down in the earth, the hurrying of nature to prepare plants and flowers for the next year. She watched squirrels scuttling to bury nuts, half of which they would never remember; she thought of the trees that would arise from the buried treasure of life, the first tiny saplings that would appear in the spring. There was a secret excitement in the quiet air, a kind of authoritarian housekeeping filled with competent voices directing how each thing must be prepared, how each ordered. Without autumn, there would be no more springs.

It was early October. There would be a note for her from Tom Sheldon discreetly enclosed in a letter to "my dear friend, Mrs. Knowles." The girl did not understand or even know of this discretion, but it had been arranged by Tom and Beth five years ago. "You never know about Mr. Ames," Beth had told Tom. "He doesn't want poor Carrie ever to have any friends. He thinks they're a waste of time."

As there was no preparatory school in Lyndon, which was an old and very poor outlying town near Boston and engaged only in industries, mainly textile, in which young children and men and women were employed, Caroline now attended a drab private school in an ancient house occupied by an elderly woman in reduced circumstances. Miss Brownley taught girls, some twenty-five of them ranging from fourteen to seventeen, and it was her positive opinion that young ladies needed to know nothing more than how to walk properly, how to play the piano with élan, how to engage in "edifying conversation," how to greet and how to depart, how to conduct oneself in the drawing room, how to adjust to something she ominously called necessity, how to dance with propriety, how not to dress "to attract vulgar attention," how to modulate one's voice, how not to offend anyone under any circumstances, and how to write the most elegant copperplate. Her young ladies were drawn from the families of rising factory managers, rather unsuccessful lawyers and doctors practicing in Lyndon, and daughters of "old" families as "reduced" as she was herself. She maintained quite a delicate but firm distinction between the girls of "new people" and those with "background." This made for cliques, backbiting, snubs and coldness, and the cruel rivalries which only women understand. Caroline was aware of cliques and inner circles; she was part of neither and rejected by all. She had accepted this as one of the peculiar aspects of her existence and bore no malice.

She was known to be the daughter of the ambiguous John Ames, who was rarely in Lyndon. He was reputed to be very wealthy. None of the girls believed it. Caroline's clothing was certainly not that of a rich man's daughter. Her shabbiness aroused laughter among her schoolmates, who did not fail to point out to her that the elbows of her drooping wool frocks and her meager coats were obviously darned and patched, that her shoes were cheap and that she wore, at fifteen, heavy cotton stockings instead of lisle or even silk. But more than all else, it was less than tactfully called to her attention that she had no beauty, no presence, no grace. None of this depressed Caroline, for so far as she was concerned the girls were only frivolous annoyances. Her realities were her father, Beth Knowles, Tom Sheldon, and the moldering library of the house in Lyndon. These were her life, not tossing curls, not dances, not gay trippings in the narrow halls of the house of her teacher, not fluttering dresses and dainty slippers, not fashion and style, not rings and bracelets, not secrets whispered in class and the exchange of notes. Above all, not carriages bringing the other girls to school. She walked the four miles to Miss Brownley's house and walked them home, and the weather was of no physical concern to her. Walking was an adventure. The girls declared she skulked and was ashamed of her wretched state and pretended to pity her.

Caroline believed herself ugly and was not disturbed by it. Tom Sheldon liked her. He did more than like her; he loved her. He was nearly eighteen now, and he wrote her of "the day when we'll be married." He never failed to write of her beautiful eyes. "A lady on one of the canal ships had a big topaz ring on her finger, and it was just like your eyes, Carrie, all full of brown light and twinkles. I sure wanted to see you again right away when I saw that ring." And Beth had told her roundly, "If men married only pretty and beautiful girls, the world wouldn't have many people in it, believe me! You have to have something else, and I call it spirit."

Caroline was not sure what spirit was. Was it what poor old dead Kate had called character? Was it intelligence? The girls at school, whom she hardly noticed, possessed neither of these things. Caroline often wondered if she did, and she would reread all of Tom's letters, looking for enlightenment. Tom loved her, though she was stocky and clumsy and could never talk very well and there was no curl in the long hair as black and fine as straight silk and her clothes were coarse and mended. Therefore, she must have "spirit." She was surprised to find that she was not entirely satisfied. Her Aunt Cynthia had recently adopted a little girl, and Melinda was very beautiful, almost as beautiful as Cynthia, for all she had been taken from an orphanage and had no family. Melinda was now four, a grave little girl who was nearly as silent as Caroline. But sometimes she would laugh, and the laugh tinkled and her gray eyes shone.

The Ames house in Lyndon stood on five acres of wooded land, wild and unkempt, for old Jim would do only sporadic gardening. He did keep an area about the house free of tall grass and fallen branches, but he never bothered with flowers; the family was away at the seashore from early June to the first of October. As he never planted seed, obstinately insisting that was Nature's job, the cleared grass was coarse, heavy, and full of pigweed with thick branching leaves. He took care of the rig and the elderly horse and used it only when Beth went on shopping errands or he was to meet "the master" at the station. Occasionally, with languor, he would wash windows grown dull with summer dust and rain or winter sleet, leaving, as Beth said irascibly, a worse smudge than before. But he was an old man; he helped Beth inside the house and complained constantly about the amount of wood she used in the ancient black iron stove and in the living-room fireplace. He liked the stable best, where he could talk to the horse and congratulate him that he was used so seldom and needed very little currying. Then he would swipe at the old rig with a dirty cloth, sit down in a rocking chair, and sleep. He disliked everyone except Caroline, whom he would entertain with hoary but fascinating stories. He was part

Negro; his stories often had the richness of rain forests dripping in green dusk under a hot equatorial sun or the mystery of those who lived half of their conscious lives in a state of awed wonder. He had been a slave.

Jim called the Ames house a mansion, which it was not and which it had never been. It was not in a good section of town; beyond the wooden fence, which was the only article Jim kept in perfect order and strength, stood shacks, working people's little homes, full of children and noise and fury and drunken shouts on Saturday nights, and gloomy factories constantly increasing. But the house lay in a kind of somber enchantment of its own among its old and rotting trees, hidden from the sight and sound of neighbors. It had been built long ago, and no one knew who had been its original owner. Of dull red brick overgrown with glossy green ivy, it stood tall and thin, three stories high, with a widow's walk on the top story, though the house was far from the sea. It had long windows as thin as splinters, and brown shutters and brown doors, all moldering. A path led from the locked gate and served as both walk and drive and was narrow and dusty and without gravel or stone, the earth hard-packed in summer and greasy with sliding brown mud in the winter. Once Jim had caught three little boys climbing the cronelike apple trees in the autumn and devouring the wormy fruit. They had evidently bolted over the high gate with its sharp points. He drove them off savagely and reinspected the gate and tested its bolts. Sometimes John Ames wondered acridly at this. A slave, of all people, should detest both fences and gates after he was free.

Caroline pushed open the well-oiled iron gate, for it was always unlocked for her near the time of her return from school. Carefully she locked it behind her. She liked to walk alone to the house, especially on warm brown-and-golden autumn days like this. It was always damp under the arching trees, now yellow, ocher, and umbrous, with a flare now and again of some scarlet maple, like the beginning of a conflagration in this moldy and silent place. Caroline could smell the poignant and atavistic heaps of rotting leaves, the primeval earth sweating in its darkness, the sharp breath of an occasional spruce. Sometimes she would sit on a flat stone and watch squirrels and birds, or catch the flash of a skunk's tail or the white fluff of a rabbit or the blur of a mouse rushing from one pile of leaves to another. It was so quiet here; the rumble of factories in the distance only increased the stillness, like thunder over a closed landscape.

Sitting on the stone today, Caroline sighed and smiled a little. A soft wind, heavy with the pungent scent of decay and loneliness, brushed her face; her hands, lying on her knees, were dappled thinly by the leaves remaining on the trees which arched over her. Her solid feet rested on the dark and oily earth. She let herself luxuriate in the thought of the letter waiting for her in the house. Though she could not as yet see the house, she could smell the burning of wood.

Poor Beth; it was warm today, but Beth, who was so fearful of the coming winter, had defiantly started fires. "You never know when the weather will change," she would say with a challenge in her blue eyes. She was approaching fifty; her crisp and curling hair was almost gray, and, though plump, she shivered in a cool wind. Old Kate was dead, and Beth knew that only she would stay in this lonely and sifting house with all the dull and inexplicable echoes in the narrow halls, the tall and half-empty rooms and bedrooms, the brick-walled and brick-floored kitchen, the black iron fireplaces, the cracked and warped doors, the primitive facilities, the ceilings broken and yellowed, the walls papered with paper so old that the original patterns had gone, leaving only spidery tracings and no color except what age had given it, the floors carpeted with rugs that no amount of sweeping would clean, and all of the carpeting of a dim brownish tint as rough to a bare foot as gravel. So Beth had her fires sulkily, even when John Ames was at home, which was increasingly at longer intervals. She had even moved some of the furniture from several of the eight uninhabited bedrooms (Jim, by choice, slept in the loft in the barn) into the rooms used by Caroline and herself, and had shaken her head over chairs slippery with age and worn of fabric, and beds with towering carved headboards that reached to the ceilings. With Jim's grumbling help she had tugged at marble-topped tables to move them into the two bedrooms and had looked with discouragement at stone cracked and filled with ancient dirt. But there were no ornaments anywhere. Eventually, out of her own money, Beth had bought two cheap green vases "in town," one for herself and one for Caroline's room, and she kept them filled with cattails, which she gilded or painted, or wild spring or autumn flowers she found on the land. When all but the cattails, which Caroline loathed, failed, Beth would make artificial flowers of coarse colored paper and dip them in paraffin to last through the dark winter. She thought it made matters cozy; Caroline would look at them and shudder, but she never told Beth, who had gone to such trouble for her.

Beth had bullied John Ames into permitting her to buy clean cheap muslin for her bedroom windows and Caroline's. These she had tinted pink, which Caroline also loathed. But all of the other windows were hung with decaying brown velveteen draperies, dejected and dusty and tattered. Finally Beth stopped her desperate work of mending them; let them rot, she would say grimly, then *he'll* notice. But John Ames apparently did not notice, and no guests ever came to make invidious remarks. The house stood in its ugly decay, its breathless isolation, its silence, its utter abandonment. It was in this horrible place, Beth would reflect, that the young Ann Ames had died, far from family and friends, far from the beautiful house in which she had been born and in which she had lived for twenty years. How could she have endured it? Beth would ask herself.

Beth could not understand Caroline's love for the house and its snarled acres, and Caroline, who could never express herself well, could not tell her only confidante what this silent isolation meant to her and what relief and surcease there were among the desolate trees. For here, where no one came but her dreams and the remembrances of Jim's eerie stories, she could be free, no longer stiff with awkwardness as she was in school, no longer frightened as she was on the streets of Lyndon. Here she could think of herself as beautiful and beloved, surrounded by creatures as shy as herself.

"It's bad for a young girl to have no friends," Beth would say crossly. Caroline would not reply but would touch Beth's plump arm quickly. She could not tell Beth that she had multitudes of companions in the small woods and endless multitudes of dreams.

After a while Caroline left the stone and absently brushed some dried fragments of leaves from her coarse brown woolen frock and went toward the house on the winding and overgrown path. Dust followed her in a golden cloud; she looked back at it with delight. A blue jay, like an azure arrow, flashed across her way and perched on a tree limb and squawked at her. She nodded and spoke to him as to an old friend, and he yawned and began to groom himself, unafraid of this human creature who never shouted or threatened. Caroline stopped to look; the red of the maple leaves behind that quiveringly alive blue being enchanted her. He was bluer than the autumn sky shining through the leaves. He and his companions would remain here during the winter, a cerulean visitation flitting above the incandescent snow, calling attention to a rare fox with an outcry that strangely increased the cold fire of the immaculate day.

Caroline pulled the brown and green wool tam-o'-shanter from her head so that the pungent wind could touch the thin black braids which she now wore bound tightly about her round skull. Her eyes were tawny and vivid under their black brows. When she smiled, her big white teeth flashed. The large freckles on her coarse nose gave a piquancy to her appearance which only Beth and Tom Sheldon appreciated. When she was alone like this, the clumsy stockiness of her body seemed to disappear; she walked swiftly and lightly. She saw a thousand shadings of entrancing color everywhere. She longed to capture them in her hands and hold them always. She wanted to fix them, not only in her mind, but in time.

Miss Brownley had taught her to paint correctly in water colors, but the tints were too anemic for Caroline, though she did not know why they distressed her. Somewhere, she knew, lived rich colors to match those she saw, colors so vivid that the soul would never tire of them. She had not as yet been to the Boston Museum. The only paintings she had ever seen were Miss Brownley's pallid water colors framed on yellowish walls, depicting curiously bloodless butterflies hovering over deathly sprays of pale lilacs, or tiny landscapes so muted that it took considerable peering to distinguish them as more than feeble blurs. Caroline's whole spirit yearned for intense hues and riot; she saw more than mere colors; she saw the joyous and powerful emotion in them. They were eloquent, singing, dazzling. All this was impossible to communicate to Beth.

Beth had bought the bow of bright scarlet ribbon which tied Caroline's flat black braids to her head. Caroline took it off now, to hold it rapturously in her hand. She would lift it to compare it with a living red leaf. But she was never satisfied. The dead fabric could not duplicate the vital hue. However, she was grateful for the ribbon; it was a tongue of flame in her hand. She swung it like a narrow pennant about her.

Ugly and monstrous though her home was, Caroline, oddly, did not find it so. The browns and stained whites did not revolt her. Her father lived here, and he was enough to give all this a passion of its own. So the girl was humming and smiling when she opened the cracked door that led into the boxed hall with its gloomy oak staircase winding upward to the second, and then to the third, floor. There was no carpeting here, and Beth had long ago given up trying to polish the planked wood. There was a smell in the house like old raspberries, musty and pervading. The light of the autumn did not reach here; all was brown, chill, and dim. Caroline ran into the kitchen, where the heat from the huge black stove almost suffocated her. But there was a fragrance of soup and boiling meat and newly baked apple pie and cheese. Beth had become chronically sulky these past years, but when she saw Caroline her round face with its network of fine wrinkles smiled. She turned her plump body and waved at the girl with a big wooden spoon.

"You're late, dear," she said.

"Oh, I stopped in the woods for a while," Caroline hesitated. Her eager eyes searched Beth's face, and Beth stopped smiling. "There wasn't a letter today, dear," she said with regret. "But sometimes they're late. There'll be one tomorrow, you'll see."

"Tom must be up near Syracuse by now," said Caroline, the hope gone from her strong young voice. She put her books on the bare wooden table and looked down at them.

"I've just made a pie," said Beth encouragingly. "Our own apples." She grimaced. "The birds and the bugs got at them worse this year than ever. But I did save a few, and the pie's nice. Sit down and have a piece while it's hot. And there's some cheese for it. I bought the cheese to catch the mice, but it isn't too bad. Old Tabby's too rheumatic now to help out much."

Caroline sat down. The sad lump in her breast was very heavy.

"I forgot to tell you," said Beth grimly, though she had not forgotten at all. "Your dad's home; got in unexpected an hour ago. He's in the library. He wants to see you at five. Precisely, he said," and Beth mimicked, without charity, John Ames' sharp cold accents.

Joy broke over Caroline's face like a brilliant wave, and for a few moments she was beautiful, her eyes like tawny light. "Papa!" she cried. "But he wasn't expected back from New York for a week!" She paused and clutched the edges of the scarred table. "You said he *wants* to see me? He *wants* to——"

"That's what he said," replied Beth with dryness. But she was full of pity.

"I wonder why," Caroline marveled. The sadness was gone. "Beth, I do want some of that wonderful pie of yours; it smells like perfume."

"And I have some hot coffee," said Beth, glancing at the girl tenderly. "And even some cream." She stopped in her bustling to touch Caroline's big head. The braids had slipped when the ribbon was removed; now they fell down Caroline's broad back. The high-buttoned collar of her brown frock obliterated what little there was of her short strong neck. The fold under her chin was as browned by the sun as was the rest of her square face. Caroline beamed at Beth. "How good you are to me, Beth. You're just like a mother."

Caroline felt with certainty that there would be a letter for her from Tom tomorrow. It was good to have another happiness waiting for her as well as the one in the library. She did not see the easy tears in Beth's emotional eyes, nor hear her sigh. She ate the good pie and sighed with pleasure, for it was spiced with cinnamon and laced with honey and had a sugary crust. "Papa will like this," she murmured through a mouthful.

"Papa's going to Boston after he sees you," said Beth shortly. "About six. On the train."

"Oh," said Caroline. She put down the fork and felt surfeited. "He has so much business in Boston," she said valorously. "And he does so much for poor Aunt Cynthia and Timothy and Melinda." She reflected that her father seemed particularly fond of Melinda, who was so beautiful.

"Especially for poor Aunt Cynthia," said Beth wryly.

Caroline nodded vigorously. "That's because she reminds him so much of poor Mama, Beth."

"Of course," said Beth.

Caroline glanced repeatedly at the old wooden clock on the brick wall. It was a quarter past four. Had it stopped? No, it was ticking loudly. The fire in the stove crackled; Caroline could see its redness in the cracks about the iron plates. "I haven't seen Timothy since last Easter," said Caroline, who was afraid of her cousin.

"Good thing," said Beth, who had seen the boy several times. "I never did like that one. He's like an ice splinter."

"Well," said Caroline. "I guess we just don't understand people like Timothy. And doesn't he look like Aunt Cynthia? Melinda does too."

"Yes, doesn't she?" muttered Beth, slapping the lid back on the soup. "You'd think she was her own daughter."

"Even her eyes and the color of her hair!" said Caroline, who admired Melinda very much. "Aunt Cynthia dresses her beautifully."

"Just like she was her daughter," said Beth with an angry knot in her throat. "Yes indeed."

"Melinda looks like the portrait of Mama and Aunt Cynthia in Aunt Cynthia's house," said Caroline, thinking of the lovely little girl and how wonderful it would be to paint her in living color.

"Yes indeed," said Beth, and slammed the spoon on the iron sink which had a pump attached.

"I like Melinda," said Caroline, drinking her steaming coffee. "She goes to a nice school, too."

"The very best. Miss Stockington's, Carrie. It would be nice if you could go there too."

"Oh no," said Caroline, shocked. "I'd be out of place." She added, "And Papa can't afford it."

"Yes indeed," said Beth sullenly, and crashed the oven door. "Papa can't afford it. But Mrs. Winslow can afford Groton for Timothy and Miss Stockington's for little Melinda, who isn't yet five years old."

"I saw Melinda in the school play last Christmas," said Caroline. "I wish I were an artist! I'd paint Melinda in green light, with her yellow hair and her big gray eyes, with a black kitten on her lap, and there'd be sunshine sloping down through the trees and making the trees look emerald and very dark green with bright flecks of gold."

Beth thought of the portrait lying in an old trunk at Lyme, and she turned and stared at Caroline, who was sipping her coffee and smiling.

"And Melinda would wear a dress of deep rose color," said Caroline. "Not a sick, miserable pink. A rose like velvet, with a bright blue sash, and a rose ribbon in her hair." Her face took on a dreaming expression which was close to ecstasy.

"All those colors wouldn't match," said Beth. "They'd clash."

Caroline shook her head. "Oh no. Not the way I'd like to see it done. Not just painted on the—the paper. Laid on, Beth—you know, with a kind of knife or something, so it would be thick and radiant. Oh, I don't suppose people paint like that. It would be sort of crude."

Beth had been listening. She shook her head as Caroline had done. "I suppose you're right," she said slowly, thinking of the portrait again. "Only amateurs would do it that way."

"No elegance," said Caroline wistfully. "It—it would be like a shout." She clasped her strong hands on the table. "It would be something different; it would mean something. It just wouldn't be a pretty picture. But paints are so faint; do you know what I mean?"

"You mean water colors," said Beth. "But water colors aren't the only things there are. You've got to go to the Boston Museum."

"Yes," said Caroline vaguely, imagining endless rooms filled with dim paintings like Miss Brownley's.

Beth threw a dish on the sink with violence, and Caroline jumped at the noise. Beth swung about, and her round face was flushed and full of emotion. "Carrie! Do you know you aren't even educated, going to that miserable school? It's a shame! A girl with a father like yours, going to Miss Brownley's! You don't know anything, Carrie! What do you learn there, anyway?"

"I don't suppose I learn a great deal," said Caroline, startled. "I learn history, and some things, and how to write nicely."

"You are wonderful, Carrie, you're wonderful!" cried Beth. "You are the most wonderful and the sweetest girl in the world!"

She ran to Caroline and gathered the girl to her breast fiercely. Caroline was accustomed to Beth's occasional outbursts and patted the woman's shoulder. "Um," she murmured. "I don't think I'm wonderful. You're awfully good to me, Beth, and there's no way I can tell you what I think about you."

"Don't try," said Beth, wiping her eyes and going back to the stove. "Carrie, if I'd ever been blessed with a child I'd like her to've been like you. And I'll never leave you, Carrie, never!"

John Ames looked at his big daughter as she came timidly into the room. He thought, I'm always surprised at what a monster she is, uncouth and uncivilized and as ugly as *he* was. He said in a distasteful voice without even first greeting her, "Why is your hair hanging down your back, Caroline? You're a great girl now, going on sixteen. Aren't you a little old for such things?"

He had not seen his daughter for nearly two months. Caroline, who could never accustom herself to her father's abruptness and who always blamed herself for irritating him, turned red and looked at him humbly. She murmured, "I'm sorry, Papa. I took the ribbon off, and I was so glad to see you that I didn't wait to comb my hair again."

"I expect, at the very least, that my daughter should be a lady," he said. It was painful not only to see Caroline but also to feel that sharp compunction when he was most disagreeable to her.

"Sit down, Caroline," he said. "I have only an hour to talk to you. Then I must leave for Boston. But first I want to tell you that I've arranged for you to go to Miss Stockington's school in Boston; you'll stay with your Aunt Cynthia for five days, arriving at her home on Sunday night and returning the next Friday night. You'll be a woman in about two years; it's time for you to learn something more than you're learning at Miss Brownley's."

Caroline, who had seated herself on the edge of a chair, was so stunned that she glared at her father. Always attuned to all things, she was even now aware of the damp and moldering smell of the long old library with its sifting books, its narrow windows dark with velvet draperies and the quick night outside, the odor of dust and soft decay and ancient carpet and the wan fire of soft coal in the grate. They intensified her overwhelming dismay. The cracked black leather chairs glimmered in dull lamplight and seemed to jeer at her from every wrinkled plane.

"You mean, Papa, that I'll not be here for five days every week?" she stammered.

Not to walk any longer, except for two days a week, in the warm bronze autumn, in the lustrous white winter, in the golden spring—it was not possible. Not to see old Jim every day, and Beth, her only companions, was something she could not bear.

"You don't have to look as if you're about to be executed," said John Ames with annoyance. "After all, it's very kind of your Aunt Cynthia to offer this; in fact, she persuaded me that Miss Brownley isn't adequate. Your aunt has a beautiful home; her son is away at school and Melinda"—at this point his face changed subtly—"is only a child. Perhaps she's lonely. And she does have your interest at heart."

Caroline wanted to burst into tears, but she knew that her father would then stand up in disgust and walk out as he had often done before. She put her hand helplessly on the heavy walnut table beside her; in spite of

Beth's efforts, the dust gathered daily like shifting sand. Caroline began to trace her initials in the dust and swallowed her tears and made her throat stiff. "It's kind of Aunt Cynthia," she murmured huskily. She kept her head bent.

"Listen to me, Caroline," he said in a rising voice. "And don't take up my time with foolish remarks." He took out his big gold watch, glanced at it, and replaced it. "You are old enough to know some things, and I am here now to tell them to you, for tomorrow is Saturday and I want you ready that night to leave for Boston. Jim will drive you to the station. You don't know what a sacrifice I am making," he said, as if to himself.

"Yes, Papa." Caroline lifted her head and looked at her father obediently, with the tears hanging on her long thick lashes and the lamplight shining in her golden eyes. John looked aside, and she thought how handsome he was and how he never grew any older, and how incredible it was, and marvelous, that she was his daughter.

"Caroline, you're my only child, and it's not likely that I'll ever marry and have other children. I don't think you're a fool, though you always act like one. There were never any fools in my family, and there's no reason for there to be one now.

"I've never told you about my family and yours. You know only that your mother was Ann Esmond of Boston. But my own mother was of a family much more distinguished than the Esmonds; one of her ancestors was a Virginian, a general in the army of George Washington. Don't ask me her name; I won't tell you. As for my father——"

He stopped. Caroline was giving him her full and bewildered attention. She had never thought of her father's having any family or even of his ever having had any parents.

John Ames stood up and went to the fire and kicked a coal back onto the hearth. The rug was sizzling, and the wet harsh smell of burning wool filled the air. John stamped at the smoldering spark and muttered. He said without turning to his daughter:

"My father was of an even better family than my mother's or your mother's. He was educated not only at Harvard but at Oxford, in England. He specialized in international law. He could have been a great man. Eventually he would have been a Supreme Court justice. The President knew him, and so did many more. But—he died. Quite suddenly, he died."

Caroline thought: Poor Papa, he must have loved his father so much, and I never knew. She wanted to go to him and put her arms about him and console him, but she had never kissed him in her life except at Christmas, when he permitted it.

"My mother and I lived alone in the country, in a farmhouse near a village," said John, as if he were reading aloud a page and not speaking of himself. "Your grandmother's parents had expected a lot of my father; unfortunately he didn't come up to expectations in spite of his prospects. He decided, when I was ten years old, to throw up a whole lifetime of work and study and to do something else."

"What, Papa?"

John frowned. It was intolerable to listen to that meek and yearning voice, that innocent voice. He said, "It doesn't matter now. It happened a long time ago. He never succeeded in what he wanted to do. My mother's family wanted her to leave him and come home. She would not. When her father died he left his money to his nieces and nephews and not to his daughter. So she and I lived alone in that farmhouse."

A house like this, thought Caroline with deep affection. A house with trees about it and a little brook. Papa must have loved it.

"I won't go into details," said John, "about my life and my mother's when my father decided that what he had wasn't enough for him and when he turned his back on all his friends and made us exiles. But from the time I was ten I knew what poverty was."

He came back to his chair and looked at his daughter. "You've never known what it is to be poor, Caroline. Fools say that poverty is no crime. But it is. The world impresses that on you very severely. It treats you much worse when you're poor than if you were a murderer or a madman. I know. And the poor are even more vicious toward the poor than the rich are; they never forgive you for being one of them. When you're poor, your poverty-stricken neighbors are afraid that you'll ask them to share what little they have with you. And when they refuse, or have to refuse, they hate you for making them uneasy. Do you understand?"

Caroline did not. But a confused picture rose before her, terrible and frightening, filled with hoarse and repudiating voices and the sound of slammed doors and the look of a desolate brick wall in winter. She nodded speechlessly.

"Money," said John, "is the only thing that can stand between you and hate and persecution and hunger. It's the only fortress a man has. People may talk stupidly about family and position and name. These are nothing if you are poor. For when you are poor you have no family and no position and no name. You're wide open to the world and what it can do to you, and what it does do to you is the most contemptible thing imaginable. It takes your humanity from you. And it exploits you much worse than if you were an animal. But even worse than all these are the faces——"

Caroline looked at him, affrighted.

Is it possible I've reached her? thought John Ames. He was pleased.

"The faces," said John Ames. "You have no money. You go into a shop and try to buy food on credit, and the shopowner shouts at you as if you're a mangy cat and drives you out and everyone who hears laughs. Do you know what it means to hear people laugh at you when you have no money? I've heard many ugly sounds in my life, but none as ugly as the laughter of those who hate you because you haven't a penny to buy a loaf of bread or a piece of meat."

His cold and controlled voice did not become emotional. He spoke like a schoolmaster, without emphasis, and each word was a stone thrown at his shrinking daughter.

"There's nothing as hideous," he went on quietly, "as the faces that look at you when you're ragged and cold and hungry and homeless. They're all black open mouths, laughing, jeering, hating. You have no status. You have no place. You're fit only for a kick or a blow. I've gone through all that, Caroline."

Again Caroline nodded. She looked down at her clenched hands knotted together in her woolen lap.

"I'm not blaming the world," said John Ames. "When it treats a man like a dog, it is because he's become less than a dog for having no money. He deserves his punishment. It's despicable to be poor."

Caroline had never known what it was to hate. But the world of men had treated her father with hatred and derision. There was a convulsion of emotion in her, a withdrawing and yet an attack. She felt very sick; nausea clawed at her stomach. Then terror took her again, and she looked about the room. We're poor! she cried inwardly.

John Ames looked at the violation of innocence which he had committed, and he was satisfied.

"I want you to understand these things," he said almost gently. "I want to make it impossible for you ever to have to suffer as I suffered."

Caroline raised her head as at the sound of a reprieve. There was some money, then, to stand between her and the world, the enemy of all who are poor. "Yes, Papa?" she whispered. "We're not poor, Papa, not really terribly poor?"

"No," he said, smiling slightly. "Not terribly poor. And that's why I had to talk to you tonight, so it won't happen to you."

Her father loved her. She had never doubted it, she said to herself with a huge inner melting. She began to cry, her big shoulders heaving. John frowned.

"Stop it, Caroline. I haven't time for childishness. Stop it, I said. What? Haven't you a handkerchief? What a careless girl you are. Here take mine."

Caroline held the soft smooth linen to her face and smelled the delicate fragrance of the lavender bags Beth put in her father's chest of drawers. It was the most comforting perfume in the world to the girl; she would never smell it again without a wrench of longing and tenderness and love. For the first time she was conscious of the sweetness of good linen, its reassurance, its promise of safety.

John watched her as she pressed the handkerchief to her eyes and moved her full wet cheeks against it. He shifted his long and elegant legs uneasily and for an instant he thought of his mother. Only once had he ever seen her stern; it was strange that her remembered face, rising before his recollection, was stern now, almost forbidding.

"Caroline, even the Bible warns that the poor, the blind, the childless, and the lepers shall be counted as dead. And the poor are all that, for their very children come to hate them for their misery, and they have no eyes to see anything of the beauty your poets talk about there"—and he pointed to the silent books dying on the walls—"and they're lepers as far as their lovely fellow men are concerned. You've lived an isolated life here and in Lyme, and it's my fault, and now I am correcting it." He did not add that it was only when Cynthia had insisted that the girl be better educated for her position, in order that she would be able to manage the money which would inevitably be hers in time, that he had even considered giving Caroline a good education. "After all," Cynthia had said to him, "the girl is my sister's child, and she is very intelligent; don't be such a monstrous person, John."

Caroline as a child, through neglect, through some innocence, he was determined to destroy, for it was the innocence of his father which had led to so much anguish. Ugly women, he had discovered, were very sharp about the world, and he respected nothing more than intelligence. If the greater share of what he had and what he would have in the future were to pass to Caroline, she would have to know at what a cost it had been bought.

"Yes, Papa," said Caroline. The old obedience was still there, but now he detected resolution as well as fear in her voice.

"My mother," said John in a flat tone, "died of starvation. Do you hear, Caroline? My mother died of starvation."

It was many years ago, but he could feel the lightness of his dead mother's body in his arms, and when Caroline looked at him with fresh horror she saw that he was very pale and that his eyes gleamed in the dull lamplight. She thought, What if Papa died like that—of starvation? And she glanced about her quickly in terror, as if an enemy had entered the cold and bitter room. Like an answer to her emotions, the wind rose in an autumnal thunder and crashed against the windows, which rattled like old bones.

John went on so quietly that Caroline had to strain to hear: "When she died I was alone with her in a farmhouse, in the winter, with only a small fire in her bedroom. There wasn't anything to eat in the house; there wasn't any money for food. I was more than a year younger than you, Caroline. After she died she was buried in what they called the poor corner of the churchyard; grave, hearse, and minister cost twenty dollars. My father"—and he stopped a moment—"returned home two days later. He had been trying to get some money. He climbed the hill in the snow; he dropped dead in it before he could reach the house."

Caroline, always so insulated by neglect, gazed at her father, aghast. Her tears began again, and again the soft luxury of the handkerchief soothed her and promised her that she was safe. She knew that Beth was poor, and old Jim. But she had not visualized poverty as utter despair, starvation, and absolute cold.

"Oh, Papa!" she cried. "I don't want to be like that! I'd rather die."

"You won't be like that, Caroline," said John. "And I'm telling you these things so that one day, when you inherit what I have, you'll be able to guard it well and increase it, and you'll never spend a penny but what is absolutely necessary. Never a penny, Caroline. Each penny is a brick in the wall that'll keep you safe from the world, safe from everything."

"How did you get a little money, Papa?" She leaned eagerly toward him to hear, and he saw that the innocence was gone at last and he knew it would never return. He tapped his hand on the arm of the chair.

"I'll tell you, my dear." He had never called her that before, and she was one warm bubble of joy to hear it. "I'll be brief just now; you'll probably hear all about it when you're older—from others. When I left the village for a larger town I worked hard. I was fourteen, and a big strong boy. Binghamton, Albany, New York. I could forget my degradation, the degradation of poverty, and the wretched shame of it, when I went away. For you see, I was determined never to be poor again. I was determined to get money.

"I did every kind of work you can imagine. I sailed on clippers; I worked in hotels and in private mansions. But I never took a job among middle-class people. The money wasn't there. I put myself in the way of rich men; I preferred to earn as much as three dollars less a week among the rich than among just the middle-class and provincial, and I can assure you now that the rich knew the value of every penny they have, whether they earned it themselves or inherited it. When a rich man spends, unless he's an absolute fool, he makes sure that he'll get his money's worth, and more. And—I found friends. It takes intelligence to make money, and to keep it if you've inherited it, and I never worked for fools. They had nothing to teach me."

He stood up. "Tell Beth to call the rig for me. I have just five minutes to reach the Boston train for New York. Someday I'll tell you the rest of the story. You are too young now to understand it, and I have no time to try to make you understand."

Caroline blew her nose and stood up also. There was an atavistic smell in the room now. She did not know this acrid pungency was the smell of her own new fear and the smell of her father's old fear. But it affected her tremendously. She was never free of it again.

She went toward the door, but her father called her back. She stood before him, large and square, and he looked down into her reddened eyes. He saw her fright and the two little white lines about her big red mouth. He never knew why he bent his head and kissed her and then patted her shoulder. She suddenly flung her strong arms about his neck and kissed him over and over, as if protecting him fiercely; he stiffened. Then the door closed behind her.

"What is wrong with you, Carrie?" asked Beth in a worried voice as she helped the girl pack her meager belongings. She glanced at the heavy profile and was alarmed to see a new sullenness there. "You know how wonderful it'll be for you to go to Miss Stockington's, where you should have gone a long time ago. So don't pout."

Caroline carefully folded a long and yellowish flannel nightgown, as rough as sand, and placed it in her tin trunk. She said absently, "I'm not pouting, Beth." She picked up the flannelette drawers which Beth had made for her; the bulky top was fitted with tapes, but Beth had ruffled the ends of the legs prettily where they met the knees. Caroline's large hand smoothed the ruffle; the edges had been embroidered in a gay pattern of red and blue cross-stitch. "Beth, are you poor?" asked Caroline with abruptness.

The question startled Beth, and she looked up in the gray barrenness of Caroline's room. October wind and rain marched past the windows. Beth was about to answer, then she stared thoughtfully at the girl, her eyes puckered. Simple, but astute, she felt something dangerous and alien in the room, something that had never been there before. "Well, no, not really. I save almost all my wages, and I have a pension, and the government's just increased it." Then, as her alarm sharpened, it suddenly drifted away. She smiled at Caroline, and easy tears came to her eyes; the girl was worried about her because she loved her. She put her scarred hand on the girl's arm.

"I didn't think it would mean anything to you, dear," she said, "but poor old Kate left me all she had after her simple funeral expenses. I never told you. You never cared about money; you never even thought of it."

Caroline did not smile. It was only the grayness of the day which gave her face a somber hardness, thought Beth. Caroline said, "I didn't know. Was it much?"

Again Beth's eyes wrinkled, and uneasiness returned to her. "Why—considerable. I thought she'd leave it to her sister's children in England, but she left it to me. Why?"

"Perhaps she thought you'd save it or use it sensibly. Kate was very saving, Beth."

Beth folded a knitted skirt very slowly. "I didn't mean that, Carrie. When I asked you why, I meant why did you ask."

But Caroline did not know herself. She only knew that since last night she had been afraid and that the fear was beginning to shape and solidify in her heart, like iron. "I'm glad you're not poor, anyway," she muttered. She looked about the room vaguely. "It must be terrible to be poor."

Beth did not know what made her say sharply, "I don't know that it's so terrible. My own family was always poor. There were ten of us, and the farm wasn't too good. Papa always had a very hard time grubbing up enough for us to eat and fill the silo for the horses and cows. But we were awful happy. Awful happy."

"How could you be happy without money, Beth?"

Beth sat down on the edge of the bed and looked at her scarred palms. She felt a little sick as well as utterly baffled. What had happened to Carrie? Earnestly she lifted her eyes and gazed at the girl.

"My papa used to say that money helped everywhere," she said, "whether it was when a new baby was born, or the cows got sick, or there was scarlet fever and we had to have the doctor, or whether anyone died. It was like grease on an axle wheel, Papa would say; it made the going smoother. Papa wasn't one of those silly people who pretend that money doesn't mean anything; he knew what it was to need it, you can be sure of that. But what he meant was that money made things roll better. Why, there was a family down the road with a good farm, a real rich farm, four times as big as ours, and there were only three big healthy boys—they went to school with our mess of children and they'd never speak. They never got sick. Mrs. Schiller always had a fine silk dress on Sundays, and India shawls—that pretty Paisley pattern, you know, Carrie—and a fur cape in winter. They had a surrey, too, all shiny and fringed, and it could seat all five of them and room to spare, and a horse kept just to pull it. They'd jingle up to church in fine style, and we'd pull in behind them in one of the farm wagons and all over hay.

"But the funny thing about it," said Beth, "was that you never saw any of the Schillers smile, and nobody ever heard them laugh, and they had sour faces, thick around the nose, as if they were always mad at everybody all the time. They had a girl working for them, and they'd bicker every time they paid her her six dollars a month, and they'd lock up the food-safe at night and the pantry door so she couldn't have a bite if she got hungry at night after working from dawn to dark. Bessie would tell us; she was a friend of my oldest sister. 'It's like working in an icehouse,' she'd say, and we'd all laugh at her stories about the Schillers. They never got a single mite of happiness out of their lives, Carrie. They'd never speak to anyone who didn't have as much money as they had, or more. Nobody liked them, but our house was full all the time with children, and on Sundays friends would come with fresh pumpkin pies or mince, and there was always a turkey on hand at Christmas, or a goose. And Papa never spared the fires; the boys always kept a lot of firewood ready."

Caroline smiled slightly, but it was a sober smile. "Do you honestly think all the poor are happy and all the rich miserable, Beth?"

"No, no," said Beth shaking her head. "I'm not that simple, Carrie. I mean, you can be happy without money and you can be wretched with it. It depends on what kind of a person you are. The Schillers were just awful people, that's all." Now she was becoming confused. "Carrie, I just don't know! But I do know that our family never had any money and we were happy, and maybe we'd have been happier with it. I don't know!"

"You see," muttered Caroline.

Beth shook her head emphatically. "I don't see, Carrie. You read my Bible sometimes. God is no respecter of persons, it says. There's more to living than money. I'm not educated, Carrie. I can't think very deep. But I do know that God isn't interested more in a rich man than a poor one, except He expects more of the rich."

Beth was perturbed when Caroline gave her a sly golden glance out of the corner of her eye.

"'A rich man's wealth is his strong city,'" quoted Caroline. "That's what it says in the Bible. And the Bible classes the poor with the other dead: the blind, the childless, and the lepers."

Beth sat upright on the bed. "Carrie, the Bible often comments on things as they are in the world. That doesn't mean that it approves classing the poor, the childless, the lepers, and the blind together as dead. Carrie! I have no children of my own."

Caroline turned away from her trunk and ran to Beth and knelt down before her and took her hands. "Beth, I'm terrible sorry. Please forgive me. Please——" And she began to cry. Beth pulled the large head to her breast. "Carrie, Carrie darling, what is it?" she asked. "What's hurt my girl? Why, Carrie, you're all the child I ever wanted. Don't cry like that; you'll be sick at your stomach. What's the matter, Carrie?"

"I don't know, I don't know," said Caroline, and clung to her friend with desperate arms. "I wish you were going with me, Beth. I'm awfully afraid."

Beth sighed and smoothed the coronet of long thin braids. "Yes, dear. I understand. You don't want to leave home."

After Caroline had gone and the lonely, empty house thundered with dull far echoes, Beth discovered that the girl had not taken the Bible which she had bought for her three years ago. It was a fine Bible with a black leather cover stamped with gold, and Caroline's name had been engraved on it, also in gold, and the pages were of thin silky India paper and the small print clear and sharp. It had cost Beth a whole month's wages. Beth wrapped it up carefully and sent it to Boston to Caroline. The girl never opened the package. She put it away in her tin trunk. It was found forty years later, the leather moldering away, the pages matted, the gold obliterated, and what had cost Beth so much in love and money was thrown out.

CHAPTER SIX

"You're a difficult girl," said Cynthia Winslow to her niece. "There was a time when I thought you had the disposition of your mother. You don't look like Ann, of course, but you did have many of her traits of character. I must have been mistaken after all; children change. You're seventeen, Caroline."

"I can't help it if I'm not stylish, Aunt Cynthia," said Caroline sulkily. She looked at the portrait of her aunt and her mother.

"We aren't talking about the same things," said Cynthia with pettishness. "Dear me, Caroline. You are becoming more like your father every day. You are stiff like him and cold and too silent, and you keep yourself from any contact with people. Why? No one has ever hurt you, to my knowledge, to make you so distrustful and withdrawing. If you'd been hungry or homeless or lost or beaten or brought up in some dreadful slum, then I could understand. Dear me. I thought I was a very perspicacious person and understood people. But now I am beginning to think I'm really a fool and don't understand anyone at all."

She was exasperated. Her long and delicate hands were folded together on her blue velvet lap. She looked more Florentine than ever before, cool, polished, and chiseled, in her forty-first year. Her hairdresser came once a week to arrange her bright hair and to instruct her maid; if he brought a tint to conceal any gray, the maid never betrayed that fact to the other servants.

There were no lines in her long porcelain neck, no wrinkles about her pink lips. The smoky color of her eyes was as ardent as ever.

"What is it you want to know about me, Aunt Cynthia?" asked Caroline. She looked at her aunt warily.

"I don't want to know anything, Caroline. What a person is, is God's business and his own. But I do wish you'd be more cordial to the girls in your school. You've been going there two years, yet you never invite them here. Why can't you laugh more? You're a young lady, and though you say you aren't stylish and I must admit that your figure could be improved—what a pig you are about chocolates and bonbons!—you do have a nice face when you smile, and your eyes are simply beautiful. Your complexion is sallow. That comes of being burned brown every summer at Lyme. Why don't you go home to Lyndon more often? You used to count the days to the weekends, but in the last year you've never wanted to go there, and you hardly read poor Beth's letters and hardly ever answer them. Never mind. I am, in a way, talking to myself and wondering. You must have your reasons, and I never pry.

"But I am interested in your making the best of yourself. I made your father give you a generous allowance. You could dress well, and a little restraint over the sweetmeat dishes would do wonders for your figure, even though your bones are broad and heavy. But you are tall enough and broad enough to be imposing. You could have presence. But what sort of clothes do you insist upon? Ugly dull browns, which call attention to your freckles; dark blues, which make you appear more sallow than you are; maroons fit only for old ladies. And your boots! Like a stableboy's."

"I'd look foolish in ruffles and fluffs and bangles," said Caroline. She looked at the diamond bracelet on her aunt's arm. Cynthia had told her that John Ames had given her the bracelet when she had adopted Melinda.

"I don't mean such things," said Cynthia. "They aren't for you. But you could wear pleasant colors. You could be statuesque in the proper shaping and style of your clothes. Impressive. Even your father complains."

Caroline, who was bored and resentful at this lecturing, became interested. "What does Papa want me to do?" she asked eagerly.

"He wants you to look like a young lady who will inherit a tremendous amount of money," said Cynthia.

"But there isn't a tremendous amount of money!" cried Caroline.

Cynthia was taken aback. There was more here, she reflected, than met the eye. She studied Caroline. Then she smiled a little. "Oh yes, my dear, there is an enormous amount of money. Your father is one of the richest men in America. He could buy up half the gentlemen in Boston. He can touch rubbish and it turns to gold. It's a gift, and a very convenient one, though it must be dull at times."

Caroline's eyes glowed as though she had had a message from a lover, and Cynthia frowned.

"But why didn't Papa ever tell me that, Aunt Cynthia?"

"Possibly because he is afraid you might get extravagant ideas," said Cynthia dryly.

"Such as you have," said Caroline with a candor that removed the innocent bite from her words. Cynthia laughed. "Very true," she agreed. "Your papa is always accusing me of extravagance, as you know, it seems. Dear me, I am a Bostonian born and bred, as was my own papa, but I don't have the Bostonian's reverence for money. I consider that vulgar. The really fine and aristocratic families of Boston have disappeared, have gone away, or have been extinguished by poverty or no male heirs. Now we have the merchant princes and an absolute money society; your worth, in Boston, is judged by how much you actually weigh in gold. And what irritable people, and how truly mannerless and brutal! My papa would never have admitted them to our house.

"It's very odd," said Cynthia, meditatively looking at her pretty foot and apparently examining it. "The Bostonians adore the English, who at least pretend not to use money as the sole criterion of a man's worth. But the Bostonians, except for their everlasting and tedious afternoon teas and an affected accent, are not like the English at all, who have manners and graces. There's nothing so distinguished as a mannerly Englishman, and there's nothing really so undistinguished as the Bostonian who loves the English and makes very little effort to imitate them."

Cynthia paused. Caroline was restlessly playing with the wool fringe about her throat. The older woman laughed and shook her head. "My father didn't really have a tremendous fortune. The clever diminished it very neatly for him. But he never let anyone know! He was of a great and gentle family, and he was very intelligent, and he loved his daughters. So he pretended to be extremely rich, knowing his neighbors, and he let them pretend to him that they admired family background. You see, he was kind, too, and he was sorry for them."

She looked at Caroline briskly. "But here we are in Boston, and there are the Assemblies to consider and your presentation at a proper tea. I know your father doesn't consider them important; there are times when I believe he is an authentic gentleman. Don't stare that way, Caroline. It's most disconcerting. What I am trying to say is that you live in Boston, and you will probably spend a great deal of your life here, and if you live in a certain society by your own choice—and it is your father's choice—you should at least abide by some of their rules even if they appear ridiculous to you. As your father's heiress you will have considerable importance in Boston, and you will meet young men— Do move back from the fire, my dear. You have suddenly turned a quite fiery red, and your eyes are watering."

"Excuse me, please," Caroline muttered, and jumped to her feet and ran heavily out of the room. Cynthia was accustomed to the girl's sudden awkwardnesses, but they still annoyed her. Only all that money would get her a suitable husband; even then the effort would be formidable. Cynthia sighed, then smiled, thinking of Melinda. Cynthia reached out her beautiful rounded arm and pulled the bell rope, and Melinda came in as at a signal.

Cool and sunny spring wind had brightened Melinda's cheeks, had ruffled the pale ashen gold of her hair, had made her gray eyes brilliant. She was a most beautiful child of nearly seven with a tender pink mouth, a dimpled white chin, and a forehead of touching purity. All her actions were graceful; she was grave by nature, but when she laughed everyone listened. She ran to Cynthia and kissed her and put her chilly cheek against Cynthia's and murmured lovingly and wordlessly in her ear. Cynthia forgot the elegance of her dress and pulled the child on her knee and kissed her passionately. The resemblance between them was remarkable.

Though many frequently spoke of the child's lack of "background"—and this was spoken of the most frequently by those who had no true background at all but only one invented after the acquisition of money—all loved Melinda, the nameless, the adopted, who had lived for nearly four years in a very exclusive "home" called "Miss Christie's Nursery and Children's Shelter" much esteemed in Boston. It was not entirely an orphanage, though many of the children were of old and impoverished families. Boston society felt itself obligated to help care for these children, offspring of lifelong friends, and very often adopted them later or made themselves responsible for their higher education and "good" marriages. Others were truly nameless but well financed from mysterious sources abroad as well as in Boston. It was a never-ending source of spirited conversation as to whom these children could really claim as parents, but tact and certain discretions did not permit of any real probings. Melinda was one of these children. Miss Christie, if she had sealed records, never mentioned them. Her high cold serenity when referring to "her" children intimidated even the most curious and malevolent. Her standards were meticulous and inflexible, so few had any dubiousness when adopting a nameless child of unknown parentage.

Cynthia Winslow was on the Board which assisted the home, as were many of her friends. (But even the Board never had access to Miss Christie's sealed files.) She had ostensibly first seen Melinda when the child was three years old. She adopted her a year later. "I could not resist the darling," she had said to her friends with tears in her eyes. Others had wished to adopt Melinda, but in some way, never disclosed, John Ames had secured the child for Cynthia. Miss Christie answered no questions.

Timothy Winslow, to everyone's surprise, loved Melinda. It was quite unusual for a young man approaching eighteen to care for a child, and especially one adopted by his mother. Timothy was called "aristocratic" by his mother's friends, with the after-remark "that of course it was to be expected, with the Esmond and Winslow blood." No one particularly liked Timothy, in spite of the "blood," for his monetary prospects were poor and he was at the mercy of his uncle's well-known aversion to spending money. Moreover, he had a silent personality and a look of perpetual but polite disdain which others, while affecting to admire, found annoying.

It was one of the major delights of Cynthia's day when Melinda returned from Miss Stockington's. She carefully recorded in her memory any unusual remarks the child would make so as to repeat them to John Ames, who would listen to them and smile. Only Cynthia and Melinda knew how much he loved this graceful and beguiling child.

"Tell me, darling," said Cynthia today as she smoothed Melinda's curls, "did anything interesting happen at school?"

"Everything," replied Melinda with enthusiasm. "Miss Stockington has the very first hyacinths. Ours are just green leaves; she puts glass jars over them when they first push up. Why don't we do that, Mama?"

"I like things in their season," said Cynthia, smiling. "Why hurry them? They know better than we do when they are ready."

She looked over her shoulder at the long windows leading to her narrow garden. The crab apples were still chill and empty of the many-colored blossoms they would display in a few weeks; sun lay golden on the branches of the maple tree, and its buds were like small and wrinkled garnets, darkly red in the wide spring light.

Melinda chatted softly. It was a sweet and murmurous sound to Cynthia. John Ames had wanted a governess for Melinda, but Cynthia insisted upon Miss Stockington's. "I am not bringing up a recluse like Caroline," she would say, and her large eyes would become less smoky and take on the hard brightness of an implacable stare. When Cynthia looked at him that way John always retreated.

The child, who liked to please others, not to gain their approval, but because she was instinctively tender, talked to Cynthia about some "new" children from New York whom she had met at Papanti's dancing school. They were nice, said Melinda, but only two of them could be called First Families. "Their grandfathers came from Boston," said the child.

"Truly?" murmured Cynthia, abstracted. She was examining Melinda's profile. The profile was exactly like her sister Ann's, and Melinda had Ann's gentle spirit and great sympathy even at this early age.

"The others are only rich," said Melinda.

"That should not stand against them in Boston," said Cynthia wryly. "It depends, of course, just how rich they really are. Or if they have committed the unpardonable sin of having anything else but an English ancestry."

Melinda was puzzled. She leaned back in Cynthia's arms to look at her closely, and Cynthia laughed. "I am a wretched cynic, darling," she said. "I hope you won't be. It's salvation to be a cynic, but it can sometimes be very sorrowful too."

"What is a First Family, Mama?" asked Melinda.

Cynthia hugged her. "That depends on the locality. In England it has something to do with the Normans; you'll learn about that later. In France, with the nobility. In Germany, with the high military class. But in Boston it means being rich for two or three generations and never spending your capital, as I do always, and getting richer all the time. And being constipated."

Melinda blushed vividly. Cynthia was delighted. "Ah, I've said an improper word, haven't I, pet? You see what it means to be a cynic? You are always improper and always at the wrong time, deliberately."

"Are we First Family, Mama?"

Cynthia shrugged. "My status is in chronic doubt. My ancestry is impeccable—you must ask Miss Stockington what that means—but my finances are deplorable. I am afraid I am a great trial to my friends and occupy a lot of their anxious conversation. Fortunately Uncle John is very rich. Does it matter to you, love, if we are not First Family?"

Melinda considered. She knew she was adopted; she remembered the pleasant years at Miss Christie's very well. She took her life and all the love which was given her for granted, for she loved in return. "Do you mean, Mama, if we weren't First Family no one would love us?"

It was on Cynthia's tongue to say, "Of course they wouldn't." But she looked into the eyes so like Ann's and she could not say it. She kissed Melinda lightly. "No one could help loving you, dear," she said. "And love makes a first family of anybody."

Caroline was crying in her room.

She hated this room where she had spent the past few years. It had little color, and this alone would have been offensive to a girl who was moved unbearably by passionate hue and strength of line, and to whom the scarlet flare of trees in the autumn was an exquisite and joyous anguish. The room was excellently proportioned and quite large, and looked out upon a garden which Caroline always thought too pale and restrained, and its walls were of smooth ivory faintly touched with silver at the moldings and along the panels. Caroline, who never spoke of what she felt to anyone except one person, would have preferred walls of a deep and singing yellow, a ceiling of strong blue, and furniture simple and upholstered in intense colors of crimson and green and gold. She disliked the dim Aubusson rug with its muted soft tints; she would have liked a floor of black lacquer strewn with little carpets of absolute luminosity. She had never seen a room such as she imagined, full of light and vigorous color values. But she imagined it with a nostalgia that became agony to her. Everything in this room she occupied was a misery to eyes yearning for ardent vigor and emotion, for graphic affirmation. Its cool bed of neutral wood with its spread hangings of faded blue velvet seemed to suffocate her. Here in Boston she lived in what she believed to be a designedly blanched house in a city of brownness.

Her father wished her to be here. That was enough for her. He appeared to have respect for her Aunt Cynthia, of whom she was afraid and whose wit tortured her spirit and whose humor was beyond her understanding. All that was earthy and powerful in Caroline was repelled by the cool sophistication of Cynthia Winslow which affirmed nothing and denied nothing and regarded raw feeling as something offensive. Cynthia was too civilized, and in many ways too attenuated, for Caroline's comprehension. Cynthia's laughter bewildered Caroline, who saw no humor in what Cynthia considered humorous. The older woman's love of clothing baffled

Caroline; what did it matter what one wore? An orange sunset glittering behind black winter trees was surely more important than the proper way of waltzing. Cynthia, with some sardonic wrinkling about her eyes which Caroline never appreciated or even saw, had explained that someday Caroline must "take her place." Caroline had no desire to take any place whatsoever. Had she been articulate enough to tell this to Cynthia, she would have found instant sympathy. But she was not articulate. Between the woman and the girl there lay an area of exasperation bounded by the impassable walls of semantics.

Caroline was now always afraid. Her foremost and overpowering terror was the terror of being poor, of being at the mercy of relentless horrors in the shape of men. She remembered a certain day last December, and the memory never left her; it woke her in a nightmare in the middle of the night. It haunted her life without surcease. The experience removed forever any doubts she may have had about her father's convictions concerning money.

It had been a few days before Christmas. She had found, to her surprise, that her father did not particularly object to gift-giving in Cynthia's house and that he gave gifts to her aunt, her cousin, and Melinda. (In her simplicity she had not as yet asked herself what status her father occupied in this cool and well-bred household on Beacon Street.) So Caroline was confronted with the fact of Christmas-giving beyond the gift she usually bought for Beth Knowles. She had saved the greater part of the allowance her father grudgingly gave her. She had assigned one dollar for her aunt, seventy-five cents for Timothy, from whom she shrank in real fear, and the same for Melinda, whose beauty and grace alarmed as well as entranced her. But she would spend two dollars on Beth, thriftily and sensibly, buying her some black cotton stockings and a box of the tea Beth especially liked.

Shyly one day she told Cynthia that she would do her Christmas shopping in town after school. Cynthia immediately made plans. Both Caroline and Melinda would be brought home as usual from Miss Stockington's in the carriage. Melinda would be dropped off, and the carriage would then convey Caroline to Boston's "nicest shopping district." Caroline was not so unworldly as to be unaware that shops recommended by Cynthia would be fearfully expensive. She knew the shops Beth patronized, in a very sleazy neighborhood, where gifts could be bought cheaply. So she hurriedly told Cynthia that she particularly liked to ride in the horse cars and that the carriage would bring Melinda home alone. Cynthia had wrinkled her brows at this and thought of the dangers to unaccompanied young girls in the crowded streets. Then she studied Caroline, her clumsy clothing, the broad strong face which only the beautiful hazel eyes saved from absolute unattractiveness, and the occasional charming smile, and decided that Caroline was plain enough and appeared poor enough not to draw hostile or thieving glances. She was certainly old enough, thought Cynthia. "It will be a long walk to the best shops from the streetcars," she had warned the girl, but

Caroline, who knew it was only a very short walk to the shops she preferred, had only smiled.

Caroline had saved seventy-five dollars over a year from her allowance. She carried her money with her always, in a deplorably cheap and battered bag made of coarse carpeting and snapped together with a brass-plated lock. Caroline, in spite of paternal neglect, had never really been much alone for a considerable period of time until she had come to Cynthia's house, and even there there were servants all about her when Cynthia was away attending many parties. So she was unused to isolation, in the full sense, and quite unused to being alone on the streets of a city. It was this which had partly led Cynthia to give her permission to this lonely shopping. It was time that Caroline developed self-confidence.

A feeling of freedom came to Caroline when she boarded the horse car for downtown Boston and the area of cheap shops in a frowzy neighborhood. Not even the strange and resentful faces about her in the car made her shrink too much. She found a secluded rattan-covered seat over the rear wheels and huddled herself together for warmth. Her ugly brown coat, too short, too tight, hardly met across her body; her long plaid skirt just brushed the tops of her buttoned boots, and as she sat an area of coarse black stocking was revealed. Her velvet hat, too wide for her face, its blackness too old, was tied down firmly under her thick chin with cotton ribbons, and her gloves were of black wool made by Beth. There was nothing in her clothing to distinguish her from the others in the car; she was as poorly dressed as they, and as dun-colored. She had the aspect of a strong kitchen maid on a half day's outing. Nothing that Cynthia had been able to do as yet had brightened Caroline's wardrobe, nor had Cynthia been successful in persuading the girl to abandon her old clothing. "They are still wearable," Caroline had said stubbornly, surprised at Cynthia's suggestion.

A dull, brownish mixture of sleet and rain was falling over Boston. Out of this disheartening murk the buildings emerged in chocolate shapes; the brick walks glimmered wetly; the cobbled streets appeared smeared with grease. Umbrellas bobbed everywhere; the horses clopped wearily. The stench of wet hay, wet old clothes, and wet wool pervaded the horse car; the windows steamed from the miserable little heat emanating from the passengers. Aunt Cynthia, reflected Caroline, might call Boston a sherry-and-topaz city. To Caroline it appeared liverish and snuff-colored, with an overtone of rust. Caroline's thoughts were not happy. She was homesick for Lyndon at this time of the year, where Beth, in John Ames' absence, would keep fires going, and there was a gaiety in running from icy narrow halls into a firelit room, and a pleasure in dashing down from a frigid bedroom into a warm kitchen full of the smell of porridge and hot bread and coffee. Caroline had discovered the harsh joy of contrasts which Cynthia would never understand in her uniformly warm and pleasant rooms, in her guarded and comfortable life.

Caroline's thoughts turned to Beth, to whom she hardly wrote any longer but whom she still loved. Beth was too sharp; she sensed too many things, and her tongue was too ready. She would, given time, understand from Caroline's face and even from letters, the sorrowful transformation which had taken place in the girl. Caroline did not think of the transformation as sorrowful; she thought it sensible. Yet she did not want Beth to know of it, Beth who would argue and try to convince her to the contrary; Beth who loved. As yet, Caroline had no arguments of her own to counter Beth's arguments; she had only the fearful instinct born in her on the night her father had spoken freely to her. Loyalty to her father also prevented Caroline from seeing too much of Beth now or writing to her regularly; everything that Beth said was a refutation of John's philosophy of fear, mistrust, and penuriousness.

The horse car came to a stop with a clang of bells, and Caroline started, jumped to her feet, and ran out of the car on her strong young legs. She was in her chosen neighborhood. Here the sleet and the rain seemed to have concentrated in a muddy downpour. The little murky shops winked feebly in the gloom; they were like evil old men loitering under streaming eaves. Caroline had no umbrella. She was jostled by dubious throngs who never gave her a second glance. No lecherous young laborer winked at her. Her head bowed against the icy sleet, she scurried into her favorite shop, one larger than the others, where one could buy anything from cotton and lisle stockings (seconds) to used coats and dresses, men's fusty suits, rough cotton and wool underwear, children's cheap toys, some groceries, and mended ancient furniture long thrown out of servants' attics and rudely repaired here. Gaslights, yellow and unshaded, blinked down on the heaped and scarred counters, and shopgirls and salesmen, shivering and chapped and white with hunger and cold, hovered about, waiting like starved spiders for customers. The wood floor was slippery with mud and damp; the few windows were blurred with filth.

Caroline paused in a crowded aisle for a moment and was promptly and profanely pushed aside by a woman with a following of many starveling children. Caroline had a problem. She had decided quite suddenly to send a gift to Tom Sheldon, who would be home this Christmas in Lyme. She had not answered Tom's last three letters; he, like Beth, was a threat. But he seemed beside her now, a vital presence, and she saw him as clearly as if he were actually there, and her young heart rose poignantly. She would buy him a secondhand watch. It would not be a new dollar watch; that was too much to spend. But somewhere in this shop she would find a repaired nickel watch for seventy-five cents or even fifty cents. She remembered having seen these watches before.

She was methodical. There was a rule in this shop that one could gather up his own purchases, take them to a counter near the door, where they were itemized and counted and paid for. It was a very efficient arrangement, invented by the proprietor, who could then hold only two clerks responsible for any losses. It also minimized stealing by both clerks and customers. He had strong men—three of them—patrolling the aisles, men with brutal faces whom he had recruited from the docks. Sudden cries and screams were not unknown in this shop; in fact, the customers barely looked around in curiosity to see who was caught in the act of thievery, for thievery was a way of life in this neighborhood. The men were armed with short clubs which they only partly concealed in the pockets of their coats. It was not customary to call the police; the guardians of the wretched stock were quite sufficient either to seize the stolen goods and beat the customer thereafter with dispatch or to force payment. Caroline did not know of this arrangement; she never knew that it was the voice of a thief which was occasionally raised in dismal fear or pain. She knew only that the prices here were "reasonable."

She was shy and afraid of strangers. So she kept her head down and only mumbled at clerks as she purchased three pairs of black cotton stockings for Beth, a sewing box with a japanned lid, all chipped and crocked, for Melinda, a box of tea also for Beth, and an anonymous little wicker basket for Cynthia. It would be handy for buttons, thought Caroline. She admired the basket. A bunch of flowers had been painted on the uneven lid, and their colors were vital and alive. This part of her shopping concluded and the unwrapped purchases in her arms, she looked for the counter where the secondhand watches were for sale.

It was then that she became aware that in her meanderings she had lost her purse, which contained every dollar she owned. The purse, in truth, had been deftly cut from her arm during her preoccupation. This did not occur to Caroline, to whom theft was only a word. Her first panicked thought was that she had left it on the counter nearest the door, where the stockings were sold. Her purchases jostling in her arms, she raced back to the first counter, and in so doing attracted the attention of one of the burly men, who followed silently but swiftly on the heels of a girl whose clothing proclaimed her a servant wench, a kitchen maid lowly and badly recompensed.

Caroline, gasping and quite livid with panic, reached the stocking counter and stammered out her loss to the cynical clerk. "Seventy-five dollars!" cried Caroline as the clerk stood immobile and grinning into her face. Still clutching her purchases, Caroline began frantically to paw at the heaped stockings with her right hand. The purse was not there. "But I must have left it here!" she sobbed, frightened by the loss of the money. "It must be under something!"

A hoarse voice spoke easily beside her. "And where would you be gettin' seventy-five dollars, miss?" Caroline swung to see a huge and ugly man beside her, teetering on his heels. "Maybe stole it, eh, from your mistress?"

"What?" faltered Caroline, shrinking instinctively. "I—— You don't understand! I must have left my purse here when I was examining the stockings. You must have seen my purse!" she exclaimed to the clerk.

"No," said the clerk, languidly patting her "waterfall" of dirty yellow curls. "You didn't have no purse. I was watchin' you."

"Then," said Caroline, her panic growing, "I must have left it on the horse car!"

Blindly, urged again only by instinct, she turned and ran to the door, past the checker who tried without success to seize her arm, thrusting her way in terror through the staring mobs. Her one thought, glazed by anguish and so blurred beyond real thought, was to reach the street and somehow find the horse car, long gone over half an hour ago. She was caught at the very door by the burly man, who swung her about savagely, and even while she glared at him dazedly in her despair, still thinking of her purse, he slapped her face so brutally that the slap was heard above the hubbub of the customers.

No one had ever struck Caroline before in all her immured life. She staggered back under the blow, feeling the pain less than the stupefied bewilderment. Uppermost in her thoughts there still remained the loss of her purse. Recovering almost instantly, and never questioning why she had been assaulted—that was unimportant in view of her loss—she tried again to reach the door. She was seized by the shoulder and torn away and flung headlong into an aisle. Before she could fall she was caught by a powerful hand whose fingers clamped like crushing iron about her arm.

"Dirty, s——g thief!" said the burly man, shaking her furiously. "I'll learn you! Yessir, I'll learn you!"

He fumbled for his club. The gaslights, the staring eyes, the giggling faces, the curses of the mob of customers, the joyful shriek of anticipating children dazed Caroline. And reality poured upon her with one appalling throb and roar. She stopped struggling. She saw the upraised club; she knew it would descend upon her head, crushing her to the floor. A vomitous fluid rushed into her mouth, and her legs stiffened, and sweat broke out on her pallid face. She stood rigid and waited for the final terror, the final ignominy, the final horror. She did not even tremble.

Perhaps it was the look in her eyes, wild and startled, or the fact that she did not fight and try to evade the impending blow, or perhaps it was the alien aura which hovered about her that made the burly man pause in the very act of bringing his club down upon her. A glove had fallen from her hand; he saw that her hand, though large and broad, was well shaped and smooth, not the hand of the usual servant girl. He saw that she was well fed. Glaring at her with mingled perplexity and hate, he pushed his club into his pocket and began to drag her toward the rear of the shop, parting a way for his passage with oaths and kicks. Caroline, gulping desperately and trying to keep her footing, began to cry feebly. But she had no words. It was a nightmare; she would wake up soon.

The burly man, who had a considerable retinue of the avid now, urging him eagerly to beat the girl, reached a double door and kicked it open and pulled Caroline inside. He flung her into the center of the room, where she fell heavily on her hands and knees. He shut the door against the hungry faces pressing toward it. Caroline remained in her fallen position, dimly shaking her head, a dimness in her mind and eyes. It was not until some moments had passed that she became aware of the gigantic boots and trunklike legs beside her. Then in abysmal fear beyond any fear she had ever known, she fell over on her side, sprawling, to put as much space between her and those menacing boots and legs as possible. She saw then that she was lying on a dirty floor smeared with the spittle from chewing tobacco and that everything about her was hot and stinking.

Trembling violently, she looked around her. Two other men were in this room, which was intensely heated by a pot-bellied black coal stove in the center. Large gaslights hanging from the ceiling filled the room with a light fearful to the girl. One man sat at a scarred roll-top desk heaped with papers; he was in his shirt sleeves, and Caroline, with the clarified vision of unrelieved fear, saw that his shirt was striped in red and white, that he was scrawny, withered, and wore steel-rimmed spectacles, and that he was old. Another man sat at a rickety table, also heaped with papers, and he was younger and had a pale, bloated face and mean little blue eyes. Green steel files lined the walls.

"What's this, what's this?" protested the old man in a querulous voice. "Can't you handle thieves alone, Aleck?" He chewed, coughed, and spat on the floor.

"Mr. Fern, I don't know about this one," said Aleck, and made as if to kick Caroline. When she shrank back on the floor, he bellowed with laughter. "No sir, this one's new to me. Kind of funny."

"Funny, eh?" said the young man at the table. He got up languidly; his body was swollen.

"Sure is, Mr. Johnny. Maybe an amateur or something. But look at her hands. No kitchen drab or sewing girl from some factory. Don't want to make mistakes, y'see. There's always the police."

He bent and grasped one of Caroline's hands and displayed it to the two men. "See what I mean? Smooth. No burns; no pricks. No calluses. Like a lady's hand. You'd think she was a lady 'cept for her clothes and the looks of her."

The young man giggled; it was a high and feminine sound. He bent over the cowering Caroline and stared at her. "That ain't no lady," he blatted. "And maybe she's in some other work besides the kitchen or the shop. Maybe she works where she don't have to use her hands. See? Maybe she uses somethin' else, if you follow me."

The old man cackled, and the burly man roared and slapped his thighs. Johnny lifted his hand in modest deprecation of this applause. "Corrected. She ain't the type; look at her. Not my type anyways. But there is no accountin' for tastes, as the old lady said when she kissed the cow. Get her up on her feet, Aleck."

Aleck obligingly tugged at Caroline's arm and pulled her upright. She made no sound. She had heard of nothing in her life that could act as a frame of reference for her now. She did not know why she was here, nor what she had done, nor why these evil men smirked at her. She had heard the word "thief" but did not, in her dazed state, connect it remotely with herself. She knew only that she had been struck, that she had been prevented from trying to find her purse, that she had been dragged into this place. Was she to be murdered? And if so, why? Tears of primitive fear began to roll down her face; her voice was locked in her throat as in a nightmare. She tried to scream; the sound emerged as a whimper.

The men were listening to Aleck, the burly man. She heard his voice as from a far, vague distance and could not distinguish the words. Her staring eyes fixed themselves on him. And then he was pointing at her face. "Y'see what I mean, Mr. Fern, and why I brought her here? She's funny; don't act like the other thieves. And when I find somethin' funny I don't mess around with it. Had one bad experience, makin' a mistake, and ended up behind bars. Aleck's not goin' to make another one. It's right in your hands, Mr. Fern."

Johnny came up to Caroline and took an edge of her coat; she shrank back from him. He roughly lifted the hem of her skirt and examined the cheap wool material. He pulled up her petticoats and looked at her cotton stockings. He fingered her old black velvet hat. He shook his head.

"Cheap-jack clothes," he said. "We got better right out on our counters. Even the whores wouldn't buy things like this; got more self-respect." He lifted his hand and slapped Caroline's cheek. It was an easy gesture, but it stung like a wasp, and Caroline put up her hand to shelter the spot. "All right, Katy," said Johnny in a gentle voice, "let's have your story. Why'd you come here to steal?"

"Steal?" repeated Caroline in a stupefied tone.

"Steal!" said Johnny, lifting a threatening hand, and Caroline stepped back. "See here, Katy, I'm losing patience. Be quick about your story or I'll call the police and you'll rot in jail."

"My name isn't Katy," Caroline stammered. "My name is Caroline Ames. I wasn't——" But she could not say the infamous word.

Aleck had listened intently to her few words, and he shifted uneasily. "There's her voice," he said. "That ain't a regular voice. Funny accent. Used to hear it on the docks. Beacon Hill accent. When they was goin' on the big ships for Europe."

"Now you hush, Aleck," said Johnny, shaking his head at the other man. "You just imagine it. If this girl got a Beacon accent she picked it up. Now look here, Katy. We don't want no trouble. You just pay up what you owe, and you get your nice packages, and you just leave nice, and we'll forget it."

"I haven't any money," said Caroline. She paused, and the abysmal terror roared in on her again, shouting in echoes, "No money! No money! No money! I haven't any money!" She covered her ears convulsively with her hands but could not shut out the increasing thunderous and mocking chorus: "No money! No money! No money!"

"You see?" said Johnny to Aleck with resignation. "Just a plain thief. Came in here to steal and couldn't get out with the things. She needs a good lesson."

Aleck scratched his ear. "Eh, I don't know, Johnny. She's scared; people don't use accents they picked up somewheres when they are scared. But, as you say, look at her clothes."

"I think," said Mr. Fern in a dry old voice of precision, "that I'd better talk to the girl. Now look, my dear"—and he turned on his wheezing swivel chair to look at Caroline directly—"you just tell the truth and you can go home. What's your name? Where do you live?"

Caroline, in a shaking voice, told him. "My name's Caroline Ames. I live on Beacon Street with my aunt, Mrs. Cynthia Winslow, and my father is John Ames."

Johnny giggled, and Aleck scratched his ear and thrust out his under lip. Mr. Fern nodded encouragingly at Caroline, and his eyes twinkled behind his glasses.

"Very nice," he said. "Mrs. Winslow gives nice parties; sometimes read about them in the newspapers. Very select. On all kinds of charity boards, too. Great lady, as my dad used to call her kind. And who doesn't know about Mr. John Ames, him with his fleet of ships and clippers?" His cackle was a modulated shriek. "Reckon they'd be surprised, though, to find out they got a niece and a daughter. What do you do in their house, eh? Make beds and empty slops, maybe? Just tell the truth."

"I go to Miss Stockington's school," said Caroline, her voice fainting. Why didn't they believe her? What was wrong?

Johnny became hysterical. He stamped about the room, slapping his hands together in uncontrollable mirth. He leaned against a wall and gasped, "Miss Caroline Ames, she calls herself, in those clothes, goes to Miss Stockington's delicate, exclusive school! And lives on Beacon Street. God, the girl's got imagination, you've got to admit that!"

"Uh," said Aleck, more and more uneasy. One of Caroline's braids, loosened by the brutality inflicted upon her, had loosened and was now lying on one of her sturdy shoulders. It was clean hair, well brushed and cared for, Aleck noticed. "Say," he said, "if you don't mind, Mr. Fern, I'd like to keep out of this. I've heard about some of these rich folks. They don't care a damn about fine clothes; wear worse than their servants. But still," he added doubtfully, "what was she doing here, in this rat hole, and without any money?"

"That is exactly the point," said Mr. Fern, shaking an admonishing finger. "She just wouldn't have been here. Where's her carriage? Where's her money? Girls from good homes don't run around loose like this and try to steal secondhand trash."

"I lost my purse," said Caroline feebly. "I had seventy-five dollars. I saved it from my allowance. I came to buy some stockings for our housekeeper in Lyndon, Beth Knowles, and some things for my Aunt Cynthia and my cousin Timothy, and Melinda."

"Here in this place?" asked Mr. Fern in a fatherly tone of resignation. "Now, Katy!"

"Beth comes here," said Caroline, crying again. "Our housekeeper. And I used to come with her."

Aleck suddenly shouted, clenching his fists, "I tell you, I don't like this! There's something wrong! Keep me out of it!"

"You brought her here," said the giggling Johnny. "We didn't. You find something wrong now, but you didn't find it when you dragged her back from the door when she was trying to run out with the stolen merchandise."

"Johnny has a point," sighed Mr. Fern. He turned to Caroline again. "Don't you know it's wrong, Katy, to steal things, to take things when you don't have the money to pay for them?"

"Yes, yes," said Caroline, looking with terrified longing at the door. "Of course. It's wrong. But I did have money. I just lost it, on the horse car or somewhere in the shop."

"And you came here on the horse car and not in a nice carriage?" asked Johnny, wetting his lips and grinning evilly.

"I—Aunt Cynthia wanted me to use the carriage," Caroline stuttered. "But——" She could not remember just now why she had refused the carriage. There was a dreadful rolling and shouting in her head. She put both hands up to her temples.

It never occurred to her, for she was so innocent, to ask these men to call a policeman or to send a messenger to her home. She was caught in something monstrous. She could not think. The chorus had begun again: "No money! No money! You have no money! If you had money you would not be here now! You would be safe at home! No money!"

She thought of something. Cynthia had given her a beautiful ring for her birthday, a large and fiery opal. The colors had entranced Caroline; she never wearied of holding the jewel in her hands, cupped under lamplight. The hues soothed her lonely spirit, gave it the flush of glowing life, filled her with the sense of promise beyond any promise in book or poetry or music. It was too magnificent for her to wear on her hand, for others to look at. She had it hung about her neck on a strong cord. She fumbled at it now, her golden eyes burning with dread and fear. She brought it out but held it tightly in her fingers. These terrible men might take it from her.

"My Aunt Cynthia gave this to me," she whispered. "It's mine. So, you see, I am telling you the truth."

The men came to look at it. Even Mr. Fern got up from his desk to examine it. Caroline was never to know what thoughts occurred to two of them now. But Aleck knew. He put his hand on Caroline's shoulder; it was a hard hand and she did not know it was protecting. He saw the rim of canary diamonds curving about the large stone. He, if not Caroline, knew the worth of this marvelous ring.

Then Mr. Fern and his son looked at each other inscrutably. As at a signal, Johnny rushed to his desk and began to write with scrawling haste. Mr. Fern gave Caroline his chair, tenderly. "Sit down, my dear. You must be tired. It is all a mistake. You understand this? We're poor men, Johnny and me. We just try to make a living. And people come in and steal. We have to protect ourselves. You understand that?"

"Yes," Caroline whispered, but her eyes were still large and bright with dread and shock. It was late. Night already pressed against the smudged windows. "I must go home," she said. "They'll be worrying about me."

Mr. Fern looked at Aleck, who stood there near the door, huge and stolid, and exchanged hard look for hard look. There was to be no help from Aleck, Aleck who knew all about the police.

"So you'll just sign this little paper," said Mr. Fern. "Just a little paper showing it was all a misunderstanding. Between you and us. A mistake."

"Yes, yes," said Caroline hurriedly. Hope came to her.

"And as a token of our esteem, we'll give you your purchases," said Mr. Fern. "Gifts. From us to you." He put the pen in her hand. "Just sign here, my dear Miss Ames. Just a formality."

Caroline signed. She did not even read the paper, which absolved Fern and Son of any responsibility toward her, which agreed that Fern and Son had acted only in accordance with law and that an error had been made on her part. She had attempted, read the paper, to leave the shop without accounting for her purchases and had been questioned. All had been resolved to the satisfaction of all parties concerned. Signed, Caroline Ames.

They put her in a hack and paid for it and sent her on her way. Caroline knew she fainted in the hack. She came to when the old hack pulled up abruptly before the house on Beacon Street. But it was drawn before the servants' entrance, at the side. "A little farther," said Caroline in a new and shrinking voice. "The front door."

"What?" growled the driver, who knew nothing but that an ill-clad girl had been thrust dazedly into his hack and that he had been given a fee and a meager tip.

Caroline scrambled from the cold and broken vehicle. If she did not move very fast, she thought numbly, something more terrible might happen to her. "Yes, yes," she murmured, and fled up the flagged path to the servants' entrance, and there she huddled in the shadows, not feeling the sleet and the rain or the bitter wind in her white face. It was not until the hack had moved on that she crept to the front door and rang the bell. She almost fell into the warm and luxurious hall, and the maid stared at her, at the dusty clothes, the bare hands—for Caroline had lost both her gloves—the battered hat, the streaked face and distended eyes, and the mean parcels that tumbled to the floor. Caroline said something incoherent and stumbled up the stairs with a kind of animal desperation which looked only for shelter. When she reached her room she closed the door behind her, then leaned against the door and panted audibly.

She looked about her calm and pleasant room—at the fire burning discreetly behind a brass screen, at the draperies, the rug, the bed, the desk, the chairs—and her slow gaze had a sudden searching in them, a wild relief, and, above all, a hungry fear. She was safe at last; she had been rescued from horror, the implacable horror of not having any money. But she was only momentarily safe from the world, which hated those who were poor and tormented them. Unless she had a great deal of money, and always had it, she would be open again and again, forever and forever, to what her father had called "the faces," the loathing, the ignominy, inflicted on those who were destitute, who were helpless, and who had no golden armor to protect themselves even from their own ravenous kind.

For the first time in her own life Caroline now truly hated, grimly, icily, and with powerful revulsion. She clenched her hands into fists. What her father had told her had frightened her; she had believed him without doubt. But sometimes vague dissatisfactions and humble questionings had invaded her mind. She despised herself now. Her father had been only too right; he had known the truth. He had tried to teach her the truth, for her own protection, and she had not fully believed. Not until this frightful day, this frightful night.

Then she thought, "But we don't have much money! What shall we do, Papa and I? We must have a lot of money, all the money we can get, or they'll kill us, as I was almost killed tonight. A lot of money, all the money in the world—if we can get it. Then we'll be safe."

She began to cry without tears, and only with great heaving sobs of fright. She felt an almost crushing pity for her father and for what he had endured as a young boy and a young man. She remembered vividly all he had told her, all he had suffered, and only for the crime of not having money. "But it *is* a crime!" she cried to her elegant room and its subtle furnishings. She put out her hands and groped toward the bed and then sat on the edge of it, shuddering, feeling cold ripples on her flesh.

The door opened, and with a quick and pretty rustling of blue silk Cynthia entered, her well-bred nose wrinkling fastidiously as she looked down at the newspaper-wrapped parcels in her hand. "What on earth, Caroline!" she exclaimed. "Where did you get these, for goodness' sake! Where have you been so late? I was almost frantic."

She stopped at the sight of the silent girl sitting on the bed, shivering as if with influenza, still dressed in her hat and coat, her hands clenched on the woolen knees. "Caroline! What on earth! Why, you are wet and streaked with dirt! Caroline!"

The big hazel eyes regarded her silently; the dry lips were parted. Cynthia stared back. Then she placed the parcels on the floor and pushed them aside with her foot. Something had stricken the poor girl, something had most evidently scared her out of her wits. Where had she been? Why was she so late?

But Cynthia was a sensible woman and knew there was a time for questioning and a time for not questioning. She came to the bed and said gently, "Let me help you off with your things, dear. It is an awful night, isn't it? Have you a chill?"

"Yes," whispered Caroline. "I've had a chill." She had never been sick in her life before, but now she felt physically broken, cold to the heart. She did not protest when Cynthia, who concealed her distaste, helped her to remove her clothing and to find one of her ugly flannel nightgowns. Cynthia considerately averted her head when Caroline, trembling, stood naked before her—a large, smooth, and impressive young statue—and slipped the nightgown over the big shoulders.

"There, there," said Cynthia soothingly, as one speaks to a frightened child. "Now, we'll just turn back the counterpane and we'll get under the warm blankets and the puff and we'll have our dinner in bed, a nice hot dinner of soup and a little fish and some chicken. We'll just be quiet and see how we are tomorrow."

Caroline lay stiff and straight in her bed, and silent, and looked at the fire. She said in a weak voice, "I lost my purse—somewhere. I had seventy-five dollars." But she did not turn her head to her aunt.

"Oh, how unfortunate," said Cynthia, bending over her anxiously and studying the girl's pallor and the fixed bright distention of her eyes. "Well, it isn't too much money, is it? I will give it to you tomorrow."

"You don't understand, Aunt Cynthia," said Caroline, and her eyes fastened on her aunt's face with what Cynthia almost believed was sharp dislike and aversion. "Seventy-five dollars is a lot of money. It is the difference between—between——" But she could not tell Cynthia of what she had experienced.

"Certainly it is quite a sum of money," said Cynthia, trying to smile away that afflicted expression on the girl's face. "But if it is lost, then it is lost. Dear me, why do you wear that ring I gave you around your neck and not on your hand? Won't the cord choke you in bed?"

"It's too expensive to wear," Caroline muttered. She had always been afraid of Cynthia's sophistication and had always been shy with her, feeling clumsy in her presence. But she had never hated her before. Her aunt was a silly, spendthrift woman who did not know that money was the difference between ignominy and respect, slavery and freedom, life and death.

"One doesn't hide beauty," Cynthia said with kind seriousness. She smoothed the girl's tangled hair, and Caroline shrank from her, and Cynthia was startled. But she continued without a change in tone: "Beauty is to display, to decorate, to make the world a lovelier place." She looked at the dun-colored heap of Caroline's discarded clothes on the floor; Cynthia had not laid them upon a chair because of the filth and bits of straw and dust all over them.

"There's no beauty without money," said Caroline, and turned her head away.

"Oh, Caroline. Nonsense. You really don't mean that." Cynthia smiled again. "Why, I have very little money, but I do have a lovely house and I live well, if not grandly."

"We're not talking about the same things," said Caroline in a mutter. But Cynthia heard, and her face became thoughtful. "I don't know," she said. "Perhaps we are."

Caroline made no protest at all when Cynthia ordered that the girl's clothes be taken from the room "and given away to someone."

Cynthia, who was rarely inquisitive, did not ask why Caroline later became interested in better, if not handsomer, clothing. For a few years at least Caroline wore excellent material, even though it was badly draped and poorly cut, for Caroline would not employ Cynthia's expensive seamstress. And always, Cynthia noted, Caroline was never without a good, strong leather purse, and she held it in a clutching grasp.

What had happened to Caroline on that destroying day remained her own secret. She had no words to give it substance. It stayed with her always. The note she had signed for Fern and Son was, many years later—two generations later—incorporated in a witty book about her life by the grandson of old Fern, and it was considered very risible and multitudes greedily laughed, and the book was translated into many languages. But no one read of raped innocence in that book, and the dark terror of a young girl, and the sad ruins of a whole life.

Caroline was crying because of the letter she had received from Tom Sheldon.

It was spring and Tom was with his elderly parents now. His father had bought, with Tom's earnings on the Erie Canal and on harbor ships in Boston, some scrubby land in Lyme near the sea and, going largely into debt, had built a number of small summer homes upon it. These he had sold at considerable profit a year ago and had been encouraged to buy more land for the same purpose. During the summer months Tom helped his father, who did most of the building, and was investing in the venture.

He wrote in his letter to Caroline: "I know we couldn't spend much time together last summer, Carrie, but you knew how it was, with all the work. But even when I did have time on Sundays you didn't often meet me on the beach and in the back of your house, the way we always did, and only once did you go down to the village with me for some ice cream. Don't you like me any more, Carrie? You know how much I love you. Why, I never saw a girl as nice as you anywhere, and I've seen some beauties, too. Nobody has your eyes and your ways and your pretty smile; you're the only girl for me. It's because of you that I began to read so much. Now I read for my own pleasure, and when I'm in Boston I go to the Museum and sit in the balcony when they have concerts. Once it was just to be worthy of you; now I know that a man has to do things for his own soul, as well as for the girl he wants to marry. I go to church whenever I can, for, as I've told you, there is more to life than success, and more to life than death or just living from day to day.

"You haven't answered my last two letters. I was on the move, though. Perhaps I missed your replies. Did I, Carrie? I reread all your letters; I've kept every one. The last one I had disturbed me. I thought you were merely thinking on paper when you wrote the previous ones, but now I am wondering. Why do you always write about money and ask me if I am saving as much as I can? You sounded so afraid of something in your last letter. Now, I've worked hard enough as long as I can remember; my parents were poor and I did what I could. I know the value of money. I'm not improvident, and I'm not a spendthrift. But I know, too, where the value ends. We weren't born for the sole purpose of acquiring money and saving it and worshiping it. There is another reason why we were born, and that reason isn't cash.

"I've known what it is to be hungry and alone and shabby. You write me that the world hates those who have no money and tries to destroy them. Carrie, that's going too far! I've had my share of knocks and punches and other things when my pockets were empty. Does that matter? That, too, is a part of living. And I've met kind people almost as poor as I was, who shared what they had with me. Wicked people can be found anywhere. I'm not foolish enough to say that there are more good people than bad; there aren't. The devils are ten to one more than the angels, and I have scars to prove it. But even that doesn't matter. It's only your own soul you have to consider, and your own justness to others, and your own determination to be decent.

"Money can bring you a lot of peace of mind, and I'm trying to get it as fast as possible, Carrie. A man's an idiot if he says money is nothing. But he is a worse idiot if he thinks there is nothing else besides money. Why, Carrie, there is the whole world. Don't you remember how you used to point out things I might have missed without you, the way the light lies on the ocean just before a storm, and how the trees look in the early morning, just as if they're shaking themselves awake and spreading out their green clothes to catch the wind? Hundreds of things, Carrie dear. You gave me eyes. I was always too busy to see before. Now I know that you don't have to have a lot of time to look at the world; you just have to look. What has happened to you, Carrie?

"I love you; I love the way you smile, and the soft way you have of laughing. What troubles you, Carrie? Can't you tell me? You've changed. Don't change, Carrie. Wait for me."

But how can I explain to Tom? Caroline asked herself, holding Tom's letter in her hands tightly and seeing the strong and controlled writing through her tears. I never could explain to anybody; I just don't have the right words. Tom, I love you; I wish I could see you every day. Perhaps I wouldn't be so frightened all the time. Sometimes, for weeks on end, I see nothing at all but my fear, and no other faces but those in that awful shop. Tom, you are wrong. Yes, you are wrong. My father was right from the very beginning. But still, I love you.

CHAPTER SEVEN

"You really must help me with Caroline," said Cynthia to John Ames in early June. "She shows absolutely no interest in the things which absorb young girls. She isn't yet eighteen. It's time for me to give her her presentation tea—boring, I admit, and I do loathe tea, a fact I keep discreetly to myself. The tea is only the beginning for a Boston girl, and especially for the daughter of John Ames. You will have to give her a fine ball at her coming out. Do be quiet, and let me finish. You think it ridiculous; perhaps it is. I never had such a wearisome time as when Ann and I were presented to society—old haughty dowagers we'd known all our lives and who had been present when we were christened. Nevertheless, one has to conform sometimes. It is much less wearing to conform to the unimportant things than to oppose them. Perhaps I don't have the stamina of other Boston ladies. Please stop kissing my arm and listen, for I am quite serious.

"If for no other reason but sound logic and shrewdness, Caroline must go through these things. After all, she will have to deal with these people later. (Much later, I hope, my love. What should I do without you? I really love you dearly, though I can't think why.) Unless, of course, you are intending to appoint a Board of Directors or something to manage Caroline's affairs in the future and let her drift along in this dull and aimless way all her life. And she must meet young men, the sons of the dowagers who are already asking when Caroline is going to be presented to them. The dowagers have seen Caroline fleetingly, one might call it, and I think they rather approve of her sturdy appearance, being so sturdy themselves. Are you sure there is no Boston blood in you, sweetheart? But then, you never did tell me anything about yourself, which makes you mysterious, and I love mysteries. Don't ever tell me.

"Caroline goes dutifully, but miserably, to dancing school. The boys, when at home from college or spending an afternoon or evening away from their blessed Harvard, show considerable interest in Caroline. We don't deceive ourselves that it is her fragile appearance which attracts them. It's your money. And I do believe that they, like their mothers, approve of Caroline's sturdiness; she has a no-nonsense figure and manner to which they are accustomed; it seems most proper to them. But she isn't interested in riding or charities or good works and all the other tiresome things. She ought to pretend, at least, for her own sake." Cynthia paused.

They were sitting together in Cynthia's suave little sitting room next to her bedroom. The rose-and-silver draperies moved in the warm June night wind, and there was a scent of tearoses and peonies from the garden below. Cynthia's dressing gown, of a silvery material, flowed gracefully about her beautiful figure and parted softly to show her white throat and part of her white breast. She sipped an excellent cordial; her lovely hair rippled loosely about her shoulders and down her back.

"You've seen me many, many times before, John," said Cynthia affectionately, and touched him lightly on the knee. "And how handsome you still are, in spite of being an elderly gentleman in your fifties; hardly any gray in your hair; you look so distinguished. I like to see you smile. Do you know that you rarely smile except when we are alone together, or when you look at Melinda before she goes to sleep?" Cynthia's voice dropped.

"Before I talk to you about Caroline, I want to ask you a question," said John.

She shook her head again and sighed and smiled. "And the answer is still no, dear. Not even for Melinda's sake."

"Now that the usual formalities are cleared away, we will talk about Caroline," said John. "I don't agree with you. I'm not afraid of offending the Boston biddies and their sons. I doubt if Caroline will ever marry. There is something missing in her. She probably understands this very well.

Give your tea, Cynthia, if you wish, and I'm sure you'll be sorry for Caroline afterward. But, no ball. If it's money only that interests the ladies of Boston —and I know it is—their interest in Caroline won't decline because she wasn't presented at a ball. And they will invite her to the Assemblies, and she won't go. I won't say a word to her. Let her alone, love. I am about to begin a much more important course of education for her. Beginning tomorrow."

He looked gloomily at her swinging foot. "She will learn. She has great capacities. She understands many things. I've had talks with her. And tomorrow the intensive education will begin."

"How?" asked Cynthia, alarmed.

"I am going to take her down to the docks and show her my ships and clippers. That is only the beginning."

"I try to remind myself," said Cynthia sadly. "I try to tell myself that if you were completely a wretch you'd never have brought Caroline to me and sent her to Miss Stockington's. You see, I like to believe that I'm incapable of loving a man who is an absolute beast. So I tell myself that in spite of what you say about Caroline you do have some love for her."

"Oh, God," said John, and stood up impatiently. "If demonstrations of selfless love are so important to you, Cynthia, you'd have married me years ago. You'd have some consideration for Melinda."

"You make me sound like a fool," said Cynthia sharply. "Of course I have consideration for Melinda. She's my precious darling. And it's partly because of Melinda that I won't marry you, and I wish you'd stop bringing up the tedious subject. Very well. I won't argue with you about Caroline any longer, though the very sight of the poor girl breaks my heart sometimes. I've never seen anyone so desolate-looking; the only time she glows a little is when you're here, and you hardly speak to her about the casual things a girl loves to hear from her father. I'm very vexed with you. No, you cannot stay with me tonight. Be understanding and go up to your own room. I'm tired."

Caroline, as usual, had been inarticulately joyful when her father had returned to Boston that afternoon from an unusually long absence. While she did not feel the curious and inexplicable security she felt when with Tom Sheldon, she always had the sensation that when her father was present he represented some kind of desperately needed shelter for her. She never doubted he loved her; she believed he was only as inarticulate as she in expressing his emotions, and as shy as she. In return, her love reached adoration, unquestioning, absolute. John Ames, to his daughter, was all-wise, omniscient, beyond good and beyond evil, to whom everything had been explained and to whom nothing was strange and without an answer.

It was this fixed idea which Beth, in her simple way, and Tom Sheldon, in his love and anxiety, and Cynthia, in her wise sophistication, had tried to shake. They had failed. Beth thought Caroline's adoration piteous; Tom recognized it as dangerous for the girl; Cynthia had considered it a crippling of the spirit and an absurdity. It was Cynthia who had given Caroline a copy of *Dombey and Son*, with the subtle hope that Caroline might find there something resembling herself and the tragic heroine who loved her father without reason, and stupidly. When Caroline had finished the book Cynthia asked her how she had liked it. To Cynthia's wry despair, Caroline had answered seriously, "Poor Mr. Dombey!"

It seemed quite natural to Caroline for John Ames to occupy the large and pleasant apartment on the third floor. She did not even ask herself how long he had occupied it or if he had been there before her own removal to this house. She was his daughter; for him to go to a hotel when in Boston would have been ridiculous. Moreover, Cynthia was his sister-in-law. Caroline had a jealous eye for evidence of affection; she saw that while her father had respect for Timothy, and interest in him, and advised him when the young man was at home—Timothy was to go to Harvard, of course, in the autumn—John Ames showed no other sign of any attachment. But Caroline, to her dismay and lonely fear, saw that her father loved little Melinda. A dull, sick resentment began to fill Caroline at the sight of the little girl. More and more, she avoided Melinda and muttered only short answers to the girl's remarks. Sometimes she thought that Melinda was as trivial and as mindless as Cynthia; certainly the two enjoyed incomprehensible jokes together which bewildered her.

She was not quite as naïve as both John Ames and Cynthia believed. Her wide reading had left her with a very solid idea of sensual attachments, and she had some dim understanding as to why she felt a throb of joy at the sight of Tom Sheldon and why his kind touch on her cheek was electrifying. She was innocent but not uninformed. There was a lack of specific detail in her mind, which often engrossed her wonder and conjecture at night, but that there were very specific details she had no doubt. Cynthia, in spite of her suavity and worldliness, was still of her era; she had attempted with what she had believed to be the utmost tact and delicacy to enlighten Caroline in some fashion. She had been quite astonished to see Caroline turn a bright, confused red; Caroline used to terminate these sessions abruptly. She was curious, but her dislike for Cynthia, which had become aversion since that malignant night last December, rejected Cynthia as a confidante.

When John had returned that afternoon they had had what Cynthia referred to as an intimate family dinner. She and John spoke together politely and with friendly interest, avoiding any sign of intimacy in the presence of the obdurate Caroline, whose shining eyes were almost entirely fixed on John's face, and in the presence of Melinda, to whose every childish remark John listened with faintly smiling attentiveness. The dinner, as usual, was loathsome to Caroline. She detested the taste of sherry in the fowl, the mushrooms on the fish, the exquisiteness of the little cakes, and the wine-flavored prepared fruit. One of the maids, who was almost a friend of hers, would leave a slice of cheese and some bread and milk on her bedside table and a round apple. These Caroline would devour with a lustiness that would have interested, if not revolted, Cynthia.

John, admonished by Cynthia's sparkling eyes, spoke to his daughter a few times at dinner. He remarked coldly but with approval that the last report received from Miss Stockington had indicated that Caroline was extremely proficient in mathematics. "The Apollonian Art," he had added. "And the most utilitarian."

"I doubt bankers know it is an art—or anyone else connected with money," Cynthia had said. But Caroline did not hear her. She was overwhelmed with joy at her father's approval. She wanted to tell him how mathematics fascinated her, how there was a tempo, flow, and precision in it that were intensely musical, and how its order and clarity reminded her of color and harmony. But she could only stutter and look at him adoringly, and he turned away.

It was then that he decided he must now undertake Caroline's education himself. She had been expertly taught at her school; she spoke German and French well and with good accents. History had been another of her best subjects. If nothing else, Caroline had been an excellent scholar.

Caroline was so happy over her father's approval that she wished to talk to him after dinner, but he indicated that he was tired. He disappeared upstairs after a short interval in the drawing room. Caroline's disappointment was very visible. Cynthia said, as she began to work on another square of gros point for her dining-room chairs, "Your father is a very busy man, you know, Caroline. He is going to stay for a few days, so don't be too disappointed that he couldn't remain with us tonight."

"I'm not disappointed," said Caroline with hard coldness. Even the faintest criticism of her father outraged her. "I know he's tired. And he has many responsibilities."

Cynthia shrugged. She knew that John was now with Melinda in the child's bedroom. Caroline showed indications of leaving the room. She must not encounter her father leaving that pretty room with all its flounces and bright lamps, nor must she hear the muffled laughter. When Caroline began to pull herself to the edge of her chair Cynthia said coaxingly, "Dear, would you please refill my glass with that crème de menthe? My digestion is a little out of order tonight."

Caroline obeyed sullenly, but she watched the smooth green fluid flowing from the carafe into the crystal glass with pleasure. Lamplight flashed on it, deepening its running hues to emerald. "Won't you try some, Caroline?" asked Cynthia. But Caroline put down the carafe with such speed that it clattered on the silver tray. "I don't like spirits," she mumbled.

Cynthia sighed. "It isn't 'spirits,'" she said. "Dear me, why do you always try to make me look like a drunken trollop, Caroline?"

Caroline was shocked, which was what Cynthia had intended. "Aunt Cynthia!" cried the girl, and flushed darkly.

"Well, you do," said Cynthia, smiling and sipping the liqueur.

"You drink whiskey sometimes," Caroline blurted.

"So I do. I have a theory that many people would go mad without an occasional indulgence in alcohol. The world isn't exactly a Garden of Eden, you know, Caroline, and there are some people who must retreat from it sometimes or lose their minds."

"You live in a kind of Garden of Eden," said Caroline bluntly.

"Do I?" Cynthia lifted a humorous eyebrow. "I'm glad you think so. I try to give that impression. It is very ill bred to show your troubles or your doubts or your illness or worries to the world. It is like undressing in public—indecent. Thank you, dear, for reassuring me."

Cynthia's little witticisms always confused Caroline, who never knew whether her aunt was serious or not. She stared acutely at Cynthia and decided that the older woman was mocking her gently, and she colored again. "I've never known you to be ill, Aunt Cynthia," she said in her somewhat loud and very direct voice, "and if you have troubles I've never seen any sign of them, and I've lived here a long time. What worries could you have?"

Cynthia put down the square of canvas and looked at Caroline thoughtfully. She shook her head a little. "My dear child," she said, "I do hope that you won't be one of those obtuse women who see only the obvious and insist that there is nothing else in life but the obvious."

"I don't," said Caroline with harshness in her voice.

Cynthia was surprised. She was also bored. Talks with Caroline were frustrating and unrewarding; they never seemed to be talking about the same thing. Besides, she had heard Melinda's door open and close and John's footsteps going to his room.

"Good," said Cynthia absently. She took up the gros point again. Her dress, of silk exquisitely printed in pale lilac and gold, was like a spring garden. Diamonds glowed and winked about her neck, her wrist, and her fingers. Her throat was white and smooth, her hands pearly. Caroline looked at her, her strong black eyebrows drawn together in a newly formidable fashion.

"I'm not as stupid as you think I am," said Caroline suddenly. Cynthia, again surprised, glanced up. "I never said you were stupid, Caroline," she replied, "and I certainly never thought so. That's another bad habit you have: you put things into people's mouths and then accuse them of your own imaginings. You're a very difficult girl."

"So you often say," said Caroline. She got to her feet clumsily and left the room without another word. Again Cynthia shook her head. The ormolu clock on the mantel chimed half-past nine, tinkling musically. A carriage or two rumbled by on the cobbled street. The spring wind sighed at the windows. In half an hour Cynthia would go to her own rooms and John would join her.

Caroline, in her bedroom, took up her schoolbooks. There was a sensation of tight excitement in her. Her father had remarked with approval on her scores in mathematics. She must apply herself even more intensively to them to gain more approval. She smiled a little, and a tender look appeared about her mouth and a brightness in her eyes. She stood up with an unaccountable restlessness and went to the window. The light from her father's room shone down upon her. He would be busy with his papers tonight. All of the girl's senses were acute; the spring night air blew into her face, stirred her dark hair, flowed on her cheeks. Her young body was suddenly and mysteriously aroused. All at once, powerfully and involuntarily, her thoughts turned like an eager face to Tom Sheldon, and her eyes filled with tears. A sensation of joy spread from her heart over all her flesh and nerves.

She ran to her dressing table and stared at herself. Her cheeks were softly colored; her big mouth was red and unusually full and moist. And her large and beautiful eyes looked back at her with a startled and joyous expression, the irises swimming in gold. Her face was strongly molded; her artist's eyes found a greatness and splendor of earth and vitality in it, and she marveled and thought again of Tom. Her fingers fumbled at her hair; she pulled down the long narrow braids, unwound the strands. Her hair flowed over her shoulders and down her back like rippling glass.

I am not pretty, she thought. I'll never be pretty, as people call it. But I think I see what Tom sees in me! I am not ugly at all!

Without illusion she saw her broad shoulders, her large full breasts, her thick waist, and the outline of her heavy thighs under her brown foulard dress. But even these had a splendor to her critical appraisal. For the first time in months she thought longingly of canvas and paint, and her fingers arched and trembled. If only I had them, she said to herself, I'd paint my own portrait and send it to Tom.

She forced herself away from the mirror. She had work to do. Her vital mind had infinite strength, and so she sat down and opened her books. She became engrossed, forgetting the fine, flowing cascade of her hair, and even Tom. She looked about for a volume of Pythagoras which she had brought with her from Lyndon, but she could not find it. There was an advanced problem she wanted to solve. Then she remembered leaving it in the little exotic library downstairs and ran to the door. She flung it open and looked cautiously down the hall, her hair spilling forward across her shoulders.

She heard a murmur of voices from somewhere. She did not want to encounter any servants on her way downstairs and waited. Then she became conscious that the voices were those of her father and her aunt. She frowned. What had he to say to frivolous Aunt Cynthia that would give his voice that deep and murmurous sound, that deep and caressing sound? He was laughing; he had never laughed that way before, to Caroline's knowledge, and then his voice sharpened. Caroline heard his footsteps nearby, and then she knew that her father was not downstairs. He was in her aunt's room.

For a moment or two her thoughts were stunned, and she stood there helplessly in her doorway. Then the thoughts came jumbling back. Of course, her father had been going over Aunt Cynthia's household books; that sharpness was familiar to his daughter and was always connected with money. But Caroline's hand was cold and a little damp as she pulled the door almost closed. She heard Cynthia's voice quite clearly now, raised as if in vexation:

"No, you cannot stay with me tonight. Be understanding and go up to your own room. I'm tired."

Caroline was freshly stunned; the dryness in her throat turned to parched sickness. "No, you cannot stay with me tonight." But men "stayed" only with their wives or, in the case of esoteric females in far countries, with their mistresses.

Stay! With Aunt Cynthia! Caroline, clutching the edge of the door, leaving it ajar but an inch or so, leaned against the side and closed her eyes tightly. She was wrong. She was stupid. She was evil. Her father . . . She heard Cynthia's light laugh, and it sounded strange to Caroline, intimate and warm and mocking. The door to Cynthia's room opened, and Caroline glanced through the small opening of her own door, her legs trembling.

A gush of light flooded out into the quiet dark hall. Cynthia believed her servants to be cozily in their beds, Melinda asleep, and Caroline absorbed in her solitary thoughts or asleep also. She stood on the threshold of her sitting room, all sparkling silver and bright hair, and John Ames was facing her and her arms were about his neck and she was kissing his chin, slowly, teasingly, deliberately, and avoiding his mouth archly. Caroline could even see the dancing flash of her eyes, the warmness of her evading mouth, and her half-naked breast. She could also see that her father was clasping Cynthia about her slender waist and pulling her close to him. Then he put up one hand, caught the teasing face, and kissed the laughing mouth hard and long.

Caroline slid her door shut. She felt weak and deathly ill. Bent like an old woman, she crept, one foot after another, to her bed and fell upon it. She buried her face in the rose-scented linen; it sickened her and she sat up, gasping. She pushed her hair back from her wet face; her fingers felt like wood.

Her Aunt Cynthia was not only a perfumed and spendthrift woman, she was also a bad woman. Mistress. She was John Ames' mistress. She was not married to him. She was shameless, polluted, corrupt. In some way she had entangled Caroline's father, against all his uprightness, his integrity.

Caroline's violent thoughts immediately absolved her father, who had become involved with an unspeakable woman. For what else but money? That made her—a strumpet, a drab, a dreadful creature who sold herself like a trinket. Did she sell herself to other men also, like the women in Zola's books? (Caroline had found those books in Cynthia's small and cherished library and had read them with shrinking disgust and fascination.)

The specific details were still beyond Caroline; Zola had more than hinted at them, but they had slid over Caroline's virginal mind like harmless aspic. There were things men and women did together; she averted her mind from them, feeling some curious disloyalty to her father.

We must get away from here, thought Caroline in numb shock. I must get Papa out of this house.

She jumped up. She was desperately sick. She vomited for a considerable time. Later, exhausted, drained of body, scarlet of eyelid from tears, she pulled a blanket from the bed and slept on the floor. But before that she braided her hair tightly into hard thin ropes.

CHAPTER EIGHT

As John Ames and his daughter drove off the next warm morning to the harbor in Cynthia's smart victoria, John glanced sideways at Caroline and with his customary distaste. Caroline's dress, very primly draped and somewhat too tight for her heroic figure, was of dull silk in an unbecoming brown printed over with large white roses. Her small bonnet of brown straw rode on the top of her tightly coiled braids. Her hands, in brown gloves, clutched her big leather bag. Cynthia had sighingly assured John that all that Caroline had was now expensive, except for the seamstress, who had no sense of style at all. John glanced down at Caroline's feet; she did not wear the soft slippers now very fashionable; her shoes were hard and brown and stiff. John frowned, and then he was struck by a kind of heavy familiar sorrow which he never investigated.

Why did Caroline have to resemble *him?* John asked himself now, as he had asked himself thousands of times before. She had inherited nothing of the physical or mental features of her parents. In appearance, in character, she resembled only David Ames, who had starved his wife to death and had left his young son a pauper.

Caroline, as usual, was shyly silent. John was accustomed to this. He was also accustomed to large and adoring glances. Caroline was not looking at him as they bowled over the cobblestones of Commonwealth Avenue and the sun shone down upon them. She did not look at the ladies on the proper "sunny side" of the avenue, who strolled together, enjoying the soft gentle air with its hint of the sea. And John noticed that his daughter was even paler than usual except for blotches about her mouth, and that her eyes were red-rimmed and cast down, the lids swollen.

"Are you sick?" he asked irritably.

"No, Papa," she said, almost in a whisper. "I think I'm just a little tired." He saw that her throat moved as if she were gulping on tears, and her thick black lashes glistened.

"I thought you would enjoy seeing something of what I have and what will be yours," he said, folding his gloved hands on the top of his cane and trying to control his annoyance and the odd sadness that invariably followed it.

"Oh, I am enjoying it," said Caroline. Now she looked at him for the first time, and in spite of their swollen appearance and red edges her eyes were arrestingly beautiful in the sunlight, and piteous. "It's just—— Papa," she continued on a desperate burst, "I want to go back to Lyndon and then to Lyme!"

"So you shall," he said. "Don't you always in the summer? You'll be going back next week for a little while. I have plans; I'll tell you about them later." He paused, then asked curiously, "Don't you like living with your aunt in Boston?"

"No!" Her tone was so violent that John turned to her with deeper curiosity.

"I thought you did. You haven't shown much anxiety to go to Lyndon on the weekends these last few years. And Beth worries because you seldom write to her."

Caroline was silent. Her hands twisted on the purse which perched on her lap. "Don't you like your aunt and Melinda?" asked John.

Caroline turned her eyes on him imploringly. "Papa," she said, "I don't have words to say the things I often want to say. No, I don't like Aunt Cynthia. It's not that she isn't good to me. It—it's just that we don't understand each other; I feel a stranger in that house. I used to like little Melinda; I know it's wrong not to like a child. But I don't like Melinda any more. I'm terribly sorry, Papa."

John's face became cold and stiff, and he warily studied Caroline out of the corner of his eye. She was desolately struggling not to cry. He moved away from her a little on the soft cushions of the carriage and then stared before him. Cynthia was an astute woman; she had assured him that Caroline knew nothing of her relations with him. Then he was angry. How dared such a big lump of an unattractive girl dislike Melinda, who was not only lovely but of an almost angelic disposition? His anger became more intense, for it was spreading to Cynthia also, Cynthia who would not marry him and give him another acknowledged daughter in Melinda.

"I've offended you, Papa," said Caroline miserably.

"Yes, you have. You express your dislike of two people who have never harmed you and who have tried to love you. I suppose you don't like Timothy, either?"

"I detest him," said Caroline helplessly. "That's wrong too. But I really have reason not to like Timothy. He makes fun of me; he's cruel in that smooth way of his. He doesn't like anyone but Melinda. I want to go away before he comes home from school. Do you know what he calls me, Papa? The Gargoyle."

John pressed his lips together to keep from smiling, then was annoyed at the recurring sadness that came to him increasingly when he thought of Caroline or talked to her.

"Frankly," he said, "you're not alone in disliking Timothy. I respect his mind; he will be a great lawyer, and I'll have use for him later. But that is all. I'll do what I can for him for his mother's sake. Beyond that, nothing. At least you and I understand each other on that point, don't we?"

Caroline was so grateful that she smiled, and her smile was brilliant and for an instant or two she had an intense charm. John was startled, and he frowned thoughtfully. With those eyes, he said to himself, and with that smile, if she'd just practice it more, there could be a husband for her, and children. Moreover, Boston men preferred money to beauty. He felt almost fond of Caroline and patted her hand.

"I, for one," he said, "never underestimated your intelligence, Caroline. You are sometimes awkward, and you're too shy and afraid of people. After all, you'll be very wealthy someday, when I am dead."

Caroline looked at him again with her eager and fascinating smile. "Papa, I know I'm very afraid of people. You see, I keep thinking that you have to have a lot of money so they can't hurt you."

"So you have," he said, and smiled at her in return. "No one can hurt you if you are rich. Did you think we were poor? I think you're old enough to know that I am a very wealthy man now."

"So Aunt Cynthia said," replied Caroline. "But I didn't believe her."

John meditated on this sardonically. "You can believe her," he said.

Caroline gave a deep sigh; some of the rigidity left her body. She was like one who saw a threat removed.

John went on: "In your position it is very necessary to know many people. It will be even more necessary when you are alone. Not that I intend to die soon, so don't look so stricken. Caroline, you aren't a child now. Have you ever thought of the day when you'll want to be married?"

He was taken aback at her sudden blush and the dropping away of her eyes.

"Have you?" he insisted.

"Oh yes, Papa. Oh yes," she murmured.

John stroked the golden head of his cane and watched her narrowly, his interest increasing. "Anyone in particular, Caroline?"

"Yes, Papa." She bent her chin until it almost touched her wide chest. "Please, Papa, don't ask me any more just now."

"Well, well," he observed. "But I must ask you a few questions. I won't ask the young man's name, seeing you're so disturbed. I only hope, though, that his family has plenty of money. Girls like yourself are often the victims of fortune hunters, men who marry for money and have no money of their own. That is one thing you must be on guard against. Now what is wrong? Why are you so pale?"

"Papa"—she spoke as if her throat pained her—"not every man who doesn't have money marries a girl because she has money. Perhaps he may like her for herself."

John was genuinely worried. "Caroline," he said sharply, "don't be a fool. And let's be candid with each other. Men, poor or rich, often marry penniless girls if the girls are beautiful. But you are not beautiful, Caroline. A man without money would marry you only for your money—my money. You'll see; you'll be surrounded by paupers who want to marry a fortune rather than try to make fortunes for themselves. And paupers have a way of ingratiating themselves with girls who have money and no beauty. On the other hand, there are dozens of young Boston men who have a proper respect for property and wealth, having both themselves, and who will marry girls like you of good family and will make excellent husbands and increase both fortunes. Caroline, have you been having dreams of any particular young man who has no money and who is already flattering you in the hope of marrying you in the future?"

Caroline could not speak. She thought despairingly: Not Tom. Tom loves me.

John, seeing her face, was alarmed. He said in an even sharper voice, "Caroline! I want you to remember something. If you have any young man in mind, and I can't think of any of the sons of the people who visit your aunt who are poor—First Families in Boston are never poor—just tell him this as a test. Tell him that you will inherit not a single cent of my money if he doesn't have a fortune of his own. Promise me you'll test him that way."

Caroline lifted her head, and her father saw her profile, which had suddenly acquired both pain and dignity. "Yes, Papa," she said. "I'll tell him that. You see, I'd want to know, myself."

"Good girl," he said, relieved. He looked at her closely. She was no fool, his daughter.

"When you put him to the test he'll run off as fast as his legs can carry him," said John, smiling somberly.

Not Tom, Caroline repeated to herself with deeper despair. And then: Not Tom? Tom? A sick lethargy began to spread over her body, as if she had been poisoned.

She felt a strong cool wind on her face. She became aware that considerable time had passed and that she had not known it. The sunny streets and trees and pleasant houses had disappeared.

The sea, the harbor, the wharves, and the docks were nothing new to Caroline Ames. Miss Stockington, one of whose ancestors had been a pirate of no mean accomplishment who had been hanged in Liverpool when the Spaniards had tiresomely complained too loud and too long of him to the English government, insisted that her young ladies take a yearly expedition to the harbor "to see their inheritance." Caroline considered Boston Harbor somewhat overwhelming, harsh, noisy, and too exuberant and too clangorous. She preferred the ocean at Lyme, with the cold blue waves leaping upon the black rocks and sprawling in white abandon over the bitter shingle, and with its thunderous voice which strangely seemed the very voice of silence. There was an order in wildness which was absent in the human order of the harbor, with its massed ships, its vessels waiting at anchor, its steam, the dirty grayish sails of clippers dipping in a sea which also appeared dirty, its warehouses dripping with a kind of salty black oil, its smells of fish and sweat and pungent spice and bananas, its stinking, tarry freighters, its coils of harsh rope, and its filthy stanchions. And, above all, its clamor of tongues.

She had expected to be here now, and she had some vague idea that her father owned, or partly owned, a clipper or a freighter. But her eyes opened on an unfamiliar scene. The ocean rolled beyond, uneasy on this June day, as if it carried with it memories of storms and battles far in the distance, and its swells glimmered as if oiled and its color was dull green. It did not thunder; it hissed. Two huge docks extruded into it, and everywhere stood the few familiar things: the great black freighters dripping and vomiting bilge, their decks slippery and filthy, their smokestacks rusty and oozing, and the unquiet clippers whose sails were being lowered. There was also the smell of tar and rope in the warm sunshine, and warehouses loomed near the docks, and there were the customary wagons and drays wheeling about on the quivering wood, the horses stamping.

But the unfamiliar things caught Caroline's immediate and shrinking attention. Here there were no good-humored bawlings of seamen, no whistles, no singing, no laughter, no running of strong legs. A curious quiet hung over the docks, for all their busyness, a quiet that was swift and orderly but also dimly sinister even to Caroline. There were no regular dock police here, idly moving about and raucously chatting with the seamen. There were men—and now Caroline trembled—exactly like Aleck in the shop of Fern and Son, burly and savage men with brutally alert eyes and swinging clubs and quick, feline steps. Similar men, big and bulky, yet tensely aware, stood on the decks of the freighters, chewing tobacco and watching everything, and if they spoke it was in undertones to each other. They leaned on railings, spat, and muttered, and their eyes were sharp and watchful. Caroline, feeling exposed and vulnerable and open to attack, looked toward her father, but he had alighted from the victoria and was looking at the many great ships. The vehicle seemed grotesque on the dock, like a flounced lady in a foundry. Caroline, with a sensation of again being abandoned to violence, glanced over her shoulder to the warehouses. Their windows were barred and shuttered; only their great doors, like hungry mouths, stood open to receive the swift freight being carried into them under the eyes of the private police, who swung their clubs for instant action. And on the warehouses there were no familiar merchant names. Only one was painted on them: AMES.

John Ames stood near the victoria, elegant and as watchful as the private police he employed. His right hand idly swung his cane. His black bowler glittered in the sun. For all his fine clothing, his distinguished air, he was part of this scene. He was at one with his employees. The latter were not furtive; they had a look of savage arrogance, which was reflected in John himself in a more polished fashion. The men saw him, and the quiet muttering stopped at once, and a single bell sounded over the uneasy hissing of the water. Police and seamen came to attention, and even the wagons and the drays halted.

"Papa," Caroline murmured, feeling panic. John looked at her impatiently. "Well?" he said, and his voice was resonant in the quiet. "Why don't you get down?"

The coachman sat on his seat like a stuffed image, blind and deaf. After one glance at this homely figure, which did not even get down to assist her, Caroline scrambled from the vehicle, her sturdy shoes thumping on the hot wood of the dock. She rushed to her father's side, instinctively clutching her purse, her shut parasol dangling from her wrist, her tired and reddened eyes blinking, baffled, in the dazzling sun. A freighter belched smoke and steam and cinders, and Caroline flinched. It was like a huge, ugly, derisive voice raised against her, calling attention to her unlikely presence in this place, demanding action and ridicule against her. John looked down at her, amused.

"Well?" he said again. "What's the matter, Caroline? Don't you like all this? You should. It belongs to me. It will belong to you. It is all mine— the warehouses, the docks, the ships."

"Yours, Papa?" asked Caroline.

"Mine. All mine." Several of the private dock police were now approaching the two on cat feet, and Caroline moved closer to her father. They were all Aleck of Fern and Son. Caroline's mouth became as dry as paper; she could not take her eyes from the clutched clubs. But the men were smiling obsequiously; they were removing their battered hats; they were touching their red foreheads; their feet were scraping now as they stood before their employer. They bowed to Caroline. The men on the ships stood as rigid as carved wood, their sea-and-sun-darkened faces expressionless, their ferocious eyes remote.

Then Caroline, with one of her blinding flashes of intuition, understood. Money was not only a defense against the world, the strong Chinese Wall that kept out the barbarians who lusted and destroyed. It was power over the barbarians, over all the world. It was the invisible but mighty club over all the Alecks, over every man. It made humankind grovel and smile with servility as these brutes were smiling. It was power. Her eyes still shrank from the Alecks, but she did not fear them any longer. Her father owned them. In time, she would own them also. For the first time in her life she felt a hating exultation, born of her old fear.

"Yes sir, Mr. Ames, yes sir!" one of the Alecks was exclaiming with the fervor of an abased slave. The other Alecks joined in, in a chorus of servility. Everything was in order. Captain Allstyn was on the *Queen Ann*. No, there had been no trouble. The Alecks snickered and scraped. Everything had been taken care of; not a single boat of the harbor police had even been sighted. No government official had appeared within a mile. Everything was taken care of, sir, if you please.

John Ames put his long hand in his pocket and drew out a handful of glittering gold pieces. The police stretched out their hands eagerly, wetting their brutal mouths. They bowed; they scraped over and over. They bowed very deeply to Miss Ames and hoped she was well.

"Can't you say something to these men?" asked John with irritation.

Caroline stared at them. They lifted their eyes reverently only to her chin. She wet her dry lips. "How do you do?" she murmured in the best Miss Stockington manner.

The brutes became ecstatic. They bowed almost to her knees, their coarse hair tawny or black in the sunlight, their hats held against their thighs, their clubs dangling impotently from their thick wrists. It was one of these who had threatened to crush her skull in the shop of Fern and Son. She said to herself that if she struck one of these bobbing heads with her parasol the victim would chortle with delight and be happy to have been singled out from his fellows by the "little lady."

A piping sounded from somewhere in this sinister but urgent quiet. A man in a kind of disorderly uniform was bounding down a gangplank from the nearest freighter, which was also the largest and the blackest. The man had a huge bald head, like a ball, that glittered in the sun, and a huge red face like a baboon's, and eyes like blue fire. He was short and immensely broad. His uniform, of a dark gray with brass buttons and braid, wrinkled about his body. As he ran, clumping, on the dock toward John Ames and Caroline, his cap in his hand, he fastened the last of his buttons. Caroline, accustomed to the military neatness of the captains of Boston Harbor far to the left, could not believe this man to be a captain, for he lacked compactness, tidiness, and stern precision. The Alecks fell away meekly. He grinned at John Ames, and his teeth were like the teeth of a shark, and his gums were red as the gums of a dog are red. He saluted casually, and John Ames, smiling, gave him a negligent salute in return.

"Caroline," he said, "this is my best captain, Captain Allstyn. An Englishman, and a veritable Union Jack."

Caroline had no way of knowing that Captain Allstyn was an illegal captain, that he had been permanently barred from all employment in the legitimate lines for murderous brutality to his crews and drunkenness and smuggling and general larceny. She had no way of knowing that her astute father had picked up this man in a state of poverty and sullen despair in a Liverpool public house, and that John Ames, having rescued this man from starvation and having restored him to the sea with an immense salary, had bound Captain Allstyn in gratitude to him forever. Moreover, Captain Allstyn shared in the spoils, for John knew that one might bind a man briefly to one by saving his life, but one bound him for all time with money and opportunities for loot.

"You are very kind, sir," said Captain Allstyn, and Caroline was startled at the man's pure well-bred English accent, so strange in comparison with his lumbering appearance, his gross red face, his Vandal's eyes, his stained uniform. She was also impressed by the fact that he did not bow or scrape to either her father or herself.

Captain Allstyn turned to Caroline. "I trust," he said in that patrician accent, "that Miss Ames' first visit will be pleasant for her."

Caroline could only stare at him mutely. He was deferential, as all gentlemen were deferential toward ladies. He stood with his hands at his sides in the exact posture of the young men at the dancing school, waiting for any remark she might care to make, his head inclined slightly and attentively.

"Oh—yes," stuttered Caroline. Captain Allstyn considered her. A lump of a girl, a frightened girl, but a girl of family and breeding. An innocent young thing, like the horsy girls in Sussex who prattled and blushed and stammered and loved dogs and the paddock and trembled when they were presented at Court and rushed home at once thereafter and married bumbling young men like themselves. Captain Allstyn had once been one of those bumbling young men after his short career in Her Majesty's Navy. He had even married a girl like Caroline. But the sea had called him back, back from the hunts and the horses and the dogs and the awkward young girls and the sunny quiet fields and the rosy brick houses and teatime.

He often heard it remarked that John Ames was a "nobody." But Captain Allstyn felt this to be untrue. Those ostensibly aristocratic were too frequently plebeian; the true aristocrat cared nothing for the opinions of others nor for any impression he might make. He lived, an individualist, for himself. Even if the aristocrat engaged in nefarious activities, he did so without pretense to virtue and with no anxiety to hide what he was. Quite often he was an adventurer, but he always led and never followed. John Ames was an aristocrat, as was his captain, and that was the secret they both recognized in each other. For this reason Captain Allstyn was not only commander of the *Queen Ann* but the captain of John Ames' mighty fleet of ambiguous ships.

The captain looked curiously and openly into Caroline's face. He saw the intelligent eyes, the glint of shy fear, and behind them both he saw the shine of young power and dignity. He had expected a pretty girl, for John was handsome. But prettiness did not particularly affect Captain Allstyn, who preferred it in the better bordellos, where it could be sampled in variety. No one would dominate this girl who had no charm but her uncertain smile. Captain Allstyn was relieved. He expected to be with the Ames Line for many, many years, and it was excellent to know that his next employer would be this sturdy girl grown to womanhood and to impressiveness.

Caroline was confused. It had overwhelmed her to know that her father owned all this; she needed concrete evidence, such as the money in her purse, to reassure her that she was not vulnerable and that never again would she be exposed to what the world could and did do to the helpless. She like Captain Allstyn immediately, and this also startled her. She was not accustomed to liking people. Totally inexperienced though she was, her intuition enlightened her considerably concerning the captain.

"Are you coming aboard, Mr. Ames?" asked the captain.

"Yes. Of course. That is why I brought Caroline," said John. He looked at the captain intently. "I thought there were things she should know."

The captain smiled briefly. Caroline stared at the freighter. "We are boarding that, Papa?" The freighter appeared formidable to her, like a long black shark, filthy and weather-beaten. John took her arm. "Certainly."

Caroline had never been aboard any ship in her life. She hesitated, fearful again of the brutish police, the ominous dark faces of the men on the ships. But she saw no derision, no ridicule, no slyly exchanged glances of amusement. She went on with her father, the captain following just behind her left elbow. She could hear their footsteps, loud against the uneasy whispering of the sea, sharp against the sinister quiet. They might have been proceeding against an immense stage-set of painted ships, painted sky, and painted men, with only the ocean to relieve the silence.

Sturdily she climbed the gangplank, lifting her unbecoming dress, the sun hot on her face. All the air was filled with strong smells steeping in the heat. She looked about her when she reached the deck; it heaved a little; the wood was dark with water and stained. She was disappointed. The beautiful clippers she had seen against the sky in the main harbor had enthralled her, their sails white and lofty in the sun, like pulsing and gigantic birds. While the other girls exclaimed about their "prettiness" she had felt their wild grandeur, their solitude, their air of leaving the world and rising into light.

The *Queen Ann* had masts for sails, as well as smokestacks. The sails were down. The ship was ugly and even repellent. The deck was slippery. The whole vessel had a look of decrepitude, and one thought of derelicts. The hatches were open and the cranes in place. It smelled of oil and tar and leather and bananas and wet wood and fish. It was very large; the men in the bow appeared diminished. Caroline wanted to please her father. "It's big, isn't it?" she murmured.

Captain Allstyn answered her in his gentle and cultured voice. "It is one of the biggest on the seven seas, and about the fastest, Miss Ames. It is your father's flagship."

"Come, Caroline," said John, and took her arm again. He led his daughter down a flight of narrow stairs to the deck below, where lanterns were hanging from walls to give light. Here the smells were intensified, the floor only slightly cleaner than the deck. A feeling of secrecy came to Caroline; she saw that the passageway ended very close at hand, and a big locked door, braced with iron, faced her. John took out a bunch of keys and fitted one in the lock and opened the door.

The long passageway beyond was still closed and without portholes, but the lanterns were now fixed lamps on the walls, the oil burning behind glass shades of many colors ornamented with gilt. The walls themselves, smooth as brown satin, were hung with fine engravings and paintings set in gold frames, and the floors had been covered with rich oriental carpets, narrow and brilliant as woven jewels. A fragrance hung here of perfume and spice and rich food and wine. Along the inner wall stood many carved doors, polished and urbane, with gold-plated handles. The farther door, similar to the one they had opened, now swung back, and two young men in gold and brown livery appeared. They hurried toward John and his amazed daughter, bowing neatly at almost every step.

"No, no," said John. "We need nothing. Except, perhaps, in about half an hour, you may bring us some brandy and a little madeira, and wafers."

The young men halted immediately but continued to bow. John opened one of the doors to the left and motioned Caroline to go through it.

She had often heard some of the girls in school rapturously describe their staterooms after their parents had taken them to Europe, so Caroline had some slight idea of what staterooms were. But she doubted, as she looked at the sudden splendor of the room beyond the door and as her feet sank into deep, colored carpets, that any stateroom ever resembled this for luxury. It was large; it had three square portholes across which had been drawn thin, glittering golden tissue. It was a room for a potentate, for a prince, with its gilded lamps, its small marble tables, its crystals, its gold-painted carved furniture upholstered in satins and velvets and damask, its carved pale ceilings and walls touched with gilt, its divans and love seats, its little marble fireplace, its small buhl cabinets filled with *objets d'art*. She had a glimpse of a room adjoining, a bedroom with a swan bed, with furnishings to match.

The outside light, drifting through the golden tissue at the windows, filled the room with a warm yellow glow. Caroline looked mutely at her father. He smiled a little, unpleasantly. "Sit down, Caroline," he said. She obediently perched on a French settee, her feet and knees pressed together, her clutching hands tightening about her purse. Her father sat opposite, near the windows, and the yellow light rippled over him and heightened the bitter blue of the eyes that fixed themselves upon her.

"There are several rooms like this on this deck," he said. "You see, it is not only a freighter, Caroline."

"It is locked," she murmured. "To protect—all this," and she made a clumsy gesture with her gloved hands.

"To protect more than this," said John. He looked down at his right hand, which lay on the arm of his chair. Damn it, the girl had to know, if she was to act intelligently in the future. But he evaded her eyes and frowned.

"These are your quarters, Papa?" she asked, and smiled, thinking of her handsome father in this room when at sea.

"No," said John. "I never travel on my own ships, and particularly not this."

"Why?" she asked in astonishment.

He turned a large signet ring, very old and very precious, on his finger. Some of his friends in Boston smiled at that ring and talked about it when he was not present. It was an heirloom, they said, which he had bought somewhere and to which he was not entitled. John never enlightened them that the signet ring had belonged to many generations of his mother's family and had been given to the first notable Hollingshead by George II.

"Caroline," he said at last, "I want you to listen to me carefully. The docks outside are mine; the freighters and the ships are mine. This is mine. I have many other enterprises; I keep them only as long as they pay me a profit. This fleet of ships is paying me larger profits every year." He paused and frowned again. Caroline listened attentively. "I never travel on any of my own ships, particularly not this, as I've told you, because in the event of any trouble it would be best that I not be here. The ships are registered, yes, in the Ames name, but that is all. My captains, and especially Captain Allstyn, are responsible for the cargoes. I have nothing to do with the cargoes; they are the responsibilities of others. There is not a port in the world which they do not touch regularly."

Now Caroline was utterly baffled. The wide openness of her eyes and innocent face were turned to him, trying to understand.

"For instance," he said, watching her, "this freighter, while carrying cargo, also carries much more precious merchandise. The rooms on this deck are used exclusively for passengers who wish to leave their respective countries for a time, or for life, and who must do it without delay, without clearances, without public notice. The *Queen Ann* has carried bankers, princes, merchant chiefs, great industrialists, noblemen of many nations, even a petty king occasionally, and their ladies, to countries far from their own. The last occupant was a jewel merchant with a large personal cargo. The price of their passage is paid to me. I find it very lucrative."

Caroline, still looking at him with that calm innocence, was silent. He waited. He let her think. Then all at once she dropped her eyes and stared at her purse.

"I see you understand," said John.

"I understand," she said.

"But there is something else you do not understand," he said. "Great fortunes, immense fortunes, are rarely made honestly, and certainly not very fast. It was not my intention to start a dynasty slowly and carefully. And legitimately. That would have taken too long for my purposes. Besides, what is 'legitimately'? Some of the mightiest fortunes in America, now honored and scraped to reverently, were made in a fashion similar to mine. The Delanos, for instance, made their fortune through opium, the Astors through their exploitation of the Indians and their furs, the Vanderbilts through their ruthless manipulation of railroads and stock market. Yet who despises them? Presidents and kings are delighted to entertain them, and as delighted to be entertained in turn. One of the really tremendous fortunes in America was made by gun-running to the South during the war; another, equally tremendous, was made by blackbirding, the running of naked black savages from Africa to America in spite of intricate and punitive laws. The heirs of all these have married into some of Europe's noblest families; their children are now aristocrats. Their marriages and their deaths and their births make notable headlines in the newspapers.

"Murder of the helpless, ruin of the weak, theft, exploitation and despair and death have attended the making of these fortunes for a few. Not to mention, of course, the subornation of politicians, princes, and statesmen, who profited by glancing the other way or by quietly assisting.

"Yet who cares? Who denounces? Only last month the daughter of one of these men, who had been admitted to the most elegant schools in the world and whose debut cost countless thousands of dollars, was married to a British duke, and all the world applauded, and the newspapers went mad in their ecstasies and their stories of 'the little duchess,' and the very exploited mobs themselves became delirious with joy, though it was on their own suffering bodies that the fortune had been made.

"Caroline, there is only one crime which the world will not forgive, and that is poverty. And long ago, as I told you, I was determined never again to commit that unpardonable crime."

All the color had left Caroline's face. Only her golden eyes stood in that face, wide and staring and mute. John stood up and began to pace about the room, his head bent, his hands in the pockets of his striped trousers, his long black coat hanging from his lean shoulders.

"The penalty of failure, honesty, and weakness is ignominy, degradation, and obscurity, as well as hunger and despair. Did I make this world? No. But I met it on its own terms. Money, or your life. The prattle of clergymen and philosophers does not change these things. It was always so. It will always be so. Laws may be passed in the future, as they've been passed in the past, to restrain the immutable law of the world, to change it, to modify it. These will never succeed. The giants will always ignore punitive and restraining laws; laws were not made for giants, but only for pygmies. You see, the giants can buy anyone, anywhere, or if they can't buy them they can destroy them. Revolutions have been instigated against princes who defied the giants and tried to protect the weak; Presidents have gone down under shameful accusations when they opposed the giants. Calumny can be bought and used as a weapon. The politician, backed by the giants, will always win elections. For to whom do the people really listen? They listen to the man or the organization with cash. You see, there is no virtue in the people, either. They are just as hungry and as ruthless and as terrible as their masters."

Like jetsam and flotsam, broken phrases from the Bible rose to the surface of Caroline's mind. The virtue embedded in her character, the simplicity which was part of her nature, the honor which was her very spirit was outraged, terrified, and sickened. A passionate revolt stirred her, and a loathing, not for her father, but for the world which had made him what he was. He had stopped before her now and was looking down at her still and stricken face and averted eyes.

"Well, Caroline?" he asked with gentleness.

"I think," she muttered, "that I'd like a drink of water."

He pursed his lips. "I think a little brandy would be best," he said. He pulled a bell rope. Caroline did not move; she was staring at her shoes, a large figure as motionless as stone. She was not even aware of the entrance of the young man with a silver tray holding brandy and wine bottles and crystal glasses. When a glass, very slender and thin and filled with a golden liquid, appeared before her eyes, she started. She made a slight gesture of repugnance and rejection, but her father's hand remained insistently before her. She could see its long white firmness, the signet ring on the finger, the tight knuckles and clean pale nails, as if in a glaring and hurting light. Then she took the glass.

"Drink it," said John. "Slowly."

She automatically put the glass to her lips and sipped. The stinging brandy touched her tongue. It reached her stomach. It lay there like a burning coal, and tears crept about her eyelids from the sensation. When she looked at her father he was sitting opposite again and slowly and morosely drinking.

"Papa," she said, and coughed.

"Yes, Caroline."

"Papa," said Caroline, and her voice shook. "I know—knew—there were bad and wicked people in the world. I've read about them in history. But I always thought they were—strange. Unusual. I thought they didn't resemble—all the rest of us. I thought—conscience—— I thought even the bad people had a conscience and that at times they were ashamed, or frightened, or disgusted with themselves." She stopped and looked at him despairingly.

John raised his eyebrows and sipped a little. "Conscience?" he repeated. "What a child you are, Caroline. Man is an animal, Caroline; he is different from the other animals because he has intelligence, which makes him all the worse because it gives him a larger outlet for his savagery, his terribleness. I know hundreds, perhaps thousands, of men who have no more conscience than a tree or a stone. Are they unhappy, or do they accuse themselves? No. Not at all. They are the happiest, most contented, most satisfied, and most serene people in the world. They enjoy living, and they live, not merely exist. Many of them are absolutely charming. I believe even the Bible says that the children of darkness are wiser in their generation than the children of light. As for those with a conscience—Caroline, they are the most miserable of people. They are the failures, the unhappy, the incomplete, the despised of their families and their neighbors. They die, as it has been said, unwept, unhonored, and unsung. Very few even attend their funerals. I don't think there are many of them, anywhere, so they aren't a problem. Caroline, if you are thinking of religion, I will tell you this. One of the worst scoundrels I have ever known, who had caused the deaths of scores of men while he was getting his fortune, died only a month ago in New York. It was almost impossible to reach the church where the funeral was being held. I had to leave my carriage several streets away and proceed on foot, though the police were out in platoons to keep order, riding on their horses, swinging their clubs against the heads of the urgent but reverent mob, and whistling all over the place.

"All wheel traffic was halted several streets in a square around that church. Thousands of shabby people filled pavement and street like trees, men and women and children. They surged like waves about the church, breaking under the onslaughts of the police so that dignitaries from Washington could climb the steps, and statesmen and giant fellow thieves and ambassadors from a dozen powerful nations. Even the President was there, flanked by senators and generals. Flags hung at half mast all over the city. The big church was like a flower garden and stuffed to the walls with men and women who had come to do that scoundrel and murderer the last honor and obeisance. The choir thundered and wept. The clergymen—and there were five of them—knelt before the altar and prayed for that man's soul, and women pressed handkerchiefs to their eyes.

"It was as if a great and mighty and heroic king had died, and not a giant thief from the gutters of Pittsburgh, a murderer and a liar, a suborner of statesmen and rulers, a man who had helped to make a whole nation, China, desolate and opium-ridden, among many other crimes. Yet one had the feeling that the very seraphim were present in that church where the cross hung over the bronze and gilt coffin in which that man lay in state."

Caroline moistened lips that felt heavy. "Perhaps," she said in a very faint voice, "he tried to do something good before he died. Charity?"

"Not a penny. His fortune went to his sons and their families, and they were even more rapacious, if possible, than he was. He had left nothing to servants who had worn out their lives in their long service to him."

John looked broodingly at his glass. "I knew him well. He was a devil. And the very happiest of men. He lived to be very old and enjoyed every minute of his life. He had thousands of devoted friends."

Caroline felt as though she were hearing the most monstrous and most insane of blasphemies.

"But why, Papa? Why all this for him?"

"Because he had money. Because he had the enormous power which only money can give. And that is all the people ever worshiped. Christianity is over eighteen hundred years old. It has never been able to remove the people's true god from them, nor cast out the devils who serve it, nor throw down the temples which house it. The people are responsible for their satans.

"You've seen the men on my docks and on my ships. There isn't one there who wouldn't lay down his life for me and who wouldn't thank me for the honor. Yet if I should suddenly lose all I have there isn't a man there who wouldn't crush my skull with his club."

Yes, thought Caroline. All the Alecks everywhere. They had made her father what he was. They, and not their masters, were the true devils. They deserved their demons. It was the people of England, she remembered, who had loved their horrible king, Henry VIII, and his enormities against them, and his crimes and his murders, and his executions of his wives. He had been Good King Hal to them, this monster, this vile creature. They had even adored Cromwell, who had brought drab dismalness and terror to them and who had had them whipped in their very streets and thrown into prison. History abounded with the adored demons whose tombs were now shrines.

"Are you ill?" asked John with sincere anxiety. "Poor girl. I hope I haven't frightened you."

"I do feel a little sick," murmured Caroline.

"I think you've had enough for today," said John.

"What have you done to Caroline?" Cynthia asked John that night. Her gray eyes stared at him inimicably.

"Don't be a fool, Cynthia," he said. "I did nothing but take her down to my docks."

"And that is why she didn't come down to dinner and why she lies like a deaf-mute on her bed. Is that it, John?"

"Perhaps," he answered. "I think she is just a little tired."

"Don't touch me," said Cynthia. "I think I am a little tired, myself."

CHAPTER NINE

A year later on the last night she was ever to spend in Cynthia Winslow's house, Caroline was called into her aunt's sitting room. She came with sullen reluctance, and sat down in her usual fashion on the edge of a little chair while Cynthia half lay on her chaise longue in a drift of white silk and lace.

"Caroline," said Cynthia, "you are now going home to Lyndon and to Lyme; you've left Miss Stockington's school forever. You are my sister's child, my dear Ann's girl, the daughter of my twin. You don't know what it is to be a twin; a person's twin is her other self and not apart from her as with just another sister. So, in a way, you are also my daughter."

Caroline did not reply. Cynthia took up her silver brush and began to brush her long loose hair. Then she flung the brush from her with a crash and sat up. "Caroline! I wish you wouldn't sit there like a lump and just stare down at your hands. I used to think you were fond of me until just a short time ago. No matter. But you must listen to me. It's very important."

"What is it?" muttered Caroline. She could never meet her aunt's eyes any longer without blushing and feeling hot and hating.

Cynthia studied her with despair. "Caroline, I must talk to you. You've been seeing a lot of your father this year. He has been taking you about; he has been talking to you. And each time when you've come home you've been ill and white, and you look like death. I know your father. I knew him before you did and before he married my sister. I have a great deal of respect for him; he's a man, which is much more than you can say of many men these days; I know all about men."

"You should," Caroline muttered.

Cynthia paused and frowned. "What did you say?"

But Caroline was silent. Cynthia rolled up her eyes and pressed her lips together for a few moments. "Though your father hasn't told me, I have some pretty shrewd ideas of what he has been teaching you. He has a distorted view of life, and no doubt he has reasons to have that view which seem valid to him. He trusts no one; he dislikes almost everybody; he hates too much. I am not going to be a bonbon and say he is entirely wrong. I know what the world is. But it is not exclusively filled with liars, thieves, scoundrels, murderers, vipers, ingrates, slanderers, and brutes. Not every man and woman is detestable and loathsome; not everybody is spiritually diseased and cruel and merciless. And there are some who are so good that it is a joy to be with them and listen to their voices. They're rare, but they do exist. In a larger measure than your father suspects. I've met them. My sister, your mother, was one. I had an aunt and an uncle who became Romans, one a nun, the other a priest, and they went away on foreign missions and died of awful diseases, trying to help the unfortunate in other lands. Just to be in their presence was to feel holiness. I've met devoted people all over the world who spoke nothing but truth and goodness. I've known heroes who would betray no one, not even a dog. Some of the most blessed people I've known had no money; some had a great deal. It is your father's misfortune that he will not see these people or, if he sees them, he does not recognize them."

Caroline was outraged. She had heard nothing beyond Cynthia's criticism of her father. Her cheeks burned and her eyes came up to meet her aunt's with absolute ferocity. She jumped to her feet and cried out: "How dare you say such things of my father? You, you especially!"

Cynthia got up slowly and moved a step or two closer to the girl.

"Caroline," said Cynthia. "Caroline, what is it?"

But Caroline swung heavily about and ran from the room. When she reached her own room she sat down on the edge of her bed and beat the pillows fiercely with her fists and said over and over, aloud and passionately, "I hate her! Oh, how I hate her!"

Caroline Ames sat on the boulder on the wet black shingle, where she had sat for so many summer mornings and days and evenings. The vast stone-colored Atlantic stretched before her, heaving sluggishly, and the pale opaline sky of pre-dawn sloped down to mingle with it. A cold salt wind gushed from the water and pressed like an invisible wall against the girl's chilled body. She shivered and pulled Beth's thick gray shawl over her shoulders and stared at the east, only half seeing. She listened vaguely to the dull lap and gigantic breath of the ocean. Now the opaline sky brightened far over the water, flushed into delicate pearl and rose and clear green, and long streamers of it touched the farthest waves so that they quickened into color. Then a golden crescent of light lifted over the rim of the ocean, grew larger, more brilliant, and the sun strode over the sea toward the western land, and all about him pennants and banners of a hundred hues heralded him.

Caroline did not know why she cried, why she always cried at seeing this ever-changing victorious march of the dawn sun over the water, and why she was always so stunningly moved. She fumbled for her handkerchief and found none in the pocket of her brown cotton frock. She wiped away the tears with the backs of her hands, childishly. It was foolish, she thought, to feel such sorrow, such yearning, and such passion at the sight of a phenomenon that had occurred every morning through the ages and would occur monotonously for ages more. But she continued to cry even while the shingle, black and wet, began to glimmer with pink and blue and heliotrope all about her, and the wind warmed and sea gulls chattered and shrilled and caught all that color on their wings and skimmed over the surging water.

"Caroline," said a man's voice near her, and she started, then turned red with embarrassment. She did not turn. She knew that Tom Sheldon was here; her hands tightened together in her lap and she did not answer. She felt him move closer until he was at her shoulder.

"You've been here over a week, and I haven't seen you," said Tom. "And so I thought you might come here in the early morning, and so I came."

Caroline was silent, but something in her leaned with a fierce and tender eagerness toward him, like thirst and hunger combined. He stood there; she could see, out of the corner of her eye, the height and strength of his tall body, his rough brown shirt and workman's trousers, his tanned arms bare to his elbows, his big worn boots.

"Didn't you want to see me?" asked Tom.

"Yes, yes," she murmured. The last tears were icy on her cheeks. She turned to him now. He smiled down at her gravely. She had not seen him for a year, and her first thought was that he looked much older and that he was no longer a youth but a man of nearly twenty-one and that she loved him. Simply, like a very tired child, she drooped her head sideways and rested it against his upper arm and tried to keep from crying again. "Oh, Tom," she said.

He put his arm about her shoulders and held her to him tightly, and she said again, "Oh, Tom."

He kissed the top of her head, and then her forehead, and for the first time she turned her lips up to him and very gently he gave her the first kiss of love. She felt the kiss not only on her mouth but in her heart, and then through all her young body, and now she could not prevent sobbing.

"Hush, dear," said Tom, but he let her cry as she clung to him, her arms tight about his waist, her head on his chest. "Poor little Carrie. What's wrong? You wouldn't cry like this if there wasn't something terribly wrong. Here, let me wipe your face and your poor eyes." He pulled out a dark blue coarse handkerchief and lovingly patted her cheeks and her eyes, and she looked at him as if she could not get enough of seeing. She moved to give him room on the boulder, and he rested one buttock on the stone, and their arms clutched each other. His strong black hair ruffled in the wind, his blue eyes smiled, his browned face was all planes and angles, and his dimpled chin was hard and firm. A deep peace came to Caroline; she dropped her head on his shoulder and held off the pain which she felt climbing in her.

They watched the sea and the sky and the sun. Behind them, in the old beaten house and behind a discreet old curtain, Beth Knowles watched them and smiled and cried a little herself. She had done the right thing to tell Tom in the village yesterday when he could find Caroline. Thank heavens, she thought, *he* wasn't here; in a little she would call the children to come in and have a hearty breakfast of flapjacks and pork sausage and syrup and good hot coffee, and again there would be young voices in this dreadful house, and young laughter. Poor Carrie. How wretched she had been this past week, how lonely, how sad, how desolate, peeping through the window at sundown at Tom as he restlessly strolled up and down the shingle, waiting for her. Caroline no longer "talked" to Beth; her remarks were few, her answers monosyllables, her face heavy and sullen, her mouth sulky, her eyes always shifting away. She spent most of the time in her room with endless books and went out only at dawn and at night, walking in loneliness up and down as Tom walked. What had *he* done to Carrie, that horrible monster, that fiend of a man? Carrie had been changing for a long time, but the change was more awful and more definite now, as if Carrie had been covered invincibly with stone.

"Tell me all about it," said Tom to Caroline, his arms warm and protecting about her.

But I can't tell you, thought Caroline desolately. How can I tell you that among so many other things my father is a smuggler, that he corrupts government tariff officials so that they don't see what his ships are bringing in, that all his enterprises are built on people's greed and hatred for each other, whether it is gun-running or opium or money manipulations or gaining control of them so that they are either ruined or pay him a huge profit, and that there isn't a nation anywhere that doesn't know my father or a government that doesn't try to destroy him or court him, and that he knows generals and senators and kings and statesmen who help him at a price, and that he buys so many of them? Tom, you wouldn't understand that my father could not be what he is unless others wanted his services or his money or his help. They corrupted him; he didn't corrupt them. He only supplies what they want—for a profit.

"Don't cry again, dear," said Tom, and again mopped with clumsy love at her cheeks and eyes. "Not unless you tell me what's the matter."

Caroline thought of the promise she had made her father a year ago, and she cringed. She pushed aside the dabbing handkerchief, lifted her head from Tom's shoulder, and dropped it on her chest. The wind stirred little wisps of her fine black hair about her cheeks and forehead. There were grayish shadows under her eyes and under her cheekbones. Tom looked at her with concern. "There's something really wrong, isn't there, Carrie?" he asked sternly. "And that's why you've kept away from me."

"No, no!" she exclaimed, lifting her head but averting it from him. "There's nothing wrong. I'm not a child any more, Tom. I have things to think about."

"Am I one of them, Carrie?" he asked in a softened voice. "Please tell me I am."

She waited, then nodded.

"I see," said Tom, and he sighed. "Well, that doesn't matter. Just as long as I know you love me. And you do."

Caroline said, "How are you and your father doing, Tom?" Her voice was dull and low. Tom looked at her with sharpness. Then he made himself smile and speak with enthusiasm.

"Oh, fine. Wonderful. We have orders for six more houses this summer, Carrie. We're even hiring carpenters and bricklayers from Boston. All these new summer houses between here and the village. We've bought up most of the ocean-front land, and I can tell you they'll bring a big price when the houses are built. Big for the kind of people who buy them. They're people from all around who couldn't afford the sort of houses real rich people buy, like at Newport and Marblehead, but they're people who would like to have a place away from Boston for their wives and children when it's hot in the city. We're even thinking of buying land at Cape Cod; I'm sure there's a future there for the houses we build, good sound summer houses, nicely designed and comfortable and airy, with plank floors and cool plastered walls, and porches and little gardens behind, and a little beach in front or on a bluff looking out to sea. America's changing, thank God. Now we have a lot of small merchants and businessmen and manufacturers with nice shops or small factories of their own, and they're thriving. There are a lot of people who don't like industry. But what would they have, anyway? The old aristocratic society of great landowners and people who just worked the land for them and were paid practically nothing?

"Not," said Tom, one arm dropping from Caroline, "that I like a lot of the mills and foundries and factories, full of poor Hungarians and Poles and Italians brought over by the boatload from Europe to live on compounds like cattle and eat and sleep and die behind the big wood-and-iron fences. And half starved; practically prisoners in this big land of the free! But we already have people in government raising howls about this contract labor. They're talking in Washington about passing an alien contract labor law, and the big fellows can shout and curse and threaten, and we'll have the law just the same. If not this year, then the next, or the next."

He paused, and his young face became stern and hard as he looked out over the sea, and he muttered something profane under his breath. He did not see Caroline shrink; he did not know that she was remembering that some of her father's clippers brought hordes of the wretched and the starving to America for service in the monster mills and foundries. They were huddled in the holds, far below decks, and were delivered—for a price —to their new oppressors and exploiters.

"Well, anyway," said Tom, "we have all those new smaller merchants and little factory owners buying our snug houses so they can come here from Boston, and even from New York, in the summer and pretend that they are rich with their summer homes, just like the families who go to Newport and Europe and the Mediterranean in the hot months, and their wives and their kids get a little sun. And they're nice people, too, very ambitious." Tom chuckled indulgently. "The village doesn't mind; the shops do good business, and the owners don't care if they're patronized by people who have just as many calluses as they have and who only ten years ago worked in shops and mills, themselves."

This was a phenomenon that Caroline had not known existed, the rise of a sturdy middle class in America. Her father had never spoken of them; she had confusedly believed that her country was composed exclusively of merchant princes, owners of vast mills and foundries, Wall Street financiers, and then, under them, squirming like a faceless mass of unhuman maggots, the people who worked for them and served them and made their fortunes possible. Now she had a glimpse of the yeomen, the small competitors of the giants, the resolute challengers of mighty fortunes, the unlearned and independent strong who had the power, the character, the innate force and ambition to climb also, if only for a short distance. They were something new in the world. Caroline did not know why she felt a sudden pleasure, a sudden relief. She turned her face to Tom and smiled and said, "I'm glad, Tom. I'm very glad."

"What?" said Tom. He was delighted at her smile. "Oh, you mean about the houses Dad and I are building. We ought to clear at least two thousand dollars this summer. Two thousand dollars! We cleared about a thousand last summer; next summer it ought to be three, or perhaps four!"

Caroline's smile went away. Just that little bit of money. Again she remembered her promise to her father.

"What's the matter, Carrie?" asked Tom. "You look like a thundercloud."

Caroline pressed the palms of her hands together and looked at the shingle. Little frills of white foam burst on it. The sun was climbing higher and higher; it was very warm. Then she began to speak, steadily and without intonation:

"Tom, you keep writing to me about the time when we'll be married. I told my father some time ago that I was thinking— Tom, he wants me to get married someday. You see, there's a lot— Tom, I don't know how to say this, but my father told me that if I married a poor man, a man without a great deal of money, I'd never inherit anything he has."

She waited, watching the little bursts of foam near the boulder. Tom was silent for a long time. She felt a beginning wave of sickness climb within her, smothering her, choking her.

"Carrie," said Tom at last, "look at me."

Reluctantly she turned her face to him. He was smiling. He took her chin in his hand, and the warmth of his brown fingers spread over her flesh.

"I'm not a poor man, Carrie dear. I'm making money. I'll make more."

His fingers no longer warmed her. She closed her eyes. "Tom, you don't understand. My father is very rich; he is one of the richest men in America. He wouldn't consider what you are making to be real money, Tom. And if I married you I would be cut out of his will entirely."

Tom stared at her. His hand dropped from her chin. "Oh, Tom!" she cried, and caught his arm between her hands. "Oh, Tom, try to understand what I'm telling you! You hate me now, don't you, Tom?"

"No," he said slowly, without moving. "I love you, Carrie. Why, there isn't anything else in the world for me but you. And now you're crying again. Here, blow your nose. Don't cry like that; you'll be sick."

He was full of rage against John Ames, and disgust. He had never thought of Caroline as a rich man's daughter. She had been only Carrie to him. Her father! As if his damned money mattered one way or another to him, Tom Sheldon!

"Listen to me, Carrie," he said. "I want you to listen very carefully, dear, and I want you to know that I'm speaking only the truth. Are you listening, Carrie?"

"Yes," she murmured.

"This is very important to both of us, Carrie, so be sure you hear everything I say. I won't speak about your father; you'll only be offended. Carrie, I never thought about you as having any money, either now or in the future. An intelligent man with guts and hope and health and determination will always be able to make enough money to be comfortable. It doesn't take a fortune to be happy, just as you can't be happy unless you have some money. One way or another, it's bad. Extremes are always bad.

"Carrie, I'll never be a very rich man like your father. I've heard a lot of rumors about how he made his money and how he is still making it. I never want to see him, Carrie! I mean that. He hasn't been the right kind of father for you—not like my father. What's the matter?" he added sharply.

For Caroline had pulled away from him and had pushed his arm from her waist.

"Don't talk about my father that way!" she cried, and her cheeks were red with anger.

"Carrie!"

"You don't know what you're talking about!" she shouted, and made as if to slip down from the boulder. Tom watched her. And then he knew that if she escaped from him and ran off into that damned old house up there beyond the dunes and the tangled and bearded tall grass he would never see her again. So he caught her arm roughly and held her to the boulder.

"Listen to me!" He shouted louder than she. "You've got to listen, Carrie! I'm sorry if I hurt your feelings about your father. Listen, Carrie."

She perched on the edge of the boulder, breathing heavily, her eyes staring at him with animus. Then, as she saw his face, both tender and firm and yet outraged, she stopped struggling.

"I just want to say this, Carrie. You don't need anyone's money. I'll have enough to take care of you comfortably; probably more than comfortably. I can't promise you a fortune. After all, I'll make my money honest— I just want you to know that you'll be safe with me; I'll take care of you. You don't need anyone but me. I never thought about you having money of your own, and I swear it solemnly. I only love you."

She believed him. She knew he was speaking the truth. She slumped suddenly on the boulder and let him put his arm about her again.

"You believe me, don't you?" Tom asked her, rubbing his chin over her velvety braids.

"Yes, Tom." She wanted to cry again.

"So perhaps next summer we'll be married," he said, stroking her cheek. "You and I, Carrie, we'll be married. I'll build a nice home for us, not too far from the village, and overlooking the ocean. A pretty house, Carrie. Why, I'll start it this August! There'll be a garden, and perhaps some chickens, and flowers and vegetables. We'll be happy, Carrie, just you and I."

"I'm going away soon," said Caroline, her throat full of knots. "Next week. I'm going with Papa all over the world to see his friends."

He turned his head away and looked at the sea, cold and bounding now in the fresh morning light. The sea would take Caroline from him; it would take her away in the custody of her father, his enemy.

"I'm sorry," he said slowly. "I looked forward to this summer, Carrie. I thought we'd be together, making plans." He glanced at her profile. "Don't worry, darling. It doesn't matter. I'll be building our house. It will be ready for us next spring. Carrie?"

But Caroline was not listening to him. She was thinking of the day her father had taken her to his docks. She was remembering the wild and passionate sense of power she had felt, the power over the Alecks of the world, and not only her safety from them. This power did not come from love, from tidy walls, from little gardens and chickens, from warm kitchens, from the voice of any man, no matter how beloved and how needed. It came only from money.

She wanted to make him understand, and she was full of desolation again.

"Tom," she said, "I've listened to you. I want you to listen to me now. A little money isn't enough for me. I'd always be afraid with just a little money. I can't bear to think of not having a lot. It frightens me."

"Why?" he asked, astounded.

"I can't tell you. I can only say that at one time I didn't have money — I'd lost what I had. And—people—thought I was poor, or something. They treated me as if I weren't a human being, Tom. That's what frightens me."

"Oh, hell," said Tom. "The world's full of bas— I mean, Carrie, the world's full of all kinds of people. I'm not like that; you aren't. Millions of us aren't like that. You don't have to be frightened, Carrie."

No, he'd never understand, thought Caroline with despair. Then in the midst of her despair she smiled. Tom did not want her for her father's money. He wanted only her, Caroline Ames. Tom, watching her, was surprised at the change in her face, the softening, the growing color. When she leaned against him again he sat very still, afraid that she would inexplicably draw away as she had done before.

"When I'm with you, Tom, I'm not afraid," she said.

"Good. You see, Carrie, that it's all right?"

Her head fell on his chest, and she could hear the potent and reassuring beat of his heart and she was filled with love. There was nothing else but love, and with love you had the strength of armies, and the protection of walls. She nestled closer to him, and he held her tenderly.

"And I'll build our house," he said, his lips against her forehead.

A little house. A house open to the sea. A house open to enemies. A house open to the Alecks of the world. There would not be much money.

She pulled away from him. "Not yet, Tom," she said. "Don't speak of it yet. I knew you wouldn't understand. I just haven't any words!"

He stood up very slowly. He moved away a short distance. He took out a short squat pipe, filled it very carefully with tobacco. He struck a match against the side of its box and lit his pipe. Caroline watched him, blinking and fearful.

Tom folded his arms on his chest and looked at the brilliant horizon. Caroline crouched on the boulder, her palms pressed against its roughness.

"What do you want, Carrie?" asked Tom. The smoke from his pipe rose bluely in the clarified air.

"What do I want?" she stammered.

"Yes, Carrie. What do you want?" he asked gently. "Your father's money or me?"

She rubbed her hands on the roughness of the boulder.

"Tom," she said, "I want both."

"You can't have both," he said, as if reasoning out a very simple problem. "Not while he's alive. You can't have both—until your father's dead."

She jumped from the boulder.

"How can you say that?" she cried. "How dare you say that?"

"What did I say? I told you the truth. Does the truth hurt you that much, Carrie? And didn't you tell me as much, that your father will disinherit you if you marry a poor man? What decent man would say that to his only daughter?"

"You hate my father!"

Tom turned to her. "Yes, Carrie. I hate what he's done to you. And so I suppose I hate him. Carrie——"

But Caroline was flying away from him, leaping over small dunes, brushing aside the rustling dry grass, her shawl blowing behind her like a forlorn banner.

"Carrie!" he shouted. "Come back, Carrie!"

She did not turn. Her arms were flung out under the shawl, propelling her. She was in flight, a winged albatross struggling to rise and leave the earth.

"Oh, Carrie," said Tom, and his body felt so weighty that he believed it would sink in the sand.

When Beth Knowles heard Caroline rush into the house with the crash of a door she came out from the kitchen, her kind and comely face webbed over with smiling wrinkles, a dab of flour on one plump cheek. "Well," she exclaimed, "I thought you two would never come in for breakfast, and the flapjacks are ready for the skillet——" She stopped smiling and looked beyond the breathless girl. "But where's Tom?" she asked.

Caroline threw the shawl on a rickety chair and looked about the long, wretched room as if desperately searching for something. "He didn't come. He went away." Her voice was sullen, and she would not look at Beth.

"Gone away?" repeated the woman, bewildered. "Why?"

"I sent him away!" cried Caroline angrily. "That's all. I sent him away. And I am hungry, Beth. It's late."

Beth stood in silence and stared at the girl. She sat down slowly. "You sent Tom away, Carrie? Tom? Why?"

Caroline, feeling as if her throat and chest were filled with cutting stones, turned aside. "He said some things about my father. My father!" She swung toward Beth. "Don't you understand? Why do you look at me like that? I sent him away. He never understands anything. He's a fool."

"Tom," said Beth. Her eyes filled with tears. "You can say those things about Tom? I don't believe he'd ever say anything mean about anybody, even your father."

"Even my father," shouted Caroline. "Do you hear how that sounds? 'Even your father'! How dare you, Beth?"

Beth clasped her hands tightly together. She gazed at Caroline earnestly. She wondered how she had not seen until now the power and the strength which were Caroline's, the formidable expression, the rigid pale areas about her mouth. This was not the child she had brought up and had cared for and had loved as her own child. This was not the shy girl who had once cried at leaving her. This was a woman, tall and mature, and the eyes that looked at her, Beth, were not the young Carrie's eyes.

"I see," said Beth, and put the back of her hand wearily against her forehead. "Yes, I think I see."

"You don't see. How could you see? You and Tom, you're alike. You both hate my father. And why? Because he isn't like you, soft and weak and not caring about money? He cares for money because it's the only thing in the world. It protects him from people like you!" The derisive voice lashed at Beth.

"Everybody hates my father!" Caroline continued ruthlessly. "Because he has force and intelligence and can command what he wants. And do you know what I want? I want to be just like him."

Beth dropped her hand, and Caroline saw her eyes and for an instant she was a little girl again, wanting to burst into tears and run to Beth and hide her face in her lap.

"Yes," said Beth. "I suppose you do." She stood up tiredly.

Caroline's voice stopped her. "And what's wrong with that? What do you know about anything?" The stricken look was gone from her; her face appeared congested.

Beth paused in the doorway with her back to Caroline. "I suppose I should have expected it eventually," she said. "There's nothing else I can do for you, Carrie. Now I can go away. I can't bear staying here and watching what is happening to you and knowing it will get worse."

"What are you talking about?" demanded Caroline roughly. "You—go away? You can't! You have to take care of my father's houses; you have to work for him."

"No," said Beth, shaking her head. "I don't have to do anything, Carrie." She looked over her shoulder at Caroline and shook her head again. "You think that you can buy people, don't you, Carrie? Just as your father thinks. But there are some things you can't buy, and I'm one of them. I have enough money. I have a pension of my own. And so I'm going away when you leave next Thursday with your father. There's nothing for me here any longer."

Caroline was angry and alarmed. "After all these years you've worked for my father, taking his money! You'd be that ungrateful?"

Now Beth turned fully around. "Are you out of your mind, Carrie? 'Ungrateful'! You're very ready to call others fools. You're a young fool yourself. Your father has paid me less than a third of what I could have gotten many times over. Why did I stay? I could have married Mr. Bentley, the Boston shopkeeper where you buy your dress materials; he's a rich man, rich enough for me, and I liked him, and he wanted me. That was four years ago. But I didn't leave. Why? Just because of you, Carrie." Her voice broke.

Caroline took a step toward her. "I don't believe it," she said flatly. "If you're telling the truth—I don't believe it! Nobody would be stupid enough to stay when she had a chance to better herself."

"I would. I was stupid," said Beth, spreading out her hands. "I agree with you, Carrie. Now it's too late. Mr. Bentley married somebody else, and I didn't care. I thought I'd stay here and protect you."

"From what?" cried Caroline.

"From your father. From what he is; from what he's already done to you. I wouldn't be regretting it now, Carrie, if I'd only succeeded. But I failed. Didn't I?"

Caroline was silent. She peered at Beth in confusion.

"Didn't I?" repeated Beth.

"I don't know what you're talking about!"

"No. I don't suppose you do, Carrie. I don't suppose, now, you'll ever understand. It's too late." Beth's voice broke again. "Oh, Carrie. Is it too late?"

Caroline sat down heavily in a chair and put her hands to her cold cheeks. "I'm tired. I'm hungry. I'm——" Her muttering tone halted. There was such a wild and chaotic yearning in her, such loss, such anger, such bewilderment. She raised her voice. "Beth, you can't leave my father. He needs you."

Then she burst into agonized tears, and Beth ran to her and caught her head in her arms and held it to her warm breast. "Don't leave me, Beth, don't leave me!" the girl sobbed. "Oh, God, don't leave me!"

"Hush, my love. Hush, my dear child. Hush, sweetheart. Of course I won't leave you. How could I leave a poor child like you? Who would ever help you but me?"

Carrie clung to her, and said over and over in a dull and aching voice, "Oh, God. Oh, God. Oh, God." It was too terrible for Beth to bear, and she pressed her cheek against the tormented young mouth and cried.

But Caroline would not see Tom again. Nor did he come to the shingle near the house. He wrote to Beth: "When Carrie wants me I'll go to her, but not until then. I'll wait for her, but she'll have to call me first. Stay with her, Beth. You're all she has."

CHAPTER TEN

"So this is your girl, eh, Johnny?" asked Mrs. Norman Benchley Broome in her hoarse and vulgar voice, as baritone in tone as a man's. "Not a very pretty specimen, I'd say. You'll have to buy her a husband." Her laughter boomed out thunderously, and her raddled cheeks, painted and dry, swelled out. "A pretty price, too, or, damn me, I'll be mistaken."

Mrs. Norman Benchley Broome (she insisted upon the full name) had been a whore long ago in one of New York's better bordellos, where her wit and rough glee and delight in her profession had made her extremely popular and had resulted in a high demand for her specialized services. She had captivated the delicate and attenuated Mr. Broome of one of New York's oldest and most distinguished families. He had been an elderly widower, extremely wealthy, and a renowned auctioneer, and had recouped family fortunes long dissipated by his father and his uncles. He had no children; he had only numerous nieces and nephews who lusted for his money and whom he detested. So he had married Maggie Spitzler, partly because she amused him tremendously and he was fond of her, and partly to spite his hungry relatives.

New York had not turned its haughty back on Mr. Norman Benchley Broome. He was so rich, his fortune in the high multimillions, and he entertained lavishly and with taste and distinction, and his white-fronted Fifth Avenue house was famous for its parties and excellent company. But New York had approached his bride with scandalized tentativeness, for her past was no secret to the gentlemen, who had been titillated by her, and no secret to their ladies. It was not that Maggie ever pretended she had led a different life. It was even a matter of pride to her, and in drunken and taunting moments she would even embarrass the blushing but avid ladies with accounts of more florid episodes. Maggie, as she would say herself, didn't give a damn for the proprieties. She gave a damn for nothing but herself, and she had such a love for living, such a dedication to life, and such a boisterous joy in it that eventually she drew all to her as a great fire draws the cold and thin-veined. She was cruel, rowdy, forthright, and blasphemous, and full of wit "and the very devil," the gentlemen would say, thinking of their proper wives and dull daughters. On her husband's death she had inherited every penny of his estate, his vast holdings, and the hatred of his relatives. She was now in her late sixties and as vital, avaricious, and conscienceless as she had been on the day she had run away from home at fourteen with a "drummer."

John Ames was one of Maggie's favorites for many reasons, though he was, she would say with hearty and unwinking blatancy, "a nobody." So he had brought his daughter Caroline to visit his very old friend this hot July day when she was on the eve of leaving for Newport.

Caroline had not been impressed by the five-story white and marble-fronted house on Fifth Avenue, for nothing really impressed her except natural, wild, and savage beauty. The gilt and silver, the crystal and bronze, the thick oriental rugs, the statues and the mirrors, the damask and the carved wood, the great alabaster and marble fireplaces, the imported velvet and silk brocades oppressed her rather than inspired her respect or her wonder. They were only on a bigger scale than those in the houses she had infrequently visited in Boston. She thought it dull and dark, for the silk-shrouded windows kept out the blaze of fervent light that palpitated over New York. Her nostrils were offended by the mingled odors of incense and stuffy perfume in the great and crowded rooms. Mrs. Broome, to Caroline, was not only vulgar but disgusting. The girl gave her hostess several long if furtive glances and dismissed her as a detestable, nasty, and unclean old woman. Maggie, who had not reached her present eminence without astuteness and perception, felt Caroline's cold hostility; however, so great was her vanity and her power that she ascribed it to the fact that Caroline was only a "bumpkin," a raw and unattractive creature who was probably overawed or jealous or frightened.

Caroline sat stiffly on a carved chair with a red velvet seat. It was a thronelike chair; Caroline's feet barely reached the floor; her dark hair did not touch the back of the chair. Her hands were folded tightly on her purse; her gray silk frock was most unbecoming. But a thin shaft of light creeping through the draperies lay across her eyes, so that Maggie, who could be very imaginative, thought they resembled the eyes of a young lion.

The old woman and the girl of eighteen sat opposite each other. John sat near his old friend, for whom he had an amused affection, much respect, and tolerance. They both drank whiskey, John with distaste but with an expression of appreciation, Maggie lustily. Caroline had refused even sherry, in a cold low voice. She had finally, at a reproving look from her father, accepted an ice, a lemonish drink which she did not like. It floated with bits of strawberries, and its foamy, creaming top nauseated her.

What an old, vicious harridan, Caroline thought, listening to the booms of ear-tearing laughter and the coarse, mannish voice. Mrs. Broome frequently slapped John Ames on one of his immaculate broadcloth thighs and then would let her enormous fingers remain on it a little overlong. She was unusually tall, as tall as John, and lathelike in figure, which a somewhat soiled bright pink brocaded dress with an exaggerated bustle threaded with gold did not soften. She wore slippers to match, and her big bony ankles swelled out over their fashionable narrowness. Once she had had a mass of naturally yellow hair; when it had begun to darken and to gray she promptly had had it dyed, though no other woman in New York would have been so daring. Now it was the color of a brass doorknob or knocker, but not as polished. She wore it piled in bunches of untidy curls and waves on the top of her cranelike head, with quantities of short ringlets, like dyed string, streaming down about a raddled neck. Though Maggie had never, since childhood, been exposed directly to the sun, it was odd that her skin should be so brownish, so coarsened, so resembling large-pored canvas, so grossly withered. Her profile, Caroline thought, resembled one of the less attractive buzzards, with the low slanted forehead, the huge predatory nose, the painted and crinkled large mouth surrounded by merciless clefts from nostrils to corners, the pointed but receding chin. But what really revolted Caroline were the very tiny and depraved black eyes between the bronzed lashes. They resembled varnished raisins and glittered restlessly and never softened, and never expressed anything but brutal amusement or rapacity.

Maggie loved jewelry and had enormous quantities of it. Today she wore her emerald necklace, gigantic stones, dirty and soiled, each surrounded by a halo of precious canary diamonds, and all hung on a jeweled gold chain. Matching bracelets marched up each strong but scrawny brownish arm, and her fingers glittered with rubies, diamonds, emeralds, and sapphires, and long earrings of the same pulled down her ear lobes. Her ears, Caroline noticed, stood out from her head, sinewy and unusually large.

Caroline could feel her power, but her young stubbornness, newly aroused, pushed resolutely against that power. Maggie had met aristocrats like Caroline in the past; she had always demolished them, because under the layers of breeding, courtesy, and good manners lay what Maggie called weakness. She wanted to demolish this girl also, a poor thing in her opinion, gawky, young, ignorant, and without any light or wit. It was unfortunate that she was dear John's daughter, but one had to put people in their places immediately.

Maggie pondered. She was sixty-eight. John was much younger, but men had a way of dying, sometimes violently, and there was much in John's past that could bring about violence. His heir would be this bumpkin in her frightful gray dress, "like a Quaker's," thought Maggie. The round white silk collar made the thick short neck even shorter. But she was John's heir. The shrewd Maggie felt Caroline's stolid strength. In the meantime, vexed and insulted by Caroline's indifference and her hostility, Maggie used raillery delivered at the top of her voice.

"I don't think I'll have to buy Caroline a husband," said John Ames, amused and not irritated by Caroline's large and weighty silences. "She'll be able to manage that herself. Don't underestimate my girl."

Maggie sniffed, produced a grayish and widely laced handkerchief from her sleeve, and blew her nose like a longshoreman. Dirty old hag, thought Caroline resentfully. Maggie looked at her and caught the expression in the girl's eyes, the icy disdain, the cool withdrawal, the fastidious eyebrows. She grinned. The late afternoon sunshine took a reddish tinge. "I don't underestimate anything belonging to you, Johnny boy," said Maggie, having discerned that Caroline winced at this affectionate nickname. "Somebody like her daddy, eh? Do you remember, Johnny, my love——?"

Caroline, in spite of her aversion, listened intently. Her father had told her little of his connection with the Broomes. Maggie enlarged on it with gusto, much thigh-slapping, many winks, nudges, and sly grins. The falling sun began to make a pattern on the crimson damask wall opposite; the fabric shone like rubies, and Caroline noticed it with the inner eye of the artist and thought how it might be reproduced in paints. But her attention was unwillingly grasped by the roaring and insistent voice of her hostess and its very vitality, and soon she heard and saw nothing else but this woman.

"Let me see, Johnny pet," said Maggie, tapping a big and crooked finger against her lip. "I had been married to that Old Bastard five years; that made me thirty-five. You were about twenty-one, and more handsome than any of the vaudeville boys who used to slide in to see the cheaper girls at

Madame de Plante's. But in those days you didn't have a flat dollar, did you?"

Caroline's thick black brows drew together, puzzled. John looked at her out of the corner of his eye. Then he smiled at his old friend. "Not a dollar," he agreed. "That is, none I could spare just then."

"Ah, me, I got top price!" sighed the old beldame reminiscently. "And enjoyed it, too, and that's more than the other trollops did. But never give anything for nothing; never found that bad advice at any time. Yes, you were about twenty-one and you'd been working for the Old Bastard for nearly a year, and he brought you here for dinner one night, and in you came in your secondhand, threadbare broadcloth coat—way out of style; they were wearing coats short that year, just about reaching their asses—and I thought, 'What's the old fool dragging in this time, something out of an alley cat's litter?' And there you were, looking like a million dollars. And I didn't care if everything you had on didn't cost two cents. You had me, Johnny, you had me."

"Eight dollars," said John Ames. Caroline was staring at Maggie, hardly understanding a word except that what she had heard was shameful. She could tell that from the sliding grins, the nudges, the chuckles of her hostess. What horrified Caroline was that her father was smiling, as if at a pleasant memory. "I bought it at Sam the Gentile's in Chatham Square. And I still owed him four dollars for it when I came here, and he trusted me."

"Hah!" exclaimed Maggie. "That showed a lack of sense on his part— Sam the Gentile! Did you pay him? Don't tell me. I'd rather believe you didn't. Where was I? Yes, Johnny, you had me two minutes after you walked in. The Old Bastard said: 'Maggie, my dear, here is a young man who is going far, and he's right under my wing.' I didn't worry. Being under the Old Bastard's wing didn't mean he'd give you a cent you wouldn't earn five times over. Johnny," she said with a hideously languorous look and leaning toward him, "do you remember what I wore that night?"

"Certainly. A Worth gown of woven silver, and turquoises."

She slapped his upper thigh resoundingly and beamed at him. "You never forget anything! You know, Johnny, I said to myself, 'I'll have that boy in bed with me as quick as a wink, as soon as I can get rid of the Old Bastard some evening.'"

Caroline turned a brilliant pink. John cleared his throat. "Now, Maggie. You never did, you know."

"But I tried though, didn't I?" She grinned at him archly. "But you were all loyalty to the poor old sod, and I never minded it a bit. I knew you'd be loyal that way to me, too, someday, after I'd put him down under the old six feet. I was a fine figure of a woman, wasn't I, Johnny? The Old Bastard, heaven rest his thieving soul, got his excitements from watching me comb out my long yellow hair at night and brushing it over his big bloated belly; it was like a big toad."

John cleared his throat again. He would have preferred that Maggie be more restrained; Caroline might have indigestion over this. If she were older, reflected John, I'd be afraid, with that color, that she was on the point of having a stroke. "Now, Maggie," he said with a slightly quelling glance at his dear old friend.

She tossed her head. "Oh, I forgot Miss Stockington, in person, was here." She chuckled. "But, what the hell, Johnny! She's got to learn someday, if only secondhand like your old suit. Doubt she'll ever learn any other way. Truly, Johnny, the girl doesn't resemble you at all, though I must admit that's a fine pair of eyes there. Does she ever smile or laugh?"

"Not often," said John. "Young people are always very serious, you know."

"Never anything to be serious about in this world, except money." Maggie was enjoying herself. She continued with her reminiscences.

John Ames had begun as a stock clerk in one of Norman Benchley Broome's warehouses. Broome at that time practically controlled the auction business in New York. He also financed traders who sailed to far places for various commodities, such as copra, hemp from India, teak, tea from Ceylon and China, ivory from the Belgian Congo, sables, lambskins and squirrel furs from Russia, priceless shawls from Kashmir, silks from China, spices, velvets from Italy and France, carved alabaster from Spain, works of art from a dozen different ports, stolen from famous galleries, and a thousand other things avidly desired in Europe and America. John was in the accounting department of Broome and Company. Auctioneers; there had been three brothers then; Norman outlived his two younger brothers.

John's initial salary had been five dollars for seventy-two hours' work every week, and often on Sundays without extra pay when a special shipment was due to dock. He paid three dollars of that a week to his landlady in the Bowery for rent of a back room and two meals a day. He worked furiously and apparently without fatigue, not only because he hoped to earn more money, but because he had decided after two weeks that here lay the beginning of the fortune he was determined to have. Other clerks dropped out from sheer exhaustion; others found better situations; others were discharged upon a timid request for more money. John stayed on, making friends among superiors with his industry and willingness. Within four months he came to the attention of the eldest Mr. Broome. Mr. Norman then moved John to his own personal offices. "I trust you, my boy," he had said. "And that's more than I can say of even my own brothers. Remain with me and you'll make your way."

John remained. For several years, since he had been fourteen, he had learned not only to work in a superhuman fashion and under incredibly terrible conditions but also how to ingratiate himself with the powerful. They asked nothing, he had observed, but that a young man be polite, work all the hours possible without complaint or demands for higher wages, be absolutely loyal and always at hand, anxious to serve, and give all and ask nothing. Such a young man, they would say, had character. They highly approved of character in inferiors. If besides character they were also personable, well spoken, and appeared to have education, the approval became stronger and a personal interest was taken. But John had known. He possessed two hundred dollars, which he had earned and saved, and that was no small accomplishment, considering that in these years he had never earned more than eight dollars a week and had had to live on it. Quite casually one time he brought this to Mr. Broome's notice after asking Mr. Broome, who was unusually expansive that day, what he would suggest as an investment. Mr. Broome was surprised, pleased, and full of approval. He himself had inherited an excellent name and exactly fifty dollars when his father had died full of integrity and debts, and what he had now he had earned in the way John had earned his first two hundred dollars. John, Mr. Broome decided, was the son he ought to have had. Moreover, the young devil had the appearance of a gentleman.

Good blood there, Mr. Broome had reflected, looking for the first time at the long and narrow hands which were serving him so well and so perfectly, at the narrow feet in worn but polished boots, at the clean if threadbare clothing and the precisely folded cravat. So he, Norman Benchley Broome, had been at John's age, with two younger brothers to educate and a fortune to make. Indifferently, to disguise his interest and sudden affection for one so like his own young self, Mr. Broome had tentatively inquired as to John's parentage. Only to Mr. Broome had John then confided that his father had been a promising young lawyer, a friend of Supreme Court Justice John Marshall, who had prophesied a seat on the Bench for him in the future, and that his mother had been a Hollingshead of Albany. Mr. Broome, who instinctively knew when a man was telling the truth, knew that John was telling it now, reluctantly and only because both of them knew it was necessary. He felt less uneasy about his interest in John now; it was never good to encourage the low-born too much, in spite of ability. John had birth and character too. Excellent.

He took John under his wing, with no increase in salary. But he did advise John to invest in Broome and Company, which John did at once. More and more often John was called into the old gentleman's office, not only for discussions about the business, but for cautiously friendly talks about his future. In spite of himself, John began to feel some affection for this old patrician. He studied Mr. Broome's manipulations. Mr. Broome had a seat on the Stock Exchange, and John learned quickly and well.

In time, Mr. Broome entrusted him with various missions dealing with the piratical traders with whom he did business and with the disposal of the merchandise. He was charmed with John's knowledge and astuteness and passionate interest. He had, by now, increased John's salary, without being requested, to twenty dollars a week, a large sum. He watched John narrowly after this for any signs of profligacy. But John continued to live and dress as frugally as ever and to save even more money, which he invested in Broome and Company and in some other enterprises upon which John had consulted his patron. When John was nearly thirty Mr. Broome had come to rely upon him implicitly and to put him "in the way of things." "Make yourself ready, John," the old man would say, "and fortune will find you." By this time the two younger brothers had died, leaving sons and daughters the oldest Mr. Broome detested for their lavish habits and frivolity. He had bought back his father's house, where he had been born; he had filled it with treasures.

When John was thirty-one his salary was the unbelievable amount of one hundred dollars a week and he had his desk in the pleasant room adjoining Mr. Broome's office. His investments were growing rapidly. He was comparatively well off. He moved closer to Broome and Company, so that he could work longer hours, but he spent little if any more money than he had spent eight or more years ago. He was asked to dine at the Broome house at least twice a week. Maggie had become fond of him and praised him mightily to her ancient husband. She spoke to all her friends of "Norman's boy, John Ames," without the slightest jealousy or anxiety. She tried to find a wife suitable for him; that is, a girl with financial prospects. Mr. Broome's best friend was Mr. Esmond of Boston, with whose father he had attended Harvard; the disparity in ages had meant nothing to the decrepit old aristocrat.

On one occasion Mr. Broome and his wife had been invited to the debut of Mr. Esmond's daughters, Ann and Cynthia. Maggie had suspicions of aristocrats, especially when they were not multimillionaires, and she had declined. "Take Johnny Ames," she had said jokingly. But Mr. Broome thought it an excellent idea and had taken John, and John had met the beautiful young Ann and had fallen in love with her at once. But he had to wait.

He did not have to wait too long. Mr. Broome died in his sleep one night. Maggie was forty-eight years old and one of the richest widows in the world. It was no surprise to her that John was made one of the executors of Mr. Broome's estate, in conjunction with his firm of old family lawyers, and was appointed chairman of the Board of Broome and Company, received a salary of eight thousand dollars a year, investment advantages, a stipend of five thousand dollars a year as joint executor, and an outright legacy of one hundred thousand dollars from the estate of his late employer. He was a rich man. He married Ann Esmond and took over her fortune, and he was well on his way.

After consultation with Maggie Broome and after even longer consultation with the family lawyers, and with their consent and Maggie's, John Ames liquidated fifty per cent of the Broome holdings, invested them in sound stocks for Maggie, and so relieved her of any concern with the business. He managed the remaining interest and within a few years had built it up to power and position. (He now owned fifty-one per cent of it.) John was extremely active in numerous other enterprises as well as the Broome interests at the time of his wife's death and was regarded with respect and admiration by wealthy men twice his age. Five years ago he had gone into the importing-exporting business himself. If the manipulations he undertook and his personal business were highly suspect, it did not diminish the admiration and respect of his associates. He was a multimillionaire this day as he sat with his daughter and his old friend, Maggie Broome, in the Broome mansion.

The sun had long since set. The summer twilight had set in, gray and hot.

Both Maggie and John had talked to the girl, and she had listened soundlessly. Servants came in to light lamps, to murmur to their absorbed mistress, who waved them away impatiently.

She bellowed hoarsely to Caroline, "And the rascal has every penny he's ever earned, damn him!" She beamed at John with open affection and admiration. "Why, he could have a dozen houses like this, on the Mediterranean, in London, Paris, Berlin, Budapest, Newport, just like I have! But not him; dear me, no, not Johnny-boy Ames! And it'll all be yours one day, my girl, all yours! Lucky little bitch!"

Caroline flinched, but almost absent-mindedly. She had not missed a word of what to her was a touching saga. She wished she had known Mr. Broome. Without him, her father might never have succeeded. "Damn me, but the girl *does* have beautiful eyes, like yellow-brown velvet in the sun!" exclaimed Maggie. "And she almost smiled a couple of times, and it was real pretty, Johnny boy. Maybe you won't have to buy her a husband after all."

"Well, Caroline?" said John.

"I think it was very interesting," murmured Caroline, speaking for the first time. (Oh, this frightful old woman! How could her father bear her even for a moment?)

"Interesting, she says!" shouted Maggie, thumping John hilariously on the shoulder. "Interesting, the silly minx says! Why, that's like calling—— What's that damn big tomb in India, Johnny?"

"The Taj Mahal."

"The Taj Mahal—calling it nice and pretty. Or maybe like calling that cursed big stone lion-thing in Egypt——"

"The Sphinx."

"The Sphinx—kind of sweet. Hell, but what can you expect of a mincing schoolgirl?" Maggie was disgusted.

"I meant," Caroline said clearly and loudly, "that anything concerning my father is interesting to me."

"Um," said Maggie, cocking her head in the lamplight and studying Caroline narrowly. "Maybe the girl isn't a dunce after all. Spirit. I love spirit; I had lots of it in my day; had to. And now, come to think of it, she's a big girl, and there's something about her that's familiar. What d'you think it is, Johnny?"

"The scent of power," said John.

"Could be. Yes, could be. Hope you're right. After all, this girl'll be working for me as you've worked for me, Johnny. Someday. Think she can do it?"

"I know she can," said John, and gave Caroline one of his few smiles. She instantly felt a warm glow of joy and smiled in return.

A soft gong, which had already sounded twice, now sounded again. Maggie snorted and moved her bony shoulders restively. "Let 'em pound!" she screamed in the direction of the hall where a servant hovered. "Who's paying their damned wages, anyway, the scum?" Her voice dropped to a growl. "I don't know what the world's coming to these days. They cost me a fortune, all nine of them, and live like kings and queens at my expense, and are they grateful? No, they pound that goddamn thing in my ears when I'm not ready."

She shouted at the hovering servant, "Bring more whiskey and soda! Bring more glasses! And shut up!" She turned to John. "God! I wish these were the slave-owning days! I'd teach them manners!"

Caroline never answered Tom Sheldon's letters, though she cried over them and kept them until the ink was almost obliterated by her tears and the cheap paper blistered. She kept them to the end of her life.

He had written her only a few days ago and had given his letter to be enclosed with one of Beth's.

"I'll wait for you, Carrie, forever. No matter how long, I'll wait. There will never be any other girl for me but you. Now you're gone, I walk in front of the house every morning and at sunset, after I've quit working, and I pretend you're walking with me and talking to me. Why, I can even hear your voice and the way you laugh and see the sunset in your eyes.

"Don't forget me, Carrie. Don't forget me, my darling. I'm here. I'm waiting."

CHAPTER ELEVEN

Little love, little darling, thought Timothy Winslow as he watched his adopted sister seriously cultivate about the rosebushes of Cynthia's long and narrow garden. The girl's pale yellow hair streamed in ripples and waves down her back, but the smooth locks were tightly controlled about her head with a blue ribbon. She sat on her heels, her blue dimity frock spread all about her and protected by a ruffled white apron; her hands were gloved. But she did not work daintily; she had a thoroughness and a disciplined manner of working which alone would have commended her to the diligent Timothy. The warm June sky was already deepening in tint as the sun sloped westward. Cynthia's garden, like herself, was trim and formal in appearance, with curving graveled paths among ornamental trees and shrubs, and flower beds that were always in bloom and always changeful in color and always sharply defined and neat. It was not a large garden; there were many much larger on Beacon Street and more elaborate. But none had more charm and grace.

Timothy sat in the shade of a tree on a white bench, long and precise in his black broadcloth, his fair head bare. He watched Melinda. She was not a chatterer; what she undertook, she did earnestly and gave all her efforts to it. She moved about easily in her squatting position, merely shifting her pretty feet in their black slippers, her legs protected by long white silk stockings. She was not quite thirteen, but her profile, grave and thoughtful, the posture of her head, and the warm hints in her slender body told of approaching womanhood.

"Aren't you tired, Melinda?" he asked. He was pale and weary, for he had just been graduated from the Harvard Law School, where he had worked with a quiet and controlled intensity and so had earned a number of honors and the respect if not the liking of his teachers and fellow students. In two weeks he was to join the staff of John Ames' lawyers in New York—Tandy, Harkness and Swift—as a junior law clerk. His salary was to be eighteen dollars a week and he intended to live on it alone, for since childhood he had known why John Ames had settled a trust fund on his mother. He did not castigate his mother in his mind for a single instant; having no real moral values of his own, though sparing in his own private life, he thought the whole arrangement rather clever of her. Coldly analytical of everyone, and especially of himself, he had not yet reached a satisfactory conclusion as to why he would no longer take money from his mother. Certainly there were no virtuous scruples attached, he would think.

He loved no one but Melinda, his adopted sister. Two years ago, when he was twenty-one, he had decided that he would marry her someday. She would be eighteen in a little less than six years. In the meantime he would begin his delicate and careful courtship. He knew she loved him also, in her childish fashion. He resented it when he heard others remark on Melinda's resemblance to Cynthia. He saw no resemblance at all, except perhaps for the coloring. The girl was grave, serious, and full of tenderness for everything, and her gray eyes were deep and thoughtful. To Timothy Winslow she was the most beautiful, most precious, and most delightful creature in all the world. He loved her because she possessed what he lacked.

It had enraged him for years that John Ames dearly loved Melinda also. He felt that in some way this love violated the young girl. But he kept his rage to himself and never expressed it. No one had told him, but he felt sure that John had provided very generously for this child in his will. He had one fierce hope: that John Ames would die before Melinda was eighteen and before John became aware of the attachment between Timothy and Melinda. Otherwise he might change his codicil. There was no valid reason that John should dissent to his well-born, diligent, and ambitious nephew's marrying a girl without a name of her own, but still Timothy's exquisitely acute and keen mind suspected that John would indeed object.

Another obstacle was in the way: Cynthia, herself, who did not like her son even if she did love him maternally and was proud of him.

Melinda looked up from the roses and smiled. Then she took a pair of scissors and cut a white rosebud and ran to him with it across the grass. Her shadow flew behind her, elongated. It was the shadow of the woman she would be, graceful and flowing. She knelt on the bench beside Timothy, kissed his cheek shyly, then pushed the stem of the rosebud into his buttonhole. "There," she said in her sweet, clear voice, "that is all you needed."

Timothy put his arm about her slender waist, and his fingers stroked her back. "Needed, in what way?" he asked.

"I don't know," she said, and leaned back contentedly in the curve of his arm. "But it does seem to complete you, somehow." She bent her head to sniff at the rosebud, and he looked down at the smoothness of it and the tender way the gilt hairs glimmered on her temples. She had a soft and immaculate profile, firm and pure. She would be an exceedingly lovely woman, Timothy thought with detachment. But he loved what she was more than her appearance. His arm tightened about her, and she knelt upright to examine his face seriously.

"Is there something the matter, Tim?" she asked. She was the only one who used the diminutive form.

"No, why should there be? I was just enjoying watching you dig around those silly roses."

"They're not silly," said Melinda reprovingly. "They're beautiful. They have the most wonderful odor."

He playfully rubbed his knuckles against a soft cheek colored like a tea-rose. "You're much prettier," he said. "And you smell nicer."

She had an endearing chuckle. "Oh, you! You always say good things to me," she said in her pretty child's voice. "You're a flatterer, as Mama would say."

"I never flatter anyone," replied Timothy with absolute truth. "Puss, will you miss me when I'm in New York?"

"I always miss you," she answered. They looked into each other's eyes. The shadow of the future woman was in Melinda's, with no coquetry. "After all, you're my brother, and I do love you so much, Tim."

Timothy frowned a little. "I'm not really your brother, you know, Melly." He watched her closely.

"No, not really. But more than other people are brother and sister."

"What do you mean by that?" asked Timothy.

The child shrugged helplessly. "I don't know! I suppose it's because you never tease me the way other boys tease their sisters, and never ridicule me the way they do, and never want me to leave the room. Other girls' brothers do all that, and so they often don't like their brothers. You're so awfully kind to me, Tim."

Tim paused. He made his first definite move. "That is because I love you, Melly."

He had said this to her scores of times, lightly, affectionately. But now he spoke as a man. The girl, so sensitive, heard the change of tone. She leaned again against his arm and studied him. The large gray eyes moved over his face. Then all at once she blushed deeply, and she jumped down from the bench and ran to the roses. But she did not squat down or take up the trowel. She looked at the flowers in absolute silence and without moving, her hands hanging at her sides, her head bent. Warm shadows ran over her face; an evening wind lifted the glittering cape of her hair and blew it briefly.

Timothy waited. Something had changed between them, and both were conscious of it, though what had been said was only the apparently playful exchange between a brother who was a man and a sister who was still half a child. He knew a poignant moment had been reached. A great deal now depended on what Melinda would say and what she would do. If she suddenly laughed and ran into the house, he would know that he had been deluded, that he had not touched her at all, and that she was still only a child and thought only as a child.

She turned her head and looked at him, and there was trouble in her eyes and a searching, too. He looked back at her with the same gravity. The wind made a murmuring in the trees and the shrubs. Clouds of golden bees rose from flower beds and drifted away. A robin let his clear and melancholy evening song roll like drops of silver down the blue slope of the sky. Swallows chittered, gathered together, and flew into the sun. Shadows deepened and lengthened, and the warm air subtly changed and filled with a thousand sweet scents. Melinda looked at Timothy in silence, and for a long time.

Then she slowly moved toward him again, not running as a child runs, but as a woman walks, half reluctant, half eager. Reaching him, she stood before him. Carefully, tenderly, so as not to frighten her—for he knew that any vehement move would now frighten her—he lifted his hand. She looked at it and moved back a small step. She looked into his eyes again.

Timothy had never been so intent, yet in appearance he appeared negligent and casual. The girl's eyes fluttered from his face, then to his hand, then back again. She reached out and took Timothy's hand. There was no childish pressure now, no childish grasping. It was a woman's shy touch, a woman's half-fearful reaching.

"Melinda," said Timothy gently.

"Tim," she answered.

That was all, but it was enough for Timothy. He smiled. He stood up and, still holding Melinda's hand, he went toward the house, and Melinda walked sedately beside him and did not look at him again.

Cynthia that night spent her usual evening hour with Melinda in her bedroom before saying good night. There was a deep tenderness between mother and adopted daughter, a sure confidence, and an artless trust. Melinda was never loquacious, nor did she speak easily and carelessly. Every word, Cynthia was certain, was well thought out before Melinda spoke.

To Cynthia, Melinda was still a beloved child, and only a child. She was not yet thirteen. She had reached puberty and was changing day by day. Cynthia was aware of this; it sometimes alarmed her and made her uneasy. But she knew her mother had felt so about her own daughters. It's just that we know we are going to lose them someday, and perhaps sooner than we wish, Cynthia would think. It's quite a tragedy—for us. But as long as I can, I am going to keep Melinda a child.

"What is it, pet?" she asked Melinda, who sat near her in a ruffled nightgown of the softest Egyptian cotton, her long hair braided neatly for the night. Was it possible that she, Cynthia, had never noticed before the increasing firmness of the child's features and the budding of her young body? Where has the time gone? Cynthia asked herself with a mother's familiar pain.

The girl's bedroom was in her favorite colors, blue and ivory, with a dainty tester bed and ivory rug. Melinda rocked in a chair near Cynthia, and Cynthia impulsively reached out and smoothed the girl's head with love. "You're so quiet, darling," she said. "Don't you feel well? Is something bothering you?"

"No, Mama," said Melinda slowly. "It's just that I'm thinking. I'll be thirteen in October, won't I?"

"So you will," agreed Cynthia.

Now Melinda's face glowed, and Cynthia saw it. "Don't be in a hurry!" she cried. "You are only a child, still. You look like Alice in Wonderland, dear," she said somewhat incoherently. "There's nothing much in a grown-up world, Melinda. It's all disillusion, and worry, and pain, and anxiety, and very little pleasure. Be a child as long as you can."

"But I'm not a child," said Melinda. "Not really, Mama."

"You'll always be a child to me," said Cynthia. "A mother," she went on, trying to smile lightly, "never does want her children to grow up. She wants them with her always. Of course, darling, you'll be a woman someday, and then I suppose you'll marry and leave me. Well, we don't have to worry about anything for many, many years yet, do we?"

"Mary Ann's sister is seventeen, and she hasn't come out yet, and she's engaged," said Melinda. "She's really been engaged since she was fifteen, and that's less than three years older than I am."

"Oh, heavens," said Cynthia, and laughed a little. "Have you been reading romances behind my back?"

"The Mother of Christ was only fourteen when He was born," said Melinda with a stubbornness Cynthia had encountered several times before.

Cynthia sighed. "I suppose that is what they say," she admitted. "But we aren't living in the old times, dear, and girls don't marry so young. Not in America, at least. They don't even get engaged then." She paused. "What little boy has charmed you, pet? It seems to me that Amanda brings that big hulk of a thirteen-year-old brother around very often these days. No wonder; you're so pretty. Is it Alfred?" She smiled indulgently, thinking of her own long-past and childish infatuations. "Alfred Bothwell has a long way to go before he becomes a man. Many, many years. Is it Alfred?"

Harper Bothwell, finally becoming certain that Cynthia would never marry him, had married a cousin twelve years ago, a widow with a boy about a year old, and had adopted him, and he now had a daughter of his own in addition.

Melinda was silent. Cynthia smiled again. So it was Alfred, that big hulking boy. The love affairs of children! But one had to manage them wisely or the little souls were extremely hurt, and the hurt could last all one's life. Cynthia remembered her own young years. She had been frightfully infatuated with—now, what was his name? She could not remember. But he had had a beautiful pair of big brown eyes. Like a cow's, she thought now wryly. She had been thrilled to the heart when he had sent her a bunch of tight little hothouse roses when she was Melinda's age. Where was the poor creature now? He was a fat old banker with a belly, in New York.

Melinda said, "Mama, do you still not know who my parents were?"

The girl had asked this many times before, and Cynthia, respecting her, had always answered: "Darling, no one knows. The records are always sealed." So she repeated this again tonight, expecting Melinda to accept it as casually as she had done in other years. Melinda was not satisfied.

"I wish I knew," she said wistfully.

"Why?" Cynthia demanded.

"I don't know, Mama. I wonder if they are dead."

Cynthia bit her lip. She had been about to say, "Of course they are not dead." She shivered at the thought of how close she had been to saying that. She drew her light lace shawl closer about her. Really, these June nights could be deceptive.

"Are you dissatisfied, Melinda?" asked Cynthia with some sharpness. "Haven't I been a good mother to you?"

"Oh, Mama," said Melinda with remorse, putting her hand on Cynthia's knee. "I've hurt your feelings. I'm so sorry. But a girl, adopted like me, often wonders about her real parents. Don't be hurt, Mama. I love you so much."

Cynthia held out her arms to Melinda, and the girl came to her and sat on her lap, and they clung to each other. Cynthia murmured over and over, "My darling, my darling, my darling."

They rocked together, and Cynthia thought, as she had thought many times before, that she would literally burst with her passionate love. She murmured endearments against the girl's temple and cheek. "Melinda, Melinda," she said.

Then Melinda said, "Mama, I'm sorry Tim's going away so soon to New York."

Cynthia stopped rocking. She smoothed Melinda's head. "Well, dear, after all, he's a man now. He has his own way to make. He can't stay home forever."

"I suppose not," Melinda sighed.

"You two have always been so fond of each other," said Cynthia. "But never mind. He'll be home on the holidays, no doubt."

"Yes. Yes," said Melinda. "But I'll miss him so much."

"There's always Alfred Bothwell," said Cynthia, smiling.

Melinda did not answer. Cynthia rocked again with the girl in her arms.

"I've always loved Tim so much," said Melinda.

"And that makes you a majority of one," said Cynthia. "Look at the time! My chick should have been in bed and asleep half an hour ago."

Cynthia came down to the sitting room, where Tim was reading a dull financial paper. She had refused to have gaslight installed, saying it smelled bad, flickered too much, and was too harsh and glaring. Timothy knew that she preferred the softer light of lamps because of the filmy webbing about her eyes and the one small cleft between them. Otherwise she was as stately and graceful as in her youth, with a slender and supple figure; she moved lightly, and her native polish was enhanced by the years as silver is enhanced by use and becomes more satiny. She sat down in her favorite chair near the fireplace; the aperture had been filled with a basket of red roses, and the scent filled the room. It had been raining a little; an odor of warm dust and freshness and heated stone came through the tall opened windows.

Timothy had risen automatically when his mother came in, then when she had sat down he took up his paper again. They had, as yet, not exchanged a word. Cynthia picked up her embroidery. The clock chimed ten.

"Why don't you wear spectacles, Mother?" asked Timothy idly from behind his paper. "You're in the bosom of your family and there's no one to peep. It is almost painful for me to watch you holding your work at arm's length and squinting. That's a fine way to acquire the wrinkles you loathe, you know."

"One can always trust you, Timothy, to say the kindest things," said Cynthia.

"One remembers that on his mother's next birthday she will be forty——?"

Cynthia could not help smiling. "Forty," she said. "I've been forty some time now and I don't intend to be any older even when I have grandchildren. Don't be impertinent, Timothy." She sighed, looked at her work impatiently, and put it down. "How time flies," she said.

"I've heard that remark before," said her son.

Her restless thoughts moved on. "Really," she said, "I don't see how you can subsist like a gentleman in New York on eighteen dollars a week. It's ridiculous."

"I'll subsist, if not necessarily like a gentleman. I'll be as rigorous as my dear Uncle John was at my age."

"You never mention him without a sneer in your voice," said Cynthia. "What has John ever done to hurt you? He has been more than good to me, and without any obligation on his part, and good to you, too."

"But, dear Mama, he isn't a gentleman, and you are always speaking of breeding. Never mind, don't frown. It only makes that mark between your eyes go deeper. There are some who can afford to be gentlemen; I am not one of them yet, due in great part to the profligacy of both you and my dear dead papa."

Cynthia's cheeks colored. She looked with animus at her son, and then she saw that he appeared strained and pale and that his light eyes were tired. She could not help it: he was abominable and merciless, but he was her son and she loved him even if she disliked him heartily as a person. "You've said that before," she remarked in a milder tone than he expected. "Your father's expectations were exaggerated, and neither of us had ever had a reason to be prudent. We weren't trained in prudence. But at least you've had a beautiful home, an excellent education, and you are a gentleman in spite of what you say."

Timothy shrugged and rattled the paper. Cynthia became exasperated. "You surely will allow me to send you a sum which will double your income," she said. "Why, I believe you're proud! It's good to be proud, but not at the price of cheap shirts, poor lodgings, bad food, and coarse boots. Especially when it isn't necessary."

"It won't be necessary long," Timothy assured her. One of his feet moved restively. For a moment she was deeply moved. She wished he had been a less difficult child, but even as an infant he had resented coddlings and kissings and murmurous sounds against his cheek. "He's like a little thistle," she would complain. What did she know about Timothy? she reflected. Absolutely nothing. He had been an unloving baby, an unloving and self-assured child, and now he was a withdrawn young man.

Timothy continued, when she remained silent: "I expect to start at eighteen dollars a week, yes. But I hope—I know that I will be getting much more than that within a year. And I hope that I'll be a junior partner within five years. Dear Uncle John has hinted as much; he practically owns that law firm. At least he frightens the devil out of the whole office when he appears. A rich, tidy firm. I remember an old Scots saying to the effect that lawyers are the devil's race, and I'm sure it is true."

"Why do you always ascribe villainy to everybody?" Cynthia said with renewed exasperation.

"Probably because everyone is a villain at heart," he replied, pleased that he had annoyed her. "Except, of course, Melly."

"Don't call her 'Melly'!" Cynthia cried. "What a vulgar nickname."

He put down the paper. "She calls me Tim, and that's a nickname," he said.

"But she's only a child. She's growing up. At least she will soon begin to grow up," Cynthia added hastily. "And it's time for even you to call her by her right name." She clasped her hands in her mauve silk lap and smiled. "The child is in love! Imagine that, she is in love."

Her large gray eyes dreamed, grew brighter, as if a little tearful. "Is she indeed?" Timothy said. "With whom?"

"A silly schoolboy just a little older than herself. Harper Bothwell's adopted son, his nephew. That big uncouth boy, Alfred."

"Did she say so herself?" asked Timothy.

"I think so. Yes, I think she did. At least when I teased her about Alfred—he's always coming here with Amanda and standing around looking ill at ease and staring at Melinda. Like a stork, on one foot."

"Did she say so herself?" repeated Timothy. Cynthia was startled.

"Dear me," she said, "you are actually sounding like an outraged father." She was pleased. "Or the very much older brother you really are. What does it matter? Those children! Now I don't recall that Melinda really did say anything."

Timothy carefully folded his newspaper, then smoothed it neatly. The ring his mother had given him on his fifteenth birthday, a deep ruby set in bright gold, twinkled in the soft lamplight.

"However," said Cynthia, "I agree with you that it's ridiculous even talking about such a thing in connection with those children. It'll be years and years. I myself was married too young. I wasn't quite twenty-one, and very inexperienced, practically a dolt concerning worldly matters, and no doubt very stupid." She glanced at the portrait on the wall.

"Melinda," said Timothy, "will be eighteen in less than six years. And that horror of a boy is only a little older than she."

"But he's going to be handsome. All the Bothwells are handsome, and he is a Bothwell by birth as well as by adoption, you know. He has really lovely Irish eyes, deep blue, and such long black lashes, and his hair is black and curly. He is pimply just now, but he'll be a fine-looking man. Melinda could do much worse—with all that money, too. Ah, well, it will be centuries, and it's foolish even to talk about it now."

"You are so particular about breeding," said Timothy. "I've often wondered why you adopted Melinda."

Cynthia took up her embroidery, held it at arm's length, and pretended to scrutinize it. "How tiresome," she said. "I think I took too large a stitch there. It will have to come out. What did you say, Timothy? Oh yes something about Melinda's parents. Well, one has only to look at the child to know that she didn't come from a mean line. And when I saw her for the very first time I said to myself, 'Why, if dear Ann had had another daughter she would have looked exactly like Melinda.' It almost killed me when Ann died."

"Of neglect," Timothy reminded her. "Dear Uncle John was too parsimonious to call a physician in time."

"I know, I know," said Cynthia in distress. "In a way, it's not entirely his fault. I know how hard he had to struggle. He wasn't sure of himself. He still isn't, even now."

"I think it was Frederick the Great who said, 'Nothing is enough for a man to whom everything is not enough,'" Timothy replied. "Or something similar. Yes indeed, I think poor old Uncle John should be pitied. But not for wanting more and more money. I want it myself, and I'm just as determined as he is to get it. I just pity him for having such a gargoyle of a daughter."

"Oh, Timothy, how unkind. Caroline is becoming, in a way, a very impressive young woman. Is it possible that she, like you, is twenty-three? How time flies. And she's gained considerable poise during all those travels with her father. Her eyes are really remarkable; they grow more beautiful every time I see her, and her smile is charming. She has such pretty teeth— a little too large, but pretty just the same. And she dresses almost stylishly after spending nearly a year in Paris. Yes, very impressive. She is certainly old enough to marry. I must speak about it to John when they return from Switzerland. And she has a marvelous mind. You ought to appreciate that, at any rate." She stared long and thoughtfully at her son and smiled teasingly. "Have you ever thought of marrying Caroline yourself? You do love money, you know, and she will inherit so many countless millions."

"Good God!" exclaimed Timothy. "What grotesque ideas you do get!"

But Cynthia had become a trifle excited by the idea. "Do let's be practical," she said. "You are so cold-blooded; you are determined to be as rich as John. How better, and how much more expedient, to get it by marrying than merely drudging along year after year in hope. You can't really detest Caroline as much as you imply. What has the poor girl done to you? She'll be a grand old lady. No Boston man ever let a woman's appearance stand in the way of a good marriage. And Caroline will not only be immensely rich, but she's my sister's daughter and she is well bred. Really, Timothy, you could do much worse."

"I don't think so," said Timothy with an elaborate shudder. "We hated each other from the first minute."

Cynthia pursed her lips. "It's hard to say what Caroline ever thinks. I doubt she 'hates' you; she's indifferent to anyone but her father. It is I she dislikes intensely, if anybody. She won't even stay in this house when they're in Boston. Timothy, you've always been practical, perhaps too much so. Your marrying Caroline will keep the money in the family, where it belongs. And if you really can't stand Caroline after you marry her, there are other consolations."

"Such as a mistress," said Timothy pleasantly.

Cynthia laughed. "Why not? There, you'll think I'm shameless."

"Nothing to me is shameless," said Timothy, "provided there is cash concerned in it. But Caroline really sticks in my throat. Shall we drop the horrible subject?"

Cynthia nodded, but she was becoming even more excited. What a solution for poor Timothy! She must speak to John. She had very little, herself, to leave her son.

"Don't forget, I'm giving a dinner for you to celebrate your graduation before you go to New York," she said. "I've invited all my friends. They can be helpful to you." She yawned suddenly. "Is it actually eleven? I remember when that was only the beginning of the evening for me. I must indeed be becoming—middle-aged." But she glanced down with satisfaction at her smooth white hands which showed no rising veins, no mottling, no withering. "You seem so tired, Timothy," she said in a gentle tone. "It's been very hard on you. But you do have your key, and I'm proud of you. Why don't you go to bed?"

"I will," he said, standing up. "Shall I ring for the maids to put out these dingy lamps?"

"In a moment. Good night my dear."

She stayed alone for a minute or two. She did not know why she felt so suddenly depressed. Then she rang the bell and left the room. She floated up the graceful stairway, then stopped on the last step. Timothy was standing at Melinda's door, his head inclined in its direction. Cynthia smiled sadly. How he loved the child! Her son moved on, his head bent.

CHAPTER TWELVE

Caroline had seen Tom Sheldon briefly but once during her two weeks in Lyme in 1878. He had later paced up and down the narrow shingle but did not glance at the house. She had cried, then had resolutely turned away. In 1879 she had not seen him at all, for she was constantly traveling with her father. In 1880 he had come upon her at dawn on her boulder in front of the house at Lyme, and he had sat down beside her and they had not spoken, and then he had kissed her cheek gently and had gone away. In 1881 she had spent only one week at Lyme and encountered him once in the village, where he had bowed soberly and had gone about his business. In 1882 she had remained in Lyndon for the short time she and her father were in America, but that year, on her twenty-second birthday, she had received a little gift from Tom, a small baroque pearl set in a coil of old silver.

But he wrote her constantly, though she did not reply, except once to thank him abruptly for his gift. (She never knew that he had half expected her to return it. Had she done so, he would have known it was hopeless.) She read his letters, deeply and darkly stirred. Always, she looked for his last words: "I will wait for you, Carrie darling. Don't forget me."

She wrote Beth long letters, which often confused and baffled that simple and aging woman, but Caroline knew that Tom would be the next to read them. She described the countries she had visited and the people she had met. She did not mention her father. But her letters were unconsciously filled with her cry of bewilderment, fear, and loneliness, which grew year by year. So Tom's letters to her were full of reassurance and love and understanding. Her loyalty to her father prevented her acknowledging the passionate gratitude she felt. It was impossible for her to marry Tom; she must avoid him forever. And then she would watch the post for Beth's next letter in which Tom's letter was enclosed.

She had met multitudes (it seemed to her) of people in these years, mostly associates of her father's, and sometimes she and John dined at their London, Paris, Berlin, and Geneva homes. Sometimes, when John thought she seemed especially silent and dull and pale, he would take her to the French Riviera for the sun and air. She would walk in loneliness, averting her eyes from the bathing and sunning men and women, and avoiding the gay *salles à manger* and eating in her room. She shivered at the sound of music. She cared nothing for the exotic food and ate plainly, as did her father.

It had taken Caroline several years to come to the horrified conclusion that all the Alecks were not confined to the gross and ignorant working classes, to the brutes on docks, to the drivers of hacks. They lived and had their being among her father's friends. They had the same fierce expression as the original Aleck, the same imperviousness, the same lustful greed, the same solid brutality, though their exteriors were clothed in broadcloth and they spoke in cultivated voices and smoked rich cigars and drank fine wines and lived in magnificent homes. They were as merciless as Aleck, and as exigent, and resorted to gigantic exigency when they considered it necessary. She had always believed that the less desirable traits of the human race were forbidden entry to good homes and were unknown among people of breeding and education. She had believed that the animal traits of cruelty, avarice, and opportunism, of hypocrisy and falsehood, of treachery, of rapacity and barbarousness, were limited strictly to the Alecks. When she discovered that these traits existed among those who did not have to work for a living with their hands and who had tremendous fortunes, it was a violent experience for her. Illustrious names, lofty bearing, education, charm, and worldliness did nothing to change human nature, she dismally concluded.

However, there was a distinction, she observed: The Alecks frequently were assailed by the law. Their counterparts among her father's associates were not only not assailed by the law but were decorated by governments and received many honors and spoke easily of czars and kaisers and emperors and kings, and lesser but still august ranks. They were accepted everywhere. It seemed, to the appalled girl, that one had only to be a monster on a tremendous scale to be honored.

As she sat now in her suite in Geneva, she recalled one man in particular whom she regarded with silent but furious loathing and terror. He was an Englishman, Montague de Valle Brookingham, and when his father died he would become Montague Lord Halnes. Forty-four years old, he had been more than considering asking John Ames for his daughter. Caroline could do worse, John would think, and Brookingham was on his way up and had come a long way from being a younger son—his older brother had died two years ago—of a noble but impoverished family. There was nothing Brookingham would not do, and he had done almost all of it. Though he had been young at the time, he had made a fortune through the Franco-Prussian War and had received the ribbon of the Legion of Honor from a government which had apparently been unaware of the fact that he had supplied arms to the Prussians also. Like John Ames, he was a formidable adventurer and had a nose for money, and enormous liquid assets, most of which he kept discreetly in the banks in Switzerland. The crumbling family home in Devonshire had been restored by him after his brother's death. Had his brother not providentially died, the house could have rotted for all he would have cared, he had said to John laughingly. Fortunately his brother had also died without an heir. The title would come to Montague, and the old lord was now in his seventies and "doddering." Queen Victoria, it was said, regarded Montague with much favor and thought him witty and captivating, and Mr. Gladstone and Mr. Disraeli, though disliking and suspecting him, had to be polite when he called upon the monarch. Prince Albert had privately thought him despicable, but the Queen remembered that he had been of excellent service in the Affair of India. He had dreams of an earldom, and his dreams were not without substance.

He was now in Switzerland, as were numerous other friends of John Ames. Caroline sat alone, dreading the evening. Mr. Brookingham would be present, as always. He was at least two inches shorter than the tall young woman, with a large head covered with thin mouse-colored hair, a clean-shaven face, and a somewhat chubby body and a small bulge in his belly. The head was quite out of proportion to his general size. When he was serious or in repose, his plump features were ordinary and undistinguished, even commonplace, his light blue eyes faintly reflective, his nose broad and shapeless. In cheap and ordinary clothing he could have passed as a semi-skilled artisan or poor shopkeeper on the streets of London on his way home to a meager fire, small crowded rooms full of cheap bric-a-brac, a sleazy rug on the floor, and to a tea composed of boiled eggs, toast, and currant jam. But even in his well-tailored and expensive clothing he had a look utterly without distinction or flair. He faintly resembled a valet dressed in discarded garments from the wardrobe of his master.

It was when he smiled or laughed that he terrified Caroline. Immediately his face, and even his features, changed amazingly and actually took on different contours. Then the light blue eyes darkened, tilted, and became demonic under faded brows that flashed upward from the corners. His quiet mouth was then diabolical. His nostrils flared, his ears peaked, his plump cheeks became angular. A portrait of him in repose and another in amusement would have convinced any viewer that this was not the same man at all.

There would be others present tonight, but they did not seem to Caroline to be half so dangerous, evil, and ruthless as this man. In a way he fascinated her; she was always watching for his face to change, for the rather dull quietness to take on a preternatural quality of pure and laughing malignance. She had heard others say he was charming, and she had been dumbly incredulous. Her father relaxed in his company, and his other friends enjoyed his witticisms and his delicately depraved remarks and his way with a joke. He was always extremely courteous to Caroline, and thoughtful, and she thought he mocked her. The innocence in her was startled in his presence.

So, drearily this evening, she shrank from the thought of the man who wanted to marry her for his own reasons. She did not like Switzerland, and she thought longingly of Italy, and especially of Rome, with its smooth white grandeur, its eternal immovability, its waiting air of timeless power. She had been in Switzerland three times, and it had always remained alien to her, which surprised John Ames, who thought the gray starkness of the country resembled his daughter's character.

Caroline remembered her first journey to Switzerland. Italy had overwhelmed her with its exuberant beauty, its flashes of almost intolerably lovely color, its lush untidiness which was part of its enchantment, its harmonious and flashing landscapes, its humming repose and murmurous silences. John had believed his daughter indifferent to these, just as he was indifferent. It was in Milan where she had secretly bought a tiny painting of the Bay of Naples for Tom Sheldon; it remained in her luggage under layers of paper. She knew that hundreds of artists had made the Bay of Naples almost as banal and blasé to millions of eyes as copies of the Venus de Milo. But this painting was different; the usual purples and blues and scarlets had not been used. The unknown artist had captured a noonday view in one blinding moment of gold—gold every tint, shade, and hue; mountains, rocks, and water—so that the painting lay in the hands like a shimmering rectangle of living gilt, changeful and pulsing.

It was also in Milan where a subtle change came to John Ames, a kind of gray darkening over his flesh, over his eyes, and over his fading hair. He was not a complainer, but with the intensity of absorbed love Caroline fearfully saw the change. She asked herself dozens of frantic questions: Did John's appetite, always spare, become even more spare in Milan? Was he less decisive of movement; was his voice slower; did he appear faintly exhausted? She timidly suggested a physician. "Here?" he had said contemptuously, dismissing the wisdom and the glory of Italy in one word. Then, seeing her face, he had added kindly, "There is nothing wrong with me. You must remember that I'm not young any longer, Caroline, and I've been busy in Rome, and the climate is enervating. I'll be glad to be in Switzerland, and so will you. You'll like everything about it."

That had been three years ago. She had never given the little painting to Tom Sheldon after all. She had become almost accustomed to the change in her father; at least, since no other symptoms of any disorder developed, she reluctantly came to the conclusion that if there was any change at all it was due to his age. She rarely saw Cynthia and even more rarely spoke to her; she did not know that her aunt was apprehensive also and that Cynthia "nagged," as John called it, about eminent Boston physicians.

Father and daughter had stayed overnight in Stresa before Caroline's first visit to Switzerland. This was north Italy, but spring was vehement everywhere, though with less passion than in the south. Caroline could see Lake Maggiore from her bedroom window, silvery and glistening, afloat with two islands of vivid green. At her left stood an arm of the Alps pitching down into the water in a broken chaos of purplish gray under a dim sky of lilac. Caroline stepped onto her narrow balcony and looked below her at the grounds of the hotel, at the bursting colors of azaleas, the wet coolness of palm trees, the greenness of sloping lawns. A soft rain began to fall, rustling. The air filled with a thousand faint fragrances. I should like to live here! thought Caroline. She wrote to Beth: "I can't describe Stresa. It is so still and calm and great, a study in grisaille, greens, and faint lavenders."

One of Caroline's teachers had once told her: "There are no real boundaries in the world; there are only artificial ones made by greedy governments. People, countries are all the same, and only governments keep them apart. There are no such things as race and national temperaments; you would see that if presidents, kings, czars, and kaisers didn't divide people for their own purposes." On seeing Switzerland, and on other occasions in other countries, Caroline knew that her teacher was a milky fool, had either never traveled or had done her traveling through dull minds who saw no variety in mankind and preferred to see all men as of one dun color. Men's spirits, in spite of their detractors or their adulators, remained superbly isolated and deeply different one from another.

The next day she and her father left for her first visit to Switzerland. She stood at the border while her luggage was examined by kindly Italians, and she looked at the grave and motionless faces of the Swiss officers. Then with only a few steps she was in a nation entirely different from Italy, and among people who had nothing in common, temperamentally, with the

Italians. She boarded the excellent Swiss train and read the admonitions in Italian, French, and German concerning the dire penalties inflicted on those who destroyed or defaced or dirtied the shining cleanliness of the conveyance. The exhortations irritated her. She remarked on it to John, who shrugged and said, "They are a very strict and rigorous people. Unlike the Italians." Caroline added to herself in rebellion, "They have no color." She glanced down at her dull dress of brown wool and for the first time in her life she thought, "I too have no color." She saw her broad face in the glistening windowpane and was sadly affronted by her lack of beauty. She did not see that she had a kind of large majesty and that her face, in spite of its broad shape, had a Gothic quality.

Even the Italians on the train—businessmen from Milan and Rome—appeared subdued in the reproving atmosphere of the Swiss train. Their mustaches seemed to lose a measure of their stiff pugnacity, their manners some assurance; their attitudes became less melodramatic. They stopped talking vivaciously and applied themselves diligently to papers, which apparently pained them. "Why do you stare?" John Ames asked his daughter. She did not answer for a moment; she was thinking of the little painting she had bought, of blue Vesuvio and Soma against a scarlet sky, of flower markets incredibly blazing, of painted buildings and red roofs. She looked through the window at Switzerland. She had no words and merely smiled deprecatingly.

The mountains in Italy had appeared green and violet and soft. Here they had frozen into vast and granite forms, with only an occasional steep emerald meadow among pines and boulders. The day was dim and somber, enhancing the awesome landscape of narrow valley and looming stone. Vapor gushed through high passes, and an infrequent waterfall, slender and the color of illuminated lead, broke from rock. Swiss hamlets stood diminished in the little valleys, the houses built of slate-colored stone and dark wood or of some stark-white mortar with black roofs curiously shaped and curving, and all dominated by grim little churches, pale and harsh and pointed. The mountains climbed higher, white and dark gray, ribbed and striped with white slashes of snow, though this was the middle of May. Caroline could feel the icy wind along the window sash, and she shivered and pulled her brown traveling shawl closer over her shoulders. A lake, steel-blue and surrounded by purple cliffs and crags, wheeled into sight, and Caroline thought of the Bay of Naples at sunset. She had glimpses of streets, chill and barren and winding and very neat, and little tidy carts and carriages, and children so covered with heavy brown clothing that they appeared shapeless and nublike.

Her thoughts shifted. It was only the hard gray light that made her father appear wan and desiccated and very tired. Timidly she asked whether he would like some chocolate. A waiter was coming into the car with a linen-covered tray of cups and pitchers and little plates of cakes. John said impatiently, "No, but have some yourself. Swiss chocolate is the best in the world." Caroline sipped her chocolate mournfully.

"We will soon be in Geneva," said John, shuffling his papers together and replacing them in his brief case. "I always stay at the Hotel Grande. Economy doesn't pay abroad. All Americans are supposed to be rich; if you're as sober as most Europeans, except for the Italians, the Parisians, and the Austrians, they think you are poor and so you lose authority and influence with them. We're alleged to have dash, at least when it comes to spending." He smiled a little grimly.

Caroline no longer said to her father, "I am afraid," though she was always frightened. She had acquired a quiet, monosyllabic kind of conversation which added to her dignity, so that people said, "She is still quite a young woman, but she isn't foolish. Solid and firm and observant." Not only Bostonians thought this; New Yorkers approved of her, and she had been especially respected in London. She was, on this first visit to Switzerland, only twenty and appeared ten years older. Strangers often believed she was her father's wife, to be sure, but one eminently suited to him.

Geneva, on this first visit, did not impress her. It had a kind of purposeful bustle, orderly and hard and excessively clean and dull. The confidence of the people awed Caroline. The manager, surrounded by servants, received them with restrained cordiality and no excitement. He conducted them to their suite, gave Caroline only the slightest of curious glances, and inquired after Monsieur's health. Even the Swiss of French origin, thought Caroline, had taken on the cold stoniness of their country, and the intonations of their voices were frigid. Later she was to encounter the owner of the hotel, a Swiss of German origin, and she thought him stiff and unfriendly and his look at her father glacial.

To Caroline, the suite appeared very luxurious and, as always, she compared new places to her Aunt Cynthia's house, which she privately and disdainfully referred to as a "boutique." These rooms could under no circumstances inspire thoughts of a "boutique," and Caroline liked them. She liked the long double windows opening onto a stiff iron balcony; she could see small and geometrical gardens below, then a cold rigid street, then the flat, grayly shining lake, and always the omnipresent and gloomy mountains. The sun came out briefly as Caroline looked at the grayish-white houses across the lake; it gave no life or vivacity to the landscape, but rather a strange sullenness, like a reluctant smile forced onto an impersonal face. She turned back to the rooms, to the heavy walnut and mahogany furniture and lumbering carved tables and chandeliers and thick crimson carpet. Everything was on a large scale, and Caroline felt no cramping as she had felt in the elegance of her aunt's home. She fingered draperies of spongy red or dark blue velvet, tasseled and brushed, with valances and gilt hardware. She surveyed her bedroom with its four-poster bed, its marble-topped commode, its cumbersome rocking chairs or tufted dark green seats, its tall wardrobe. A girl in a navy-blue linen uniform and white apron and cap came in, curtsying, to help "Madame" unpack and assist her.

"Mademoiselle. Mademoiselle Ames," said Caroline awkwardly. "I am Monsieur Ames' daughter."

The girl lifted a polite eyebrow, curtsied again, and turned her attention to Caroline's small amount of baggage. Caroline had learned not to interfere. But she watched uneasily as the girl deftly unpacked her meager wardrobe, and she thought this servant, as did the others in London and Paris, expressed by the set of her shoulders the poor opinion of the expensive but poorly designed and poorly cut frocks and gowns.

The girl finished unpacking. Caroline fumbled in her purse. She found some French and Italian coppers. She put them on the table. The girl ignored them, curtsied, and left. They should be grateful for anything, anything at all, from an American! thought poor Caroline hotly. Her tips in Italy had been accepted with a humor which she had considered gratitude. She decided she did not like Switzerland. In fact, with the exception of Italy, she did not like Europe. Proud and mighty London offended her belief in her father's importance—there was no Englishman as important as John Ames. Shrewd and laughing Paris had frightened her; Vienna had appeared cynical and uncaring. Rome, indifferent to passing ages, had only tolerated her.

John had smiled at her oddly. "We are still a young frontier country, and these countries are old. Give us time, my dear. We'll not always be young and naïve. And good," he had added. "No, no. We'll not always be good and kind and just and free. We'll be the greatest despot and murderer of them all. Just be patient."

Caroline had been startled and puzzled at this extraordinary remark. That night she had met her father's friends, had found them ambiguous, frightening, and too adult for her youth and inexperience. There was something about them that repelled and appalled her, though she did not know what it was. Her father changed in their presence, and this frightened her more than anything else. He became one with them. She listened to them acutely when they spoke in German or French or Italian. Something was astir in them that was terrible, and her father was part of it. She had tried to get him to explain later, but he had said wearily, "It will come to you in time. At present, you need only listen."

"But, Papa, they were Englishmen and Germans and Italians and Frenchmen. Yet they didn't seem, really, to have any country——" She looked at him helplessly.

"They don't," said John Ames. "They have no country, just as I have no country."

She had nothing to say to that. There seemed nothing adequate to say, nothing to question.

She knew now, three years later, on another May night in Geneva, in the very same suite, a great deal more than she had known earlier. These men and these women—English, German, Swiss, American, French, Austrian, and Italian—had indeed no country, no allegiances, no nation, no honor, no principles. They had but one loyalty: money. In the presence of money they were one nation, one people, one mind, and one soul. They respected and liked each other and used each other. When they spoke of their native countries it was with objectivity and no patriotism. They would betray and plunder if it brought them fortune. A Russian banker had joined them but two years ago; he was smoothly enveloped in their bland and watchful anonymity. His face had taken on the contours of theirs; he spoke French without an accent. He was a small, rotund man with a jolly expression and brilliant black eyes, and they called him Alex, and Caroline had never quite been able to pronounce his surname. He was as American, or as French, German, Italian, Austrian, English, Swiss, as any of his colleagues.

The women were few; there were only three of them—one, from a place she vaguely described as Mitteleuropa, the wife of a German, another the French wife of Alex, and still another the English wife of an Austrian. The Englishwoman was very soignée and reminded Caroline smartingly of Cynthia, the Frenchwoman was dowdy, and the lady from Mitteleuropa was dark and wicked and very suave. Caroline feared and disliked all of them, but she really detested the women who, though so aware of all that was transpiring and so involved, were still women with women's malices and private little pettinesses and tendencies to exchange mirthful and personal glances at another's expense. They murmured to her affectionately, brought her small expensive gifts, and spoke of her "future," but she knew they considered her ugly and gauche and a very bad mistake, indeed.

These people would also be here tonight. Dinner would be served in the large sitting room of the suite, and the servants would be impeccable and chill. The guests were always the same: the Slebers, the "Alexes" (Monsieur Alexander Polevoi and Madame), Mr. Montague Brookingham, Herr und Frau Gottfried Ernst (the Austrian banker and his English wife). Madame Polevoi, the French lady, would, as usual, appear even more dowdy than Caroline, but she would have a grace and a charm which would bring the eyes of the gentlemen more often to her than to Frau Ernst, who bought all her gowns from Worth and whose jewels were astounding.

There would be nine of them tonight, with Caroline and her father. Caroline restlessly moved to the sitting room, where the waiters were already setting up the long white table. The linen glistened in the cold May light which was reflected back from the ash-colored mountains and the gray lake. The silver sparkled icily, and so did the crystal. The waiters appeared unaware of Caroline's presence; they murmured to each other in French, German, or Italian as they smoothed and arranged. The centerpiece was of jonquils; unlike the American flower, these had a poignant and sorrowful scent which pervaded the room with funereal sweetness. The two long windows were open to the gelid air, and Caroline, in her bunchy crimson wool, felt tendrils of invisible cold moving over her face and hands.

All at once she wanted to be part of this homely if efficient ritual. She moved hesitantly to the table and pretended to be absorbed in the flowers. She meticulously moved a perfectly set arrangement of silver. She suddenly shivered in the hard cold of the mountain air. She said to one of the waiters, "I should like a fire if you please," and she pointed to the black marble fireplace and its mantel covered with elaborate German beer steins and a pair of sentimental porcelains. The waiter, bowing, pulled a bell rope for the man who cared for the fires. He came in, in his uniform of white and blue stripes, with a cap of the same material on his head, and laid the fire. The tops of the formidable mountains turned a faint scarlet as the declining sun touched their glaciers and white caps.

The usual Swiss guests would be absent tonight, and so would the Italians. These bankers—they were always bankers—were in Russia, John Ames had explained to his daughter. No matter what else they did, or what their obscure affairs, they were always bankers, he would say wryly. "There is much more to banking, Caroline," he had once said, "than the taking in of money, letting it out on local mortgages or farm loans and enterprises, and paying it out with interest." "Banking" was the power behind the throne of the Czar, the thrones of Austria-Hungary, Germany, France, the British Empire, Spain, Scandinavia, the obscure palaces in South America, and, of course, the chair of the President of the United States. Caroline was now well aware that the bankers had only to raise a delicate forefinger, to nod disinterested heads, and thrones would fall, armies would march, the thunder of arms would shatter the peace of the skies, kings would be deposed, empires and nations rearranged or blasted, and the destiny of millions changed irrevocably.

There was one thing that John Ames, among many others, did not know about his daughter, the tall, impressive, silent young woman with her meager coronet of fine black braids. She had a year ago come to the strong and passionate decision that she herself would never be engaged with these people, would never speak to them again when her father died. Intrigue sickened her, but she exonerated her father. After all, he had suffered; he had been desperately poor and had been persecuted for his poverty. He used these people. In a way, she thought naïvely, it was a retribution.

She knew that her father was enormously wealthy. She had been taught all about the stock market. It appeared to her to be exciting, part of the growth of the industrial world, and contained opportunities for the discreet and affluent. If there were men who manipulated the stock market in New York, London, the Bourse, Berlin, and St. Petersburg, it was very well. It was a splendid game, and profitable. She would keep her father's fleet of ships, for legal cargo only. Again, she exonerated John; he had been forced to do as he had done. He had had no choice in a ravenous world.

Reality and her natural integrity, simplicity, and honesty were, unknown to her conscious mind, having a grim battle in the corridors of her spirit. Reality attempted to show her that the majority of men, perhaps all of them, had much of the "Aleck spirit" or had less; but they had it. Reality had shown her that men had their price, and not every price was cash. Once she had read a book written by a distinguished Jesuit priest which defined very clearly man's naturally depraved state and his dark insistent nature, from both of which he could be delivered only by God. Caroline had been outraged and frightened by this confrontation of reality, and she had torn the book to shreds with a passion she had not known she possessed. But secretly she had agreed.

She who had never been ill in her life had taken to having violent headaches and bouts of nausea over the past few years. She could feel the dull premonitions of one of the headaches now as she cowered close to the fire which had been built in the sitting room and absently watched the placing of chairs about the table. Her big, well-formed hand moved to her throat and touched the pin Tom Sheldon had given her.

The door of the suite opened, and John Ames stepped over the threshold in his English derby, his fine English broadcloth, and carrying his English umbrella, tightly rolled.

"One of your headaches, Caroline?" asked John, as he stood by the fire and looked down at his daughter. He had bathed and dressed; he smelled of good soap. "I hope not. Did you take the powders Dr. Brinkley gave you in Boston?"

"Yes, Papa," she murmured.

"I hope you aren't going to become one of those languid and elegant young ladies who have fashionable headaches," said John. His hand moved restlessly over the steins on the mantel.

"No, Papa," said Caroline.

"Perhaps you need spectacles."

"Dr. Brinkley said not."

"It can't be rich food, for you don't like it," said John. He spoke absently. The great gas chandelier had not yet been lit; the room was pervaded with an ashen light, dull and cold and melancholy. But beyond the windows the mountains had taken on their vast menace again and loomed nearer.

"I hate these mountains," said Caroline.

"I thought you liked mountains, Caroline. You were always dreaming over them in Italy."

"These are different," said the young woman.

John shrugged. He frowned as he saw Caroline's dark crimson wool with the simple pin at the high puritanical neck. "Haven't you anything—gayer —than that frock?" he asked.

"This is my best, Papa. And it's very stylish."

"Bustles don't become you," said John. "I don't know why you can't have a touch of elegance, Caroline. I dislike dowdiness."

"Mrs. Alex is dowdy," said Caroline, and her headache, which had been only in the background, suddenly sharpened.

"Madame Polevoi," said John. "A comparatively simple name, for a Russian one. I wish you wouldn't call her 'Mrs. Alex.' Is she dowdy? I never noticed. She is charming."

"She looks like a monkey," said Caroline as her head throbbed sickeningly. "Madame Pol—Polev—I just can't pronounce it!—has an apelike face. With all those big white teeth. I often wonder if she retracts them when she isn't smiling."

John laughed and glanced down at his daughter approvingly. "I never knew you had wit," he said. "Or some natural human malice. Good."

Caroline was confused and baffled. She looked up at her father, wondering if he was mocking her. And then she was frightened. She had not noticed before: he was even more ashen than the light. He appeared gaunt and exhausted and very gray, and his blue eyes, always so dominant in his face, had become sunken.

"What is it, Papa?" Caroline exclaimed, and got to her feet. "You're ill!"

"Don't be silly," he said with impatience, and moved backward as Caroline attempted to peer more closely at him. "I had a very heavy luncheon; these Swiss lunches! And I tried to walk it off near the lake. I'd like a little soda if you don't mind. I have a touch of indigestion, and that's all."

He had never confessed to any physical inconvenience before, to Caroline's knowledge. "Indigestion? Yes, I have some soda. I'll mix a little with Vichy water, Papa." She ran into her bathroom, and her hands trembled as she prepared the effervescent drink. She brought it back to John; he had seated himself and she thought he was breathing too rapidly. He appeared not to notice her and the extended glass for a few moments. He seemed absorbed in some intense inner communication, some deeper reality. "Papa," said Caroline. He turned up his eyes to her and she saw the dark shadow in them and his momentary bemusement, as if he were wondering who she was and where he was.

"Oh yes," he said, and his voice sounded as if it came from a distance. "Damn these heavy meals! I don't like them, but you can't insult your hosts." He smiled; Caroline, in that uncertain light, thought that his lips had a bluish edging. He took the glass and drained it. Then he held out his hands to the fire. "I'm glad you thought of this," he said, and rubbed his hands. The sound was dry, like the rustling of paper.

He had never approved of heat before. He bent forward to the fire; his shoulders had an unfamiliar aspect of fragility, of weariness. A servant came in and began to light the chandelier; moment by moment the room brightened yellowly. But Caroline noticed nothing but her father. Was it only today that his temples had become concave, his ear lobes darkly mauve? He looked older, smaller, as if he had suddenly shrunk. Caroline's fingers tightened on the brooch at her neck. "Papa," she said. "You really are ill. Let me call a doctor."

"What are you talking about?" he said. "You're becoming an old woman, Caroline." But he held his hands closer to the fire. All at once he fell back into his chair, and his breathing quickened again. "Damn those lunches!" he repeated. "I never have one without dyspepsia afterward."

"The soda isn't helping, Papa?"

"A little," he said impatiently. "Do stop fussing, Caroline." He had closed his eyes; the lids were wrinkled, like those of a very old man. "I have things to think about, my dear. A matter is coming up tonight; I don't approve of it. You probably won't understand, but I want you to listen carefully. I not only don't approve of it, I think it's insane. . . ." His voice trailed off. Then his breathing quieted and he smiled. "There, the pain's gone. No more lunches, thank heavens."

"Yes, Papa," she said, nearly blinded by her headache and fear now.

"You've seen Brookingham many times. He's one of my best friends and associates. An excellent family, too. He's a very wealthy man and will very shortly have a distinguished title."

Caroline pressed her palm against her forehead. "Perhaps it was that ham at breakfast, Papa," she said. "I do have an awful headache, and a pain in my——" She paused. "We ate the ham; perhaps it made us both sick."

"Perhaps," said John with more impatience. "Do let's stop talking about our physical inconveniences, my dear. I think I mentioned Montague Brookingham to you. Well?"

"The Weasel?" said Caroline without thought.

"What? What did you call him, Caroline?"

The girl blushed. "I'm awfully sorry, Papa. But that's what I call him in my mind. A plump weasel."

John looked at her. Then, to her bafflement, he began to smile faintly. His exhausted eyes brightened with amusement. "So, you call him the Weasel, eh? You have a lot of imagination." He considered, then smiled again. "Definitely a weasel, in more ways than one. But a very intelligent man and, as I said before, wealthy and of a distinguished family."

"I don't care," said Caroline, happy that she had made her father smile.

Then he was no longer smiling. He was staring at her in his usual formidable way. "He isn't hateful to you, is he, Caroline? He admires you, you know."

Caroline considered. Mr. Brookingham was her father's friend. She did not want to antagonize her father, so she said quickly, "I suppose it was nasty of me to call him names. Admires me, Papa? Oh, he doesn't. He thinks I'm very stupid. And ugly."

"On the contrary," said John. "He thinks you are very brilliant and attractive."

She only waited, perplexed.

"He wants to marry you, Caroline," said John abruptly.

Caroline's mouth fell open in utter astonishment and disbelief. "Marry? Me?" she stuttered.

"It's true he's about twenty years older than you are, my dear. But I was quite a bit older than your mother too. You look considerably older than you are, even now. I think," said John, studying his daughter ruthlessly, "that you'd easily pass for thirty-five."

But Caroline, shocked, heard nothing of this. "Why, Papa!" she cried incredulously. "He's a monster! A monster!"

"What are you talking about? 'A monster.'" John was angry. "What do you mean by a 'monster'?"

But Caroline had no words to explain. She was overwhelmed by her horror and incredulity.

John's face became darker, and he looked at his daughter probingly. "He's done nothing more monstrous than I've done," he said. "One lives with the world on its own terms. You've been traveling with me all these years. I'd thought by now that you understood how I made my money, and how you will continue to make money after I'm dead. I'd like to have the security of knowing that you and my money are safe in the hands of Montague."

Now the color left his face and he looked faint. He gripped the arms of his chair.

"You mean," said Caroline, "that you want me to marry him, Papa?"

"I don't mean anything. I am merely defending a friend whom you called a monster. I am only suggesting that you consider him as a husband. Did you intend to remain unmarried all your life?"

"No. Oh no," said Caroline, and thought of Tom, and her eyes filled with tears.

"Well, then. There's no one else but Montague. I think it would be a fine arrangement. I know a dozen women who'd scream with joy at the thought, and titled ladies, too, in England and on the Continent. You aren't young any longer, Caroline."

"Papa," she said feebly, "if you want me to marry him I will."

John was silent. Those damned lunches! The room had tilted to an angle, and it had become dim. He looked with annoyance at the chandelier and was surprised to see that it was burning. There's probably fog in the room, he thought.

Then, as if he had heard an echo, he became aware of what Caroline had said. It was a great effort to speak. He said, "There is no question of my 'wanting' you to do anything against your will. What I 'want' and what you want may be two different things." He stopped. There was a painful choking in his throat, as if he had been grasped by a spiked and iron hand. He shook his head with more irritation than alarm. He coughed a little. "Some years ago you mentioned a girlish infatuation. You haven't spoken of it since then, so I assume that is past. You are a woman now. Ah," he added as a waiter came into the room. "You may bring in the buckets of champagne if you please."

CHAPTER THIRTEEN

It was Alexander Polevoi whom Caroline called the Giggle, for he had a soft and chuckling laugh and was always smiling, and he appeared to find life very amusing indeed. His French wife (the Teeth, in Caroline's category) bounced at his side, all vivacity and charm and magnetism, though she was even shorter and stouter than her husband and her dress was careless and her jewels less than immaculate. Both were in their fifties, and both possessed, quite vividly, an avid interest in all things, particularly money. Both were well-born and came from substantial and even illustrious families. Their eagerness for money puzzled Caroline, for neither, it was evident, had ever been poor or had suffered adversity. Monsieur Polevoi, in fact, had been a cadet in His Majesty the Czar's personal guard, and he had an aunt who was distantly related to the Empress.

"Dear, dear petite," said Madame Polevoi with a flash of her great and famous white teeth. Her head hardly reached Caroline's shoulder, and so she embraced one of the girl's large arms emphatically. Her gay monkey face twinkled. "How charming you are tonight."

Helpless as always when among people, Caroline could only mutter incoherently. She was more dazed than usual; all her thoughts were in confusion, smoldering with terror and disgust and fear. When the Slebers entered she could only move her lips silently. Franz Sleber resembled a bat, with his pallid short face, his naked head, and his big pale ears; and his wife (the Simper) appeared actually beefy in contrast and much more alive, with her wicked dark eyes, her sentimental air and smile, and the generous girth of her lavish figure. She had dyed her hair an improbable black with rusty highlights, and it was drawn back from her square face in a huge tight bun. Yet she had style. If she mentions Mitteleuropa to me tonight I'll scream, I really will, thought Caroline. "Dear Luzy," said John, kissing her hand.

"Are you well, dearest?" asked Luzy Sleber with a languishing look of synthetic concern. "You seem pale."

"The Swiss luncheons," said John Ames. "I see the Ernsts are here."

Caroline loathed the Ernsts a little less than she did the others, for Herr Gottfried Ernst (the Bower) had a gentle way with him, and he was younger than the others, in his middle forties, and he was handsome and dark and slender and had a sweet smile. If he constantly bowed each time a lady addressed him, Caroline thought, it was because he was less sure of himself than were the other men. He was of a noble but very poor Austrian family, and Caroline fancied that his faint lack of complete assurance probably came from early poverty. His English wife (the Glitter) had brought him a fortune which had been derived from an excellent beer. She wore a simple black gown tonight, caught under the small bustle with a pin of diamonds; there was an enormous glittering necklace of rubies, emeralds, and diamonds about her long white throat, matched by earrings at her small ears. Her figure was superb—tall and slender and of lovely proportions—and her delicate white arms had a certain translucence. When she spoke, and always in English, for she knew no other language, there was hardly a trace of the born Cockney in her speech.

Two waiters filled glasses with champagne and served them from a silver tray. These were for Caroline and John Ames. The others preferred dubonnet for a reason inexplicable to the unworldly Caroline, who had not yet learned that champagne was a dessert wine. The ladies chattered in English, in deference to Babette, who had resolutely resisted learning a "foreign" language even though she lived in Vienna and liked it with supreme British tolerance. Caroline managed, as always, to skulk near the fire in order to avoid direct attention. She kept a painful small smile on her face. Her hazel eyes were bright with misery. Let him not come tonight, she prayed, and would not look at the door for dread of its opening. Nevertheless, it opened and Montague Brookingham beamed plumply on his dear friends, who greeted him with pleasure.

The ladies adored him. Caroline shrank closer to the wall, but she looked with hopeless terror at the man she believed her father wished her to marry. She had never been able to endure the touch of his hand; she had never been able to turn away when he spoke for fear of missing that changeful aspect of his which both fascinated and paralyzed her. It was not until this very moment that she realized the enormity of her father's suggestion and understood, at last, that it actually concerned her.

He came toward her, and she spread out her palms on the wall, as if trying to dissolve into it. He had a way of gliding, for all his plumpness; he walked as precisely and as lightly as a dancer. Now he faced Caroline, smiling his captivating smile, and the top of his head reached to her eyebrows.

"How are you, Caroline?" he asked in a charming voice. But Caroline stared at him fixedly, and he could not miss the naked loathing and fear in her eyes. He was startled. His smile disappeared. "I hope you are well," he said tentatively. Damn it, had Johnny Ames spoken to her in his usual abrupt way? The girl needs finesse, not a bludgeoning, he thought. She was really not in the least handsome, he thought. However, there had been times when she had smiled involuntarily and her eyes had shone with astonishingly beautiful golden lights, and the smile itself had had loveliness in it. The Queen, he had thought, would be pleased with this girl, who was respectable, wealthy, well bred and quiet, and impressive in her height and her slow, deliberate movements.

Caroline could not speak, so he bowed to her with a smile and joined the animated group surrounding John Ames. The girl sank down weakly on a chair near the wall and put her hands on her knees. It was impossible. Not even to please her father could she do this terrible thing. Her headache became nauseating. She pushed herself to her feet and groped and sidled along the wall to her room and bathroom. There she drank a glass of water. She rubbed her arms; she felt as cold and stiff as stone. She began to cry a little and wiped away her tears childishly with the backs of her hands.

She would tell her father tonight about Tom Sheldon. Nothing mattered now but Tom. Perhaps her father would permit her to leave for America at once, she thought frantically. She must see Tom; she must feel his arms around her. She had a frightful sensation that she was in danger and that only Tom could give her protection. She looked at her face in the mirror; it was as pale as her father's and as ashen. What have I been waiting for? she asked herself, and did not remember. What kept me silent all these years? She had no other fear tonight but the stark fear of Montague Brookingham and all that he was. I'll go to Tom; only Tom matters, she told her face in the mirror. Warmth moved over her body; her shivering stopped. She dried her face, lifted her head, and returned to the sitting room.

Her seat at the table was between Brookingham and Herr Ernst. The former had decided "to leave the girl alone" so that she might recover from what had frightened her. Herr Ernst, always kind and considerate, spoke to her in German with his soft Austrian accent. He had just returned from Paris where, he said, he had had the privilege of viewing the private collection of paintings owned by a friend. Unlike the others, who frequently thought Caroline ridiculous and wondered how so handsome a father could have so dull and spiritless and unattractive a daughter, Herr Ernst thought Caroline had much character and interest, and he liked to look into her eyes, where he detected no conceit, no cruelty or cunning. She reminded him of his grandmother, whom he had adored in his childhood.

"As a traditionalist," he said, "I am not moved or inspired by the Impressionists. They paint only for themselves. If art has a function beyond its own beauty and power, then its function is to communicate with others and give to others its own emotion. My friend, Fräulein, is also a traditionalist, but he was fortunate enough to acquire three modern paintings of tremendous power and beauty, and I confess that their color and vitality moved me greatly. Here was modern art that cared very much for the viewer. The artist was no exhibitionist, concerned only with his own thoughts and dreams and full of arrogant vanity. Never have I seen such colors! They seemed to leap from the canvas; traditionalists may say that certain colors are inharmonious with others. Nevertheless, this artist combined the inharmonious colors with astounding effect, and all was harmony."

Herr Ernst had learned from Caroline herself her secret interest in art, and he was rewarded now by a sudden eagerness in her face. She nodded.

"One canvas absorbed me," said Herr Ernst. The table conversation had not yet reached anything important, so he could devote himself to this silent girl who unaccountably charmed him and aroused his pity. "It was not a striking subject in itself. It showed only a bleached and barren plain, like a forlorn desert. But in the near distance was a high and pointed hill, and on that hill stood a ruined tower of crumbling stone with shattered battlements. That was all: the unfertile, blanched plain, the flowerless hill, and the tower. But as I looked at it I became despondent. Did the artist intend to say that this strongly painted scene suggested the inevitable fruitlessness and loneliness and defeat of power? I do not know."

He laughed gently. He meditatively sipped a little wine. "There was not much color in that scene, yet it conveyed vehemence and passion, as well as terror. Some guests thought it blank and distasteful and undisciplined. One said, 'Ah, these Americans! They know nothing of art and culture.' You see, the artist was an American who died many years ago. David Ames."

"Ames?" said Caroline.

"Yes. The same name as yours. A relative, perhaps?"

"No," said Caroline. She glanced at her father at the head of the table. He had been listening. "You have no relatives, Papa, who were artists?" she asked timidly.

"No," he said. "I never had a relative who was an artist." He resumed his conversation with Madame Polevoi. Caroline thought: He had been listening. Why? He is never interested in art of any kind.

"Another impressed me greatly," the Austrian entrepreneur continued.

"Yet it was only a scene of a mean little street which can be found in any European or perhaps American industrial city. Little drab shops dimly lighted, with small grim windows, and a wagon here and there. The narrow pavements glistened as if a recent rain had fallen, and the street wound into the distance to where an old dark church stood. Extraordinary! The church steeple bore a cross, and it was painted the color of fire, the very color of anger. And above it all was a tremendous sky of many colors, suggesting doom and retribution. There were figures on the street, but one could not tell the sex. They had been reduced to anonymity, featureless and without color. One's eye could not leave the fiery cross and the furious skies. The artist must have been a man of sensitivity and pain and foreboding."

Caroline could feel it in herself, as if she had seen the canvas personally. Then the lady from Mitteleuropa simpered, and Caroline became aware that all at the table had listened. "How ugly," said Madame Sleber. "I prefer beauty, for itself alone. Why do these self-styled artists paint ugliness, without grace and tranquillity?"

Herr Ernst smiled in a peculiar way. "Perhaps they are honest, madame," he said.

"Honesty probably did not pay, in the artist's case," said John. His weariness marked his face as if painted by gray paint. "Do we have to discuss art any longer? I mean no offense," he added in his meticulous German, "but I believe we have business to discuss."

"Yes," said Monsieur Sleber quietly. "I wish to discuss what has been interesting us so intensely the past few days. Karl Marx is dead. But his influence on European politics is increasing, even in England, where he died a short time ago. We have entered into an era of what he called prehistory. We must advance it.

"Marx's followers and disciples are not persecuted in England, where all his papers and writings are now being gathered together. These will be important, perhaps even more important than *Das Kapital*, which is outlawed in France and Germany and other countries. But persecution, as history has shown repeatedly, does not extinguish a doctrine, a religion, or a theory. From this time on Karl Marx will be the most significant power in the world, perhaps greater"—and Monsieur smiled his amiable smile—"than one Jesus of Nazareth. Forgive me a little musing, but there will come a time, I am certain, when Marx and Jesus will fight the final battle for mankind in the minds of men."

Caroline was listening, her dark brows drawn together. She had heard much of this the last few days, and mostly with indifference. Of what importance, she had asked herself, was a newly dead German philosopher to her and her father?

"You are exaggerating, Franz," said John Ames abruptly.

Sleber spread out his hands deprecatingly and inclined his pale bald head. "I think not, John. You said yesterday that there will be no more revolutions in the world and that all has reached a static place where the fight among nations will be only for profits and not for mere territory and subjects. But you will remember that it was because of Marx's ideas and teachings that the French revolution of 1848 broke out."

He put his hands, dainty as a woman's, on the tablecloth and sent his slow glance about the table.

John Ames stared down at his plate. He looked alarmingly ill.

Franz Sleber continued. "The bourgeoisie is not the enemy of Marx's proletariat. It is our enemy. Cicero's 'new men' are rising again all over the world, which was once comfortably divided between the aristocratic wealthy and the laborers and the serfs, as it should be."

"It is a confused picture," said Herr Ernst doubtfully.

Franz Sleber smiled. "All that concerns man is inevitably confused, for man is intricate. But one thing can be said simply: Greed and envy and the desire for power motivate all men to a larger or lesser degree. And, as the power of the State was challenged by the new middle class in France, so now this class is challenging—us. It is challenging our wars for profits, our absolute liberties, our power. The middle class suspects power of all kind."

"And so," said Montague Brookingham, "the middle class must be destroyed before it grows too strong. You have seen them in England, with their ugly brown town houses and their fat vulgarity and their bee-like industry. And their uncompromising support of religion and what they call their virtues."

Herr Ernst said in his gentle and hesitating voice: "I understand the middle-class threat to us. It was the American bourgeoisie who challenged the aristocratic wealth of England. It was not the little accounts keeper or the worker in the mill or the man who tended sheep and cattle in America who made America free. It was the owner of shops, the owner of mills, the comfortable farmer, the proprietor of newspapers and businesses, who challenged England in the name of liberty, which the masses neither understand nor want."

John Ames was silent. His face was still shadowed by his hand. Caroline watched him anxiously. But she was also thinking, and a powerful repudiation of what she had heard was resolutely becoming stronger in her mind. She would never have anything to do with these suave and amiable and ruthless people who wanted money, not merely to protect themselves, as she and her father did, but as a thing in itself, as a personal power!

"You'll be taking a tiger by the ears," said John. "Again, as for myself, no."

He looked suddenly at his daughter. "Well, Caroline," he said, "what do you think of all this?"

Caroline shrank when everyone looked at her. She faltered, "I think you are right, Papa. I've been reading about revolutionaries since the last discussion we—you—had here. I think they're wicked men. I think they're insane too. If they ever have control of governments they'll make slaves of everybody, without exception. They did that in France in 1795."

They all smiled, including John. "Gentlemen and ladies," he said, "you have heard the voice of innocence, and there are times when I think innocence is very perceptive."

When Caroline was alone with her father she said impulsively, "Papa, let us leave Switzerland at once."

They were sitting by the expiring fire, and the ice-laden air from the mountains seeped into the room. Caroline had wrapped a blanket around her father's knees as he sat on the hearth. He was a man who went to bed early. Tonight he sat in silence long after the clocks of Geneva rang midnight over the city. He had not even noticed when Caroline had covered him.

"They don't understand," he said, as if speaking to himself. "There's something horrible loose in the world now, and they're only too eager to help feed it. Well, I'll probably not be here to see it."

Caroline was frightened again. "Papa! You'll live a long time."

"They're in such a hurry," he said, as if she hadn't spoken. "They won't succeed soon. It will be a long time, if ever. I don't want to see it."

"They're only a few people," said Caroline, attempting to soothe him.

"Immense wealth is not 'only a few people,'" said John with irritation. "They'll have their 'holy wars,' which will be wars for profit, as usual. They will feel satisfied."

He turned his haggard face to his daughter, and his eyes were looking at far places. "Think of it—madness in control of the world. Who will challenge madness?"

Caroline did not answer. The room was becoming very cold. John rubbed his lips with his hand. "If my mother were alive she would have the answer, which is no answer at all. She would say that God will challenge madness."

Caroline wanted to tell her father about Tom Sheldon, but he stood up then, feebly, the blanket falling from his knees. He stared down at the huddle of cloth at his feet as if it were a profound puzzle and he was wondering what it was. Then he raised his eyes to Caroline.

"What is it, Papa?" Caroline exclaimed.

He put his hand on the mantelpiece. "That food," he muttered. "I think I'll go to bed. It's late."

He walked toward his bedroom slowly and carefully, like a drunken man, and Caroline helplessly watched him go. When he reached the door she called out to him, "Papa. Good night, Papa."

He turned and looked at her bemusedly. With an effort he finally said, "Good night, my dear. Good night." He entered his room and closed the door heavily after him.

Caroline stood and looked at his door for several moments, full of lassitude and sick anxiety. She did not want to go to bed. She pushed aside the draperies at the windows and looked out at the shadow of mountains under a polar moon and the flat, faintly luminous plain of the lake. The bridge to her right flickered with yellow lights, which reflected themselves like amber blurs in the water. The city rang with the iron tongues of bells proclaiming the hour of one in the morning. If only we could leave now! thought Caroline under the pressure of some vague but insistent premonition. The palms of her hands began to sweat under her growing fear. The cold air struck her face like a wall of ice. She thought of Lyme, and a powerful yearning for Tom Sheldon made her throat and chest ache. She would write him tomorrow and tell him that she would be in Lyme in July! She would tell him that she loved him. For a moment she cringed at the thought of expressing her emotions on paper. No, she would not tell him that she loved him and that she would marry him. She would merely write an impersonal letter, and she would send him the little painting of the Bay of Naples. He would understand. "Dear Tom," she said aloud, and was startled at the sound of her own voice in the silence. After a little she smiled joyously.

Homesick, warm with longing for Beth and Tom Sheldon, she went to bed, noting as usual that the tepid bed warmers had hardly softened the stiff cold white sheets. Remembering Beth, she brought herself to pray awkwardly and to repeat the Lord's Prayer. When she arrived at "And deliver us from evil," her thoughts quickened. She shivered under the blankets and the eider down and thought of her father's guests. But there were others! Yes, there were others like Beth and Tom and old black Jim who had been a slave. There had been a kind and weary teacher or two at Miss Stockington's. If she knew such people, then there must be many in the world, after all. She opened her eyes, startled, in the darkness and thought of this deeply, and a free and joyous sense of release came to her and washed away her chronic fear.

She fell asleep, feeling deliverance, not only from the evil which was her father's associates and friends, but from the iron prison of herself and her terrors. It was some time before she began to dream. She was on the blanched and broken plain of the painting that had been described to her, and she could smell its barrenness, which was the very odor of sorrow and loneliness. There was no end to the plain; it heaved and rose and fell to every horizon under a sky like stone. And there was the tower on the treeless pointed hill, black and gray and crumbling, with the ruined battlements and the empty door. It plunged high into the air, throwing a black shadow before it. Caroline, in her dream, was afraid. She looked about the plain, on which nothing moved, but she felt menace behind every boulder, every dip and fall. She ran to the tower, stumbling, falling, her legs as heavy as the trunks of trees. There was shelter in the tower; she would hide in its broken recesses and no one could find and hurt her. She had almost reached the door when she saw the tall figure of Tom Sheldon standing before it, his arms outstretched to bar her way. "No!" he cried. "No, Carrie!"

"I must! I'm afraid!" she cried back to him. But he left the door, smiling, and took her hand and pointed, and she glanced fearfully over her shoulder. The plain was full of warm trees and light and flowers, and it was not barren at all.

But from within the tower came a terrible groaning as of a man in agony. "Who?" asked Caroline, clinging to Tom. "No one can hurt you now," he said, and tried to draw her away. But the groaning became louder, more helpless, more beseeching. "It's my father!" she screamed. Tom instantly drew her hand, but she held back. "Don't go in there, Carrie," he pleaded.

She was more frightened than ever before in her life. She snatched her hand from Tom and ran to the door. The groaning was all about her. She awoke, gasping, and sat up. She had not dreamed the groaning at all. It came from her father's room.

She jumped from the bed, and immediately the bitterly cold air pierced through her cheap flannel nightgown. She struck a match and lit the gas lamps on the wall, calling out desperately, "Yes, Papa, I'm coming!" She snatched up her worn old brown dressing gown with the patches on the elbows and flung it over her shoulders and ran into her father's room. The yellowish glare from her own lights fell on his bed. He lay on his pillows, and his face was livid, his eyes closed, and he was groaning deeply. She went to him, trembling, then lighted the wall light. John Ames was unconscious; streams of sweat ran from his forehead like tears; he was gasping for breath. And then Caroline, who had never seen death, knew that he was dying.

She had faced a few crises in her life, but not one as awful as this, so what she did next was born of panic, inexperience, and inability to think. She had only to pull a bell rope for help. This did not occur to her in her blind frenzy. She ran back into her room and pulled a pair of boots over her bare feet, and her gasping was as loud as her father's. "Yes, yes, yes!" she cried. "Just wait, Papa." She flung open the sitting-room door and rushed out into the wide carpeted hall, in which only a single light burned. She fled down the wide marble stairs. The clocks of Geneva struck three. Caroline reached the dim lobby, where a clerk slept behind the counter. She did not see him or think of him. She had remembered seeing a doctor's home down the street from the hotel; she would bring him to her father. She dodged around the brown marble columns of the lobby, her boots clattering on the white marble floors. The bronze doors were bolted; her wet hands tore at the bolts with a savagery and strength born of her despair and urgency. She pulled the doors apart and rushed into the silent dark street full of moonlight and shadows.

She found the doctor's house in a minute or two and leaped up the brown stone steps and pulled wildly on the rope again and again, frantic with her need. The windows in the tall gray house remained black for endless moments, then finally an upper one flickered. She continued to pull on the rope, and the house echoed with the clangor. The door opened and the sleepy bearded doctor in his dressing gown stood on the threshold, shaking his head.

"Come! Quick!" she clamored in French, and then as he began to stare at her she repeated her agonized plea in German. The doctor continued to stare. He saw a tall and frenzied girl on the steps, with dark and disheveled braids on her shoulders, an obviously poor girl in miserable night clothes. Her aspect was so strange and her cries so piercing, he moved back a step. She caught his arm and repeated her pleas in both languages.

"But where?" he asked, noting more closely the poverty and coarseness of her clothing and the wildness of her eyes. "Who are you? What do you want?"

"My father!" she moaned. "In the Grande Hotel, there!" And she pointed with one hand as she continued to clutch the doctor with the other. The doctor's arm stiffened. Geneva was a lawful city, well policed, orderly. But still, there were criminals here also, and the ugly poor. He looked down the street at the Grande Hotel with its dim lower lights. Was this wretched girl a servant there? But, if so, why had she not summoned help in the hotel, who would then have sent for him or the house physician? He looked again at the lumbering unbuttoned boots, at the blowing flannel nightgown, at the patched robe. This was no guest of the hotel! He struck down her hand, moved back, and tried to close the door. She, this animal, was either a drunken prostitute or mad.

"Go away!" he shouted. "I'll summon the police!"

Caroline flung herself against the door and held it open with the strength of extremity. The hall light shone on the doctor's face. He had the eyes of old Mr. Fern in Boston, and for a moment she was sick. But her necessity overcame her fear. She began to cry out incoherently: "Please, please! My father! Mr. John Ames. We're Americans. Guests in the Grande Hotel. My father is dying! Come, come, in the Name of God!"

Her French was excellent, and this alone made the doctor pause. He glared at her. "There is a physician in the hotel," he said. "Call him if you speak the truth."

She clung to him. "Come, come!" she prayed, not hearing his words. "My father!"

"Can you pay?" he demanded accusingly. The girl would break his arm, curse her. "My fee. Can you pay—you?"

For a single moment Caroline was dumb at this universal and terrible question. She blinked her starting eyes. Then she panted, "Yes, yes! We're rich Americans. Americans! Come, for God's sake!" A ball of nausea rose in her throat, but she still held the doctor's arm with a powerful grip.

"You can pay in Swiss francs?" he demanded. Rich Americans. *Nom de Dieu!* What rascality was this?

"Yes! Please!" Caroline began to sob dryly.

The doctor cursed under his breath, but he reached for his ready bag on the table. He went with Caroline down the steps, then became angrily aware of his night clothing. He pulled his arm from hers. "Wait, I must dress," he said roughly. "Give me your name again. I will come in a few minutes."

"It will be too late!" Caroline almost shrieked. "My father is dying!" She understood, even in her red panic, that if she left him now he would not come at all. He wanted to be rid of her, this man with old Fern's eyes and Fern's accusing voice.

"Mad, mad," he muttered to himself, but went with her. She dragged on his arm, trying to hurry him. He glanced fearfully into shadows, expecting a crouching form to leap out and strangle him. He thought of his unprotected home and his wife and children. The street echoed with the girl's footsteps; his own feet wore only slippers, and he felt the cold air on his ankles and cursed her. Now the hotel seemed a place of refuge to him, and he hurried also.

The clerk had been awakened by Caroline's opening of the doors and the sound of her running. The owner, Herr Schloesser, had been summoned, and he was gravely regarding the unbolted doors when Caroline and the doctor burst through them. He stared and started. "Fräulein Ames!" he exclaimed. "What is wrong? Fräulein!" He recognized the doctor, who was an old friend. "*Herr Doktor*," he said. "What is this?"

The doctor flung off Caroline's hand, and she immediately seized him again. "You know this—this—creature, Adolf?" he said.

"But certainly! She is Fräulein Ames, one of our cherished and frequent guests," said Herr Schloesser helplessly. "Fräulein, what is it?"

The doctor relaxed. He turned benevolently to Caroline. "My dear child," he said, "let us be calm." He patted the stiff fingers on his sleeve and turned with an air of worried importance to his friend.

"The lady says that her father is dying," he said. "Will you lead me, Adolf, and obtain some assistance for this poor, frantic lady?"

"Herr Ames? He is ill?" The hotelkeeper was alarmed. "Why did she not summon help here?"

"That I do not know. She apparently lost her wits," said the doctor with more and more benevolence toward Caroline. "Dear lady," he said, "calm yourself. I will go to your father at once."

"The elevator," said Herr Schloesser. "Good God, this is frightful. I will take you up myself."

Caroline was sobbing weakly now. She had released the doctor; she wrung her hands over and over as the ponderous elevator drew them up past sleeping floors. Once or twice she coughed chokingly; the doctor's arm was now on her shoulders with solicitude. (But whoever would have thought!)

"I have summoned my wife," said the owner as he opened the lacy iron door of the elevator. He glanced with concern at the girl. "Poor Fräulein," he murmured. He forgot the bad treatment in the matter of tips for his employees. This young lady was on the verge of collapse. His sentimental Teutonic heart made tears come to his eyes. But how strange this was! Why had she not called for help here in the hotel?

Caroline ran to the open door of her suite, and the two men hurried after her, the gaunt bearded doctor and the tall fat Herr Schloesser. She ran into her father's room. It sounded with his groans, which were fainter now. Herr Schloesser lit more lights. Caroline fell on her knees beside her father's bed, then merely rested there, her eyes on John's face, her white lips twisting in incoherent prayer. She did not feel the presence of Frau Schloesser, who knelt beside her, rosary in her fat fingers. She did not hear the woman's mumbled prayers. The doctor examined his unconscious patient carefully. He began to frown as he listened to his heart. He was very important and in command of the situation now and very tender toward both father and daughter.

He said, "We shall need nurses. This is very bad. The gentleman has had a serious heart attack. He must not be moved for an instant." He reached into his bag for a hypodermic needle and fussily asked for water. Herr Schloesser brought it in a clean glass, and the doctor dropped three little gray pellets in it. When they were dissolved he injected the liquid into the thin limp arm of his patient. "That will relieve his pain," he said, and studied the livid face, the blue lips, the sweat, the heaving chest.

Herr Schloesser murmured, "He is—he is——?"

"Possibly," said the doctor in rich tones of commiseration. "But one cannot tell. I have seen worse recover. It is a matter of extreme quiet. Please wake a servant and send to the hospital for nurses, in my name."

He sat down beside the bed. There was nothing to do but wait. He looked at Caroline and shook his head sympathetically and motioned to Frau Schloesser with his hand. Obediently she pulled Caroline to her feet, saying, "Dear little one, it is in the hands of God. Sit down here in this chair at the foot of the bed. Adolf, send for some brandy."

The hall outside was now quietly humming with servants, who brought in hot pans to be put at the sick man's feet and against his icy hands, and heavier blankets. Caroline was now in a state of mute stupefaction. She crouched on the chair, and her eyes fixed themselves on her father's face. She continued the dolorous wringing of her hands. She had no thoughts. She was only stunned. When the glass of brandy was put to her lips she was not aware of it; she only swallowed, then coughed briefly. Cold was all about her, cold in the room, cold immobilizing her body, cold in her heart, and the bitterest cold in her soul.

Don't die, Papa, she whispered in herself. Don't leave me, Papa. I'll do anything, if you won't leave me. I'll marry anyone you want. Don't leave me. I am all alone. There is no one else in the world, only you, Papa.

The lights in the room were, to her, only a yellow mist in which floated her father's unconscious face. It looked like a face of gray granite on the white pillow. But he was breathing easier. The sweat had dried. He appeared to be sleeping. The doctor examined him again and nodded with a slight satisfaction. "I believe the heart is rallying," he said. How large a fee should he charge these rich Americans? They had money to throw away in handfuls, these millionaires. He glanced furtively at Caroline. But why should a rich young lady dress in such ragged clothing? He shook his head. Everyone knew that Americans were quite mad and had peculiar ways.

He cleared his throat as he felt his patient's pulse. Caroline started, as if something had crashed against her ears. She looked at the doctor, who was bending over her father, this doctor with Fern's eyes, this man who had asked that crushing question, who had believed she was very poor and so would not come to a dying man without assurance of his fee. He would have let Papa die if they could not have paid, if Herr Schloesser had not come to her rescue. She had had to drag him through the street; she had had to plead with him as a dog would plead. Because he had thought she had no money. No money, no money, no money, clanged the iron tongue in her mind. If we had no money Papa would have been left to die. No money, no money. "Oh, God," she muttered aloud.

Frau Schloesser was now holding a cup of hot fresh chocolate to her lips. But the sight of it nauseated her, and she gulped and shook her head. She put her hand to her mouth to control the retching. Then she felt the doctor's solicitous fingers on her own wrist. His eyes were still Fern's eyes, but they were also beaming as Fern's eyes had beamed when Caroline had shown him her aunt's ring. She snatched her wrist from him.

The bells of Geneva proclaimed the hour of four. A ghostly glimmer quickened in the east, and the black mountains stood against it. The lake murmured restlessly. Two tall nuns in the white of nursing Sisters came into the room, accompanied by a priest. All rose but Caroline, who looked only at her father.

She felt a gentle touch on her shoulder. A Sister was bending over her. She asked, "Mademoiselle, has your father been baptized? He is a Christian?"

"What? What?" she muttered. The Sister was patient. She said slowly, "Your father—he has been baptized, he is a Christian?" She spoke in French, and then as Caroline looked at her uncomprehendingly she repeated the question again, in German. Caroline stared, her broad face a deathly color. "Christian," she repeated. "No. No, I don't think so."

She put her frozen hands to her face. The words meant nothing to her at all. They were foolish. Her father was very ill, and this woman asked questions. "No," she said again, for she had been educated to be polite even in the face of irrelevance. "I remember. He told me he hadn't been baptized, and my aunt said he wouldn't let me be baptized." Then she became conscious of the white linen of the Sister and understood she was a nurse.

"Will my father live?" she asked piteously, and caught the snowy robe.

The Sister said gently, "It is in the hands of God. But the Father is here to baptize your father, to administer Extreme Unction, in behalf of his immortal soul, should he die. Are you willing, mademoiselle, that this take place?"

"Die!" cried Caroline wildly, and clutched the robe tighter.

"There are things worse than death," said the Sister with compassion.

"No," said Caroline, and then was silent. After a moment she murmured, "It is much worse to be poor." She paused, then said lifelessly, "Baptize him if you wish."

The priest sighed. Frau Schloesser had removed articles from the bedside table and had spread it with a clean white cloth and had brought water. One of the Sisters lit a candle in a ruby glass. Caroline watched, hardly seeing. The priest was putting on a strange strip of cloth, embroidered, over his thin old shoulders. He had opened a book. All fell on their knees, and the priest intoned in Latin. There was a little dish with oil in it and two or three little balls of white cotton. What is it? whispered Caroline in herself. A Sister was raising John's head, a thick white napkin covering her hand and part of her arm. The priest lifted the water, murmuring, and let the water flow over John's unconscious forehead. "In the name of the Father, and of the Son, and of the Holy Ghost," said the priest. He anointed the unconscious man with oil. The others, kneeling, lifted their voices in prayer, including the doctor. Caroline watched and listened dumbly. She leaned back in her chair and closed her eyes, and all sound and sight receded from her.

When she opened her eyes—and it seemed to her that a long time had passed—the priest had gone and the two Sisters were sitting beside her father. The doctor was leaving. Caroline could not move. A window had been opened; the sharp mountain air invaded the room. Somewhere swallows chattered, and a frail gray light came through the windows.

Then John Ames said, "Caroline?"

Caroline started to her feet, but she was so cold, so shattered, that she stumbled and fell against the bed. There was no one in the room now but her father and herself and the Sisters. She dropped on her knees beside John Ames. His eyes were open and sunken far back in his head, and there was an awful searching in them. "Papa," said Caroline. "Oh, Papa." A Sister compassionately put her hand on the girl's shoulder.

"Caroline," he repeated, and his voice was dry and whistling. "Listen to me." The searching brightened in his eyes.

"Yes, Papa."

"Go home," said the dying man. "Forget—— Caroline. Go home. Don't remember—— I was wrong." He paused and struggled for breath. He shut his eyes.

"Papa," pleaded Caroline. "Papa, I'll marry Mr. Brookingham for you."

Again his eyes opened and became intense. "No," he said. "No, no. Go home. Forget. I was wrong. Remember, I was wrong."

"Yes, Papa," said Caroline, not understanding.

Once more he seemed to sleep. Caroline took his hand; it was as cold as stone. She pressed it to her cheek. Then he said in a loving voice, "My darling, my little daughter, my Melinda. Melinda. My daughter." He smiled. "My pretty child."

Caroline stiffened. Her mouth opened soundlessly.

Then John Ames spoke for the last time in his life, and all his passion and longing were in his final cry. "Cynthia! Cynthia!"

And then he died.

PART TWO

Love is to the moral nature
what the sun is to the earth.

BALZAC

CHAPTER ONE

The small hotel on Beacon Street in Brookline was not old, but it had been designed deliberately to look old from the very moment it had been completed. Otherwise it would not have appeared respectable and so would have been avoided by those for whom it was intended: the elderly dowagers, the decrepit widowers, the spinsters and the aged bachelors of good family who were possessed of something which was now much more important in Boston—money. This is not to say that wealthy nobodies of no "connections" would have been tolerated in the Beverley, but neither would ancients of excellent name but uncertain income have been welcome.

So the Beverley gave solid and discreet service to those who were childless or without immediate relatives or who had found that an impertinent government had cut off, through immigration laws, a constant flow of cheap servants willing to live in a cold attic room for a few dollars a month and work at least fifteen hours a day in the kitchens and parlors and dining rooms of huge mansions and be always at call no matter the hour.

Cynthia Winslow thought the Beverley equally as bad as the other small resident hotels now springing up in secluded Brookline and even in Boston itself. Why they had to be so ugly, if comfortable, she thought, was beyond her. Almost invariably they were constructed, as was the Beverley, of soft-looking muddy-brown stone, with tall, thin arched windows, gloomy little lobbies full of rubber plants and desiccated palm trees in tubs, dark corridors, and dining rooms calculated to chill the blood even in the summer. They all smelled of wood and wool and old bodies and peppermint and polish and varnish and lemony cologne and Pears soap and, in the vicinity of the gloomy dining rooms, of lamb stew and tea. Noting the dark crimson velvet draperies and lace curtains and the dull brown-patterned rugs in the lobby, she had no doubt that this depressing décor existed in the bedrooms and private little sitting rooms also.

Normally she would be at Newport now, looking at the blue sea of July. But Caroline Ames had written her a stiff little note that she wished to see her aunt at four, precisely, in her sitting room, for tea "and certain matters which need discussing." Cynthia, thin and tall and very white and strained in her black silk mourning, sighed as she was assisted from her handsome victoria by the doorman, a comparatively young man of thirty-five whose brown livery and general demeanor tried to hint that he was at least fifty-five. He glanced respectfully and with approval at the bright hair under the small frilled black bonnet and noted the white chin above the black satin ribbons. "Mrs. Winslow," he murmured, and led her preciously

162

to the glass-and-wood double doors, making her feel at once like some tottering dowager of eighty. Good God, thought Cynthia as she always did when visiting the Beverley and similar hotels, why do people consider that only *age* is respectable, and the smells of age? You would never think, her thoughts would run, that America is a young country when you encounter Boston and the Beverley hotels. Cynthia was not only weary and sad, but heavily depressed. She had almost decided to move to New York, which was electric and passionate and gay and utterly disreputable and lively and young. My heart is only partly dead, she would tell herself; if I remain here, I will utterly die. I will eventually retire to a Beverley.

But Melinda belonged in Boston—grave, sweet, and gentle Melinda.

As she was conveyed up two floors in the elevator, which groaned heavily, as was proper, and whose ropes squeaked distressingly, Cynthia became more downhearted and her grief sharper. She had experienced grief many times in her life; one should become accustomed to it eventually, she thought. But sorrow was always fresh, always new, and always wore a new and unfamiliar face. If only John had listened to her three years ago and had consulted a physician; if only he had not driven himself so hard; if only he had refreshed himself with constant little joys and pleasures in a life like a desert; if only he had not been obsessed beyond the mere need of money; if only he had learned to laugh and to be flexible in a measure. If only . . . It was always the lament of the grieved. Even Melinda and I could not keep our darling alive, thought Cynthia, forgetting to be irritated because the liveried old man, old enough to be her father, carefully assisted her from the elevator.

She even smiled drearily at him when he insisted on accompanying her down the narrow dark hall with its smells of old bombazine, asthma remedies, arnica lotions, and gas jets to the gleaming walnut door of Caroline's suite. He knocked on the door importantly; Cynthia's thin black silk rustled and exhaled a fresh odor of lilies of the valley. Beth opened the door, and a hot gush of sunlight poured into the hall, and the old man bowed and retreated. "Beth," said Cynthia, unaware of the gratitude in her voice. She did not want to see her niece alone. "Mrs. Winslow," said Beth in a muted voice. "Please come in." She sighed, and Cynthia, passing her, touched her arm comfortingly, though why Beth needed comforting she did not know.

The suite, as Cynthia feared, carried on the brown and dark crimson and navy blue of the lobby below. But it had a still and sterile smell and was hot. In the very center of the sitting room sat Caroline in very heavy black clothing with a silver and pearl pin at her throat. Cynthia saw her silent profile, forbidding and impassive, and her straight tall back and her coronet of coiled braids and her large folded hands. The older woman's heart was filled with pity; she had not seen her niece since the funeral of John Ames some weeks ago, nor had she heard from her.

"Caroline," said Cynthia impulsively. She was not a woman of easy tears, but now her beautiful gray eyes filled with them. She went to her niece and put her gloved hand on the young woman's shoulder. But Caroline did not move. She merely said in her strong voice, "Please sit down, Aunt Cynthia," and indicated a stiff chair opposite her. "And, Beth, please leave us alone." Beth sighed again, retreated to a bedroom, and shut the door. Cynthia sat down opposite her niece and looked at her earnestly. Then she was shocked. This girl was still stunned with grief; her features appeared wooden, her hazel eyes without life.

"This won't take long. I won't detain you," said Caroline. The folded hands tightened. "I've been in Lyndon and in New York. I've been consulting with Papa's lawyers."

"Of course," murmured Cynthia helplessly. "Did you see Timothy too?"

"Yes," said Caroline. She looked down at her hands. Cynthia said, "Caroline, why don't you come and stay with me and Melinda for a while? Let us go to Newport together."

For the first time Caroline looked at her, and the hatred and revulsion on her face shocked Cynthia. Cynthia could not help crying out, "Caroline! What have I done to you to make you look at me like that—you, my sister's child!"

But Caroline could not accuse her of her sins, for that would be involving her dead father. She could not speak of Melinda, for that would disgrace John Ames, who had been the victim of this shameless woman, this extravagant and foolish strumpet, this trollop, this middle-aged woman who had the audacity to flood perfume upon herself even now and curl and color her hair and wear fashionable mourning clothes!

"I have work to do," said Caroline. "I can go nowhere. I'm not an idle woman."

"Yes," said Cynthia, and wondered why she spoke at all. Only pity held her here; she must make another effort to help that grief, that crushed immobility. John would want her to do that, and this was Ann's daughter. There was no trace of the mother in Caroline, nor a single trace of John Ames; Cynthia had never considered Caroline really ugly. But now she was ugly in her sorrow and hatred and seemed years older. Her dark skin was thicker and heavier, her chin more massive, her large head actually giving the illusion that it was sitting squarely on her shoulders without the benefit of any neck at all. This gave her a fold under the chin, though she was not stout. Rather, she had lost much weight; the hideous thick black mourning of some undetermined cloth hung on her body.

Caroline looked at the tall and narrow windows swathed in lace curtains and crimson draperies. She spoke without emotion, "My father left—left your adopted daughter—nearly one million dollars. Well invested, secure, sound."

"Do we have to talk about this?" cried Cynthia. "Caroline, you're my niece. I want to help you. We both loved your father," she continued recklessly. "I'm grieved, too, though possibly not as much as you are, for he was all you had. You've avoided me; you haven't answered my letters. You're flesh of my flesh and blood of my blood. Let us console each other and not talk about money just now, please!"

"You knew about my father's will?" said Caroline inexorably, as if Cynthia had not spoken. "Before he died?"

"Yes," said Cynthia, sagging in defeat.

Caroline looked at her again, directly, seeing her aunt's beauty and style, her slenderness and her jewels.

"You think that will was fair?" asked Caroline.

"Fair?" repeated Cynthia faintly. Then she colored and became vaguely indignant. "My dear. Your father left you all he had, many, many millions of dollars. If he wished to spare a little for Melinda, that was his privilege. Did you want it all?" she exclaimed, flushing even deeper. "I never thought you were greedy, Caroline! Why, you couldn't even begin to spend a tenth of the income from the money and property he left you!"

"I don't intend to spend even a tenth," said Caroline, still speaking without emotion. "I intend to use the income to increase Papa's fortune, as he would want me to do. I see there is no use in speaking of fairness to you— about your adopted daughter." She paused. "I did think, though, that you'd be willing to refuse that money. You have no right to it."

"It is not mine. It's Melinda's," said Cynthia, and there was a sharp constriction in her throat. "I have no legal right, or any other right, to refuse money left to my daughter."

She was filled with cold alarm. Did Caroline know that Melinda was her sister? But how could she know? "Do you hate Melinda?" asked Cynthia angrily. "And if so, why?"

Caroline was silent. The fold of flesh under her chin became a dark pink. Then she said dully, "Yes, I hate her. I never did like her, and I never knew why. I wasn't jealous of her; why should I be? But——" She paused, lifted her hand, and dropped it.

"Hatred is a wicked thing," said Cynthia, and now her lovely voice was hard. "It is even worse than greed. Are you greedy, Caroline?"

Caroline's mouth tightened in a bitter half smile. "Aren't you?" she said. "I see you won't give up that money left to—to your adopted daughter. I've talked with the lawyers in an effort to break that will. They tell me I can't. I could put you through years of litigation, they tell me, but you would probably win in the end. My father, they said, had the right to leave his money as he wished. I only thought you would see that justice was on my side. I was foolish, wasn't I?"

The small and burdened room became intolerable to Cynthia. But she controlled herself. "It was very kind of your father," she said, measuring out her words carefully. "We are all grateful. Don't look at me so terribly; you aren't intimidating me. Melinda will keep her money. Is there anything else?"

"Yes," said Caroline. Cynthia could not know that the girl wanted to burst into wild and desperate tears. "There is the matter of the twenty-five thousand dollars a year left you in trust, for life, by my father. I'm sure that now he's dead you'll be willing to give it up."

"No," said Cynthia quietly. "Why should I? It is all I have. Would you wish me to starve, Caroline?"

"You'd receive an income from Melinda's trust," said Caroline. "It wouldn't be that much money, but it would be enough, until Melinda is twenty-one, when she will be able to manage Papa's money herself. And surely she wouldn't let you starve!"

Cynthia was really angry now. "I have no intention of giving up my twenty-five thousand dollars a year for life, Caroline. The trust was established many years ago, when you were about ten years old. It is not part of your father's estate at all. It was money set aside, as you know. Upon my death the trust will revert to his estate. Can't you wait that long, Caroline? Do you want everybody to die so you will have everything?"

She stood up, rustling and sweet with perfume. "Have you no respect for your father's wishes? For the provisions he made from his own money? I thought you loved him."

Caroline's large breast moved and trembled. She could not speak. She could not say, "You exploited my father, for yourself and your daughter, and I only want to right a wrong. You cheated and robbed him for your own wicked purposes, for you are without shame and decency." To speak so might invite fresh revelations, and to have them spoken would defame her father and disgrace his memory.

Helplessness and suffering thickened her tongue and kept her silent. Cynthia drew on her gloves. She was very pale. Then Caroline could speak, and only in a low voice:

"I see it's all hopeless. But I can ask one thing, and I wish you would grant it. I go often to Papa's grave. And I see you leave flowers on it all the time. I wish you wouldn't."

"Why not?" asked Cynthia. "I was very—fond of your father. And so was Melinda. Why do you want to deprive us of a little consolation?"

Caroline lifted her hand, then let it fall. How could she explain that she thought her aunt's and Melinda's visits and flowers desecrated that grave?

"I'm sure that your father doesn't mind," said Cynthia sadly, picking up her purse. She looked at the big and inarticulate girl, and she was full of pity again. "Caroline, you've led a very unnatural life, and you're still young, only going on twenty-four. You were deprived all your young years, and I quarreled with your father about it. Now you are rich. In a way, you're free. Take up your life, Caroline, if you can. And, if you will, I can help you."

"To be like you?" asked Caroline with loathing. Cynthia was horrified. She felt naked and unclean. She wanted to strike Caroline, and never had she wanted to strike anyone before, not even Timothy.

"What a dull and stupid fool you are, Caroline," she said in a shaking voice, her hands clutching her black silk purse. "What do you know of living? Of love and enjoyment, of happiness and laughter? Of being young and gay? Of liking people and music? You've lived like—like a—beast, Caroline. A miserable big beast in a zoo, fed and sheltered adequately, but that is all. You know nothing of the world and mankind. Oh, my God!" she cried. "It isn't your fault, I know! It was your father's fault, and I can never forgive him for that, never! I only wanted to help you."

She began to cry. Then she ran to the door and went away.

Hearing the departure and the slam of the door, Beth came into the room. Caroline was sitting soundlessly, her hands over her face. Beth had not been ashamed to eavesdrop on the conversation. She stood and looked at Caroline, and she was disgusted with her, and outraged. But she loved the girl. She said, "Carrie, Carrie, my child?"

"Don't, Beth," said Caroline, and she stood up and went into her own room.

Beth wrote to Tom Sheldon: "We'll be in Lyme for a week or two beginning next Tuesday, dear Tom. Please help me with Carrie. Sometimes she seems to be going out of her mind with grief. She hardly speaks at all. She just wanders around the house in Lyndon, and then she goes to New York to see her lawyers, alone. She won't even let me go with her. She looks like she's dying, Tom. And she will die, I'm sure, if someone doesn't help her. Her aunt tried, and she drove her away. I try, and she won't answer me. She does love you, Tom. She wears your brooch all the time. It's the only jewelry she does wear; she never touches the jewelry her mother left her and which is now out of the bank. Never mind if she acts like she doesn't want to see you or talk to you. Just be there, Tom dear. She needs you."

Tom had written many times to Caroline since her father's death, but she had not answered. He had even gone to Lyndon, to find that she was in New York. He left urgent messages for her, which she had ignored. Now he read Beth's letter and shook his head. He would try once more, and if he failed, then it would be the end. He would have to try to forget her. Perhaps he wouldn't. But he had a life to live too. He held Beth's letter in his hand and reread that portion of it referring to the brooch he had bought for Caroline. Then all at once he was desperate, and he saw himself as a ridiculous figure, a buffoon, an ignoramus. What had he, Tom Sheldon, who had never had a formal education and who was now twenty-six years old and only a builder of good little houses in obscure places, to offer a woman whom the newspapers were still referring to as "one of the richest girls in the world"? He had always thought of her only as Carrie Ames, a sad, shy girl, a shabby, frightened girl, a girl he loved and had to protect.

On reading of her father's death in Switzerland he had sent her an expensive cable, offering her consolation and assuring her that he loved her and prayed for her. But his real emotion was one of thanksgiving that a sinister presence had been removed from a terrified girl who had been restored to life. He felt continuing dismay that the newspapers had not as yet stopped writing of her; he looked at Boston, New Haven, and New York newspapers, and invariably her photograph was there, accompanied by articles concerning John Ames and speculations about his daughter, "whom he had kept secluded while he prepared her to take his place in the world of finance." Tom would look at the severe photographs of Caroline, and beyond the cold, impassive expression he would see her soft hazel eyes, her smile, and hear her hesitating voice and sometimes a rare, confiding laughter. The full realization of what and who Caroline Ames was did not reach him until this very moment, on a July day, as he sat on his father's porch, facing the sea and resting after fourteen hours of vigorous work.

Never before had he considered money in connection with Caroline. "How could I have been such a fool!" he said aloud and with bitterness, looking at the evening sea and watching the rise of the golden curve of the young moon. He remembered that the newspapers had even hinted that such-and-such a personage—a European nobleman, a count, a prince, or sons of mighty fortunes in America—was being conjectured as a possible mate for Caroline Ames. At first this had not disturbed him. Carrie was "my girl." The woman in the newspapers was not Carrie at all. It was not until John Ames' body had been brought home and laid in the Esmond family plot in Boston that sharp uneasiness had come to Tom. He had actually gone to the cemetery. Caroline knew so few people, he had told himself. Only her aunt and her cousin Timothy and her adopted cousin, little Melinda, and perhaps a few friends would be there to console and help her. He would not go to the church, of course; it was better for the bereaved to be alone there, looking at the face of the dead for the last time. He arrived at the cemetery gates an hour before the burial.

Then he received his first shock. A cordon of police was at the gates, and the captain on horseback coldly asked him if he had "a ticket" or if he was visiting the grave of a relative. "No," said Tom, bewildered, his hands holding the strong thorny roses he had cultivated himself in his sea garden behind his father's house. "I'm just a friend of—of Miss Ames." It took a moment or two for him to realize that he could not attend the funeral of John Ames unless he had a scrap of cardboard and had been invited!

The captain was kind. He looked at Tom's neat cheap clothing, at the black cravat he had bought only that morning for fifty cents, and at the sturdy workman's boots. "Are you a servant of the family?" he asked. Tom glared at him. "Well, then," said the captain in his Irish voice, "you'll not be at the funeral, I'm thinking, my boyo. It's very exclusive, that it is, and all the big lads and their ladies will be here, even from Washington," he added importantly, flicking a speck of dust from the harness with an elegant touch of his gloved finger.

"I'm a friend of Carrie's—that is, Miss Ames," repeated Tom, growing angry and bewildered. "But it is not a ticket she sent you," said the captain, shaking his head. He liked Tom's appearance, his height, his lucid eyes, his well-brushed black hair, and he thought the roses very beautiful. He bent down from his horse to sniff them. He was sorry for Tom. The "big ones" were always forgetting; they had money to think about, and it was money that was important to them.

"The President of the United States," said the captain, "is sending an important personage to represent him at this funeral, and there'll be a few senators and congressmen and the governor and many of the big ones from New York, itself, and their ladies, and politicians with the sticky hands of them. Oh, many a famous one will be here! And so the funeral is private, with three ministers and a procession."

He nodded at Tom. "But there's no law," he said, "that'll be keeping you, lad, from standing back there, outside the gates, and watching. Best to take your place; the whole town will be coming out to see the grand funeral, all with black horses and plumes and silver harness. Boston gentlemen spare their five-cent pieces, but they do love their funerals!"

Tom Sheldon did not believe that John Ames ever loved anything or anyone and would certainly not "love" his funeral. He became despondent. He could not connect Caroline with such a funeral and such a display. Yet all that he had been reading lately in the press, all the adulation for Caroline and all the guesses about her tremendous inheritance and her position, came back to his mind, and he was more and more depressed. The broad road leading to the cemetery was empty. Tom peered through the tall iron bars under the close supervision of one of the policemen. He saw, near the bars, a raw brown grave decorated only by a cheap wooden cross which was already leaning and discolored. All about it lay the crowded graves of the insignificant and the obscure and the glitterless, some with cheap funeral urns upon them, some covered with ivy or ferns, and some with fading flowers. The lonely and abandoned grave moved Tom in his own personal misery. He went back to the captain and said, "There's a grave in there with no flowers or urns or ivy, just an old little cross. May I put these flowers on it?"

The captain looked at the beautiful vital roses, then peered at the grave, and then he looked at Tom. "You'll be coming out at once?" he asked doubtfully.

"Yes, I have no ticket," said Tom, smiling slightly.

"Well, now, and you may go in and say a prayer for the poor soul," said the captain. "But it's ten o'clock and the funeral is at eleven, and the rascals who have nothing better to do on a Chewsday working day will be running after the fine funeral, or in front of it, to see a rich man buried and gape at the horses and the famous people. So go in, but be quick about it, lad."

He waved Tom inside the gates. The unsheltered sun beat down on the hard earth and shimmered over the graves. Tom could feel the lumpy soil and stones even through his thick boots. The silence that only cemeteries possess lay about him palpably; he had tucked his cap under his arm, and the sun struck his bare head like a hot hammer, and his eyes were dazzled. He stood and looked down at the abandoned grave, at its grasslessness, its loneliness. He bent to read the name: "Alice Turney, 1864–1883." The painted words were already faded, burned by sun, half washed away by rain; the cross leaned. It would soon fall and would rot unnoticed and uncared for. Alice Turney was a name; there was no "sister of" or "wife of" or "daughter of" mentioned on the cross. She had been only twenty, this nameless and unloved and unwanted Alice Turney. Had no one loved her even for an hour? Had she died of loneliness and sadness, a girl from some back street, a servant, a seamstress, a shopgirl?

"Hello, Alice," said Tom. "I've brought you some flowers." He wished he had a glass pot and some water so that the roses would not die too soon, as this girl had died. He took some moist earth from a broken old urn and arranged it on the grave and stuck his roses in it. They stood up bravely, red, white, and yellow, with brilliant green leaves. The sentimental captain, watching, sighed, blinked his eyes, and coughed.

Tom, looking down at the grave, suddenly thought of Caroline, and he did not know why. He walked away. When he reached the gate he saw that the broad street was full of dust and running and fast-walking figures of men and women. He smiled his thanks to the captain and struck off on a side road. He would not be able to see Caroline; she would be surrounded and immured and veiled. In fact, she would not be his Carrie at all.

He remembered all this as he read Beth's letter. He remembered the letters he had written Caroline after her father's burial. She had not answered them. He had made excuses for her: she was sick with sorrow; she had a great deal of responsibility and many papers. There would be people who would have to consult her and whom she would have to consult. But she would be alone. She had lost the father she had loved; she had only Beth and himself, Tom Sheldon, now. Surely it was only natural that she would remember this.

Tom's mother had died a year ago. He lived alone with his old father, who had developed, very late, a marvelous talent for designing little homes which were spacious and peaceful and full of modest loveliness. He and Tom loved each other devotedly and, in spite of the fact that fifty years lay between their ages, they had been like brothers. Now, for the first time, Tom wondered why he had never spoken to his father about Caroline Ames, not even when he was only twelve years old. Had he known, even then, as he knew now, that his father would not have understood? Had he known that his father's reaction would have been based on solid reality and not on dreams and hopes? Old Thomas Sheldon was a man of sense as well as kindness. He would, with only a few pragmatic words, have destroyed something that was as intangible as a breath.

Caroline's money was a golden wall that would keep them apart. Tom had never seen its power and its height and its invincibility before, and its awe-inspiring glitter. Caroline had been more intelligent. She had not answered any of his letters. What if she did wear his brooch? She probably never gave it a thought. He would never see her again. To him, her money was nothing. As her father's daughter, Caroline would know that her money was everything.

But it isn't, thought Tom. Or is it?

CHAPTER TWO

Beth Knowles, who was kind as well as shrewd, and was growing old and tired, could not understand why Caroline Ames rarely if ever spoke of her father. To Beth, the dead were not far away; she had a vague conviction that they still loved the living and that they craved remembrance and love in return. Her family had been simple; almost all the people she had ever known had been simple. The complex and mysterious ones, like John Ames, were, in her opinion, hardly to be considered human at all, and certainly not normal. Once or twice before her father's death Caroline had tried to tell Beth of the people she had met in the great American cities and abroad, but Beth had only gaped wonderingly, had shaken her head, and had expressed her sturdy incredulity. "Now, dear," she would say coaxingly and with a hint of rejecting fear in her loving eyes, "aren't you exaggerating just a little? Why, the governments would do something about them. Christian folks would rout them out or put them in prison or something." She wanted to be reassured that the majority of people were like herself, intrinsically good, full of simplicity, loving, kind, and brave.

To Beth, Caroline was as simple as herself. Her inexplicable moods and withdrawals, her broodings and sullenness and sudden outbursts of incomprehensible passion, were only symptoms of the misery her father had brought into her life from her very birth. Now that John Ames was dead, Beth told herself, the girl would be a prisoner released, and she would be "like every other young lady." It would take a few weeks, perhaps, and then the wings of her spirit would lift. Being simple and normal, she would soon speak of him with sad affection, as Beth always spoke of her own dead. But Caroline never mentioned him or gave any indication that she was thinking of him.

Unlike Tom, Beth did not connect Caroline with money and power. She had avidly read of Caroline's great fortune; she had cut articles about the girl from the Boston newspapers and had smiled knowingly at the conjectures of the reporters about whom Caroline would eventually marry. No one but "important folks" got their names so lavishly printed in the newspapers almost daily. But the Caroline Ames of the newspapers and the fortune and the "little Carrie" whom Beth loved did not actually mesh into one fabric in Beth's thoughts. After all, she would say to herself when some uneasy and unwelcome thought came to her, hadn't she always made Carrie's flannel nightgowns and petticoats and drawers, and hadn't she wiped the little girl's nose and sopped away her tears and held her in her lap and told her of "Jesus, meek and mild," and instructed her in the Ten Commandments and the Sermon on the Mount? To Beth, Caroline was still a child, needing protection and love. The money was mysterious and not quite real to the affectionate woman.

Beth was delighted when Caroline told her in Lyndon that they would go to Lyme on Sunday rather than Tuesday. Ah, thought Beth delightedly, she is thinking of Tom! So Beth sang as she packed her own clothing and Caroline's. Old Jim was long dead; they would take a hack to the station.

Caroline had never been loquacious, not even with Beth. Now she was almost invariably silent. She sat with Beth in a dirty coach in the train and looked blindly through the smudged windows. They had always traveled like this, in a welter of crying children, the stench of oranges, urine, straw, and ham sandwiches. The crowded aisles, filled with opened wicker baskets of coarse food, running infants and milling adults in shabby clothing, were familiar and reassuring to Beth. Nothing had changed. She looked at Caroline's large profile, impassive and darkly pale, with the broad nose and the heavy folded lips. Sunlight occasionally struck her eyes; they were cold and yellowish between the thick black lashes. A sharp uneasiness struck Beth. She moistened her lips and said, "I hope that Lyme won't bring too many sad memories back, dear. One must go on."

She eagerly waited, in her simplicity, to hear Caroline sigh and say gently, "I'll try, Beth." That was the acceptable reply in Beth's world. But Caroline did not answer for several moments. Then she said, "I'm going to sell the house in Lyme."

Beth considered this statement for a few moments. Then her heart was touched deeply. The girl did not want the house in Lyme any longer because it would remind her too much of her father and she could not bear it yet. So Beth said with tender complacency, "Well, we'll not be hasty, will we, dear? The house has a wonderful view. It does need some work done on it badly, but I imagine we can get Tom to do it for us very reasonably." Caroline did not reply.

They got into a hired hack at the depot, and after a few moments the summer sea came into view as they trundled down the rutty road. It was a blue plain, filled with bright shadows. A few fishermen's boats studded the horizon like black periods, accenting the emptiness of water and brilliant sky. Beth pointed to the high land to her left and cried with pleasure, "Look, Carrie! Those lovely little houses up there which Tom built last summer! And so reasonable, too." Caroline did not look or answer.

The Ames house stood stark and gray and rotting beyond its shingle, its dusty windows blind, its wooden walks heaped with dead leaves and rivulets of sand, its chimneys leaning, its clapboards and roof curling. Beth was more depressed than usual when she saw the house. Really, it should be taken down, she thought, thinking of the barren rooms, the dirty stone fireplaces, the kerosene lamps, the frayed matting, the crumbling furniture, the dark attic, the cold kitchen with its old wood stove and uneven floorboards, and the outhouse behind. Even when first built, Beth thought, it must have been ugly.

There was a pile of stove and fire wood near the rear door, and Beth immediately built a fire in the kitchen stove and put on a large boiler for hot water; she also built a fire in the wretched living room. Caroline said nothing. She sat in a dusty chair whose upholstery was torn, the cotton stuffing revealed dirtily, and apparently watched Beth building the fire and apparently listened to Beth's heartening chatter. "I'll clean your room first of all, Carrie," said Beth. "I'm glad I took down all the curtains last year and stored them upstairs after washing them. In one of the trunks. Would you like the Paisley-patterned ones for your room, or the ones with the big red roses?"

Caroline, all at once, could not bear Beth's loving chatter. She stood up, looked about her aimlessly with blank eyes, and said, "It doesn't matter." Beth was kneeling on the ashy hearth, and Caroline saw her weary plump shoulders, her slowed movements. She said, "I'll go to the attic and get the curtains." Her voice was almost gentle.

Beth looked over her shoulder with a happy and wondering smile. "Why, how nice of you, dear. They're in the trunk with the round lid, the wood one with the brass hinges."

Caroline went up the creaking and gritty bare stairs, indifferent to the dust she collected on her black skirts. Beth could hear her heavy and sure steps mounting to the attic. She began to hum to herself. One just had to have patience; one just had to work; everything would be good soon. All things came to one in time. Caroline, in the webbed and rotting attic, closed the door, then leaned against it, shutting her eyes. It was very warm here. She did not notice the stifling air. When she opened her eyes again she did not see the soft thick carpet of old dust on the floor. Why had she come up here? Then she remembered, through the haze and agony of pain which never left her.

She pushed herself away from the door with extreme effort, for she was always exhausted these days. Her feet sank into the soft thick dust, and a cloud of it rose about her. She coughed. She found the trunk and lifted the rounded lid and looked listlessly at the faded curtains Beth had placed there last fall. Poor Beth, she thought vaguely. Compassion was an unusual emotion for her, she who was always engrossed in her own fear and now in her own anguish. She paused, looking down at the curtains. All at once, and for the first time since her father's death, tears came into her eyes and she bent her head against the lifted lid of the trunk and sobbed chokingly. She could not stop and she did not know why she cried. Her uncontrollable sobs shook her; her efforts to restrain them made sweat burst out over her face and join her tears.

Finally she could control herself. She fished in her skirt pocket for her handkerchief and rubbed it dazedly over her eyes and then blew her nose. For only a few instants there was a calm cool place in her mind, full of peace. Then it was gone, and there was only cold pain again. She picked up all the curtains and was about to close the lid with her elbow when she saw a dim package at the bottom of the trunk, covered with dull gray newspaper—a flat package, like a picture. She stared at it, frowning, seeing the sifted fragments of paper and the outlines of a frame. A picture? But her father never bought pictures. He had never gone with her to the various art galleries in Europe.

What? thought Caroline, and felt the smallest thrill of interest. A portrait of her dead young mother? Her father must have valued it, to keep it. She put the curtains down on the top of a flat trunk and lifted the picture in her hands. The paper drifted from it; she saw the dimmed gilt of the frame. Then she carried the picture to the attic window that looked out on the sea, and she held it to the light, brushing off the fragments of paper.

For a stunned moment or two as she stared down at the portrait she thought she was seeing a painting of herself or that she was looking into a mirror. She blinked furiously; she smudged her handkerchief again over her face. Her ears began to ring. She brought the portrait closer, and then she saw it was not a painting of herself or a mirror. It was a man. The large golden eyes smiled up at her; the large full mouth was curved slightly in a smile. There was a wide eagerness in the expression. A fragment of the sifting newspaper clung to the top of the frame. "April 4, 1839, Genesee, N.Y." The print was barely legible. Now it drifted to the floor. Then Caroline, whose heart was beginning to hammer, saw the artist's signature on the painting: "Self-portrait. D.A. 1838."

Without wonder, without amazement or conjecture, she knew at once. She leaned against the webbed wall near the window. She began to sweat again. She looked at the portrait almost fiercely. D.A. was David Ames. She knew his style well; she had, only two weeks ago, gone to a private showing of eight of his paintings in Boston, remembering what Herr Ernst had told her that terrible night in Switzerland. She had hoped to see the painting of the tower, of the awful apocalyptic painting of the church with its fiery cross against foreboding skies. But they were not in this loaned collection, which was from New York and London. She had walked mutely from one painting to another in the small but select art gallery in Boston, unaware that other people had recognized her from her photographs and were now whispering discreetly behind their hands to their friends.

She had only known that this David Ames was a great artist, that his pictures glowed and palpitated and teemed with the color she loved, no matter the subject. They lived on the walls; they were like windows rather than paintings; they opened out on strange scenes full of emotion and vivid life. One was a young girl, very young, with a dark swarthy face and long lank black hair lying on bare shoulders the color of copper. She wore a scarlet dress with a bright blue apron, and her legs from the knees down were bare, as were her feet. She was seated on a rough wicker chair in a garden crowned with burning hues, and there was a bare table near her elbow filled with curious fruits like large jewels. The black eyes gazed at the viewer with strange but composed interest; the red lips were serious and grave. Caroline's finger, without her volition, had reached out and touched the painted fruit; the paint was thick and had apparently been laid on with a knife.

And now she was looking down at another painting of David Ames. He was her grandfather, the man her own father had hated, whose crimes against him and her grandmother had been hinted at in the very few times John Ames had mentioned him. He had spoken only when he had been very tired. Caroline leaned more heavily against the wall, moistening her lips. Then, without knowing why she did so, she suddenly clutched the portrait against her breast and held it there tightly in a passionate embrace.

Her emotions almost shattered her. Why had her father saved this portrait? She would never know anything at all about her grandfather, whose face, the replica of hers, lay against her breast. Slowly she held out the picture again, studying her very eyes, the very formation of her face, the very texture of her hair, and her own large ears and short neck. Only the expression was different. It was an older face, but in all ways it was also a much younger face than hers. It was a face without fear. Caroline did not know that she was beginning to smile; a sensation of deep knowledge and love was invading her for her grandfather. She did not hear her own soft weeping. David Ames had not been a vicious and wicked man, a cruel and heartless man, as her father had said. He had been a great artist, lonely and despised before his death.

"I wish I'd known you," said Caroline aloud, and she held the portrait to her cheek so that it touched the cheek of the dead man.

There was a movement far below on the wet shingle, which was reddening under the declining sun. She looked down through the window and saw Tom Sheldon standing on the shingle, staring at the house. He was smoking, and the gray trail of the smoke lifted straight up in the warm air. His blue and white striped shirt was open at his throat; his arms were bare and brown. He stood tall and solidly on the gleaming sand, his sun-darkened face thoughtful and serious. He smoked idly, but he was watching the opened door of the old house. Then he turned away.

If Caroline had not found the self-portrait of her grandfather she would not have done what she did now. The emotion she had been experiencing quickened to a storm. She put the portrait of David Ames on the pile of curtains, caught up her dragging black skirts, and ran out of the attic. Beth heard the rapid tumult of her running feet on the stairs, the desperate clatter, the smothered crying. She came hurriedly out of the kitchen in time to see Caroline, her skirts flying, her arms outstretched, racing toward the door. She had a glimpse of Caroline's face, laughing, weeping, distracted, and of her disheveled hair. "What is it?" screamed Beth, terrified. But Caroline fled across the sagging boards of the living room and through the door, and she was calling, "Tom! Tom! Wait for me!"

Beth stumbled to the door, watching that turbulent young figure rushing down the wet shingle. And there was Tom, turning, startled. Then he was holding out his arms and he was laughing and the gulls wheeled about him. A moment later Caroline was in his arms, and she was clutching him, and Beth could hear her incoherent cries. Then she was still, and Tom was smoothing her hair and holding her to him as a father might hold a child.

"Oh, thank You, Father," Beth said. "Thank You." She threw her apron over her eyes and burst into tears.

Tom held Caroline a long time in his arms until he had quieted her. When she lifted her head from his shoulder and looked up into his face shyly, he thought that she was the most beautiful woman he had ever seen. Her olive cheeks were wet and flushed with apricot; her hazel eyes shimmered; her smile was charming beyond description and childishly innocent and joyous. The soft sea wind brushed wisps of her black hair over her low forehead. "Oh, Tom," she said.

Arm in arm they went to their large boulder on the gleaming shingle and sat down side by side. The evening sky reddened, and the sea was the color of ripe grapes. The water hissed and murmured against the black rocks; a freighter fussed busily along the horizon, and sandpipers scampered about scallops of foam, and gulls circled with light on their wings. Caroline's hand began to tighten on Tom's with rising hysteria, and he only waited. He was her first confidant; she did not know how to begin or what to say; her life was like a huge rock on her shoulders, pressing her down; she did not know how to shift it, but shift it she must. Awkward and taciturn, with no apt words but only her need to explain, to cry for help, she began to speak hoarsely and with sudden incoherent blurts, and Tom listened. He kept his face still and gentle, knowing that she was looking at him intensely and imploringly, begging him to understand. She began with the finding of her grandfather's portrait a little while ago, then she moved back in time, her words stammering against the background of wind and water. Always, vehemently, she absolved her father.

A less perceptive and loving man than Tom would have found the jerky and breathless story incomprehensible, for it was delivered in bursts, with no connecting links. Always, she insisted piteously, her father had been the victim of villains and exploiters; he had done only what he had to do. The others had no excuse for their rapacity and their evil. An unknown and appalling world emerged before Tom's disgusted and outraged inner eye. Occasionally Caroline paused out of exhaustion, searching for fresh words, and she looked emptily at the slow darkness rolling over the sea. She told of that night in Switzerland, and her voice quickened with terror and grief and rage, and she pulled her hand from Tom's and clenched them into fists on her knee and beat her knee with them. Her face became charged with suffering and hatred. Tom listened until she was done.

Tom saw very clearly that John Ames had been no victim—instead, he had been his own mortal enemy—and that in his distortion of spirit he had martyred and victimized his own daughter. He had also hated her, it was evident, because she resembled his father. He thought of David Ames and the discovery of his identity by Caroline, and he was full of pity for the dead artist and a deeper pity and love for the girl who had been proxy for her grandfather. He hated John Ames dead more than he had hated him living. Once his father had told him, "It's this way, Tom: even though some of the bully boys in the pulpit say we make the events, all of them, in our life, that just isn't so. I can't make folks like me if they're dead set against me for one reason or another. And if somebody wants what I have, even if he's unjust, he can cause me a heap of trouble without my having anything to do with it.

"There's only one good thing we can control, though, and that's the way we take the miseries of life, and all the injustice and malice and cruelty, and the sickness and death and failure. It's what we do in our souls that counts."

John Ames had answered his own challenge, from boyhood, with vengefulness and hate. His choice had been his own. It was piteous to hear his daughter declare that he had done only what he had to do. Tom waited and knew that Caroline was watching him eagerly in the warm salt darkness, with the sea growing louder in their ears.

Then he spoke slowly and gently, the fire in his pipe a low ember. "That's an awful experience you had in Switzerland, Carrie. No one can doubt it or excuse it. But let's look at it this way, without excusing the doctor who wanted to know if he'd get paid. You run out to his house in the middle of the night, in your night clothes, out of the hotel, when there're servants there. You woke him from a sound sleep; he had a house and a family behind him, and you scream at him to come to your father, when he knew very well that you just had to pull a bell or something and get all the help you needed.

"Let's say, though, that he was all bad and wrong and greedy and cruel. You aren't the only one who comes up against such people all their lives, Carrie. We all do. Why, I deal with them every day, sweetheart. The banker down there in the village; he practically wanted our eyeteeth on the first loan and insulted us. He didn't have a right to insult us.

"When I was on the canalboats I ran into many rotten people who did rotten things to me, sometimes as bad as what was done to you. What should I have done? Hurt them back? That would have been a waste of time; it would have crippled me too. Why should I let such people break my spiritual legs and put out my eyes? I didn't let them do it to me. I kept thinking, too, of the good people I'd met who'd helped me, often when they couldn't have afforded to. The world's a hard place and a dangerous one, and nobody's going to be able to change it. There's no security or peace in it.

"I never had much schooling, but I've read all I could and I never stop reading. I wanted to be—right—for you, Carrie. There's nothing in the Bible, Carrie, that promises us much more than pain and struggle. We're supposed to have the courage to forget, and even to forgive, and go on, on our own straight way. You were hurt, sure. But suppose all of us, including me, answered back the way you've been doing, poor girl? We'd——" But Carrie pulled her hand away from his. He did not attempt to take it again.

How can I explain to him, thought Carrie despairingly, that it's all tied up with money, and that if you don't have money, a lot of money, the world will tear your throat out and destroy you? She said, "Perhaps I haven't explained it properly, Tom. It was because that doctor thought I had no money, and that's what frightened me."

Tom nodded understandingly. He knew what it was not to have money. But he could not know how money affected Caroline, for he had not lived her life and had not had her father as his own.

He said, "I won't let anything ever hurt you again, Carrie, or at least I'll try. You've had to stand too much. But now there are only you and me. Let's go on from there, shall we?"

Caroline wanted to believe that Tom understood and that she had come to a safe place. She put her head again on his shoulder and cried, huddled in the warmth of his arms.

She said, "Tom, I must go to New York the day after tomorrow to see my father's lawyers again—Tandy, Harkness and Swift. My father owned fifty-one per cent of Broome and Company stock. Did you ever hear of it? No? It doesn't matter. There's a frightful old woman—Mrs. Broome—she will be there; there is going to be a discussion. Tom! I don't want anything more to do with her kind of people, here or in Europe or anywhere!"

"Good," said Tom warmly. He had only a faint idea that Caroline was about to withdraw from her father's associates and friends. The ramifications and enormous enterprises behind Caroline's fortune were unknown to him. He had been reading of trusts and monopolies in the newspapers. He did not connect Caroline at all with trusts and monopolies and cartels, which were the preoccupations of unhuman and faceless giants in top hats, Prince Albert coats, and striped trousers (as shown by cartoonists). Caroline had a lot of money; he was aware of that. But the source of that money was nebulous to him. His farthest journeys had been to Boston and the small towns along the coast, and his direct small contacts were with little lumber mills, brick manufacturers, and slate dealers.

"I am also going to conduct my father's fleet of ships and clippers in a legal fashion," said Caroline. "It's what he'd want me to do."

"Legal?" murmured Tom abstractedly, kissing her cheek. Then he laughed. "Keep a little boat for us! Mine is about done." He paused and said again with more alertness, "Legal? What do you mean?"

Caroline, without feeling in the slightest that she was betraying her father, told him. Tom blinked, incredulous. He knew the world of small evil; the monster world was still beyond his understanding or acceptance. He felt the sea wind on his throat and bare arms and he was suddenly cold. Was it possible that in free and honorable America there were actually such men as John Ames who could buy governmental officials, who could bribe higher and presumably better than ordinary human beings in positions of lofty office? But Caroline was naming men with whose names Tom was familiar through the newspapers, and she spoke of them casually. She spoke of the White House, the State Department, in the tones of one who knew them well. This stunned Tom. For the first time he was afraid.

"Or I'll sell the shipping business," said Caroline.

My God, thought Tom simply.

He said, "Carrie, did you really meet President Hayes?"

She was surprised. "Why, certainly, Tom, many times." Her voice was weary. "I've told you. We had dinner with him on several occasions in the White House." She waited, then said timidly, "Is something the matter, Tom?"

He squeezed her hand. After a moment he asked, "I wonder if the President knew what and who your father carried on his ships, and what countries he dealt with."

"I don't know," said Caroline. "But nothing mattered to the people in Washington. It was just money. Papa supported Mr. Hayes before and after he was elected."

Tom lit his pipe with uncertain and fumbling fingers. The world was not simply composed of a few undeniably evil men and many undeniably good men. It was not composed almost entirely of men who loved and honored their country, as he, Tom, had believed. He thought of himself bitterly as a provincial numskull, a fool, an ignoramus. He had actually believed, in his stupid simplicity, that in spite of a few incompetent rascals the men who controlled his government were of the race of the Founding Fathers. America's integrity, honor, and courage were beyond question. Now something more terrible than the account Caroline had given him of the people she had met abroad struck Tom's dazed mind.

"Is something the matter?" Caroline repeated with more timidity.

"My God," said Tom aloud. Then he put his arms tightly about the girl. "I'll take you away from all that," he said. "You can't have anything more to do with it, Carrie," he said.

"No, never again," said Caroline, and kissed his cheek like a child. "Tom, you'll go with me to New York? You'll help me?"

Tom could not help it, but he cringed. He saw himself in his coarse country clothing lumbering beside Caroline in an elegant office, face to face with the pale countenance of evil, face to face with smooth enemies. What would they think of him?

"You'll help me!" cried Caroline.

"Yes, yes, of course," said Tom.

It was very dark. A lighthouse blinked, faded, blinked again. A gull cried in the night. It was very dark.

Tom's father died that night in his sleep. He had not made a sound. Tom was sitting in the little parlor of the house; his father's bedroom door was slightly open, but Tom heard nothing. He had sat there until dawn, thinking with growing fear of what Caroline had told him, thinking of Caroline herself, and wondering in despair how it would be to be her husband. He smoked, let his pipe grow cold, then relit it. He went into the dark kitchen for a drink of water. He stood there looking out into the rustling night, thinking, thinking. I never even thought! he told himself with disgust. It was just Carrie, the little girl I'd known since I was twelve. Then he thought of Caroline clinging to him on the boulder, and her mournful kisses and her trust and her tears. He shook his head and groaned softly and went back to sit and smoke and think.

Would love be enough for Caroline? Would she actually be content to live in the small house he had designed for her? He must ask her to consider everything. He must try to show her exactly what he was and what she could expect. For the very first time he saw the power of her fortune. It was stupid, he said to himself, to chatter that it meant nothing at all. He considered his own little and uncertain income. Would Caroline expect more from him than that? She was the mistress of one of the mightiest fortunes in the world. He looked down at his worn trousers, his worn workman's boots, his calloused hands. Why should Caroline love him? It seemed impossible that a Caroline Ames could love a Tom Sheldon. A sick premonition grew in him as the first shadowy light of dawn and the first blue shadow touched the parlor windows.

He would talk to his father. He trusted old Thomas. I should have talked with him years ago, thought Tom, rising wearily to go into the kitchen to grind the breakfast coffee and cut the breakfast bacon. How was he to explain to old Thomas? His father would stare at him with his faded eyes and then he would say . . . What would he say? "That I am a shambling country fool," said Tom, working the handle of the kitchen pump. "I must have known that all the time, and that's why I never told him about Carrie."

He built a fire in the stove and put the blue granite coffeepot on it, and then the iron skillet. Long shafts of rose and green lifted in the east. Tom went to call his father just when the bacon began to splutter. But his father was serenely dead.

CHAPTER FOUR

The boy who delivered their morning newspaper from Boston and their groceries from the village brought the news to Beth and Caroline, who were eating their usual uninspiring breakfast of oatmeal, milk, stewed apricots, and coffee.

When Caroline had come into the house the night before after leaving Tom, Beth had thought with sentimental joy: Why, how beautiful the child really is! She eagerly wished for confidences; a young woman in Beth's world would have been full of shy bubblings. Though Beth had known the Ames family for so many years, she instinctively and stubbornly held to her conviction that, given the opportunity and the circumstances, Caroline would behave exactly as all other young ladies.

She was extremely let down and disappointed when Caroline only smiled at her awkwardly and said, "I've been talking to Tom. It's very late, isn't it? I'm sorry, Beth." She had pumped some water into the sink and washed her hands.

"Why didn't you bring Tom in?" asked Beth, hurt and perplexed.

"He had to go home; his father was waiting for him." Caroline dried her hands on the coarse towel.

"Is that all?" cried Beth.

Caroline blinked at her. "All? I suppose so. What do you mean, Beth?"

"What did you and Tom talk about, for heaven's sake, all that time?"

Caroline appeared taken aback, and her tone changed and became colder. "I think that's my own business." She paused. Beth's depressed and searching expression surprised her, then vaguely touched her. "Oh," she said, and then she colored. "We were talking about getting married. In about six months."

At this point, in Beth's uncomplicated world, a young lady would have blushed very deeply, run to her only friend, cried and stammered and laughed and murmured, held tightly in that friend's arms. But Caroline was puzzled by Beth's silence and stared at her. "Do you think that is too soon after——?"

"Oh, Carrie!" exclaimed Beth. "I don't understand you! You know how I love you and Tom, and now you're getting married!"

"Yes?" said Caroline, more puzzled than ever. "What's wrong, Beth?"

Beth slammed the skillet of pork chops on the kitchen table. "There's nothing wrong!" she shouted. "Nothing at all but you, Carrie!"

Caroline was honestly astounded. "What have I done?"

"Nothing," said Beth, then burst into tears. Caroline sat down and stared at her in total bewilderment. They ate their dinner in silence. Caroline, still silent, went up to her room, and Beth washed the ironware dishes, completely frustrated. And Caroline, in her room with the window overlooking the dark ocean, gave brief consideration to Beth. The poor thing was growing old; her words and manner tonight were very strange. Then she put Beth out of her mind and thought of Tom and smiled in the darkness. For at least half an hour she did not think of her father at all. When she did, she remembered the portrait of her grandfather. Years and death stood between her and David Ames. Yet never, even with Tom, had she felt such oneness of communication. "I must find some of his paintings and buy them," she said aloud. "They belong to me." She would hang them in her own room; she would never let others see them; they would be her own.

No one needs me, especially not Carrie, thought Beth in her bed. Here Carrie is going to marry Tom, and she didn't think it would affect me at all or whether or not I'd be happy over it. I'm just a servant to her. After all these years!

The heavy silence of the next morning afflicted Beth, but Caroline, absorbed in her own plans, did not feel it. Tomorrow Tom would go with her to New York. They would conclude many things together. She said, "Beth, I'm going to New York tomorrow, and of course you'll have to go with me, as Tom is going also."

Startled, Beth swallowed the hard lump in her throat and smiled. "To buy the ring?" she asked coquettishly.

"The ring?" repeated Caroline, frowning. "Oh, the ring. No, we didn't speak of that. It's a little soon. No. This is business."

The boy brought the paper and the groceries then, and Beth, hearing the news, cried. Caroline sat at the splintered table with a dull expression. She had never seen old Thomas; he had no reality for her.

"Oh, poor Tom!" Beth wept. "Poor, poor Tom! How terrible for him! Of course his father was very old. But still, how awful!" She stood up briskly, tying on her apron, her face dripping with tears. "As soon as I have cleared up, Carrie, we'll go to the village to give Tom our condolences."

Caroline shrank. She was incapable of relating anyone outside her immediate sphere with herself. All warm impulsiveness, all natural human sympathy toward mere acquaintances or strangers could not be felt by her. Humanity at large had no meaning, no actual reality. She was like one born blind, or made blind in childhood, who was only disturbed by any discussion of color or form or appearance.

"He'll be waiting for us," said Beth. "There'll be many people there, to be sure, for everyone loves Tom and loved old Thomas, but he'll only want to see us, really."

Caroline shrank even more. She thought of the day following her father's death in Switzerland, of the swarms of his associates who had come to the hotel, of Montague, who had easily and smoothly made all arrangements, of the curious faces turned to her, of the words of sympathy that made her stunned darkness even darker. She had sat in that darkness, alone, a stranger in a strange land, and had wanted only silence.

"Oh, Beth. I can't go to see Tom! All those people!"

"What did you say?" asked Beth. "Not go to see Tom—now? Don't you understand? His father is dead, Carrie! Just as your father died!"

"This is entirely different!" exclaimed Caroline, infuriated by Beth's lack of understanding. "Tom's father and my father—this is entirely different!"

"Different? What did you say?" asked Beth, her hands on her apron strings. "How different?"

But Caroline could not explain. She sat stolidly and sullenly in her chair and compressed her large pale lips.

Beth carefully folded her apron with her worn hands. She put it on her chair. Then she tried again. "Tom loved his father, just as you loved yours. He'll need comforting; he'll want our sympathy."

"Why?" Caroline demanded. "He'll want to be let alone, just as I did." It was shocking to her that Tom, who loved her, should love his father also. Thomas Sheldon had not been John Ames, who could move governments. He had been only an old man, unimportant and faceless. So she repeated now with deep annoyance, "This is entirely different."

Beth sat down heavily. "Carrie," she said, "I don't think you have any human feelings, have you?"

"I don't know what you mean," said Caroline. "Certainly I have human feelings. Beth, you just don't understand."

All the warmth and sweetness which had comforted her during the night had gone. All the shy joy she had experienced had been destroyed by this old man's dying, an old man of whom she had never spoken and whose existence had never reached her conscious thoughts. More and more exasperated, she considered Beth, whose lined face was very white and whose fixed eyes made her uncomfortable. Then something stirred in her impatiently. Something was expected of her, and she always winced from the expectations of others.

"I never knew Mr. Sheldon," she said, trying to be patient with this old foolish woman. "Tom knows that; he'll understand why I can't go to him. He'll want to be alone. I'll write him a note," she added with a clumsy animation which she hoped would appease Beth. Tom could not feel the same sorrow for his father which she had felt for hers. The very idea was affronting and stupid. Beth was frightening her. She stared at the older woman with mistrust. She added sulkily, "Perhaps you can buy some flowers in the village."

But Beth was crying, her plump shoulders shaking, her face in her hands. It was as if she were crying for her own dead, and Caroline was overwhelmingly bewildered. How could Beth cry for an old man she had never known?

She stood up, disturbed by Beth's weeping, and put her hands on Beth's shoulders, more to silence her than to comfort her. Then Beth looked up, her tired face bloated with emotion, and she saw Caroline fully and with terrible perception.

"Oh, Carrie, my child. Oh, Carrie, God help you."

While Beth, still weeping, hastily dusted the hopelessly dusty house and prepared to leave to visit Tom, Caroline slowly went to her arid room, which smelled of grit and mustiness and dank bedding. She was accustomed to wait for Beth to straighten this ancient and ugly room as a matter of course. But now, with inept hands, she did it herself, moved by an uneasiness as well as a growing feeling of resentment. She opened the grimy window and looked down at the shingle and the morning sea and the fishing boats on the radiant and heaving horizon. The clean salt air, sharp and pure, blew on her face. Caroline's feeling of uneasiness grew. Only in very early childhood had any sympathy for others, except her father, stirred or agitated her. Once Beth had touched the periphery of her consciousness with love and solicitude. But that was long ago. Since that time she had lived in a world whose tight little circle had revolved about John Ames. All her deep impulses had been stifled and blunted. She had been like a young and tender tree, growing between two narrow walls, which found its growth circumscribed and increasingly narrowing as its little branches grew, and increasingly stunted, so that eventually it had no contact with anything but the crippling walls and stone and never was able to bend its deformed branches to embrace anything outside itself and could never send its roots down to a common pool of life.

Nevertheless, though she did not know why, she had a shadowy sensation that in some way she had failed Beth and Tom. Her spirit was like a fossilized seed whose vital element had been killed.

As she looked down at the blue tide rising on the shingle she thought, "Everything has been spoiled." She had taken Tom fiercely into her life, out of her awful need. For the first time she had been able to look at the death of her father, not as a calamity which had utterly destroyed her, but as an event, still agonizing but now bearable. Tom was utterly hers, once she had seized him. She was angry that the death of an unimportant old man should concern him, for it showed her that Tom was not entirely hers but could actually be wounded by something which had nothing to do with her.

A little girl, a stranger, ran barefoot along the shingle. This portion of the beach belonged to Caroline and was private. Her first impulse was to call down to the girl to go away. But the little girl touched the rising scallops of foam with bare toes and squealed, and her hair was a blowing golden vapor in the wind. With sudden shock Caroline thought of possible children she might have. She had always feared and hated children. Normal children had not understood her at school and had derided, mocked, and tormented her for her silences, her inability to communicate, and her wretched clothing.

But she, Caroline, would have children. John Ames had spoken of them; they would be his heirs and Caroline's. He had spoken without warmth or expectation, but only as one speaks of an unpleasant reality. Caroline leaned on the window sill and stared at the child. She would have children; they would be hers and her father's, as well as Tom's. For an instant or two the deformed tree which was herself felt new wind on its branches, its feeble dusty leaves. The child ran away; Caroline followed her with anxious, questioning eyes.

She sat down. She remembered that mothers loved their children. Her father had said with a disagreeable smile that this love was only an extension of egotism, that mothers and fathers loved their children only because of selfishness.

Caroline shook her head as if to shake some baffling thoughts from it. After a little she brought out her secretary, a shabby leather case full of paper and envelopes. She put a bottle of ink on the chair nearest hers and dipped her pen in it. For the first time in her life she was about to write a note of comfort, and she did not know how to begin. She wrote in small sharp letters: "Dear Tom." Then she stopped. What should she say? That she was sorry about his father's death? But she was not; she only resented it as a bitter intrusion in her own affairs. She chewed the end of the pen and frowned. Suddenly she got up, carrying her secretary, and climbed to the attic and found the portrait of her grandfather. She looked down at the gentle and accepting eyes, and the rushing sense of release came to her again. Sitting on a trunk in that dim, webbed half twilight of the attic, she wrote rapidly: "I'm sorry about your father. Beth will bring you this note. I must go to New York tomorrow. I'd hoped you would go with me, but I understand that the funeral will prevent you. I will have to manage alone. I will return the next day." She reread the note. It did not satisfy her; even her deformed spirit understood its coldness, but she did not know what else to say. So she signed her name. Then all at once, under her name, she wrote, "Dear Tom!"

She went downstairs to find Beth, still crying quietly and bonneted and shawled, pulling on black cotton gloves. Caroline dropped the note on the kitchen table. She was very uncomfortable, and because she was uncomfortable she was vexed. She fished in her black serge pocket for her purse, unsnapped it, and put a one-dollar bill on the note. She said surlily, "The market sells flowers. This dollar will buy a lot of them."

Beth looked at the note and the money, still weeping. Her impulse was to embrace Caroline and again attempt to reach her. But though Beth was a simple woman she realized it was all too late. There was only the hope that Tom could do that. Beth, without speaking, left the old, leaning house, and Caroline was alone.

She walked through the hideous rooms, hearing the squeaking of her footsteps. She went outside and looked at the rise of the ground far beyond the house, now overgrown with tall sea grass and brambles soughing in a lonely wind. She was overpoweringly restless. She walked to the shingle and looked far out at the incandescent sea and the bulk of Marblehead lifting its grassy top and stone and little white houses to the sun. A large ship pushed along the horizon, and Caroline thought of her father and was again bereft. Tell me what to do, she said to his ghost.

Tom's house was filled with sad-faced villagers, for he and his father were loved and respected. Every small hot room was crowded; his father's coffin, plain pine covered with a sleazy black silk cloth, lay in the parlor, and Thomas Sheldon slept in it peacefully, flowers surrounding him. The scent of them choked the air. When Beth arrived Tom showed her his father in silence. His face was haggard and lined, but he smiled at her a little, then led her outside.

She gave Tom Caroline's note. She was very surprised when he did not comment on it or Caroline's absence. He stood beside Beth in the hot sun on the little porch and he reread Caroline's note. It did not sound cold and stiff to him, nor selfish. He saw that the sharp writing had wavered a little here and there. He read the impulsive exclamation under her name.

"She wouldn't come," said Beth, sighing. "She's very strange, Tom. I suppose you should know that."

"Would you ask a woman with broken legs to walk?" said Tom. "Would you ask a blind person to see? Would you ask a deaf girl to hear?"

He put his hand on Beth's fat shoulder and said, "Don't worry, Beth. It's all right, really it is. Are you coming for the funeral tomorrow?"

"Oh yes, dear Tom."

"But Carrie will be going to New York alone, then. Isn't that dangerous for a young woman?"

"Nothing is dangerous for Carrie," said Beth with some bitterness. "She can handle anything."

"I don't know; maybe I don't agree with that," said Tom. He looked beyond the village to the hill where the poor cemetery stood.

Beth cried again. "Oh, Tom, I don't know! I don't know what happened, but all at once I kind of got a glimpse of the real Carrie, and it was awful. I mean everything about Carrie was terrible. Why couldn't that hateful man have died when she was a little girl? It would have been better for her!"

CHAPTER FIVE

Caroline left the next morning for New York on the seven-thirty milk train. It would be a long and gritty ride, full of discomfort. She settled herself on the lumpy black leatherette seat and put the basket lunch Beth had packed for her beside her. It was covered with a white napkin. The train had lurched along only a few miles when the folds of the napkin were befouled by the black soot belching through the open window. The heat wafted along the crowded coach, and the passengers coughed when clouds of smoke and steam rolled in.

Caroline sat stolidly in her black mourning dress, with the black shawl Beth had knitted for her over her shoulders. A two-dollar black bonnet, severe and plain and draped with a wisp of mourning veil, perched on top of her coronet of braids. She opened a ledger on her lap, removed her black gloves, and studied the figures of Broome and Company to refresh her memory. Her dark face misted with sweat, and grit clung to the area between her large nose and her heavy mouth. Her short neck became damp; her broad shoulders dampened under her clothing. Her expression became brooding and thoughtful and intent. She even forgot Tom in her concentration. Her feet, in thick boots buttoned and severe, rested on her purse, protecting it.

Caroline was thinking of old, depraved Maggie Broome. Her fear of Maggie had long passed. Maggie needed her as she had needed John Ames. Caroline smiled grimly. She possessed fifty-one per cent of the Broome stock. There would be no mocking airs and graces from old Maggie this time, no jeerings, no raucous laughter, no winks and grins, taunts and elbow-nudgings. The letter Caroline had received from her a short time ago had been flighty and vainglorious, but under the scrawl and under the words Caroline had detected uncertainty and even some anxiety. I can ruin her, thought Caroline. I can sell out the stock; it's low now; I can throw it on the market. If the stock were thrown on the market, the other shares would immediately fall and Maggie's income would be greatly decreased. Caroline let herself feel the pleasure, then shook her head. It would not be practical. Her father had taught her that a sensible man, no matter how goaded, never took petty revenge if it meant a loss for himself. When talking to Tom, Caroline had cried that she wanted nothing more to do with the Maggie Broomes, that she was withdrawing from her kind. But Caroline did not think of this now. There was too much money involved. There were future heirs to be considered, just as her father had considered his own daughter.

Caroline thought of her cousin Timothy, junior law partner of Tandy, Harkness and Swift. In the past Caroline had shrunk from the thought of Timothy, but now she gave him all her attention. He was her age. Cynthia did not like her son, and her son did not like his mother. Caroline had not been particularly interested before. Now, suddenly, she was deeply interested. She thought of Cynthia, the polished, the idle, the parasitic, the frivolous woman who had unaccountably seduced John Ames. Extravagant, wicked woman, thought Caroline, feeling again a savage clench in her heart.

Nothing, thought Caroline, would so disconcert Cynthia Winslow as some good fortune coming to her son. Never for a moment did Caroline understand that a mother might not like her children but that she could still love them. Cynthia's frank aversion, openly and laughingly expressed many times, had convinced the young Caroline that Cynthia wished no good for her son and that she detested him.

She was hot, dirty, and tired when she arrived in New York. She was driven in a hack to the Gentlewoman's Pension in the lower Thirties where she always stayed when alone. The French conceit did not extend beyond the name, for the pension was owned by two middle-aged spinsters, sisters, of indubitably Anglo-Saxon origin, who spoke no French at all. They had bought four elderly three-story brownstone houses, had connected them, had established a deplorably tasteless but clean dining room for their guests, and had bullied a staff of young girls and middle-aged women into keeping their establishment immaculate. They had a permanent clientele of old ladies and spinsters like themselves and accommodated transients like Caroline, who was deeply reverenced. She expressed the "tone" of the place; on this humid day it smelled of hot wool carpets, laundry soap, polish, and gas. There was always a large front room available for her, looking out on the narrow, quiet street and showing a glimpse of a religious seminary across the road enmeshed in tall old trees. Few carriages or other vehicles disturbed the heated quiet, the silence of brick and stone.

Caroline bathed from the large china bowl and dried her hands on plain linen towels. One of the spinsters brought her tea and hot muffins and strawberry jam, inquired about her health, murmured her sympathy. Caroline listlessly drank a little tea and ate a muffin, washed her hands again, picked up her ledger and purse, and went out to the hack, which had returned for her. She was driven to Tandy, Harkness and Swift on hectic Broadway, but she did not look at the brawling city seething under its burning blue roof. She had the power of absolute concentration.

Tandy, Harkness and Swift occupied two genteel floors in a somewhat new building with an elevator. They were lawyers of substance, power, rectitude, and considerable repute and managed a number of excellent estates in conjunction with their regular legal work, which was never concerned with anything the least reprehensible. Everything was conducted soberly and with distinction; no raised voices had ever been heard in their offices, for they did not accept clients of excitable disposition or tangled affairs. In a city which teemed with colorful dubiousness, they were a cool aridity of elegance and probity. Cousins, the sons of three sisters (two had been born in Boston), they had, of course, been educated in genteel Harvard. Their fees were exceedingly substantial.

As relatives, they had a strong family resemblance, all being small and slight and impeccably groomed in long black coats, striped trousers, and spats, even in hot weather. After all, they had a standard to maintain. They all had deceivingly large limpid eyes of a clear brown, which concealed their intelligence and astuteness, and smooth brown hair. All were clean-shaven; all wore white cravats with black pearl stickpins; they had small white hands and were very precise. They had accepted John Ames as a client on the recommendation of other valued clients, though they had on many occasions disapproved of him. He was not a gentleman; he was not really a Bostonian. But, as Bostonians, they had the customary reverence for large fortunes, and as John had always behaved in a gentlemanly fashion and had never become heated or emotional and had always listened to their advice, they had given him a measure of their dignified approval.

Each occupied a large quiet room with a separate waiting room and a tiny office containing two clerks. Timothy Winslow worked in a little office which he shared with another junior and a clerk. There was also a conference room, the floor covered with an Aubusson carpet, several palms in tubs, heavy mahogany chairs, and a cabinet in which waited bottles of excellent sherry and crystal glasses. The walls were paneled with mahogany, and there were draperies of blue velvet at the two long thin windows. A funeral quiet hung in the room even when it was occupied, for grave affairs concerning finance and estates were discussed here. The firm was co-executor of John Ames' estate, with Caroline. They approved of Caroline; after all, her mother had been an Esmond and she was a young lady of no flamboyance and had a proper respect for money, a dignity of her own, and was a Bostonian who possessed all the virtues of Bostonians.

She was led with real affection, concern, and solicitude into the conference room. Her nose was immediately assaulted by an expensive but rank scent, for in that place of austere virtue and unsullied affairs sat old Maggie Broome—Mrs. Norman Benchley Broome—as haggard, as soiled, as bejeweled, as depraved and overdressed as always. She was like a gaudy and lascivious parrot with a raucous voice in that paneled and subdued quiet. Five years had not changed her. She was still erect and bony, mottled of dry skin, still heavily painted, still yellowish, still raddled, disrespectful, lewd, and dyed. Worse, she was dressed in a violently pink silk suit and wore pink slippers with gemmed buckles, and her shirtwaist, though obviously expensive and flowing with handmade laces, was dirty. She looked at Caroline with her varnished raisins of eyes, noted her dress and general appearance, and her mouth twisted and the red grease upon it wrinkled. But she shouted, "Dear, dear Caroline! God! I haven't seen you since poor old Johnny's funeral! With all the nabobs there with their tall hats! God, child, you look healthy!" Her bangles rattled.

Messrs. Tandy, Harkness and Swift did not handle the Broome affairs, for which they were thankful. They wore sober expressions; they could not express any distaste for Maggie, for as Bostonians it would have been inconceivable for them to reveal aversion in the face of money. After all, old Norman had been of a fine family even if he had married this harridan. They were quite pleased that Caroline's impassive face showed no pleasure and that she bowed in cold silence and seated herself stiffly and looked only at the gentlemen. The effect was somewhat spoiled by Maggie's hoarse chuckle and the swish of her pink silk skirt as she crossed her legs.

"I should like my cousin, Timothy Winslow, to be present today," Caroline said to Mr. Tandy.

"Who?" demanded Maggie, cocking her head, which was roofed by a large Milan straw hat burdened with blue and pink silk roses. Caroline ignored her and continued to regard Mr. Tandy with massive expectation.

"Oh!" said Maggie. "Winslow. Son of Johnny's fancy lady, eh?"

The gentlemen's mouths opened. Caroline continued to look at Mr. Tandy.

"Pretty gal, for her age," continued the malicious old woman, grinning. "Saw her a couple of times in Delmonico's with Johnny. Style. Flair. Excellent taste. Drank champagne like it was water and ate sherry lobster. All the men couldn't stop looking at her. She wasted her time on Johnny, and I say that even if I did love him."

She had been enraged at Caroline's ignoring of her and at the minx's glacial attitude. Now she was creating a sensation, and she basked in it. The gentlemen were clearing their throats and looking at the backs of their hands with distressed expressions.

"Your aunt, eh?" said Maggie. "Oh, he never told me she was his doxy. Never a word out of him, no ma'am. She was always, when I saw her, 'my wife's sister, Mrs. Winslow, Maggie, in New York concerning her affairs.' But there was a look on his face. Mad for her, and she for him. Charming gal. Looked at me and we laughed together; no hypocrite, she. Pretty as a Gainsborough picture."

It was inconceivable to Caroline that her father ever patronized Delmonico's. She had always thought of him as living as austerely in New York as he did in Lyndon or Lyme, and as obscurely. After all, New York was not Europe, and he did not need to impress Americans. Her first fierce thought was that Maggie was lying. But Maggie was chuckling and nodding with delight, and Caroline suddenly believed her. "And he dressed like a dandy, too," said Maggie with admiration.

Caroline looked down at her gloved hands. She felt sick and betrayed.

Mr. Tandy pulled a bell rope and murmured to the answering clerk that Mr. Winslow's presence was requested. Then he sat down and looked helplessly at his cousins, and the twitching of their eyes answered his distress. Maggie swung her big pink foot and regarded Caroline with enjoyment.

"No secret he left his lady's adopted kid nearly a million dollars," she said. "And no secret in New York about what the government did to his ships and clippers yesterday. Everybody's talking about it. Kind of a jolt to you, wasn't it, Caroline?"

Caroline was startled. For the first time she looked at the old woman with bitter hazel eyes. "What are you talking about?" she demanded rudely.

Mr. Harkness cleared his throat. "I'm sorry, Caroline. I sent you a telegram last night. Didn't you get it?"

"No," said Caroline. She was frightened. "Please tell me."

But before he could answer, Maggie laughed resoundingly, and she showed all her yellow fangs. "The boys in Washington just confiscated everything, that's all! All the ships and schooners and sloops and clippers. Just like that!" And she snapped her fingers with a crack. "Seems like Johnny was up to nothing good; God, girl, you must have known that! And then he died and the bribes weren't handy any more, and they got a fit of virtue in Washington and came to life all at once and they grabbed everything. Opium and other contraband, they said, as if they hadn't known it for years and years all the time! But, no bribes, no protection. No Johnny, no campaign funds; no Johnny, no funds for the Department of Commerce and the customs boys and the Cabinet officers. Simple as that. Now they'll all share in the loot when the government sells Johnny's fleet, and everybody will be happy and put an extra dollar in the collection plates on Sundays and buy themselves handsomer doxies. The boys in Washington never sleep."

"You have no proof—er—of all that, Mrs. Broome," said Mr. Swift.

She screamed with mirth. "No proof! Good God, sir, you don't need proof. Everybody knew all about it."

"When everybody knows all about anything, you can be sure it isn't true, madam," said Mr. Harkness.

Maggie uttered an obscenity. Caroline shrank. "Tell me, please," she pleaded. "Is it true that all Papa's ships have been seized by the government?"

"I'm afraid so, Caroline."

"But it doesn't belong to them!" Caroline exclaimed, turning a dark red with fury. "It belongs to me! They'll have to pay me for it!"

"Ho!" laughed Maggie. "You'll be lucky, gal, if they don't take away half your fortune in fines out of Johnny's estate! There's one thing about the Washington boys: they've got big teeth and big bellies, and when they take, they take everything. Never any bottom to their bellies."

Caroline was terrified.

"I don't think it will be as bad as all that," said Mr. Swift. "You know, Caroline, we did not manage that part of your father's affairs. That was his own. But it is true that the government has seized the fleet and that they will sell it. We hope—we have reason to hope—that they will be satisfied with the proceeds and not demand any fines from you. In fact," he said compassionately, "I can almost assure you that they will consider the confiscation sufficient."

Maggie narrowed her gleaming eyes at him. "Um," she said. "Seems like I remember that three congressmen owe you a lot, sir. Yes, it seems to me. Good luck."

"My property!" cried Caroline. "It is my property!"

"Not any more, dearie," chuckled Maggie, shaking her head so that all the silk roses danced.

"The Constitution guarantees the right of property!" said Caroline.

"Not when the Washington boys want it," said Maggie. "There ain't no Constitution when Washington wants something and its paws are sticky. Constitution, hell!"

"Please, Mrs. Broome," said Mr. Tandy. "I think Miss Ames has had a severe shock. Caroline, would you like some sherry?"

"No," she said. "If this is all so," she stammered, "then America is no better than any other country."

"Much worse," Maggie assured her. "Really foul, dearie. Always was. You can buy anybody here; old Norman used to say so, and by God he ought to know! Your money or your life: that's the government, if you've got any real cash behind you. You got to buy your safety, and buy it regular."

Caroline thought suddenly of Tom Sheldon and Beth. She was distracted. "I don't believe it!" she cried. "Not everybody's filthy and a thief and a liar!"

"Yes, not everybody's like poor old Johnny and the government," said Maggie, vastly enjoying herself. "You got to be poor here to be let alone. Once you got enough to grease hands, they're pounding at your door. Think I don't grease palms, myself? And all the Vanderbilts and the Belmonts and the Astors too? Sure they do! They couldn't operate if they didn't. How do you suppose they get laws passed to protect 'em? Answer me that."

Timothy Winslow had entered silently a few minutes ago and had closed the door behind him. Maggie suddenly became aware of him. "Hah," she shouted. "Who's the silver boy, eh?"

"Allow me," murmured the anguished Mr. Tandy, conscious of the shocked and frozen girl in her chair. "Mrs. Broome, this is our junior partner, Mr. Winslow."

"Well, now, there's a handsome one for you," said Maggie with admiration. She held out her hand and Timothy shook it, and she openly inspected his slender height, his ascetic face, his eyes and hair. She ogled at him.

Caroline, overcome with her thoughts, did not look at her cousin. Mr. Tandy indicated a chair at a little distance, and Timothy sat down. He too was enjoying himself. The Gargoyle was definitely in a whirl, he was pleased to see. He wondered why she had wanted him here. He could see her pale and sweating face, her stricken eyes, her dry lips; he could see her gloved hands trembling. Maggie continued to study him with pleased fascination. Fine face there; a little cold, but interesting. She knew these cold and quiet men; underneath, they had twice the strength of the noisy boys.

"Shall we consider what we are here for?" asked Mr. Harkness, committing one of the first grammatical errors in his life. He was deeply upset.

"By all means," said Maggie gustily. "I've got a party tonight; couple of government fellers, too. Time for the August pay-off, y'know. Big fellers."

"Well, dear Caroline?" asked Mr. Swift, more and more concerned for the girl. "Or is it too much for you today?"

Caroline pulled up her sagging body. Her eyes were dull and heavy. "No, it won't take long," she said. "There is the matter of my owning fifty-one per cent of the stock of Broome and Company——"

"Right," said Maggie. "I want to buy it. Johnny as much as promised me. He's not chairman of the Board no longer. You don't aim to be that, do you, Carrie?" she cackled. "Not that you'd have a chance, being a female."

But Caroline looked only at the lawyers, who smiled at her hearteningly. "I'm going to retain the stock," she said.

Maggie scowled, and all her evil years immediately webbed and distorted her face. "You trying to go back on Johnny's word to me?" she screamed. "A promise is a promise!"

Caroline turned her head slowly and looked at her. "He never told me of any promise," she said coldly. "Nor was there any such promise or a document among his papers. I would respect a promise made by my father —if there had been any. I therefore do not believe there was."

"You're calling me a liar, you trollop?" Maggie cried.

Even Tandy, Harkness and Swift had to suppress involuntary smiles at this epithet. But Timothy smiled openly.

"I am saying," said Caroline, her voice clearing, "that I found no such promise. My father was very meticulous; all his affairs are in absolute order. Therefore, I will go on the—assumption—that there was no promise. I am keeping the stock."

"The hell with you," said Maggie, breathing hard. A purple tint spread under her rouge. "The very hell with you, you ugly numskull. I want that stock."

"You are not going to have it," said Caroline. A little color returned to her lips. "I have other plans. I know I cannot be chairman of the Board or even a director. So I will appoint a director."

The lawyers were immediately interested. They cleared their voices in anticipation.

"My cousin, Mr. Winslow," said Caroline.

An astounded silence fell over them all. Timothy sat up very straight, electrified. He stared from Caroline to his employers and then at Maggie. He turned very white.

"At a salary of twenty thousand dollars a year," Caroline continued.

Again they were very silent. Then Maggie breathed, "The hell you say."

Mr. Tandy stirred. "Caroline," he said. "Your cousin is very young.

Hardly twenty-four. Oh, I know that even younger men are appointed to boards. But have you considered all the circumstances, my dear?"

"I have," said Caroline. "I have given it a great deal of thought."

"Ah," said Mr. Tandy, stupefied.

Maggie began to smile. She tilted her head at Timothy. She almost forgot her own fury. She licked her cracked and painted lips.

Then Timothy spoke properly and in a subdued voice to his cousin. "Caroline, you know this is a startling, a wonderful, offer. I can't be grateful enough. It's true"—and he bowed apologetically to the older lawyers—"that I have been studying the Ames estate lately. After all, Mr. Ames was my uncle. Perhaps I should not have let my curiosity, my natural curiosity——"

"Perfectly natural, dear boy," murmured Mr. Harkness, dazed.

"Perfectly natural," echoed his cousins.

"Damned natural," said Maggie vigorously. "Who's going to marry this lump of a girl, anyway? So, who's her heirs? Got to keep money in the family."

"Twenty thousand dollars salary," said Mr. Swift.

"Of course," said Timothy with a generous smile at his employers, "I will hope to remain with you, sirs."

He concealed his exultation, and his really wild astonishment as to why Caroline should do this for him, Caroline who had always feared and hated him and had been hated in return. Little beads of sweat appeared on his forehead.

He said seriously, "You are sure you want this, Caroline?"

"I am." The girl spoke firmly.

"Why don't you give him some of the Broome stock too?" asked Maggie.

Caroline's loathing eyes turned to her. "No," she said. "He might sell some of it to you, and I'd no longer have the fifty-one per cent."

"Don't trust him, eh?" Maggie chuckled. "Think he might sell it to me, eh?"

Then she was infuriated again. Her face became utterly repulsive in its ancient malice. "You are a bitch," she said. "A nasty bitch. Going back on your father's word. I won't forget it. One of these days you'll find hot coals in your drawers, and Maggie'll have put them there. I don't know Washington for nothing."

"Nor do we," Mr. Tandy was forced to say sternly. "Mrs. Broome, please do not threaten our client."

Maggie jumped to her feet, swishing and rattling. "This girl'll regret this day, and I don't say such things without knowing 'em!"

Before any of them could answer her she uttered a really blasting obscenity and trotted to the door, opened it, and slammed it behind her.

"Can she really injure me?" Caroline asked her cousin much later.

"There's no doubt she'll try," Timothy said. "But you must not let that worry you too much. The old boys in the office have their connections, too, and some of the connections are a great deal more formidable than old Maggie's. Not that they do raw blackmail and bribery. Oh no. That would be barbarous. Gentlemen are above such things." And he smiled his slight, cold smile.

"They could not prevent the government from seizing my father's property," said Caroline, freshly enraged.

"They didn't manage that part of your father's estate," said Timothy. "Besides, dear Caroline, you must know that your father was engaged in something very illegal, and Tandy, Harkness and Swift won't touch that sort of thing. But they could have advised you; they could, I think, have told you of the nice gold stream that went from your father to the men in Washington. Then you could have kept it up."

"No," said Caroline. "I would not. No, not under any circumstances. Timothy, do you think there is any possibility of demanding some financial consideration from—Washington?"

"No," said Timothy. "You see, there is an investigation under way of people like your father. I'll be frank about it. There are periodic investigations. A few of them are begun by really honest tyros in Washington, newly elected, who are out to save the country, and so on. But the majority are begun by men who want larger shares of the loot. If the loot doesn't come to them fast enough they instigate investigations or they allow those already begun to proceed."

Caroline and her cousin were having dinner in the dining room of the Gentlewoman's Pension, and Timothy, who had accepted Caroline's awkward invitation, thought the food and the general surroundings completely deplorable.

"You can be sure, however," said Timothy, looking with suspicion at the sliver of dried halibut on his plate and the wilted slice of lemon, "that my dear employers won't let anything happen to the rest of the estate."

He glanced abstractedly around the dining room, which was beginning to fill with elderly fat or thin women tottering to their stark white tables. A hot dun-colored light seeped into the room through small windows hung with chintz in shades of sickly dark green and pale purple which fought feebly with the wallpaper of dull cabbage roses and viciously blue leaves. The Brussels carpeting was crimson and exhaled a dry if clean smell. Every table was centered with a glass bud vase filled with a single wax rosebud. An excellent place for a vacillating suicide to make up his mind finally, thought Timothy. But he could not be depressed.

He could not understand it; he could not fully accept it. He felt a unique emotion as he looked at the big young woman opposite him, with her sad face and sullen eyes and tight coronet of braids. This emotion was very close to profound gratitude; he had never been grateful to anyone before, and the sensation confused him a little. Cautious, as always, he continued to wonder why she had done this for him. He could not ask her directly. Then he had another thought and he put down his knife and fork and considered it with much agitation and disgust. Was she hoping to marry him? Good God! But why else?

"Don't you like the halibut, Timothy?" asked Caroline, startled by his expression.

He reflected for a few moments. Yes, that was it; she wanted to marry him. Dear Mama, in some way, had suggested this to her. The tip of his tongue touched his lips. No marriage, and all this unbelievable good fortune would drift from his fingers and he would again be a mere junior law partner of those old pious dogs, Tandy, Harkness and Swift.

"Would you prefer the stew?" asked Caroline, who had never before cared what anyone else ate. Moreover, what did it matter? "It isn't like your mother's table," she added, and the sullen eyes darkened.

Timothy watched her. "No," he said warily. He carefully moistened his mouth again. "Mama has her own tastes. Have you dined with her recently?"

He was immediately interested to see that she colored deeply. Then he was certain that she intended to marry him; she had been talking to dear pretty Mama, whose neck he lusted to wring immediately.

"No," said Caroline, so loudly and so harshly that several old ladies glanced at her with disapproval. She became aware of this and dropped her head, and her big, well-shaped hands clenched on the table. Then she said in a lower voice, "You must really know, Timothy, that your mother and I were never—never——"

"Fond of each other," said Timothy.

Caroline shook her head. She looked at Timothy, as if pleading for his forgiveness. "Forgive me, but I never liked your mother. You mustn't ask me why, please."

She picked up a slice of bread, regarded it blindly, put it down again. "Please don't be offended, Timothy, but I can't ever again visit your mother. It has nothing to do with you."

What a mystery, thought Timothy with a little contempt for this fumbling girl, but now with some hope. Mama certainly was gay and frivolous; she was also charming. She had charmed everyone all her life except her son and her niece. So marriage was Caroline's own idea. Timothy drank a little tepid coffee and wondered with a not inconsiderable despair how he was going to reject any offer so that it would not injure him and cause Caroline to change her mind.

"I wonder," said Caroline, stammering a little, "how your mother will accept the offer I made to you, Timothy."

Timothy lifted his eyes quickly. He waited. Caroline played with the silver beside her plate. "I hope," she murmured, "that your mother won't be too—annoyed. I've known almost all my life that she disliked you. I hope that her—annoyance—won't be too hard for you to bear, Timothy."

So that was it! Caroline had made him this offer, not because of his indubitable talents and his intelligence, but because she hated his mother and believed that her son's sudden good fortune would enrage and frustrate Cynthia! What a crippled mind the girl has! thought Timothy. He smiled involuntarily. (Of course this raised another problem. Caroline must continue to believe that Cynthia would be disconcerted. He, Timothy, only hoped that his mother would have the good sense not to write Caroline a grateful letter when she received the news. He began to frame a cautioning letter to his mother in his mind; she was subtle; she would understand.)

"Will it be too hard, Timothy?" asked Caroline, wondering at his silence.

"What?" Timothy brought his attention back to her. "Oh, my mother. Well, Caroline dear, you know that Mama and I never have been congenial."

Caroline smiled; it was not a pleasant or beautifying smile, and, seeing it, Timothy knew he had been right. His elation returned. He quite impulsively reached for her hand and briefly pressed it. "You're very kind, Caroline," he said.

Was she absolutely out of her mind, the poor thing? Timothy asked himself. Had she so little sophistication at her mature age, and after all that travel and all the complex personalities she must have met? She was not ignorant; she was not stupid; she was not without some perception. But she knew nothing, after all, of humanity. She was like a withered nutmeat in its fossilized shell. Thanks, of course, to lovely Uncle John.

He let himself meditate on the reason for Caroline's hatred for Cynthia. He was perfectly sure that Caroline was too virginal, too innocent, to have guessed at the relationship between her father and aunt. Like all malicious people, he was intensely curious. The reason for Caroline's hatred engrossed him, stimulated him. He wanted to know.

But before he could speak Caroline said, "How terrible it must be for you, Timothy, to have a mother who dislikes you so and who would resent any good fortune coming to you. It must have made all your life so barren. You see," she added, "my father loved me. I have that to remember, that he loved me."

Good God, thought Timothy with contempt. Can she really be that idiotic? He sighed. "Yes, dear Caroline," he said gently, "you, at least, have some consolation."

"Yes," agreed Caroline.

Timothy delicately wiped his damp face. Caroline thought he did this to conceal his emotions properly. "I ought not to have said that to you," she said. "It must be painful." The dull black of her dress moved as she sighed. Timothy had a wild urge to laugh. "Would you mind changing the subject, dear Caroline?" he said in a subdued voice.

"Of course, of course!" she cried, and she smiled, and as so many others were affected, so was Timothy by the sudden beauty and shyness of that smile. He had never seen it before. It had such radiance; it was like quick and brilliant sunshine on a carved face of dark granite. He had not known she had such beautiful teeth. If only she knew about that smile, he thought with considerable astonishment, she'd practice it regularly just as other women would, and with amazing effect. He was a little taken aback. What if some other man were ever treated to that smile? With the fortune, Caroline would then become irresistible, and what of all that damned money then? It would pass to strangers instead of, rightfully, to Caroline's blood kin. He was terribly disturbed. Marriage, for Caroline, had been taken for granted by him as an impossible contingency.

Caroline said, with the radiance of the smile still lingering at the corners of her mouth and eyes, "There are so many things I want to discuss with you, Timothy, for I will be leaving tomorrow morning. You see, I am not retaining Papa's offices in New York any longer. Tandy, Harkness and Swift will dispose of all Papa's enterprises here for me and will put the money into trusts and investments and liquid assets. You will, of course, help in these matters. I intend to concentrate on investments; Papa taught me thoroughly about them. He knew I wouldn't care about the business enterprises, which are too much for me to supervise. But I do intend to keep the Boston office, which deals with the financing of local New England enterprises, such as textiles and shoes and fishing, and the collection of rent from property in Boston. Papa has a staff of seven men there in that office. I hope, Timothy," she said with a return of her usual shyness, "that you will help me occasionally in Boston."

"Indeed! How kind of you, Caroline," said Timothy.

"There will be a percentage for you," said Caroline. "I hope it won't all be too much for you, Timothy."

Timothy wanted to laugh again. He remained properly and seriously sober.

"Before I left," said Caroline with that touching simplicity which always amused Timothy and made him contemptuous, "I had a quiet talk with Mr. Tandy and Mr. Harkness and Mr. Swift. We all agreed that you could not, with your new responsibilities, be only a junior partner any longer. You will be a full partner."

Timothy was speechless. His moods were not vivid or quick; they moved slowly and inexorably and without passion. But now he actually wanted to get up and kiss Caroline with fervor.

"They had the greatest confidence in you," Caroline continued, beginning to eat her execrable rice pudding and unaware of the painful joy and ecstasy her cousin was feeling. "Mr. Tandy did remark that you were still only twenty-four, but I reminded him that I am going on twenty-four, too. Besides, you are my only male relative." She paused. Her natural honesty then made her blurt out, "I wish I'd understood about you earlier, Timothy! I always thought you were—— I was afraid of you, Timothy. Truly. I thought you were just like your mother! You see how stupid I was? I didn't understand."

"I am not in the least like my mother," said Timothy gently, thinking of Cynthia's natural sympathy, kindness, joy in living, love for all that was beautiful and graceful, her foolish generosity and instant warmth. He shook his head and repeated, "I am not in the least like her, Caroline."

"And Melinda's just like her," said Caroline, and she was ugly again.

Timothy was startled, seeing that abrupt change of expression and the naked hatred. He wanted to say, "You are wrong. Melinda is a love." But his remarkable intuitiveness warned him that everything would be ruined if he said that. It was only too obvious that Caroline hated the young girl. This made him reflect again. Would Caroline destroy him when he married Melinda? Yes, she was capable of any recklessness, he now discerned, to satisfy her furious loathings.

Caroline, blushing, was murmuring, "I am going to be married, Timothy."

"What!" he exclaimed. "What!" The old ladies muttering and complaining about him stared at him, aghast at his male vehemence in so genteel a setting.

Caroline was blushing even more; worse, that damned beautiful smile was on her face again. Timothy pushed back his chair, and his pale eyes sparkled. "What are you talking about?" he demanded rudely. (All that money! In the hands of an unknown, accursed stranger!) "Who is he?" said Timothy, and he was so agitated and so incredulous that his usually smooth and controlled voice was rough with rage. "Some European fortune hunter?"

Caroline was immediately reminded of Mr. Brookingham. "No, no," she said hurriedly. (How kind Timothy was.) She added soothingly, "Dear Timothy, I'd never do that. I thought you understood that I am no longer interested in European affairs, except as they affect the stock market. I dislike Europe intensely, and Europeans. They frighten me. So knowing. So ruthless. Please don't look so worried, Timothy. The man I am going to marry—I have known him since I was about ten years old."

A Bostonian! Timothy, a Bostonian himself, knew these Bostonians. Let the swine once get control of all that money, and he, Timothy, would be out in the cold.

"Who?" said Timothy. (God damn the bastard! The sneaking, sly swine who had done this to him, probably laughing behind his back!)

"You don't know him," said Caroline apologetically. (Dear Timothy, how concerned he was for her!) "But when you know him you will like him immensely.

"Please don't worry, dear Timothy. Tom is so good, so kind."

"Tom who?" he almost shouted. "Tom Adams, Tom Graves, Tom Winthrop, Tom Burnett?"

"Tom Sheldon," said Caroline, suddenly aware of the avid attention of the old widows and spinsters about her. "Please be calm, dear Timothy. You don't know him. He lives in Lyme."

"In Lyme?" Timothy repeated, stupefied. No one lived in that wretched seaside village! Timothy began to sweat. "We don't know anyone in Lyme, Caroline!"

"I do. He builds houses, Timothy. His father was a handy man, and then he and Tom began to build little summer cottages and houses. You can see them all over."

Timothy was absolutely dumb. He could only stare at Caroline; a dull and sickening ache struck the back of his head. Then he muttered, "Sheldon? I don't know any Sheldons."

"Of course you don't, Timothy," said Caroline. "You were only once in Lyme, if you remember, and it was only for a day, and you were about fourteen then. And Tom was about sixteen and helping his father, doing chores in the village."

I'm not really hearing this! Timothy thought. I'm going mad. He said faintly, "Doing chores in the village?" And then louder, "A *handy man?*"

Caroline stopped smiling. She looked aside and frowned anxiously. The horror and disbelief in Tom's voice had finally impressed themselves upon her. She remembered now her own thoughts about old Thomas Sheldon. She had thought this, she recalled very clearly; she had thought it even this morning on the train, and she had been full of anger against Beth.

She looked furtively at her seething cousin; she had never seen Timothy so disturbed. His coolness was completely shattered.

"You aren't serious, Caroline! This is impossible!"

She murmured, "I suppose it sounds so. I didn't really understand how it would sound to you; I never thought of it. Do try to be patient with me, Timothy, while I explain." And in that uncertain stammering voice which she always used when disconcerted or ashamed or frightened, she told Timothy of Tom Sheldon. He listened intently, never moving his pale eyes from her face. There was no pity in him now, no gratitude, no exultation.

When she was done, he passed his hand over his smooth light hair and then stared blankly at the table. What else could one expect, he asked himself, of the daughter of a wretched nobody, a tramp from nowhere, possessing no family, no background? One could expect precisely this, a comedy of vulgarity, of lewd barnyard scuffling and clutching, of a mating between a village dolt and a lumbering female fool. They would breed a horde of ugly, featureless brats who would inherit all that money. All that money!

"Caroline, please listen to me." He made himself smile at her like a brother, full of indulgence and patience. "I am now the only male relative you have; I have a responsibility for you. You are alone in the world; you are a female, still young and unprotected. But you are a traveled, educated woman. You are the heiress to one of America's greatest fortunes." He thought he would stifle in that hot room full of its odors of wax, peppermint, old bodies, and heated wool. A thin shaft of hot copper sunlight struck his arched fingers where they were pressed on the stiff linen of the tablecloth.

"You could marry any distinguished man in the world," he went on, clearing his tight throat. "You could marry a prince if you wished. Yet you now tell me——" He paused. He could not speak Tom's name or talk of his background; his white eyelids dropped over his eyes, and he squeezed them together so that they were parched wrinkles in his face. He shook his head over and over.

"Have you thought, Caroline, what your father would think of this madness?"

Caroline's large mouth wavered. She said, "Yes, Timothy. I've thought. The night Papa died—there was a meeting in our suite in Geneva and all the gentlemen were what you would call distinguished, and their wives were of excellent family, or at least they had fortunes. They wanted to embroil Papa in something infamous—I must tell you of it sometime—and Papa rejected them and their plans. He despised them." She stopped and then pressed the damp palms of her hands together in an urgent gesture, almost passionate. "One of the men was a Mr. Montague Brookingham. You may have heard of him. His father died recently and he is now Lord Halnes. He wanted to marry me, Timothy; he had spoken to Papa about it. He was abhorrent to me. And just before Papa died he indicated that he didn't want me to marry that man; he wanted me to go home and forget all of them, all those you speak of as distinguished. So Papa would have understood about Tom." She looked at him pleadingly.

"Your father knew about him; he knew this feller?"

"Timothy, please. Don't call Tom—that. No, Papa never knew anything about him. I was going to tell him that very night. And then he died." Tears came into her eyes, and she swallowed.

He did not speak; the arched fingers curled on the tablecloth as he struggled for control. Caroline continued: "But I had already made up my mind earlier in the evening that even if Papa objected I'd go home, back to Tom. Tom is clean and good. I love him, Timothy."

The simplicity of her final words would have moved a less relentless and rapacious man than Timothy Winslow. But they only infuriated him.

"Your father would have disinherited you, Caroline. I knew him very well; I have studied his whole career almost all my life, and especially since I have been in that law office."

Caroline shook her head. "No, Timothy, you are wrong. I know it now."

He wanted to say to her, "You can't do this disgusting thing. Do you know to whom your money rightfully belongs? To the Esmonds, who have had to endure your contemptible nobody of a father for too long! It was the money of an Esmond lady which he confiscated, a full two hundred thousand dollars."

He was hardly able to control himself, and it was a curious emotion for Timothy Winslow, who had never before permitted any human being to outrage him like this. But even in his sickening anger he knew that a wrong word now would wreck all his future, would send Caroline from him forever. So he said, "Caroline, you are really so inexperienced. This—this man—he knows who you are and all about your fortune."

She interrupted him eagerly. "Yes, Timothy, he has always known. It isn't of any consequence to him."

He gaped at her. He put both smoothing hands over his head now.

"Tom isn't interested in my money," Caroline went on. "He wants to build a little house for us in Lyme. We'll live very quietly. That is why I am putting so much of my money into investment trusts which my bankers and your partners will take care of for me. I never intend to touch the principal of Papa's money; we'll live simply on what Tom earns as a builder of little houses and some of the interest on my fortune. And I do plan to increase that fortune, as Papa would want me to do."

Oh, God, thought Timothy. He studied Caroline with sharp intensity. Nothing would change that bovine mind; nothing could convulse that lump of stolid flesh. She would have her peasant, and all that money would be his and a brood of animals'. The money would never be Timothy's and Melinda's, Melinda who had grace and beauty and intelligence and who deserved this fortune and whose children would deserve it. Melinda deserved mansions and castles, homes in New York, Boston, Paris, London, on the Mediterranean. But this creature would keep it locked in her milkmaid's hands, then give it to her faceless cubs.

He had to conceal his face; he knew that; he shadowed it with one long hand. Caroline was touched. "Dear Timothy, it will all be well," she said. "Please don't be disturbed. I want you to meet Tom very soon. I want you to be at our wedding." When he did not answer, she added timidly, "You may have thought I was impulsive today, Timothy. But I wasn't. You see, for many years Papa talked of you; he admired you so much. You are my cousin, and I only wish I had known you better before."

Timothy dropped his hand to the table with the exhaustion only great emotion can bring. But he could not bear to look at her. He forgot what he now owed Caroline; he felt as one feels who has been irretrievably robbed. He accepted this fact; nobody could persuade Caroline from this disaster, which was his own. He knew her stubbornness, her rocklike immovability.

He thought of his mother. What would she think of this? If only she had some influence over her niece! Damn her, why had she inspired such hatred in Caroline?

He said, "Caroline, take some time to think about this—matter. Don't be hasty. It's all your life, you know. If later you find you've made a mistake, it will be a calamity for you."

Caroline smiled with gratitude. "I'm not making a mistake, Timothy. I know Tom too well. I want you two to be friends."

When Timothy returned to his hot but austere room that night he found a letter from his mother. He did not want to read it immediately; he knew her annoying vivacity, the way she had of making something trivial into an enthusiastic adventure, though her letters, since that dog had died, had been somewhat subdued.

Listlessly he dropped the letter on his bedside table and walked up and down his room in the fervid twilight. He told himself repeatedly that there was nothing he could do. A wrong move, and he would only destroy himself. If he went to that bumpkin rascal, Sheldon, who was licking his lips in anticipation over the Ames fortune, Caroline would be hopelessly offended. A gentleman would listen to a gentleman, but what could a gentleman say to a cowherd? There was nothing he, Timothy Winslow, could do about it.

Then he picked up his mother's letter absently. He lit the oil lamp near his narrow bed and tore open the envelope. He recognized from Cynthia's handwriting that the old girl was vivacious again; there were all those loops and twirls. He made a contemptuous sound and began to read. It was a short letter for Cynthia, and, as he feared, it scintillated.

"Darling, you must come home immediately! I have the most marvelous news for you! I have so much to tell you!"

"And I, madam," said Timothy grimly, and aloud, "have so much to tell you too."

CHAPTER SIX

A few days before the meeting between Caroline and her cousin, Timothy Winslow, something very remarkable indeed happened to Cynthia.

She had been very restless and suffering from what was fashionably called "the vapors." She sat in her warm and silent little garden one day, dressed loosely in a white silk-and-lace robe; she had rolled up the sleeves, and her ivory arms were translucent in the green light that fell through the trees. She was considering her life with unusual sadness. She thought of John Ames with pain and loneliness and a sick longing. She had never loved any man but John in this particular way. Now it was as if her life, pleasant, full of flowers, music, laughter, beauty, and grace, had been convulsed, shattered, darkened, abandoned. She had not been John's wife; she endured the secret anguish and torment of a widow. Her friends were sympathetic, but after all, they would say to her consolingly, he was only her brother-in-law and not her husband. It is quite different, the widows would tell her with sighing significance. For the first time Cynthia wished she had married John Ames. She could then be honestly and openly grieved.

Cynthia, who held many moral laws lightly, knew bitterly now that a woman in an ambiguous situation must hide her emotions and must permit those emotions to fester in her silently. She controlled herself as much as possible, not for her own sake, but for the sake of Melinda, whose young life must not be ruined and despised. But it was almost too arduous for the sorrowing woman. Three months had passed since John had died. Cynthia longed to weep openly, to let her grief be known so it would not poison her in the dark nights.

She was a woman to whom the intimate presence of a man was absolutely necessary. Her nature was ardent and graceful, and in many ways dependent. Her bed was not a new widow's bed; it was nonetheless empty. She might be middle-aged, but her passions were young and had been aroused only by John Ames. Her beautiful body was as urgent as a girl's. Care and coddling of her flesh, her naturally vivacious and interested personality, good health, and eager awareness of living had kept her unusually young for her forty-five years. Moreover, there had been little stress in her life, and much love and affection. These had prolonged her youthfulness. In all but actual years she was like a woman of thirty.

So, in spite of herself, she thought of marrying, in her hunger. But the desirable men were already married; the widowers were cautious and were looking for younger women; the bachelors were beyond desire and unhealthy. She was also a woman who, though the beneficiary of a life trust, would have nothing substantial to leave a prudent man. She was beautiful and desirable, but in the eyes of Boston men these were not enough. She was condemned to be an observer of life from this time onward and no longer a participant. There would be no nights of excitement, no confidences in the dark, no smothered laughter and kisses, no warm turning in arms, no sense of being of the first importance to any man. She had no desire for another liaison, though the opportunities were there among disgruntled husbands and a few wary bachelors. It must be marriage or nothing, and the nothing was terrible to Cynthia Winslow.

She had not kept Melinda in town this hot and steaming summer. The young girl was sorrowful enough for "Uncle John." So Cynthia had been persuaded by a close friend to let Melinda accompany the family to Newport. The friend was Mrs. Bothwell, who was fond of the girl and who frequently thought of the fortune left her by John Ames. After all, there was her son Alfred. Cynthia was alone in her house; the idea of going to Newport was distasteful to her. Had there been any opportunity of meeting a strange man of substance and charm she would have gone. But she knew there was no such opportunity. She could see the dreary years ahead, years of discretion, emptiness, loneliness, and deprivation. Melinda would marry and have her own affairs. She, Cynthia, would live virtuously and in desolation in this house, bored and silent. She highly regarded those who were engrossed in good works, but good works as the sole aim of life repelled her. The world was made for joy, also, and pleasure and intimacy. I should really go to New York, she thought restlessly in her garden on this hot, still day. But she knew she could not. A lone woman in New York was in a most anomalous position.

Locusts sang in the crab-apple trees; a wet, hot wind blew over the flower beds. Large yellow bumblebees hummed stridently in the silence. A bird drank from a distant stone bath. A rabbit timidly poked its head from the end of the garden, a leaf in its working mouth. "Go away," said Cynthia listlessly. "I don't plant petunias for your supper." She lifted the weight of her lovely hair from her neck and threw it over the back of her low chair. She fanned herself and fluttered a perfumed handkerchief over her moist forehead and cheeks. Nothing, she thought, could be more oppressive than Boston in August. Yet when she instinctively caught the shadow of autumn in the hollows under the trees, in the frantic exuberance of the flowers, in the light of the vivid sky, in the color of the little crab apples, in the faint browning of the grass, she was unbearably depressed. She hated winter; she now even hated the topaz deepening of autumnal Boston. Melinda, it was arranged, was to go to school in England in late September.

Not Switzerland! Cynthia thought of those five months she had spent in Switzerland, immured in a luxurious villa near Lucerne, awaiting the birth of Melinda, when she was ostensibly supposed to be traveling all over the Continent as a gay widow.

"Darling John," she murmured now, "I should have married you. It might have been awful, but then again I might have been able to do something with you. I am no poor little Ann. Besides," she added with a faint and mournful smile, "as your widow I should have had a great deal more money and so should have been much more desirable."

A perspiring maid came from the house, gliding over the grass as if she had no legs at all. She has forgotten the brandy, thought Cynthia irritably, aware that she had been drinking too much since John died. The maid carried a card on a silver tray, and Cynthia, yawning, picked it up. There was really no one in town, except some very elderly and tiresome widows who lived on back streets. Had one of them really emerged in her rusty black and decided to pay Cynthia Winslow a visit? Cynthia read the card: "Montague Lord Halnes."

"Who on earth?" Cynthia murmured, frowning, then remembering not to frown. She could not afford wrinkles. She knew no Mr. Montague Lord Halnes. She said so, very shortly, to the maid. But the maid was an Englishwoman, and she was awed; she curtsied, to Cynthia's astonishment, not to Cynthia, but to the card. "It is Lord Halnes, Mrs. Winslow," she said with a touch of superiority in her voice. "A very famous family in England. The old lord died nearly two months ago, and the present lord came into his title and the estates. I read about it in the papers from home."

"Oh?" said Cynthia, sitting up and vaguely excited. "But why should he come to see me?" She shook out her hair, and the long bright curls fell down her back.

The maid smirked importantly. "Indeed, Mrs. Winslow, I do not know. But Lord Halnes was a Mr. Montague Brookingham, and I do remember overhearing that he was a friend of Mr. Ames."

Cynthia sat up even straighter and was more excited. Of course, Montague Brookingham. John had spoken of him often and admiringly.

"His lordship is awaiting Mrs. Winslow," said the maid with some reproof. Americans did not keep nobility waiting; but then, Americans were very ill bred and ignorant.

Cynthia felt the first prickling of animation she had felt for months. She examined the smooth white card and its fine engraving. "Oh dear," she said. "I am not dressed. I do wish he had written first. Why, I might have been out of town!" The very thought was calamitous. Then she paused. "Lady—Halnes—she is not with him?"

"I believe his lordship is not married," said the maid coldly. Cynthia smiled at her. "Do you study the Almanach de Gotha in your spare time, Jordan?" she asked mischievously.

"Certainly, madam," said Jordan, whose accent was becoming more and more British each time she spoke. Cynthia thought she was covertly sneering at her, but a sharp glance reassured her that the woman was entirely serious. "There is a whole page devoted to the family in the Almanach," added Jordan. "They go back to King John."

"I must dress," said Cynthia. And then she saw herself as a man would see her, in thin white silk and lace, with loosened and warmly disheveled hair, with bare and pretty arms, and with a face flushed delicately in the heat. The maid stood apart to let her mistress stand, but Cynthia leaned back indolently in her chair and smiled.

"On second thought, bring Lord Halnes out to me in the garden," she said.

Jordan was horrified. She looked closely at Cynthia; the white silk and lace only half obscured the handsome high breast, and it was obvious that the lady wore no stays and that there was little under the loose gown, if anything. It was indecent! Nobodies—and Jordan was convinced all Americans, including the President, were nobodies—did not receive nobility like this, half nude in little city gardens. It was shameful. Had Mrs. Winslow no sense of the proprieties at all, no self-respect, no pride? She was dressed for the boudoir, like one of those creatures one spoke about only in whispers and behind one's hand.

"Don't stand there gaping," said Cynthia impatiently. "Didn't you hear me? Bring Lord Halnes out to me here. And fetch brandy. You might consult with Cook; it is possible that his lordship will have dinner with me."

"You don't wish tea, madam?" asked Jordan desperately. "It is teatime."

"Brandy," said Cynthia with emphasis, waving the woman away with her lace handkerchief. "Do I ever have tea when I am alone?"

Crushed and appalled, Jordan sailed leglessly over the grass to the back door of the house. How does she manage it? thought Cynthia, shaking out her soft and luminous laces and observing with pleasure how her long thighs and calves were lovingly implied under the thin silk. She became excited again. A rich and unmarried nobleman! Englishmen were tall and slender and handsome and very ruddy, especially the nobility. They were charming. Cynthia's heart began to beat rapidly. Why was he visiting her? For what purpose? Had he a secret message from poor John? She moved her chair a trifle and let two long curls flow over one shoulder.

Jordan appeared again, leading the way for Lord Halnes, practically genuflecting at each step, thought Cynthia. Then she looked at Lord Halnes and was sharply disappointed. What an undistinguished, rather short, and obviously portly man! He resembled a dull stockbroker or upper bookkeeper or obscure businessman. His quiet face was plump and expressionless, with a small double chin, unremarkable features; he was partly bald, also, and his clothing was entirely too heavy for this climate. Why, he's not even as tall as I am, thought Cynthia, depressed, and he's probably very tedious. She made no move as he came toward her over the grass, visibly perspiring.

Lord Halnes, wearing an appropriately grave expression and not appearing to see anything about him, was really acutely aware of and astonished at the beauty of the woman half reclining under the trees. Well, well, he thought with pleasure. Johnny did himself well, after all. What a handsome creature. She looks hardly more than a girl. And a devil, if I'm not mistaken. Good old Johnny!

John had not spoken very much of Cynthia; he had not even hinted of his affair with her. Yet when he had spoken, and with reluctance, his face had warmed, the color of his eyes had become actually human, and his abrupt manner had softened. It needed a very perceptive man—and Lord Halnes was most acute and perceptive—to understand that men like John Ames did not suddenly change at the mention of a woman's name if inspired only by a brotherly and distant affection. Moreover, there was that package in his, Lord Halnes', pocket.

He had come to within about eight feet of the silent Cynthia before he smiled, and Cynthia was suddenly astounded. Not only was this man charming, but he was clever and fascinating also. The satanic light in his eyes, the curious expression of subtle evil, the virile power stirred Cynthia and delighted her. He bowed to her and murmured in a voice that sounded marvelous to Cynthia, "Mrs. Winslow? I am sorry to intrude. I should have written you first. But I am here only until tomorrow, and to see you in behalf of my old friend, John Ames."

What a lovely vixen, he thought agreeably. What great gray eyes and gilt lashes, what a long white throat, what distracting hair, and what a figure. Has she anything on under that silk and lace? Possibly not. But she is a lady of breeding, that is very obvious, even if she is careless. Johnny had taste, at least.

The silk and lace whispered softly as Cynthia held out her hand, and they exhaled a hint of intriguing perfume. Cynthia murmured, "How kind of you to come, Lord Halnes. A message from John? How thoughtful. Please sit down in that willow chair; it is quite comfortable. How kind of you." She said to the bedazzled Jordan, "Brandy. At once, please. You will have brandy, won't you?" she added to Montague.

"Indeed. A great pleasure," he said, sitting down. His eyes danced on her with approval and enchantment and secret teasing, and Cynthia's heart danced also. It had been a long time since a man had looked at her like this, with appreciative boldness and naughty inspection.

"Of course the English prefer tea. Perhaps?" said Cynthia in seductive tones, as if imparting a meltingly improper suggestion.

"I detest tea," said Montague, leaning back in his chair and continuing his enjoyable inventory. He had dropped his pleasant voice to a warm intimacy.

"I do too," said Cynthia with a soft laugh. They were conspirators in a delicious comedy. They smiled happily together. Cynthia's lashes drooped; between them the smoky gray of her eyes sparkled.

"This is such a surprise," said Cynthia, her voice still murmurous.

"Indeed. Indeed," agreed Lord Halnes, implying a deeper meaning.

"You must forgive me for not moving this hot day and being so—undressed," said Cynthia, indicating her clothing.

"I should not have forgiven you if you had done otherwise," said Lord Halnes with a long slow glance over the graceful length of Cynthia's body.

"How kind. How understanding," said Cynthia, relaxing even more.

"How delightful," said Lord Halnes.

"So good of you," murmured Cynthia. She daintily applied her handkerchief to her forehead; the lace and silk fell back along her arm, revealing it almost to the shoulder. The action hinted of the cleft between her breasts. Lord Halnes was more appreciative than ever. He leaned forward a little. That was really a remarkably slender and supple waist and not the result of whalebone, and that curve of hip! Good old Johnny! If he was not mistaken this would be a wonderful baggage in bed. He was enchanted by the white chin, the fragile pulsation in the lovely temples. Give him an ardent lady in the bedroom rather than a voluptuous trollop. There was considerable skin visible, but this did not embarrass Lord Halnes in the slightest. He was suddenly in love, and the realization shocked him and made him silent for a few moments.

What a wicked man, thought Cynthia, who was not unsophisticated. What a marvelously wicked man. Still murmurous, as if the comedy of naughtiness were now in full stride, she asked him where he was staying, and when he told her the name of his hotel she made a gay grimace. "Appalling," she confided.

"Very," agreed Montague. "As bad as London. Do you know, Boston reminds me of London." How could he arrange to get this dazzling creature into bed? It seemed a most urgent matter. He had never felt this urgent before, and it was not only exciting but an absolute necessity. If she was mourning for old Johnny it was certainly not evident.

"Dear London," sighed Cynthia, who loathed London. They looked intensely into each other's eyes and then suddenly burst out laughing together. It was the first time Cynthia had laughed since John had died.

Jordan brought the brandy; her face had a fixed and reverent expression. Lord Halnes took the tray easily from her hands and placed it on the wicker table near Cynthia. Jordan retreated. She could not understand. His lordship had not appeared in the least shocked at the madam's dishabille, nor disturbed by her shamelessness, her immodesty. Ah, these were new and distressing times. "Allow me, dear Mrs. Winslow," said Montague, bending over the tray. He poured a little brandy into one crystal glass. Cynthia said languidly, "A trifle more, please. I do enjoy brandy."

"Excellent," said Lord Halnes, filling her glass and then his own. He gave the glass to Cynthia; their fingers touched; it was electrifying. There was no doubt of it, thought his lordship. He was in love. He was absolutely bewitched. This made him thoughtful. There were always complications in life, but he was accustomed to dealing with them. He had not even the most passing doubt that he could get Cynthia into bed. She was attracted to him; he knew those mischievous and languishing glances well. It would be a miraculous interlude in a country almost as dull as England. Interlude?

Oh, not an interlude. There must be some permanent arrangement, satisfactory to both, but with no responsibility.

Lord Halnes, mused Cynthia. Wonderful man. A really wicked man. He would never be tedious. There was an excitement about him, even if he was English. He was also very, very rich, enormously rich. There was possibly a castle in England. Cynthia said as she sipped her brandy, "I never see an Englishman without remembering the frightening time when I was presented to Her Majesty."

Montague was surprised. "Yes?" he said.

"I was an Esmond," said Cynthia. "Of the very old Esmond family in Surrey. Of course we have been here at least a hundred years. My great-great-grandfather was a younger son. We are distantly related to Lord Baltimore."

Montague was silent; he sipped his brandy also and mentally commented that it was extraordinarily fine brandy. But he was really considering the new gentle note in Cynthia's voice—what an adorable voice! An American lady was distinctly different from an English lady. But this lady had been an Esmond. He knew the English Esmonds very well. Improvident, if charming. Mrs. Winslow was not only distractingly beautiful, she was intelligent and very subtle. This was somewhat unnerving. She had caught a hint of his thoughts. This would not be an easy matter. Montague became serious and put down his glass. He must have her, at almost any cost, except marriage, of course.

"Your niece, Miss Ames, is the daughter of your sister, I understand, Mrs. Winslow."

Something had gone wrong, thought Cynthia, deeply vexed. She said, sighing, "Yes. My twin sister, my dear Ann. Isn't it unfortunate that Caroline doesn't resemble her? You have met Caroline, certainly."

"Yes," said Lord Halnes, feeling genuinely despondent. But there was nothing else for it. "You see, old Johnny was quite sympathetic to the idea of a marriage between me and Caroline."

Cynthia was so jolted that she sat upright abruptly, spilling some of the brandy in her slender lap. Lord Halnes immediately sprang to his feet and, murmuring, used his handkerchief to mop up the liquid. His fingers and the back of his hand came into contact with the thin silk, and he felt the warm and velvety flesh under it. His head quite whirled; a hot thrill ran through him. "Oh, pardon me, pardon me," he stammered.

Cynthia watched the trembling fingers with a faint smile of sudden satisfaction. The fingers were not anxious to leave her. She found a tiny fold or two of silk that needed attention. The handkerchief slowed, dragged, almost halted. Cynthia's perfume filled the air as an early breeze quickened. She let her right arm lean briefly against Montague's shoulder. His face was brilliantly scarlet now and considerably bloated, and there was a congested look about his nose. He sat down, panting a little. "So sorry," he said.

"Really nothing," murmured Cynthia. "So clumsy of me." She paused and looked at him with delicate incredulity. "You were speaking of Caroline?"

"Yes," said Lord Halnes reluctantly. He was having some difficulty with his breathing. Muttering an apology, he passed his handkerchief over his chubby face. Now that he was not smiling he looked again like a respectable upper clerk in a banking house. "It was Johnny, you know. He and I were very close friends; he thought the match very suitable."

Cynthia sipped reflectively at her glass. This gave her an opportunity to display her captivating profile with the finely carved nose, the full rosy lower lip, the clear white brow. She let Montague dwell on that profile for a little. "I see," she said. "But Caroline is hardly twenty-four. And American girls are quite immature compared with European young ladies. She is so inexperienced; I am her only close relative." Cynthia sighed, and her breast stirred. "It is only natural that I should feel some responsibility for my sister's daughter."

"I understand," said Montague. He refilled his glass with some agitation. Damn the beautiful devil; she was deliberately seducing him. Under other circumstances he would have been elated. This was a bad spot; he must get over it quickly so that more important matters could be tenderly explored. "In America," he continued, "marriages are romantic. It is all love, isn't it? But in England and on the Continent"—he did not like England to be considered part of Europe—"things are a little more sensible. Money and a good match are the thing, though it is not true for America."

Cynthia laughed musically. "Perhaps not. But it is so in Boston. A man doesn't expect, in Boston, to be lucky enough to get beauty and money together. In fact, an attractive face is somewhat of a drawback to a Bostonian and just a trifle suspect. And what more does a man need but money?" She turned a bland yet sparkling face upon Montague, and her eyes were innocent.

He could not look away. Cynthia smiled gently, showing her small white teeth; she nibbled her lower lip thoughtfully, and this distracted Montague to an inner frenzy. "Have you seen Caroline in Lyndon or Lyme?" she asked, having detected the frantic gleam in his eyes.

"No. Not yet. After all, she is a young lady, alone. I thought she might be here."

"Oh dear, no. Caroline and I are not very good friends, I am afraid. It is not my fault, I assure you, Lord Halnes."

"Please call me by my Christian name. Please."

Cynthia raised her eyebrows.

"Montague," he pleaded.

"Then you must call me Cynthia, now that you are almost a member of the family." She tilted her head on her long neck and gave him a dazzling look.

"Cynthia," he repeated. He was certain he had never heard a lovelier name. He was becoming fatuous, he thought. If he did not control himself he would find himself groveling like a clodhopper. He regarded Cynthia's elegant hands; he remembered the satin touch of them.

"We were speaking of Caroline," said Cynthia.

"Eh? Oh yes," said Montague a little stupidly. "So we were. You have no objection to my——"

"Becoming my nephew?" interrupted Cynthia, dimpling. "As I am forty-three, and you, I believe, are a little—a very little—older, the situation is amusing."

"I can't believe you are forty-three," said Montague sincerely.

"How kind of you! Frankly, I am not yet forty-three. I was married very young. I was only eighteen when my son Timothy was born." Again she turned a bland face on him. He did not doubt her word at all. His infatuation was increasing at an alarming rate. He had seen more beautiful women before; he had possessed more beautiful women. But he knew, as a judge of womankind, that Cynthia not only was pretty but possessed wit and brains. She was not only a lady but perfectly cultivated and sweet as honey. John Ames had been her lover, yet she exuded a kind of purity and tantalizing virginity. This is no woman of light virtue, thought the unhappy Montague.

"May I ask how Caroline regards your offer?" asked Cynthia seriously.

"I haven't made it yet. But Johnny, poor Johnny, told me a day or two before he died that he would extend my offer to Caroline. I have reasons to believe that he did so."

"Oh?" Cynthia's tone was cool and abstracted, but she felt sick. How intolerable this was, how frightful. This man was not only wealthy and titled, but he was a man she understood; she was already helplessly attracted to him; when he had mopped the brandy from her clothing she had experienced the blissful response she had thought she would never know again. And Caroline—Caroline!—stood in the way. For the first time in her life Cynthia knew violent hatred. It caused her to flush, to become prettier, for her eyes flashed. Then she was sick and abandoned again, and only her training prevented her from bursting into tears. Anyone but Caroline, she thought, anyone but that dreadful, sullen lump of a girl who had insulted her so grossly. How cruel life was, how brutal, how disgusting. She had never thought this before, but the repellent aspects of life now overwhelmed her. I will go to New York! she vowed silently. I couldn't stay here and see him with her—that dreadful, sullen lump of a girl. Lady Halnes—Caroline! It was only the money. Montague did not need that money, but when did a man of his kind not want more even if it were attached to a Caroline Ames? He needed it for wider power; the very quality in him which fascinated her was the quality that would prevent him from marrying a fortuneless widow.

"And?" she murmured, fighting the tightness in her throat.

He started. "And?" he repeated dully. "Oh yes. I must admit that Caroline did not seem entirely pleased. This is only a conjecture of mine, please forgive me. But when I saw her just a few hours before poor old Johnny died I was certain that her father had mentioned the matter to her."

Cynthia became sharply interested. "Were you, indeed? I am deeply attached to Caroline; I am her aunt. I should like her to be happy. What was her response? This is all very subtle, it seems."

"Not very," said the dejected nobleman. He was very certain now that Cynthia would not be easy to capture; she might not be captured at all, under the circumstances. But that would be intolerable. He must not let himself think it. "Caroline, as you may know, isn't subtle. She is silent, but very direct." He paused. "I always felt that she detested me."

Cynthia's eyebrows rose in a splendid imitation of disbelief. "Surely you were mistaken!" she cried. "How could that be so—Montague? Even Caroline would know that you were offering her a great honor!"

He was delighted and as flattered as a schoolboy. He was lighthearted again. He smiled. "I don't think Caroline considered it an honor. We haven't exchanged any real conversations, you know. She is a trifle difficult to understand."

"I do know," said Cynthia sympathetically. She let her eyes become large and humid. "Poor child. She has had a most wretched life. I must tell you of it someday. It was all her father's fault. I did my best, truly I did."

"I am sure of that!" he exclaimed. He pulled his chair closer to her.

"I'm afraid that I wasn't very successful. Ah well." Cynthia let herself muse again. Then she held out her glass to be refilled once more. She laughed sweetly. "In a way, this is very amusing. You see, I am considering remarrying; a Boston gentleman. I have known him from childhood, and he is now a widower. You must really give me a little time! It would be absurd for you to marry Caroline before I marry, wouldn't it? A little improper." She fluttered her hands and gazed at him appealingly. "You will wait, won't you, for at least a few months? It would be much better if it were at least a year from the time John died." She was suddenly shocked; she had actually forgotten that she had loved John Ames. She turned quite pale. Montague felt a spasm of vicious jealousy. He thought that Cynthia had paled with remembered grief, that she mourned.

But what had she said? That she was going to be married. He said with actual rage, "You are marrying? But, as you have said, Cynthia, it would be proper to wait a year, wouldn't it?"

She heard the anger and she saw the male fury and hostility on his plump face, the utter refusal to believe her, to tolerate this thing. Contentedly she eyed him with softness. Really, she thought, he may be a great man, a powerful man, an extremely brilliant man, but a woman of finesse can manipulate him as easily as if he were a miserable shopkeeper. As easily as if he had been John.

"You've forgotten," she said gently. "I am not John's widow. I am only his sister-in-law. It would not be in the least improper for me to marry in November."

"In November!" he cried. "Impossible!"

"Impossible?" She pretended astonishment. "Why should that be? After all, I am almost forty-three. I am no schoolgirl." She assumed hauteur and let her eyes show incredulity at his presumption, and a measure of outrage. "But we were speaking of Caroline," she said coldly. "Not of me. I was wrong to confide my private affairs to one I have just met; please forgive me. You will see Caroline, of course, before you leave Boston?"

He did not answer her; in fact, he had hardly heard her. His undistinguished features appeared swollen, and he looked at her as if he hated her. She was attracted to him; he knew all the signs. She had led him up the garden path and then had coolly abandoned him. She was an elusive devil; she was after something. He wanted to pull her from her chair and kiss her roughly. He moistened his lips.

"No?" said Cynthia in a fragile tone.

"I'm sorry," he muttered. Then, "I see. You were asking if I were going to see Caroline. That is why I came." He fell morosely silent, his eyes still lustfully on her face.

"She refuses to come to this house," said Cynthia, now very satisfied. "She will not see me. I believe she was a little jealous."

"Why?" he asked bluntly.

"She thought I had some influence over her father."

"Did you?" he asked more bluntly. He refused to dance any longer in a silly minuet. So she was raising her eyebrows again, was she, and becoming haughty? Be damned to her.

Cynthia smiled and showed her white teeth. She understood. She played with the long lace on her arm and looked at him frankly. "Caroline thought so. And perhaps I did. But not to her hurt, I assure you. You see, my sister and I were twins. John adored my dear Ann."

He shifted restively on his chair. The heat had lessened in the garden, but his complexion was fiery. "Did he adore you also, Cynthia?"

"How dare you?" she exclaimed, really angry now.

"I adore you," he said heavily. "And I've known you less than an hour. Please. Please, Cynthia. Listen to me. My God, I suppose I've been an insulting blackguard, and you are quite right to be outraged. If you wish, I'll leave at once. I deserve to be dismissed."

Cynthia was silent. But there was a rapid exultation rising in her. She kept her face cold and aloof, however. "It is unlike an Englishman to insult a lady," she said finally. "But considering that you are going to marry Caroline, that you will be my nephew"—she let him think of that for an instant—"I feel constrained to forgive you."

"Thank you," he said gratefully, and Cynthia smiled in herself. "I don't know what possessed me; it is not like me at all. What in heaven's name did I say to you?"

Cynthia let herself show amusement. "You said you adored me. How kind. If I did not know you were an Englishman I should consider you a French gentleman."

His color became even more fiery.

"I must tell Edgar," said Cynthia. "Now that we are to be married I am afraid he is taking me a little for granted. After all, we were children together." She paused and gazed at him with mischief. "I was a trifle hasty. I should really be flattered."

"I don't know what possessed me," repeated Lord Halnes, feeling as if he had been rescued.

Long blue shadows slowly crept over Cynthia. It had been a long time since she had known happiness and bliss. She bathed in them luxuriously. Poor Montague. She had really been very naughty, she reflected. She had deliberately led him on to commit that appalling rudeness. Once a man became helplessly rude, a woman became the victor. Perhaps it would have been a little more tactical to wait for another occasion. But there was no time to be lost, no time for approaches and retreats. He was much more difficult than John.

What was he taking from the pocket of his long coat? It was a flat parcel. He said almost humbly, "You must understand, Cynthia, that John was—fond—of you. A few days before he died he bought this gift; I was with him. He told me that you liked jewelry; he said something about your birthday. He left the gift in the shop to be lengthened and paid for it. Then he died. I went to the shop, where I am well known, and took the gift, and so I have brought it to you. It is little enough to do for poor old Johnny."

Tears came into Cynthia's eyes, and she was more beautiful than ever. Her hands trembled as she opened the package. On a bed of rose velvet lay a brilliant diamond necklace garnished with fine rubies—a slender necklace all intricacy and fire and light. "Oh," said Cynthia with a sob, "dear, dear John." She bowed her head and cried. Her bright long curls fell over her face, which she had partly covered with her hands. She was like a young girl, weeping.

Neither ever knew how it had happened so quickly, but Montague's chair was now beside Cynthia's, and her head was on his shoulder, and he was wiping her wet eyes and face with the first tenderness he had ever known in his life, and he was smoothing her hair lovingly, and he was murmuring the most idiotic things. He knew they were idiotic; he knew that he had been expertly lured and that he had followed, like an absolute maundering fool. He also knew that he loved Cynthia, that she was the first woman he had ever loved, and that he would never let her go. He kissed her flushed, moist cheek almost reverently. "Hush, my love," he said. "Hush."

Some part of himself, objective and cynical, laughed at him. He smiled back at it. He kissed Cynthia again. And then she timidly lifted her full red lips and returned the kiss, and she was all joy, even though she continued to cry sincerely, and the necklace slipped from the smooth silk of her lap and fell into the grass.

Less than an hour and a half had passed since Lord Halnes had stepped into this enchanted garden. He kissed Cynthia and dried her tears. He could not have enough of her kisses.

CHAPTER SEVEN

When Timothy Winslow left the train on this hot day in Boston he was surprised to find not only the family victoria waiting for him, as usual, but his mother also. This was unprecedented; Cynthia had not done this since he had been a child returning home from Groton. She waved a scented handkerchief to him gaily as she sat in the carriage, and he was freshly surprised and intrigued. With the engine hissing and steaming behind him, he came across the boards of the platform, carrying his own light luggage, being a prudent young man and a Bostonian who did not believe in unnecessary tips to porters.

When he had last seen Cynthia she had been very pale and drawn and dressed in deep black and looking all of her forty-five years and even more. Now she appeared hardly more than thirty, and she wore a light blue silk dress, all ruffles and jeweled buttons from breast to ankle, and a few choice gems and blue satin slippers. Even more frivolous was the pretty rose hat perched on her blond head, a hat in the new small "hunting" fashion, with an impudent dip of the brim over one eye, a high crown heaped with bluebells and a single blue plume fluttering in the heated breeze. A wisp of blue veiling hung over her eyes, increasing their gray bright sparkle, and Timothy, after one quick, expert inspection, decided that exuberant nature, rather than paint, was responsible for the color on his mother's fair cheeks and lips.

She reached over the side of the victoria and embraced him with sincere affection and said fervently, "Dear Timothy! How glad I am to see you! Do get in; I have so many wonderful things to tell you!"

He did not doubt it and was highly curious. A demi-widow had been miraculously transformed into a joyous and gracefully ebullient young woman, and, knowing Cynthia, he thought that could only mean that she had a new liaison. Or, at the very least, that some rich old widower had unaccountably left her a fortune, to the scandal of Boston. His mother, he reflected, was a very scandalous woman at heart, in spite of her impeccable reputation and discretion.

The horses, as if infected in their elderly age by Cynthia's obviously high spirits, trotted off briskly through the steaming streets. Cynthia had removed her gloves; her discerning son saw the huge glare of an awe-inspiring diamond on the ring finger of her left hand. He had never seen such a fine gem in all his life. He mentally calculated the cost. He glanced at his mother's radiant profile, as neat and purely cut as a young girl's. There was not a single wrinkle visible about the eyes or the mouth. Aha, he thought, more and more curious.

"Please do not tell me," he said with his chill and knowing smile. "I can guess. You are going to be married, Mama." And he took her long white hand and stared at the ring. "May I ask who is to be my stepfather?"

Cynthia had one deep narrow dimple near her lips, and it deepened as she withdrew her hand. "You'd never guess in all the world," she said. "How clever of you to know, though, dear Timothy, that I am engaged to be married."

"Only a blind man could miss it," said Timothy. Cynthia candidly lifted her hand and pressed the ring to her cheek, and her eyes glowed humidly. "I suppose so," she sighed with a contented smile. She leaned back against the velvet cushions and gave herself up to a brief dream of delight. She was in no hurry to speak; her mouth curved blissfully.

"Who? Where? When?" asked Timothy, thinking over the few eligible men his mother knew.

Cynthia actually giggled. She clasped her hands together tightly and looked at her son with such happiness that he was startled. But she spoke with deceptive demureness. "Who? Ah! You never met him, dear boy, but I'm sure that you must have heard of him. He was one of John's friends."

"Another pirate?" asked Timothy disagreeably, but wondering how large the scoundrel's fortune was and whether he was utterly impossible socially.

"In a way," laughed Cynthia, not at all offended. "But such a distinguished one!" Her voice dropped dramatically. "On September tenth, darling, I will become Lady Halnes!"

"Who?" cried Timothy, actually stunned out of his customary poise.

Cynthia was delighted at his reaction. "Lady Halnes," she repeated, uttering each word deliciously, as though it were completely and totally sweet. "I will be the wife of Montague Lord Halnes, the most adorable man in the world!" And she cried just a little and smiled.

"I don't believe it," murmured Timothy. He took off his straw hat and wiped his face.

"I hardly believe it myself," Cynthia almost whispered.

Timothy felt that he was dreaming. It was only a week ago that this man's name had been mentioned by Caroline Ames with loathing. What had she said? That once her father had wished her to marry him. Timothy, from his close and secret inspection of John Ames' affairs and papers in the safe at Tandy, Harkness and Swift, knew all about Lord Halnes.

"How did you manage it? And where did you meet him? And how long have you known him?" asked Timothy incredulously.

"Is it really less than two weeks ago?" mused Cynthia dreamily. "Why, I seem to have known him all my life. He came to see me in Boston. We were engaged almost immediately. I am having a little dinner tonight, dear Timothy, for just a few friends who are actually coming in from Newport to attend. I wrote them such intriguing letters, they couldn't resist returning to find out! Then you will announce our engagement."

"Good God," said Timothy in a hushed voice.

"Of course," said Cynthia, "my friends must not know how short a time I have known dear Montague. I am going to hint that it has been for many, many years."

"Good God," repeated Timothy.

"You aren't annoyed?" asked Cynthia with sudden concern.

"Annoyed? No. Just stunned. What a remarkable woman you are, dear Mama. To manage this. He must be very susceptible, or something."

"I'm not sure I like that remark," said Cynthia, turning fully to him and regarding him coldly. "He is not in the least susceptible. He hadn't the slightest idea of becoming engaged to me until two hours after we met."

Timothy could not help it. He was not a young man who laughed easily, but now he burst out laughing, and after a moment Cynthia joined him. Cynthia could not remember that her son had ever kissed her spontaneously, but now he leaned toward her and kissed her smartly on her perfumed cheek. She was deeply moved and put her sparkling hand on his shoulder briefly. "Dear Timothy," she murmured.

She said in a more sprightly voice, "Of course I have deducted two or three years from my age, dearest. I was hardly more than eighteen when you were born."

"Interesting," said Timothy. "And you didn't marry my father until you were twenty."

She struck him coquettishly on the arm. "Don't be tiresome, dear. I am merely exercising a woman's prerogative; I am deducting only two or three years. I am telling you this so you won't commit a faux pas when you meet my darling Montague."

"I see," said Timothy, still more than slightly dazed. Why, the man's fortune was even greater than John Ames'. And what would that mean for Timothy Winslow? He would be the heir to at least a portion of that formidable fortune. Then he felt less exultant.

"I seem to recall that he was the youngest son of three and that he inherited the title and the estates very recently after his father died. But titles and estates descend to rightful heirs, don't they? Such as living children, second cousins, and what not. That's British law. And how can it be that a man like Lord Halnes would marry someone who can't give him a rightful heir to hold onto the booty?"

Cynthia was shocked. "My dear boy, I'm not obsolete, even if I am your mother! Old Mrs. Brewster had her last child when she was almost fifty! Dear me!"

Timothy looked at her with admiration. The old girl was quite capable of presenting Lord Halnes with an heir, and no doubt a son at that. He was certain that she would not only try but would succeed superbly.

"I will forgive your crudely youthful remark," said Cynthia graciously. "But then, I am realistic myself; that is why I agreed to an early marriage."

"'Gather ye rosebuds while ye may,'" said Timothy, "'for Father Time is flying.'"

"Lewd, but true," said Cynthia placidly. "There is no time to be lost."

Timothy wondered whether any experiments in that direction had already taken place. He would not put it past his mother, who was delightfully exigent and practical for all her apparent frivolity and irresponsible ways. Looking at her more sharply, he saw the bloom on her face and decided that in all probability the experiment had been embarked upon. He silently congratulated her. But he was still faintly puzzled. From what he knew of Lord Halnes, he could still not accept that such a man had been so expertly seduced into rapid marriage to a middle-aged woman almost immediately upon meeting her. It was vaguely out of character. Then his respect for his mother heightened. He had known, he told himself, that despite her apparent softness and lack of character she had a will that overcame everything and a charm that brought her everything she wished.

He studied her, not as a son, but as a man. He had always admitted his mother was beautiful. Now she appeared extraordinarily seductive and beguiling. He could well imagine how Lord Halnes, the terrible and the ruthless, had been easily and complaisantly led to this agreeable conclusion. Dear Mama! He hoped that any impending child would be a son. Then Mama would indeed be formidable in her influence over her husband and would not forget her first son and her adopted daughter, Melinda. Timothy quite loved his mother now. One had, after all, to bow to superior finesse and astounding genius.

"I love him so," sighed Cynthia.

"Excellent," said Timothy.

"And he adores me," said Cynthia, blissful again.

"No doubt," said Timothy. "I feel that way about you myself."

The green and fretted trees threw their cool shadows on Cynthia's lovely face. She tilted her parasol and breathed deeply. "In some way," she said, "I have come to love Boston lately. But I'll love England even more."

Timothy had forgotten this.

"Dear Montague has a wonderful town house in London," said Cynthia, dreaming again. "And the family seat in Devonshire and a home in Scotland. How marvelous it will be for darling Melinda."

Timothy sat up. Cynthia went on: "We will keep our house in Boston, though. Montague comes at least once a year to America. And he does seem to like Boston, though why, I don't really know. So dull. He is charmed by my house. He hasn't met my dearest Melinda yet, but he will shortly. He has seen her portrait and has fallen in love with the little dear. Do you know, he may possibly adopt her! Wouldn't that be fortunate?"

"You will be taking Melinda to England?" asked Timothy.

She stared at him with astonishment. "Dear Timothy! Where else? She is only thirteen. Did you think I could leave her here when we go to England? And with whom? Dear boy!"

Of course she was right. The carriage drew up before the house on Beacon Street. Timothy said as he helped his mother from the carriage, "I, too, have many things to tell you. And you won't like some of them." He could not keep a vicious note from his voice.

When Timothy left Cynthia alone in her little sitting room, where they had talked for a long time, Cynthia found it necessary after all to resort to the paint pot. She had dressed abstractedly and then had coiled up her hair in the new Grecian fashion. She looked searchingly into her pier mirror; she wore a magnificent Worth dress of pale ivory and gold brocade which revealed bare shoulders and slim white throat. The small train just touched the floor but was draped sufficiently to show golden slippers. She put on John's necklace and her betrothal ring. But I look like a ghost, she thought, sighing, and dipped a slim finger into the paint pot and touched up her cheekbones and then her lips and blew a cloud of perfume upon herself with her atomizer. She had sent a maid for Lord Halnes, and after a soft knock he came in, dressed formally.

"Ah, my love," he said, looking at her with intense pleasure. "You look like a shining bird." And he kissed her lingeringly, just barely standing on his toes.

"Dear Montague," she said, and blinked back her tears. "Do you know, Papa always called me that? And he called my sister a dove."

"Is anything wrong, Cynthia?" he asked after they had seated themselves on a love seat that overlooked the garden.

"A great deal wrong, and a great deal very good," she replied. "That is why I asked you to come here where we can talk in privacy before dinner. Do give me a glass of brandy, dearest. Thank you." She was very serious, and Montague knew that when Cynthia was serious she was not to be taken lightly. She was not a trivial woman.

He listened in silence while she spoke of Caroline, her son, and Caroline's prospective marriage. Then, when she had come to the end of her story, he asked her permission and lit a thin cheroot and smoked quietly for a considerable time, thinking. Cynthia waited anxiously and thought how marvelous it was that she was no longer alone and had such a man to protect and help her and share her worries. His mobile eyebrows moved up and down; various muted expressions drifted across his respectable face; a thin blue smoke rose above his solid round skull.

Then he said, "Well, old girl, there is nothing you can do, is there? Caroline is more than of age. She never struck me as a fool; on the contrary. Dull, but not a fool. She has shown considerable acumen in her choice of your son, who, from what you have already told me, I should judge to be an extraordinary young man."

Cynthia smiled a little. "John always called him pernicious, which was really quite unfair."

"I met him below after he left you," said Lord Halnes. "We introduced ourselves."

"Oh? Good," said Cynthia with a faint question in her pretty voice.

"I think both his mother and his uncle to be good judges of character," he said.

"How ambiguous, darling."

He took her hand and kissed it. "I think not. I'm pernicious, myself. Well, then, I repeat, there is nothing you can do about this unfortunate marriage your niece is about to make."

"I feel so responsible, Montague, for she is my sister's child."

"But she feels no responsibility toward you or to anyone but herself. I repeat, she is not a fool. The clodhopper she will marry may have redeeming qualities, seen through the girl's obstinate eyes. She has known him from childhood; I thought very often that she had a most sensitive eye. Perhaps that is why she always shrank from me."

"How ridiculous! Caroline shrinks from everybody. Unfortunate girl. I never did know why she hated me so. And now she has done all that for Timothy because she thinks it will put me out of countenance! Really! And you say she is no fool."

"She has a single eye, though it is a very sharp one. She sees, in a large measure, what she wishes to see. You should console yourself with the thought that at least she has made an overt gesture to one member of her family. I doubt that she did it only to vex you. She isn't a petty young woman. Clumsy, maladroit, but not petty. I haven't the slightest doubt that she will increase poor old Johnny's fortune. In a way, I pity the young man who is going to marry her. Who would not be wealthy? But, to paraphrase Lord Acton, money corrupts, but absolute money corrupts absolutely. The young man will be corrupted, for all he is a nobleman of the soil, as I think one of your poets put it."

"You are not corrupt, Montague," said Cynthia, smiling again.

"No?" He tilted an eyebrow at her. "My darling, would you love me if I were not, and if I were as I appear to be in sober moments?"

"Of course not," she agreed. "You are quite satanic, and that makes you irresistible. I could never marry a dull man, even if he had your money. I haven't the faintest idea how you got your money and I don't want to know. It is sufficient for me that I love you." She was serious again. "But, Montague! My sister's child. A girl who has great advantages, who would be considered a desirable catch in Boston or anywhere else in the world. She has presence, really. She could look majestic if she weren't so afraid and sullen and suspicious all the time. She will make a heroic dowager if she does not prevent herself. And she's so very, very wealthy, and an Esmond, and I am sure that her dear father was a gentleman born, even if he denied it."

She could never mention John Ames but that Montague felt a hard spasm of jealousy. "There, now, you are frowning," she murmured, and absently kissed his cheek. "Poor Caroline. I had thought perhaps you and I could do something."

"We can do nothing at all," he said decisively. "Any attempt at interference on your part could injure Timothy too."

She nodded. "But such a scandal, Montague. Tongues will be wagging all over Boston. No one will believe it!"

"Then we will give them more reason to wag," he said, smiling once more. "And no one will believe it. How long have we known each other, sweet Cynthia?"

"Twelve—no, thirteen—days," she said.

"Twelve years," he answered. "Didn't you say we should remember that? But it has really been much longer; I've known you all my life. I was simply waiting for you."

He reached to her throat and deftly removed John's necklace and without comment put it on the table. I will save it for Melinda, thought Cynthia, oddly comforted.

CHAPTER EIGHT

After her evening with Timothy Winslow in New York, Caroline went to bed early in order to catch the first train back to Boston the next morning. She had inherited her father's faculty of putting all thoughts out of her mind at will which were not connected with the immediate issue. She had only to think as she lay down: I will take care of that in its season or at such an hour or day, and then she would sleep at once, and usually without dreams or uneasiness.

But tonight she dreamed again of the tower which Herr Ernst had described to her. There was one difference, however. It was her grandfather, David Ames, and not Tom Sheldon who entreated her not to enter the tower and to ignore the groaning of the hidden man inside. She looked at him with wondering recognition and then with trusting love. He took her hand; his head hardly reached her tall shoulder; he smiled up at her and led her away into a landscape throbbing and vibrating with color and beauty. He said, "Here is life. Don't go back, my child." She looked over her shoulder and saw the tower crumbling into dust, its battlements turning into wisps of smoke.

She awoke to early morning, and someone was knocking softly but insistently on her door, and she threw on a cheap calico wrapper and opened it. It was one of the maids, who had a letter in her hand. "It was delivered by a messenger, who said it was urgent, Miss Ames," said the girl, looking curiously at the wrapper and the coarse cotton nightgown that peeped from under it. Caroline closed the door and opened the letter and found that it was a message from Mr. Tandy. He had written, "It is most necessary, dear Caroline, for you not to return to Boston immediately but to meet us at our offices as soon as possible." It was only half-past six, and Caroline's train left at eight. She reread the short message, frowning. Then she began to bathe and dress.

She was at the office building at half-past seven. The hot morning streets were already filled and scuttling with weary clerks who had spent a hot and airless night in their rooms; the first blinding sun flashed on the rooftops. Horse cars rumbled, and drays and wagons full of goods and food clattered over the cobblestones. But the office building was cool and dusky, and the offices were shaded, quiet, and discreet. Caroline thought of what her father had once said of Tandy, Harkness and Swift: "They rarely offer advice or an opinion, but they officiate in their Temple of Law, murmuring a quiet prayer before entering the Consultation Chambers." Though it was very early, clerks were at their desks, green eyeshades cutting into their foreheads. Mr. Tandy was waiting for Caroline, and he appeared to be slightly agitated; he conducted her into his own office, seated her with his usual affectionate courtesy, and sat down behind his desk.

"A contingency has arisen, dear Caroline," he said, and picked up an envelope which was covered with foreign stamps.

"Yes?" said Caroline. If Mr. Tandy spoke of "a contingency," that was equal to another man speaking of an enormous disaster or unheaval. She felt a thrill of fear.

"Otherwise I should not have disturbed you," said Mr. Tandy. His small neat face appeared much less composed than usual.

"Please!" exclaimed Caroline.

"Of course, my dear. May I give you a glass of water?"

"No," said Caroline abruptly. "Mr. Tandy, there is another train to Boston in an hour. If there is something I should know I'd appreciate it if you'd tell me at once. I don't want a glass of water!"

"Very well," said Mr. Tandy a little stiffly. One did not rush into matters of importance without first, and properly, approaching them in the correct atmosphere, and Caroline was creating an atmosphere that was decidedly not correct. She was staring at the letter in his hand and was leaning forward. Mr. Tandy dropped it on the desk and half covered it with his small fingers, rebukingly.

"You will remember the terms of your father's will, Caroline," he said in a cool and reverent voice. "Half his estate was left to you outright; you had the disposition of it only during your lifetime. There was, of course, the possibility of any residue or increase. We know that you will increase the residue. No matter. The other fifty per cent was held in trust for you by Tandy, Harkness and Swift and the Bankers Trust Company of New York, to be invested discreetly by them, you to receive the income, only, during your lifetime."

"I know," said Caroline impatiently.

"Your father asked that within four months of his death you should make a will disposing of a part of your outright legacy of fifty per cent. You have not done so."

To his surprise and mild interest, she turned very pink and suddenly appeared years younger. "I intend to draft my will very shortly, Mr. Tandy. In fact," she added, "I can make my will now, though I don't intend to die soon, I assure you."

"One never knows," sighed Mr. Tandy. "But let us hope, dear Caroline, that you will live many, many decades. I will go on. You may remember that your father's will states that in the event of your death without natural and legal issue—which means only children, not a spouse—what remains of your outright fifty per cent, if any, is to be added to the invested trust. With the exception, of course, of what you have made your own through investments or other avenues."

"Yes? Yes, I understand."

"Do you, my dear?" he asked in a peculiar tone. "If you have no natural and legal issue, all will go to another heir. Surely you must have understood there must be another heir or heirs?"

Then she was deeply frightened. "I never intended to use any part of my outright legacy, Mr. Tandy. I intended to use only the income, to increase the legacy."

"Very good," he said approvingly, understanding that this was precisely what a proper Bostonian would do. "One does not dispose of principal recklessly. But still, without your natural and legal issue, there would be another heir. And you did not think of that, my dear?" he demanded with less approval and some shock.

She fumbled with her purse, then exclaimed, "Mr. Tandy, who is the other heir if I have no issue?"

Now she was greatly alarmed. Mr. Tandy leaned back in his chair. "One understands your sad condition after your father's death, my dear, and one understands that, after all, you are a young female. It is understandable that such things may have skipped your mind briefly."

"Please, Mr. Tandy, I must know! Who is the other heir?"

"That, my dear, is what we could not tell you. You may remember that the will states that in the event of your death without natural and legal issue a secret codicil, carefully sealed, should be opened. It was only to be opened—a copy of it is in Surrogate's Court and another copy in our safe—on your death, whether a week from now or sixty years from now. But in no other event. Do you remember that we told you of that codicil?"

"Yes," said Caroline faintly. "But I gave it very little thought. Besides, I intend marrying."

"Indeed?" said Mr. Tandy with very deep interest. "Soon, my dear?"

But Caroline was flushing again.

"Under those circumstances, and under your resolution to marry—I assume you have someone definite in mind—I can well understand why you did not consider the codicil," said Mr. Tandy. (His mind inventoried the young Bostonians Caroline might possibly know. Or was it some foreign fortune hunter?)

"Please. The codicil?" said Caroline in a stifled voice.

"I believe I have mentioned that it was not to be opened except in the event of your death without natural and legal issue."

Caroline snapped and unsnapped the clasp of her purse. She considered this with confusion. She opened her purse again and touched her plain cotton handkerchief to her lips.

"And you cannot tell me, Mr. Tandy?"

He paused gravely. "Until this letter, my dear"—and he smoothed his hand over the letter on his desk—"I could not, under any circumstances."

"What is the letter?" cried Caroline, moving to the edge of her chair.

"I don't understand it," said Mr. Tandy. "It should have arrived many weeks ago. Your father wrote it, my dear, two days before he died, and I still do not know why he wrote it. Perhaps it was that he had some premonition—— He must have come to love you very dearly."

"Papa?" said Caroline weakly, and her eyes filled with tears.

"I can only believe," said Mr. Tandy, "that after writing that letter Mr. Ames permitted it to remain in his desk in your suite in Geneva, so he could give further consideration as to whether or not he should send it to us. He was never a hasty gentleman. We shall never know if he did intend posting it. We shall never know if he actually posted it or if some servant, during cleaning, found the letter and posted it on her own volition. The Swiss are very correct about these matters," he added with approval. "Had it been found, say, in France or Italy, it would never have arrived.

"In any event, the long delay may be due to the fact that it was not found until comparatively recently—the postmark is very blurred and unreadable—or it was lost in the post for some time. The European posts are very incompetent, I have discovered. It arrived last evening among much other mail. I did not discover it until half-past nine last night; I had remained in order to dispose of accumulated matter. I then wrote you and had the message delivered to you this morning. Very urgent."

"What did Papa write you?" asked Caroline in a loud voice. The heat was rising here even in this shaded office, and her forehead and face were damp.

"You may read it yourself, dear Caroline," said Mr. Tandy, and rose with ceremony and came around his desk and gave it into her hand. "You will notice he dated it two days before his death."

Caroline's trembling fingers fumbled with the envelope. Her eyes blurred at the sight of her father's handwriting. She unfolded the stiff white paper. Her father had written: "Under circumstances which have arisen, and under the impression that I may not live much longer, I have decided to authorize you to open the codicil and reveal the contents to my daughter, Caroline Ames, immediately after my death."

Caroline, after reading, looked mutely at the precise little lawyer who had again seated himself. "I cannot open the safe except in the presence of Mr. Harkness and Mr. Swift. That is our rule. But I will make an exception in this case and tell you the contents of the codicil, Caroline." He paused and regarded her solemnly. "In the event, my dear, that you die without natural and legal issue, the estate is to go to the adopted daughter of Mrs. George Winslow, Miss Melinda Winslow, without any restrictions whatsoever. Remarkable, that! And Mrs. Winslow is to receive ten thousand dollars a year from that bequest, in addition to the life income of twenty-five thousand dollars a year, which she already possesses. Moreover, Mr. Timothy Winslow is to receive an outright bequest of five hundred thousand dollars."

Caroline stood up, and her purse crashed to the floor. She caught the edge of the desk. Mr. Tandy actually ran to her and put his arm about her. But she stared before her blankly.

Then she cried fiercely, "I don't believe it! I don't believe Papa ever made such a codicil! No!"

"Caroline, you must be calm." The little man, with supreme strength, forced her back into her chair. Then he stood over her; she sat stiffly and rigidly, her hands clenched on her knees, her eyes glazed, and she repeated over and over, "I don't believe it! He would never have made such a codicil!"

"You must be calm," said Mr. Tandy, alarmed at her appearance. "Caroline, certainly he made such a codicil. He made it in the presence of the three of us, during the time he made the body of his will. There were four other witnesses, also, in accordance with law. I thought it strange, myself. But then, he had no other family but you, no nephews, no nieces, apparently, no brothers or sisters. To whom else would he leave his money if you died without issue? In a way, it is to be expected that he would leave it to Mrs. Winslow, or at least that he provide more money for her, and to her son. Frankly, I expected that Timothy would inherit in the event of your death, for he came to regard Timothy with considerable esteem." Mr. Tandy coughed. "But the naming of Miss Melinda Winslow, who is only the adopted daughter of Mrs. Winslow, did strike me as extraordinary—she, a stranger, and not connected with your father by ties of marriage or family."

Caroline had never felt so ill before. A sensation of huge and shameful betrayal came to her. She dropped her head on her breast and sobbed.

"Be calm, my dear," said Mr. Tandy soothingly. "I know it is a shock. But you must remember that your father reconsidered. He wrote this letter. We'll never know why; we only know he wrote it. It is authentic; it is in his own handwriting. No one else could have known about that codicil but your father and ourselves."

But Caroline said, "It still remains that if I die—without natural and legal issue—the money—all that money—will go as written in the codicil?"

"Certainly. We are not authorized to change the codicil; we are only to tell you of its contents."

"He left it all—to Melinda! To Melinda!"

"To you, Caroline. You are the heir, not Miss Winslow. Unless you die without——"

"I know, I know," Caroline interrupted. The tears ran down her cheeks.

Mr. Tandy, though he would never have admitted it, possessed normal human curiosity. He watched Caroline wipe her eyes, and his expression was thoughtful. He cleared his throat. "Er, my dear, you would have no opinion as to why he made that—most unusual—codicil?"

Caroline was silent. She twisted her handkerchief in her hands. Her feeling of betrayal was still huge in her. But now it was brightened with furious hatred for Melinda. That dreadful woman, her aunt, had been responsible for this!

"No?" murmured Mr. Tandy.

"No," said Caroline with loud firmness. "I can't imagine why." It was the first falsehood she had ever spoken.

"Extraordinary," said Mr. Tandy. "We wondered, at the time." He was disappointed.

Then Caroline said with even more firmness, "I must make my own will today, Mr. Tandy. I wish to leave my outright fifty per cent of Papa's money to Mr. Thomas Sheldon of Lyme, Massachusetts, whether or not we are married at the time of my death."

Mr. Tandy sat down abruptly, and he was quite pale. "Mr. Tom Sheldon?" he repeated. "I don't believe we know any Sheldons, Caroline."

"I know him. That is sufficient, Mr. Tandy."

A most remarkable day, this, reflected the lawyer. He cleared his throat again.

"It must be today, this very minute," said Caroline. "For, if I should die, Melinda would have that money also."

"True," said Mr. Tandy. "And, as your father's will stands now, even after your marriage to this—Mr. Sheldon?—and if there is no issue, Miss Winslow inherits, with the exception of what you have invested of your fifty per cent outright legacy during your lifetime and your marriage. Ah, here are my partners now. You wish Timothy to be present?"

"No," said Caroline at once. "I do not. Mr. Tandy, another thing: if after my marriage I die, the terms of my father's will remain, and my balance is to go to Miss Winslow, in spite of any will I make?"

"I thought that was clear, Caroline. Legally, you can only dispose of what you have personally invested of your outright bequest—to Mr.—er— Sheldon. Unless you have natural and legal heirs."

"And the other invested fifty per cent, in trust, will go to her, in spite of any will of mine or even if I am married, unless I have natural and legal heirs?"

"Correct, my dear."

Caroline said in a loud, harsh voice, "I will marry very soon, as soon as possible! I do not intend to wait, as I originally intended."

"Let us go into the conference room, then," said Mr. Tandy. He paused. He had thought that Caroline would marry Timothy Winslow. This was all very disconcerting.

He said, "My dear Caroline, I don't believe you are imminently about to die!" He attempted a jocular smile. "Please consider what you are about to do. Would it not be best, as you are almost alone in the world with the exception of your aunt and your cousin, for us, your co-executors, to meet this—this Mr. Sheldon—and let us consider him well and give you our advice, our best advice, of course?"

"No," said Caroline.

Mr. Tandy was hurt. He said, "Your aunt and your cousin know him well, then?"

"No," said Caroline.

"But, my dear! *Who* knows him?"

"I do," said Caroline, standing up.

"But what is his background, his family?"

"He hasn't any," said Caroline.

Caroline arrived at Lyme at nine that night and found an anxious Beth

Knowles waiting for her with a station hack. "Carrie!" exclaimed the old woman. "I've been so worried about you!"

"Foolish," said Caroline curtly as she climbed into the hack. "You know that sometimes I'm late returning from New York." She settled her shawl about her shoulders. "When we get home I am sending the driver of this hack for Tom Sheldon. I must see him immediately."

"What?" said Beth. "Tom? Tonight? Why, Carrie, his father's just been buried! On the way to the depot I passed his house and it was full of people!"

"No matter," said Caroline. "I want him, I need him, and this is urgent."

"Carrie, use some common sense," said Beth. She had seen Caroline's stern pale face in the lamplight at the depot. "His friends are with him; it's very late; he's probably thinking of bed; it's been terribly tiring, and he did so love his father. He won't come, Carrie."

"Yes, he will."

"Carrie, you may be a very rich young lady, but Tom has his feelings too. Can't you think of that?"

"No," said Caroline.

"Why, you're shaking, dear. You must have had a chill, though it's so warm."

"On second thought," said Caroline, "we'll stop near Tom's house and you will go in, Beth, and ask him to come with us back to our house. At once."

"Why, people will think that we are both out of our mind!" said Beth.

"No matter," said Caroline. "What is their opinion to me?"

"He won't come," repeated Beth. "He has some respect for his father, even if you don't. He won't come."

Caroline was silent. A little later she ordered the driver to stop on the village street near Tom's house and nodded to Beth, who after one last protest left the hack and obeyed, muttering to herself. Caroline waited, still staring fixedly ahead of her. The night was soft and warm, and she could hear the sea beyond the village. She did not turn her head when Beth, clucking distractedly, appeared with Tom. She said, "Get in, please. There's enough room."

"Carrie," said Tom gently, standing near her. "I can't leave a house full of good friends. Don't you remember that my father was buried today?"

"Please get in," Carrie said. "This won't wait, Tom."

He had never heard that tone in her voice before. He took her hand; it was cold and stiff. He said to Beth, "Would you please tell my friends that I've been called away for a little while? I just can't face them myself."

"Yes," said Beth, subdued. They waited in absolute silence until she returned. Then they drove off to the desolate and shattered house, and no one spoke all the way. Darkness surrounded them; there was no sound but the trotting of the old horse and the mutter of the ocean.

Beth ran into the house to light more lamps while Caroline, still in silence, paid the driver and gave him his meager tip. Then she walked ahead of Tom up the shifting wooden boards to the house. He could see the shadowy outline of her, tall and straight and formidable. He was exhausted with his grief; his head ached and he felt profoundly numb. He could not even find the strength to wonder why Caroline needed him at this hour.

Beth, as usual, desperately tried to make matters look normal. She said brightly, "I'll make some coffee right away, and I've made some fresh doughnuts." She looked at Caroline anxiously.

"No," said the girl. "Go away, Beth."

Tom dropped wearily into an old rocker. "Yes," he said. "I need it. Please, Beth."

He looked about the room, which he had never entered before, and he was dully disgusted. Caroline threw aside her shawl and her purse and sat down on the other side of the cold and ash-filled hearth. The uncertain light of the kerosene lamp struck her face, and then Tom was greatly concerned. She appeared ill and, in spite of her silence and stillness, distraught. "Carrie," he said. "What is it? Has something happened to you?"

"Yes." Then she added bitterly, "Do you think I'd come after you like this, Tom, if it hadn't?"

She had become harder, older. She sat stiffly in her chair, looking before her, her profile massive and fixed.

"It's so important that even tonight you had to see me, Carrie?"

"Yes. It's the most important thing in the world. Why do you have to have coffee and those ridiculous doughnuts?"

"Possibly because I haven't eaten anything today," said Tom. He did not know this girl, this pallid and unyielding stranger. He said in a gentler voice, "And you look as if you need something too, Carrie."

"I only had breakfast," said Carrie. Now she looked at him, and her eyes blurred.

"Carrie! Are you sick? Has something terrible happened to you?"

"I told you, yes. Please, Tom, sit down. Don't touch me. I couldn't bear it just yet." One large tear ran down her right cheek, and she mopped it away.

Tom, who had stood up to go to her, sat down again. She had offered him no consolation; she had expressed no sympathy; she had not even mentioned his father. For the first time Tom thought: Why, she doesn't act human. This isn't my Carrie. She thinks of nothing but her own will.

He stared at Caroline and then again saw her misery and her muteness, and he almost forgot his own sorrow. Beth bustled in with a tray of steaming coffee, three cups and a plate of fresh doughnuts. She gave Tom a comforting look and said, "Here, now, I think we all need it, don't we? Such a terrible time. Dear Tom, I——"

"Go away," said Caroline. "Leave us alone, Beth."

Beth looked at her helplessly, then at the three cups. Tom stood up and poured coffee from the battered pot. He gave a cup and a doughnut to Beth and looked at her kindly. "Well, I never," said Beth feebly, the easy tears on her eyelashes. She glanced at Caroline, then seemed afraid. She took her coffee and doughnut and left the room and closed the door behind her.

"Drink some coffee, dear," said Tom, giving Caroline a cup. But she waved it away with a fierce gesture.

"Tom," she said, "I want you to marry me tomorrow. I've thought it all out."

Tom put down his own cup on the splintered old table near him. He stared at Caroline as if she had suddenly gone mad. Her eyes were wide and blazing now in the lamplight.

"What are you talking about, Carrie?"

"You want to marry me, don't you? Or have you changed your mind?"

Tom had no words. She smiled at him, and it was an ugly smile. "I made you my heir today, Tom. Whether you marry me or not. Will that change your mind?"

Tom clasped his hands slowly and looked down at them. "No," he said quietly, "that won't change my mind. But I think you have lost yours, Carrie. Don't you want to tell me anything?"

"No."

"I don't want your money, Carrie."

"And you don't want to marry me, after all you've said?"

"I want to know what's happened to you. Yesterday and today. Something has. I love you, Carrie, and so I know something has happened. You must tell me."

"I can't. Isn't it enough that I've made you my heir?"

"This is crazy, Carrie. What's wrong with you?"

"I can't tell you. Don't you trust me, Tom? There are some things I can never tell you. Never!"

Then he saw her anguish and her fear.

"No!" she said. "Don't touch me. Not yet, Tom. Will you marry me? Tomorrow?"

"Carrie, I thought you wanted to wait a decent time after the death of your father. You were the one who said that. And now my own father just died."

"It doesn't matter, Tom!" she cried. "Nothing matters now!"

"And there was the house I was going to build for you. We were going to wait for that." He was confused, in his exhaustion. "You wouldn't want me to live here—here, in this house, Carrie—until we built the other, would you?"

"What does it matter where a person lives?" She stood up and wrung her hands and looked about her as if she had never seen this room before. "Tom, we can't wait. Who knows what will happen to me?"

Tom walked up and down the room, heavily and tiredly. "You've forgotten, Carrie. You're Caroline Ames. You aren't just an obscure working-class girl. You have a position. I've been thinking too. A Caroline Ames can't marry a nobody. I wanted to talk about it to my dad. And then he died." He paused. "What am I, Carrie? A nobody. A village builder of summer houses. I haven't even had an education. I've been out of this village only twice in my life, and then only to Boston. What will everyone think of you if you marry a man like me? You've traveled all over the world; your father was one of the richest men in it, and now you have his money. Carrie, don't you know yet about the newspapers? They'll make fun of you; all the reporters will be swarming out here, laughing at you. Caroline Ames and the village hayseed! If you aren't thinking of yourself, I am. That's because I love you."

"You don't want to marry me," said Caroline in a dull voice, as if she had not heard a word he had said.

"I had no right to ask you, Carrie. I must have lost my mind, somehow."
"Why?"

"If I'd given it a minute's thought I'd have known how stupid I was. Carrie, can't you think of your own position?"

"You don't want to marry me," Caroline repeated.

"Oh, Carrie. Don't you have a sense of proportion?"

They looked at each other.

"I know only one thing," said Caroline, trembling. "You don't want to marry me."

"I don't have a right to marry you. You could marry anyone in the world."

"I don't want to marry anyone. I want to marry you."

"Why?"

Caroline walked to a dusty window and looked blindly out at the ocean. She said, "I thought you knew why. I love you, Tom. I want to marry you. Isn't that what we arranged only a few days ago? Have you forgotten?"

He went to her then, looked earnestly into her face. And then he took her into his arms and kissed her gently.

"All right, Carrie. I'll marry you tomorrow. It's all wrong, but I'll marry you tomorrow if you want it that way."

And then she clung to him and burst into wild sobbing, and the sound filled the house with mournful echoes.

"Don't leave me, Tom!" she cried, her lips against his throat. "Don't ever leave me! Oh, God, don't ever leave me!"

"I won't, Carrie. As God is my witness, I won't." And then, "Carrie, why are you so frightened? Carrie?"

They were married the next afternoon in a small fishing village, with only Beth and the wife of the justice of the peace as witnesses. The justice was a dull old man; he had heard of Caroline Ames, but he did not remotely suspect that this plainly clad, plain-faced young woman who appeared to be a servant or a shopgirl had any connection with the daughter of the great and powerful John Ames. He discussed the marriage that night, yawning, before going to bed. "Now, I've seen that girl before," said his wife. "But where?"

"I don't know," replied her husband. "It'll come to us, I reckon, sometime."

It came to him several days later when newspapermen descended upon him vociferously and demanded details. A clerk in the county office in which the marriage certificate had been filed had noted the name and had consulted his superior. But no one could find Caroline and her husband, Tom Sheldon. Beth, in the house in Lyme, disclaimed knowing their whereabouts. "Perhaps New York, or maybe Europe," she said, shamefaced at lying, and thinking of Caroline and Tom all alone in the wretched house in Lyndon without a cook or a servant. Hiding as if they are criminals, Beth thought resentfully. She had been left behind to deal with this contingency, and she repeated her lie over and over.

The marriage was a sensation. Cynthia Winslow and Lord Halnes and Timothy read of it the day after Cynthia's engagement had been announced. "Oh, heavens, it's shameful," Cynthia murmured, shocked. "Yes, Timothy dear, you told me of that man, but I just couldn't really believe it. After all, dear John's daughter! And how ruthless she is, not even to let us know, not even you, Timothy."

"I told you she was her father's daughter," said Lord Halnes. "She will never be anything else. Unfortunate young man! I am more and more delighted, my love, that you rescued me from her."

"Poor Caroline," said Cynthia. "Poor, wretched little girl."

PART THREE

He that maketh haste to be rich
shall not be innocent.

PROVERBS 23:5

CHAPTER ONE

"Just one more firecracker, John," said Tom Sheldon, looking up the long sea path to the great house. "It's breakfast time. Let me light the cracker, this little one. You'll wake the babies."

But the little boy insisted on striking the wooden match himself and lighting the fuse. It hissed, and then the firecracker went off with a pleasing noise. John's eyes glowed with excitement and satisfaction. He pleaded for another, but Tom shook his head. "It wouldn't be fair. You must wait until Elizabeth and Ames are dressed and brought into the garden. Remember, you promised last night."

"But that was last night," said the child, scowling. "What's a promise, anyway?" His large hazel eyes were discontented.

"A promise is a man's word," said Tom reprovingly. "Come on, now. Your mother will be looking for you."

"No, she won't. Not even on the Fourth of July," said the six-year-old child. "All she cares about is her old papers and books and such stuff."

"That's enough, John," said Tom sharply. "You're being very disrespectful and impertinent."

"She don't care for nobody," the child muttered, following his father up the wide flagged walk from the beach. "No sir, nobody."

Tom turned. "She loves us all, and so that's enough, John."

The boy stopped and kicked at one flag. He looked mutinous. "She never even sees us, hardly. Always in her study with her old books and papers, and then she goes to Boston and New York all the time. Why can't she be like other mothers?"

"Because she isn't," said Tom. "Stop pitying yourself. You have everything you want."

"That's because of you, Daddy," said John slyly. "All she gives me is five cents every Saturday. She don't know about what you give me!"

"You're making me sorry I give you anything," said Tom, stopping to fill his pipe. "It isn't fair to your mother. Go on, Johnnie; I'll follow you in a few minutes."

"I just want to know one thing," said the emphatic little boy, planting his sturdy legs in front of his father. "Why can't I go to school like the other boys?"

Tom thought: How can you tell a child that his mother is chronically frightened and mistrustful of everything and particularly everybody, that she sees the whole world as a personal threat and deadly menace to herself and her family? You can't tell a child that; you will only frighten him too.

So Tom said, "Your mother thinks that a tutor is best at your age. It will be different later. You'll see; go on, Johnnie."

But John gave him that glinting, upward glance again and said, "She's scared. That's what, she's scared!" And then he ran up the very wide flagged walk from the sea, and Tom, disturbed, watched the agile and powerful little body race along.

Tom had built this house with his own hands and the help of his devoted stonemasons, bricklayers, and carpenters. He had borrowed the money from Caroline and had insisted upon giving her due notes; half of what he had borrowed, with interest, he had already returned to her by 1892. She had said, "But, Tom, my money is yours." And he had replied, "Yes, dear, and my money is yours. But I'd prefer it this way just now." He knew that she had spoken out of affection but not out of her deepest convictions.

There had been no question of a cozy little house in Tom's mind, for Tom had experienced almost from the start the subtle but cogent corruption of his wife's wealth. Caroline did not care where or how they lived; she had, at first, insisted that "with a little paint here and there and perhaps a few bricks and some wood" the houses in Lyndon and Lyme would be quite satisfactory. Who cared for "display," and why? Who wished for "grand" furniture and rich rugs and molded ceilings? Who would be their visitors? "I know no one and care to know less," said Caroline. "We'll never entertain."

"Don't you want beautiful things around you?" asked Tom, puzzled. (A Caroline Ames should have a proper setting.)

"Not vulgar things," Caroline had replied. And Tom had thought with love: She's very simple and unaffected and austere, my darling. She cares only for things that are truly beautiful. Tom was certain of this when he discovered that his wife was buying as many of the canvases of a David Ames as possible and paying enormous prices for them. She did this while they lived in Lyme and Lyndon, waiting for the new house to be ready for them. She locked the paintings away. She would have a room for them all, Tom thought, or perhaps scatter them about the house. When the house was built Caroline did indeed have a small gallery for the pictures. But she locked the gallery door and kept the key and would not permit even her family to enter. Her daughter was later to refer to the gallery as "Bluebeard's Closet."

Though Caroline did not want a new house, and particularly an expensive one, Tom insisted it was "due" his wife and that she "deserved" it. He bought twelve acres of sea front and sandy land some ten miles from Lyme with his borrowed money. The land rose on a steady swell from the beach, so that the house finally stood on a considerable headland and was connected with the beach by a twenty-foot-wide flagged walk bordered by hardy bramble roses which formed a colorful hedge almost the entire season from spring to fall. Tom had designed the house in its entirety; Caroline could have shown no less interest than she did.

It was a very large house, three stories in height, built of yellow stone and yellowish brick. Tom did not like the pretentious houses of Newport—which he had visited for inspiration—or other homes along the ocean, also pretentious. He did not like round towers and turrets and foolish battlements and empty piazzas. He chose building materials the color of the sand, and his house rose strongly on its headland, rectangular, proud and unornamented, broad and high of shining window, tall and impressive of door. It appeared not to be superimposed on the landscape but as if the landscape itself had given birth to it. The main rooms—the parlors, the dining room, the breakfast or "morning room," as Tom had enthusiastically called it—and all the major bedrooms looked out upon the changing sea. Caroline had neither admired nor protested; her only comment was when the servants' rooms, on the third floor, also faced the sea and had large windows. "But, Tom, why bother about what the servants see or can't see? They'll be only too busy working and won't have time to waste looking at the water. What will they want with 'a view'?"

"They're human, aren't they?" Tom had asked. Caroline's large mouth had moved just a little in an expression of contempt. "We'll need no other servants," she said. "We have Beth. Perhaps one of the local women can come in occasionally to help her if necessary."

"Beth? With all these rooms, Carrie?"

"There, you see, Tom? I told you such a big house was totally frivolous and unnecessary. We'll be putting ourselves in bondage to menials. I used to hear my aunt's friends complain of how they were the slaves of their servants. I never wanted that. Beth is quite enough; oh, don't talk to me about her age! She's very lively, really; she can manage. With occasional assistance, if any."

It was Tom, in his first act of treachery toward his wife, who went to Beth and told her. Beth, who was delighted by the thought of the rising house, became dismayed. "But, Tom, I'm getting old, really. Do you mean that Carrie honestly expects me to take care of that big house and do the cooking and everything and look after the baby that's coming, all by myself?"

"She does, Beth. And so you must tell her that it's impossible."

Beth had studied him. "Why can't you tell her yourself, Tom? You're the master, you know."

This was in January 1886, just prior to the birth of little John. But Tom had learned enough by now to say to Beth, "I may be the master, Beth, but it's Carrie's money. I'm building those new little houses all the time, clear up to Marblehead, but I put everything I make into new land and new buildings and have almost no cash on hand. And then I'm paying for this house, too, on borrowed money."

With considerable prescience, he had insisted upon the house directly after the marriage. Had he waited even a year the house would never have been built, and he had known that somehow. But Caroline, fiercely and desperately in love, willing to listen if even only reluctantly, had consented to the house. If Tom wished it, he could have it, though it was so extravagant and wasteful an idea. She was so grateful to him for loving her. By the time they had been married one year she was much less pliant; had not the house been half built by then, she would have refused the whole thing. Even so, the Christmas before her first child was born she had actually hinted that they could make a profit if they sold the house when completed or just as it was.

On the quiet advice of Tom, and with indignation, Beth had gone to Caroline and had said, "Carrie, we'll be moving into the new house in April. We haven't much time; do you want to talk with agencies in Boston about a cook and kitchenmaid and at least two housemaids and a gardener—there's all that land, you know—and a coachman and a stable boy? And the baby will be born soon, and I do wish he'd be born in the new house instead of this awful old Lyndon place! You'll need a nursemaid."

Caroline was sitting by a warped window, wrapped in heavy shawls. She was weighty with her child, and a little languid. She had drawn a table to the window, and a chair, and here she would sit, going over her investments and her ledgers and her papers, making notes for the office in Boston. She worked endlessly from morning until evening. Now she lifted her large head, glanced absently at the snow-filled grounds about the old house, and said, "What are you talking about, Beth? We won't use all the rooms in the new house; that would be ridiculous. We'll need only the kitchen, three bedrooms and one bathroom, and the smallest sitting room. And as it will all be new, there will be little dust. Why, you won't have even as much work to do as you have in this house!"

Beth said quietly, "I think you're wrong, Carrie. Tom's been down to New York a lot, and he's buying furniture and he doesn't have any intention of building a big house so that we can all crouch in a couple of rooms like ditchdiggers. I'm getting real old and tired, Carrie. I can't take care of a baby——"

"I intend to take care of my own child," said Carrie coldly, waving her hand in dismissal.

But Beth stood there, fat and weary and white. "You haven't the slightest idea of how to take care of a baby or all the work there is, Carrie. All the washing, all the night feedings, all the watching and caring. You'd be so tired you wouldn't have time to fuss with all those books and ledgers and papers of yours, and you wouldn't be able to go in to Boston at all, what with the nursing and such. Or perhaps," said Beth angrily, "you'll attend those meetings of yours and nurse the baby right in front of all those men!"

Caroline had stared at her, but Beth, very angry now, stared back. "Very well, then," said Caroline at last, "I don't want to burden you too much, Beth. We'll hire a nursemaid for the first few months. Get a girl from the country; eight dollars a month will be more than enough for the time we'll need her."

Beth was almost defeated, and then she remembered what Tom had said: "Don't back down, Beth. Carrie is only a young woman, after all, and very inexperienced."

So Beth said resolutely, "No, Carrie. Not just a nursemaid. We'll need all the other help too."

Carrie narrowed her eyes at the old woman, and for the first time Beth saw John Ames in his daughter. She was so startled that she stepped back a little in fear.

"No," said Caroline, and bent over her books again in the fading winter light.

Beth pulled in a deep breath and remembered what Tom had told her to say. "All right, Carrie. Then I'll give you a month's notice right now. I'm sorry I'll be gone when the baby is born, but it's too much for me."

Caroline carefully laid down her pen. She could not believe it. She stared at Beth incredulously and with contempt. "Are you out of your mind, Beth? Where would you go?"

"I have enough to buy a little house, and with the rest of my savings and my pension from the government—and I just got an increase, too—I can live easy somewhere in Boston. Have you forgotten that your father left me three thousand dollars, too?" She turned away and added in a lower voice, "A month, Carrie. You'd best get busy right now to replace me, and when you do you'll find that no other woman, even if she's real stupid, will work as I do or go to the new house all alone."

"You'd leave me, Beth?" Caroline's voice had changed to that of a fearful and bewildered little girl; Beth's first impulse was to run to her, pull her head to her breast and say, as she had said hundreds of times before, "Of course I'll never leave you, dear!" But she thought of Tom again. So she turned near the door and looked at Caroline and did not move.

She said, "I really will, Carrie. I've made up my mind. I raised you and cooked and washed for you and made your clothes for years and was like a mother to you. But there comes a time when a person's got to think of herself, too, and the time's come for me."

Caroline was silent, but she lifted her hand to detain Beth. Then she said slowly, "The house is costing a large fortune in itself. More servants will be a constant drain. I can't afford it, Beth. I can't even bear to think of losing all that money every month."

Now Beth was angry again. "Carrie! Do you think I'm a fool? Maybe the papers exaggerate, but if you have only half of what they say you have you'll never be able to spend a half of the income, let alone the principal you're always talking about, not even if you lived like Mrs. Vanderbilt. That's what the papers said. You're one of the richest girls in the world, Carrie."

"What my father left me," said Caroline, trying to control her vast fear and rage, "is a trust. A sacred trust. It can't be spent criminally on frivolities and stupidities. It's money, Beth, it's money! Can't you understand that?"

"I certainly can. And what's money for, except to enjoy it?"

"It's to be kept and increased."

"What for?"

But Caroline could not explain to this simple woman that money in itself was sacred and inviolable and a place of secure refuge from the world. She exclaimed, "What for? To have, just to have!"

Beth shrugged wearily. "That sounds crazy, Carrie. I believe in saving; I've saved all my life. You've got to have some security in your old age. You can't be a beggar or go to the poorhouse if you have any pride. Why, I'd rather starve, myself. You can't expect others to do for you what you should do for yourself. Even a little child knows that. But money, just to have! That's crazy, Carrie."

"Then thousands of wealthy people all over the world are crazy too," said Caroline with a grim smile. "I've met many of them. They are very careful and thrifty, even with their children; they teach them proper respect for money. They're not extravagant and heedless fools. They know what money is and what it means, and they never spend a penny they don't have to, under any circumstances."

"Then they're crazy too," said Beth. "I don't believe in being extravagant, either. But I believe in using some of your money to enjoy life, too, after you're sure you have something to leave your children. Carrie, I'm tired. I don't want to talk any longer; we don't understand each other any more, though I've tried to teach you since you were little. So you have my notice. I'll be sorry to leave you, for you were like a child to me. But I've got to look after myself, now that I'm old."

She left the darkening room. When Tom came in after spending cold hours upstairs in a dusty, bleak room over his own prints and designs for his house and the small houses he would start in the summer, he found Caroline silent and crouching over the small fire. She cried to him hysterically, "Tom, you must talk to Beth! I think she's lost her mind, at the very least!"

Tom listened. His body was cold and his hands red and stiff, for there was little wood in the woodshed, and the fire upstairs did not draw very well in its ancient chimney, and the bitter winter wind crept through every crack in the old house. He knew what poverty was. But his parents' little house had never been as poor and as cold as this one, and he had never been so thoroughly chilled before, not even on the canalboats in a blizzard.

He knew that a crisis had arisen in this house. If Caroline had her way, if he took her part and pleaded with Beth to stay under the present circumstances, then the future would be frightful. It was hard not to comfort Caroline, heavy with her child, and with her tear-stained face turning confidently to him now for his reassurance and promise to persuade Beth to accede to Caroline's stubborn blindness and desperate penury. There was more at stake here than Beth alone. There was Carrie herself, and her husband, and the baby about to be born, and future children.

So Tom said very gravely, "I'm afraid that Beth is right, Carrie."

Carrie was aghast, and she pulled herself from Tom's arms. "But I can't get along without Beth!" she cried.

"Yes, I know. So you must have Beth. But you've got to meet her terms, Carrie. I'll go to the agencies in Boston myself tomorrow. And now I'll have a little talk with Beth about how many servants we'll need."

Caroline's love for her young husband had a slavish and unhealthy quality in it. She was still young; deprived of love all her life, she had given love to Tom with a kind of helpless frenzy and devotion. That love, after a year of marriage, was still strong enough to make her say now, though with dread and reluctance, "Very well, Tom. But it does make me worry so, spending all that money. I'll never really forgive Beth. We shouldn't have built that house at all! Sometimes the very thought of it makes me frantic."

Tom knew that she was not speaking extravagantly, for Caroline was as economical with words as she was with cash. For the first time he, too, was frightened. He said, "You mustn't be frantic, Carrie. You must be sensible." His tone was so stern that she became silent again and later tried to appease him. She was like a child who has been unjustly and cruelly punished and is bewildered, and when she shyly and timidly caressed and kissed him, Tom felt his first despair.

During all these later years he had tried to change Carrie, relieved now of the terrible influence of her father. He had tried, not for his own sake or the sake of their three children, but for Caroline herself. But each necessary purchase had sincerely shocked her; on several occasions she had become ill with fright. She haggled with the cook about the food the household consumed. If she succeeded in reducing expenditures for the food by only a single dollar a month she was radiant and triumphant. If she replaced a servant with one willing to accept a little less she was as joyous as a young girl on her bridal morning and could not understand why Tom did not share her joy. She would even spare time from her work and expend endless energy and hours in shopping in Boston for a cheaper article. She became extremely interested, almost absorbed, in Tom's own business. She would pore over blueprints with him; she would point out that a little more sand in the concrete mixture, "just a tiny little more," would save him at least ten dollars on a small house. "It wouldn't harm the quality," she would plead. "But it would harm my opinion of myself," said Tom, and she would stare at him, baffled.

She actually found a place where he could purchase slates for less than he was paying. "But the slates are thinner and weaker," he said. "They would have to be replaced constantly after the winter." "Who cares?" cried Caroline. "But I advertise lifetime roofs," Tom replied. "I am not a cheat, Carrie."

"I am not a cheat, either," she said angrily after the argument had continued many months. "I resent your implication, Tom."

"No, you are not a cheat, Carrie. You are scrupulous about your affairs. But I don't want you to make me a cheat. I have to live with myself."

She thought the prices of his fine little homes too low. "If they can pay two thousand dollars for a house, they can pay one hundred more."

"But why should they? I get a reasonable profit, and a reasonable profit is all I want."

"That's foolish. You should get everything you can."

"Why?"

The arguments always ended on that, with Caroline glowering and perplexed and Tom despondent. They had been married almost eight years now. Caroline still did not understand her husband. He understood her only too well, and his compassion was still strong and protective. But his fits of despair and hopelessness had shorter intervals between them. He knew now that Caroline was becoming less confiding in him, less trustful. Once there had been some communication between them, but as Tom did not know the source of that communication in Caroline he could not help it increase. He had thought it came only from love. A fearless man himself, he was bewildered by the demonstrations of Caroline's terror, which seemed utterly senseless to him. When a stock she had purchased dropped a few points, she was frenzied. "But it'll rise again," he would say, disturbed. "But, Tom, if I needed to sell now I'd lose a lot of money!"

"But you don't have to sell, Carrie," he would say patiently.

"That's not the point, Tom! They'll have to pass the next dividend if the stock doesn't rise again."

"You won't starve," Tom would remark with indulgence.

Then Caroline would stare at him, thunderstruck, and appalled that he did not understand; and, seeing that look, Tom was also appalled that she could be affected so violently. She would retire into sullen silence and would sleep only fitfully, and Tom, lying beside her, would be afraid that she was losing her love for him. He had no way of understanding that her love was as strong as ever and even more possessive, and that her diminishing communication with him was not due to loss of love but increase of fear. She was becoming distrustful of him, not as a man and her husband, but as a person who did not understand that money must constantly grow, must double itself, must be viable and dynamic, and that it was the most important thing in the world. Her distrust increased her fear; she often thought: If I should die Tom would squander everything. And so she changed her will. Tom would have only an income from her estate in the event of her death, an income to be predicated exactly on what his own business earned, year by year.

But all this had taken over seven years, almost eight, to happen.

The house had been built, had been comfortably furnished by Tom out of his own funds and the money he had borrowed from Caroline, and was adequately staffed at least part of the time. There was also a house in Boston, where Caroline stayed when it was necessary to spend a few weeks there on business or even a few days. It had a single elderly servant in charge. It took many years for Tom to realize that Caroline was more comfortable in that penurious house in Boston, old, drafty, and molding, like the abandoned house in Lyndon, than in her great mansion by the sea. When she went to New York she continued to patronize the shabby pension of her unmarried years. Here, too, she was safe. It cost so little money.

They lived an isolated life. Tom had no friends but the villagers and his workmen; Caroline had no friends at all. She never saw her former schoolmates in Boston. She had never been part of the living world of warm humanity; she was not part of it now. Her world was her money, her husband, her children. Her associates were her bankers, her stockbrokers, her lawyers. She saw no reason to broaden her horizon, to chop down the weeds and underbrush and fertilize the wilderness which had surrounded her all her life. Those who had another kind of living evoked her scorn and contempt. They were light-minded, without value, full of frivolity, and spendthrift. She loved art galleries and visited them in Boston and New York—on free days. She liked music and would take Tom with her to Boston and New York for concerts and operas. They sat in the highest and cheapest seats. She bought secondhand books for pennies, to fill the fine library at Lyme. She and her children were clothed less extravagantly than her servants. The clothing was of good sturdy material, without beauty. She employed a seamstress to make and remake it until it was worn out. She was pleased that her last child, Ames, was a boy. She had put away John's outgrown clothing in moth balls in large trunks in a separate room, to be made over for the youngest child.

Quite often the dark isolation of his home made Tom desperate, and he would drive down to the village to meet his workmen in a saloon and drink beer with them and laugh a little. Or he would visit his old friends in the village. They never asked him why he brooded so silently, why he laughed so seldom now, why he appeared to forget them in some desperate thoughts of his own as he sat among them. They would say among themselves, "Poor Tom. He ain't been the same since he married that rich Ames woman."

Part of his misery came from the fact that he thought Caroline loved him less and needed him less. He turned hopefully to his children. He would cultivate them, play with them, love them extravagantly, indulge them. The great tragedy of his life deepened. He did not know that his children, young as they were now on this Fourth of July, 1892, respected and feared their mother and had no love for him at all. They had caught the infection of Caroline's mistrust of him. Their corruption was already firmly established, though John was hardly more than six, Elizabeth only four, and Ames just three. They romped with him; if they thought of him at all it was as someone to be exploited, to be cajoled for advantage, to be slyly manipulated. A buffoon; a simple person; a big playmate.

Tom's taste did not run to the magnificent, the exquisite and precious, or the ponderous and heavy in furniture, which was now so fashionable. His mother had been able, through some special genius of warmth and love, to make even her poor house comfortable and kind and peaceful. It was in this manner that Tom had furnished his house, of which he was so proud and which he had believed would bring tranquillity to the beset Caroline. There was not a room in his house which was not sunny for at least part of the day and filled with light even in the gloomiest weather. He had chosen pleasant furniture. The morning room, paneled in glossy pine, was filled with Pennsylvania Dutch pieces, unpretentious yet comforting. When Caroline had seen the furnishings of the drawing room and parlor she had said doubtfully:

"Sheraton? Weren't they terribly expensive?" "No," he said doubtfully, "they aren't Sheraton. I think the dealer called them replicas."

Caroline was appeased. Then she saw the furniture in the dining room, more ornate and graceful, and she had exclaimed: "Chippendale! The Chinese period!" And Tom had said, "I don't know. But I thought of us and our children looking at this furniture three times a day, and it seemed beautiful to me. I admit it was very expensive."

Caroline hated the dining room. It reminded her of her Aunt Cynthia.

The bedrooms were very simple but had the solid elegance of poster beds, canopies, good plain rugs, small mahogany commodes, and easy chairs. Tom had not neglected the servants' rooms, to Caroline's outrage. She did not like the draperies in the house, bright and colorful and silken. "No privacy," she said. "Anyone outside will be able to see our lamps through them." "And," said Tom, "if they do they will know that people live here and are a family."

Caroline had shrugged. The outer world of people was of no importance to her; they had no verity in her world. She insisted upon dark velvet draperies for her bedroom, and Tom, listening to the hidden sea at night, would feel stifled. But they had no quarrel until Tom bought an authentic Aubusson rug, all pale gold, dim blue, and muted crimson, for the drawing room, and Caroline immediately recognized it for what it was and was infuriated. "Why, it must have cost my dividends for a year on my New York Central stock!" she cried. "How can you be so profligate with my money?"

"I borrowed that money from you," said Tom. "I'm repaying it, with interest."

He came into the morning room this Fourth of July morning in 1892 and found Caroline studying some of her interminable papers and frowning. She ate her frugal and tasteless breakfasts here; Tom's dream of the children about the table had never been fulfilled. Caroline had insisted from the very beginning that they eat alone in the upstairs nursery with their nurse-maid. She did not wish to hear their chatter. She did a great deal of her work in the mornings, before the stock market opened. She had the first telephone in Lyme, with a direct line to her brokers, and the telephone was in the morning room, on the smooth Pennsylvania Dutch table. "I think you should be interested," she told Tom, who had protested. "When you have surplus funds, if ever, you should give some thought to the stock market yourself."

"I'd rather put any surplus funds into more building," said Tom, "and more land." He had looked at Caroline earnestly. "Oh, you've explained, Carrie, that your money is alive and invested in growing industries and railroads, but it isn't the kind of life that appeals to me."

Caroline was not interested even in the "life" of industry and the railroads. She could not translate them into flesh and blood, into workers and producers and executives and businessmen. To her, they were figures that rose and fell and brought profits, and without any human animation at all.

Caroline was deeply concerned about her children, though she would not have them "underfoot," as she explained to the baffled Tom. He thought her tremendous anxiety about them, her fear for their safety, arose from love. It did not. They were merely her "natural and legal heirs," protecting her father's fortune from those she hated. She had no actual love for anyone but Tom.

This morning, as usual, Caroline was carelessly dressed in an ugly cotton wrapper, which swathed her majestic figure meagerly and fell open to reveal the plain white cotton nightgown she always wore in the summer. She lifted her wide blunt face to Tom when he entered, and immediately her smile made her beautiful, brightened the childish freckles on her strong nose, gave radiance to her lovely hazel eyes and a glisten to her big red mouth and clean large teeth. Her braided black hair hung over her shoulders, and some of it had loosened about her olive cheeks, so that she appeared almost girlish. When Tom kissed her she put her hands about his neck and held him to her fiercely and briefly, then pushed him away.

"Why are you working on this fine morning, and on a holiday, too?" asked Tom, seating himself near her and awaiting his breakfast. He looked about the table and, as always, he wished the children could be here, laughing and chattering.

"I detest holidays; they're so dull, and they're a waste of time, and they get in the way," said Caroline. Then she frowned. "Didn't I hear firecrackers a little while ago? Did you actually disregard my wishes and buy John some fireworks? You know how dangerous they are! He could get lockjaw."

He looked at her carefully with his kind eyes, then lit his pipe. His thick black hair had been ruffled by the sea wind, and his face was brown from the sun.

"Yes, dear, you heard firecrackers. I bought some for John, and I have Roman candles and other things, such as sparklers, for tonight. Why should you deprive him? Dangerous? Of course they are. But life is dangerous; it always was, it always will be. Children must learn as soon as possible that danger is everywhere and that death as well as life is everywhere too. Then they'll be able to guard themselves. You can't create a secure world for children; that's foolishness."

"You mean you are deliberately exposing the children to death and danger?"

"I mean I am exposing them to natural hazards so they'll be conscious of them and be careful. They must learn that they aren't going to live forever, either, and that someday, sooner or later, they'll die."

"How can you speak of death to children?" cried Caroline.

"Because it's here," he said patiently. "Sometimes you aren't very realistic, Carrie."

"You always say that," said Caroline sullenly, and she lost her fugitive beauty, and her face was heavy and impassive again.

"As for lockjaw," said Tom, as if she hadn't spoken, "I've already explained about that to John, and he understands that a firework's burn isn't a trivial thing. I've bought some fresh iodine, and he knows how that smarts and he'll be careful." A maid brought him some bacon and eggs and coffee, and he began to eat.

"You always have such a careless approach to life," said Caroline.

"Not careless. Accepting. You and I aren't going to live forever, either, Carrie."

She was silent. He ate with pleasure, but she was frightened. She could think of death for herself and even for her children, but not for Tom. Never for Tom, who was all she had. He was thirty-four, and so no longer young. He climbed about his houses and worked with his men and chipped stone and laid bricks with them. He could be hurt. She visualized Tom dead, for the first time, and the old familiar terror took her.

"You take all kinds of risks!" she said harshly. He was startled at her tone and looked up.

"We all do," he said, wondering at her strong change of mood. "We take the worst risk of all when we draw our first breath. We're surrounded by risk."

Caroline did not reply.

"What's the matter, Carrie? You look very white."

"Nothing." Then she bent her head and laid her cheek on the back of his hand.

"Carrie dear," he said with concern, "what is it?"

"I wish," she mumbled, her lips now against his hand, "that you'd just stay here with me and the children and not go out and away."

"You mean," he said, laughing a little, "you want to lock us up to keep us safe? That's silly. There are stairs to fall down inside this house, floors to slip on, fires that could burn us all to cinders, food that can go bad and poison us, dusts that carry infections. There's no safe place anywhere, Carrie."

He looked down at her head and tried to see her face. He suddenly remembered her face on the morning after their wedding night, as it lay sleeping on the pillow beside him. It had had such a clean yet shining look, as pure and quiet as the face of a statue, purged of fear and recoil. He had raised himself on his elbow to look and to wonder and to feel fresh love. She had not been afraid of him, he remembered. He did not know that in a very dangerous sense she had actually taken him.

He bent and kissed her hair, and he wondered if he would ever be able to rescue her from her chronic fear.

"Let's go and see the kids," he said, smoothing one of her ears with a gentle finger.

She sat up abruptly. "I have some work to do," she said. "I'll get dressed and go into my study. Children are very boring, at least to me."

"They're fond of you, Carrie."

"Are they? I never noticed. If you want to go, Tom, don't let me detain you."

He hesitated. In some odd way he felt that he should not leave Carrie at once. Carrie could be very foolish sometimes, he reflected. But still he hesitated, and though she bent over her papers again she watched him out of the corners of her eyes. Then he sighed and left the room. Caroline's hand clenched over her pen with ferocious jealousy. How could Tom prefer the company of young and stupid children to hers?

Tom went up the broad and curving stairway to the second floor. As always, he kept pausing to look with pleasure and contentment at the sunlit rooms full of the flickering shadows of the leaves on the trees he had planted years ago and the far, faint glimmer of the ocean light. The house was quiet. To him, it was a peaceful place. He liked the distant clatter of dishes and pots in the kitchen and the voices of the servants; he could smell their morning coffee. He had a sudden desire to go into the kitchen and sit at the table and talk with the servants, whose customary sullenness lightened at the sight of him.

But he went up to the big nursery. Here were different voices, quarrelsome and pettish. The nursemaid scolded; old Beth pleaded. Tom opened the door. Little Elizabeth was firmly seated on John's big rocking horse, and he was trying to pull her off, and little Ames was whining on the rug and discontentedly smacking a toy animal. The room blazed with sunlight and gushed with warm air. It was a pleasant room, the walls papered with delicate flowers, the floor polished, the soft draperies blowing.

"Well, well," said Tom. The children immediately raised their voices in a shrill and protesting chorus. John ran to him, a tall sturdy boy, large for his age, with crisp dark curls, his mother's broad face and hazel eyes and blunt nose. "Make her get off, Papa!" he screamed, pulling at Tom's hand. "She won't get off!"

"Let her ride a little," said Tom. He smiled at his pretty little daughter, who had such big, staring blue eyes, long and satiny fair hair, and delicate features. But she did not answer his smile; her expression was dogged and determined. She rocked more vigorously.

"It's my horse!" shrieked John in rage, and stamped.

"But you've got to share a little," said Tom soothingly.

"I never saw such children," sighed Beth, sitting down and fanning herself with her hand. She had aged, had lost much weight, and seemed always tired. Even her eyes had faded to a weary, almost colorless tint. "They have everything, but they're never contented or happy like other children."

"I don't think children are very contented or happy at any time," said Tom.

"I want fifty cents," said John, forgetting his horse.

"Why, Johnnie?"

"Just because."

Tom considered him. "There must be some reason, dear. Tell me."

"Just to have," said John, impatient at his idiocy.

This sounded unpleasant to Tom. "For candy? To save for a present?"

"No! Give me fifty cents."

Tom's healthy impulse was to refuse. But if he did John would get into a temper again and remember his horse and would pull his sister's hair and make her cry. Elizabeth was Tom's favorite, his darling. So Tom gave his son a silver piece, and John smiled up at him slyly and clutched the money in his brown little fist. Elizabeth, watching, suddenly crowed as if in triumph and rocked harder. When Tom came to her she ignored him and continued her crowing. Her blue eyes glistened, and she did not stop rocking even when Tom kissed her. The nursemaid watched, disapproving. Mr. Sheldon was certainly foolish over these ill-behaved children who needed thrashing more often than not.

Tom picked up the squalling little Ames, who was a fat and bouncing child with slate-gray eyes and blond flat hair and a curiously triangular face, broad and wide at the top and tapering abruptly and sharply to a very pointed and receding chin. He was once the least healthy of the three children; as an infant he had been scrawny and had constantly whined and had had the croup. Now he was fat, but his color was pale and delicate, and his flesh lacked firmness.

"Candy!" he cried, avoiding Tom's kisses and wriggling in his arms.

Tom glanced at the nursemaid, who shook a disapproving head and firmly folded clean clothing. "Well, now," said Tom. "You've had candy, haven't you?"

"Too much," said Beth, rocking and fanning herself. "That's all he ever wants; he hardly eats anything. Don't give him any, Tom."

"Candy!" screamed the child.

Tom put the boy down. Ames waddled furiously to Beth and kicked her leg. Immediately the elderly nursemaid swooped on him and smacked him hard on his bottom. "Bad boy!" she cried. "Bad, wicked, spoiled boy!"

Tom wanted to interfere, but he was wise enough not to, knowing that Briggs was very competent. Ames howled; Elizabeth rocked silently; John ran vigorously up and down the room in sheer animal restlessness.

"They'll be all right, Mr. Sheldon," said Briggs, giving the father a sharp smile. "It's time for them to go out now and work off their spirits on the beach."

So Tom, somewhat depressed, though reassuring himself that children usually managed to grow up to be presentable adults, went down again to the morning room. Caroline was not there. He walked through a wide hall to her study. She sat at her desk, straight and upright, dressed in a dull brown frock with a ruffle of yellow lace at her throat. The ruffle held the silver pin Tom had given her so long ago.

"How are the children?" she asked indifferently when Tom entered.

"As lively as usual," he said. "Carrie, I wish you'd give them a little more of your time."

"Why? They have Briggs and Beth."

"But they need their mother."

"Nonsense. That's sentimentality." She held up the morning newspaper. "I thought you might like to see this; I find it amusing."

It was a Boston newspaper, dated the day before. There was a photograph of a young woman on one of the pages which recorded the events of society, a large and prominent photograph. The girl had a beautiful face, slender, composed, but sad. Her light eyes looked from the page with an expression of mute longing, and her fair hair was drawn simply back from her fine cheekbones and the excellent contours of her face and folded into a chignon at the nape. Her sensitive mouth, exquisitely shaped, expressed sorrow and resignation, and her throat appeared long and vulnerable. Tom read the column beside the portrait:

"Miss Melinda Mary Winslow, daughter of Lord and Lady Halnes of Paris and London, arrived in Boston last Sunday with her parents for a short visit. She is a member of the Assemblies and made her debut in London and Boston four years ago. It will be remembered as one of the most brilliant debuts of the season of 1888. Miss Winslow is the adopted sister of Mr. Timothy Winslow of Boston and New York, who married Miss Amanda Bothwell in June 1890, an occasion Boston will long remember."

Tom studied the portrait and was touched by the expression on the lovely face. "Oh," he said. "Your adopted cousin. I never met her. She's not married, is she? Do you know why?"

"Yes," said Caroline with a most unpleasant smile. "I know."

She would say nothing more. She dismissed the subject and said, "No one believes me, but we're on the verge of a financial panic."

CHAPTER TWO

Tom Sheldon had met Timothy Winslow for the first time less than two years after he had married Caroline Ames.

Caroline rarely spoke of her relatives, and Tom had come to the conclusion that there was something malign and disreputable about them all. When she had read of her aunt's marriage to Montague Lord Halnes she had at first been silently shocked and then had flown into a bitter rage. After Tom had calmed her a little he questioned her, but she became as furiously silent as she had been furiously vocal and incoherent. She said only, "That unspeakable woman! And my father dead not even four months! And that man!"

"But, Carrie, she wasn't your father's widow."

Caroline would say nothing then. A few days later she spoke of Melinda with contempt and mysterious hatred.

When they had been married a month Caroline mentioned her cousin Timothy, and he was surprised to hear her speak with some warmth and kindness. She told him of the arrangements she had made for Timothy, of her father's belief in him. Later she went to New York with Tom, but did not suggest that he go with her to her lawyers and bankers, and though he was relieved he was also hurt. Was Carrie ashamed of him? He asked her that question later, and she had looked at him with absolute surprise and had said, "Tom, don't be silly!" It was not until much later that he discovered that his wife was naturally secretive; she would seldom talk about her investments and holdings to him and merely mention that she had bought or sold.

Once, he remembered, she had begged him to go with her to see her lawyers and help her. Now that they were married she never suggested it. She kept her papers locked in a big safe in her study; she also kept her desk locked. He had discovered this accidentally a year after their marriage. He did not ask her why she did this; he had learned much of Caroline by this time.

When John was born in the old rotting house in Lyndon, in the deep of an exceptionally bad winter, she had had a severe ordeal. She did not recover quickly; she retained a certain listlessness. Then matters needed her attention in New York, but her doctor forbade her to go while the weather remained bitter, and so she had sent for Timothy to come to her. They had just moved to the house near Lyme, and Timothy arrived one day, carrying his brief case.

Tom, usually kind and tolerant and ready to like anyone, did not like Timothy Winslow, that sleek, quiet, fair young man with his calm and elegant ways, his pale and observant eyes, his low voice, his fine features. He was courteous, listened politely when Tom spoke, and subtly made Tom feel stupid, ignorant, clumsy, and totally irrelevant. He and Caroline stayed all day in her study, and it was tacitly understood that Tom's presence was not necessary. Just before dinner they had emerged, and Timothy had remarked with the utmost agreeableness about the pleasant rooms of the house and its excellent form. But it was quite evident to Tom that Timothy did not really like the house. Tom thought it boorish of Caroline to remark, when Timothy admired the drawing-room furniture, "Oh, it's not really Sheraton, none of it. Just replicas Tom found somewhere."

"Replicas?" Timothy had repeated, raising his light eyebrows.

Then Tom had said with hard coldness, "I don't know what's wrong with good replicas."

"There's nothing wrong," Timothy had replied too quickly. "If Caroline hadn't told me I doubt that I'd known. It's remarkable what they can produce in factories these days, isn't it?"

His voice dismissed both Tom and factories, and during dinner he had talked almost entirely with his cousin. He had admired the new baby. He had remained overnight and then had left early. When he was gone Tom, still smarting, said to his wife, "Your cousin despises me. But I can tell you one thing, Carrie. He hates you."

Caroline seemed vaguely interested. "Really, Tom? Well, what does that matter? I don't like him, either; I admire him for his ability, and he'll serve me well so long as it's to his profit. And he's given me some excellent advice about my investments, even when my lawyers and bankers and brokers thought him wrong. So, you think he hates me? We detested each other when we were children. Now we can use each other, and so we're friends."

"Perhaps you trust him. But I don't," said Tom. "If he can ever find a way to injure you or exploit you, he will."

Caroline was amused. "He never will," she said.

She mentioned Timothy later when she heard in a letter from him that his mother had presented Lord Halnes with a son in London and that his infant half brother's name was William Alexander Albert George Alistair. Caroline was disgusted. "A woman that age, a woman that old!" she said. "Why, she must be forty-six or so." Then she added with an unexpected malevolence, "I wonder how Miss Melinda likes to be replaced?"

"What did the girl ever do to you?" Tom asked. "She's very young, isn't she? About sixteen, seventeen? And she's an orphan, isn't she? Carrie, you're not like your cousin, are you? Looking down on the poor girl because of her birth or something?"

"Oh, Tom," she said, "if I were like Timothy, would I have married you?"

"Thank you," Tom answered wryly. Caroline looked genuinely confused. Then she returned to the subject of Melinda. "I never liked that girl; in fact, I think I really hate her. She is nothing but curls and smiles and precious little ways and thinks herself very aristocratic. I hope she is smarting. My aunt was fatuous about her; now she has someone else to be fatuous about, and I'm pleased."

When the family came to Boston for Melinda's debut Caroline read of it morosely. She muttered over the account of Melinda's presentation at Court. But she did not discuss the matter with Tom. That was in December 1888. In the meantime Timothy Winslow had made himself indispensable to his cousin and visited the house near Lyme at least half a dozen times a year with his bulging brief case, and Caroline frequently met him at her office in Boston and in New York. Timothy remained bland and courteous to Tom. He did not speak of his mother or Melinda. Even when he returned from his yearly visit to England he did not mention his family. By this time Caroline had had a telephone installed, and there was hardly a day that she did not speak to her cousin at length and in private. She had come to trust his judgment absolutely. In 1889 she had been able to make him executive vice-president of Broome and Company, with increased responsibilities and a larger salary and profits.

"That's a lot of money," said Tom, still smarting over Timothy. "And he's not quite thirty yet, is he? And he's still with your lawyers too?"

Caroline did not like even Tom to question her judgments. "You may not like Timothy, but I have absolute confidence in him now, and I made a wise selection. He represents me at meetings of the Board of Broome and Company; I could hardly be on the Board myself, as a woman, and that's very tiresome. Well, it isn't too much money for Timothy, considering what he does for me. I wouldn't know what to do without him."

One day early in 1889 she returned from New York strangely excited. She was then pregnant with Ames. Tom had protested her going in her condition, but she had refused to listen to him. He thought when she returned that she was sick. But she had given him a darkly exultant smile and had said impatiently that she was quite well and there was nothing wrong.

He was certain there was, but he knew how obstinate Caroline could be and that she became even more so if pressed.

She had stayed on that occasion, as always when alone, at the Gentlewoman's Pension, which was becoming exceedingly shabby; it was in its final year. She and Timothy had dinner there, also customary after a day or two of long, hard discussion and consultations. The food was more execrable than ever. Caroline noticed that Timothy hardly touched his plate and that he appeared tense. His smile was absent; there were lines of nervousness in his pale face. But he seemed more than usually solicitous about his cousin and unusually deferential. She was quite pleased.

"Should you, Caroline," he said delicately, "be coming to New York so often—now?"

Caroline said bluntly, "Why not? You mean about my being pregnant? I don't believe in all that silliness about retiring, Timothy, and keeping out of sight, with the dainty pretension that nothing is about to happen. What is so shameful concerning pregnancy? Queen Victoria used to preside at Parliament and at Court on the very eve, I've heard, and no one commented on it."

Timothy had laughed quickly, though he thought her gross and common.

"Does it show?" asked Caroline in her forthright manner.

Timothy glanced about him furtively. He tried to be as forthright as Caroline and let her see that he admired her, which he did not. "No. No, Caroline. What an extraordinary woman you are! I wish more of our ladies were so honest."

"I haven't time to be anything else," said Caroline. She paused. "I'm grateful to you, Timothy. Against all other advice, but taking your advice about that harvester stock, I made a fine profit on it."

"Twenty-five thousand dollars," agreed Timothy. He relaxed a little. Now for it! "These old men are too conservative; they distrust modern inventions and our powerfully rising industry all over the country. But we are still young, and we have faith in the future."

She nodded. "I won't forget this, Timothy. It's been my biggest profit in three months, and even the last big profit was due to you."

He sipped a little vile coffee. Then he leaned his elbows on the table and looked at her with flattering seriousness. "Caroline, I must protest your check."

"Nonsense. You earned it," said Caroline, wincing only a little.

"I've come to admire you over all these years, Caroline. I've come to think of you as my best friend."

She was more and more pleased with him. She was sorry she still could not like him very much.

"And so," said Timothy, "I want you to be the very first to know." He hesitated and made his pale eyes more serious than ever and more flattering. "I'm going to be married this summer."

"Are you?" Caroline appeared interested. "That awful Bothwell girl, Amanda, who has been pursuing you for years?"

"Oh, Carrie." He lifted his hand deprecatingly and then let it drop on the table. "It wasn't very gallant of me to tell you, was it? I thought it would amuse you. How old was she when you last saw her? Well, she's twenty now, and one of those big, hearty Boston girls. A man eater, brisk and ruddy, and addicted to long walks and museums. There, I'm being ungallant again."

"She has a lot of money," said Caroline thoughtfully. "The Bothwell fortune is one of the largest in Boston, and they're very clever in their investments, I've heard. You could do worse, Timothy. Then it is Amanda?"

"No." There was no retreat now. "Caroline, I know how you feel about the other members of our family, and in many ways I don't blame you. I've revised my opinion about one. In fact, I have come to love her, if I may speak frankly. And I want you to think of her kindly, too, as my future wife."

Caroline knew instantly. The "one" could only be Melinda. She was so shocked that she turned deathly white. Her eyes widened, became huge and full of extreme horror. She pushed her chair back from the table, looked about wildly, as if searching for an exit in an urgent emergency.

Timothy was frightened for the first time in his life. He could see only anger and repudiation in Caroline's face, in the way her eyelids jerked spasmodically, in the way she had put both hands to her large breast. He had never seen her so shaken. What if he had ruined himself?

"Caroline, please," he said pleadingly.

Caroline caught her breath. Then she whispered, "Oh, not Melinda! Timothy, not Melinda!"

His acute ear caught something strange in her voice, and his eye something even stranger in her appearance. She was not angry, after all. She was only extremely shaken.

"Caroline dear, please listen," he urged. "I know how you feel; you think of my mother in connection with Melinda. But Melinda isn't the least like her, believe me. I wish you had known her better; you would now love her too. I am going to marry her this summer and bring her home with me. The English climate isn't good for her; she's quite frail, you know."

Caroline found her voice. She repeated, "Oh, Timothy. Not Melinda! How could it be Melinda?" And then, to his amazement, he saw that her eyes were large with tears.

"It is Melinda, I'm afraid," he said with more courage.

Then she cried, "That's impossible!"

"Why, dear? Do you hate her so much?"

She wanted to say, "You can't. I never told anyone before, but I know she is my sister. And yours." But she held back. To tell him this devastating fact would be to degrade her father, to heap filth on his memory. Yet something must be done. Then another thought came to her and sickened her almost beyond bearing.

"Does your mother know about this?"

Timothy, though excessively puzzled about Caroline's reaction, was relieved. "No, Caroline. Melinda is going to tell her. I've just had a letter from her today. She has possibly told Mother by this time. And that is why I am sailing for England the day after tomorrow."

"Oh, Timothy," said Caroline in despair for him. "Why didn't you tell your mother before?"

"Mother's never liked me, as you know, Caroline. And she adores Melinda. I've always been afraid that if she knew prematurely she would do all she could to keep Melinda from marrying me. I've had the astute idea for a long time that she would consider me unsuitable for Melinda, not only because I am more than ten years older, but because she distrusts me and never concealed the fact. She's wrong. I never cared for anyone before Melinda or since. Melinda insisted on telling her now; she is a girl who can't bear deceit. She's devoted to my dear mama."

"That terrible woman!" cried Caroline.

Timothy was silent.

"You can't marry Melinda," said Caroline, and her eyes filled with tears again.

"Why?" he insisted.

"Your mother should have told you."

"What should she have told me? Is your objection, Caroline, because Melinda is an orphan of unknown parentage?"

Caroline wanted to say yes, but falsehood was almost impossible for her. She could only shake her head mutely.

"Well, then." Her strangeness made him uneasy. "What else, Caroline?"

She tried to drink water, but it splashed over her hand, and she put the glass down. Then she stared at him blankly for several moments. Wicked woman! Let her tell her son herself, in faraway England. Let her suffer as she had made others suffer with her wantonness. Let her feel shame and agony. Let all know what she was.

She said in a clearer voice, "Please don't think, dear Timothy, that I am objecting. But you must tell your mother. You say Melinda has probably already told her by now. I doubt she will give her the reason why you cannot marry Melinda. And she must tell you!"

Now Timothy watched her alertly.

"What can she tell me, Caroline?" he asked.

"It's not for me to tell you."

Timothy considered all possibilities but the true one. "Melinda's father or mother was a criminal, perhaps?"

Caroline hesitated. Then she said loudly, "Yes! Yes!"

"How do you know?"

"I—heard, Timothy. Perhaps I heard. Don't press me; I won't tell you."

So Caroline was as haughty about the family as he was himself. Yet she had married that familyless bumpkin. Was she regretting it? Timothy hoped so.

"Let your mother tell you," she said.

"But even if there was something despicable in Melinda's background, it will not make any difference to me," said Timothy. "All that is behind her."

Caroline stood up. "Let your mother tell you." Timothy rose with her. She had a sudden thought. Was that horrible woman capable, for her own sake, of keeping silent before this dreadful situation? Would she permit incest?

Caroline said, "Write me. If she doesn't tell you, write me and I'll tell you, Timothy. Be sure to write me before marrying Melinda."

"I will," he promised. He would have to do that, for his own sake. Otherwise Caroline would never forgive him. But whatever this mysterious thing was, it meant nothing to him. Caroline had been immured most of her life. She was making something of a thing that was of no consequence to him. He would return with Melinda as his wife, and Caroline, who now needed him, would have to be reconciled.

They parted in a subdued atmosphere. Later Caroline felt her first exultation. She had finally been avenged on her aunt.

CHAPTER THREE

Though Timothy had frequently heard his friends and others contemptuously refer to Caroline as "that stupid Ames girl," he had always known that Caroline was neither stupid nor a fool. She, more than anyone else in all his life, had the power to alarm him, and for this alone he was never to forgive her.

So when he sailed for England in June 1889 to marry Melinda and bring her back with him to America, he began to feel uneasy on the second day out. He tried to dismiss Caroline's strange words and expressions. He did not succeed. By the fifth day his uneasiness had become sharp tension and anger. Why had not Caroline told him what she thought he should know? He no longer believed that Caroline was inspired by some female dislike of Melinda, or jealousy, or resentment, or anything equally trivial. She had been horrified, genuinely aghast. She had said it was his mother's place to tell him, not her own. Perhaps so. But as he had acquired a feminine characteristic or two of his own, he was angry at his cousin. She trusted him in other ways; she should have trusted him in this.

On the sixth and balmy day he became excessively restless and walked the pleasant promenade deck for hours. He stood at the rail and urged the ship on with his will. He thought of Melinda constantly, but the memory of her grave sweetness, her gentle voice, her artless mannerisms, and all the other characteristics which had charmed him since she had been a child of four only tormented him now. He had seen her at least twice a year since his mother's marriage, a month in the summer and often at Christmas. They wrote to each other more than once a week. He could not remember a time when he had not planned on marrying Melinda. Now she was eighteen, and it was all understood between them.

She had promised to speak to Cynthia. If anything was wrong, Cynthia herself would have cabled her son. But her last letter, received only a few days before he had sailed, had expressed her pleasure over his visit and the things she had planned for his amusement. She had enclosed a photograph, pridefully, of her son William and her daughter Melinda. On the last night out, just before going to the captain's ball, Timothy took out that photograph and studied it again, as if it would tell him something. He looked at the faces of the young girl and the child. The boy had a round and sober face, somewhat resembling his father's, but he had his mother's and Melinda's large light eyes framed in thick and silken lashes. The photograph told Timothy nothing, yet he felt some premonition of calamity on looking at it.

He did not sleep that last night. He was almost the first passenger to disembark at Southampton on this hot June day. He was more than usually irritated by the solemn delay of the Customs and the fact that as his name began with one of the last letters in the alphabet he had to stand, fuming, under the large W for too long a time. The last train to London was already puffing restively when he had finally closed his luggage, found a porter, and jumped into a first-class carriage. A fastidious young man, he was abnormally sensitive to the presence of others; he was glad to find that his compartment contained only himself and a deaf elderly man engrossed hungrily in English newspapers. He sat and looked out at the green English countryside, the placid cattle, the tall hedges, the profusion of buttercups and ferns, the little blue streams, the larches and oaks and willows, the small hamlets. England was peaceful and tranquil, in spite of the distant smoke of great factories and glimpses of dull workmen's streets and attached houses behind dusty hedges. In London he took the waiting train for Devonshire, for the family was in the country. The heat and smoke and rushing crowds in the glass-covered station suffocated him; his face and hands became gritty and moist.

Three old ladies in shawls and bonnets and carrying old-fashioned reticules occupied his compartment, and they glanced at him quickly over half-glasses and compressed identical withered lips. "Not English," they communicated with each other silently. They took out shapeless lengths of gray knitting the color and texture of their own hair and knitted busily and murmured together in far, high English voices. Timothy did not feel his usual empathy for the British. He knew the old ladies expected him to smoke and were ready to ring for the trainman in that event. He looked impatiently through the dusty window and swung one lean leg over the other. When the train stopped to pick up fussy families, he detested the clipped treble voices of the children, the dowdiness of the women, the authoritarian manners of the men, the clucking nannies, and the inane young girls with their fair rosy skins and the heaps of fair hair under large straw hats. Why did the English always travel with so many shawls and plaid blankets and mysterious packages on hot summer days?

The train growled, bleated, and smoked its way south, and now the country broadened, became wide and sedate, yet mysterious in its velvety green, its parklike hills and knolls and isolated giant trees, its moors purple under the sun, its villages and cathedrals faerie-like, its cloudscapes enormous and changeful over the quiet earth. Scents of grass and flowers and water invaded the compartment. There were some who spoke fondly of England being "pretty, lovely." But Timothy could feel the monolithic heart of British power under all this pleasantness, this serene smile, this passage of little stone bridges and quiet river and stream. The spirit of Empire lay under the deceptive calm and order, and the spirit of Empire had not only an imperial quality but a ruthlessness. One of these days, thought Timothy, we in America will feel that ageless stirring. An old if powerful Europe was bad enough and menacing enough for humanity. But a young American empire with no traditions, no caution, no experience, no wisdom, no craft, no wily diplomacy to control it would be a terror, even more terrible than ancient Rome.

Timothy usually spent these hours agreeably, either in studying his companions or in taking pleasure in the scenery. But now his thoughts were not only irritable but apprehensive. His leg swung faster and faster. He could not read or rest. The sun was hotter than he remembered from last summer. When he caught glimpses of the sea it shimmered with colorless intensity. Country roads seemed too crowded with dogcarts and carriages and other vehicles, villages too teeming. The old ladies waddled off the train and he was alone, and the long transparent English evening was beginning. Lonely houses appeared, buried in green shadow. The moors took on a threatening silence without horizon.

Then he was at the last station, and the train emptied. An evening wind was rising, pure and fresh and scented, with a hint of wilderness. He climbed the long wooden steps rapidly. He would be met, as usual, by a family carriage and he hoped the coachman would be young and brisk and not potter over the road. A porter struggled behind the young man, who ran up the stairs two at a time. He reached the platform and found himself met not by a coachman but by Melinda. She cried out his name as his head and shoulders appeared and ran to him lightly. She was in his arms, repeating his name over and over in an ecstatic whisper.

Laughing a little in his relief, he held her off and looked at her. She was tall and slender, like his mother, and had a delicate figure set off by her white duck skirt which flared about her ankles and by her white blouse with its rows of exquisite lace. She was hatless; her curling hair hung down her back, restrained only by a blue ribbon, in the English fashion. Her white slippers and silk stockings enhanced her appearance of fragility. "You are thinner, darling," said Timothy with tender accusation. She laughed softly and patted his cheek, and her young face was full of light and her gray eyes shone in the evening radiance. Now his last apprehension was gone. Melinda was all joy and serenity. She took his hand and led him to a dogcart drawn by a fat pony. The porter was informed by the girl that a carriage would pick up the luggage at once. "I wanted us to be alone on the way home," she said to Timothy.

She sprang into the dogcart and Timothy followed, taking off his hard hat to let the evening breeze cool his forehead. Melinda gathered up the reins, clucked to the mottled pony, and they drove away. For a while Timothy was content to sit in silence beside the girl as she deftly guided the pony down the cobbled hill to the village. He looked at the high and quiet sky, the walls, the little gardens, the thatched roofs, the children at gates, the blowing curtains at tiny leaded windows, the curving hedges, the traps and the occasional carriage, the drowsing cats on window sills, the hollyhocks and the ancient twisted chestnuts and the white-limbed birches.

Melinda was smiling gently; sometimes she glanced at Timothy and a quick happiness darted across her face like a soft light. Her long silken curls blew about her shoulders; he looked at the touching line from her chin to her ear, so vulnerable, so sweet to him. He took her hand and said, "Melinda, I'm not going home without you, you know."

"I know," she said. The dogcart left the little hamlet and swung between high hedgerows blowing with buttercups and ferns and little white flowers. From the meadows above came the lowing of home-going cattle and the tinkle of their bells. Swallows rose against the falling sun; the scent of salt water mingled with the perfume of warm grass. Somewhere church bells rang, their infinitely melancholy and nostalgic sound falling over the countryside, and birds clamored in the trees and a distant dog barked.

Timothy said, "Have you told Mother yet, dear?"

Melinda hesitated, and she was grave again. "No, Timothy. I don't know why, but I thought I should wait until you came. I didn't want her to think that it was all—stealthy."

Timothy sat up, and his apprehensions were sharp again. "You should have told her," he said. And then, "Never mind, dear. Perhaps you are right."

She smiled at him timidly. "I hope so. And I do think you are wrong about Mama objecting. Why should she? My friend Lady Agnes married a viscount eighteen years older than herself, and everyone thought it was a fine match, including Mama. As for Uncle Montague, I'm sure he'll approve; he's so fond of you, Timothy."

"Pernicious, like me," said Timothy, laughing a little.

"Oh, Timothy," said the girl, "I couldn't live without you. And I do so want to go home. It's beautiful here, and I love London, too, but it's not home."

He was very moved, and he held her slender elbow. "What? You prefer old dowdy Boston and the fusty old ladies in bombazine and the dry Common and all the imitations of England and the respectable vulgarity? But then, we'll be living in New York too."

He told her of his progress with Caroline as the dogcart climbed up the winding and silent road to the headland, and Melinda smiled again, her sweet and affectionate smile. "Once," she said, "Caroline really loved me; that was when I was a little girl. I never told you, but one day she brought out a box of water colors and she tried to paint me in my pink frock with a blue sash. She was terribly discouraged; she said the colors were so pale."

"Caroline—paint?" said Timothy in astonishment.

"Why, yes. She was fierce about the paleness of the colors. It was a lovely little portrait of me; I wanted to keep it, but she tore it up at once. I cried, and she cried too. I couldn't have been more than five, a year after I came from the orphan home."

Timothy thought about Caroline. She had many aspects, and he suspected that there were many which would even make him uncomfortable, but art was one he had never considered. Then he said, shrugging, "All the girls at Miss Stockington's school were taught to dabble in water colors. You did, yourself."

"Yes. But Caroline's work was different. I was so little, but even at that age her painting looked strong and brilliant to me. It reminds me of a painter whose work I saw in Paris. Ames! Yes, that was the name. Isn't it strange that he should have the same name?"

But Timothy was already tired of Caroline. He wanted to look at Melinda and talk about her. The dogcart reached the high green headland, broad and filled with blue evening shadows, silent and full of peace. Far beyond lay the bay, sparkling like silver fire and streaked with scarlet below the setting sun. And now they saw Lord Halnes' country seat, a house of gray stone under heavy trees, without gates or walls, and surrounded by deep gardens. The road was private, soft with dry dust.

Melinda and Timothy ran into the stone hall together, and stained-glass windows threw jeweled light down upon them. The paneled walls were lined with armor and pennants, and a low fire burned in a wide fireplace against the rising evening chill. Timothy looked about him with pleasure; it never smelled old and musty here, or damp or unfriendly, though it was an ancient house. There was a warmth and wideness in the hall, in the curve of the great stairway, in the breadth of oaken chairs and settees filled with bright cushions. Timothy knew that his mother had brought her charm to this old mansion, and air and grace, and he was always glad to arrive and be part of the gracious household.

Cynthia came down the stairway in a light blue dress, a string of fine pearls about her throat, and in that mellow air she did not appear to be more than fifty years old. Her hair was as soft and vivid as ever, though discreetly dressed now, and her skin was still fine and clear, her chin line still distinct. She was leading a little boy by the hand, and he climbed slowly and carefully down the stairs beside her. "Dear Timothy!" she cried. "William! Here is your brother!"

Timothy kissed her, patted her shoulder in his usual bantering manner, picked up his small brother, and kissed him. The child gave him Melinda's own serious look and her timid smile, and when he smiled he lost his resemblance to his father, for his smile was not quite Montague's. "You've forgotten me, haven't you, William?" asked Timothy. He was fond of his brother, who amused him with his solemnity. The child shook his head mutely and stopped smiling, and Timothy put him down.

"Let me look at you," said Cynthia, taking Timothy's thin shoulders in her hands and looking up at him searchingly. "Good heavens. It seems preposterous that such a big young man is my son! You make me feel old, dear."

"Age cannot wither nor custom stale her infinite variety," said Timothy with some malice.

"I hate that phrase," said Cynthia, smoothing her dress about her excellent waist and exhaling perfume. "It isn't in the least gallant; it's usually said of old ladies who are fat and rich, and it's always said by their hopeful nephews who hopefully count their aunts' years. But tell me all about New York and Boston. We haven't seen you since Christmas. Do come into the sitting room; tea is waiting."

"Where's old Montague?" asked Timothy as they went into the wide and pleasant sitting room where a fire rustled invitingly and windows stood half open to the evening breeze and looked upon the gardens.

"Don't be disrespectful, dear," said Cynthia with her old coquettish way of tapping him on the arm. "Montague will be here for dinner; he's in the village about something. He becomes quite the country squire in Devonshire and potters about and discusses crops and has beer at the inn."

"Square, rugged, homespun Montague," said Timothy. "I love to see him in his country boots and with his brown stick and his walking gaiters. Honest Montague, and his pipe and his old dad's big gold watch and chain which he never wears in London. I've often wondered if it still runs."

"Now you are mocking again," said Cynthia, and smiled her gay and charming smile. "Montague's just like every other Englishman; he's a different man in the country."

"That's good," said Timothy. "If the old boys in these parts ever saw him as he is there'd be another hanging on the village green, title or no title."

"I thought you were fond of him!" cried Cynthia, beginning to pour tea. "Melinda darling, do give Timothy some of these sandwiches so he can chew them and stop his nasty remarks."

"I am fond of Montague," said Timothy. "It's just that I envy him. I would like to be a ruddy Englishman with a title and a country seat and a house in London and a shooting box in Scotland and an ermine cloak and coronet for coronations and practically all the money in the British Empire —that is, all the money the Queen hasn't snatched for herself."

"Well," said Cynthia, "she has all those children, you know, and then the grandchildren too. Just swarms of them."

Timothy laughed. He refilled little William's cup himself; the child gazed at him with great wide eyes.

"Melinda, you look so pale," said Cynthia. "Timothy, do tell me it's my imagination."

"She needs to go home permanently," said Timothy. "It's wrong to leave me there all alone while the three of you nest cozily in England. I'll have to change it."

He looked at her closely as he said this, but her happy smile did not alter. "I suppose it is lonely for you," she said. "But how nice it is for all my family to be with me here. It makes up for everything. Besides, dear, you'll be marrying one of these days. By the way, how is Caroline?"

He told her of Caroline, and she regarded him proudly and nodded her pretty head and poured more tea. "I always told you the poor girl was no fool; she's proved that by appreciating you, dear. Is her third baby born yet?"

"No, but imminent," said Timothy. Cynthia laughed; she waited for Melinda's laugh, but the quiet girl seemed to be abstracted. "Melinda," said Cynthia, "is something wrong?"

"No, Mama," said Melinda. "I was just thinking about Caroline. I don't know why, but I was thinking."

"Poor thing," said Cynthia. "How is that country boy, her husband, Timothy?"

"As boorish and dull as ever," answered her son. "We hate each other heartily; he'd like to boot me out of his frightful house whenever I'm there."

The long English twilight set in, clear as water, and as still. Lord Halnes came into the sitting room in his tweeds, his respectable face cordial as he saw Timothy. They shook hands, and Cynthia rang for more hot tea. The fire brightened; one last bird sang to the coming night, and the song was infinitely sweet and sad and close. The family chattered, but Melinda was silent, listening to the bird. She did not know why, but tears came to her eyes and a faint pain to her heart. When she turned her head she saw Timothy watching her.

After dinner that night Timothy and Lord Halnes were left alone to drink their brandy together. The two men talked in low and serious voices now that Melinda and Cynthia had left them.

"And you are really convinced, sir," said Timothy, "that we are actually about to enter the age of prolonged and universal wars?"

Montague nodded. He looked at his pipe distastefully. "I don't know why I smoke this thing," he said, "but it seems expected of me in the country. Yes, Timothy. These are the last years of peace. And grace. We're all preparing for the new century and what it will bring us. My father told me that his father was certain that the year 1800 would mark a change in the world, but my father had at first thought him merely elderly and full of crochets. But my grandfather was quite right, you know. The world changed violently. The Age of Reason, or the Age of Enlightenment as they liked to call it, passed with extraordinary suddenness after the turn of the century. There was old Bony and his wars; there was also Waterloo and the Congress of Vienna and the industrial revolution and a tremendous change in mores and the solid rise of the middle class and a new Puritanism. They blame the last on poor old Victoria, but she is the symptom of her times and not its cause. She is the living symbol of the middle class, and now we have mean middle-class virtues, middle-class dullness, middle-class obstinacy, middle-class determination to have its day, and all the other dreary matters. Dash and joy, grandeur and aristocracy, intellect and pride and privilege, glory and passion—all these, my boy, began to pass away with extreme speed after 1800.

"I'll probably never see these things again in my lifetime; I only saw their passing. When your southern states lost that war of yours, your country also lost its last grace, poetry, spaciousness, and the charm of living. No wonder we English loved your South. It was not all greed for profits, I assure you, which sent England to the aid of southern gentlemen."

Timothy listened with sympathetic alertness and nodded over and over.

"There was a time," said Lord Halnes, sipping his brandy and looking at Timothy over the glass, "when money and aristocracy were the same thing, for it was inconceivable in a civilized society that an aristocrat should be poor and that the barbarian should have money. It made for intellectualism and the privileges of intellectualism. Where is there a Voltaire today in the world? Unless he owned a factory, a Voltaire of today would starve to death. There is only one god today, and his name is industry and Marx is his prophet." Lord Halnes smiled. "I am not averse to industry, my boy. It brings me a pretty profit, I admit. But it is also in the wrong hands."

He stood up, and Timothy saw his undistinguished profile. Lord Halnes poked the fire.

He smiled pleasantly at Timothy. "Do you know, I had this same talk with old Johnny Ames one time, just before he died. He would not join us."

"Could you expect otherwise?" asked Timothy. "He was a low-bred rascal."

But Lord Halnes frowned thoughtfully. "No," he said slowly, "I don't think so, Timothy. He never spoke of his family, but I'm certain he had one and it was of no small reputation. There was something about him; you can't mistake good blood. Yet he refused us."

He sat down. "And now we'll have wars. There are many reasons for wars. As many reasons as men have vices. What was it your Benjamin Franklin said? 'There was never a good war or a bad peace.' He was not a gentleman, but he was shrewd and intelligent. He knew his humanity and despised it and feared it and he had no hope that the American Republic would survive. And it will not.

"And now," said Lord Halnes, "tell me more about your cousin Caroline."

CHAPTER FOUR

Cynthia let her son into her private sitting room, which was as graceful and charming as herself, and full of firelight and the scent of roses and expensive perfume. She had had the dull oaken walls painted old ivory with touches of gold, and her furniture was definitely French in origin and light and airy. She was dressed in a white satin robe, and her hair hung free and she looked like a young woman. "Dear Timothy," she said, yawning, "what on earth were you and Montague talking about so long? We go to bed early in the country." She smiled; her contentment had made her flesh silky and vibrant.

Timothy sat down near her where she had reclined on her chaise longue. "I won't keep you up, Mother," he said. "Just give me five minutes."

"Darling, I'm not the Queen," she said. "Dear me, you must have had a tiring journey. You look positively wan; if you keep the muscles in your face so tight all the time you'll be old before your time. I never saw you so serious! What is it, Timothy?"

"It's very simple," he said, and he clasped his hands tightly between his knees. "It's possible you've already guessed it. I love Melly."

"Why, dear, we all do," she replied with tenderness. "Now, Timothy, don't be tiresome again. You are always saying that the English climate doesn't agree with her. The climate in Boston is much worse than in London and just as dank and steamy. And we intend to spend much more time here in Devonshire, for Melinda's sake, and I hope that satisfies you. Surely you must admit that the weather here is perfect, so balmy and mild. Melinda enjoys herself here; she has many friends in the country and is a great favorite. There is a certain family—you haven't met them yet—but one of the sons——"

Timothy broke in, "Mother! You didn't hear me. I said I love Melly, and she loves me. We want to be married; we always did, since she was twelve years old."

It was not possible. His mother had sat up abruptly as though struck, and she had become old, older than her years, old as death in her color and the starkness of her face and the bright terror of her eyes. Her hair fell back from her face. She caught the arms of the chaise longue, and her hands clung to them, and her mouth opened and her jaw dropped.

"What?" she muttered, and then swallowed. Then she cried out, "What? What did you say?"

"Good God," replied Timothy. "Is the idea so horrible to you? I'm your son, remember? You never liked me, but I never thought I was repulsive enough for you to hate. I'm sure you love me, in your way. Didn't you hear me? I love Melly. I can support her in even your extravagant style, even without her own money. I will give her anything she wants." As the expression on his mother's face became even more startling, he almost began to plead. "Don't talk about the difference in our ages; it doesn't matter to us. We've spoken of it often, knowing that it might disturb you. It shouldn't. Mother? Are you listening?"

She stood up and caught the back of the chaise longue as she retreated from him. He also stood up. Then he remembered what Caroline had said to him, and he was sick with the very first awful dread he had ever known. But he tried to smile.

"Why are you running away from me? Do watch out; that window behind you is wide open. Oh, for God's sake, Mother! Calm yourself. I'm not the scoundrel you think I am; if you had ever taken the time to learn about me you'd even have liked me. I really love Melly; I never loved anyone else.

I promise you solemnly I'll be good to her and take care of her and cherish her and all the other things. I promise you; I'll swear it to you, if that'll help."

Then Cynthia whispered dryly, "Oh, God. Oh, God. Oh, dear, dear God!" She put her hands to her face and stood there, trembling.

"Please don't be dramatic." Timothy tried to speak reassuringly. He took a few steps toward his mother. "Melly loves me. This isn't something new. We've talked about it for years. Now she's eighteen. We want to be married. With your consent or without it. We made up our minds, you see, long ago. I am taking her home."

Cynthia dropped her hands. Wrinkles had webbed her face; her eyes had sunk. She put one hand to her throat.

She whispered, as though her voice had been taken away from her, "You can't marry Melinda, Timothy. You can't marry her. Don't even speak of it. In the name of God, I beg you, don't even speak of it!" She took a step toward him, and he waited. Then she flung out her arms distractedly, "Timothy! Don't even speak of it!"

"Why?"

She was silent. They stood and looked at each other, Timothy pale and relentless, Cynthia shivering.

"I should have told you," she said at last, humbly, brokenly. "Oh, Timothy, I should have told you! But I was thinking of Melinda; I always thought of her first. I never wanted her to know; I never wanted anyone to know. I took such care. Timothy! I can't bear it for you to look at me like that! I'm your mother, and I can't bear it!"

She was staring at him, not only with horror, but with anguished pity and love.

"Is it something about Melly's background or family?" He tried to smile contemptuously.

She thought, then said in a broken voice, as if some hope had been given her. "Yes, yes! It is that. And so you can't marry her."

"I thought all the records at that orphanage were sealed." He was convinced that his mother's objection was not her objection to him, personally, after all, and he could really smile. "But I suppose you found out. Were Melly's parents idiots or criminals or hanged, or something? It doesn't matter. You only have to look at Melly to know her for what she is herself. Mother, I swear that Melly's background means nothing to me. I love her too much."

He waited, but she did not answer him. Long slow tears ran down her face. Over and over, she shook her head.

"You didn't think Melly not fit to marry some nobleman's son here, Mother. Why do you think she isn't good enough for me?"

She appeared to diminish before his eyes, to become bent and withered and ancient. "Believe me," she said, and her voice was whispering again, "you can't marry her. If I'd ever have thought—I'd have told you, Timothy, long ago. But I thought you loved Melinda as your sister. Your adopted sister. That was all."

He put his hands in his pockets and looked at her narrowly.

"Well, I don't love her as my sister. I love her as a woman, as the girl I am going to marry in spite of everything. You can't stop us."

He remembered all at once that Caroline had had a similar reaction to his announcement. "Caroline said I couldn't marry Melly, either. What is it? I have a right to know."

"Caroline said that?" Cynthia cowered against the back of the lounge. "Caroline—knows?"

"Apparently. She told me that she couldn't tell me, that it was up to you to tell me. Tell me!" His voice rose viciously. "I've got to know!"

Cynthia was even more stricken. She looked about her wildly, as if looking for a place to hide, to bury herself, to forget. Then she pressed her hands to her cheeks and resumed her fearful litany: "Oh, God. Oh, God."

"Tell me," said Timothy.

Cynthia's body shriveled in her wide white robe. She looked down at the pretty carpet which covered the floor. She faltered, "She's your adopted sister. There's a law——"

"Nonsense," he said, recovering some of his surety again. "I'm a lawyer. And I'm not a Catholic and neither is Melly, and the impediment of a kind of consanguinity doesn't apply to us. I can tell you. in full honesty, that there is no law in America which prevents me from marrying Melly. None. Well?"

"You don't understand!" Her voice was a thin wail. "Why, it would be a kind of—incest!"

"Oh," he began impatiently. "Incest! Have you lost your mind, Mother?"

The soft evening wind blew out the brocade curtains of the window, and they seemed to wrap themselves about Cynthia, as if to protect and hide her. She clung to the folds desperately to hold herself upright. She looked at Timothy, and then her head dropped on her breast, and she only stood there.

She became aware, in her torment and her sickness, that a long time had passed in silence. Her head felt as heavy as a stone; she had enormous difficulty in raising it. And then when she saw the terribleness of her son's face she fell back again.

"Dear, dear Mama," he said softly. "Would it be incest?"

She folded her arms in the draperies and held them to her breast. She could not look away from him. But she said, as if expiring, "Yes, Timothy. Yes."

And then, "Forgive me, Timothy. Forgive me."

"Who is her father, dear Mama?"

His voice was still soft, and she lifted her face and closed her eyes and could not answer.

Again there was silence in that pretty room, and the wind rose and a night bird cried.

"Why, that was a foolish question, wasn't it?" said Timothy. "Her father was John Ames. John Ames. I just remembered. You were his mistress for a long time. You were, and are, a trumpery woman, dear Mama."

"Oh, Timothy," she said, and her tears began again. "Oh, forgive me. I'd rather have died than told you. I love you, Timothy."

He did not move. He, too, looked old. His hands were clenched.

"And Melinda," she murmured. "Poor child. Poor children. What can I do? What can I do now to help both of you?"

"It's very simple," he said. "It won't really matter to you, Mama. You will laugh about it in a few days; I know you. It will be a joke between you and your husband. How you will laugh in your pretty way. You can tell Melly yourself, like the good sweet mother of both of us."

He paused, then said, "But wouldn't this be better? I'll tell Melly myself."

She started toward him, but he flung out his arm. She stopped and cried, "You can't do that, Timothy! You said you loved her. You can't break her heart by telling her and shaming her. You wouldn't do that to Melinda, would you? Oh, God, you wouldn't!"

"She'd hate you," he said meditatively. "Yes, she'd hate you. And that's what you deserve."

"You'd kill her, Timothy! You'd really kill her! I'm all she has. You would even take that away from her, because you hate me. Hate me, I deserve it. But don't hurt Melinda. Don't hurt my child."

"You've hurt her. You've destroyed her, dear Mama. You've destroyed me too."

He tried to breathe against the choking desolation in his throat and the dreadful loss he was suffering, and the hatred. He thought of Melinda waiting to hear even now what his mother had to say, waiting for him to knock on her door and tell her. "Melinda," he said aloud. "Melly." He still could not think of her as his sister. He could only think of leaving her, of never seeing her again, of never having her for his wife. She had wanted to come with him tonight to his mother, to be with him when he told Cynthia. What had made him refuse? What had made him say he must see his mother alone? "Melly," he said again.

"Timothy," his mother cried.

He turned away from her. He spoke in a flat dull voice. "I won't tell her. I couldn't, not even to do to you what you've done to us. If only you'd told me when she was a child. But that was beyond you; you had to hug it all gleefully to yourself. I can't tell Melly, and you can't, either. I can see that. Yes, I can see that. She's waiting in her room for me to come to her. She's waiting."

He went to the door. "I'm going to the inn in the village. I'll stay there overnight and take the first train to London. And you can lie to Melly; you can say whatever you want—that I changed my mind. Anything. It doesn't matter. Nothing matters any more."

Lord Halnes, who was reading comfortably in bed in his large cool bedroom, heard a tap on his bedroom door and then his wife entered. He looked up smilingly and in welcome, but when he saw her face he stepped out of bed in his long nightshirt and was as disturbed as it was possible for him to be. "Cynthia," he said. "What is wrong, my dear?"

She stood near his bed and was speechless, so he put his short and pudgy arms about her and forgot that she was taller than he and even forgot, as usual, to stand on his toes when embracing her. Then he drew her to his bed and was shocked to feel how feebly she moved. He put her down gently and sat beside her and picked up her hand, which was cold and lifeless. Then she bent her head and cried soundlessly and shivered. He took his woolen robe and wrapped it about her and waited. Cynthia was no light-minded woman; if she was in this state at almost midnight, then she had experienced some disaster.

"What is wrong?" he demanded more insistently, and rubbed her cold hands.

"Timothy," she said, and her voice was so low and hoarse that he had to bend his head to hear her.

"Oh?" Lord Halnes frowned but was relieved. He knew Timothy very well; he was certain that so discreet a young man would do nothing very vital to jeopardize his position with his mother and her husband. So Montague's alarm disappeared. He said almost indulgently, "Why don't you get into my bed, my dear? It's warm with hot bottles, and you are so cold."

But Cynthia did not move. She finally looked up. "He wants to get married," she began.

Oh, so that was it. Was the young fool about to marry some impossible trollop and make an ass of himself in public? But that was not like Timothy, the fastidious and cool-eyed and exigent. "Who?" asked Lord Halnes.

Cynthia wet her lips. She looked at her husband imploringly. "Melinda," she whispered.

Lord Halnes dropped her hand and his eyes bulged. "Well," he said, and then added with rare vulgarity, "That's a bloody contretemps, isn't it! Good God."

Cynthia stared at him dazedly, and then she saw his sympathy and amazement.

"What?" she murmured.

"Do you mean, my dear, that Timothy didn't know Melinda is his sister?"

Cynthia clutched the nightshirt at his chest with both hands. "Did you know, Montague, did you know?"

He put his fingers over her hands very tightly. "But certainly, my poor love. I knew from the instant I saw the girl that she was your daughter and that her father was poor old Johnny." He paused. "Is it possible no one else knew? In spite of the resemblance and the circumstances?" He was incredulous.

Cynthia was so relieved that she burst out crying and put her head on her husband's shoulder. "And you didn't mind, Montague?"

He patted her cheek tenderly. "Certainly not, dear Cynthia. Do you mean that you thought I didn't know and were afraid that I'd find out someday? What you must have suffered and feared. Yet I thought that you knew I knew."

"Oh, Montague," she cried, and he tried to comfort her. Now she could speak coherently and tell him of the interview between herself and Timothy, and as she spoke his expression became menacing, though he continued to smooth her wet cheek. That damned young rascal, to speak so to his mother, to Lady Halnes! When Cynthia had finished he held her to him and thought. Then he asked, "You haven't talked with Melinda yet? You must do so at once, since she's waiting. And I'll have a word with Timothy myself."

He paused and considered. "You know, it might have been best not to say anything, Cynthia. After all, the Egyptian chaps, all the Pharaohs, married their sisters. It was the law. Full sisters, too. Well, don't shudder. The truth might have come out someday when real damage had been done through a marriage. Let me give you a little brandy before you speak to Melinda. I don't think she should know the truth; no, I truly do not. You must be very inventive and very calm, my poor girl."

He gave her a glass of brandy, and she humbly kissed his fingers before taking the glass from him. He touched her gently on the head, put on his robe, and went to Timothy's room. He found that Timothy had packed a valise and was ready to go.

He was not particularly moved by Timothy's controlled but very apparent suffering. He shut the door behind him and said, "Were you thinking of walking to the village inn at midnight, three miles away, Timothy?"

"Then you know," said the young man.

"Certainly, I always knew. I am surprised that a man like you didn't know all the time. What blind eyes you have. Now, concerning that inn and that walk, for of course you haven't rung for a carriage?"

Timothy sat down on the bed as if exhausted. "No," he said. "It isn't a long walk; I don't want to disturb anyone, and it's all downhill." He looked at Lord Halnes and could not keep the gleam of hatred from his eyes. "You knew all the time and you never told me."

"Why should I have? Did you take me into your confidence? I do admit now that I should have been suspicious of your obvious affection for Melinda all these years, knowing you as I do. A man of your kidney doesn't love anyone merely for family reasons; had you had a brother or a sister you had known as your sister, you would most probably have hated them and considered them impediments to your own fortune and inheritances. Yes, I should have been suspicious."

He paused. "I have no intention of providing you with a carriage. I also have no intention of permitting you to create scandal in the village by appearing past midnight with your luggage. You are not going to cause tongues to wag about your mother. And about me. Is that understood?"

"Are you threatening me?" asked Timothy, roused from his sick apathy.

"Of course I am, if you wish to be so blunt. And I don't threaten weakly. I can ruin you. I will certainly ruin you forever, my dear boy, if you do anything rash tonight. I think you will consider that, for you are no fool. I say this in warning, so that you will never scandalize your mother's name, anywhere, or at any time. Again, is that understood?"

Timothy was silent. Lord Halnes smiled coldly. "It isn't that I do not sympathize with you," he said. "But you are a man, after all, and not a whining girl or a child. What is done is done, and there will be no revenge for you."

He waited, but Timothy said nothing. The young man's fair hair gleamed in the lamplight. Lord Halnes said, "There is a morning train to London at half-past seven. You will spend what is left of tonight in this house, then a carriage will be ready for you at the door at seven; before that you will be served breakfast in your room. You will indicate to the coachman—confound servants!—that you are needed urgently in London, at once. Good night." He hesitated, then held out his hand to Timothy. Timothy looked at the warm plump hand, that most powerful hand. And so he shook hands with his stepfather.

"Good night," Lord Halnes repeated. "I assure you I am sorry, but often things like this cannot be helped." He looked at Timothy again. "I prescribe a stiff drink of brandy. Ring for it."

Never in her life had Cynthia been so devastated as she slowly crept to Melinda's room and saw that there was light under the girl's door. She had seen her beloved parents dead and had thought she would never suffer so again; she had lost a husband, and then, much more agonizing, John Ames. Yet all that was nothing to what she was enduring now. Three times she lifted her hand to knock on the door, and three times her hand fell down helplessly. But she must have made some sound, some catch of the breath, for the door was flung open eagerly and Melinda stood there, the light shining in her hanging curls, her beautiful face smiling. When she saw her mother the smile disappeared, and her eyes opened wide and she felt disaster. She stood aside, and Cynthia moved into the light and pretty room, found a chair, and fell into it silently.

"Mama?" asked the girl, pleading.

She studied Cynthia, and what she saw was even more disastrous. She sat on the edge of her bed and dropped her slender hands between her knees. "You told Tim no, Mama?"

Cynthia nodded, the tears heavy in her eyes. Then she held out her arms to her daughter. Melinda, who was very white, did not move for a few moments. Then, crying out a little, she went to her mother, knelt beside her, and permitted Cynthia to put her arms about her and hold her close. But she did not respond to the caress.

"I'm so sorry, Mama," she murmured. "But we are going to be married just the same. We've talked about the possibility of your objecting; I'm so sorry, for I love you so much. But we are going to be married."

Cynthia pulled the girl's head to her breast. She said, "No, my darling. Uncle Montague and I have just talked about it. You see"—and she had to swallow the dryness in her throat repeatedly so that she could go on—"we know all about Timothy. He would make you very unhappy. When I—when I talked with Timothy I found out something else. He can't love anyone, really. If you had no money of your own—over a million dollars now—and prospects of much more, he would not want you."

Melinda pulled away from her, and her gray eyes flashed. "That is not so, Mama! Timothy loves me; he always did. I will ask him to come in here now and let him say so to your face!"

Cynthia clasped her hands tightly together. "He's already gone, Melinda. He left for the village half an hour or more ago. That was because we told him that if he—married—you, we would both cut you off from the family, and you would have no prospects of an inheritance, and neither would he."

Melinda sat back on her heels. She was very white, and her eyes fixed themselves in such intense pain on her mother that Cynthia could not bear it. "Tim has gone?" said the girl. "I can't believe it! He left me because—because of money?"

Cynthia nodded. "Oh, Melinda, listen to me. He knows how rich and powerful Montague is. Montague was very frank with him; marriage to you would mean that Timothy would be ruined forever."

"Uncle Montague did that to me?" cried the girl in bewilderment and shock. "I thought he was fond of me!"

"It is because he is fond of you that he did it, darling. Please try to understand. We know what Timothy is; he would break your heart. If Timothy had really loved you and were willing to defy Montague and sacrifice his prospects, then he would not have left this house and left you without a word or even a note. Isn't that clear to you? Surely you can see now that you are less important to him than his future!"

Melinda put her hands over her face, but she did not cry. Cynthia watched her; she felt very weak and prostrated and her knees were shaking.

"He's my son, Melinda, but he is a bad man. He was a bad boy. He never cared for anyone. He is using his cousin Caroline now, and she should be warned about him. He uses everyone, Melinda. I am his mother, and it almost kills me to tell you this. If I'd only known sooner! I should have told you, and this would never have happened."

Melinda dropped her hands. Her young face was lost and stricken; she looked beyond Cynthia. "Oh, Melinda," said Cynthia, but the girl did not appear to have heard her.

She said, "It isn't possible. No, it isn't possible. I'm sure he loves me." She stared at Cynthia now. "I'm sure he loves me!" Her voice was a cry of suffering.

"No, darling. He doesn't. He never did. Don't look like that, Melinda; it breaks my heart. But it's all for the best. You are young. You will meet someone else who will really love you and make you happy. You will forget."

"No," said Melinda, shaking her head. "I'll never forget."

A month later, in New York, Caroline said coldly to her cousin Timothy, "You surely realize that it wasn't my place to tell you about your mother! And Melinda. I never interfere with anyone's affairs; it was your mother's affair. I could not tell you."

Timothy looked at her a long time. He was very thin and appeared extremely tired. Then he smiled at the hostility and umbrage of his cousin. "No," he said gently, "you couldn't really have told me. You are quite right. We'll just have to forget all about it, won't we?"

But I'll never forget, he said to himself even while he was placating Caroline. I'll never forget, as you'll see for yourself one of these days.

CHAPTER FIVE

It had taken many years, but now there was a confidence and sympathy between Tom Sheldon and his wife's lawyers, Tandy, Harkness and Swift. When Tom had written Mr. Tandy that he wished to have a confidential discussion with him Mr. Tandy had replied, under discreet blank cover, that he would be glad to make an appointment for the tenth inst. So Tom went to New York, after explaining uncomfortably to Caroline that he was in search of some particular lumber which was exceptionally cheap.

Before he left for New York, however, he had gone up to the servants' quarters for his daily visit with old Beth, who was now in her eighties. She had been confined constantly to her bed for over two years, since she had fallen and broken her hip. The servants liked her; she was in good hands, and Tom had made sure of that. He no longer plagued Caroline to visit Beth daily, and so Caroline very rarely mentioned Beth except to say once, sullenly, "I'm sorry for the old soul, of course, so don't look at me as if you think me a monster, Tom. But it is so tiresome; we wouldn't need Gladys if it weren't for Beth, who requires such a lot of attention."

"We seem to need fewer and fewer servants, Caroline," Tom said, looking at the furniture, which was showing many signs of wear, and at the wallpaper, which had needed to be replaced five years ago, and at the dusty carpets.

"They want too much money these days!" Caroline snapped in answer. "Why, even my aunt never paid more than eight dollars or so a month for a housemaid, and she was very extravagant. She had an excellent cook, but she paid her only twelve dollars a month. Now these creatures are demanding five dollars a *week*, a cook seven! Do they think we are made of money?"

Tom had wanted to replace the servants who unaccountably left. (He suspected that Caroline had discharged them behind his back.) But Caroline would not permit this, even though he said he would pay them himself. "You can't spend our children's inheritance," she had said with real anger. "What you have and what I have belongs to them."

"You mean," Tom said bitterly, "that it belongs to you. Everything belongs to you. Well, Beth isn't going to suffer. She's served you all these many,

many years; she's treated our children as if they were her grandchildren. She deserves all we can give her. Don't say anything, Carrie. This time I won't listen to you."

He went upstairs this cold November morning and was enraged to find that no fire burned in Beth's room and that Beth's old wasted face appeared chill and blue. She coughed when he spoke to her, and said she was quite comfortable. But Tom brought coal himself and built a fire, then called for young Gladys, who sulkily told him that Mrs. Sheldon said not to waste fuel on unnecessary fires and that Mrs. Knowles was always in bed anyway, warm under blankets and quilts. Tom said, "I want a fire in here day and night, Gladys." And he gave the girl a ten-dollar gold bill, which made her beam and wink at him.

Beth's voice was croaking and feeble now; it was hard for her to talk. "When did you get this cold and cough?" Tom demanded, sitting beside her in the tiny high room and taking her hand. He was disturbed to feel its heat.

"Tom dear, you musn't worry," said the old woman, turning her head restlessly on her pillows. Her thin white hair was only a wisp over her pale skull. "Old people get colds very easily. I'm really very comfy, dear."

"I'll have the doctor for you at once," said Tom, more and more concerned as he listened to Beth's cough. He patted her hand. "Where's your tonic?" He poured the brown medicine for her, and she took it obediently and gave him a long and faded look of love and sadness. The room was becoming warm. Gladys was a good girl; she kept the room neat, and the little window was clean. Which is more than can be said for the rest of the house, Tom thought, angry with himself that he always let Caroline have her way. But it was easier than confronting her indomitable stubbornness. Besides, he loved her. Had he loved her less he would have opposed her more.

He went downstairs. The trap was already waiting for him. But first he went into Caroline's study, where she was, as always, surrounded by papers and ledgers. She looked up at him, frowning for an instant. There were no gray threads in her fine black hair, though she was nearly forty. Her face had changed little; it merely seemed stronger and harder and squarer. The perpetual large freckles on her broad nose never failed to charm Tom, and the sudden smile which quickly replaced her frown had never lost its ability to touch him, to make him think of her as a young and vulnerable girl. He kissed her, and she clutched him to her and kissed him over and over. But she said, "Do try to make a good bargain this time, Tom. People always cheat you."

"No, they don't," he said. "You mean that I never cheat them, and that's a different thing entirely. Carrie, Beth seems very sick this morning. Send for the doctor at once."

"Why?" She stopped smiling.

"I told you. She has a bad cough. Promise me you'll send for the doctor."

Caroline's big pale mouth, no longer red and uncertain, set itself in hard lines. Then as Tom continued to meet her eye determinedly she shrugged.

"Very well," she said. "But if you had your way you'd be calling the doctor daily for Beth, which is ridiculous."

She added, "Will you be seeing Timothy in New York?"

"No. Of course not. I detest him more and more."

She smiled again. "I can't see why. He made a lot of money for all of us during the Panic of '93. Oh, stocks were very low then, but even so you had to know just what to buy and have some judgment about which would be the first to recover and rise. He was almost invariably right. Now that he's president of Broome and Company he's making money hand over fist for me."

"And for himself."

"That's to be expected. I wish you didn't resent him so, Tom."

"Don't pity him too much," said Tom ironically. "He's done marvelously well since he married that Bothwell girl, as you know. With that nice fat trust from her grandfather, old Bothwell."

Caroline was scowling blackly again, and Tom knew that she still felt much hostility toward him for "daring" to sell Alfred Bothwell a large tract of land five miles away on the sea for a home after the young man had married Melinda Winslow six years ago. He had never understood Caroline's real and open hatred for the pretty young woman, who now had two children, twins, a boy and a girl. He had seen Melinda often and had been fascinated by her grave beauty, the large sadness in her lovely eyes, her sweet voice and gentle manners, her air of simplicity and trust. Once he had seen Lady Halnes at the Bothwell home and had marveled at how young she still appeared. She was a widow now and rarely came to America. There was some rumor that she and her son Timothy were not particularly friendly and that she seemed indifferent to his two sons and his little daughter but was fond of his wife, Amanda.

"If people are lucky enough to have family they should cultivate it," he had said to Caroline, who had given him a cold, dark look in silent answer. He guessed that some mystery was involved here, but Caroline never enlightened him. He had built the comfortable house for Alfred Bothwell, for Tom was well known for the excellence of his houses along the coastline. It was during the building of the Bothwell house that he had first met Melinda, and later he had come to like not only the young woman but her husband. He visited them occasionally, without mentioning this to Caroline, with the vague thought that someday his children would know theirs and lead a normal life.

Mr. Tandy, Mr. Harkness, and Mr. Swift were very old, yet they seemed to have changed little over the years, except to become thinner and more desiccated, parched of clever face, and very yellow of teeth. But their brown eyes sparkled just as brightly as always and rarely missed anything of importance.

Mr. Tandy was waiting for Tom in his office, and he greeted Tom with real affection. He had once said to his cousins, "That young man, I might say, is the type of an emerging American race. He is more truly American than are we Bostonians, for it is evident that he is a mixture of bloods. He has the strongly boned facial structure of the Scot, the long head of the Englishman, the shrewd and intelligent long lip of the Irishman, the pugnacious nose of the German, and the dark skin and prideful look of the Spaniard. Indeed, truly American, the consolidation of many races into one new race."

"What can I do for you, my dear Tom?" he asked when they were both seated in his office with the door firmly shut. "I gathered from your letter that it was something very important."

"It is, sir." Tom hesitated. He rubbed his temple where the thick black hair had grayed. "But it's still the old story—Carrie."

"Ah, yes." Mr. Tandy studied him reflectively. "She seems in excellent health."

"That isn't what worries me. I thought we'd have another talk about her. My boy John is thirteen, Elizabeth is eleven, and Ames is ten. They aren't young children any more. You will remember that when I talked with you last time you promised to try to persuade Carrie to let them live a more natural life. John goes to the village school, which isn't good enough, with only three overworked teachers; he'll have a hard time in Groton next year. Carrie never permitted him to make friends among the other children and visit them at their homes or bring them to ours. He goes in the buggy and comes back in it, and that's all. He had a tutor until he was ten, and the same old tutor teaches Elizabeth and Ames. She won't let the younger children go to John's school; it was he who raised such a smoke that she finally permitted him to go, and that surprised me." Tom paused and smiled ruefully. "Carrie never wanted the children to leave the house and the grounds. But even Carrie understood that he must go away to school next year. I've tried to persuade her to let Elizabeth go to Miss Stockington's. And there's Ames——"

Tom frowned. "Ames is a peculiar little fellow. He isn't robust like John. He's secretive; you never know what he's thinking. Sometimes he's very unfriendly to everyone. In some ways he resembles——"

"Timothy," said Mr. Tandy. "Ah, yes. In some way."

But Tom, who had meant exactly that, shook his head. "I hope not, sir. By the way, I hope I can get out of here without running into him. He has a lot of influence over Carrie, and that's funny, because she really doesn't like him. Do you know what I actually did? A year ago I asked him to talk to Carrie about sending Elizabeth away to school and getting a better tutor for Ames. I was reduced to that." Tom reddened.

"I see," said Mr. Tandy. "I did talk to Carrie, you know, and she refused."

"When I ask her why," said Tom, "she either pushes the subject away or she looks frightened. Frightened about what? She stands at her study window when it's time for John to be home and is restless until he's inside the house and the door is bolted. She always bolts doors, summer and winter, and would keep the windows bolted in hot weather if I permitted it.

"I might understand a little if she were devoted to our children, but she isn't. She is apprehensive about them, concerned about them, and worries about them. But she doesn't love the boys and the little girl. She doesn't love anyone."

"Except you," said Mr. Tandy kindly.

Tom was not embarrassed but only more disturbed. "Yes. If I were a man who is easily frightened I'd be frightened by that. What if I die? What will become of Carrie? She has no friends; she won't have anything to do with her family, except for Timothy Winslow, but even so she never visits him and his wife in Boston, nor will she go to their house in New York. I've met Amanda once or twice, you know, and she's a nice young woman and very friendly, but Carrie will not see her.

"I'm in my forties now, Mr. Tandy. I may live a few more years or die in a year. Or live to be a hundred. For Carrie's sake, I hope so; I often pray so. I'm her only link to life, and not a very reliable one at that. She never had the children, and they never had her."

Mr. Tandy murmured sympathetically and looked at his clasped hands on the desk. Tom tried to laugh. "At one time I thought they loved me as I love them, but they don't. I've given up trying to find the answer."

Mr. Tandy murmured again. Tom nervously took out his pipe and filled it with tobacco and lit it. Mr. Tandy was moved to see those big brown hands trembling a little. Tom continued: "If I didn't have my old village friends and my workmen I'd go out of my mind. How can Carrie live without some human associations, some little friendship, some affection from others besides me? And so I come back to being afraid for her. She's a recluse; she's getting worse every year, and she isn't old yet! She never steps out of that house except to go to her Boston office twice a month and to New York. If she loved our home I'd understand a little. But she doesn't. It's falling into rack and ruin, and I have to do the repairs on the sly—the outside, I mean. But the interior needs renovating; she hires only the cheapest and most slovenly farm girls, and so the house is actually dirty. I tried to hire better, and though you will hardly believe it, she became hysterical. She looked then as if she were being—threatened. Please don't laugh, sir."

"I assure you, Tom, that I am not laughing at all," said Mr. Tandy seriously. "You've known Caroline since she was very young, haven't you? I did not see her at all until she was a young woman. About eighteen or nineteen. She was almost, at that time, the way she is now. How was she when she was a child?"

Tom thought about this, frowning. "She was frightened even then. But she was a sweet, shy child. Then she changed; I don't quite remember just when or how, except that she seemed afraid of her shadow, and she grew away from me, and later I didn't see her for several years. Mr. Tandy, I thought I knew all about Carrie. I'm sure I'm the only person she ever confided in, but that was a long time ago. Just before we were married. Since then she hasn't confided in me at all. I don't know what I did to ruin her confidence in me, but I must have done something. She's interested in my work; she's very excited about it sometimes and she's given me some fine advice. But still, when I try to talk to her or get her to talk to me, she withdraws as if I had struck her, and she's short with me for days afterward."

"I see," said Mr. Tandy, thinking. "You never knew her father, did you?"

Tom said shortly, "No, I never knew him. I would see him occasionally in the village, at the depot. I don't know why I hated him, but I did. Perhaps it was because I thought he was injuring Carrie. I still think he was the worst influence in her life. You never saw the filthy old house they lived in in Lyme during the summer. We all wondered how it survived each winter; it was falling apart. Yet Mr. Ames was rich even then, but he never did anything about his house, and Carrie lived like a beggar with a very old woman she called Kate, and Beth Knowles. If a man hated his child he couldn't have treated her worse than Mr. Ames treated Carrie, if you can judge from appearances. Yet she loved him, and that's what I don't understand."

Mr. Tandy did not answer immediately. Then he said, "I knew John Ames a long time; I met him shortly after he married Ann Esmond. A lovely girl. Since then we've handled his affairs and, as you know, we are co-executors with Caroline. She has that small bank on Thirty-fifth Street and a very competent staff, and so they will take care of Caroline's affairs after we in this firm are all dead." He showed Tom his long yellow teeth in a brief smile. "I hope I am breaking no confidences when I say that she will not appoint Timothy as her executor."

"I'm glad to hear that," said Tom. He went on: "I've tried all our married life to draw Carrie out, to make her more human. Once I said to her, 'What if I die, Carrie?' She almost went out of her mind. It took me hours to calm her, and you wouldn't expect that of such a woman, would you? She walked up and down, wringing her hands. Perhaps I was wrong to say that to her, but I thought she should realize how friendless she is and how alone and so do something about it. But it was worse than ever after that. You wouldn't believe it, but she made me stay in the house for three days! I had to humor her. I'm not exaggerating, sir. It isn't good or healthy for a woman to be wound up in anyone like that, not even her husband. Yet she doesn't trust me and doesn't confide in me, and that's what I don't understand. She'll go for days, and sometimes weeks, without hardly speaking to me, all wrapped up in her investments and her money. I get damned lonesome, sir. She won't let the children have their meals with us; we must eat all alone. And there are times we never exchange a word at the table. It gets—weird. But if I cough or look tired, I see her watching me like a hawk, and then she doesn't sleep at night until she is convinced I'm all right again. Do you know something, sir? She makes objections about getting a doctor for the children or the servants or for herself, but if I have the slightest cold the doctor is sent for immediately. The man must think that Carrie is a little queer."

"Caroline's eccentric, yes," said Mr. Tandy. "Let me be candid, dear boy. Caroline led a very secluded life while a child. Then she traveled with her father. She met many famous people internationally. Her father entertained them, and they entertained him and Caroline. Had she been—ah—capable of forming friendships in those young years she would have done so. But she did not. There are some people who are constitutionally incapable of making friends. They are recluses by nature. Caroline is simply wise enough to know her incapacity."

Mr. Tandy felt he was being mendacious, but he wanted to comfort Tom. Besides, John Ames had been dead a long time, and it was bad taste to arouse the dead, to confront them with accusations, to denounce and judge them.

Now Tom was coloring again, and he smoked and looked at the window, where the November light was ashen and dull. "I don't know how to say this, sir, but I must. I've been reading some books about a doctor in Vienna, a Dr. Sigmund Freud. I don't understand his theories, but then I'm not an educated man. But from what I have read, he has cured people like Caroline through some sort of hocus-pocus. And I understand that there are some of his pupils in New York now. I have the address of one or two of them, which I got from the newspapers.

"I thought," said Tom, "that you might talk to Carrie and persuade her to see one of them. He might cure her of her terrible fears and her obsession for me and make her more normal and pull her out of herself. Something must be done quick for Carrie."

"My dear young man!" exclaimed Mr. Tandy. "Are you speaking of alienists? They are for mad people. Good gracious! Caroline's not mad. Did you actually think that an alienist, by some sort of hocus-pocus, as you call it, could help Caroline? I've read about their theories, too, quite extensively. They are of the opinion that every quirk of human nature is in some way connected with—ah—with intimate relationships. Can you conceive of Caroline talking artlessly and confidentially to such a man, when she won't even talk to you, whom she loves? The idea is ludicrous! Caroline!"

Tom was silent. Mr. Tandy became agitated and shook his head. "There's nothing wrong with Caroline; she's mentally and physically far superior to most members of her sex. Her mind is absolutely clear and sharp, like a man's. And I'm certain she had no—ah—twisted thoughts about her father, as those men would imply. Certainly John Ames had a powerful influence over her, but not that! How could you think that of her? Good gracious!"

"I didn't!" shouted Tom, ashamed and red-faced. "Good God! Don't you understand? I thought one of those alienists could help her, that's all."

"Well, then," said Mr. Tandy, "Tom, let me tell you this: Caroline is a strong individualist. She is not like other women. She is herself, and as a human being and herself she deserves her dignity, which these men would violate, even if you could get her to go to one. She would have every right to be insulted at the mere suggestion. Why, I'll wager she has twice the intelligence of that Freud himself! And a great deal more character and self-discipline. If she is peculiar about money and has fears about it, that isn't unusual. We call it the fetishism of money. It doesn't represent to Caroline what it represents to others, and she isn't the only human being with that peculiarity. It represents, I think, security to her, and the slightest loss of it makes her frantic, for her security is threatened. Why she has this fear, I don't know, but again it is not unusual. I know half a dozen people in Boston alone who are that way. We call them 'eccentrics.'"

He added with more gentleness, "Don't be alarmed. God can help her. But only God. I am an old man, and I never gave much thought to God in my youth, but I do now. If we all prayed more and tormented ourselves less, this would be a happier world. A more peaceful one. If you can, at any time, turn Caroline's slightest thought to God, you will help her to her own individual salvation, for men aren't saved by themselves but only by the power, the merits, and the grace of God. Caroline is in His hands."

It was bitterly sleeting when Tom arrived home the next morning. After he dismissed the station hack he walked around the side of his great house and looked at the sea walk leading to the shingle. More huge boulders had been washed up upon it. He shook his head. The ocean roared and hissed in the storm and was hidden behind the steely curtain of the sleet. Caroline would not let him, despite his strength, move the boulders himself, and she was always promising to get "the man" to move them. "You have to watch your heart at your age, Tom," she said. "The man" rarely appeared. Caroline called him shiftless and spoke of the hard-working servants in her aunt's former home in Boston. Tom suspected, quite rightly, that Caroline would not pay him enough.

Tom listened to the howling and screaming of sleet and water and watched the faint dull light that hardly lifted the desolation. A strong odor of salt mingled with the furious wind. Tom said aloud, "Somehow, this makes me think of my own life." He pulled his coat up around his ears and went into the house. He encountered Gladys in the dark hall, and as she helped him remove his wet coat she sniffed and gasped audibly. With his usual kindness he asked what troubled her.

"Oh, sir!" she sobbed. "It's awful! Poor Beth died late last night! All alone, too."

"Oh, my God," said Tom, feeling heavy and old and full of grief. "Well, she wasn't young, Gladys, so don't cry like that." He paused. "What time did the doctor come, Gladys, and what did he say?"

Gladys paused portentously, Tom's coat dangling in her arms. "After she was dead, sir. Oh, ain't it awful? Poor Beth!"

Tom stood still. "Why wasn't he sent for before she died?"

Gladys hung up the coat in the hall closet before she answered. And then she said in a muffled voice, "The mistress didn't send for him, sir, until I came down after looking in on Beth at ten o'clock, just before I was going to bed, and there she was, dead. I'd seen her last at six when I took up her supper, and she was very sick, sir, indeed she was!"

"Did you tell Mrs. Sheldon that?" asked Tom.

"Yes, sir! And she said that Beth would be all right, and if she wasn't the doctor could come today."

"And—no one—was with her when she died?"

"No, sir. Nobody. I wanted to look in on her a couple of times, but I was busy with Miss Elizabeth and Master Ames. They do get out of hand, and old Mr. Burton can't handle them alone."

"Mrs. Sheldon didn't go up at any time?"

"Not that I know of, sir. She was busy, like always, in her study."

"Yes," said Tom. "Like always."

Gladys had drawn the shades in Beth's room, but Tom opened them. He was conscious of the profound silence of death in the little chamber and the sound of wind and sleet battering against the small windowpane. Beth lay in her bed, which had been neatly remade, and she appeared asleep, her sparse white hair around her withered face. Tom stood beside the bed and looked down at the dead woman, and even in his inner rage and grief he was aware of the sadness and loneliness of her expression, the abandonment of the folded hands on her sunken breast.

He looked at the forlorn old woman for a long time. Then he said aloud, "Good-by, Beth. I loved you very much. God be with you." Then he went downstairs. The silence of death appeared here also; the children's voices could not be heard. To Tom, this was stealthy and guilty and sly. He went to Caroline's study and flung open the door with a bang. The room had been lit against the darkness of the day, and Caroline was at her desk, frowning, her new spectacles on her nose, her pen in her hand, and heaps of neat papers before her, and ledgers. She was not yet dressed; she wore one of the flannel nightgowns Beth had made for her and her ancient brown dressing gown, and her feet were in slippers. She started at the noise of Tom's entrance, looked up, removed the glasses, and gave him a sober smile, waiting for his usual kiss. But he stood in the doorway and looked at her, and all at once she was aware of his anger.

"Tom," she said. Then, "I'm so sorry about Beth."

"That's a lie," he said. "A filthy, conscienceless lie. A contemptible lie. You aren't sorry at all. You let her die alone. You didn't even send for the doctor until she was dead, though you gave me your promise. She served you all your life, loving and caring for you when no one else cared for you or loved you, and she wouldn't leave you. She was better than most mothers to you. But you couldn't spare five minutes to see her yesterday, to speak to her kindly, to show her any concern, to let her know that you loved her. But you never loved anybody, did you, Carrie?"

She jumped to her feet. Terror filled her eyes, and even now Tom could wonder confusedly at it.

"Tom! Beth was old and sick. Very old, very sick. She'd been this way for over two years. She had every comfort! Gladys waited on her hand and foot. And Beth knew how busy I am; she understood."

"Did she? Does anyone understand when they're dying and no one comes or cares? Will you understand, Carrie, when that time comes for you?"

(The terror became a stark brightness on Caroline's face, and she was a girl again, listening to paternal reproaches she did not comprehend but which threatened her.) "Tom!" she cried again. "I'm going to have Beth buried tomorrow near your parents. I'll put up a big stone for her. I've ordered the nicest coffin from Boston—it cost three hundred dollars. And a lot of flowers from Brewster; they'll be here tonight. Tom!"

"A coffin and a stone and flowers for an old dead woman who had just wanted to know that you hadn't forgotten her," said Tom. "Just think how much that's going to cost you, Carrie. A few dividends for November from New York Central Railroad! How can you bear it?"

She held out her hands to him, and her face was blank. She had the bewildered attitude of one who is blind and waits for attack.

"I'll never forgive you for this, Carrie," said Tom, and stepped back over the threshold and shut the door behind him.

He could not stand the house yet, the silent, guilty house. The dead old woman on the top floor seemed to dominate it, to fill it with her forlorn and seeking presence. He put on his coat and went outside into the wind and dimness and salt sleet and walked down the sea lane to the shingle, which was wet and black. The wind tore at him; the sleet stung his face; the scream of the ocean deafened him. But he stood and did not care or even know. He was one wound of sorrow.

Then he felt a hand on his shoulder and heard someone panting beside him. He looked and saw Caroline. She had flung one of his old coats over her dressing gown. Her ankles were bare, and her loosened hair whipped about her face. "Oh, Tom," she cried. "Come in! You'll catch lung fever out here. Please come back, Tom."

"I'll never come back," he said.

"Listen!" cried Caroline in despair. (She was fifteen years old again, and she had not heard from her father for several months and she was afraid he was ill or dead in some foreign city, and she was lost.)

"I can't listen, Carrie, because you can't say anything that would mean something to me. You've ruined your own life. You're ruining the children's lives. I can't help you. I've tried, all these years. You're beyond help. But I can help the children because they're still young. They never had a father like yours, God damn him!"

(The young Caroline had no words. She was heartbroken; no one cared for her; there was no one in the house but Beth, who could not comprehend her few incoherent words and cries.) "Listen!" she pleaded. "Please listen." The loneliness, the forsakenness, was a thick aching in her heart, and the inability to communicate was a stone in her throat.

"To what? What can you say, Carrie? I can only tell you that I've loved you so much that I've become less of a man because of it and let you have your own way all the time so you wouldn't be hurt. But I'm going to take a hand in things now, myself, about the children."

(She was now the Caroline who had heard her father cry out, not for her, but for his other daughter. She was the forgotten daughter, and only the other was remembered.)

"Oh, God, listen," she groaned. "I'm here. Don't you hear me? Please listen. Don't you hear me?"

"I hear you, Carrie," said Tom, unrelenting. He pushed his hands into his pockets and turned his face from her, and it was the turning away of her father's face. She grasped his arm with both hands and clung despairingly to him. Her wet loose hair blew about her like a long dark banner.

"I'm trying to tell you about Beth. It isn't the way you think. I'm not that bad. Beth——"

"I don't care what you think, Carrie. But I am thinking of Beth and all that Beth means. And I'm thinking of the way you won't have anything to do with your family, and especially with Alfred Bothwell's wife, Melinda, who never hurt you."

(The storm howled about them and shook them, but Caroline was the girl who had first seen her aunt in her father's arms, in warm lamplight, and she was hearing Cynthia's soft, seductive voice. And she herself was betrayed.)

"Listen," she whimpered. "Please listen."

"What you have, Carrie, in money means nothing to me. It never did. What is money? You gave your life to it, just as your father did. You're nearly forty, and you worship money and put all your humanity in it, as if it meant anything at all."

(She was the young Caroline crouching on the dirty floor of Fern and Son, robbed, beaten, dragged, thrown down.)

"Listen," she sobbed, and shrank back from him. "You don't know what money means to me, Tom."

"Yes, I do," he said in a hard voice above the storm. "It means your life, doesn't it?"

"Yes. Yes. But not the way you think. Please listen."

One of her hands clutched him again, and he pushed it off, not feeling its icy wetness. "I'm going in," he said. "And you'd better too. Doctors cost money, you know." He paused. "You've even made our house ugly and dirty because it costs money to keep a house clean. You've bought all those expensive pictures, but you keep them locked away and hide the key. Why, Carrie, why?"

(She was the young girl who had sat in the woods near the old house in Lyndon in the autumn, with the trees fiery about her and the sky brilliant through and above them, and there was a scarlet ribbon in her hand.) "They're mine," she said, her voice rough and hoarse. (They were hers, secret and loved, and they loved her in return, and she was not alone but was communicating in fullness with beauty and tenderness.)

"Yes, everything's yours, Carrie. Everything. But not everything now. You can have your money. That's where your treasure is, as the Bible says."

(But her treasure was in love, and there was no love and no security now.) "Why don't you listen?" she said. "Let's go in and I'll try to tell you." Her voice died away futilely.

"You don't have anything to tell me any longer, Carrie."

He stood apart from her, and there was no love, no concern, no softening on his face. Her thin slippers had sunk into the wet sand; a wavelet of the incoming tide dashed over her ankles. He said, "You hate people. You always did. I don't know why. Maybe you think that friendship will cost you a little cash. You never give anything to charity. You care for no one but yourself. And your money."

(She was beating again on the doctor's door, and then the doctor was there and she was pulling at his sleeve and he was resisting her and regarding her with scorn and detestation because he thought she had no money to pay for help for her dying father. She heard the last echoes of the clanging of his doorbell.)

"You can't live without money!" she cried. "They'll let you die, without money! They'll let you die!"

"You let Beth die, and you had money enough to give her a little ease at the last, but you didn't. She died all alone."

(But her father had not died all alone. She had been with him, and there were tall kind women in white with cowls about their faces. They had helped her through those terrible days. She felt again their gentle hands, the comforting of their arms. She had forgotten. She must remember them—today —tomorrow.)

"I forgot," she mourned, and clasped her freezing hands together piteously. "I'm so sorry. I forgot. I should have remembered."

"It's too late now," said Tom, and he turned away from her and slogged through the wet sand of the shingle to the sea walk and the house. (He was her father, leaving her forever, forgetting her, and she uttered so terrible a cry that Tom was struck, and he looked back at her.)

"Come in, Carrie," he said uncertainly. The faint gray light lay on her face, and he was horrified at its expression, its blindness, its complete agony.

(But there was no place for her to go any longer. There had really never been any place to go. There was only a dark wilderness in the world, and she was all alone.)

That night she moved from their bedroom into a "guest" chamber which had never sheltered any guest, and she never returned. She was alone as she had never been alone before. She began to spend long hours in her gallery, looking at her grandfather's paintings, and only there, walking from one to another, did she feel communication and understanding. Tom later tried to reach her, but it was impossible. She had mistrusted him earlier with regard to money, but now she mistrusted his love, on which she had leaned and by which she had been warmed and consoled. The wall had been broken; the fire had been quenched. She loved him but did not feel that he loved her. He had left her, and though he had half carried her to the house on that dreadful morning and had dried her hands and her hair and her face tenderly, she never again believed in his love, never again believed that he was truly, warmly concerned about her. She confronted the world alone, and all the terrors in it.

As for Tom, he was stricken by Caroline's coldness, her shrinking, the way she averted her face and head when he approached her, her silence, her indifference. She did not speak to him of her affairs after that day; she showed no interest in his. He prayed for her, and often he would stand at her closed bedroom door. She had shut him out; she had left him. He loved her, but she had left him. It was not his fault that he could not hear her weeping, for she cried silently, as the lost cry, as the abandoned mourn.

CHAPTER SIX

Mr. Tandy walked very rapidly into Mr. Swift's office, and his old face was tense with consternation. He held a letter in his hand. "Good heavens!" he exclaimed. "Has Caroline Ames gone mad or become a Roman? Look at this! She has ordered me to send a cashier's check for—this enormous sum!—every year, to something called the Sisters of Charity in Boston! And she's adding a codicil to her will to make it perpetual as long as her estate exists! Good heavens! She never gave anything to charity before, though there's Phillips House, the Humane Society, the Boston Park Commission, and a dozen other proper charities! And listen to this from her letter: 'The Sisters are never to know the donor.' She was circumspect in that, at least!"

A few days before Christmas the new young priest of St. John the Baptist Church in Boston walked through his warm and silent church, smiling here and there at a young boy or girl kneeling before an altar or at an old woman saying her beads or a tired man sitting with his hands folded on his knees. The yellow candlelight flowed and bent a little; the door boomed its echoes along the nave; the Gothic ceiling trembled and moved with the faint sunlight that filtered through high stained windows; the crucified Man dropped His head above His altar; the statues, in that fragile illumination, seemed to stir behind their candles. It was silent and peaceful, pervaded by the ghost of incense, by all the thousands of prayers which had been whispered here, and by the Most Holy Presence.

A woman was sitting alone, with empty pews all about her, and there was something in her aspect, her rigidity, which made the priest hesitate and then pause near her. She was staring at the crucifix, and her hands were clenched tightly on her large and ugly purse. She was like one in catalepsy; she was not praying and seemed hardly to breathe, and the priest could see her eyes shimmering in the soft gloom, empty eyes like glass. She was evidently a poor woman, for her clothing was black and unfashionable, though neat and severe, and her black buttoned boots showed cracks under the polish. She wore a black bonnet in the style of at least fifteen years ago, and her gloves were black. But she had dignity. She reminded the young priest of his Aunt Marie, who had lived in Cincinnati until she died when he was still a child. He had been fond of Aunt Marie, a widow, and proud and poor, who had been a seamstress and had known the bitterness of sorrow and loss and privation.

The priest genuflected, then slipped quietly into the pew beside the woman. She did not appear to notice him. She was still staring emptily at the crucifix, her eyes unblinking. Again the priest hesitated; he saw one tear run down her broad cheek, then drop onto the plain black of her winter coat.

"Is there something wrong?" he whispered. "May I help?"

She did not move for several moments, and he had just come to the conclusion that she was either absorbed in some awful agony that had deafened her to the human voice or she had not heard him, when she stiffly turned her head toward him. She regarded him silently, no expression on her features, and he was startled at the clear yellowish gleam of her eyes.

"Something wrong?" he whispered gently.

She shook her head. She did not move, yet he had the impression that she had shifted away from him.

"Are you sick?"

Again she shook her head.

"Won't you let me help you?" he insisted.

Her face changed, and he saw that she was not as old as he had believed and that she still had some youth. Again he thought of his aunt, who had, years ago, received the news that she was losing her sight and would soon be blind. His aunt had sat so, immobile in her tiny hot little parlor, too stunned to speak, too anguished with her thoughts. The priest put his young hand on this woman's shoulder impulsively and said again, "Won't you let me help you?"

Her big pale lips parted, and her throat trembled, as if trying to reply. The priest glanced again at her black clothing and said, "Are you a widow?"

A widow. Yes, she was a widow, she thought. She could finally speak, but only in a hoarse, far whisper. "In a manner of speaking, yes."

Her tone, her words surprised the priest, and he looked more keenly at her. She had not spoken like a poor and ignorant woman, but like a lady of family and substance.

"I'm sorry," he said. "I will pray that you will be comforted."

Again her face changed, and he saw the dark shadow of bitterness on it.

"Please don't bother," she said. "There is no comfort for me any longer; there never was; there never will be."

"There is comfort here," said the priest earnestly. "God never forgets His children."

She smiled very slightly. She stood up and he stood up also, and she passed him and did not bend her knee at the end of the pew. She marched solidly toward the door, and he watched her go, her black skirts swishing about her, her back rigid. The door boomed behind her as she opened and closed it.

It snowed heavily and wetly just before Christmas, dropping down in big fat flakes and burying trees and shrubs and sand dunes. Tom Sheldon drove his sleigh to Alfred Bothwell's home. He did not hear the merry tinkle of the harness bells; he had long forgotten the sound of merriment. The road was packed with thick alabaster and the pale sun shone on it, and even the old horse felt the briskness of the air and recalled how it was to prance over the snow. "Steady, boy," said Tom, and the bells rang and the sleigh glided smoothly and the sea was a bright gray and the sky was opalescent, like the inside of a shell.

Alfred Bothwell was a member of his father's law firm and lived in Lyme rather than Boston because he preferred the freedom and the lack of constraint. There were quick half-hour trains in the morning and evening. He was a kind and carefree young man of thirty-two, with an open manner and a generous lightness of disposition, and his father's friends often said meaningly that it was lucky he had a rich adopted father and would inherit half that father's wealth and had not had a start "from scratch." His lightness extended to law, and his good humor toward all things and all people, and Bostonians recalled severely that his mother had never had any reverence for anything.

"It's not as if we're missing anything of importance," Alfred would say. "We go to Dad's house frequently for a weekend and to Newport for a while in the summer, and we attend anything worthwhile, such as a concert, a charity ball or musicale or opera, and the Assemblies. But I don't want to keep up the formal dance every hour I'm not sleeping or doing something else as private! Talk about the British! They're lax compared with Bostonians; they're indecently limp. One of these days everyone who can afford it or really wants it will live outside the big cities and go back and forth every day."

Because he was by nature beneficent and had what his mother-in-law considered a ridiculous trust in people, he was always eager to help others and was overjoyed when they succeeded. He genially called the fine house Tom Sheldon had built for him "illegitimate Regency with all the amenities," but he recommended Tom to his friends, and so Tom had an excellent business now, building not only the small comfortable houses he preferred but also sound and handsome homes for the summer, along the beach, for Bostonians of good fortune. In fact, he was making Lyme and other suburban small villages and towns very popular for summer residents.

The two men had one fast thing in common: absolute honesty, and an honest way of looking at the world, without illusion but also without cynicism. This alone would have made them friends, and they had been friends from the very day Alfred had bought his land from Tom Sheldon.

As Tom had hoped, he found Alfred and Melinda at home and happy to see him. There was always such serenity in this large and pretty house, and even on dark days it appeared full of light. There were also contentment and good humor and much laughter and affection. But Tom often wondered why, when she thought she was not under scrutiny, Melinda's expression would become so sad, her gray eyes so absent and full of longing. He had been attracted to the young woman from the very first for this thing alone, for in some way she reminded him of Caroline. Unlike Caroline, she was engrossed in her pretty five-year-old twins, Mimi and Nathaniel, and would glance repeatedly at her husband with an affectionate smile and placidity.

Every room in the house was fragrant with flowers, scent, and polish and was filled with excellent furniture and oriental rugs and decorated in good taste. Tom found some peace when he came here and was happy in the genuine warmth of Alfred's pleasure. Alfred was a tall and somewhat plump young man with lively large blue eyes, curling black hair, and features which could not, even in the eyes of charity, be regarded as aristocratic. His mouth was too full, his nose too nondescript, his color too high. He loved the table. He loved almost everything and everyone, and the affection seemed reciprocated.

"Well, well," he said jovially, "glad to see you, Tom. Whiskey, as usual?"

He served Tom and himself very generously and gave Melinda a glass of sherry. They sat together in the morning room, which had a wonderful view of the sea and the snowy beach and the shining sky. Melinda did not speak very much; she had a silent poise which was sympathetic and gentle. Tom smiled at her and thought how beautiful she was, so tall and slender in her red merino frock with white lace at her throat and about her wrists, and with such a touching line from ear to delicate chin. She was twenty-nine, but in spite of her dignity and sweet reserve she appeared much younger.

Alfred told Tom some amusing things about nameless clients and Tom listened, smiling. He did not know that his friends were a little concerned at his pallor and the haggard expression about his eyes. He had not seen them since October, and they found a change in him, an aging, a hint of misery. Alfred was too sensitive to pry, to ask personal questions, but he understood that something besides friendship had brought Tom here today after the snowstorm. He saw Tom looking at the wreaths of holly at the windows, at the holly fastened along the molding, and then at the tall Christmas tree glittering with tinsel and ornaments in one corner.

"We're having our holidays at home this year," said Alfred, watching Tom. His father's old friends may have disapproved of him and thought him insensitive, but he was in fact very perceptive. "Dad and Tim and Amanda and their kids are going to be with us, and best of all old Cynthia and young William will be here three days before Christmas. Superb as ever, old Cynthia, though she never did get over that rascal's sudden death. Think he was murdered, myself."

"Now, Alfred," said Melinda with a slight smile. "You know very well he had a stroke and died in Mama's arms."

"Somebody poisoned him," said Alfred. "I'm hearing a lot about these international fellers. Sinister devils. Became interested in the subject about ten years ago and did a lot of reading about it. You'd be surprised. We have presidents and kings and czars, but those old boys pull the strings, and the others dance to the tune. Probably old Johnny Ames was murdered too. Always suspected the bastard, and pardon me, Melinda."

He had been quite right, he thought, watching Tom's face become hard and closed. It was something about Caroline.

"Alfred, you do have such an imagination," said Melinda. "If they are as powerful as you always say, they'd take very good care to protect themselves."

But Alfred was serious. "That's exactly what they want you to think, my pet. Who said that the greatest triumph Satan had ever had was convincing the world that he didn't exist? When everybody was so excited about the Spanish-American War and freeing Cuba and what not and nearly went out of their minds when Admiral Cervera's fleet was destroyed in the Battle of Santiago de Cuba in July last year, I thought, 'Well, the boys are probably licking their lips now, having pulled it off, and are making plans to exploit not only Cuba now but the Philippines and then Central America and then all of Latin America.' I was right about the Philippines but expected it to happen earlier than February of this year. Just watch from now on. We're never going to have any peace any longer. The boys are up and doing. I have friends in England and Germany and France who are sending me undercover material."

"And who, knowing all that, applied for an officer's commission immediately?" asked Melinda teasingly.

Alfred touched her hand and grinned. "Just an escape from domesticity. Besides, what man doesn't like a show, and Teddy Roosevelt is better than Barnum. It's America's naïveté which is going to get her into one hot pot of trouble in the next few years. All drums and flags and freedom and nobility. Why, they're already teaching the brats in the first form that the day of kings and 'despots' and czars are over, and we'll all soon be wallowing in brotherly love together and kissing each other wetly all the time, and that the Century of the Common Man begins exactly on January 1, 1900.

"And that's what interests me, funny enough," said Alfred with unusual thoughtfulness. "The 'Century of the Common Man.' What does that mean? Who is the Common Man? Never met a common man, myself; everybody you meet—your barber, shoeshiner, grocer, clerk, cook, blacksmith, tailor, lawyer, doctor, professor, merchant, or whoever—is a mighty uncommon feller, and he knows it and is proud of it. Stick a 'common man' label on him and he's going to buck; everybody thinks he's better than his neighbor, and so he is, damn it. I don't like this Common Man thing; it smells like brimstone. And who's behind it, I want to know?"

Tom was thinking of Caroline's wild and incoherent revelations just before they were married, and his own revulsion and partial disbelief. He had come to believe in the truth of what she had told him; he had studied newspapers and publications for all these years since then.

"I think you're right," said Tom. "I haven't any grounds for my belief, and you probably don't have much more. But you can feel it in the air."

Alfred refilled his glass and Tom's, and he was extremely sober for so lighthearted a young man. "A funny thing has just occurred to me. I was at the Harvard Club in New York last week. Now, you know the Bristow, Kellem and Bishop law firm in Boston; one of the best; old family; all the money in the world. Well, I met young Bishop in New York, son of old Bishop, junior member of the firm. A brainy feller, but mean and sharp. Somehow he isn't doing well in his dad's firm; old man's disappointed in him, if you can believe the rumors you hear. Was graduated summa cum laude and all that. I remember him from Groton; always thought himself better than anyone else; high and mighty. Quietly vicious and superior. After the summa cum laude, great things were expected of him. They fizzled out. He's disgruntled. Looks at people with sparkling eyes, as if he's thinking of something nasty only he knows.

"Well, I don't like him, but after all, our families have always known each other and it's noblesse oblige, you know. So I'm genial with him in my fatuous way and invite him for a drink, and the surly so-and-so accepts and then stares into the glass. I'm not noted for exceptional tact—at least Melinda is always saying so—so I ask him how the law business is doing. And he looks at me contemptuously and says, 'A bourgeois occupation. There are more important things in the world now, and they'll be more and more important in the next century. You'll see.' And he gives me a yellow smile, looks me up and down, and then without another word he gets up with the drink I'd just bought him and goes away.

"I can't," said Alfred, "get him out of my mind for some reason. He's a failure and he knows it, even if he has a great big mind and tries his hand at poetry every once in a while. Heard he gets some of it published, too."

"You are making me uneasy, Alfred," said Melinda. "I'm thinking of Nathaniel. He's only five years old, but what if there are any real wars—not like the little opéra bouffe, the Spanish-American War? Oh no! America hates war; we've never had a real war since the War between the States, and that wasn't with a foreign country. Why," she said with more gentle cheerfulness, "the world hasn't been so peaceful in centuries. And there's The Hague, and all you hear is everlasting peace."

"That, my sweet, is what is making me very, very uneasy," said Alfred. But he touched her hand affectionately and smiled at her.

Tom thought of all the money Caroline had made in the Spanish-American War and the Philippine war through her munitions stocks. He had told her he considered profits from wars immoral and in violation of every decent principle, and she had looked at him coolly and had said, "Don't be simple, Tom. My profits come from investments; I have nothing to do with war and war makers. If men want to kill each other for something or other, which is none of my business, then why shouldn't I make a profit from their activities?"

And this was the woman who as a girl had expressed her wild loathing of the men who had been her father's associates!

He became aware that Alfred and Melinda were looking at him, and this brought him back to himself.

He said, "I've been thinking. We've never had a Christmas tree at our house. Carrie never wanted one." He paused. "So I am going to ask you if

I can bring my children here a day or so before Christmas to let them see yours."

"Why, yes. How nice," said Melinda, who had never seen Tom's children. Her gray eyes became as bright as the illuminated sea beyond the house. "And I do hope Caroline will come too. Timothy often speaks of her." A subtle change came over her face for a moment.

"You know Carrie," said Tom bluntly. "She doesn't care for family or holidays. I've given up trying to change her. But we both have rights in our children. John's going to Groton next September; Elizabeth is going to Miss Stockington's. Ames is only ten, but I'm going to get him a young tutor; Carrie won't listen about him going to the Lyme public school. Poor Mr. Burton is old and tired. Think of all the kids he's had to manage and teach! So I am going to give him a pension for life, the same salary he's had with us."

"How kind of you, dear Tom," said Melinda.

"Not kind at all," said Tom. "He's had a time with our kids. I'm only trying to compensate him." Then he said, "We don't appreciate teachers, any of us. They give their lives trying to make animals into men."

He had announced to Caroline, after Beth's death, that he would decide the future and the education of his children. She had said nothing. He had expected anger and arguments. He had been vaguely alarmed. He had sensed Caroline's withdrawal from everything that concerned him. That she had also totally withdrawn from her children had dismayed him, and he had wanted some discussion, but it had not come. It was as if her children had no existence for her beyond their actual being. She will get over it, he desolately tried to reassure himself. Carrie would return to their mutual bedroom—sometime. Carrie would become radiant again at the sight of him, would lift her face for his kiss and cling to him. Sometime. She surely would forget his anger about Beth! After all, he had had reason to be angry and disgusted, and any reasonable person would understand that. It was just a matter of a little more time.

Alfred began to chuckle. "I can't help remembering from time to time, for some totally malicious reason, what it must have meant to Caroline when that old lady, Mrs. Broome, left all her stock to Timothy Winslow. No offense, I hope, Tom, but in an adopted way Caroline's my sister-in-law. I thought that would crack the cozy business relations between Timothy and Caroline, but it didn't seem to, did it? She's got the controlling stock, I hear from Timothy, but he's sure got a nice fat lump himself, so I guess she couldn't do anything else but make him president after she'd elbowed the Board a little. There, now, I've made you angry."

"No," said Tom, "you haven't made me angry. You've always known what I thought of her cousin, and Carrie has too. He isn't fooling me; one of these days he'll knife Carrie, and I've told her so."

He glanced at Melinda, remembering that Timothy Winslow was her brother through adoption, but she seemed abstracted and unaware of the conversation. The sunlight was dimming before another storm. It is probably that, he thought, which makes her mouth take on such a sad expression.

"He'll try, anyway," said Alfred agreeably. "I haven't seen Caroline since I was a kid, but from what I remember and from what I've heard, she's more than a match for our avid boy. Never did like him."

Melinda spoke in a constrained voice. "Dear Tom, please give my love to Caroline. I've written her often, you know, but she doesn't answer. I understand that she's very busy; all that responsibility. Sometimes I feel sorry for her."

"Well, we all choose how to look at life," said Alfred philosophically. "I guess Caroline's as happy in her way as we are in ours, so don't get sentimental, pet."

He said to Tom, "Which party do you belong to, the party that insists that 1900 is the end of the nineteenth century or the party that insists it is the new century?"

"I never gave it a thought," said Tom.

"The bigger party wants it to be considered the new century," said Alfred, "and I'm with them. This one is all threadbare, though I suppose historians will find it interesting. The industrial revolution, you know, right after the so-called Age of Enlightenment. I have a theory that that age was directly responsible for the materialism of the industrial revolution. Voltaire; Rousseau; all the rest of the 'reason' boys. 'Set high Reason in your heart and die with her.' Who said that, Melinda?"

"I'm sure I don't know," replied his wife with a faint smile. "I sometimes suspect you make up aphorisms yourself and ascribe them to someone else so that nobody will think you are really very intelligent."

"I'm just the tripper of the light fantastic," said Alfred. "Very helpful. You get some of those old legal boys believing that you, their opponent, are a gay half-wit, and they fail to pull up the heavy artillery until it's too late. They've just been coasting along and yawning along, and there they are, suddenly looking at the heels of the defendant or the plaintiff and watching you thanking the jury and bowing to the judge. Well, anyway, we're going in to Boston for the big once-every-hundred-years celebration. Even Boston will be excited, I hope."

He went to the door with Tom, but in the hallway he stopped suddenly. "I've just thought of something else. After I'd had that drink with young Bishop, I went for a walk and I passed a Salvation Army band singing their hearts out and vigorously banging away and tooting horns and ringing their what-do-you-call-them. Good, hearty sight, earnest boys and girls really believing in something. And then an old gent, dressed up like an officer, began to speak, and he had a voice like William Jennings Bryan, all emotion and throbs and louder even than the band. He was shouting that we were coming on new and terrible days and that the 'abomination of desolation' mentioned by Daniel was at hand, and the nineteen-hundreds were spoke of by Matthew—the end of the world as we know it. 'And ye shall hear of wars and rumors of wars—nation shall rise against nation, and kingdom against kingdom—famines, earthquakes, pestilence.' And great 'tribulations,' too, and the sun and the moon not giving their light, and pillars and clouds of fire, and practically everybody being killed off except the elect, or something. I was fascinated."

He paused. "And then I remembered young Bishop, though for the life of me I can't understand why I did. Funny thing. I can laugh at it now."

"I'm not laughing," said Tom.

They shook hands, and Tom went away. Alfred returned to his wife. She was sitting very still and looking out over the sea, and he could see her profile, quiet with a sorrow he could never understand and in which he only half believed. She turned to him and gave him a bright smile. "Perhaps the coming of Tom's children will mean a reconciliation with poor Caroline," she said as her husband came to her and took one of her hands.

"Don't count on it, dear," said Alfred. "I think this is all Tom's idea. When he breaks the news to Caroline she'll have a convulsion." He bent down and kissed her cheek and thought, as he did so often, how lucky he was to have so lovely and gentle a wife. It had taken him almost three years of constant pursuit to make her marry him. Even then she had said, "I must be frank with you, Alfred. I think I love you, but I'm not in love with you. I'll do the best I can, but don't expect more of me than I can honestly give, will you?"

Alfred never expected more than that of anyone, and so they had a serene and contented life together. Alfred was very happy, for it was his nature to be so. He believed Melinda to be happy also, and so he always laughed at himself when he caught her in a grave mood, absent from him for a few moments.

Caroline said in a cold and bitter voice, "I've given in to you, Tom, about everything you decided for our children. But I must not permit their going to that house to meet their dear cousins! I want nothing to do with that family."

"You want nothing to do with anyone," said Tom. "But we've said these same things many times before, haven't we? I've given in before, but not now. Alfred and Melinda are wonderful people; their children are kind and nice. I want my own children to have some experience with kindness and niceness even if you don't. So I will take them."

Caroline clenched her hands on her desk, and suddenly her face was extremely ugly. "If you knew!" she exclaimed. "But I shall never tell you. I don't want them to see that woman or her children!"

"But that is just what they are going to do," said Tom. "I mean this, Carrie."

Then he said in a pleading and gentle voice, "Carrie. Can't we both forget what happened to us for just that one day? I've told you a dozen times I am sorry. You never listen. How can you keep resentment alive so long? I'm your husband, Carrie."

"Are you?" she said. She drew a new pile of papers to her. "I suppose there is nothing I can say to keep my children from that house and those people. Very well. I'm very busy."

"Do you really hate me now that much, Carrie?"

Hate you? she thought. Oh, my God. "Don't be absurd, Tom. I really must get to work." When he had left her study she dropped the pen on the desk and put her hands over her face and sat there like that for a long time, desolate and alone.

Tom said to his son John, "Come outside with me and help me and Harry move some of those boulders from the sea walk. It'll do you good."

The boy was big, almost fourteen, of a heavy and clumsy build which did nothing to hinder his natural agility. He had a large round head covered with crisp curls as black as jet, and his eyes looked at his father with an unfriendly hazel glint. He had Caroline's features, and they were usually either surly or malicious. Though naturally intelligent, he was careless of scholarship and impatient; he was also selfish and egotistic. Tom hoped Groton would improve him, for Tom naïvely believed much in environment.

John was at his desk, reading, when Tom came in and made his suggestion. "Moving boulders? I don't want to." Tom had once believed that children should not be forced to do what was not entirely necessary in the way of work and discipline. He had changed his mind. He said in a new hard voice that John had never heard before, "What does that matter? I said I need your help, so put on your coat and cap and come running. Hear?"

"But that's Harry's work," John protested.

"And I say it's yours too. Come on."

John looked at him, and Tom saw his animosity and was saddened. Perhaps it was too late to change the boy's opinion of him, but it was not too late to make him assume responsibility. "Come on," Tom repeated. "I'll be waiting on the sea walk, so hurry."

Elizabeth, too, was in her closed room, and Tom reflected that everyone in this house seemed to live behind shut doors, secret and alone. He believed in privacy; he also believed in family love and exchange. A few weeks ago he had insisted that the children have dinner with their parents, and Caroline had contemptuously yielded. It was a fiasco. The children knew their mother's disapproval, so they instinctively conspired to make the dinner a wretched hour. John sulked; Elizabeth made little sharp and goading comments to the housemaid and her brothers, and Ames sneered and merely mashed up his food. Tom's hearty and affectionate remarks were not even noted by Caroline, who was reading the evening Boston newspaper at the table. John glared at him, Elizabeth raised her eyebrows, and Ames regarded him chillily. Tom did not ask for their presence after that; the children had made it very plain that they preferred to eat upstairs together.

Tom knocked on Elizabeth's door. She did not answer; he knocked again, and she murmured distastefully and Tom pretended to take this as permission to open the door and enter the extremely tidy and rather austere room.

The maids dusted and cleaned indifferently, for they were badly paid and ignored by everyone but Tom, whom they pityingly called "soft." Elizabeth invariably cleaned after them, brightening smeared windows, scrubbing sills, rubbing the few pieces of furniture she would permit in her room. Her tester bed had a starched white counterpane and a white canopy; she insisted that they be washed every week. The floor was polished and bare, with only one small rug near the bed. Everything was cold and neat, and the fire was low.

Tom had seen John Ames a few times in Lyme village. It was strange that he did not recognize John Ames in his granddaughter. Yet in appearance, in light brown hair, in fineness and rigidity of feature, in the color of frigid blue eyes, in height and stiffness, in manner and in way of short and repelling speech, Elizabeth was the young John Ames who had looked at the world closely and had not found it good. She was nearly twelve years old now, and as she had only just achieved puberty her body was as featureless as a boy's. Her long hair was tied back from her excellent bony cheeks and pale forehead and face with a blue ribbon; she wore a blue serge dress over which she had tied a plain white pinafore; her stockings were white and her little slippers glistened. She gave an impression of asceticism, of self-control and restraint, and she regarded her father now with a faint and reproving frown.

"Aren't you cold in here, Elizabeth?" asked Tom with concern, looking at the low fire.

"No. I like it cool," said Elizabeth in her precise light voice. She did not stand up. "Is there something you wanted, Father?" She did not call him "Dad" as did John and Ames.

"Yes. It's a nice sharp day, with a little sun." Tom glanced at the white ruffled curtains over the windows. "You rarely go out, dear. John and I and Harry are going to push off some of those boulders on the sea walk, and I thought you'd like to watch us."

"Why?" said Elizabeth. She was seated at her desk, on which stood a neat pile of books and some lesson papers.

"To get some fresh air," said Tom with irritation.

"I walk every afternoon, alone, along the beach. I just came in, Father. And now I have all my studies to do."

"You study too much," said Tom lamely. "It isn't too good for a child."

"I'm not a child," said Elizabeth with such dignity that Tom could not smile. She waited for him to leave. But he stayed, uneasily. He loved Elizabeth more than he loved his other children; she was his daughter; she would be a pretty woman, and probably charming, for her eyes were so large and so bright even if cold. He had tried to reach her from babyhood, to soften her natural constraint. He had never succeeded, not once. Tom blamed this on Caroline's lack of maternal coddling and affection.

"You'll be leaving for Miss Stockington's in September," said Tom, and he meant, "I'm lonely, and I'm your father and I love you, and I'll be more lonely when you're gone." He did not say this, but Elizabeth guessed it and she smiled faintly and looked at her books. She said, "I must do a lot of work before I'll be ready for that school."

"Then you don't want to join John and me?"

"No, Father."

He could only retreat. Elizabeth had already forgotten him. I've failed someway, Tom accused himself miserably. But how? I've loved them with all my heart and always tried to spend a lot of time with them. But they never wanted me.

He went to Ames' room. Ames was suffering from a cold and was in bed. One of the maids, under protest, was reading to him. He liked to be read to; he was ten years old and could read very well himself, but he preferred to inconvenience people. The maid was reading Dickens' *Bleak House* to him, and Tom listened on the threshold for a few moments. What a book to be reading to a child! But Ames was absorbed in it, and occasionally, with icy patience, he would correct the maid's stumbling pronunciation. The bedroom was pleasant; Ames collected agreeable objects and spent his allowance on them in Boston. He liked Dresden; a few precious figurines stood on a table near a window. His brushes were of polished silver; he had spent four months' allowance on the excellent antique little chair near his bed. Tom did not know what an "exquisite" was, and so he did not know that his son was such a one.

Ames had evolved from a fat pale baby into a thin pale boy with fair hair and hard-slate colored eyes. His features were not as delicate as Elizabeth's, but they were much more finely drawn than John's. He resembled his cousin Timothy Winslow in many ways. Tom loved Ames less than he did his two other children, and for that guilty reason had been even more gentle with him than with John and Elizabeth. He always felt a little fear when with him.

"How are you this afternoon, dear?" asked Tom. "Less feverish?"

Ames took time to blow his nose nicely. Then he said, "I feel terrible. Stir up the fire, will you, Dad?"

The maid slumped in her chair and stared at the window gloomily. Damned kid! She'd just love to lay hands on him and beat some respect for his father into him! Tom stirred up the fire to a hot glow.

"Mr. Ames," said the maid, "I got to go to the kitchen to get the vegetables ready. Cook's grumbling right now."

"All right," said Ames. "You read to me, Dad." He gave Tom a small and secret smile.

"Well, go down and help, Elsie," said Tom. He looked regretfully at his son. "I'd like nothing better than to read to you, Ames, but I'm going to move some boulders with John and Harry."

"With John?" Ames sat up on his pillows and laughed in nasty glee. "You mean John's going to help?"

"Why, certainly. Why not?"

Ames chuckled. "I'd like to see old Johnnie doing something he doesn't have to do! I'll bet you had to drag him by the scruff of the neck."

Tom refused to believe that his children did not like each other. It was unnatural for children not to like their brothers and sisters, and Tom believed that in some way the very isolation in which the children lived had made them "close."

"No, I didn't," said Tom. "He's a big, active boy, and it'll be good for him and he'll like it."

Ames chuckled again. Then he said, "Turn the gas up a little, will you, Dad?"

"Why not daylight? Why do all of you like to skulk behind curtains and not let in the sun sometimes?" But Tom turned up the gas over Ames' beautifully modeled head.

"I hate the sight of the snow and the water," said Ames. He picked up the book Elsie had left on her chair and turned a page.

"I'll ask Mr. Burton to come in and read to you," said Tom, lingering.

"Oh no. Please don't, Dad. He has a voice like an old woman's. I hate old people."

Tom thought of Beth, and unwillingly he remembered that his children had never liked her and had tormented her. My God, we're a guilty family, he thought. Ames was regarding him secretively over the edge of the book. Old Johnnie was right, he was thinking. Dad's a fool. No wonder Mama despises him.

Tom left the room slowly and walked down the stairs as if he were an old man himself, sick with years, sick with experience. Then his natural optimism returned, not quite as readily as once it did, but eventually, as he reached the outside door. The children were in the process of growing; it was a difficult age; it would be all right—sometime.

The air, the sky, and the sea seemed formed of bright silver. But there would be another storm tonight, thought Tom with the countryman's intelligence of nose and eye. John, who seemed almost a man in height and bulk, was huddled silently near the handy man who was listlessly prodding at one big boulder with a crowbar. "Well, well," said Tom heartily, "that's a big fellow, isn't it? It'll take all three of us to push it off the walk. Where do they come from, anyway?"

Harry whined, "No use trying to get rid of 'em. They just come back. Fool thing, anyway, this walk. I told you that, Mr. Sheldon."

"I like it," said Tom, without being offended.

"But every time there's a storm they're out here bigger'n ever. Water rolls 'em in."

"We'll roll them out. All right, Johnnie, give a hand."

"I'll hurt my back; that must weigh a ton," said John.

"Nonsense. Less than three hundred pounds, I'd say. As for hurting your back, I'll bet you could push it off onto the beach yourself, John. You're a very strong boy."

John was not flattered. He put his gloved hands on the boulder beside his father's; Harry, muttering, inserted the crowbar under the bottom. Tom pushed. John hated work of all kinds, though he was a considerable athlete.

Tom panted a little with the effort, and John made a sneering face. Tennis was fine; he intended to make the football team at Groton and engage in all the sports. But work, and especially stupid work like this, was for peasants.

Tom did not know that Caroline was watching him from her study window and that she was frightened. What did it matter if boulders came on the walk? What did it matter where or how you lived? But Tom was very foolish about his house. He was even more foolish about his children. He would hurt himself. The silvery air made Tom look very pale even at this distance. Caroline's hand clenched on the dull dark blue draperies of her study. "Stop it!" she said with anger and fear.

CHAPTER SEVEN

It did indeed storm that night. The snow came down in formidable quantities, burying Lyme and Boston, burying the countryside, heaping itself over New York also, so that the people recalled the famous blizzard of 1888. Everything stood still in a white silence. Then two days before Christmas it thawed, and there was a flood everywhere of running deep water.

"I don't like the feel of the roadbed," said old Harper Bothwell to his adopted son Alfred. "The North Shore Railroad was always a shaky line, but it's worse now, much worse over the past four years. Why don't you tell your friend Tom Sheldon to get Caroline Ames to do something about it? She's the chief shareholder, isn't she? But trust the daughter of Johnny Ames not to allow a cent to be spent even when necessary! One of these days there'll be an accident and she'll discover that lawsuits are more expensive than repairs to a local roadbed. Damn it! That was a bad lurch there!"

He looked about the coach with disfavor, wrinkling his nose and sniffing. The coach smelled; he remarked that he suspected the coaches were rarely cleaned, with which Alfred genially agreed. "But after all, it's only about a twenty-minute or less run. Did you expect a red plush private coach, Pa? You've been on this line scores of times. Never bothered you before."

"Perhaps I'm getting old; I like my comforts. Look at this seat; the stuffing is coming out. You can scarcely see through the windows." He peered at the glass, saw the dull sheets of water not only reaching the tracks but washing over them, and saw the inundated countryside and the trees seemingly growing from small lakes and drowned fields. Beyond them, the sullen sea rolled under clouds of gulls. "Don't know why you live out here," grumbled Harper.

"Never mind, Pa. We'll be home in ten minutes. It gives me an odd feeling that this will be the last Christmas of the nineteenth century, or is it the last? Doesn't matter. But as we were saying in your office, I feel uneasy——"

Harper sighed. "When you've lived as long as I've done, my boy, you get over feeling uneasy about anything. But everything's new to you young fellows; everything's portentous; everything has significance; everything is about to change. I've seen many changes in my life. What do the French say? The more a thing changes, the more it is the same. Nations go through growing pains; they get over it in time."

"But I'm living in this time, Pa. I don't believe in laissez faire. That's an attitude that helps countries go down the drain. I don't want that to happen to America. My children have to live here."

Harper clutched the arm of his seat as the train swayed around a bad curve. "Damn that engineer. Can't he understand this is dangerous, the way the roadbed is? He could slow down." He smiled sourly. "Alfred, do you think that by taking thought you can do anything about the 'situation,' as you call it, in America? In many ways things are better than they used to be. Why, I remember that old Vanderbilt and the other old railroad boys used to have to pay out fortunes in blackmail to United States senators for every mile they laid! But they finally linked the country together, in spite of the government and its greedy, itching palm. I agree with one thing you said today: there never was a government that wasn't as corrupt as hell and just waiting for a chance to jump in and establish despotism. This is true of America, too, but we're a big country, and by and large we're a sensible country. We have the Constitution."

"So did republican Rome," said Alfred. "And look what happened to Rome's constitution when the boys really got up a head of steam."

"Well, you won't see the end of the American Constitution in your time, Alfred. Nor will I. Can't tell about the future, though. It always comes back to the people. A virtuous electorate keeps its government within bounds; a stupid and vicious people lets its government expand until the government takes over everything. Then the knouts come out of hiding, and the secret police and the ropes and all the rest of it. A people deserves its government. So far, the American people have done well; no use worrying about the future."

Alfred indeed had no cause to worry about himself and his children and the future of his country. He would never know of wars and rumors of wars; he would never see the advance of socialism in America. He would never know that his beloved little son Nathaniel would die in the Argonne Forest in 1918. He would never learn of the rise of the Communist Russian Empire, nor of Hitler and Mussolini.

For within five miles of the station at Lyme the train ran over flooded ground from which the rails had been swept only four minutes before. His final memories of his world included only a leaping and crashing and rending and sliding and tearing, of screams and cries, of the shriek of torn metal, of the upheaval of a derailed train. It was like him, in those last awful moments, when he understood what had happened, to throw himself across his father and try to shield that father with his young body and his arms. But that did not matter. Old Harper Bothwell was killed within seconds, and Alfred lived, in unconsciousness, forty-five minutes longer.

It was after three in the morning when Tom Sheldon, staggering with exhaustion, his clothing torn and bloodstained, his face gray and lined and haggard, his whole body trembling, returned to his house. He could hardly walk; his boots squeaked with water; his hands were wounded. Caroline had waited up for him, and when she saw him she screamed faintly, then shouted, "You didn't have to go! There were hundreds to help in the wreck! You might have been killed, yourself! You shouldn't have gone!"

But Tom, panting, could not speak for a while. Then he said quietly, "You own the major part of the stock in the North Shore Railroad, don't you, Carrie? The roadbed needed to be repaired for years; I heard you tell your cousin that you wouldn't approve of any expenditures. And didn't I hear you telling him on the telephone only yesterday that it was nonsense to stop service until the water went down and the rails could be examined and repaired? Yes, Carrie.

"Eight people are dead, Carrie, and forty badly injured. But you don't have to worry. You didn't spend a cent." His panting became a long, slow groan. "Alfred Bothwell and his father are dead; they were coming home for Christmas. Alfred—I got to him finally—died in my arms. He never knew. That should be a little comfort to you, Carrie, but it won't be a comfort to his sister and his wife and his children."

"Alfred, dead?" she muttered, putting her hand to her cheek and standing before Tom in her rough flannel nightgown and her slippers and with braids on her shoulders. But it was Tom who was dead, who had died in the wreck. It was Tom she would never see again. She burst into agonized tears and forgot everything, her isolation, her loneliness, her quarrel with her husband, her mistrust and desolate gloom. She held out her hands to Tom. And he would not see them.

"Yes. He is dead." He paused. "Why are you crying, Carrie? He never meant anything to you. Nobody ever meant anything to you; there was only your money. But God won't let you go unpunished for this, Carrie." And he shook his head over and over. Holding onto furniture, touching walls and doors, he left the room.

Christmas came and went, and the new century arrived, but no one in the Bothwell house knew of either of them. The gray snow came and the mourning village and mourning Boston friends cared nothing or thought of nothing but the wreck. It made headlines in the national newspapers, and it was frequently mentioned that the wreck was due to neglect and that the controlling shares were owned by Mrs. Tom Sheldon, the former Caroline Ames, daughter of John Ames, who had left her such a vast fortune. There were investigations. There were talks of suits and the preparation of suits. An old photograph of Caroline was frequently published, showing her closed and impassive face, her reluctant eyes. Many anonymous and threatening letters arrived at the Sheldon house, and Caroline silently threw them into the fire.

On January 4, Cynthia, Lady Halnes, and her son Timothy Winslow sat alone in the beautiful drawing room of the Bothwell house near Lyme. They sipped brandy before the fire; they sat listlessly with their own thoughts. Timothy said to himself: The old baggage is getting aged at last. This has done her in. He thought of his cousin Caroline with hatred. He had never liked the kind and exuberant Alfred, but he was thinking of Melinda, mute and stricken since the death of her husband and lying sleeplessly in her lonely bed. She had not said more than half a dozen words since that terrible day.

Cynthia had arrived at the Bothwell house three days before Christmas with her young son. Her bright hair was so expertly dyed that it was not obvious; she still had her fine figure and her eyes were still lovely and brightly gray. She was a little over sixty, but in a good light and in her wonderful clothes she could have passed for a woman in her late forties.

But since the tragedy she had suddenly aged. Lines webbed her face; her mouth sagged; her nose was pinched. Her whole body became limp and bent. The dyed hair was a travesty now above fallen cheeks, wrinkled brow, and livid color.

"Oh, my God," she murmured. "I still can't believe it. What are we going to do about poor Melinda? She seems sightless and deaf and hardly alive. She doesn't notice her children. She didn't seem to be present, really, at the funeral services. When I touch her or try to comfort her, she only shivers and draws away. Of course she's in a state of shock, but I can see that the doctor is worried. I do wish she would go to the Bothwell house in Boston for a while. I suggested she go to England with me, but I don't think she even heard. What shall we do?"

"I don't know," said Timothy. "But after all, she's still young. She'll get over it in time."

Cynthia sipped her brandy, cried a little, then wiped her eyes. While she was doing this, Timothy was doing some hard and disagreeable thinking. Old Harper Bothwell had been a lawyer; he had constantly urged his clients to review their wills frequently in the light of new circumstances. But lawyers were notorious about neglecting their own affairs. Harper had not made a new will in spite of the marriages of his son and daughter. It had been a short will: he had no one but Alfred and Amanda, and he had made provisions in behalf of a few proper charities. So he had left his enormous fortune to be divided equally between Alfred, his adopted son, and Amanda, provided both survived him. There had been no mention of grandchildren or surviving spouses of his own children. If Alfred died before Amanda or if she died before Alfred, prior to the death of Harper Bothwell, the entire fortune was to be given to the survivor. His whole will had been based on the assumption that his heirs would be alive on his death.

If, therefore, in that wreck it could have been assumed that Alfred had died before his father, his inheritance would have passed to Amanda. But there were many witnesses to the fact that Harper was dead when the rescuers reached him and that his son was still alive and had survived almost one hour longer. Therefore, he had inherited fifty per cent of Harper's fortune, unconscious and dying though he had been, and Alfred had made his own will two years before, leaving all he had in trust to his widow for life, his children to inherit after her death. Timothy knew that Tom Sheldon's insistence, courage, and desperation had inspired the exhausted rescuers to tear apart the small last portion of the coach. They had wanted to wait for morning; there were no cries or any evidence of life in the remaining section. But Tom had insisted.

"If someone's badly hurt and unconscious in there he could die before morning. We have to go on." They did, burned and bloodstained though they were, and they had found Alfred still breathing, still alive. It was too late to save his life, if there had been any hope at all. But he had, by that short space of time, inherited his share of his father's money.

Tom Sheldon and others had made their affidavits only yesterday. If it had not been for Tom, Timothy knew, all would have gone to Amanda, for Alfred would not have been found alive. Timothy had hated Tom before; he hated him now with an insane hatred. It was not as though Melinda would have been penniless if Alfred had not remained alive long enough to inherit. Timothy had taken care of her investments; the money left to her by her father had doubled; Alfred himself had had considerable money of his own, bequeathed to him by his dead parents, which was now Melinda's. Moreover, Timothy more than suspected that the greater part of his mother's money would be left to her daughter. Melinda, without the money which Amanda, Timothy's wife, would have inherited in full, would have been a very rich woman.

The years of his marriage and his fatherhood had not reduced Timothy's love for his sister. In fact, he did not often think of his blood connection with her. She was still his love; he could never see her without longing and pain. Nevertheless, he had wanted his wife to receive the full Bothwell fortune, which he would have managed and controlled. While his mother cried tonight he wondered whom he hated more, Caroline or Tom. He did not want them dead; he wanted them ruined and beggared, by himself. The Gargoyle would then know who had done this to her. There was no gratitude in Timothy; he had used Caroline, and she had benefited him, but he considered that he had served her well while he had served himself.

He knew that Caroline wanted money to protect herself from a world she feared. But he wanted money for power, for influence, for fame. He was considering running for governor, and governors with money always had an advantage over a man of equal or even better qualities. Timothy's lust for wealth was not innocent, as Caroline's was innocent. Her dislike for people rose from fright; his rose from contempt.

"Oh, Timothy," Cynthia said, seeing her son's expression. "I know it is very hard, but what can one do? You look so terrible."

"I hope the survivors sue the hell out of her," said Timothy malevolently, and Cynthia cried again. "I'd like to represent them! But I can't."

"Timothy, she is your cousin, the poor girl. And she's done so much for you."

It was not hard for her to realize that Timothy was past forty now, for he had never, even as a child, seemed young to her. He had always been mature. She thought it was grief over Melinda that made his pale long face so tense, his mouth so thin and tight.

Melinda, since her husband's funeral, had kept to her rooms, unspeaking. Cynthia therefore started when the young woman came wanderingly into the drawing room, her blue robe tied about her, her long fair hair hanging in disorder over her shoulders, her face far and unseeing. Timothy did not at first see her. He jumped when he heard his mother cry out and saw her pushing herself to her feet. It was not until Cynthia's arms were about her daughter that he stood up.

"I should have loved him more," said Melinda in a curiously penetrating voice. She pulled herself from Cynthia's arms. She threw back the masses of fair hair and looked at Timothy, and her eyes were feverishly brilliant. "I'll never forget that he loved me and that I didn't really love him. I can't bear to live, remembering that."

"Of course you loved him, darling," said Cynthia feebly. She glanced at Timothy. This Melinda was much more heartbreaking than the young widow who had lain in her bed, silent and staring.

"No," said Melinda, and she shook her head, and her hair flew about her. "I never loved anyone but Tim, and he left me. He left me only for money. And so I married Alfred. I shouldn't have done that. It was a wicked thing to do to him, and now he's dead and I can't tell him I'm sorry." She clasped her white hands together. "If only I could tell him I'm sorry."

Cynthia, dazed by disaster herself, blinked her eyes and dimly hated the new electric lights in the drawing room, which gave the soft hues and light tones a glaring appearance and emphasized the torment on Melinda's face. It was nightmarish to her. She murmured, "Oh, dear God," and wondered where Amanda was, Amanda who was sleeping in Melinda's room and giving her sedatives at intervals. "Where is Amanda?" she murmured to Timothy in distraction. "Why did she let the poor child wander like this?"

But Timothy did not hear her. He took Melinda's clasped hands and held them tightly and looked down into her eyes until their bright wandering stopped and he had all her attention. No one except Melinda could ever move him to a fullness of human emotion, to forgetfulness of self, to sympathy and tenderness and disinterested love; not even his wife, of whom he was casually fond; not even his children, of whom he was even more fond. He said, "Melinda dear. You did love Alfred. He knew it, and"—he hesitated only a moment—"he knows this now. Do you think it's making him happy to know you're torturing yourself?"

They were childlike words, and simple, and for this reason alone they reached Melinda. Her eyes changed. "Do you think so, Tim?" she asked. "Really, do you think so?"

"Yes," he said, and held her hands even more tightly. "I never saw two people happier, dear. I used to envy you."

Cynthia stared at them and cried silently. No one saw Amanda in her long white nightgown standing in the doorway. Amanda was a sensible young woman, and she knew when not to intrude or cause confusion or excitement or distraction.

"Oh, Tim," said Melinda, and was so exhausted that Timothy had to put his arms about her to hold her, and she dropped her head on his shoulder. She began to cling to him, her trembling arms like steel. "Oh, Tim!" she cried. "I always knew you loved me! I never did believe you left me because of money and because you wanted much more! I loved Mama and Uncle Montague, but I began to know the truth, in spite of what they said. You didn't leave me just because they said they'd cut me off—no, no, you didn't."

She lifted her head and leaned back in Timothy's arms, and her hands clutched his arms fiercely above his elbows. "Did they tell you something about my parents, Tim, that sent you away? Would it have injured you if I'd married you? But then, they were happy about my marriage to Alfred —Mama loved Alfred; she wouldn't have let me marry him if it was that! Tim, Tim, tell me why you left me? I must know, Tim, or I won't be able to stand it!"

Amanda, astounded and incredulous, came striding into the room, her cotton nightgown billowing around her strong young legs, her long black hair floating rapidly about her. Her usually round and rosy face was pale and drawn, and her black eyes snapped.

"Good heavens!" she exclaimed, reaching Timothy and Melinda. She stood beside her husband and swung to Cynthia. "Mama Halnes! You surely *told* Melinda, didn't you? You haven't let her go all these years, breaking her heart and what not, in *absolute* ignorance, have you? Why," she said louder, "you have! How could you do such a thing? Such a terrible, stupid thing! Timothy! Can you stand there with this poor girl and tell me you never told her either? Why, what awful cruelty!"

She clenched her sturdy hands at her sides, and her face blazed with anger. "I just can't believe it!" she cried. "It isn't human to have let Melinda suffer all this time. It isn't human! I wouldn't treat one of my dogs like this. I wondered what was wrong with Melinda when we visited her and Alfred or they came to us. Why, I just can't forgive you, Timothy, Mama Halnes, I just can't. And everyone in Boston knew or suspected for years and years!"

Cynthia stepped back; she became even older; she was an old, broken woman. Melinda still clung to Timothy, but his arms dropped. He turned to his shocked wife. "Amanda, I didn't know either until I went to England to marry Melinda years ago. Then dear Mama told me. I left. Then she and Montague concocted some of their lies to appease Melly—I don't know. What could I have done? They didn't want Melly to know, and they convinced me it would hurt her to know."

Amanda's face softened as she scrutinized him and saw his misery. "Poor Timothy," she said. But her round features hardened again when she turned to Cynthia. "How could you?" she said. "Why, even when I was fourteen and fifteen I heard the women whispering—Mama's friends. And tittering. But of course they couldn't ostracize you! You were one of Boston's First Families, and First Families close ranks," she said contemptuously. "Then you married Lord Halnes and were even more elevated, for heaven's sake! I can understand how you felt, but not at the expense of poor Melinda. You owed it to her to tell her."

"What? What?" murmured Melinda, her exhausted eyes moving pleadingly from face to face.

Amanda had a full round bosom, and it was agitated under her nightgown. She gently removed Melinda from Timothy and put her arms about the young woman. She kissed her soundly and tenderly. "Why, darling," she said, "Timothy could never have married you. If he had, someone would have told. The adoption records and backgrounds of the children are sealed, but if anything threatens any of them or they get into situations like this, then the records have to be opened. Melinda, Timothy couldn't have married you. He's not only your adoptive brother. He's your real brother too. You both have the same mother."

Melinda pushed herself from Amanda's warm grasp. She took a step or two toward Cynthia, then stopped. She clasped her hands together and leaned forward to look at the older woman, whose weeping face was averted. Melinda's hair fell across her cheeks. She stood silently and rigidly, as if listening. Then she whispered, "Mama? Mama?"

"Yes, love," Cynthia faltered. "Yes, my darling."

"Oh, Mama," Melinda said. "Mama, I'm so glad." She held out her arms and ran to her mother, and they held each other and there was no sound from them.

"I think," said Amanda briskly to her husband, "that we aren't needed now. Poor, stupid, damned Timothy. Come on to bed, boy. Really, half the trouble and misery and pain people have is brought on by themselves. They either talk too much or not enough." She rubbed her rounded flank. "That cot in Melinda's room is made of solid iron. You and I, Timothy, are now going to bed together, and let's have a little peace if we can."

Timothy smiled at her. "There's one thing about bread and butter, my sturdy sweet: it satisfies—occasionally." He went to the wide arched door with his wife. He looked back at Melinda and repeated, "Occasionally."

When Cynthia, moving as if every muscle in her body were torn and twisted, arrived in her room she found her son, William Lord Halnes, waiting for her in his sensible dark blue dressing gown. His respectable young face, so like his dead father's, was serious. He had his father's chubby body and air of innate strength. He loved his mother dearly and knew exactly what to do for her, as his father had known.

A decanter of brandy was on Cynthia's bedside table, and two glasses. Cynthia sank on the edge of the bed, and her son filled the glasses carefully. He did not need to look at his mother. He knew that she was about to collapse. He handed her her brandy gravely. She looked at him, and he gave her the sudden charming smile of his father. She began to cry, and he did not stop her. He sat opposite her and waited. When she finally could cry no longer he presented his handkerchief, on which she blew her nose. She said, "Dear William. You are such a comfort. Like your father. You seem to know everything."

"'Everything' is not so hard to understand," said the boy. "You make deductions. And you listen. One of the errors of humanity is that it talks but hardly ever stops to hear. Too much babbling." His English voice was very precise and clipped. "Do drink your brandy. It's very consoling."

"Boys shouldn't drink brandy," said Cynthia vaguely.

"I'm not a boy," said William. "In fact, I don't believe I ever was."

They sipped in warm silence. Then Cynthia said, "Sometimes life is too much for me."

"It always is for those who feel too much. But never for those who think, Mama."

Cynthia sipped again. William said, "There's too damned much emotion in the world. Sign of the barbarian. But then, those who think too much are dangerous. I believe Shakespeare brought that out in *Julius Caesar*."

"You are a darling, William," said Cynthia.

William considered this thoughtfully. "No, Mama, I don't think so. There are too many 'darlings' in the world. Foolish, sentimental, thoughtless people. Spraying their emotions around like cheap scents and asphyxiating everybody. We need fresh air. We need muscles and guts. But in America everything is love and embraces and slopping about and looking into each other's pockets. No privacy. The difference between man and animal is privacy. Animals run together and herd together. Man should be able to stand alone. Ibsen."

Cynthia said, "But, darling, we do need to understand each other. We can't live apart."

"We don't need to," said William Lord Halnes. "We can live with God." He was fourteen years old. He repeated, "We can live with God."

He studied the glass in his plump hand. "And once we can live with God, we can live with mankind too." He lifted his glass to his mother. "Happy New Year to you, poor Mother, or as happy as it can be under the circumstances, and may this new century be better than the last. I doubt it, though. We can only hope that God, in His infinite pity, will have mercy on our souls."

Cynthia would often say through the years, "It was never necessary to tell William anything or explain it to him, not even when he was very young. He always seemed to know. That is why he chose the life he did. There simply was no other way for him."

CHAPTER EIGHT

No one in the Sheldon household would ever have believed that Elizabeth listened at doors. She was too cool, too remote, too restrained for such a suspicion. Nevertheless, she listened with sharp avidity; there was nothing too unimportant for her, whether it was a conversation between the slatternly cook and the equally slatternly housemaid, or a short exchange between her parents, or Caroline's discussions with her cousin Timothy Winslow, or Caroline's telephone calls to her Boston office or New York or her small bank in the latter city, or even quarrels between her brothers. She eavesdropped, not out of aimless curiosity or malice, but merely in order to inform herself of all things, to see whether or not they could personally benefit her.

At sixteen she had developed the art of overhearing to a special degree. Life was evolving a pattern she could see very clearly. At the center of the pattern stood Elizabeth Josephine Sheldon (and one other), who was determined to use life and not permit life to use her. If Tom Sheldon still did not know the extent of his wife's fortunes or of what her investments consisted, Elizabeth had a very extensive idea. She also knew that she was her father's favorite, that he was bewildered and saddened by his sons, and that he lived in a state of chronic wretchedness and despair. She was not yet certain how she would manipulate these facts, but she was at least sure that she would one day.

It was a very snowy Easter, and early, and Elizabeth was home for the holidays, as were her brothers. But all the doors, as usual, were shut. Elizabeth, in her schoolgirl's navy serge with white collar and cuffs, sat and listened to the silence of the house. She was sitting in what her father had called the "drawing room." It was very shabby now, and the draperies had dimmed and had been mended carelessly. The fine carpet had lost most of its pattern under grime, owing to the languid application of brushes on the part of ever-changing housemaids who rarely stayed for more than a month. The windows were blurred, and the winter sunlight could only smear them with a smudge of light; the wainscoting needed paint, and the floor about the rug was dull and splintered. Elizabeth, the fastidious, looked at the dinginess and pursed her mouth disdainfully. She did not sit here as a rule; she preferred her room. But this large, neglected room was a good central point from which she could hear any movement or voice.

The small fire spluttered, and the room was chilly as well as drab. Elizabeth listened. She heard no voices. But she finally heard the door of her mother's study open and close, and then another door open, close. She also heard the faint click of a lock. "Bluebeard's Closet," she murmured, and put aside her book and went up the stairs like a slim and graceful shadow, her light hair on her shoulders, her hard blue eyes intent. She often listened at the door when her mother entered her private art gallery. For in that room, which no one was ever permitted to enter but herself, the lonely woman talked aloud to something, and what she infrequently said was of immense interest to her daughter.

Elizabeth paused at the top of the stairs. There was a large window at the end of the hallway, gray with dust, and the light filtered in feebly. The red carpeting had faded; it was worn and unkempt and thin. The doors along the hallway were all shut. The servants were enjoying their short rest period on the third floor. Elizabeth drifted over the carpet, which smelled of old grime, and stood by the door of the gallery.

There was no sound inside. Caroline had apparently paused. Then the whisper of her footsteps on carpet began, up and down. Then she paused again. She began to speak in a monotone, and Elizabeth pressed her ear to the door.

Caroline's voice was still strong and sonorous, and she spoke in the cultured accents of Miss Stockington's school. "I still think the tower is your best," she said. "I don't know why. The brushwork of the girl on a chair or the boy with an apple is superior. Yet I had to pay much more for the tower than for those and the others. Twenty thousand dollars. I have read that you sold it for fifteen dollars. How terrible."

Elizabeth knew, of course, that the secret room contained paintings. Her father had told her. But he too had never seen them. Once Elizabeth had suggested to her mother that she would like to see them. Caroline had looked at her thoughtfully, as if considering, and then had smiled oddly and said, "I think not. I really think not." She carried the key to the room with her always. It was never to be found lying about, though Elizabeth had searched diligently. Her curiosity did not concern the paintings in the room but only what her mother said aloud before them. Once she had read that those who speak aloud when alone were mad. Elizabeth did not believe this; her mother was obviously not mad. She was only lonely. Her daughter was the single person in the household who understood that.

The hall was very cold. Elizabeth hugged her slim body with her arms and bent to the door. Caroline was speaking again.

"I dreamed about the tower once or twice," Caroline said. "But I don't remember the dreams except that they were frightful. Was the tower frightful to you? Yes, I think it must have been. It expresses some awfulness which I seem about to grasp, and then it vanishes. I wish I could see it; I wish I could remember the dreams I had. But they've gone from my mind, as if a dark door had been closed in my face. Perhaps it will open one of these days."

The footsteps whispered again. There was a sudden curious catch in the room, such as one makes when one tries not to weep. Elizabeth had never heard it before. Caroline spoke in a lower tone, almost halting, as if speaking without real volition. "I know all about you; I read everything there was to know. Your wife, her family. But nothing about your son; nothing about your parents. No one knows. Was there a reason you never told anyone of them? Yes, it must be so. If only you had lived! If only you had lived

303

long enough to know your son. I know how you died. You were coming home and found the barn afire, with all your paintings, and you died of it. I can understand that. When your life is gone there is nothing else. Yes, I can understand that; my life is gone, and I live now because of my father and what he would want me to do. I live only for a dead man, for he was the only one who loved me. There was never anyone else; there never will be. Do you understand?"

Elizabeth raised her eyebrows disdainfully. She knew of her mother's violent obsession about her father, John Ames, for she had listened enough to furious exchanges between her own father, and her mother on the subject. "Why don't you build a shrine to him?" Tom had once shouted in despair. "Or don't people build shrines to devils?" Elizabeth had then begun to wonder about her grandfather, John Ames, and what manner of man he had been. Discreet questioning and listening had given her quite a comprehensive portrait, and she approved of him, even if she found her mother's idolatry ridiculous.

Then she listened even more acutely. Her mother was crying. She had never heard her mother cry before, had never seen her in tears.

"If there was just someone," Caroline was stammering. "Do we all really live alone like this, shut up in ourselves, unable to speak? Were you so alone? I believe you were. There is a terrible loneliness about this painting of a stream running through a mountain pass; no trees, no grass, only gray stone, and the stream is as green as ice, as if frozen. I can feel all the color in it, as if each tint were a separate emotion. That boulder looks as if it had never touched another boulder since it was thrown there. Are we all like this? I know I am. I never touched anyone but my father. How am I going to go on living, except to increase the trust he gave me?

"I thought Tom loved me. I thought he understood. But he lied to me; he didn't understand at all; he wouldn't listen. He had his preconceived frame of reference, and he thought everyone should fit into it. I couldn't, and he was outraged. Why does everyone believe his own particular reality is the only reality? They say reality is objective; it isn't; it's entirely subjective. But—if Tom had only listened while I tried to show him my own reality! But he could hear and see only himself and his own codes and convictions. It's possible that I am this way too." She paused, as if in wonderment, then exclaimed, "Yes, it's very possible! But I did understand Tom's reality, even if it made me impatient—at least, I understood a little. But he would never even approach mine. I was his wife, Carrie. He never wanted to understand Caroline Ames. Did I frighten him? Tom, frightened?" Her voice rose. "No, he was not frightened; he was only disapproving and angry. But I love him so, I love him so, and he never knows it. There are all the years in between. My children? They have their reason for being, as you know, but they care nothing for me. That doesn't hurt me. I only want Tom, and he's gone far away, and I can't reach him any longer."

Her weeping was desperate now, and Elizabeth frowned. Her mother was committing a grave impropriety and showing foolish weakness. Then she thought of her mother's reference to her children, and her cool mind worked rapidly. She and her brothers had a tremendous respect for their mother, or rather for the mind that added constantly to the fortune that would be theirs one day. Their father, in their opinion, was a fool, to be used when necessary. He could not understand how important it was to be powerfully rich. Their mother understood only too well. She was polite to her children, demanded politeness and discipline, never varied in her aloof interest in their education and welfare. She gave them little or no money, never talked with them about themselves or any aspirations they might have. As her children, they were important; as persons, they had no importance at all to her. This had given her authority and power in their minds. A loving and solicitous mother would only have aroused their contempt.

Elizabeth was annoyed now that a little of the profound respect she had for her mother had been washed away by Caroline's tears in that room. She preferred to think of her mother as far above silly emotions and sentimentality. How could her mother really love a man like her husband, who dripped affection indiscriminately everywhere, as a dog drips saliva? He sought love from his children in an eager and servile way. They despised him. It was upsetting to overhear that Caroline loved so trivial a man.

Elizabeth and her brothers knew their cousins fairly well by now, especially Timothy and Amanda Winslow's children—Henry, now twelve; Harper, eleven; and Amy, ten years old. Elizabeth considered them all ordinary and of no consequence, not only because she was older than they, but because they were kind and gentle and considerate and loved their parents, which alone would have inspired Elizabeth's contempt. She saw little Amy at Miss Stockington's, a shy child with a pink-and-white face, sparkling dark eyes, and a mass of black ringlets. Elizabeth classed all girls younger than herself as "imbeciles," but little Amy, she had concluded, had no wit or intelligence at all. She would cry over the slightest inconvenience; if some classmate spoke rudely to her she was devastated and had to be consoled in the arms of a teacher. Once she had sobbed a whole morning after finding a dead butterfly. All the teachers spoke tenderly of "the child's sensitivity," but the other children laughed at her readiness to burst into tears. There were times when Elizabeth, seeing the weeping Amy in some corner or in the halls, was angered if a classmate of her own would say to her slyly, "Isn't that your cousin—that silly little girl?" As for Mary (Mimi) Bothwell, Elizabeth had some respect for her—an independent child who possessed considerable gentle fire and could be stern in the schoolyard when faced with some injustice. Nathaniel resembled his twin sister.

Only the Winslow family came to the Sheldon house in Lyme on rare occasions. But the Bothwell family never came, though the Sheldon children did visit them on Tom's insistence. Elizabeth knew that a strong antipathy existed in her mother for all the Bothwells, and she shared it emphatically. She thought they lived aimless lives. Melinda's gravity and reserve would have won Elizabeth's admiration if she had not shown such devotion to her children and such anxiety for them. She seemed especially kind to Elizabeth, which puzzled the girl and annoyed her, for she had no respect for Melinda with her "vague ways." When Melinda visited the school and sometimes encountered Elizabeth, Melinda would think: How like her father she is! I am afraid for the girl. Elizabeth usually refused invitations to the Bothwell house, unlike her brothers, but since one Christmas when she was thirteen years old, she would call occasionally and in secrecy. For at that Christmas she had met a very old woman, Lady Halnes from England, her mother's aunt, and she had also met young William Lord Halnes.

She met him again when she was fourteen, the next Christmas, when they were both walking on the hard cold shingle between the two houses. She had said to him suddenly and loudly, "William?" Her voice had rung like a bell in the cold and silent air, and he had turned and looked at her with mild perplexity, not remembering. "I am your cousin Elizabeth Sheldon," she said, feeling heat in her chill cheeks and a throbbing in her wrists and temple. "Don't you remember?" He was nearly seventeen years old then, a mature and respectable young man, and he had smiled at her and said, "Of course. Elizabeth." But he had entirely forgotten her. They had talked a few moments; Elizabeth never remembered of what. She watched for his smile, and when it came something lifted wings in her and her young body strained almost painfully. She had last seen him again only recently. He now filled all her secret thoughts and incomprehensible yearnings. She asked herself why, when she was most hungry, and could not answer her own questions. Though she knew that she had an extraordinary beauty, she had, in some measure, discounted it. The real treasure was money. Men preferred money to beauty, for money remained and beauty did not; money was rare; beauty was quite common. Elizabeth, like her mother, could not conceive that anyone could like or love her for herself and accept her without ulterior motives.

In the pursuit of what was now the most precious thing to her but which was not yet attainable because she was still too young and had no fortune of her own, Elizabeth could doggedly put William Lord Halnes out of her mind when necessary in the pursuit of first things. As she listened to her mother's weeping behind the locked door of the gallery she did not think of William consciously at all. She started when she heard Caroline unlock the door. Usually she was warned by approaching footsteps and could then flash into her own room or appear artlessly at the head of the stairs. She was not warned now. Her quick wits rescued her. She coughed loudly and repeatedly. The door opened and Caroline confronted her, majestic, frowning.

"What is it?" asked Caroline roughly. "What are you doing, Elizabeth?"

"I was just going into my room, Mother, and then I thought I heard you talking, or something, and I thought you might be sick." She stared pointedly at her mother's reddened eyes, and it was Caroline now, and not she, who was on the defensive.

"Nonsense," said Caroline. She frowned again. "Didn't I hear you cough? Are you catching cold?"

"No. It's only the dust," said Elizabeth with a slight and meaning smile.

"What dust?" asked Caroline irritably. She looked down the long hall. "These servants. They never do their work properly." She was closing the door behind her.

Then Elizabeth said, "Mother, I know you have some wonderful paintings in the gallery. I'd like to see them. Truly I would." She was curious to know what had made her mother cry in "Bluebeard's Cabinet." The information might be valuable someday. She looked at Caroline with large and innocent eyes. Caroline smiled tightly.

"Would you? I doubt it, Elizabeth." She hesitated, then pushed back the door. She paused. "A moment." She partly closed the door, moved quickly into the room. Elizabeth tried to peer through the crack but could see nothing but her mother's rusty black skirt. Caroline came to the door and said, "Come in, then."

Elizabeth entered and looked curiously about the long, well-lighted room. Here, at least, all was immaculate, the floor polished, the walls painted blue, the wide windows well washed and uncurtained. But it was very cold and very still. There were no seats except for a single straight-backed wooden chair. The walls held several paintings of good size; one of them faced the wall.

Elizabeth moved slowly from picture to picture, examining in silence, and she thought: What hideous daubs! What impossible colors! What distortions! You'd never see anything like this in the Boston Museum or at Miss Stockington's. I suppose this is what they call modern painting. No wonder our house is so dreadful and unkempt; Mother has no taste at all for anything, otherwise she would never have bought these horrors. But she said she paid twenty thousand dollars for one! Why? All that money! She has no right to waste our inheritance so!

Caroline was standing near one of the windows, watching her daughter. She waited in silence for the girl's verdict; she saw the serious, considering profile. Then Elizabeth turned her face to her mother, and the cold wintry light shone unshadowed upon it and Caroline saw her father's face, with every plane and color and expression reproduced in the younger, softer lines of femininity. A strong shock ran through her. She put her hands beside her, against the wall, as if to support herself.

Elizabeth looked at her mother and saw only a woman of nearly forty-five, broad, tall, impressive, with a crown of graying braids and an impassive wide face with large and brooding hazel eyes. She saw only a woman she thought excessively ugly, a little grimy, unfashionable in her old black bombazine with the raveled hem that swept the floor, too big of breast, too wide of shoulder. The dark skin was not lightened by any color on cheek or on sullen, heavy lip. Elizabeth stood again before the painting of the tower and pretended to be absorbed in it, for this was one her mother had mentioned in her monologue.

"Well?" said Caroline at last. Elizabeth turned to her mother again and saw a peculiar change on her mother's face, a searching look.

"Strange," murmured Elizabeth. She searched her mind for phrases she had overheard in the Boston Museum. "Authentic drawing. Brilliant color. Disturbing realism. Passionate realization." These phrases had meant nothing to Elizabeth, but her mind had stored them up for use in the future, and she could use them now.

"Oh. Yes," said Caroline. "I didn't know you would understand, Elizabeth." The girl's acute ear heard gratitude and surprise. She smiled in herself with satisfaction.

"I've seen something like this before," said Elizabeth, and then she remembered; three years ago, when she had been in the Bothwell house, old Harper had commented about a painting he had over his Adam mantelpiece. "New dimension. Not lithographic or reproduction of obviousness. Emotion, power, intensity."

Caroline said quickly, "You saw something like this before? By the same artist? Where, Elizabeth!"

She left the window and approached Elizabeth rapidly, and then she did a thing she had never done before. She put her hand on the girl's thin shoulder and pressed it, and bent a little to look into that suddenly beloved face, so like her own father's. Elizabeth's first fastidious impulse—for she hated to be touched by anyone—was to recoil, but her calculating mind kept her still and even made her shoulder less stiff.

"Why, in old Mr. Harper Bothwell's house. A marvelous painting of a mountain and a blind man staggering among a lot of boulders. The artist was a David Ames. I asked Mr. Bothwell about it; he said he was no relation to us, just the same name. I was fascinated by the painting, Mother. Mr. Bothwell said there were only about thirty in the world now." She smiled at her mother with John Ames' own smile, and an expression of pain appeared about Caroline's eyes.

Caroline said in a low voice, "I thought I knew them all. Your cousin Timothy owns the Bothwell house now. It's strange he never spoke of that painting." She looked away. "I must have it. Is it still there?"

"No. Cousin Timothy didn't like it for some unknown reason. He took it down; I don't know where it is now. It wasn't there the last time I visited them." What had Cousin Timothy said? "Repulsive. Disgusting. My father-in-law certainly had a low taste, for a well-bred Bostonian." Elizabeth said, shrugging delicately, "I do love Cousin Timothy. But he has no feeling for art, I am afraid."

The paintings on the wall glowed and glimmered like jewels, like windows opening into strange and exotic worlds of passion and color, of delight and splendor, of terror. Caroline looked at them, and her lips trembled. She would offer Timothy anything he wanted for the picture Amanda had inherited and which he had despised. Had he sold it? No matter. She, Caroline, would trace it to the ends of the world. She had a disturbing thought. Timothy always knew the value of everything. It was not possible that he did not know that a David Ames canvas was invaluable. He must have sold it.

Elizabeth said in an awed voice, "I love them all, these paintings. But the one I love most is this picture of the tower, Mother."

"Why?" asked Caroline, and leaned toward her daughter.

Elizabeth's mind clicked with mechanical precision as it sorted out what she had heard her mother say of this particular painting. She said, "I think it has a quality of awfulness, Mother. Perhaps even a little frightful. Ominous, in a way, perhaps even threatening. Like a warning." She added the last through a prompting of her immense intuition. "And yet, when you look at it, it is as though the artist closed a door in your face—to protect himself too."

"Oh yes!" cried Caroline. She swirled swiftly to her daughter and now put both hands on those young shoulders and could not know the satisfied contempt in Elizabeth's heart. "Oh, Elizabeth! You are sixteen, and I never knew what you really are! I'm so sorry." The stress of her emotion, her joy, her craving for understanding, made her pull the girl to her breast and hug her desperately.

Elizabeth, standing still in her mother's embrace, contracted her nostrils so as not to breathe in too much of the odor of old bombazine, of the odor of her mother's disturbed flesh. It was a real agony for the young girl to be held so tightly by anyone, but she controlled herself. She even put her slender arms about her mother and made her voice murmur consolingly, as she had heard Melinda murmur to her children. Caroline's tears ran down the smooth light brown head and the fragile temple.

"Oh, Elizabeth," said Caroline, and her wretched heart expanded and she was full of love and craven gratitude.

If one picture was worth twenty thousand dollars, thought Elizabeth, enduring an embrace that sickened her, how much more were the others worth? She said, "I couldn't bear it, Mother, if you left these wonderful paintings to anyone but me. Who would care for them but me?"

But Caroline, timidly kissing her daughter's cheek, was thinking: If I was so mistaken about Elizabeth, perhaps I've been mistaken, too, about my sons. I have thought of them only as my heirs, to protect Papa's money. Perhaps I was wrong.

If Caroline, in her simplicity, was doing some innocent thinking, her daughter, standing in the center of her chill and ascetic room, was also doing some very uninnocent thinking. Like her grandfather, she had marvelous powers of induction and deduction when it was a matter concerning her own profit. She had moved and reached her mother for the first time, and it had been her deliberate doing; she had seen the final indecision and wonderment on Caroline's face and had come to a very intelligent conclusion. There was no time to waste. Elizabeth, moving in her fleet and silent fashion, went to John's room and knocked on the door. No one knocked on his door except his father, and so he thought it was Tom and did not answer. So Elizabeth said, "It is I, John. I'd like to talk to you."

"Oh, you would," he grunted. "Well, come in. You know the way. You never knocked before." So Elizabeth turned the knob and came into the large warm room. She looked at the fire distastefully. "What a furnace," she remarked. The room was very untidy; open books sprawled on every chair and even on the floor and bed. John was a fairly good student at Harvard and very popular with faculty and fellow classmates, for not only was he very athletic, but he had a burly good nature which deceived many. It was only at home that he permitted himself to be himself. He said to Elizabeth, "If you don't like the heat, just go away. Well, Miss Snoop, what are you looking for now?"

It was no secret to Elizabeth's brothers that she listened to everything. This amused Ames; it did not amuse John. She looked at John now with her gelid blue eyes and said icily, "I'm not looking for anything." She sniffed the dust in the room, saw the tangled and crumpled draperies which had once been soft and colorful.

"You never do anything without a reason," said John. "Well? What is it?"

Elizabeth sat down stiffly on the edge of one chair, pushing aside the books. She considered her brother meditatively, his broad strength, his highly colored good looks. Caroline's features in her son were attractive. John narrowed his hazel eyes at his sister. "Thinking of lending me the ten dollars I asked you about this morning?"

"Did you ask Father?"

He grunted in disgust. "Of course I did. And he said my allowance was more than enough, with what he slipped me over and above Ma's pittance. What's the matter with the old man? Is he becoming a miser too?"

"Mother's not a miser," said Elizabeth. "I know everybody thinks so, but she isn't."

"What is she, then?" asked John with more disgust.

Elizabeth knew, but she did not intend to tell her brother. She made her voice soft. "She just doesn't know how to live. We've been no help to her at all."

"See who wants to be helpful to anybody!" jeered John. But he leaned back in his chair, and he was so big and heavy that the substantial piece of furniture creaked. "Well. If she won't spend a cent unless she has to, practically at the point of a gun, and lives like a dog and would like us all to live like dogs and thinks of nothing but getting money, what else is she but a miser? Tell me that."

"I told you. She doesn't know how to live. I've learned a few things from 'snooping,' as you meanly call it. Her father made her live in poverty; she went to Miss Stockington's, and she's quite a legend there. All the girls had three uniforms for the winter; Mother had only one, and she was usually out of elbows by the end of the second term. She took horse cars; there was rarely any carriage for her. She had the smallest of allowances. She never had any luxury or pleasure or the pretty things that most other girls have. She never made her debut, never had a ball given for her, never knew anyone worth knowing. Why, the poorest girl at Miss Stockington's lived like a princess compared with Mother."

"Um," said John. "She didn't have much spirit, did she? I've heard some things too." He smiled slyly. "I had a bad time the first year at Harvard; fellows kept throwing it up to me how Ma practically murdered those people who died in the North Shore wreck four years ago. Their families and the Bothwells were all good friends, and there was no good will for Ma after that, and even the big suits Ma had to settle out of court didn't satisfy them. But I finally convinced the fellows that though Caroline Ames is my mother I wasn't formed in the same image."

Elizabeth smiled in herself. She said seriously, "John, Mother needs our help. She needs to be shown why you, at Harvard, have to have more money. What does she know about how much a young man needs over and above his actual expenses? She wouldn't want people to despise you. You don't have the clothes the other men at Harvard have; you have to travel on streetcars; you have no money with which to entertain. Did you ever try to explain it to her?"

John grunted. He twisted a pencil in his hand, his big black head bent. He did not trust his sleek and beautiful sister, but he reminded himself that Elizabeth had a lot of sense and acuteness. But why should such a selfish piece care about his needs and his craving for luxury and splendid living and spending?

He said, "Why are you interested in my personal affairs all at once, Lizzie?"

"Don't call me that," she said sharply. Then she made herself smile again. "Why am I interested? Isn't it obvious? I'm sixteen; I'll be a member of the Assemblies; I'll make my debut. I have Father's promise on all that, you can be sure. But Mother's reputation for closeness is well known. Now, if she can be shown how to live and what we actually need, she'll loosen up the purse strings. Even more important, you are at Harvard and you meet eligible young men, young men I want to meet in the future. Under circumstances as they are now, I may never meet the right men. I'll have to take anything at all."

"Like Ma did," said John, grinning nastily.

"Certainly," said Elizabeth at once. "Do you think anyone with any self-respect, even a thrifty Bostonian, would have married Mother as she was in those days? Of course not. I don't intend to make a poor marriage. I need your help. You can't give it to me unless you have the money to entertain, as other young men at Harvard do. You won't be able to interest your friends in me, as your only sister, unless they can be sure I'll have some money of my own.

"Mother doesn't know anything about our needs. After all, she is our mother, and she does care for us in her way. I'm not her favorite; if anyone is, you are. She would listen to you. She's in her study now. Why don't you go in and have a frank talk with her?"

"And after all these generalities of yours, what shall I actually tell her?"

"That you want to live. That you want money to spend as easily as other young men spend it. That it is perfectly fine to save, but it is much better to spend. She doesn't know about it. Tell her."

John narrowed his eyes at his sister and watched her closely and was silent. Old Lizzie often had very good ideas. She was also frequently up to something for herself. John was suspicious; but, examine the idea as he would, he could see only that Elizabeth was thinking of herself and the young men she would want to meet. What other reason could she have but those she had stated so candidly, and with such earnestness and open expression? Still John, who knew his sister, hesitated. He rubbed his big chin with the knuckles of his right hand.

"You're a girl," he said. "Why haven't you talked to her yourself?"

"I have. She thinks I should be satisfied with what she had in her own girlhood."

"You never spend a cent you don't have to, yourself," said John, still suspicious. "You save all you can. Try to pry a cent out of you for a loan! And you always want interest, too."

"I have to," said Elizabeth. "If I didn't I'd never have money to spend on the right occasions at Miss Stockington's. When a teacher takes us out to tea we have to pay our share. If I threw away my miserable allowance I'd have to stay behind. I have a little pride, you know, John."

"You have your own troubles," said John gloomily. "I can see that. What a mess our lives are. And they'll get worse as we grow older."

Elizabeth breathed out lightly. "Think about it, John." She stood up and sadly smoothed her plain serge dress with a slim and elegant hand. John saw the gesture. "Poor old girl," he said, but not with any real sympathy. He stood up also, stretched, and said, "I think I'll beard the old lioness in her den right now."

"Good," said Elizabeth. She moved toward the door. "Let me know your success, won't you?" She paused. "If I were you, I wouldn't mention to her that you've had this talk with me. When I've asked for extra money for some lovely frock she only talked of frivolities."

"What makes you think that she won't say I'm frivolous too?"

"She knows you are a man, John. And you know she hates frivolous women. She thought Aunt Cynthia was a trollop, or something."

"She was," said John, grinning again. "I'm not the only one who listens, Lizzie. But I can see your point. A man who needs money to spend is entirely different from a woman who wants money to spend on fripperies, as Ma calls them."

Elizabeth nodded sadly and drifted away. John combed his hair at his disorderly chest of drawers, washed his hands in water he had washed in that morning and which had not yet been emptied by the slack housemaid. Then he went down to his mother's study and knocked on the door. He had much physical courage, and he knew that in her indifferent way his mother preferred him to her other children.

In the meantime Elizabeth went to her younger brother's room.

Before she left her mother only a short time ago Elizabeth had fully persuaded Caroline of her deep passion and interest in art. She had complained to Caroline that Miss Stockington's school knew nothing of true artistry and that pallid water colors were *de rigueur* and that the Boston Museum was "stuffy" and unprogressive. "I know I have no real talent, Mother," she had said to Caroline shyly. "But I'd like to try, all alone." So Caroline, moved, had given the girl twenty dollars. It was safely in the pocket of her apron at this very moment. The money was to be used ostensibly to purchase the necessary artist's supplies. Elizabeth had expected five dollars; she was incredulous at being presented with a gold certificate for twenty dollars. But she had been taught another valuable lesson: where Caroline's deepest emotions were concerned, money did not matter.

Ames' room, unlike John's, was extremely tidy and precise. He had a large shelved cabinet for his treasures, which Tom had bought for him. He also had a smooth table near his cabinet on which he kept a record book of his treasures, their history, their age, and a magnifying glass with which he could study their smallest beauties. He kept his person well groomed, for he was excessively fastidious. He was fifteen years old, taller than Elizabeth, and had a slow elegance and appeared older than he was, with his curiously triangular face, his hard slate-colored eyes, his smooth fair hair and small tight lips and sharply cut nose. He was considered colorless at Groton. He preferred his own company. Where other students bogged at Pater, he understood almost everything instinctively.

He was examining the smallest of Meissen figures, recently purchased, when Elizabeth came in. He frowned at her coldly. "Well?" he said, and lifted the magnifying glass. He held the figurine with delicate care. Elizabeth waited until he completed his examination. He was satisfied; this was one of the best of its kind and had cost the old man seventy-five dollars and was cheap at the price. He put the figurine carefully into its cotton-lined box and looked at his shelves and wondered where he could stand the figurine to the best advantage.

"I have something to talk to you about," said Elizabeth.

"Have you? What?" He turned on his chair. He was always suspicious of his sister. They had much in common.

"I've just had a talk with Mother," said Elizabeth.

"How nice," he murmured. "How is the stock market doing?"

"Who cares?" said Elizabeth.

"You do," replied her brother. "You aren't the only one who notices things. I've seen you studying the stock-market pages in the newspaper after Ma's thrown them away. And you read her financial journals too. Do you think you'll have a seat on the Stock Exchange, if they ever permit ladies to have a seat?"

Elizabeth was taken aback. She had believed her financial studies to be her own secret. Ames saw her perturbation and smiled. "I shouldn't have let you know," he said. "You were enjoying yourself so much, and I found it enjoyable to watch you. What do you want?"

Elizabeth recovered herself. She leaned toward the large mahogany cabinet and studied the many beautiful and exquisite objects in it. Everything was so small! She hated smallness. She hated tiny and fragile beauty. She despised imponderables. She thought Ames effeminate, which was not true. She thought him concerned solely with trivialities, for to her beauty was a triviality. She tended her own dispassionately, as a possession which would serve her well in the future.

"You have a fortune here," she said.

"Indeed," said Ames. "But I'm not interested in selling. Were you thinking of buying something from me? No sale."

He smiled at her and wondered what the old girl was up to. Elizabeth did nothing without a purpose.

"Has Mother ever seen these wonderful things?" asked Elizabeth.

"Ma? Yes. She's come in here once or twice. Now, Ma is strictly utilitarian. She doesn't like frivolities, and she thinks my collection is frivolous. She knows nothing whatsoever of art."

"You are wrong," said Elizabeth seriously, and sat down on Ames' bed. "I've just had a talk with her."

"Indeed," said Ames skeptically. "Has Ma suddenly developed a taste for curios or figurines?"

"It could be," said Elizabeth.

Ames laughed; he had a very quiet laugh which contained more amusement than his brother John's loud mirth. "If she hasn't, then Dad has. A very well-developed taste, too."

Elizabeth thought her brother was referring to the little works of art Tom had bought for his son, but when she saw the laughter shining enjoyably in Ames' eyes she knew it was something else, something much more interesting.

"Don't you know?" asked Ames maliciously. "I thought you knew everything. You're always everywhere in your slippery way."

Elizabeth ignored the insult and said, "It's possible I know but didn't think it was important enough."

Ames laughed out loud now. "You'd think it important enough! Everybody down in the village is talking about it, and I've heard sniggers about it at Groton."

Elizabeth shrugged. "Who cares about village gossip," she said, lifting her chin, "or schoolboy chatter?" She waited. Ames was chuckling at her and shaking his head.

"You don't know," he said. "But as your loving brother I'm going to tell you. Dear old Dad spends a large part of his time at the Bothwell house. He stops in at least three or four times a week to see poor old Aunt Melinda, who has a nice companion lady from Boston—best of family—as chaperone, seeing both the kids are away at school. Mrs. Ernest Griswold-Smith, a widow. Grim old hag. As she is almost seventy, it couldn't be Mrs. Smith Dad is visiting so regularly for a couple of hours each time. It could only be Aunt Melinda."

Elizabeth actually blushed, and Ames was delighted. "Oh no," said the girl. "How stupid. How foolish. But Mother apparently knows; she knows everything. So it can't be important. What a nasty mind you have, Ames. What could two old people like Dad and Aunt Melinda have in common? It's possible that Dad feels guilty, in a way, for Uncle Alfred's death, though it was all Mother's fault. I remember that Dad and Uncle Alfred were close friends; Dad built his house. So it's perfectly natural, under the circumstances, for Dad to continue his visits."

"Perhaps," agreed Ames. "Dad takes gifts for the kids on holidays, too. Very expensive ones. Wouldn't it be nice for us if he left all his money to Aunt Melinda and her kids, as a sort of conscience bequest?"

Elizabeth knew that her father was now rich, probably a millionaire. She was disturbed.

"I like facts, not rumors," she said, dismissing the subject for the time being. She had a more immediate object in mind. "Let's come back to what I wanted to talk to you about. I had a long conversation with Mother this afternoon. She let me see her pictures in the gallery."

"She did?" Ames was interested. "What were they like?"

Elizabeth considered. "Unusual," she said cautiously. "Interesting, too. I don't think you'd care for them, though, because you like old rare things. They're by David Ames and very expensive."

Ames sat up abruptly. "David Ames! Why, you can't buy any of his works! They're priceless! What does she know of art, anyway?"

"She knows a lot," said Elizabeth, nodding her head. "You'd be surprised. Just because she's a recluse and rarely goes out except on business does not mean she's uninformed and ignorant. Remember, she went to Miss Stockington's, too, and then traveled all over Europe, and even South America, with our grandfather. Though she doesn't talk very much, as you know, I gather she's deeply interested in art and beauty of all kinds."

"This house proves it," said Ames.

"She isn't interested in houses. She's interested in money and art."

"I never noticed it," said Ames, "and I have a sharp eye for such things. She made some mean remarks about my collections and said they were a waste of money."

"That is because she thinks you aren't serious about your collections and that you buy them only for their intrinsic value and not for any real feeling about them."

"If she thought that, she'd approve. I know Ma," said Ames, watching his sister. "What can't be sold for a profit or what one just keeps isn't of interest to her. If I were doing a brisk trade and making money at it, she would be interested all right!"

"Mother could do quite a brisk trade, as you call it, with her Ames paintings if she wanted to," Elizabeth brought out. "But she wouldn't sell them for any money, and you know how Mother is about money. In fact, she paid twenty thousand dollars for one; she told me. She's now looking for another." She paused and widened her eyes at her brother. "Why don't you tell her how you feel about your collection and that you'd like a larger allowance so you can add to them? Why don't you tell her you aren't interested in money as a thing in itself, but only to spend on beautiful things? She'd understand."

Ames was silent. His suspicions were far deeper and more astute than John's.

"Tell me," he said at last, "just what is behind all this? Your interest in whether or not I get a larger allowance to 'indulge' myself in 'fripperies,' as Ma calls it?"

"It's very simple," said Elizabeth. "I want a larger allowance too. At this very minute John is trying to persuade Ma to increase his. If he gets his way and you do, too, I'll get an increase. It would only be fair. Even Mother will see that."

Ames twitched his sharp long nose and stared at his sister. "John's with her now? Was that your idea too?"

"Certainly. I'm not being charitable." Elizabeth smiled. "I want you boys to have more money so I can have more money."

"Nothing's simple where you're concerned," said her loving brother. But he thought: This is just like old Lizzie, hot after the cash. It couldn't be anything else.

Then Elizabeth said, "If you both succeed—and I can't see why you shouldn't—I wouldn't mind a small tip for my advice."

Ames considered again. "Did you try to hit her up yourself?"

Elizabeth smiled smugly. "Why should I tell you?"

"Of course you wouldn't. But if you had, and if you'd gotten your way, you wouldn't be here putting the thumbscrews on me," said Ames. "You'd just keep your mouth shut, except when you were licking your lips. What makes you think we'd do any better?"

"Because you're boys, and mothers care more for their sons and understand them better. Mother thinks I shouldn't have more than she had at my age."

Try though he did, Ames could not see that there was anything more to this conversation than what Elizabeth was revealing. Elizabeth stood up. She had heard John's door close loudly and furiously. She waited a moment, then said, "John just went into his room. Now you can go to Mother's study and plead your case."

"I'll talk to John first," said Ames, "to see how the land lies."

Elizabeth had a fairly good idea of how the land lay, but she did not want Ames to know it. "Do you think he'd tell you?" she asked. "You know how John is—all for himself. Do hurry, Ames."

Caroline was in her study, but not looking over her financial statements and ledgers. She was thinking of Elizabeth, and her deprived spirit was expanding more and more, and she was wallowing in remorse. But she was also hopeful. She had misunderstood her daughter; it was more than possible that she had misunderstood her sons. For the first time to her they were no longer her heirs but her flesh and blood. She was in this excited and agitated mood when John knocked on her door and then came in. His first thought when he saw her sudden and eager smile was that old Lizzie had been right, for he could not remember when he had seen his mother smile like that before.

"Well, John," she said, and he was quite astonished at the kindness in her voice. "Come in. Is there anything you want?"

The big young man sat down and studied his mother and the room. Here all was extreme order, with a wide desk, good lights, and filing cabinets.

Caroline waited. She took off her glasses, and though her eyes were tired they were also shyly beaming and expectant. John was a little unnerved; the hard cold woman, the silent, unloving woman, the businesslike woman he had always known was gone. He could not understand this woman who suddenly looked like a mother, anxious to hear her son speak and anxious to help him. He had no way of knowing the yearning that was reaching out to him, the hope, the desperation and loneliness that ached to be relieved in him, the girlish naïveté and the endless suffering. He could not see the woman who wanted so dreadfully to be reassured that life had something for her at last.

John relaxed. He was grateful to his sister; she had done a very good job, it seemed, of softening up the old lady. But he moved carefully. He gave his mother a wide and confiding smile.

"I thought you'd like to know how I'm getting along at Harvard," he said. "This is my second semester, you know, Ma."

"Yes," said Caroline. Color had come into her big lips. "Tell me, John. I do have your reports, as you know, but I'd like to hear from you, yourself."

John was quite amazed. Caroline had given him only personal indifference all his life, though she had been interested in his scholarly progress and had warned him to excel. "I want to do the best I can, Ma," he said, still moving carefully. "And I'm going to like law, so I can take my place in Tandy, Harkness and Swift, as you planned. I'm only sorry I never saw the old boys, but only their sons and nephews."

"They're 'old boys' too," said Caroline, waiting for the words of deliverance. "The youngest is in his forties. I'm glad you like law, John. Ames doesn't. It is a big disappointment to me."

John had no intention of helping his brother, so he made his expression serious. "He doesn't care for anything but his collection," he said. "Well, everyone to his taste."

"The 'boutique,'" murmured Caroline, thinking of her aunt and Ames simultaneously. Her warm expression darkened.

"What did you say, Ma?" asked John.

"Nothing, John. Just a thought of mine. It will be a great satisfaction to me to have you in that law firm; they were my father's lawyers and are mine, and I want them to be my children's."

She was still looking at John eagerly and expectantly, and this disturbed him a little. What did she want him to say?

"I'll do my very best," he said, watching her.

She nodded and she still waited. She waited for him to say, "I want to do my best so I can help you and be really a son to you, because I love you and you are my mother."

"I'll do my very best," the young man repeated. He paused. "But there's something else. As you know, times are different. Even in Boston. People respect money and want it. They know it's good to have it behind you and to save part of your income. But they also know that money was made to be spent in the enjoyment of life and not only in the getting of it."

Caroline's expression changed, and John was alarmed. What had gone wrong?

"Go on," said Caroline.

"I need a lot more money, Ma. A much bigger allowance. After all, things are expected of the men at Harvard. It's expected that you entertain in your turn and not do it niggardly. I'm the son of a rich lady and so more is expected of me even than of the others. I want to live, Ma, to spend money, to have a fine time doing it, and to make many friends. You have to buy friends, you know. What else is money for, after a decent part of it is saved, but to spend and travel and have fun and a lot of enjoyment?"

Caroline was silent. She looked at him piercingly. She thought: He cares nothing for the trust that was given me and which was to be his trust also. He is selfish and coarse and wants to indulge himself at my expense and throw away Papa's money.

She said coldly, "When I am dead, John, you'll have a lot of money. What will you do with it?"

John was cautious and a little frightened now. But he remembered what Elizabeth had told him. He put some enthusiasm in his voice. "Ma, you never lived, yourself. I know how horribly you existed when you were a girl—the poverty and all that. You never had a rich, full life. You were deprived. You once told me your father had a very hard time accumulating money. But when he did have all that money he should have loosened up and spent a lot on you, to make you happy as a young girl. If there is anything to the theory of retribution, I hope he is having some of it now." He smiled sympathetically at his mother.

"Go on," said Caroline bitterly.

Things were not going as expected. But John blundered on. "You've asked me what I'll do with all that money which will be my share. Of course I'll keep some part of it as insurance and security. But I'll spend the greater part of it, enjoying myself as you should have enjoyed yourself. I want to live, Ma, as you never lived. As my grandfather never lived. What else is money for?"

She had met men like John before in her travels, beefy men, ruddy men, extravagant, selfish men, full of wine, glittering with jewelry, carrying with them the odor of lavish living and the scent of bought women. Many of them became bankrupt. They had inherited money and had spent it heedlessly, the money so painfully and laboriously gathered by fathers and grand-fathers, the money which had been a sacred trust and a fortress against the world. Her father had said, "Worthless wretches, with no sense of responsibility. They are only appetites, gaudy and gross, ripe for picking."

"What do you know of my father, John?" she asked her son.

John was fumbling around in his mind. The pale glare of the cold sun suddenly came out and he could not see his mother's face clearly, as her back was to the windows. He said, "From all I hear, he was a miser and he made your life wretched."

Caroline felt weak and sick, and she was also filled with a cold and violent anger. Her son was attacking his grandfather as her Aunt Cynthia had often attacked him, and in almost the same accusing words. What did these superficial, wasteful people know of men like John Ames, these parasites, these appetites, these heedless spenders of what worthier people had earned?

She made a quick and merciless resolution. She would change her will at once; she would leave John not more than five thousand dollars a year from a trust. Many cautious parents in Boston did this to prevent the wasting of their money by children.

She said abruptly, "You've asked me for a larger allowance in order that you can spend as other young men spend. I don't approve of such spending. No, John."

"No?" he said.

"No. When you are a member of my law firm you will have your regular salary, very modest to begin with, for at first you'll only be a clerk. Later you will be a junior member with a little larger salary. Perhaps later you will be a full member. That is up to you and your diligence and thrift. I can promise nothing more."

She was so full of bitterness and wild disappointment that she went on ruthlessly, "Don't expect much more from me. I intend to leave you five thousand a year for life, and nothing more. You may go now."

He stumbled to his feet. His eyes glittered at her with hatred. "Is that your last word?" he said.

"My very last word. And don't expect me to change it."

He knew his mother. She would never relent.

"Miser," he said. "You were never anything else but a stupid miser who never knew how to live and who doesn't want anyone else to live. But I'll tell you this: I'll get around things someway. By God, I will!"

"I don't think you will," said Caroline. (She was terribly frightened, though she sat stolidly in her chair. Her son was looking at her with the eyes of old Fern. He was looking at her with the eyes of the doctor in Switzerland.) "Go away!" she cried.

She sat at her desk, her hands pressed hard over her face. Her pain and suffering were too terrible for tears. No one cared for her or understood her, with the possible exception of Elizabeth, who had shyly confided to her earlier that she understood about money and that she carefully read all her mother's discarded financial journals and the stock-market reports. There was only Elizabeth, Caroline thought distractedly, Elizabeth who knew that money was a trust, Elizabeth who appreciated the paintings of her great-grandfather.

A knock on the door had to be repeated before she heard it. She said dully, "Who is it?"

"Ames, Mama."

She did not reply at once. Then her incredible hope returned and she said, "Come in." She dropped her hands to her desk with a feeling of intense prostration. She looked in silence as her son entered the room gracefully, his long body moving in one fluid line. He touched the seat John had sat in and said politely, "May I?"

"Of course." What was that terrible sinking sensation in the pit of her stomach, that sense of draining away, of rapidly diminishing vitality? She put the sensation from her and studied Ames, who sat so precisely and neatly, and he reminded her, not of Timothy Winslow, but of Elizabeth. Again her hope stirred, and she could smile a little with a great effort.

"I wanted to have a talk with you, Mama," said Ames. "A special talk."

Caroline winced. "You want to have your allowance increased. Is that it?"

He raised his eyebrows and considered her. Her color was practically livid, and her lips had a purplish overcast, and she appeared tired beyond endurance. So John hadn't got what he wanted. Well, he was a silly brute and had probably riled the old lady with his first words; he had no finesse.

"It's considered inelegant to talk about money, except in Boston," he said.

"So it is." Caroline smiled again. "Am I right, then, that you didn't come here to talk about money?"

All her children had been shadowy to her, but Ames had been more so than the others. They had been bred for a purpose. Never until today had they actually impinged strongly on her consciousness as human beings with thoughts of their own, desires and ideas of their own, and dreams of their own. She had treated them as her father had treated her; she considered that she had been an excellent mother, instilling respect in them for money, insisting upon frugality, giving them the best education possible, providing for them, saving for them, clothing them. As she had been given, so she gave. It had once bewildered her that they had never extended to her the devotion she had extended to her father. When she saw that they would not, she had lost the last measure of personal interest in them as human beings. They were ungrateful; they did not understand. She did not blame herself for their awful corruption, nor even wonder why they were so different from other children.

Ames said, "I have the greatest respect and admiration for you, Mama."

Caroline was startled from her apathy. She looked with sudden earnestness at her son. "Why," she said slowly, "thank you, Ames. I'm glad." She paused. "Why have you?"

"Because you are a genius," he said, and as he more than partly believed this, his light voice carried sincerity and conviction. "There are many kinds of genius, though most people don't understand that. There are the artist, the musician, the composer, the architect, the poet, the philosopher, the scientist, the great statesman or teacher. There is also the genius for making money, and without that genius possessed by a few none of the other arts could exist. Michelangelo, da Vinci, Voltaire, Wagner, to name just a few, had to have patrons. Directly or indirectly, all geniuses benefit from the person who has the genius to make money. To despise the money-making genius is to despise all the others and make it impossible for them to be."

This was an aspect of money-making which had never occurred to Caroline before. She considered it, then suddenly reveled in it. Certainly! "You are a brilliant boy, Ames," she said in a stronger voice, and the starved girl that lived in her rushed into her eyes so that they shone and became warmly beautiful. Seeing this, Ames was startled, himself, at his success.

"You were never interested in law, as John is," said Caroline. "But, as I have already told you, it is my intention that all of you, including Elizabeth, must have a thorough education in finance, in world conditions as they affect finance, after your formal education is completed. I do not intend"—and she looked down at her tightly clasped big hands—"that my father's money, which was a trust to me and my heirs, shall be given into the hands of those who know nothing about it."

"That would be ridiculous," said Ames, inclining his head respectfully.

Caroline gave him a timid and searching glance, and he was intrigued by its unsophistication.

"When John has been graduated from Harvard and studied law and business administration, then I intend for him to go abroad. Elizabeth will also go abroad, and eventually you too."

"I understand," said Ames.

Caroline could not let herself hope again, but again she searched her son's face. "This is all I have to live for," she said.

"Yes, Mama, I understand," he repeated. Now was the time. "But that's very sad, isn't it? I've seen the old wreck of the house near Lyme where you spent your summers; I've heard rumors of the disgusting house in Lyndon too. Yet you were entitled to some of the graciousness of living, weren't you? And beauty, and the kind of nice times other girls had. What was wrong with my grandfather that he deprived you like that and made you live like a beggar when he had all that money?"

Caroline's face closed darkly; the light went from her eyes. Ames saw this and wondered where he had blundered, and was dismayed. He went on hurriedly, "Money is very, very important, but not as a thing in itself. Is it?"

Caroline said very quietly, "What would you do with a lot of money, Ames?"

"I'd spend it on beautiful things," he said. "I'd have a solid background of it, of course, to protect myself. But I'd buy the handsomest small house possible, either in Boston or New York. Probably in both places. I'd buy a villa on the Côte d'Azure and one in London and another in Rome. I'd search the whole world for their furnishings, so that everything would be perfect and in the best of taste. Not large, gaudy things, or pieces, or pictures. The delicate, the fine. You know, Mama."

"Yes," said Caroline. "I know." She thought of her Aunt Cynthia. "The 'boutique.'"

"I beg your pardon?" said Ames.

"Never mind. You were saying?"

"I wouldn't spare any expense to get treasures I wanted. And I'd surround myself with them."

Caroline remembered some of the effete men she had met in her youth who would talk for hours in lyrical voices of a piece of Dresden they had recently acquired, or a small sketch of El Greco's they had found in Spain, or a rug they had come upon in Afghanistan, or a crusted jeweled cup attributed to at least a pupil of Cellini's, or a statuette exhumed from the ruins of Pompeii, or a Shakespearean folio, or a first edition of Shelley, or a Grueze figurine, or a Van Gogh bought at an enormous price, or a "little necklace" alleged to have been worn by a princess of the Second Dynasty, or a Chippendale chair, or a Chinese printed silk or scroll. These men apparently lived for useless beauty, for the gathering of scraps and debris. They had a fragile language of their own which had nothing to do with hard reality's tongue. They often went bankrupt and had to sell their treasures for a tenth or less of what they had paid for them, or their heirs sold them ruthlessly for the money which should never have been spent in the first place, the money so painfully acquired by other men.

"So that would be what you would do with money," said Caroline.

"Yes, Mama, that is what I would do. You never had beauty in your life, but I want it as you must have wanted it. What else is money for but to decorate life? And to make it pleasant and gracious?"

Caroline smiled grimly. "I know it is inelegant to talk about money." A kind of ugly exultation came to her, as if she were confronting Cynthia without fear for the first time and throwing the words of hate and anger in her face, words which had been burning in her since she was a child.

"We'll talk about it," she said abruptly, and struck her desk with the flat of her right hand, and all at once she seemed to enlarge before her son's eyes, to become formidable. "My father and I didn't spend our lives getting money to be wasted on trash and worthless *objets d'art*. I know about your precious collection. I hoped once that you'd get over all that shameful nonsense. Apparently I was wrong."

Ames, who now knew that he had lost, came angrily to himself, and his eyes sparkled at his mother. He interrupted: "Wait a minute, Mama. You have a private art gallery of your own upstairs which you hide away from everybody. I've heard rumors that you paid plenty for those paintings!"

Caroline looked at him. "That is another matter entirely," she said. "There is a reason for my gallery, which you'll never know. Only one artist's works are there; I'd never collect another artist's.

"No matter. It seems I'm to be defeated everywhere I turn. I'm not going to let my father's money and what I've added to it to be squandered in stupidities and what you like to call the graciousness of living. You are a spendthrift by nature, it seems. And so I have to guard the trust my father gave me. I've just told your brother that he'll get nothing from me but five thousand dollars a year for life when I die, from a perpetual trust. You'll have to work for a living, as my father worked; you're no better than he. You'll have your education, and that is all. You may go now."

Ames did not fly into a rage of frustration and hatred as his brother had done. Though he had been dismissed, he sat in his chair and regarded his mother with cold curiosity. "I want to say something too," he said. "You are a miser, and there's nothing uglier than a miser. You never knew what it was to live and you want to prevent others from living. Because you never saw, you want others to be blind. Your whole life is a study in ugliness and perversion. Disgusting. Like a mole's life. What have you ever had—except money? And what has your money done for you? Nothing. Who cares about you? Not even my father. I can't blame him for what he is doing now. It must have been a terrible life for him here with you. How could he have stood it for all these years?" Ames smiled at his mother. "He didn't, after all! And I'm glad."

He stood up. Caroline's thoughts were in furious chaos, but she finally fastened on what her son had said about her husband. "What do you mean?" she cried.

Ames laughed gently. "You don't know? I don't intend to tell you. But when you do know—— I'm not sixteen yet, but I'm not the only one with eyes in this house, and ears, too. You're due for a nice fall, dear Mama, and I hope it will be very soon."

He bowed like an eighteenth-century gentleman. "All my best wishes for your unhappiness," he said, and went gracefully from the room.

When the door closed Caroline jumped from her chair and ran to the windows. The red sun stood over the gray water; the snow and the empty beach below were a picture of desolation. The tide was coming in, black and deathly cold, on the rocks and on the sand.

A premonition of loss and fear and grief came to Caroline. Where was Tom? She must talk to him! How long had it been since they had talked to each other at all? Months? Years? "Tom!" she cried aloud, and leaned her forehead against the icy window. She heard the rumbling tide come in, and the sun became a dull crimson and sank behind the water.

She forgot the years in between, and the silence, and the bitterness. She was the girl who had looked from another window, like this, and had seen the young Tom smoking his pipe on the shingle. She was the girl who had seen him move away, and she was the girl who had lifted her heavy skirts and had raced down shaking old stairs and out into the wind and the twilight, calling, crying. Tom had turned to her. He would turn to her now in her extremity, and they would understand each other again. Tomorrow.

CHAPTER NINE

Tom Sheldon came home at ten that night, haggard and silent, and thinking. He had come to the end. He had not willed for it to happen this way, but it had happened. He was past forty-six now. He had had a happy and serene life until that accursed day when he had married, not Carrie, but Caroline Ames. That was twenty-one years ago. Twenty-one years in a dark prison, among strangers! He had served his sentence. There was nothing for him here. He had no wife, no real children. He had deluded himself for years, trying to bring kindness and love and understanding to these other prisoners. They had wanted nothing of him and had laughed at what he had wanted to give them.

John. Elizabeth. Ames. His children! He locked the door behind him and smiled drearily. They were not his children. They were the children of Caroline Ames. "She's welcome to them," he said aloud as he took off his coat and hung it up in the cloakroom. It hurt him to say this, but he knew it was true. If he was to have a little of life, the little that was left, he must face facts. He had been refusing to face facts for years. He stood in the cold and unswept hall. Only one meager gaslight burned. Caroline did not like friendly lights burning "all over the house, wasting money." So the house was like a dark cavern, musty and forsaken. He had just left a house full of life and light and warmth and affection. How little it took, even in money, to have a fire and a lamp! It made all the difference to a man's soul.

Here it was, the Easter holidays, and the house full of young people! The house was as silent as though completely deserted. He glanced into the drawing room; the little fire had smoldered out; no one had drawn the worn draperies, and so they reflected blackly and meanly the one small gaslight near the mantelpiece. When he had first stood in the completed room Tom had thought of children about that fire, a big fire, and a loving wife and himself watching them and listening to them and laughing with them. He had been stupid not to realize from the very beginning. He thought of John Ames and cursed him simply in his distraught mind.

Look what you have done to your daughter and her husband and her children, he thought. I hope you are in hell somewhere and that you can see and hear and know everything now. If I thought that by staying here I could still save them and help them, in spite of what I really want, I'd do it. But it's no use; it never was.

The house seemed to listen to him. It seemed suddenly filled with alert ghosts pondering what he had thought. He shivered, because he was cold and desperate and lonely, and very, very tired. His father had never been as tired as this, though he had lived to be an old man. It wasn't work that exhausted a man and broke his spirit. It was loneliness and lovelessness and lack of hope. If there were a way out, a man should take it before it was too late. He had really known it for over two years, but he had hesitated because of his children. Those two years had been wasted.

He went slowly and heavily up the stairs, hating the worn and grimy carpet, hating the cold and the smell of dust and mice. It had taken only twenty-one years of neglect to reduce a fine house to a hovel, to destroy its beauty and comfort.

It was late, but he saw the light under Caroline's study door. The light in John's room was still burning. He heard the muttering of his sons' voices. He stood in the hall and listened. The boys seemed to be agitated about something; he heard John utter an oath, and then Ames laughed thinly. There was a feeling that something had happened here, and Tom's senses became alert. He knocked on John's door, then opened it.

A good fire was burning here, as if in defiance. All the gaslights were brightly lit. John was sprawling on his untidy bed, his arms supporting his head, and Ames was sitting near him. Tom did not shrink, as he always did, at the bold and unfriendly glances his sons gave him. He shut the door behind him and said, "Well? What is it? It must be something or you two wouldn't be talking about it so late."

It was the quiet firmness in his voice, his lack of a smile, his searching and demanding expression, that startled his sons. This was a father they had never seen before. He walked into the room, warmed his hands at the fire while they watched him in silence. He looked about and said, "A filthy mess. You should have more self-respect. Well? What is it?"

John was so surprised that he sat up, and Ames lost his faintly mocking smile. "We've been foxed—someway," John said curtly.

"Foxed? By what?"

"By whom is correct," said Ames.

"Are you going to tell me about it?" asked Tom in a hard voice. "Don't if you don't want to. But this is your last chance, boys."

"What?" asked John, alert.

"Never mind. I only want to say that I've failed with you. It was never any use. But if I can, even now, help you, I will. For the last time. Make up your minds very fast. I want to go to bed."

The brothers exchanged a quick glance. Then Ames shrugged.

"All right," said John sullenly. "What harm can it do?"

He told Tom about his and Ames' conversation with their sister that afternoon and the interviews with their mother. Tom listened silently, standing on the torn hearthrug. His dark blue eyes turned slowly from one face to the other. His lean features became hard and tight. It came to Ames as he watched his father during John's recital that his father had changed, had come to some indomitable resolution, that he was a man at last in his own right and not merely the soft shadow of his wife, imploring in the background for his children's affection.

Tom showed none of the anger and disgust he was feeling. His sons had been stupid; they should have known their mother better. He saw them sharply and clearly. They had become corrupt; their mother had corrupted them. But still, they had human minds and spirits of their own and they were old enough now to resist the corruption.

He also knew who had "foxed" his sons. Elizabeth. How could they have failed to see that? It was very obvious. He saw Elizabeth even more clearly than he did his sons, and he thought of John Ames. He wanted to say, "It was your sister who deceived you and led you into this mess." But he held it back. Any affection he had had for his daughter left him, and he was sorry for his sons.

"That is all there is," said John at last, and fell back on his pillows.

"No," said Tom. "You're wrong. I am trebling your allowance from now on, John, and doubling yours, Ames, until you're John's age. I don't need to warn you not to tell your mother."

Yes, it was Elizabeth who had slyly and deftly ruined her brothers. For what purpose? To become her mother's chief heir, to take her mother's place later. He looked at the picture of his daughter in his mind, and many things that had puzzled him about her became part of a precise and plotted pattern. He had surprised her listening at doors; he had thought it a childish pastime. He had come upon her silently standing in halls, in doorways. He had thought it part of her "shyness" and girlishness. He was not horrified at what he knew now. It had been inevitable. It was he who had been the fool.

John was sitting up again and smiling sheepishly at his father. "Why, that's wonderful, Dad," he said.

"Wonderful," repeated Ames, but he was wondering what had led Tom to this, Tom who had always admonished them to respect their mother.

"When I was in Boston two days ago, Ames," said Tom, "I saw a silver-gilt salt cup that might interest you. Go in tomorrow and look at it. It's at Wooden's. They want one hundred dollars. Very rare. If you like it, buy it, and charge it to me."

He turned to John. "What else do you want besides the money?"

John was stupefied. His hazel eyes jumped. Then he blurted, "I'd like my own little sailboat for the summer. But that's two hundred and fifty dollars."

"Done," said Tom. "I'll put my check under your door tonight."

He went out of the room. He would remake his will within the next day or two. He would leave Elizabeth exactly two thousand dollars. The balance of his large estate, including all his construction business, would be left equally divided between his two sons. "What in hell do you think's happened to him?" asked John of his brother.

CHAPTER TEN

When had he first come to love Melinda Bothwell? Tom often asked himself. Was it during those first dreadful weeks after her husband had been killed and he had visited her often and had sat with her? Or was it later, when she had remembered to smile a little and thank him for visiting her and for his interest in her children? Or had he always loved her, since the first day he had seen her with young Alfred after their marriage, when she had consulted with him about the house rising on the land Alfred had bought?

That was eleven years ago. But Tom could remember his first sight of Melinda, her large gray eyes, her soft expression, her gentle mouth, her quiet manners; he could remember her voice, thoughtful and very sweet. He had thought she looked abstracted and a little sad, just as she had appeared in her early photograph. When anyone spoke she had a way of turning her head in his direction and looking at him with kindness and understanding, and she gave all her attention. She and Alfred had stood close together on that first day, and she had touched Alfred's sleeve occasionally, with affection. It was a moving gesture; it expressed more than love. Yes, it was possible that he, Tom, had loved her then.

But it was not until two years ago that he had faced the fact that he was in love with Melinda Bothwell. There was no love in his life; he had no true wife, no real children. He was not wanted, not needed, not respected in his house. By nature inclined to be extremely optimistic, and therefore not acquainted with reality, he had always, as his father used to advise him, "hoped for the best." Against truth, against what his eyes and ears told him about his family, against all his self-protective instincts, against all reasonable evidence, he had continued to "hope for the best," to repeat to himself those glowing aphorisms concocted by those who did not see the world as it was. "Give love and you will receive love in return. Evil passes away, but good remains." Apposed to these desperate folk fictions, there was the true world of men, but for a long time Tom would not see that world.

In his opposite way Tom had been as deluded as Caroline, and with almost as disastrous results to himself. It was his wild need for love that had made him love Melinda Bothwell. At this point in his life any kind and gentle woman would have inspired him. The fact that Melinda had suffered through his own wife, was a widow and lonely, brightened his need for her as a fellow sufferer, a bewildered and bereaved one, a beautiful young woman who had created beauty around her, and peace and serenity. Above all, he could talk to her and she would listen with gentle sympathy, her eyes turned to him in compassion. That Melinda, in spite of her husband's death, had never suffered as Caroline had suffered, had never been abused, frightened, and lost, and so was therefore capable of pity and was possessed of stamina of soul, did not occur to Tom. An essentially uncomplex man, he believed that all men formed themselves alone, that a tree crowded between stone walls could grow tall and strong, that a cripple could decide one day to stand upright, whole and renewed, if he wished.

It was inevitable that he should begin to contrast Caroline with Melinda, his house with Melinda's, his children with Melinda's. He began to see Caroline as a powerfully destructive force. He had given her love, he reminded himself; that he had frequently not understood her did not cross his mind. When he cursed her father, he did not absolve Caroline entirely. At the end, he did not absolve her at all.

Years ago he had believed that Caroline loved him, was obsessed with him. He looked back on those years with derision; he remembered with mortification his talk with Mr. Tandy. No wonder the old man had looked at him so oddly! Tom no longer asked himself why Caroline had married him. He had guessed that she had needed children for her own purpose, and he had served her purpose. That she might have loved him seemed a ridiculous thought to him now. The girl who had clung to him in a blue and windy twilight and had cried out incoherently to him and had confided in him was a dream which had dissolved into the reality of a bitter woman in her forties, a silent, brooding, working woman in her study in the center of a house which reflected her barrenness of spirit. She had even taken on an aspect of evil for him.

Tom had no doubt that he must leave this house, this wife who was no wife, these children who were no children. Melinda had become his passage of escape. When he was divorced from Caroline, then he would tell Melinda that he loved her. He was certain that she loved him, for her lovely face became light when she saw him, and her hand in his was confiding and warm. But his sense of personal honor stopped him from telling her until he was free to tell her. I am past forty-six, he would say to himself. If I am to live again, it must be soon.

After the talk with his sons tonight Tom could not sleep. He had told himself for a long time that nothing that happened in this house could concern him any longer. However, he found that he was mistaken. He was sickened with anger against Caroline; he turned from the thought of Elizabeth with aching disgust. How had it escaped him until now that she resembled her grandfather physically and mentally? Once he had said to himself in a sharp alarm he did not stop to analyze: Carrie has an enemy in this house!

So, sad, wretched, confused, and frightened, Tom could not sleep in his cold and lonely bedroom. At seven he got up wearily, felt all his flesh heavy and sore. I'm worn out, he thought, and rubbed his chest, which had a sensation of oppression in it. He thought of postponing his trip to New York to see Tandy, Harkness and Swift, then shook his head. He shaved in icy water; the maid very often forgot to bring hot. He could smell the chill dust in his room, the airlessness. Suddenly he shivered violently; he hurried into his clothing. The maid was just sullenly laying the breakfast table in the dank morning room when he came in. He could smell porridge, slightly burned, and an odor of cheap coffee. He was nauseated. He looked through the large smeared window that gave on to the sea. The waters were the color of lead; the sky was leaden. He could hear the hissing of the tide and could see the dull snow. It was very cold.

He arrived in New York at one o'clock. The city stood in the stark and brilliant light of early spring, struck with sun, patched with sharp shade. He usually liked New York for its stimulation and lively air. He did not like it today, for a crushing malaise was on him. He found himself shivering in quick and passing spasms. He had used Caroline's telephone long after midnight, when she had gone silently to bed, to send "young" Mr. Tandy a telegram to expect him at half-past one on urgent business. Mr. Tandy was a replica of his uncle, and he was fond of Tom. He said when they shook hands, "Are you sick? You look so gray and drawn."

"I seem to have a chill," Tom said. "And I didn't sleep well last night."

"There is so much la grippe in the cities now," said Mr. Tandy. "Shall we lunch?" They went to a restaurant which Tom liked. He found he could not eat. He could only sip a little of the hot soup and cradle his hands about the cup to warm them. He drank two cups of coffee but could feel no internal heat. It was as if all his organs were numb and frozen. Mr. Tandy watched him with concern. Tom had aged; the dark blue eyes were dull, the cleft chin less sure, the kind mouth pale and puckered. But he talked well enough, and Mr. Tandy listened, frowning.

"Are you sure you want to write a will like this?" he asked.

"Yes."

"Caroline has her dower rights, you know."

"I've left her the house. And she isn't the kind to insist on dower rights."

Mr. Tandy wondered what had caused this drastic change of thought in Tom Sheldon. It was not a lawyer's business to protest the will of a client, but to protect it. Still, something must have happened. Mr. Tandy ate his dessert slowly. "After all," he said at last, "if you change your mind it can always be rectified—while you live."

"Carrie lent me the money to build the house," said Tom. "I've repaid every cent, long ago, with interest. I want to mention that in my will, considering I've left her the house."

They returned to the warm offices, but Tom kept his sturdy coat on, and his lips were bluish. The will was short. It was signed, witnessed, and sealed. Tom sighed when it was done. He looked about the room and said, "I've often wondered why Tim Winslow left you a year ago."

"His own affairs became too pressing," said Mr. Tandy. "The Broome Company and his wife's estates. He still has his town house in New York, but he comes in only when there are Board meetings and other necessary matters connected with the Bothwell holdings. He's had particular success with Mrs. Melinda Bothwell's affairs, as you know. She is several times a millionaire in her own right, and that is not to be dismissed as a trifle." Mr. Tandy smiled.

Tom had not considered Melinda's money. Now he thought of it with perturbation. How could he have forgotten the fifty per cent of the Bothwell money and her own inheritance from that rascal, John Ames, of which Caroline had told him? Still, it did not matter. He was no pauper himself.

"We've drawn this will very carefully," said Mr. Tandy. "Still, Caroline could contest it if she wished to. She would probably not win; the court would consider her own fortune. However, let us not worry about that now. As you say, I doubt if Caroline would contest." He shook hands with Tom and said, "I am not one of these modern optimists, in the style of Teddy Roosevelt, who are so popular these days. I don't believe that this is the best of all possible worlds, nor do I believe that tragedies or misunderstandings or evils ever right themselves automatically. It needs a great deal of co-operation between heaven and man. Man very rarely offers that co-operation."

Tom fell into a sick and feverish sleep on the drafty train back to Lyme. He dreamed that he was on a barren bank of stone sloping steeply down to black and rushing water. He tried not to fall down the bank, but something inexorably pushed him, though he cried for help. Then he was in the water, and it was choking him, and he could not swim. He awoke, to find himself breathless and gasping, and the earlier oppression in his chest was one flaring pain, increasing with each gulp of air. He knew then that he was sick. His father had one sovereign remedy for all illnesses: plentiful whiskey. Whiskey was the only thing Tom thought of during the drive that brought him back to his desolate house.

As usual, all was silent here except for the clash of dishes in the kitchen. The hall was like a cave, the drawing room like some abandoned loft. His teeth chattering, Tom went to his room, where there was no fire. He built one; he crouched over the flames, trying to get warm. His head was swimming, and now he coughed painfully and shortly. The whiskey had had no effect on him except to increase his nausea. He looked at the bed but could not bring himself to leave the fire.

Caroline had heard Tom's buggy leave that morning. She had run to the window; the buggy was heading toward the station. So Tom was going to Boston. She, too, had not slept all night; she had kept her lamp burning low, for lately when she was awake she had a fear of the dark. She had lain under a mound of quilts which needed mending and stared at the cold walls of her room, the silent and unshaded walls.

Her sons did not believe they had disturbed her very much. "Ma was always like that," John had said contemptuously to his brother. But her distraction was very deep and agonizing. Her sons had come too close to her in those short interviews. During all their lives she had thought of them as her heirs, as the guardians of the trust that had been given her. Now, for the first time, she thought of them as human beings, and she was terribly frightened. She had done what she could for them, she told herself. What else could a mother do for her children but give them health, shelter, food, education, and training in their responsibilities? She had planned for John to visit London and Paris the next summer, to meet some of her investment associates. As she had been educated, so her son would be educated.

Her plans for Ames had followed the same pattern. She had seen herself as eventually old, still the potent matriarch, still the guiding force. But her sons were to take from her the mountainous responsibilities which were now hers. They, too, would marry and have heirs, and the trust would descend to grandchildren. Elizabeth also would be part of the pattern.

There was only Elizabeth now to receive the trust. Why had she, Caroline Ames, been so betrayed by her sons? What had she done, except to guard and train them? But they had looked at her today not with the eyes of trust-guarders. They had looked at her with the eyes of mankind, and they had repudiated her, despised her, and mocked her. They were her enemies. She cried out, "Why? Oh, God, why?"

It was inevitable, then, that she begin to think of Tom, her husband, and she searched her mind. He had turned from her irrevocably on the day that Alfred Bothwell and his father had been killed. He would not listen. She had wanted to tell him that only that morning she had telegraphed the offices of the North Shore line in Boston not to let the runs take place that afternoon. The telegram was not received, the horrified officials told her later. Or it had been ignored. She would never know. It was she who had told her lawyers in New York not to haggle over death and injury settlements, in or out of court.

It was only before marriage that Tom had ever really "listened" to her or had tried to understand her fumbling and awkward explanations. After marriage he had wished her to fit the pattern he had designed for her as a wife and mother. She looked at her life with Tom in spite of her pain. All concessions, such as they were, had been on her part. She had consented to a house she never wanted. She had let Tom have his will about the children's education. She had tried, in her tragic way, to do what he wished, even if it was only after a bitter quarrel and dispute. Tom had loved his children; they had now only scorn for him. Yet he had once or twice accused her of being an unnatural mother, of withholding warm love from her children! To what end had his love for them brought him?

There had never been any use in trying to explain to him what her father's money meant to her. He could only reply, as she stumbled inarticulately, in violent accusations against the dead man. And against her for being her father's victim and not attempting to "free" herself. What had he meant by "freedom"? She never understood. The first real break between them had come with Beth's death. He would not listen to the doctor, who had later tried to tell him that even with the very best and most expensive of care Beth would have died when she did. His only furious reply was that "Beth had died alone." But, Caroline asked herself, remembering with the unhealed pain of many years ago, do we not all die alone? How had her presence comforted or eased her father?

From early childhood Caroline had always been suffused with a sense of faceless guilt, and out of that guilt she had evolved an acute conscience and absolute honesty. Invariably she always asked herself, in any situation, where she had been to blame. According to her standards, impeccable and severe, she had done her best. Tom's attitude during their married life had invariably baffled her. He had no attitudes but his own. She had examined them and found them absolutely alien to her nature and her training, and not to be understood.

One thing above all had remained steadfast in her deprived spirit: her love for her husband. Possessive, blind, eager, desperate—it had been all his. But it had remained. One day—and she had hoped each day—he would come to her and say, "Let us understand each other, or at least try." He had never truly tried; the Carrie he had married was not Caroline Ames and had existed only in his imagination.

On reaching that devastating conclusion, Caroline huddled in her bed; a dark area in her mind swelled, and she brought all the force of her will and self-control to keep it from expanding and drowning her. If her thoughts ever entered it, she was absolutely certain, the very walls of her life would drop about her and there would be nothing but loss and ruin.

Midnight came and went, and then the harsh dawn stood at her windows. With the dawn came one despairing conclusion. She must try to reach Tom, if only for the last time. After yesterday, she must have a haven again. She would tell Tom about their sons. She would go to his room and shut the door and she would force him to listen, to be still, not to interrupt, not to accuse. Now a hungry warmth came to her, and she got out of bed and went to the window—to see Tom driving away. No matter. He would return that night, and she would go to him and say, "I am your wife and I must speak, and you must try to know what I will try to tell you."

She dressed quickly in one of her rusty old-fashioned black dresses with jet buttons, went into her study, and had her breakfast there. The mail arrived, and she ran through it listlessly. Someone knocked softly, and she knew it was Elizabeth and did not reply. She could think of nothing but Tom. She wanted to pray, but she had not prayed for endless years. There was no God, she said to herself. But how blessed it would be if He existed!

It was dark twilight when Tom returned, and she heard his laboring footsteps on the stairs, and after a while she rose from behind her desk, her heart pounding. She had not run for years. Now she ran down the black hall like a girl, and she was smiling at last.

I must get to bed, thought Tom, and found himself staggering. He sat on the edge of the bed and had no more strength. He could scarcely breathe for pain; his lungs were on fire and stabbed with hot knives. He had eaten almost nothing that day, but he struggled against a desire to vomit. He was sweating, yet icy cold. He did not hear Caroline enter until he heard her voice, low and uncertain, "Tom?"

She had never once come into this room since their separation, and there she was, standing like an awkward girl near him, tall and massive, clothed in black like a widow, pale and still, her hands clasped tightly against her waist. With a great effort he raised his eyes and looked at her, at her broad face, her colorless mouth, her tight, graying braids. He closed his eyes.

"Tom?" she said again.

He must speak now and end it all forever, and then sleep. He spoke, and even he was surprised at his stifled difficulty in speaking. "Carrie. I want to talk to you."

"Yes, yes," she murmured. "I do too. That's why I'm here, Tom. Tom, is something the matter?" Her voice rose and became almost shrill and she leaned toward him. But he held her off with his hand.

"It won't take long." His hoarse voice made the words slow and weak.

"I'm leaving this house tomorrow." He had to pause for breath between sentences. "Tomorrow. I'm not coming back again. It's all ended. I want a divorce from you, Carrie."

She did not move. She blinked and was stupefied. She looked about the small room, grimy and meagerly furnished, at the lamp, at the fire, as if all of these could explain to her what she had heard. "What?" she stammered. "What did you say, Tom?"

Why was it so terribly hard to talk? Tom repeated, "I'm leaving. Divorce. There's no place for me here any longer. That's all, Carrie. I'm sick. Please go away and let me rest."

He was too exhausted even to wonder why she had come to his room, or to care. His head fell on his chest. Then Caroline uttered a great cry. "Tom! You're sick! Tom, what's the matter? Wait! I'll send for the doctor at once!"

"Do what you want, but——" Tom began with another enormous effort. But Caroline had flown from the room; the door was swinging behind her. He heard her race to her study, to her telephone. He fell back on the bed, which began to sway gently under him like a cloud. Perhaps he slept, but when he opened his eyes again he found himself undressed, under the blankets and quilts, and the fire was roaring, and Carrie was seated beside him, her hand on his forehead, her face a blaze of absolute terror.

"He'll be here soon, Tom," she said when she saw his eyes on her, glazed and dark and only partly aware. "Oh, my God, Tom, you are very sick! Oh, Tom."

"You heard," he whispered. "I've got to go, Carrie. Divorce."

She was bathing his head with cool water and a cloth. She stopped, squeezed her eyelids together. "Why, Tom? Is it because you're sick? You're very feverish. You shouldn't have gone to Boston—— What did you say, Tom? A divorce?" Her face took on again that stupefied expression, and she shook her head over and over. "Why?"

His whispering voice said, "I want to marry Melinda. I love her."

The darkness took him and flowed under him. Then he rose into light once more. Caroline was sitting beside him, rigid and staring into space. He mumbled without volition, but only out of his need: "I'm very sick. I'd like to see Melinda." His own voice sounded as if it were coming from a far distance, and the walls were rocking, and the ceiling tilted.

"My sister," said Caroline without inflection. "Did you know she is my real sister, Tom, the daughter of my father?" She put her hands to her throat.

"Your sister," said Tom. It meant nothing to him now. And then it meant a great deal. He even rose on one elbow.

"My sister," said Caroline. "My father's daughter, and the daughter of that woman I've always hated." Her face changed. "My sister! You want to marry my sister! Tom, I'm your wife. I love you. I never loved anyone else except my father. You can't mean it, Tom. You're delirious."

She bent toward him, and she was crying and gulping. "I'm your wife. I love you, Tom. I love you. Can you hear me?"

333

Tom's mind cleared miraculously, and everything was too vivid for his sight, too dreadful. Caroline was stuttering through her flood of tears. "I thought he loved me; I thought I was the only one he had in all the world. But he had Melinda. When he was dying he didn't call to me. He called to Melinda. Not me, but Melinda."

Tom fell back on his pillows again, but the clarity of his mind and his eyes increased. He forgot his sickness; he forgot his pain. He looked only at his wife, at her tears, at her wringing hands, at her anguish and her twisted features. She was trembling violently; her hands moved over and over each other in the ancient movements of utter despair and loss.

"I have only you, Tom," she said. "I think I never had anyone but you, after all."

He was being drawn away into a vast distance, but he was also in the room, a diminished but very sharp, very clear room, even though in miniature. In the very center was his wife, Caroline. His wife, Carrie.

And then he knew that he had been wrong, after all. There had never been anyone but Carrie; he had never loved any other woman but Carrie, this crying girl, this broken and heartsick girl. He could hear the sea now, soft and blue and singing, and the sky was bright and infinite, and young Carrie was sitting on the boulder in her ugly dress, looking at him, waiting and crying for him to speak, with the blueness all about her and her braids whipping in the summer wind. It was all so very small, like a vivid picture, but it was fully detailed. He was being drawn away from it but was yet in it.

"Carrie, my darling," he said. "Don't cry. I love you, darling. I always did. I'll never leave you. Don't you remember that I said I'd never leave you?"

But Carrie did not hear a word, for he had not spoken aloud in his last extremity, though he believed he had. He was beyond speaking. He had heard a story, and he had understood at last, and he thought he held out his arms to his wife.

Tom never recovered consciousness again. He died of pneumonia twenty-four hours later, with Caroline and the doctor beside him. He had left, as he had said, "tomorrow."

CHAPTER ELEVEN

It was repeated with hatred in the village that Caroline Sheldon had said on the death of her husband, "Take his body away, out of this house, and put it in the church—if his friends want to see it."

What the pallid woman had actually said to the diffident young minister who had come to her house was something quite different. "This was never his home, as it was never mine. I don't know why, but it is so. He liked your old church standing in its graveyard. That was really his home, as the village itself was really his home. He had many friends and he liked them,

and even loved a number. He would want them to say good-by to him."
Her empty, expressionless eyes did not change. "He was born in Lyme; he
died in Lyme. I can't explain it, but if his friends came to this house they
wouldn't find him here at all. So let him lie in your church, please, where
his mother and father were married. He would want it." She had given the
minister a check and had said, "I never knew any clergymen. I only know
that you do your best, but you are so few, and it doesn't seem to do any
good at all."

The minister had replied with pity, "I understand. Yes, it would be the
best for Tom to be in his church." He had hesitated and had looked at
Caroline, who was old enough to be his mother. He then said impulsively,
"God bless and help you!"

But she had not heard him. She heard and saw almost nothing these days.
She felt absolutely nothing except an arctic solitude, without thought or
emotion.

It was the slatternly housemaid who had overheard the conversation, and
it was her sly and malicious distortion which was repeated in the village.
His wife had despised Tom; she had neglected him; she hadn't even called
the doctor until it was too late—she hadn't wanted to spend the money.
The village would "show" her. The little old church, black as iron and decrepit, had very few parishioners since a "fancy" new church had been built
in the village, more convenient, brighter, and with no depressing view of a
graveyard through its windows and doors. But when Tom's body was carried
there the villagers vengefully filled the church with spring flowers; a fund
was raised to bring hothouse daffodils, narcissi, Madonna lilies and hyacinths from Boston. Candles appeared in ranks of white and gold, dimming
out the old oil lamps. The worn nave carpet was removed and a new one
installed in a matter of hours. The young minister looked hopefully at all
this and thought that God was good and that this would be the beginning
of a larger parish and more spiritual devotion.

Then on the second day the church was smothered with more sophisticated flowers from friends in Boston, from "old" families. Roses. Carna-
tions. Heliotrope. Mimosa. The trains filled with former associates of John
Ames, with business associates of Caroline. Newspaper reporters came. It
was reported that Caroline Ames Sheldon never entered the church for those
three days, though her husband lay in his open coffin before the altar. Her
sons were there and his pretty, weeping daughter. But not the widow.
Throngs came and went, but Caroline was not there.

Caroline was there alone, at dawn, for she had asked the minister to unlock the door for her. He would stand at the back, hidden by shadows and
peeling wooden pillars, and watch her with sorrow and prayer as she sat in
the first pew near her dead husband. She did not pray; she did not move.
She never took her eyes from her husband's quiet and sleeping face. When
the cold sun rose she would leave. She would return after twilight, when the
church was again empty, and take up her solitary vigil. She would pass

within a few steps of the hidden minister, and he would see her face, and he would pray again for her.

A blanket of white roses arrived for Tom from Melinda Bothwell. Caroline stood and looked at it. She made no gesture. She bought a large lot in the cemetery, which contained the graves of Tom's parents, and she ordered a huge marble monument to be marked with the name of Sheldon. She said to the minister, "I will be here one day beside Tom. I wish I could bring my father's body here." She looked at the minister emptily. She said, "I can't attend the funeral. I can't explain this, either. But I feel that Tom wouldn't want me to. I don't know why."

The minister said, "Perhaps it is because he wants you to know that he isn't in that coffin at all but is with you in prayer all the time." Caroline's face changed, became grayer and stiffer, and she shook her head and went away.

The newspapers and the townfolk and the friends from Boston were scandalized that the widow was not at the funeral. "But isn't it like Caroline Ames?" said those from Boston. "I remember that she didn't show any grief at all when her father was buried." The townfolk said: "That Ames woman! What can you expect?"

Caroline sat alone in her absolutely empty house when her husband's funeral took place, for the servants were attending the services. She sat in the icy and gritty drawing room before a very low fire. She listened to the tolling of the distant bell brought to her in the faintest of echoes on the clear cold air, and below the echoes the uneasy sea rumbled like a drum. Then the bell was silent and Caroline stood up and went to her husband's bedroom. She called, "Tom? Tom?" She lay down on his bed. When her household returned she was in her study, with the door closed.

Two days later she walked the more than three miles along the turbulent beach and then up the hill to her husband's silent grave. She looked at the raw earth, at the dead and blasted flowers heaped about mountainously. All about her stood old and leaning gravestones and high dead grass thrusting through the waning snow. She said to Tom's grave: "It was that woman who seduced my father, and it was her daughter who seduced you. It wasn't my father's fault; it wasn't yours, dear Tom. Tom? Tom!" She suddenly shrieked, tearlessly, abruptly, sharply, and it was a lost, inhuman sound.

No one came to the somber house on the hill to offer condolences. Caroline would not have received anyone in any event, and it was tacitly understood.

"Young" Mr. Tandy came with Tom's will, and Caroline listened to the reading of it in the midst of her black-clad children. It did not matter to her, but at the end she gave her astonished sons a grim smile. "So you each have, as of today, seven hundred and fifty thousand dollars apiece, to be invested, to be turned over to each of you in full when you are twenty-one. I didn't know your father had that much money. You also have his successful business, which will be managed for you." She looked at Elizabeth, who was blank with shock. "Two thousand dollars," said Caroline. She uttered the strangest sound, then got up and left the room. Tom had been quite right; Caroline never once thought of contesting the will.

The children returned to their schools, and Caroline was all alone. She worked in her study. Only the servants saw the steady dwindling of her flesh. They rarely heard her speak. But they knew that she sat up almost until dawn.

Caroline saw that her only hope of survival lay in not thinking, in not feeling. She would not even see her cousin Timothy Winslow. She did not open the cable of condolence from her aunt. It was weeks before she left her house, and then it was full spring.

Her sons had never been near her. When they asked the executors for money enough to go away for the summer together and the executors consulted their mother, she said, "They have their lives. They must live them for themselves. Let them have the money. I was not named executor, though they are under age."

Elizabeth said to her mother, "I'd rather stay home with you this summer. I want to learn all you can teach me." She spoke in a carefully subdued voice and looked at her mother with eyes deliberately enlarged. Caroline nodded. "Yes, that would be best, Elizabeth. You are all I have now." She looked at Elizabeth's face, so like the face of John Ames.

Elizabeth was exultant. Her brothers had been made briefly maudlin about their father's will and had even cried! She thought of them with contempt. Two thousand dollars. All at once she was respectful of her father as she had never been respectful during his lifetime. He had known all about her. In a way, she congratulated herself, it was just as well he was dead. He would have been a formidable enemy.

Caroline never once resented her husband's will, for she had gone beyond any personal feelings at all. Once or twice she wondered at it listlessly. Elizabeth had been his favorite, but he had cut her out ruthlessly except for two thousand dollars. Why?

It was in warm June that the maid brought a thin large package to Caroline. "I found this, Mrs. Sheldon, when we were clearing out Mr. Sheldon's things for the Salvation Army, like you told us. It's got your name on it."

The brown paper was old and crinkled. On it Tom had written: "For Caroline, Christmas, 1901." Caroline took the package and dismissed the maid. She looked at the writing again. A warning of agony started at the very tip of her heart, and she suppressed it with her powerful will. Nearly three years ago. Why hadn't Tom given this to her at that Christmas? She would never know. She opened the paper, and it crackled dryly in her hands.

It was the painting by David Ames which Elizabeth had described to her and which had once hung over the Adam mantelpiece in old Harper Bothwell's house in Boston. Timothy, Elizabeth had told her mother, did not like it. The house had been left to both Amanda Winslow and her brother Alfred. Timothy had removed the painting. Tom had known that his wife had a few of David Ames' paintings. So he had bought this from Timothy for her when he had heard of it. He had bought it in love, for her joy, in spite of the black years. He had wanted to give her what she would have wanted most. The agony rose again in the tip of Caroline's heart, and this time it took all her effort to suppress it.

She tilted the picture on her knee and studied it: the dark purplish mountains, the desolate valley strewn with boulders, the blind and stumbling man, the apocalyptic sky. A sensation of terror came to her, of desertion, of threat, of warning. She jumped to her feet, overwhelmed. She stood shivering in her sun-warmed study. "No, no," she said aloud to her emotions. "I mustn't think. If I do, I'll die." She thought of her father, and she did not know why she thought of him. She studied the vaguely malformed man in the painting. It was entirely unlike John Ames, but she thought of him without her volition. It was very strange that she had the peculiar sensation that if she turned her head quickly enough she would see her father. His presence was poignant in the room. Her fear heightened. She took the painting out of the room and went upstairs to her gallery, and there she hung it.

Then she said aloud to the portrait of her grandfather, "Why did you paint this? It's more terrible than the tower. Why is the man blind? He could remove the blindfold if he wanted to; but he keeps it on. What is the meaning?"

Her grandfather's face smiled on her gently. She looked into the eyes so like her own. She leaned her cheek against his painted cheek. "You are the only one I can talk to about Tom, about myself. You're the only one who ever understood." She dropped her voice and whispered, "Help me, please. Please help."

The roses Tom had planted so long ago and which had now grown wild spilled their fragrance, mingled with the odor of salt, into the gallery. The sea walk was filled with boulders. Caroline repeated, "Help."

Nobody could console her; no one had tried except the young minister. But now she felt a soft consolation, a sensation of sympathy and love. For the first time since Tom died, she wept.

PART FOUR

The fathers have eaten sour grapes,
and the children's teeth are set on edge.

JEREMIAH, 33:29

CHAPTER ONE

Amanda said crossly to her husband, Timothy Winslow: "I really don't understand, even after all your explanations, why we have to be burdened with Elizabeth Sheldon on our European trip. Yes, I know her mother asked you. Elizabeth must meet Caroline's foreign investment associates. But she's old enough to go alone. Twenty-one, for heaven's sake! Why does she need a chaperone, or whatever? Girls these days, even Boston girls, aren't secluded all the time. She's old enough to go on her own."

She added resentfully, "Perhaps some girls of twenty-one might get into mischief alone abroad. But not Elizabeth Sheldon! Can you imagine anyone less liable to seduction or amorous adventures than Elizabeth? Oh, I grant you she's quite beautiful, and she was the sensation of the year at her debut, and she's a member of the Assemblies and is one of Caroline's heirs and all that. But who would, anywhere, try to injure Elizabeth? She's a match for anybody. She doesn't have a single beau, in spite of her looks and her mother's money, and the money alone would attract young Bostonians."

Timothy looked at his plump and pretty wife with her lively dark curls powdered with gray and her forthright and sparkling dark eyes. He said indulgently, "I know you don't like the girl. I don't either. She reminds me too much of old Johnny Ames; she probably has his character, too. The girl's as sharp as a razor, and Caroline seems to dote on her, though I can't imagine why. A cold straight icicle. I have the funniest conviction that she'll be Caroline's real heir. Caroline's been instructing her ever since she was sixteen or less. Look at the sons! They rarely, if ever, see their mother. Mutual hate, probably. John's doing splendidly at Tandy, Harkness and Swift; junior member of the firm, but he'll be a full member one of these days. Ames is no fool, either. Spends a lot of money on his nice little bachelor establishment in Boston, and very independent at twenty, but combines an interest in miniature art with a good business sense in that construction business. Good architect, too, like his father. Do you know, he got a fine contract to rebuild one of the old churches in Boston?

"But Caroline might not have any other children except Elizabeth, as far as an outsider could judge. I owe a lot to Caroline." His long pale face became subtly malevolent. He passed his hand over his smooth gray hair, which was still streaked with the pale gold of his youth. "Please let me judge, my dear, that it is perfectly natural for Elizabeth to go with us."

"I don't like her!" Amanda said vehemently. "Why does Caroline have to burden us with that girl? I've been looking forward to this trip, and so have our children. They don't like Elizabeth, either. Amy's a delicate little thing; she told me Elizabeth gives her 'the shudders.' Henry and Harper despise her. Children do have good instincts, you know."

"You were Elizabeth's sponsor when she made her debut," Timothy said.

"So I was," said Amanda sulkily. "I thought I could do something for her. But it was a waste of time. What a family that is! Do you know that Amy has a crush on Ames? Ames! She's only fifteen, but girls of that age get disastrous crushes on young men. Never mind, she'll outgrow it, I'll see to that! You may like him and be flattered that people say he resembles you. But I just detest that imitation Voltaire. And Amy will be thrown with his sister all those weeks. I just don't like it, Timothy."

"I didn't notice that Elizabeth likes Ames," said Timothy, yawning. "I doubt that she'll try to advance any interest of her brother's. Besides, a young man of twenty would hardly consider a girl of fifteen. Amy's cow-eyed devotion to him just embarrasses him. Now, watch that blood pressure. You know what your doctor says; you're quite scarlet. I wish you'd stop stuffing yourself at the table, my dear. You're entirely too stout."

This dexterous change of subject succeeded. Amanda engaged in a heated discussion with her husband about her doctor's orders. She lost her temper, but Timothy knew that the underlying reason was that he had agreed to take Elizabeth to Europe with him and his family. Amanda's first impulse toward all people was affection and kindliness, even though she was frequently blunt. She was particularly generous to younger people. Elizabeth was one of the first who had ever aroused Amanda's hostility; she never judged prematurely.

Timothy's original fondness for his wife had increased considerably since she had inherited half a fortune impressive even by Boston standards. He was also at ease with her, for she knew all about him, yet accepted him tolerantly. "You're a scoundrel, of course," she had said to him candidly before they were married, "and I won't pretend I like scoundrels. I do not. But you aren't stuffy and pompous and self-important, and you're very interesting. It's unfortunate that these traits aren't often found in the virtuous."

To which he had replied, "You may remember that Lord Melbourne said over sixty years ago: 'This damned morality is going to ruin everything!' He was referring to the 'new men,' as Cicero called them, the middle class."

Amanda had looked at him thoughtfully. "Well, this 'damned morality' is necessary for the safety of women and children. It has its points. And we in America could use more of it in our government. Washington's full of blackguards, as Papa used to call them."

The Bothwell house, which Timothy and his family now occupied, was not in the least like his mother's house, which had been pale and exquisite. He liked its solidity, its excellent sturdy stairways, its big rooms full of fine but massive furniture, its Adam mantelpieces, its Federal doorways, its fanlight. It had the authority of wood paneling and genuine strength. Amanda had insisted upon electric lighting but had retained the old gaslight fixtures, mellow and warm. She had also retained the huge and glittering hall chandelier with its candles, lit only on special occasions. Timothy often thought his wife resembled the house in which she had been born—open, sturdy, and comfortable. He found the house easeful, as a background for his most uninnocent daily life, his devious character. No one would suspect him of anything when a guest in this atmosphere of polished silver and woodwork, this brass-clawed Duncan Phyfe furniture, these heavy cabinets full of *objets d'art* and ancient laced fans, these tassled and brocaded draperies. He was nearly fifty now, but a lean, taut fifty, and looked younger, and he was ripe for his coming excursion into politics.

He and Amanda were sitting this warm June evening in the family room with its high french windows open to the sweet air. He was drinking brandy. Amanda was enjoying whiskey and soda. It was like Amanda to prefer this, and it did not displease Timothy. "It's good for my blood pressure," she would say with a wink as she took a long and enjoyable swallow.

She drank in the presence of her children, too, and they did not respect her the less. The boys adored Mama and admired their father. But Amy loved her father devotedly, and he returned the devotion. They all resembled Amanda rather than Timothy, and the boys—Henry, seventeen, and Harper, sixteen—had her candid and easy personality, her intrepid character, her integrity, and her sense of humor. They shared her intolerance of evil and malice in word or speech or conduct. This amused Timothy, thinking of his strong, tall, dark sons. He thought them just a trifle stupid for all their excellent scholarship and attention to school and duty. Fine boys, but hardly the stuff of entrepreneurs or promoters and adventurers. They would guard what they would inherit and never touch the sacred capital, but they would live solidly and richly within their income.

Amy came into the living room just now to say good night. Timothy stood up as he would for any lady, though the girl was only fifteen. Tall and with curling black hair like her mother's and brothers', she was also slender and delicate. She had an oval face that always had a soft rose-and-white glow, and large dark eyes full of sweetness and candor, a pretty short nose, and a full pink mouth. Her long blue dress, of the softest summer silk, outlined her young figure; she would be full-breasted like her mother on reaching maturity. The ruffled edge of hem just touched her ankles.

There was not the slightest physical resemblance, but Timothy was always reminded of his sister Melinda when he saw his daughter, and so he was particularly tender toward her. He bent and kissed her warm cheek lightly. "Isn't it late?" he asked, putting his arm about her shoulders. "Almost eleven."

"It isn't school time now, Daddy," she said. "And I'm not a child any longer."

"Too bad," said Amanda. "I mean, young girls these days seem to grow up too fast. Why have you done up your hair, Amy?"

The girl had twisted her silky black hair in a big pompadour over her white forehead. She patted it awkwardly. "I'm almost sixteen," she said.

"In five months." The back of her hair was inexpertly pinned. "Do say I can wear it this way on our trip, Mama."

"Nonsense," said Amanda. "You're a schoolgirl, and you're not going to look like a young lady who has her debut long behind her." Then she relented. "Well, for evenings on shipboard and for dinners. Good gracious, why are you in such a hurry, child? Youth lasts only twenty-one years. After that you are old a very long time, and it's very dreary and tiresome and full of responsibilities."

Amanda vigorously attacked the gros point she was making for her dining-room chairs. She pricked her finger and said, "Damn." Amy sat down with the grace she had copied from her father. "I didn't say you could sit down," said her mother, sucking the wounded finger. "You're supposed to ask permission. Never mind. You'll only think I'm old-fashioned, just as I thought about my own mother. Manners are certainly going out."

"Don't be stuffy, Mandy," said Timothy, sitting down near his daughter. Amanda glared at him. "I loathe nicknames," she said, "and especially that one. It reminds me of advertisements for flour. You have a suspiciously dreaming expression in your eyes, Amy, and I do detest that moist, far-off look which hints that your mother never had dreams of her own one time." But she grinned amiably at the girl. "There was a matinee idol when I was young. All of us girls simply swooned at the very mention of his name. Very dashing and romantic, with long curly hair and burning eyes. He was a grandfather; when we found that out we abandoned him." She looked at Amy with a little sharpness. "All girls get crushes. It doesn't harm them unless they take them seriously."

Amy blushed. She tried to escape the probing eyes of her mother. "Don't worry about me, Mama," she murmured.

"Don't give me any occasion to worry," said Amanda tartly. She moistened her handkerchief with the tip of her tongue, then rubbed it on a little bloodstain that had just marred the gros point.

"Amy's never given us occasion to worry," said Timothy. "Why should she start now? Are you looking forward to our trip, dear?"

"Oh yes, Daddy." She made a breathy sound which caused her mother to glare.

"Where do you pick up these foolish habits?" demanded Amanda. "Why are you girls taking on the soft choky way of expressing pleasure? Never mind. Every generation to its silliness. At least you don't say 'twenty-three skidoo.' What slang. What does it mean?"

"I don't know," said Amy.

"I wish you'd learn not to be so shy," said Amanda. "You hardly speak at all, even to your parents, though I've heard you giggling with your friends. Are we ogres?"

"No," said Amy, blushing again. She looked appealingly at her father, who brushed her soft cheek with the back of his hand.

"You're a tartar, Amanda," he said. "Amy's at the sensitive age."

"I'll bet you never were," said his wife, eying him shrewdly. "I'll bet you were never young, either. What a generation you were!" She was a little jealous and so pointedly reminded him that he was more than eleven years her senior.

"We were very serious," said Timothy, smiling. "I decided to be a lawyer when I was hardly past ten. Life to us was very sober and grave."

"Your mother's wasn't," said Amanda. "And my mother's friends were just like her. Gay. Pleasure-loving. Extravagant. Witty. Always full of movement. Sophisticated. Lively. The young people today are grim in comparison." She paused and looked at her daughter with speculation. "You haven't seen your grandmother since you were a child, or your Uncle William. Lord Halnes. A nice, brilliant young man, though he does look something like a head bookkeeper in a going establishment. Too bad he is your uncle. He'll make some lucky girl very happy. But imagine him going into that church, the Anglo-Catholic Church. His father would have had a fit."

"No, he wouldn't," said Timothy. "Old Montague restored the family fortunes. And all English boys of noble family either go into the army or navy, or government, or the Church. At the very least, into the law, so they can become judges. Montague expected that. William will be a bishop later. He does all things properly; he'll marry an English girl of just the right family, and she'll have at least ten children, six of them boys."

"Well, I hope he'll introduce Amy to some excellent young man who'll give her some solid dreams," said Amanda. "Not some nickelodeon hero. How I hate those jumping characters, those oily, bowing caricatures. Or those rough types in western boots."

"You have a lot of hates," said Timothy, still stroking his daughter's cheek.

"So I have," said Amanda sturdily. "Good, solid, earthy hates. That's what the world always needs. Tolerance! That's a sickly thing; it demands that you love the irresponsible, the inferior, the vicious, the mediocre, the false, the meaningless—and you understand them too! What stupidity."

She said to her daughter, "Are you happy that your cousin Elizabeth is going with us?"

Amy looked down at her hands. "No," she murmured. "I don't particularly like Elizabeth; perhaps it's because I don't know her very well. Then, she's so old."

"All of twenty-one," said Amanda solemnly, winking at her husband. "Well, look. It's late. Off to bed with you, young lady." She was pleased with Amy.

The boys came to say good night to their parents, and Amanda looked at them fondly, particularly Harper, her darling. What lovely, serious boys. Kind, good, honest. She kissed them heartily. Harper, she thought, resembled her dear brother Alfred.

Caroline Sheldon was alone in her dusty and decaying house now, for Elizabeth had left for Europe three weeks ago with Timothy Winslow and his family. Caroline had thriftily disposed of the lackluster housemaid during Elizabeth's absence and had only the grumpy maid who was supposed to do the cooking and the "first-floor work." Her mistress had informed her that she would attend to the upper stories, which she did not. Dust lay like soft gray carpets everywhere, except in the gallery and the study, for even the maid had done little in revenge for her miserable wages.

Like John, Elizabeth had an acute perception of the weaknesses and sins and greeds and malice of humanity and had begun long ago to take advantage of them. From early childhood she knew that her mother needed appreciation and admiration and understanding. Because she was truly reverent before Caroline's genius for money-making, she gave her these things. That Caroline needed much more, and, above all, disinterested love, was something that Elizabeth was incapable of understanding. Like all those who concentrate only on the vices of others for their own purposes, she discounted the tragedies of the spirit and ignored them. Her mother had expressed no visible grief over the death of Tom Sheldon—therefore, to Elizabeth, her mother had not been very grieved after all.

After a few dabbles with paint soon after Caroline had surprised Elizabeth at the door of the gallery, Elizabeth had confessed with excellently assumed distress that she really had no eye for drawing. Caroline had comforted her. "I, too," she had said, "have no eye, except for color, which expresses what even music or prose can't express." Elizabeth had nodded dolefully.

Elizabeth, at twenty-one, was her mother's right hand. She had completely taken on the burden of checking rent receipts from the impressive property Caroline owned in Boston and New York. She would discuss daily, all stock-market reports with her mother, and as her interest in these was truly voracious, her discussions were remarkable for lucidity and understanding. She, too, had a reverent respect for capital. It was Elizabeth who had astutely reassured her mother during the Panic of '07 and had induced her not to sell some stocks which even the shrewdest of financiers had declared worthless. When Elizabeth's judgment—and she had been only nineteen then—had been vindicated, Caroline was so delighted that she gave Elizabeth a good portion of the formerly despised stock. Elizabeth did not even spend the dividends, to Caroline's approval. She merely used them to buy more stock. It had not taken Caroline long to understand that her daughter resembled John Ames in more ways than appearance. So her old delusion began again. Her father had loved her devotedly; his granddaughter, so like him, must therefore love her mother in the same fashion, though maintaining reserve. On this false fruit Caroline's lonely spirit fed.

Elizabeth was by nature austere, like her grandfather, and bought stylish clothing as he had bought it: to impress others only. It was she now, over the past year or so, who visited the Boston office. She also accompanied her mother to New York to consult with Tandy, Harkness and Swift. They knew she was practically her mother's sole heir, except for the five thousand each for the sons, to be paid yearly from the estate, and the mysterious legacy to the Sisters of Charity in Boston. "It wouldn't surprise me a bit," said "young"

Mr. Tandy, "if the girl had managed all this herself, young as she is. She's malign. Not a good, sound human emotion in all her character."

In this, of course, they were wrong. From the age of thirteen Elizabeth had had her deep secret emotion, of which she told no one. As her grandfather had been obsessed by Cynthia Winslow, so Elizabeth was obsessed by young William Lord Halnes, whom she had seen precisely three times. Elizabeth, like her grandfather, had never been really young. Just as John Ames had not understood his passion for Cynthia, so Elizabeth did not understand her urgent need for young William, now twenty-four. Timothy Winslow had a fine portrait of his half brother in his home which Elizabeth coveted. She visited the Winslow house merely to see the portrait and always sat where it was visible to her. He looked like a sober, respectable young merchant or junior broker or lawyer and was somewhat stout. But Elizabeth had seen him smile on those three occasions when she had met him and had been overwhelmed by his curiously changeful expression which he had inherited from his father, whom he resembled closely. But whereas Montague's changefulness had been satanic, William's was mirthful, almost beautiful, kind, and light as quicksilver. Elizabeth was never conscious of her own basic needs, which she would have detested had she permitted herself to know them, but her ascetic spirit and her barren life had been instinctively drawn to something rich, bountiful, and joyous.

It was Elizabeth who, having heard of the Winslow trip to Europe, had told her mother that as Caroline had been introduced in youth to those of great affairs and financial associates abroad, so she needed to be introduced to them. Caroline had agreed reluctantly. Elizabeth did indeed want the introductions as her mother's successor. But she wanted much more: to be in the company of William Lord Halnes. Timothy and his family would naturally visit Lady Halnes and her son, and Elizabeth would contrive some way to accompany them. The fact that Caroline vehemently loathed the whole family meant nothing to Elizabeth. Caroline had no other real heir; she would never consider letting the money leave the family; she would not cut Elizabeth off with five thousand dollars a year; she leaned on her daughter, who was taking more and more responsibility from the weary woman; she needed Elizabeth. It was as simple as that to the girl.

It did not matter to Elizabeth that William might neither love nor want her. She had extraordinary beauty, and she knew it, though it was a thin and angular beauty, cold and contained. She dressed with taste and flair when necessary. She was also an heiress to one of America's mightiest fortunes. These were enough, she believed, to entice any young man. She had wanted the money, since she was sixteen, for William.

And so she was now in Europe, and Caroline was deprived, as she thought, of the only person in the world who loved her. Daily she was aware more and more of how she had relied on Elizabeth, had trusted her, and had been relieved of many petty responsibilities. She was truly alone, as Elizabeth had nicely calculated she would be.

346

It was a very hot day in July, so hot that even the moldering house on its hill facing the water was intolerable. It was also very silent. The sea had taken on an astounding color this late afternoon, like a deep and fiery emerald, sparkling on every wave. It seemed to throw a reflection of its color on the sky, so that it was hard and polished aquamarine, utterly cloudless and still. The water made no sound except for a slight hissing on the black stones and the almost inaudible murmur of a lacy wavelet on the beach.

Caroline had received an eminently satisfying report from Elizabeth which had arrived today from London. It was indeed a report rather than a letter, precise, thorough, objective. Elizabeth wrote that she did not care to put something even more important in a letter but would discuss "a certain international matter" with her mother on her return. "One should," wrote Elizabeth, "really visit Europe at least four times a year in these significant days." She had visited Parliament during a full-dress session. "Many of our associates are deeply concerned with the invasion of British foreign markets by Germany," she informed her mother. "This was discussed in Parliament last Tuesday." She had been received everywhere with the deference due the daughter of Caroline Ames.

Caroline looked for something else in the letter, some expression of affection, some personal note, some hint of natural concern of a daughter for her mother. It was not there. It was like her father's letters. Elizabeth had signed herself "affectionately," but it had not gentled the ache in the heart of the prematurely aging recluse, the hungry woman. However, because it was so necessary, so mortally necessary, for Caroline to believe that her daughter loved her, she would not let herself think or criticize or long too much. She told herself, therefore, that Elizabeth was everything a mother could wish, and a great deal more.

But the dusty and decaying house this hot afternoon suddenly became more than Caroline could endure. She went out through the front door, dressed as always in her old and rusty black dress, her gray hair braided on top of her head, her sallow face betraying lack of sun and air and vitality. Though she had lost her old massiveness and weight, her broad bones filled the lack, and though there were hollows in her cheeks, the bones above were still wide and strong and gave her an immovable expression. The once golden eyes were now only a dull hazel, sluggish and without life. The short nose had expanded almost grossly; the big lips were fixed and had a repellant hauteur. The old charming smile had long died; if she smiled now it was with grimness, and it barely moved her mouth. Lack of exercise had stiffened her limbs and her muscles; she moved like an old woman.

The sea walk was almost completely filled with boulders. She stepped among them, holding her long skirt. She wanted to go to the beach and look at the incredible color of the sea. It had attracted her from her window. Then, from behind a particular large boulder near the beach, she saw a flash of brilliant crimson, like the ribbon she had worn so long ago. It was a small flag bobbing about against the blue of the water.

A trespasser. Caroline's anger was out of proportion. The beach and the acres about the house were rigorously posted. Yet some trespasser was here. She quickened her walk, and her joints creaked in the unfamiliar motion. She came to the boulder and looked over it. A young girl was sitting on the sand, holding a large pad of white paper and a brush. She was evidently painting the ocean.

"What are you doing here?" demanded Caroline roughly. "This land is posted."

The girl, without fear, turned her head and looked at Caroline smilingly. And Caroline looked into the wide hazel eyes flecked with gold, the eyes she had had as a young girl, the eyes of the portrait of her grandfather, shimmering and soft and welling with light and trust. Caroline, stunned, stood in rigid silence, her hand on the boulder.

The girl was about sixteen, not pretty, but with a charming and gentle face, the features somewhat plump, the mouth full and red and sweet. She was slender and apparently tall, for her long legs were outlined under the blue skirt. Her white middy blouse showed the young breasts; the dark blue collar fluttered about the ingenuous face. She had curling soft dark hair which had broken away from its pompadour and streamed about her shoulders. The slight sea air had ruffled it, had flaunted the scarlet ribbon which was supposed to restrain it. The girl stood up and brushed sand from her skirt.

"How do you do, Aunt Caroline," she said, and looked at Caroline with the eager, seeking eyes of the young Caroline Ames of so many years ago.

"What?" muttered Caroline. Her hand moved awkwardly to her breast.

"I'm your niece," said the girl. "Mimi, though my name is really Mary, which I like better. My mama is your adopted sister, Mrs. Bothwell." She smiled again, hoping for a smile. "So I'm not really a trespasser, am I? I'm painting that tree there, near the water." She pointed to a blasted, withered tree with distorted limbs near the shoreline. "I've been waiting all summer for the sea to be just this color so I could paint the tree against it." She paused, and now she looked at the silent Caroline anxiously. "I love color," she said in a lower voice. "And that tree is really——" She paused again. "It's like something that died, without anyone caring about it. You can see the salt spray on it, gray and crusted. I just needed a figure sitting under it. Somebody nobody cared about, either."

Oh, God. Oh, God. Oh, God, said Caroline inwardly. She looked at her grandfather's eyes, so beaming and soft and full of hope and tenderness.

"Painting," she said in her rough mechanical voice.

"Why, yes," said the girl. "See?" She held up the paper. The color was vivid and startling and full of intensity. The tree had taken on an anguished shape, as if it were human and despairing. Caroline's dry lips parted, and she suddenly squeezed her eyelids shut.

"Is there something wrong?" The girl spoke anxiously. "I hope I haven't disturbed you."

Caroline opened her eyes. The girl had come closer to her, wishing to help. Caroline could see her face with abnormal clarity; it was her own face of decades ago, when she had been this age, even though it was prettier, ardent, and totally without diffidence.

"No," said Caroline in a rusty tone. "You haven't disturbed me." This was her father's granddaughter, but more, the girl was the great-granddaughter of David Ames.

She wanted to be angry; she wanted to order the girl to leave. She wanted to repudiate this daughter of Melinda Bothwell. But she could not. It was herself she confronted. It was the girl who had loved Tom Sheldon, who had cried in the night, who had been abandoned, laughed at, derided, unloved. It was herself.

"Well," said the girl uncertainly. "I'm glad I haven't disturbed you. I often sit here. It's so beautiful, sitting alone and looking at the sea. Alone, but not alone, in a way." She stared at Caroline, and then something must have startled her, for she moved back a step.

"What?" muttered Caroline, and without her will she stepped toward the girl.

Mimi laughed nervously. "I never saw you before. But you look familiar. Perhaps it's because John resembles you."

"John?"

"Why, yes. He often comes to our house."

"John!" Caroline was suddenly distracted.

"Why, yes. Do you mind?"

Caroline was young again, and terrified. "He shouldn't go to your house! You shouldn't see him!"

The girl was silent. She looked at this woman in embarrassment. Had she offended her? She, Mimi, was always saying the wrong thing. And now Aunt Caroline was angry.

"If he wants to come, why shouldn't he?" asked Mimi reasonably, clutching her pad of paper. (The people in the village said that Aunt Caroline was crazy.)

"Because he isn't good for you!" blurted Caroline in a loud voice. She took another step toward Mimi, and the girl retreated again. "Not for you!" cried Caroline. "Oh, not for you. Mary."

The girl stopped her retreat. She regarded Caroline earnestly. "You mean it's because he's so much older, twenty-three?"

"Where is your mother!" Caroline cried. "Doesn't your mother care about you?"

"Certainly," said Mimi. Now she was a little offended. "Of course Mama loves me."

Caroline had never known how to conduct a real conversation except with her father, Beth, and Tom, and she had failed with them all, she would tell herself. It had always been nearly impossible for her to talk with strangers except during business, and then with curt brevity. All the years stood between her and humanity, years grown dark and rusty. Once, because of her training at Miss Stockington's, she had learned how to murmur polite and meaningless things if absolutely cornered and forced to answer. But for too long a time she had spoken only of debentures, stocks and bonds, of law and the market, for only in that field was she competent in speech. It did not seem harsh or improper for her to say with loud vehemence to Mimi, "If your mother cared for you, you wouldn't see my son John!"

Mimi blushed in her renewed embarrassment, but she kept her eyes candidly on her aunt. She knew that John saw his mother only three or four times a year, and she understood that there was some estrangement. He had mentioned it lightly and in an amused fashion, as one speaks of the very old or peculiar who must be sheltered from criticism. She had thought it very kind and good of John, and her mother had thought so too. So Mimi, a properly reared girl, murmured softly, "Oh, I'm sorry."

What a strange woman this adopted aunt of hers was! Poor thing, commented the girl, so old, so sick-looking, so gray and shabby. Then Mimi thought: Why, she's just perfect for under that tree! It looks like her. She repeated with real and mature depth in her voice, "I'm sorry."

"You mustn't see him again!" said Caroline.

Mimi murmured, bent, and picked up her box of paints. The scarlet ribbon blew in a sudden rise of wind, and Caroline was sixteen once more, in the wild garden of the house in Lyndon, looking at the autumn trees with a similar ribbon in her hand. It was that young girl she touched now as her hand suddenly shot out and she put it heavily on Mimi's shoulder.

"Promise me!" she cried.

Mimi was really disturbed for the first time. "Why?" she said.

But Caroline had no words she could speak, no cry of warning and distress. She could only stare and blink at the girl in confused pain.

Mimi, tender and gallant and unacquainted with tragedy, decided that this was an opportunity to reconcile Caroline with her son. She smiled at Caroline and stood still under the gripping hand.

"I'm only sixteen," she said. "Are you afraid about John—and me?" The bright color was high on her plump cheeks. "Please don't be. I do like John, but after all, he's twenty-three and he wouldn't even look at anyone my age." She forgot the hints her mother had given her about Caroline's hatred for the Bothwells. They had been very slight hints, and sad, at the very most, and very infrequent. "Your Aunt Caroline is a little—eccentric," Melinda had explained. "She never really cared for anyone but her father and her husband, I understand. I think she is a frightened person, and no wonder, and she's a recluse."

"You don't know anything about my son," said Caroline. She pulled the girl a little closer to her and looked down into the frank eyes.

"Probably not," admitted Mimi. She was naturally sympathetic, but true pity came to her for the first time, and she did not know why. "Don't worry," she said.

Caroline sighed, and her hand slid from the girl's shoulder, as if exhaustion had struck her. Her sunken eyes wandered to the ocean, to the tree, and stayed there.

"How did you know I am your aunt?" she asked.

"Why, John looks very much like you," replied Mimi, putting up her hand to control her blowing hair. "His eyes." She peered, then laughed softly. "Well, the color, maybe. But not the expression. I always notice expressions."

She paused; her dark brows wrinkled in puzzlement. "It's funny, seeing you are only my adoptive aunt, but I look like you too, don't I?"

"Yes," said Caroline. She looked at the girl's hair, so like her own as a child, and again at the flaunting red ribbon. Then she said, "And why not? I am really your aunt. Didn't your mother ever tell you? She—and I—we're half sisters."

Mimi's mouth opened in a red circle of astonishment.

"Honestly?" she exclaimed.

"Honestly," said Caroline. And then she smiled like a girl, and her gray lips trembled at the edges.

Mimi smiled in joyous response. But she was puzzled. "Well, I'm glad. Truly I am, Aunt Caroline. But no one ever told me! I wonder why?"

"Probably because they didn't think it important," said Caroline. She was speaking without effort now, and in the voice of a young woman. She stretched out her hand again and picked up a silky length of the fine dark hair. "This is like mine was a long time ago," she said. The hair clung lovingly to her fingers. "When I was your age."

"Why didn't anyone think it important?" insisted Mimi, much intrigued.

Caroline reluctantly dropped the strand of hair. She came to herself. She said with stiffness, "It's supposed to be a secret—for your mother's sake. We had the same father."

"Oh," said Mimi. Her cheeks turned very scarlet. She considered. Then she added buoyantly, "But it was long ago, wasn't it? A long time ago? It doesn't matter any more."

"Not any more," said Caroline. "Nothing, I suppose, matters very much after a long time has passed." For the first time in many years she thought of someone besides herself and Elizabeth and her father and Tom, and she was anxious. "I shouldn't have told you if your mother didn't. I think it best you never tell her."

Mimi considered again. Then she nodded seriously. "I think you're right. If Mama didn't tell me it was for a special reason, and it would hurt her feelings if I let her know. Wouldn't it?"

"It would," said Caroline. Again she looked at the stricken tree. "Let me see what you've painted." She held out her hand commandingly.

She looked at the painting. How was it possible for water colors to catch that emerald blaze, that empty and shining sky, that postured agony of a tree? The hues started from the paper, as furious as life, as deep as life, with a somewhat terrible emotion. Caroline looked at the girl, so young and untouched. "How can you paint like this?" she said. "You never felt what you've painted."

Their heads touched as they examined what Mimi had done. Then the girl said, "Well, yes, I felt that way when I painted it. It's very funny, but when I paint I'm a different person. I feel happy or wretched and even a little frightened sometimes. It's as if someone else were in my mind. I just can't explain it."

"Frightened?" said Caroline.

Mimi said, "Yes. Nothing ever really did frighten me in my life. I wasn't even afraid of the dark the way Nat is. He's my twin brother, you know. He looks like me. Well. I could climb even higher in trees than he could, and I was never scared. But when I paint, sometimes I am afraid. Because what I see makes me that way." She added with increased earnestness, "I don't think I'm explaining it right, but do you know what I mean?"

"Yes," said Caroline. "Of course."

Mimi sighed with relief. "I saw a print of a painting by David Ames once. Do you know about David Ames? A very famous painter. I never saw the original of that particular painting. But it was a tower, all alone on rough land that looked bleached and stony. An old broken tower. And I felt very——"

"What?" cried Caroline.

"I don't know," said Mimi helplessly. "But as if it was threatening, or something. Something to run away from, very fast. As if someone were in there—— I don't know! It was dreadful."

"Yes," said Caroline. "Very dreadful." Still holding the painting, she put her other hand on the girl's shoulder again. "I will tell you something else, Mary. David Ames was your great-grandfather. He was my grandfather and your mother's."

The girl's eyes started with amazement. "No!" she exclaimed. "Mama never told me!"

"She doesn't know," said Caroline. "Only two people who are alive know. I. You. The other who knew is dead. Your grandfather, John Ames."

Mimi was actually white with shock and wonder. Then a vivid light ran over her face. "Only you and I! And you don't want me to tell anyone, do you?"

"No," said Caroline. She paused. "It will be our secret, won't it? Our secret."

"Yes, yes!" said Mimi with immense exhilaration. "Our secret." She thought, and the vivid light ran over her face again like ripples. "Not even Mama? I shouldn't tell even Mama?"

"Not even your mother," said Caroline. "I knew I could trust you," she said, as if she were Mimi's own age and they were friends.

Mimi nodded. "I remember. It was when I was a very little girl. Uncle Timothy had one of Daivd—my great-grandfather's—paintings. Mama loved it. But Uncle Tom bought it. For you." She stared at Caroline. "I just re-membered that! Isn't it funny I didn't remember before? But then, I was awfully young. It was just after Daddy died."

The color left her face. She was remembering other things, too, that she had overheard.

Caroline pressed the paper against her breast. "Listen to me, Mary! I know what everyone thinks, but it isn't true. It wasn't my fault that your father died on the North Shore road; I had tried to stop the runs that evening, but no one seemed to get my telegram. I've never told this to anyone but you. I want you to know."

"Oh, I'm so sorry," said Mimi with tears in her eyes.

"For what, child?"

The color rushed back into Mimi's cheeks as she said simply, "For you."

Caroline turned aside and put the painting carefully on the top of a flat boulder and stood looking down at it in silence. She started when she felt a touch on her arm. Mimi was beside her, very close, and the young hand held her sleeve. Mimi was crying. "How terrible it must be for you," she said.

"It doesn't matter," said Caroline in a rusty voice. "Nothing matters any more." She studied the painting again. "You are a great artist," she said. "Do you know that?"

Mimi fumbled for her handkerchief, discovered it was lost, and so wiped her eyes on the sleeve of her middy blouse. "Thank you," she said. "I think Mama believes I do well. I'm going to study art very soon, and not just as a pastime."

Caroline glanced at her house beyond the littered sea walk, the moldering house. She was feeling a tremendous excitement. "Come!" she cried, and took the girl's hand. It was warm in hers, as her children's had never been warm, and confiding, as her children's had never been confiding.

"Where?" asked Mimi.

"I have a number of my grandfather's paintings. I want you to see them, Mary." Caroline turned and walked like a young woman, her black dress blowing about her, pulling the girl with her. They were running by the time they reached the crumbling steps of the house. Blotches of color stained Caroline's cheeks. Her eyes were the eyes of Mimi.

"But you must never tell!" she cried, stopping at the steps.

"Never tell!" Mimi exclaimed in answer, and they ran into the musty house together, and Caroline, who had forgotten how to laugh, was laughing.

CHAPTER TWO

"I really don't know," said Amanda Winslow to Elizabeth.

She wanted to be rid of Elizabeth, if even only for a few days.

"But, after all," said Elizabeth calmly, "why not? Timothy's mother is my great-aunt. My Aunt Cynthia. I've seen her a few times. And her son William too. Do you mean I wouldn't be welcome in her house?" She smiled at Amanda derisively. She knew these honest, blunt people. They were really very sensitive about hurting anyone.

"I didn't say that," said Amanda, annoyed. "Don't put words in my mouth, Elizabeth. Mother Halnes is gracious to everybody. And, as you say, she's your mother's aunt. It's just that when she invited us—she just invited us."

"She didn't know then that I'd be coming with you, Amanda."

"She knows you're here with us in London," said Amanda forthrightly. "She's written to us at least four times. She never suggested that we bring you along, though she did mention you and hoped that you were enjoying yourself in England."

"But you didn't suggest that I be invited."

"It's her house, not mine. Don't be rude, Elizabeth."

"I'm sorry if you think I am, Amanda. I was merely stating a fact. It is a fact, isn't it?"

"You have a very artful way of making a person feel guilty," said Amanda, disliking Elizabeth more and more. "I refuse to feel guilty. Your mother and her aunt are not friends; you know that. Caroline has her reasons, and I'm not going to discuss them. But your mother would be very angry if you visited her aunt." Amanda stared at the girl curiously. "Just what is your reason for wanting to go, anyway?"

"This is my first trip abroad, and I've heard a lot about Devon. I want to see all I can. Is that so surprising?"

"I suppose you could stay near there, if there's an inn or something in the village," said Amanda. "But it certainly would be considered very improper in England for a young unmarried woman."

"It would also be improper in London, too, for me to be here alone in this hotel." Elizabeth smiled.

"Not really." Amanda was beginning to enjoy herself. "Timothy's friend, Mr. Eccles, has a widowed sister. I've spoken to her, and so has Timothy. She's quite willing to do us a favor and move into this hotel as your chaperone during the week we'll be in Devon."

Elizabeth's beautiful face became almost ugly. "No, thank you," she said. "If my presence in Devon isn't wanted, I'll go to Scotland. There's a music festival there just now, I understand."

Amanda was now the one frustrated. She glared at Elizabeth, who smiled again, very sweetly.

"It's very simple," said the girl. "You could send a telegram to Aunt Cynthia, telling her I'd like to see Devon and asking her if I'd be welcome. If she says no, then I'll remain here in London with that wretched old woman to watch my morals and comings and goings and peering into my room at midnight to see if I am alone."

"You can be very crude, can't you?" said Amanda. "The delicate Miss Sheldon, at that, who is so very precise and always full of propriety. Very well. I'll send the telegram at once. If your great-aunt declines the pleasure of your visit, then you agree to accept Mrs. Stonewall?"

"Yes, dear Amanda," said Elizabeth demurely.

Amanda gave her a hard look and sent the telegram. Later, as she had feared, Cynthia replied that of course Elizabeth could come. It would be dreary for her alone in London. Cynthia added that she would really be pleased by the visit.

Timothy was very amused. "Don't be so infuriated, Mandy," he said. "I know you're loving the girl less and less each day. But, as she said herself, my mother is her great-aunt. However, it isn't like Elizabeth to be so obviously pushing. I wonder what's behind it all?"

"It could be William," said Amanda, and had to laugh, and Timothy laughed with her. Quite suddenly he stopped laughing.

"I must admit that the girl is a genius," said Timothy. "I've been in conferences with her and her mother's associates, and it's remarkable, honestly remarkable, how keen she is and how informed. Nothing escapes her."

"I'm only glad," said Amanda, "that my boys are too young for her." She smiled. "Amy actively dislikes her now. So we don't have to worry about her precious brother any longer. I think Amy has had her fill of all the Sheldons, thank God. She'll never be able to look at Ames without thinking of our darling Elizabeth, our albatross."

As Amanda had been brought up to be self-sufficient and self-reliant, in spite of her family's wealth, she was packing her own trunks. She folded one of her sturdy Irish tweed suits, made in Boston, but as properly ugly as any fashioned in England. She had a sudden thought and looked sharply at her husband, who was just lighting a long cigarette and studying the view from the hotel window. Amanda straightened up. She said slowly, "You haven't objected to Elizabeth's going with us."

"I?" said Timothy.

"Yes, you. Timothy, I love you and I know all about you. And that takes a lot of tolerance on my part. You've never been able to deceive me in whole. You're up to mischief, and I have a feeling that it is very malicious mischief, and perhaps dangerous as all malice is."

Timothy turned about and looked at his wife, and the expression in his eyes alarmed her. "I haven't the slightest notion of what you mean, Mandy," he said in his nastiest tone. "Do you feel quite well?"

"I know," said Amanda. "When a man is caught in something by his wife or any other woman, he falls back on the old bromides: the lady is not 'herself.' The lady is hysterical. All right. You won't tell me. If I knew what it was, though, I'd warn Elizabeth. I don't like her, but after all, she is only twenty-one and, in a way, at our mercy here."

"She's never been at anyone's mercy, and she has no mercy for anyone," said Timothy.

Amanda nodded, as though what he had said confirmed her suspicions of him. "I see," she said. "Timothy, has the valet finished packing your luggage?"

She went on with her work deftly and quickly, and Timothy watched her. He was very fond of Amanda, and sometimes he even liked her. He did not like her now. She was the only one in the world who had ever caught full glimpses of him. He went out of her bedroom and into his own. Amanda quietly closed the dividing door and then went and stood on the balcony of the suite. She tried to recapture her old pleasure in London, which she had visited many times as a girl.

It was really a southern city, she thought. Smoke and soot might mar its light gray and light brown buildings, but it had a southern air, balmy and vital. The sunlight seemed to be reflecting from subtropical seas. It was as hot as Rome just now. It was very possible that ancient Rome, Imperial Rome, had been like this, strong and dominant and full of the bustle of Empire. Timothy often said lightly that Amanda had no imagination. But Amanda, standing on the balcony and looking down at the streets heavy with traffic, at birds wheeling about—endlessly climbing ranks of chimney pots with the sun on their wings—and listening to the deep voice of London, thought of Imperial Rome. There was the same power in this city, the same source of destiny, the same arrogance and surety. London was not "quiet" in the sense that other English cities were quiet and subdued and dully correct. Londoners had dignity, but they laughed and were friendly, too, conscious of importance.

For a time they had been too subdued and respectable under Victoria; in this Edwardian Age they had emerged in their true nature, just a little gaudy, overdressed but colorful, splendid, gallant, rich, full of pageantry and dancing. Shakespeare would have known these merry Englishmen, these adventurers, swashbucklers, and wenchers, these admirers of grandeur and pomp, these ribald and masculine men who loved actresses and opera prima donnas and yachts and horses and wine and gaiety.

It was the men of London Town who had begot liberty. It was the heirs of Dick Whittington who had not turned back at any time but had flung their flag over every continent and over multitudes of islands. If they "exploited" the "lesser breeds without the law," as Kipling had called them, they had also brought civilization to them in their merchant ships, and Bibles and science and a code of honor and justice, and the Christian imperative. They had revitalized an ancient world; they had built a new one. It was in London where feudalism had really died in the Western world.

Amanda was not given to brooding, but all at once, looking at London, she was strangely depressed, as if with a premonition. Empires passed. They died, not from without, but from within. They rotted first at the core. Who could win over a brave, resolute, and honorable man? Not even Satan. It was the man himself who defaulted his nature and fell into the pit where lay the monuments of dead civilizations and the bones of self-betrayers. Would this happen to London and the empire of which she was the hub? Amanda remembered snatches of conversations she had heard in English drawing rooms, murmurs of misgivings. "There is something on the move in the world," she had heard. "And it isn't good." "You can just almost get a glimpse of evil faces," one gentleman said, "as they slip around corners."

"The King despises Asquith," others remarked. "Let's hope he won't be elected." "But what does the Anglo-Russian Agreement mean?" a lady asked. "Germany seems suspicious." A gentleman grumbled, "And well she should be!"

King Edward, said his loyal subjects, certainly knew what he was about when he had negotiated the Anglo-French Entente. ("Why agreements? Why ententes?" asked some. "It's been a long and peaceful time since

Britain had coolly detached herself from the Continent. Why this sudden diplomatic flurry, these visits 'abroad' on the part of the King? Did His Majesty know something we do not know? Germany——?")

The press constantly discussed the Anglo-German rivalry. "The beggars are invading our trade areas," said one of Timothy's friends.

"They have the highest standard of living in the world," said another. "You'll not find any slums in Germany, or panics. You must admit they know how to work! Yet the working people there have an eight-hour day, and we have a ten. Our people accomplish less than the German worker with his shorter hours. Our industrialists are uneasy, and envious."

"You must admit that Germany has her reasons to be suspicious," said a nobleman of ancient family. "Not only that agreement and that entente. But a general air of isolating Germany. Then we're 'strengthening ties' with Spain and Portugal. No wonder the Kaiser sat up when King Alfonso was maneuvered into marrying Edward's niece, Ena of Battenberg."

Amanda had listened eagerly, for she loved these Englishmen. Then she observed that Timothy was listening also, apparently relaxed, but intent and slightly smiling. Later he said to Amanda, "Give an Englishman his politics and his port or beer, and he's happy for hours. Men, it's been said, are political animals. Englishmen are even more so."

Something was stirring darkly underground in sunlit and happy London. Amanda could feel it as she stood on the balcony this hot July day. A pity England did not have a George Washington, who had warned of foreign entanglements as the way to war. But what had Karl Marx and the Battenbergs and ententes and agreements to do with each other? Amanda shook her head. Let Timothy laugh lightly. His English friends were not laughing.

Amanda resumed her packing. There was surely no connection, but all at once she thought of her sons Henry and Harper, kind and goodhearted American boys. And she was terribly frightened; she a wholesome woman of much common sense and no vague fears.

Timothy never took this pleasant journey to Devon without remembering, with the same pain, that long-ago June day when he had taken this exact journey, thinking only of Melinda and his hopes of marrying her. He never forgot the flight from Devon the following day and his new hatred for Caroline Ames. He knew that she had been perfectly right in not informing him before he had left New York; as a Bostonian woman, it would have been unthinkable for her to tell him of his mother and John Ames. But she was the daughter of the dead John Ames. The daughter remained, "the old gray hag." Her father had brought that misery to him.

He and his family and Elizabeth Sheldon completely occupied one first-class compartment from London to Devon. The day was very hot, and the sun had a stinging quality to the eye. The window was wide open, as well as the door to the compartment, in a hopeless effort to create a cooling breeze. As a result, everyone in the compartment, including the fastidious Timothy, was gritty with soot, choking with smoke, and was constantly fishing cinders out of eyes. All, with the exception of Elizabeth Sheldon.

Timothy looked at this daughter of Caroline without appearing to do so. He often thought of her more as the granddaughter of John Ames than as the daughter of Caroline. How the young devil resembled him! She was a young and female replica, cold, aloof, immaculate in her dark blue linen suit with the white shirtwaist and the broad yellow straw hat bound about the crown with a ribbon to match her clothing. Her gloved hands rested in her lap; there was no soot, miraculously, on their whiteness. She rarely spoke, even more rarely smiled; she appeared remote from her companions in the compartment. Her profile, turned occasionally to the window, had the rigidity of stone about it, just as her grandfather's once had had. The lips were palely pink and beautifully formed, yet gave an impression of hardness. The line from her ear to her fine chin was sharply drawn and austere. The light brown hair, slightly waving, was not disordered by the hot wind. To think of her as corrupt, as Timothy did now and often had in the past, seemed absurd.

The heat had made both Amy and Amanda drowsy; they had removed their hats and were frankly dozing. Harper and Henry yawned. They got up, sleepily restless, and went into the corridor, where they leaned over the edge of the window and watched the calm green landscape pass, and the moors and the blue ponds and little blue streams. They pointed out the wild horses to each other and craned their necks after lonely farmhouses. Timothy gave all his attention to his young cousin Elizabeth, who was apparently unaware of her companions in the compartment.

Why had the girl been so quietly insistent on visiting her great-aunt, Timothy's mother? Her own mother would be enraged when she heard of it. Elizabeth did not enrage people like her mother without a reason, and it had to be an imperative one. She had seen Cynthia only a very few times. The old woman and the young had not been attracted to each other. In fact, Cynthia had expressed both aversion and troubled sadness. The two had hardly exchanged a hundred words in those years. Yet Elizabeth had made things impossible until she had got her wish to visit Devon.

As Amanda had accused, Timothy had not actively opposed Elizabeth's accompanying the family to Devon. There had been a reason: he was powerfully curious. Precisely, carefully, he went over the last few years. Cynthia. Elizabeth. Meeting briefly, the girl without obvious interest. She had not seemed impressed by Cynthia's title and riches and position. She had hauteur. Why was it so important to her that she visit Devon and a woman who was nothing to her? Timothy concentrated again on every occasion when the young and the old woman had met so briefly. Who else had been there, connected with England, with Devon?

William Lord Halnes, Timothy's half brother.

Timothy sat up so abruptly that his elbow jogged his drowsing wife, and she murmured a sleepy protest. Now he began to remember other things which had escaped his usual alertness: Elizabeth's apparently idle and uninterested questions about William. Her voice had been polite but not eager.

So the significance had escaped Timothy until now. Elizabeth never expressed much interest in anyone. In spite of her casual and remote manner, there had surely been interest, if only in the fact that she had mentioned the young man at all. "He's very rich, isn't he? He's going into the Church? Why? He's twenty-four—twenty-five? Don't the High Church clergy marry? I thought it was something like the Roman Catholic Church—celibate clergy. I see. Is he engaged yet? No? He's entitled to be in the House of Lords? Something like our Senate? I see."

Yes, she had "seen." Timothy had not. He saw now. The questions had not been merely to make conversation, for Elizabeth detested social exchanges just as her grandfather had detested them. If she were interested in young William, then she was totally interested. She had that sort of character.

Timothy had a sudden mental image of his brother. He resembled his father in appearance but not in nature. Respectable. Inconspicuous. Round-faced, sober-faced, with thoughtful and intelligent eyes. When in repose, his expression and his face were undistinguished. When he smiled he was completely charming and could move even Timothy with that look of gentleness and mirth. Timothy loathed "goodness" in people. He did not loathe it in his brother. He was very fond of William, who was intellectual as well as virtuous, good without being boring, informed without being pedantic, religious without being dogmatic.

Was it possible, Timothy asked himself incredulously, that this young woman who he thought as ruthless as a dagger could be in love—in love!—with William? She had seen him only briefly and at long intervals. When writing to his American relatives, William had never once mentioned Elizabeth Sheldon. During this trip Elizabeth herself had not spoken of him. That, in itself, could be very significant.

Timothy's thoughts rushed rapidly from point to point. Caroline would be angered at this visit. If she became angry enough she would put a "spendthrift" clause in her will against her daughter, as she had done with her sons. Elizabeth was risking all that, coldly. A woman had only one reason for that risk, any woman. Love. There could be no other explanation.

But Timothy was still incredulous. He coughed and said in a low voice so as not to disturb his wife and daughter, "I hope it won't be very dull for you down in the country, Elizabeth."

"Why should it be?" asked Elizabeth, turning her face to him.

"Well, everyone will be either too young or too old for you."

Elizabeth was silent. But he saw that she was watching him intently.

"William, of course, is down from Oxford. But my mother mentioned he had an invitation to visit friends——"

Did her face actually change? She shook a cinder from her gloves. She said indifferently, "Then you won't see him on this visit?"

Timothy did not answer. He found this effective with others. Silence in reply to a question always brought up eyes. It did so now. Timothy was startled. He had never seen this expression in Elizabeth's eyes before, full, totally directed, and entirely unguarded.

"Oh, I expect we'll see him," said Timothy. "After all, we're brothers. I don't want him to shorten his holiday, though. If necessary, I'll run up to see him where he's visiting; very nice County people, the Havens." He smiled. "There's a hint in my mother's letters that young Lady Rose Haven and William are more than interested in each other. There may be an announcement when we're there."

Elizabeth was naturally pale. But now she became very white and very still. She said quietly, "Won't Amanda and the others want to see William too?"

"Well, we may all run down for a day; it's only twenty miles by train. Mother's arthritis is bad now, so she won't be going. You can entertain each other for a few hours." He smiled blandly at Elizabeth. "The Havens are often at Mother's house. Lovely girl, Rose. Typically English, and just twenty. The family is very old and noble, and rich, too, a little horsy, but all the English are. Who was it who said that Paris is paradise for women, Italy for children, and England for horses? I must admit, though, that Rose is superb on a horse. She's won prizes for jumping too."

"Jumping?" murmured Elizabeth, looking again at her gloves.

"Steeple jumping, I think it is called. On a horse. Yes, Rose is a lovely girl. Fine figure. Just the girl for William."

Timothy was sure now. He became excited. Was the first move in his years' old determination for vengeance going to be successful? John Ames, Caroline, Elizabeth; they were all one in his unrelenting mind.

I think, said Timothy to Elizabeth in his thoughts, that I'm going to find this visit very interesting.

It was disconcerting to see that Elizabeth was watching him closely. It was impossible that she could have read his mind. But she was smiling just a little. It was a secret smile, and she turned away. Her long fair lashes touched her cheek.

CHAPTER THREE

William was at home, as Timothy had known he would be, and he and his mother greeted their guests with love and affection. "It's been some time, hasn't it, Elizabeth?" William said to his cousin, holding her long hand in both of his warm and pudgy ones. He had the power to project his kindness, for it was genuine. He already had a priestly look in his black clothing, and his round and serious face resembled that of a young monk, until he smiled. Then his eyes shone gaily, his smile was delightful. Elizabeth found herself smiling in answer. Her chill heart lurched and quickened, and she knew for certain now that she honestly and blindly loved and that there would be no one else for her in all the world. Her childish impulse of years ago toward this man had been direct and profound. Her pale cheeks flushed and her blue eyes sparkled.

Elizabeth had never been conscious of atmosphere before. The homes of others in Boston and in Lyme never excited her imagination or longing. Only the trivial demanded pleasantness and beauty around them, and ornament and perfect coloring. But Elizabeth was deeply impressed by the casual magnificence of this English country mansion, its warm and inviting vistas, its mullioned windows open to the scent of the sea and late roses, its air of strength and endurance and dignity. She would live here; there was nothing else for her.

How beautiful the girl is, thought Cynthia, even while embracing her granddaughter Amy, whom she loved dearly; she could not help glancing over Amy's shoulder at Elizabeth standing with such quiet elegance near William, who was exchanging witticisms with his brother.

"When I look at all of you," said Cynthia, sighing and smiling, "you make me feel so old and so sad. I remember that I am over seventy and that when you go away I may never see you again, any of you."

"Nonsense," said Amanda. "You'll always be young." Even the arthritis which Cynthia suffered could not take away the quick sprightliness of her smile, though her undyed hair was white and soft now and rolled neatly at the back of her head. She had shriveled considerably and moved with slowness and caution, but her smoky gray eyes were the eyes of a girl, and she dressed with taste. Her mauve tea dress of silk had a subtle air and grace, and her profile, when she smiled, took on young contours.

They had tea. The sun was lowering over the scalloped bay. Elizabeth had never heard a nightingale before, and when the pure cry of music came to her through the windows on the first murmur of the evening breeze, she was both enthralled and startled. There had been silence in her mother's house, oppressive and secret. She had never known peace and serenity. She was like one who had gained sight and hearing after a lifetime of blindness and deafness. She saw blue shadows moving slowly over the thick lawns and settling in purplish hollows under the great old oaks and plane trees. She had not known such a transparent sky before, such light and delicate pink fingerings of sun on the uppermost leaves. The wideness of the peace here, the sweet fragrance of flowers and grass and wood and tea, the tranquillity, lay on that ascetic young spirit like a blessing. She could hear now the clear ringing of the church bells in the village below the headland, the call of thrushes, the deeper passion of the nightingale's voice. She could not remember when she had last cried, or even if she had ever cried. She wanted to cry now. She looked at William. He was gazing at her thoughtfully, and when he caught her glance he smiled as if he understood, and she smiled at him with her very first innocent smile. He lifted his teacup and bent his head a little and wondered why he was suddenly disturbed and moved.

The family went to their rooms to rest and supervise unpacking and then bathe and dress for dinner at eight. The light lingered. Elizabeth was in her large and pretty room overlooking the land and then the sea. A golden mist was invading the grounds; the lower branches of the trees swam dreamily in it, as if enchanted. She opened the windows wide and looked at the sea, crimson and gilded, far below. Little sailboats with red and blue and white sails were drifting into harbor. In copses of entranced trees the girl could see distant houses on the headlands and on sloping hillsides that ran down to the sea. The scents of southern England were almost overpowering to Elizabeth; the limitless peace crept over her, and she forgot everything except William and the joy of being here. In those moments she was only a girl, soft and hoping.

She could not leave this place. She would not leave it. Resolutely she opened the polished mahogany wardrobe where a maid had already hung her gowns and frocks and gave thought as to what she would wear that night. She found herself deliciously shivering. She selected a white silk dress embroidered with fine traceries of azure flowers, and silver slippers. The maid knocked discreetly and brought in a brass pitcher of hot water and fresh towels and opened a packet of scented soap. Murmuring, she lit the oil lamps and turned them up and then touched a light to a small fire in the black marble hearth. For, though it was southern England and July, the evenings were tangy and chill so near the sea.

Elizabeth dressed quickly. The gown showed her beautifully modeled white shoulders and her smooth white arms and clung to her narrow waist and then fell into elegant folds below the knee. Caroline had never worn her mother's pearl necklace, the necklace of the portrait of Ann and Cynthia which now hung in the drawing room below. She had given the necklace to Elizabeth on her twenty-first birthday with a strange sour smile. Elizabeth wore it for the first time. She wound up her light brown hair in soft fold on fold on the crown of her head. She stood before the pier mirror and inspected herself closely, and she felt a tumult of joy. She saw herself as William would see her, and she was full of delight and pleasure. She did not wait for the dinner bell. She ran down the great staircase to the drawing room and found William standing alone before the newly lit fire, glancing over the evening newspaper from London.

She halted in the doorway and looked at him, and she felt unsteady. He put a pipe in his mouth, struck a match, and lit it. He continued to read. His solid round head bent to an item in the paper; he exuded comfort and kind strength and contentment. Then something disturbed him. He lifted his head and slowly turned toward the doorway and saw Elizabeth standing there.

She shimmered in the lamplight, white and silvery, the pearls glowing about her throat, her blue eyes soft, her figure no longer angular but melting. The two young people regarded each other in grave silence.

Then William said, using an Americanism he had learned from his mother: "Hello, there." He dropped the paper and came toward his cousin, and he smiled and held out his hand. Elizabeth could not speak; she gave him her hand, and her fingers involuntarily curled about his like the fingers of a lonely child.

He led her to a chair and then stood before her. Gentle conversation came naturally to him as a rule; it did not come now. He folded his hands under the back of his long black coat and looked down at Elizabeth. How could he have remembered her as a hard, cold child, palely indifferent and with a shut expression? His memory had been wrong, or she had changed as she had become a young woman.

"I've just been thinking," he said, "how tangled our family relationships are. Very British; hardly American." His voice was deep and eloquent and confiding.

"Yes," said Elizabeth with a shyness her brothers would never have believed. "You're my second cousin, aren't you, William? You're my mother's first cousin. And Timothy is your brother, and he's also my second cousin. And Melinda is my mother's adopted sister. Yes, it is very tangled, isn't it?"

"Do you see Melinda often?" he asked.

"No. I sometimes meet her and her children at Timothy's Boston house. But that is all." She had always despised Melinda. Yet now, as she looked at William, she did not despise his "adopted" sister any longer. She was so very happy. Her voice, usually so modulated and almost monotonous in its indifference, was warm and young. It had a ringing clarity, as of innocence. William thought: Timothy has often mentioned that the girl and her brothers are corrupt, and I had taken it for granted that corruption always recognizes corruption. But Timothy is wrong. This girl is no more corrupt than Amy.

He thought of Rose Haven. He knew his mother hoped for a marriage between her son and this girl of whom she was so fond; Rose's family also hoped for it. He more than liked her; he was drifting into a deep affection for her, placid and accepting. But now, involuntarily, he compared her with Elizabeth. Life with Rose would be peaceful and serene. It would be gracious. It would also, he found himself thinking with dismay, be a damned bore. He was so taken aback by his own thoughts that he sat down abruptly and stared earnestly at Elizabeth.

Life with this girl would never be boring. Intelligence stood in her eyes. He knew, from reports given him by Timothy, that Elizabeth was smoothly taking over many of her mother's affairs, and with competence. She had a look of sophistication, in spite of her youth, and a charmingly worldly air. Her conversation would be stimulating and not confined to parish duties, wifely duties, and duties to children. She would never prattle nicely for hours about nothing at all until her husband yawned and furtively glanced at his watch to see if it was not time to put out the lights and forget boredom in sleep. He had never, as yet, held any real conversation with Elizabeth. But he guessed quite positively that she would not bore him and that, for her, her husband would be first above all others. He knew that he would inherit a vast fortune. Rose knew nothing about money except, as she said, "it was lovely to have." Elizabeth knew all about money. William was, after all, his father's son. He had, in fact, been studying financial news from

London, Paris, Berlin, New York, and Berne, when Elizabeth had entered the room.

"Tell me," he said, leaning toward Elizabeth, as if urgently asking to be told a secret, "how you like England."

I love you, I love you, thought Elizabeth. Her face lit up. For the first time in her life she began to speak without calculation, without guile, without indifference, without coldness. William watched her, fascinated and smiling. He was more than half in love with her when the rest of the family wandered in. He had never heard a girl speak before with such joy, with such eager simplicity, and with such ardent passion.

"How beautiful you are," said Cynthia, looking at her sister's granddaughter with astonishment. "I think that you really look like my dear Ann."

She smiled tenderly and she kissed Elizabeth gently on the cheek. Amanda, Amy, and the boys gaped at this incredible Elizabeth, so stately and so full of queenliness, with her delicately flushed cheeks and her shining blue eyes and exquisite gown. Timothy looked sharply from Elizabeth to William. The young peer was gazing at Elizabeth with an expression Timothy, the malicious, could only describe as fatuous and bedazzled.

Amanda, as usual, was somewhat dowdy in her no-nonsense gown, and Amy appeared callow and awkward compared with Elizabeth. The boys, staring at Elizabeth, appeared more fatuous than their Uncle William. We are a fine success, thought Timothy. He said, "Is it really you, Elizabeth?"

"I think," said William, "that it is."

They went into the dining room, where silver and candlelight and fragrance again enchanted Elizabeth. Her Esmond blood, so long suppressed and inhibited, delighted in this display of mellowed graciousness. It was as if she had been born only this day, had come to maturity only this night. She had no other memories but of this house, no love but this young man sitting beside her and solicitous that she should be served the proper cut of beef. When William's sleeve touched her bare arm she trembled. When he turned to her she could only look into his eyes with naked and touching love.

Timothy smiled in himself with elation. Amanda thought: Perhaps I was mistaken in the girl. Poor thing. How happy she seems away from her mother and that horrible moldering house. She is only a girl, after all. I must do more for her at home. She said to Henry, who, almost eighteen, was at the susceptible age, "Dear, you haven't touched that wonderful Yorkshire pudding, your favorite." She looked at Amy, her pretty daughter, and thought crossly that salmon pink was definitely not the girl's color. She saw Cynthia smiling at Elizabeth as at some resurrected vision and was pleased. Then she saw Timothy's face and was startled. He kept glancing at Elizabeth, and there was something in that glance that made Amanda uneasy.

"I keep early hours now, children," said Cynthia. "How I used to hate them! I never went to bed before two in the morning, even when I wasn't entertaining. I loved the night; much more exciting than the day. But now I must creep off like an old, sick child, at ten."

She added quickly, "Don't pity me! I've had a most enjoyable life, much better than most."

"We're all tired too," said Amanda. "Timothy has been attending so many meetings in London, and so has Elizabeth, on her mother's business. And this country air is making all the children yawn. I think we should go to bed early."

They were sitting in the drawing room now, and Amanda was drinking whiskey, Amy was shyly sipping a little sweet port, and the boys, defying their mother's scowl, had accepted small glasses of beer. Timothy found his brandy was giving him heartburn. He could not look away from Elizabeth and William murmurously laughing together side by side on a love seat.

When Cynthia stood up, all stood with her. But William said, "I'm not sleepy, and I'm sure Elizabeth isn't. I'd like to walk with her about the grounds. There's an uncommonly fine moon tonight."

Cynthia was very tired. She was pleased that William liked this poor, loveless girl who was taking on a resemblance to "dear Ann" more and more in Cynthia's eyes. "Oh, do," she said. "I think the sunken garden is especially lovely in moonlight."

William took Elizabeth's hand easily; they said good night and walked out together. "Dear children," sighed Cynthia sentimentally. "William is so kind. Did I tell you, dears, that I hope we'll have a Very Important Announcement to make while you are here? William and Rose Haven."

"Excellent," said Timothy, looking at the french doors through which William and Elizabeth had just disappeared. "Excellent," he repeated. He caught his wife's eye. She was frowning at him. Damn Mandy. She had a way of reading what he really meant under his words. Had she heard him gloating? His fingers as he grasped Amanda's arm just above her elbow cut into her warm flesh, and she said frankly, "Ouch! Do you have to pinch me like that, Timothy, my love?"

Elizabeth, who had been born to beauty only that day, only this night, wandered slowly with William over the thick grass which was sprinkled with shining drops of dew under the moon. They did not speak now that they were alone. They passed a fountain and paused to look at it. They walked on and on, until they left the grounds and could stand on the headland and look at the sea. It was a plain of silver. The evening wind gushed with fragrance and salt.

"What is it, Elizabeth?" asked William. "Are you crying?"

"I can't help it," she stammered. "I don't know why. But it's as if I were alive for the first time in all my life."

He took his handkerchief and wiped her eyes gently, as his father had wiped Cynthia's eyes more than twenty-five years ago. He could see the blue under Elizabeth's lashes, the soft curve of her cheek, the rose of her lips. He dropped his hand.

Then, hardly standing on his toes, he kissed the girl's parted lips, simply and naturally. She put her hand on his shoulder.

"Oh, William," said Elizabeth, and her shriveled heart expanded painfully.

"Dear Elizabeth," said William, and he kissed her again and felt her innocence and inexperience, and he was full of compassion. Her lips moved timidly against his.

Was he in love with this girl? He did not know. He was not an impulsive young man. He only knew that what he felt for Elizabeth was totally different from the affection he felt for Rose Haven. During his early student years he had engaged in what the English discreetly called "young men's indiscretions," but only briefly and at long intervals. He knew what passion was. He felt it now, and something else that keenly disturbed yet delighted him. He became overpoweringly aware of the beauty of the night.

"Do you remember the last time we met?" asked Elizabeth, leaning against his shoulder.

William thought. He could not remember in the least. He said, "It was a long time ago, wasn't it?"

It was only yesterday for Elizabeth. She had been sixteen. It was a slightly warm pre-Easter day in Boston, and the air had a sweetness in it. Even Elizabeth, the exigent, was suddenly startled by the promised fragrance of spring, and she had stopped on the steps of Miss Stockington's school and had looked about her vaguely and had as vaguely frowned, as at an imperious voice intruding upon her. Her books were heavy on her arm; her fair hair blew back from her face in the living breeze. She looked at the houses across the brick road, their walls bright and rosy in the sun, and she was suddenly excited and did not know why. Then a carriage had drawn up and her Aunt Melinda was being assisted from it by young William, and they were laughing together.

She had seen William only twice before, and always she had felt a dim stirring, and when he had gone after a few words in the presence of his family she had had the sensation of emptiness and loss. The sensation haunted her for days. But she had been younger then. Now she was sixteen.

Melinda's laughter had stopped when she saw her niece, but she gave her a kind smile and greeted her and, as always, she asked about Caroline. Elizabeth murmured something. She looked at William; he was not handsome, not distinguished, not a young man to attract a young girl's attention at first glance. He was somewhat short, pudgy, and unremarkable of face and feature. Yet when Elizabeth looked at him her excitement increased, until he was the very focus of the warm spring day. Her pale face flushed as he shook hands with her. The wind blew several strands of her pretty hair over her cheeks and into her eyes, and William laughed and pushed them behind her ears.

"I'll go in for Mimi," said Melinda, pleased at the sudden laughter of her brother. She glanced at Elizabeth and was surprised to see that cold young girl laughing also. Why, the child was actually beautiful with that color in her cheeks and her white teeth flashing in the sun. How unfortunate that her clothing was so plain, her manner usually so constrained and indifferent. Melinda smiled again and went into the school and left the two young people alone.

William remarked pleasantly on the day. He was in America for another week; he had been here a month. Then he was going to Canada for the first time. He would travel from coast to coast. "One has to keep an eye on the empire, you know," he said, pursing his mouth amusingly. Elizabeth listened with silent gravity, not to his words, but to his voice. Her right arm, pressed against her side, could feel the thumping of her heart.

Then Elizabeth said abruptly, "I haven't seen you for two years."

He was surprised, for he had asked her an amiable question concerning her knowledge of Canada. She had apparently not heard a word he had said. He stopped smiling. He looked at her intently. The Sheldon family, he had heard, was very odd, indeed, and this girl apparently was a good example. But what beautiful blue eyes she had, the most beautiful he had ever seen. Absolutely blue, so that the color appeared to fill her eye sockets. Her features were stern now as she watched him.

"I suppose not," he said.

She moved a little closer to him. She was too young to ask herself why she was so helplessly pulled to this young man, why she wanted to touch his hand, his plump cheek.

"Your parents?" said William lamely. Where the devil was Melinda? But he looked into Elizabeth's eyes again and forgot his sister.

"It doesn't matter," said Elizabeth. (Why was she staring at him like that? thought William a little uneasily.) "I remember every time I ever saw you," said the girl.

"Oh?" said William. Melinda and Mimi came out then, and he turned to them. When he looked for Elizabeth she had gone.

"I was sixteen," said Elizabeth as she stood with William, looking far down at the night sea in Devon. "I never forgot, never once. It was a day in spring, and you came with Aunt Melinda for Mimi. You and I stood talking on the steps of Miss Stockington's. Don't you remember?" she pleaded.

He did not. But he was good and kind and he said, "How a person forgets. But of course——"

He kissed Elizabeth again, and they walked back to the house.

Elizabeth did not sleep that night. As her grandfather had loved her great-aunt, so she loved William, with as much passion, fierceness, and devotion. But John Ames had been able to think of other important things beyond his love. Elizabeth, as a woman, could think of nothing else but the young man.

In spite of her sleepless night—she could think only of William under the same roof with her—she bloomed the next morning. She was gentle; she laughed easily; she was kind to Amanda and her children. She walked and moved as if unbearably exhilarated. Sometimes she would press her palms together and shiver. Only Timothy understood. Cynthia and Amanda thought the girl "was coming out of herself for the first time." They were pleased, for they were kindhearted women.

Cynthia had a riding habit which exactly fitted Elizabeth, and so the girl went riding with William. She had been taught to ride at Miss Stockington's. She sat beautifully and with grace, the long skirt sweeping the horse's side, Cynthia's postilion hat riding her shining light hair, the wind whipping color into her cheeks. She did not need to talk with William. They rode in a sweet silence. They came to a quiet glade, dismounted, and sat on the scented grass together.

Then Elizabeth began to speak. Something tight and dark and strong broke in her, and she spoke to William as her mother had spoken to young Tom Sheldon in a blue twilight so long ago. She spoke with passionate loathing of what she knew and what she had heard in London; she spoke with sudden hatred of her mother's seclusion and hostility toward the world. She leaned toward William, tense with emotion, her face paling and flushing, her eyes large. And William listened.

He listened as Tom had listened, but without Tom's incredulity and repulsion. For he knew many things himself and had heard many things in London. He watched Elizabeth, not with Tom's bewildered anger and confusion, but with sadness and understanding and with indignation that this beautiful girl had been exposed to such experiences.

"I never want to go back!" she cried, beating her gloved fist against her skirted knee. She had removed her hat; the sunlight, sifting through tall trees, gilded her hair. "I shall never go back! What is all that to me?"

William was his father's son, in spite of everything. He was also sophisticated. He knew what Elizabeth, in her profound innocence, was offering. He thought of the huge Ames fortune. He knew from Timothy that it would belong to Elizabeth if she trod softly about her mother. Would Elizabeth regret one day that she had thrown it aside? He did not know. Did people, even young people, change so radically as Elizabeth appeared to have changed? He did not know.

He understood that Elizabeth loved him. Did he love her? He brushed a blade of grass from his knee. He thought soberly. He looked up and found her face close to his, and he saw the intense wide blueness of her eyes. Then he knew that he loved her beyond any doubt.

But one did not make lifelong commitments in a single moment of passion. William was no romanticist. He despised what Londoners called "brouhaha." He had an aversion for buoyant, radiant, "sudden" people. They were invariably ineffective, in spite of their noisy leaping and their hysteria. They were like children, eager, forgetful, fast on the heels of the latest novelty, discarding as quickly as they had accepted. It was purely an American phenomenon and very immature.

So William hesitated. He held Elizabeth's hand and murmured consolations. He kissed her as he had kissed her the night before. Then she flung her arms about him and pressed her mouth against his, and he held her tightly. He felt her tears on his own cheek. All his body urged toward her. He gently touched her breast. She shuddered and pressed closer to him.

Then she was crying, "I love you! I've loved you since I first saw you!"

With a tremendous effort he controlled himself. "But you've only seen me a few times, Elizabeth." He stroked her cheek.

"You must give yourself time, darling," he said, and he took her hand and helped her to her feet. He brushed her skirt with his hand, and as he bent she put her hand on his head. It was the simplest and most trusting of gestures. He took her hand and kissed it.

"How many men have you known?" he said gently. "Very few. You must be fair to yourself. Shall we leave it this way for a few days? There are so many things for you to consider."

"Yes," she said humbly, without understanding at all. She only knew that he had accepted her and that she must wait a little. She did not know why, but he had asked it.

He would never forget that hot, sunlit day. He would remember it all his life.

CHAPTER FOUR

That night William went into his mother's sitting room, where she was preparing for bed. He often went there for a quiet good night, alone. She had brushed out her long white hair; it hung in silver over her shoulders, and her eyes were bright.

"Dear William," she said. "It's been a busy time, hasn't it?"

But their guests, their relatives, had been here only two days. Did the old feel that the slightest nudge out of their routine was a "busy time"? It made him feel sad. He sat down near his mother, and she said, "You are such a comfort," as she had said so many times.

"Perhaps not such a comfort," he said. "Mother, I know you want me to marry Rose Haven."

She put down her brush and looked at him in her mirror. "But I thought it was— You are so suited to each other, dear. I thought it was all settled."

"Perhaps too settled," he said. "Perhaps too suited. All at once I'm not sure that roast beef and Yorkshire pudding is the sort of diet I'm satisfied to eat the rest of my life."

She stared at him in the mirror.

"I don't think you liked such a diet, Mother," he went on. "You've always been frank with me. Would you have deliberately chosen such a meal yourself?"

She was distressed, disappointed, yet amused.

"No," she said. "I never did. I always liked exotic things." She paused. "Have you fallen in love with a perfectly wild actress in London or some impossible young woman? A priest can't marry such a woman!"

He smiled.

"Of course," she said briskly, "I prefer excitement and color. One can't really call Rose exciting and colorful." Then she sighed. "I'm getting very old if I forget that you are young and might have different ideas and if I can be pleased at the thought of your marrying good, sound Rose Haven. I just wanted you to be settled before I died. I never gave it a thought that Rose might bore you." She paused again. "Does she bore you?"

"Yes. But I didn't realize it until recently."

"Never marry anyone who bores you," she said with decision. "Never. That's death in life. I know. My first husband was a very tedious man. I yawned my way through the years of our marriage. I won't pretend I'm not a little disappointed, but that's because I'm old now. Who is the young lady —if she is a young lady?"

"She is a lady."

Now Cynthia was alert and excited. She swung around in her chair like a girl. "Who?" she cried.

"Elizabeth."

He stood up. It was terrible to see his mother age like this before his eyes, become so crumpled and wilted and broken and small, silently stricken. She looked at him as though he had struck her down ruthlessly.

"Mother! What's wrong?" he exclaimed.

But she pushed him away feebly with her hand, as if he had obstructed her breathing.

"Elizabeth?" she whispered. "Elizabeth Sheldon?"

"It's not settled," he said hurriedly. "Please don't look like that. I know it's very soon. I—hardly know the girl. That's true. Let me give you some brandy."

"No!" she cried. She pressed her hands on her dressing table. She was the color of old paper.

Then she cried again, "No! Not Elizabeth! Oh, dear God, not Elizabeth!"

She put her hand on her breast and muttered, "I'm too old now for these things." She closed her eyes and repeated, "Not Elizabeth."

William sat down near her. "Why not Elizabeth, your own sister's granddaughter? Is that so awful?"

She bent her head on the back of her hands, breathing heavily. Then she lifted her head. She was quieter now.

"I believe in blood, William. Please listen carefully. There is very bad blood in Elizabeth, I might even say evil blood. I loved her grandfather, as you know. But I wouldn't marry him, not even for Melinda's sake. Perhaps I was wrong. I don't think I was. He would have crippled Melinda as he crippled Caroline, his older daughter. He would have twisted her, deformed her. He was that way by nature. He told me at one time that his father had 'made' him what he was. Perhaps. But the bad material has to be there first. John Ames was a bad man; I loved him, but he was a bad man.

"William, Melinda has his blood, but I kept her away from his influence. He was very careful; he couldn't do anything about Melinda so long as I wasn't married to him. I was her protection. He constantly asked me to marry him. If I had done so, the Ames money would have belonged to me, or at least a large share of it. But the money was not enough inducement for me to sacrifice Melinda. In my way, I was an honorable woman."

"Yes," he said. Then all at once he felt the need to fight for something precious to him beyond anything else in the world. "But Elizabeth is also an Esmond. And her father was a good sort, you always said, though not of family."

"There is her mother, my niece Caroline," she said slowly, painfully. "A deformed woman, a crippled woman. Elizabeth is her daughter; she has had Caroline at her elbow all her life. Do you think, blood aside, that that influence can be overcome in a day, a year, a lifetime? No. What is bred in the bone will be born in the flesh. This is as true of the mind as it is of the body. Today Elizabeth is young and pretty. Tomorrow you would see her mother emerge in her. And her grandfather. It's inevitable. She would kill you as her grandfather killed my sister, as her mother killed the spirit of Tom Sheldon. Did you ever see a good man disintegrate? I did. I saw Tom slowly die. That would happen to you."

"Elizabeth isn't like her mother or her grandfather."

Cynthia shook her head over and over. "Yes, my dear, she is. I saw them in her when she was only a little girl. Blood—and environment. You can overcome one with the grace of God. You can't overcome both. Unless through a miracle. Elizabeth, at twenty-one, is too old for a miracle. She seems soft and pliant to you now, because she loves you, just as her mother seemed soft and pliant and trusting to Tom Sheldon when he married her. The change came, as it had to come. It will come to Elizabeth if you marry her. Her nature is already formed. She would destroy you."

She said despairingly, "I only saw Tom Sheldon a few times. It was enough. And once he told me that he couldn't understand: Caroline had changed from the girl he had married. She hadn't really changed. It was only Tom who was deceived. She was her father's daughter; she was what he had made her. And Elizabeth is what her mother has made her."

She took her son's cold hand piteously. "Oh, why did this happen? So soon? It's impossible. I'm dreaming. Oh, William."

William said, "Nothing is impossible with God. He has transformed people before. If Elizabeth has inherited anything vicious from her grandfather, and even if her mother has deformed her spirit, God can help her. And me." He spoke with deep quietness. "I will soon be a priest. If I did not believe God could do this for Elizabeth, I would have to refuse ordination."

"He can't change a man, not even God, if the man doesn't want to be changed, my dear. Elizabeth has had no religious education at all; she hasn't any frame of reference. She would never be able to understand you. Think of her as a vicar's wife in some English town or village! Elizabeth Sheldon."

"She could do it, with the grace of God," said William, still very quietly. "There is another thing. She knows that her mother will disown her if she marries me; she implied that. You know what money has always meant to Elizabeth; Timothy has told us. But she is willing to give up all that money and never return to America. For me."

Cynthia put her wrinkled hands over her face. "Poor child, poor girl," she said. Then she dropped her hands. Her face changed, became terribly frightened, and she caught William's arm.

"Listen!" she cried. "There is something else. But first, how far has this gone?"

"Quite far," he admitted mildly, and wondered at his mother's open fear.

"It can't go any further, William! If you marry Elizabeth you'll not only not be ordained, you'll be forever cut off from your friends. Forever. Technically, as you know, you are Elizabeth's uncle——"

"Yes. Technically. I am half brother to Melinda, who is Elizabeth's aunt. But in reality I am only her second cousin. There are closer relationships in the royal families of Europe."

"I am not speaking of that, William! I am Lady Halnes; I am the mother of a peer who will enter not only the Church but the House of Lords. You come of a famous old family; one of your ancestors had a morganatic marriage with a royal personage. Listen to me! Tonight, before dinner, Amanda came to this very room to speak to me. Such a good young woman. She was troubled."

"Yes?" said William, holding his mother's hand and speaking soothingly.

"Oh, dear God," groaned Cynthia. "It is quite true that old sins have long shadows. I've long known that Timothy hates Caroline and hates her children, and especially Elizabeth. He remembers John Ames; he sees him in that poor girl. Once John said that Timothy was pernicious; as a mother I resented it. Now I know it is true.

"Tonight Amanda told me privately that she had opposed Elizabeth's coming here. She doesn't like the girl, but she is fair and honest. She said that Timothy wasn't in the least averse to having Elizabeth come. He must have known something! He was always that way as a child—he learns everything he can use to hurt an enemy or someone he wants to ruin.

"If you marry Elizabeth, William, Timothy won't stop at anything. He's fond of you, but not fond enough to prevent him from striking at poor dead John, and especially Caroline, through Elizabeth. Once he wouldn't have dared; he needed Caroline. Now he doesn't need her. I am his mother; he has been plotting for a long time, trying to contrive ways. To injure Caroline or her children. Amanda has felt it too. She told me she has a 'feeling,' as she said, that 'Timothy is up to nothing good.' When someone like Amanda, who is logical and very sane, has a 'feeling,' one should listen to it.

"He'll strike if you marry Elizabeth. He'll let the whole world know that Melinda is my daughter, that I was her father's mistress for years." Cynthia's face became frantic with terror. "Don't you understand what that will mean? Melinda will be shamed in America; perhaps most people in Boston do know the truth; they are willing to overlook it if it isn't pushed into their faces.

Melinda's children will be disgraced. I will be disgraced—I, your mother. It will be an international scandal. We aren't obscure people, William. 'Questions,' as the English call them, will be asked in the House, at the very least. The Church won't countenance such a scandal. Your peers will turn their backs to you, as your mother's son. It may be that the King has given some fillip to scandal, but not a scandal like this. Never a gross, open scandal, no matter how old."

She stood up in her desperation and held William by both his arms. "My children. You and Melinda. And Melinda's children. And your future children. There's no mercy in Timothy. I have no way to bribe him; he doesn't need what I can leave him from my own fortune. There is nothing any of us can do that will stop him—not this time. Not you. Not even Melinda. In a way, he'll think he is avenging Melinda, even if he disgraces her for life.

"What of your own life, William, my son? And your children? Your whole life has been directed toward the priesthood. You speak of God. Are you willing to desert Him?"

She had never seen her son so white, so quiet. But for his sake she had to go on.

"How will you and Elizabeth endure it, ostracized, disgraced, spoken of behind hands? You would both begin to remember what you had given up. Love is sometimes not worth the price, William. If you can't just now remember God, think at least of your children and their future."

"Please, Mother," said William. He began to walk slowly up and down the pretty lamplit room.

"You couldn't live in England, William," his mother sobbed. "You'd have to go to the Continent. You'd never be free from it until the day you died. You and Elizabeth would come to hate each other."

He stood at the window, his back to her, and he stood there for a long time while she cried convulsively. Then he came to her and held her in his arms as his father had held her.

"Don't, Mother. Don't cry any more."

She looked at him through her tears and saw his suffering, and she wished she had died before he had been born.

"I'll talk to Elizabeth," she said, her voice old and trembling. "I will explain."

"No, dear." He thought of Elizabeth with despair.

During all the long night William did not sleep once. He walked his floor; he prayed; he considered and reflected. He stood at his window and looked out at the darkness. The dawn became gray-blue, like a dream. There was a large willow outside his window and it moved gently. The quickening dawn appeared between the framing fronds, and it resembled numerous painted-glass windows of rose and gold and blue and red. Then William said to himself: I must find out for certain. Mother is old and has a lot of fears which are possibly groundless.

At six o'clock, when only one servant was stirring sluggishly, William tapped on Timothy's door. It was opened at once. William wondered for a moment why it was that if someone was agitated in a house others there were subtly disturbed by it as if by osmosis. At any rate, Timothy was already dressed and alert. "I thought," said William, "that you'd like to go for a ride with me. It's a fine day."

William was already in riding clothes. Timothy paused, then nodded quickly, and William went downstairs and outside to the stables. He saddled his own mare and another horse for his brother. The morning was cool and sweet, the sky wide and full of light, the grass watery with shining dew. A wind came from the sea. The trees still swam in a rosy mist, but their tops were afire. Timothy came into the stables, and if he noticed that William was pale and tired he made no comment. He himself moved as alertly as a youth, tall and thin and, as his mother would say, "all of one color." His graying fair hair was uncovered and it lifted a little from its smoothness in the morning breeze. "There's nothing I like better," he said with jocularity, "than getting up before the world and prowling about."

"You were awake," said William in the mild voice he had inherited from his father. He turned quickly. "Weren't you?"

"So I was. I'm not a heavy sleeper; never did like the dogs who can fall asleep instantly, then give a reasonable facsimile of being dead for nine hours." He looked at the horse saddled for him, then patted the animal on its neck. The horse, a very gentle one, suddenly backed away and snorted and showed the whites of its eyes.

"That's odd," said William. "I don't believe that animals 'know,' as the country people say, and instinctively recognize a villain. I've known the worst villains to have dogs and horses and other animals devoted to them, and children too."

Timothy took the reins and sprang up onto the reluctant horse's saddle like a young man. He touched the horse's side lightly with his crop, and she became still. William mounted, and they rode away in the full dawn, which was heavy with the scent of many flowers and grass and sea and pines. They rode through the village, where only an occasional chimney pot was smoking over thatched or tiled roofs. Then a church bell rang half-past six to the clear sky, and doors began to open to the sweet air. They left the village and began to climb again to the headlands, where the turf was thick and mossy and the voices of cattle could be heard. They passed through a copse of trees, which showered them with wet splinters of light. Then they were trotting briskly down a road already warm with dust, above which hedgerows appeared thick and massed against the sky. They had not spoken a word since they left the house.

The cattle were in the luscious meadows; larks rose against the rapidly rising sun and dropped their music down to the cool earth. Timothy frequently glanced at the quiet plump profile of his brother but did not speak. They finally pulled up their horses in the shade of a giant oak which rose in lonely majesty on a low knoll. William lit his pipe, and Timothy put a cigarette in his mouth. They smoked in a little silence. Two or three times

Timothy began to speak, then stopped. William sat very still on his horse and looked over the countryside; the broken shadow of leaves moved over his face.

Then Timothy said, "May I assume this dawn galloping has a purpose?"

"In a way," said William. He turned his head and looked at his brother, and Timothy saw the sober trouble in his gentle eyes.

"Anything I can do?" asked Timothy lightly.

"I don't know," said William. "That's the trouble. I don't know."

"You're one of the very few people, Bill, that I'm fond of," said Timothy. "Thinking of giving up the Church?"

"Perhaps," said William.

Timothy had asked the question jokingly. He was so astonished at the answer that he took the cigarette from his mouth and stared at William. "You're not serious!" he exclaimed.

"I don't know," said William. "It depends on circumstances."

"The Havens been putting pressure on you?" asked Timothy. "I noticed they weren't a very reverent family."

William did not answer. Timothy reached out and patted his arm. "What does Shakespeare say? 'Men have died, and worms have eaten them. But not for love.' "

William took off his cap. Then he said, "I'm not so sure of that. Perhaps not physically, not always. But spiritually."

"I don't know about that," said Timothy. "But perhaps my family doesn't love in that way."

"Perhaps not," said William. His pipe had gone out and he lit it again. All at once Timothy was restless. He dismounted and began to walk about, idly switching at the top of the tall grass. His face had become older and had even less color than usual.

"You haven't told me yet," William said, "what your political plans are now since they refused to appoint you, in America, as senator."

Timothy stopped. He stood with his back to his brother. "I'm waiting for an amendment to the Constitution," he said. "We're working at it. We have eighteen states in line now; we'll soon have the rest. Then senators will be elected by the people, directly, and not appointed by political hacks. I can wait."

"And you think that you'll be elected?"

Timothy turned and smiled a little. "Certainly. I have the money. You need money to be elected in America. Haven't you heard? Even if my opponent were the angel Gabriel himself, my money could beat him. A baboon could be elected to any office in the United States if he had enough money. And had richly paid hirelings to promise everything."

"Indeed?" said William. He stroked the neck of his browsing horse. "I've given the subject a great deal of thought and I've come to the conclusion that the parliamentary system is much better than yours and can guard the interests of the whole people much more honestly and efficiently. A very rich man aspiring to Parliament has very little advantage over a poorer man or even one in very modest circumstances. That is because of our election laws. We can spend only so much, and it is a small amount. We can't promise patronage or favors or bribes. You can be disqualified by law if there is the slightest hint of such things. Then there are the libel laws, which are very strict. You can't abuse your opponent, as you can in America, and hint nasty things about him or attack his character. You can only attack his political ideas, and you have to be careful about them too. Yes, the parliamentary system is best."

"For whom?" asked Timothy, still smiling. "What is the use of money if it can't buy you what you want, such as high political office? You see, Bill, in America we have only money—no titles, no natural prerogatives as birthrights, no natural position because of family or birth. I could point out a dozen men and women on the streets of Boston who were born of families illustrious in our Revolution and in the forming of the Constitution. One I know is a ribbon clerk in a shop, and a daughter of another family is a housemaid. Why? Because their families had lost their money long ago and so they are no longer admitted to 'Society.' Society, in America, is a purely money-based thing, and any boor with enough money can break in after a token resistance."

"Money," said William, "is surely the lowest value of a man."

Timothy shrugged. "Perhaps. But we aren't an aristocratic people, remember. We have no tradition of aristocracy, or noblesse oblige, or high principle, or chivalry; we haven't even an aristocracy of the mind. In fact, in America, intellectualism is very, very suspect. In the early days of the Republic there was a frame of aristocratic and intellectual reference. But not any longer. The Vandals took over. I know a man in Philadelphia who was a starving bricklayer, a drunkard, a cheap gambler in a saloon, where he lost all his wages. One night he won a worthless piece of ground playing poker. That was about forty years ago. A short time after that—it was near Titusville —oil was discovered on the property, and he was a multimillionaire in two years. His children now live on the Main Line, and their grandchildren attend the very best of schools and are admitted and courted everywhere. But coming down to that, you aren't so rarefied yourselves here in England. What about stout and tea? And the big soap merchant?"

"Those men had to be something else besides purveyors of stout and tea and soap," said William, and now he, too, smiled. "They had to be men of intelligence and some taste and acceptable in other ways. Money was not the sole basis, as it is in America."

"It will be, one of these days," said Timothy. "You'll see. You, too, have the middle class."

William was bewildered. "I'm afraid I don't follow you," he said. "What has the middle class got to do with this?"

But Timothy had begun to walk up and down again, slashing at the grass, and William watched him. Then William thought. He remembered long and recent discussions he had had with old friends in London and men who had known his father. He remembered questions raised in the House and murmurs among the Lords. It was very nebulous. But something was stirring, and William had felt the uneasiness and anxiety. He wished now that he had listened more closely, for the affairs of the world were also the concern of God. What had old Lord Chetlow said? "Of course there will be a war." It had seemed absurd to William.

He watched Timothy and again felt uneasy and anxious. He said, "If and when that amendment is passed, and if and when you become a candidate for the Senate, on what will you base your appeal to the people—when they can elect their senators directly?"

Timothy stopped walking restlessly up and down. He turned to William and smiled pleasantly.

"The class struggle," he said.

"What?" cried William incredulously. "What class struggle? You have no classes in America. Any man with a little intelligence and industry and inventiveness can make money in America and keep it and add to it and make himself a fortune, for you have no personal income rates as we have. Such a man can rise to any position in America. You haven't any classes!"

"We'll make them," said Timothy, and smiled more pleasantly.

"Why, for heaven's sake?"

"For political purposes. We'll also pass an income tax law, which will prevent, eventually, any man from accumulating new wealth and will act to protect those who have inherited wealth and also to protect them from the Vandals."

"What Vandals?"

"The middle class, which is invading all parts of our national life now, as it is invading your British life. With its vulgarity and suety virtues and morality and bad taste. We'll use the working class to destroy the middle class in America; we'll give the working class such hatred and such lusts that the middle class will be so taxed to death to support the working class's greed that they'll go out of existence. Liberty, equality, fraternity! Every man as alike as every other man, if we have to chop off the heads that stand up above the crowd!" He laughed and thought that William's face, looking down at his, was utterly uncomprehending and just a little stupid.

"Then," said Timothy, "we who have the great old inherited fortunes will also have power. And we'll invent our own aristocracy. America's a republic, now. But so was Rome, for the first four hundred years. We'll have an American 'democratic empire' eventually, ruled by those born to rule, with only the contented and obedient masses under them and no challenging middle class."

"You'll never be able to accomplish that in America," said William. "You'll never be able to make the people class-conscious, not when they know that a class society means the end of freedom for them."

"But they'll never know," said Timothy. "Just as your own working class, which can become middle class with enough hard work and intelligence, will never know."

377

"You'll never accomplish that without revolution," William said. "And revolutions are born of wars."

Timothy, looking at his brother, became silent.

The young Englishman on his horse turned his head and looked at the peaceful sunshine, the green meadows, the distant cliffs, the quiet hedgerows, the placid trees. The sun was warm on his shoulders, but he felt cold. But surely, he thought, these atavisms like Timothy are few in the world. The lust for power was a latent evil in all humanity, but it was a lust which present civilization had modified to a great extent or sublimated into a desire for true public service. This was a civilized world, not a world of marching empires, not a world of soldiers and despots, not an imperial world. There was only one despotism left in the Western world now, and that was Russia, and even Russia was feeling the moderating influence of Europe and was becoming exceedingly prosperous and less suspicious of her neighbors.

"Were you thinking of going into politics, after all?" asked Timothy with deceptive joviality. His eyes were probing his brother, and he was not entirely assured now that he had been airing his views to a mild provincial Englishman who would soon retire into some shadowy and cloistered cathedral. William felt that probing. He said, "Of course not. I am not interested in politics."

He stroked his horse's neck again, but he fixed his calm eyes fully on Timothy's. "As a churchman, I am interested in the ancient problem of evil. I have discovered something. Evil men are fundamentally superficial. They are incapable of powerful emotions. And of course, being superficial, they can't love deeply or have any loyalties except to themselves, or any deep principles or convictions, even wrong ones. Their malice, though often disastrous to others, is not even based on lust or greed to any profound extent. It's mere impulsiveness—atavistic. Though they seem to have aims, they are really aimless, striking without full knowledge. I would call them petty if they weren't so dangerous to others."

Timothy could not look away from his brother. He said, "That isn't what Nietzsche said of them."

"He was speaking of an entirely different race. He was speaking of truly wicked men who were beyond good and evil. Such men have intrinsic reasoning power—Satanism. They've always been very few in the world, fortunately. I could not name them on the fingers of one hand.

"One of these days," continued William, "we'll understand the nature of evil. Its attrition. Its bleakness. Its fruitlessness. Its barrenness. Its refusal to distinguish between right and wrong. Its piteousness. What a world without song or light, without pity and gentleness, without color and contrast, without affirmation or vitality, without satisfaction and joy! Only a corroding acid malice, only a hellish loneliness. Destructiveness without a feeling of accomplishment. They are the ravenous bellies St. Paul spoke of, which are never filled."

He looked at the sky. He said, "They are the damned."

He knew that he had lost. He was dealing with an evil man. While he was sick with pain he was also compassionate. He knew what he must do, what he had known from the beginning. The Church, alone, understood the problem of evil.

He said, "Why do you hate Elizabeth? That young girl?"

Timothy's whole expression changed.

"Do you hate her because of her mother? Or her grandfather? Or are you only destructive?"

Their eyes held for a sudden long space. Then Timothy mounted his horse again. William waited. "You think I'm evil, don't you?" Timothy said. "You were coming to this question when you expounded your idea of what you consider evil."

"Don't try to read my mind, please," said William. "I have asked you the first questions."

"I couldn't explain," said Timothy, "for the simple reason that you would not understand."

"That's the answer of a man who has no defensible grounds, Timothy."

"Yes. I have. I hated her grandfather for reasons you ought to know. I hate her mother; that is a different question and has different reasons. Her father was a clod. Don't speak to me of her Esmond blood! There's very little of that in her. Her whole character——"

"A young woman's character," said William.

Timothy moved in his saddle and looked again at his brother, and he was pale and serious. But before he could speak William spoke. "Are you one to talk of 'character'? Are you capable of doing so?" His face had flushed, and his pain was on him again.

"Let me say this," said Timothy. "I have a daughter, Amy, and I believe I love her, though you would say I'm not capable of love. But I'd rather see her dead than married to one of Caroline's sons. I'd go to any lengths to prevent such a marriage. Any." He paused. "Do you understand now?"

"Yes. I think I do."

William looked for the last time at the peaceful country. He took up his reins. "I believe we understand each other," he said. "Shall we go back?" He touched his crop to his horse and she spurted away, leaving Timothy alone.

William found Elizabeth where he knew she would be, in a quiet and hidden part of the garden where they had met yesterday. She was sitting on a wicker seat in her long white Swiss dress; a blue sash was crumpled high under her breasts. When she saw William her face became subtly charged with joy and love and innocence. She moved a little, and her hair was illuminated by the early morning sun.

William came to her and took her hands and held them tightly, standing before her. He prayed that he would speak well and that this girl, younger in many ways than her actual years, would not be hurt too bitterly. She looked up at him, smiling eagerly and hopefully, and she was like a child. Dear God, he said inwardly, help me. Elizabeth, waiting, saw his expression, and her hands tightened on his.

"What is it? Oh, what is it?" she asked, and her voice became curiously shrill, compressed with fear. "William! Is there something wrong?" The gripping hands became perceptibly cold in his.

He looked down at her hands, feeling the sudden stiffness of the delicate bones. He said, "My darling, try to understand. It's impossible for me to marry you. Impossible."

What ugly, abrupt words, he thought in his misery. He made himself meet her eyes now; hers had turned wide and still.

"What did you say?" she muttered, and moved her head as if it had begun to ache. She glanced away from him. It really is quite a chilly morning, she thought. She said in that muttering tone, "It was when I was sixteen. I wanted all the money so you would marry me." She paused. Then she cried, "What did you say!"

Her face was stark; it had an expression as if she had been struck violently, and her cheekbones, shining whitely, stood out below her eyes. "What did you say!" she cried more loudly.

"Elizabeth," he said with alarm and pain. "Didn't you hear me? We can't be married. You would be hurt all the rest of your life; you'd come to hate me. We aren't alone, my darling. There are others who would be affected."

Very slowly she looked away from him and stared at the garden, moving her eyes from right to left. "I don't understand," she said indifferently, as if he had told her something incomprehensible in which she was not the least interested.

"You must trust me," he said, holding her hands firmly and trying to get her wandering attention. She had now the appearance of one in extreme shock. "There are many things you don't know, and I am not the one to tell you. Elizabeth, you must trust me."

She smiled a little. Her eyes still moved over the garden. "It was at Christmas, the first time I saw you," she said, and her voice was the voice of a child. "There was a stupid Christmas play. I was a boarder at Miss Stockington's, and so I couldn't pretend to be sick and not attend. Mimi and Amy, those silly children, were dressed like angels, and they prattled in foolish voices. I was sitting next to you. I hated all those children, the ridiculous teachers, the babbling and the carols. But when I sat there, and your shoulder was against mine, and you were smiling at the stage, it all didn't matter. I think I was about twelve. They say a girl that age can't love, but I did."

She smiled up at him with sudden brightness. "You were about fifteen or sixteen, weren't you, William? I've wanted to tell you about this before, so we could laugh together. You weren't the handsomest boy in the world; I think you were a little fat and short then. But there was something about you—something I'd never known before, and that's why I loved you. Something—good. And I never forgot you." She seemed proud and delighted.

What is wrong with the poor girl? William asked himself, deeply shaken. Her eyes were like brilliant glass. "Oh, Elizabeth," he said. He sat down beside her on the bench and bent his head in his grief and consternation. She moved closer to him; her head touched his shoulder.

"It's impossible," he said quietly. "Believe me, my darling, it's impossible."

"I had to get the money, for you," she said in a soft voice. "I see now how ridiculous that was, but it seemed very important when I was sixteen. I had, you see—I thought—to have the money so you'd marry me. I thought that was the most important thing. Who would marry Elizabeth Sheldon unless she had a great deal of money, a fortune? Who would want a girl who had a mother like mine unless she had money? So I put all my mind to it; I even tried to stop thinking of you too much, so I wouldn't be diverted. I didn't know then, William, that you could love me, just for myself, as you've said."

She stopped abruptly, then cried out wildly, "What did you say?"

She lifted her head from his shoulder. Her face had become sharp and long, almost fierce, angular in its profound terror.

"I said we can't be married," said William. "Elizabeth, try to understand. We'd injure—too many others—if we married. We must think of them too." He put his hand on her arm. Her flesh was as cold as stone.

"I'd rather be dead now than to be sitting here and telling you all this. I love you dearly; you'll never know how much, Elizabeth." His round face expressed his sober anguish. He saw she was really listening at last, bending a little toward him, as if she were confused or somewhat deaf, and trying to understand. Her nose had a blue, pinched look, and her mouth was utterly white.

"Did you say we couldn't be married?" she said, stammering a little. "What other people would be hurt? Did you say that?" she added insistently.

"Yes."

"Why should they be?" she asked anxiously. "And even if it's so, what does it matter?"

He knew there was something wrong; he guessed it from her expression, her stiff posture, the color of her lips, the petrified stillness of her eyes.

"We must think of others," he said, feeling sick and empty.

"But why?" the insistent voice demanded. "No one ever thought of me. Nobody cares about anyone else, do they? Not when they're going to be married? William?"

She was pleading for understanding, for explanation.

"I care for others," he said. And then, because he was to be a priest, he added, "And I'm sure you also care, very much. You wouldn't want to hurt those who've never harmed you. That is only human, Elizabeth."

He saw that he had not reached her at all. She was white with frozen bewilderment.

"You don't love me!" she exclaimed. "You think my mother will cut me off if I marry you! I thought you didn't care—I thought you loved me."

"I do, before God, darling, I do. Do you think this is easy for me?" He was too young to understand what he had heard from Elizabeth; he had missed all the implications in what she had said. "Your mother's money has nothing to do with it, I swear to you."

She was all tenseness, searching his face with her eyes.

"She cut off John and Ames in a spendthrift clause; they'll only get five thousand dollars a year. I'll have all the rest," she pleaded. "All the rest. What else could she do with it but leave it to me? And she's old. She loves me, too, though you would not believe that, would you? I'll have it, William, really I will."

Now she clutched his arm in both her hands and shook him a little and smiled at him, like a despairing penitent, and he was brokenhearted.

"Oh, my God!" he said. "Oh, Elizabeth."

"Don't you believe me?" she urged. "I love you, William. I never loved anyone before. I'll give you the money when I get it. I'll sign papers or something. Don't you believe me?"

He could not answer in his suffering. Then her eyes left him again, though she continued to clutch his arm painfully. She looked at the gardens. They were green and shimmering with light. But it was so cold, so deadly cold, she thought. The sunlight became a sick dazzle to her, and the trees stood as if they were tormented and crying for help.

"I only wanted the money for you," she said. "I wanted to have it. I wanted to be proud and show it to you. All that money! You don't want to let it go, do you?"

"I want you, Elizabeth," he said, and he felt the smart of tears in his eyes. "I'll never really love anyone but you. But there are the others."

He put his arms about her. It was like grasping marble, she was so stiff and taut. Then she was shivering. She shook her head slowly, over and over. "I ought to have known," she muttered. "Who would want me, after all?" Then she cried out in a penetrating voice, as if she were being torn and mangled.

"All those people in London! I didn't know—I sat and listened, and then all at once it was like—like being caught in something terrible. But if you want me to——"

He was more frightened than he had ever been in his life. For a cringing moment he regretted that he had not let his mother speak to Elizabeth, to explain, to tell her. But he had wanted to shield his mother from degradation, for she would have told the girl in her extremity.

She was watching him; he could feel the probing of her eyes. He said, "Can't I make you understand, Elizabeth? It has nothing to do with you and me. But—well, someone will hurt others if we are married. You, too, would be hurt more than anyone else."

She put her hands in her lap and, biting her lower lip in concentration, she began to make pleats in the dotted Swiss of her frock. Her head moved slowly from side to side in denial. Her profile had a tremulous appearance to it, as if she were extremely sick.

"Can't you trust me, Elizabeth?" asked William. "Trust me to know what is best for you, for others?"

"Oh no," she said with the utmost simplicity. "I don't believe a word of it. I never was your darling, was I? You never really wanted me, did you? You are really mistaken about me, William. I am Elizabeth Josephine Sheldon and I will be one of the richest women in the world. It's just that you can't believe it."

Now she lifted her head, and her face had a regal look. "I'm not like my mother. She killed my father, you know. She didn't care about him. I'm not like her. I love you. You must believe it."

"I do," he said miserably.

She stood up. She began to blink her eyes rapidly, as if clearing them. She looked down at him. She had changed again, become gaunt, and there were gray shadows under her cheekbones.

"I've just thought of something," she said. "It's Timothy, isn't it? He did this, didn't he? It was Timothy!" The wandering look, the inattention had left her. She bent a little to the young man. "Answer me! It was Timothy! He lied to you, lied, lied!"

"Hush, Elizabeth," he pleaded, "someone will hear you."

She began to laugh, a loud, abrupt laugh which she couldn't control. She put her hands over her mouth and struggled to stop the laughter. Then, as suddenly as she had laughed, she was silent and was staring down at him, not with love, but with hatred.

"You could believe him! You could humiliate me like this because of what Timothy said. No, don't stand up. Don't touch me. I hate you. And Timothy—he'll suffer for this."

Her words were full of ferocity; there was no sensation in her at all except hatred. She smoothed her frock and lifted her head. For the last time she looked at the gardens, slowly, carefully.

"You made no promises, I remember that," she said in a voice that was totally mechanical. "That should console you, shouldn't it? You've decided against marrying me because of Timothy and something he has told you. You are a coward, aren't you? But the English are all family, aren't they? I am only Elizabeth Sheldon, and I may not have any money, and what am I to you?"

She turned so swiftly that her frock swirled, and then she was running from him, away from everything that had meant life to her. William could only let her go. He sat on the bench long after she had gone and he prayed for her, and though he tried to suppress it he was wild with the first fury he had ever experienced. Finally, as he was intrinsically very sensible, he told himself that Elizabeth would forget. She was beautiful and rich, and someday he would not even be a memory to her except a vague mortification.

The family was in the dining room when Elizabeth entered the house, and she could hear them laughing and talking, and the clatter of breakfast dishes and silver. She had eaten nothing as yet. She went upstairs and packed her bags methodically and swiftly. She was not thinking any deeper than her decision to leave this house at once. She knew that there was a train for London leaving within the hour. She put on the linen suit she had worn on her journey here, smoothed her hair calmly, placed her hat on her head, and caught up her gloves. She was ready. Then she rang the bell for a servant.

"Please ask Mr. Winslow if he will come up to see me for a moment," she told the maid. She smoothed the gloves on her hands and waited. Timothy came immediately. She turned her quiet face toward him, and he saw no expression at all in her eyes.

"I am leaving," she said. "I have asked for a carriage. I don't want to say good-by to your mother or Amanda. Or anyone." She paused. "Have you anything to tell me, Timothy?"

"Nothing," he said. They looked at each other.

"I think you have," she said, and waited again.

Now he felt exultation. "It's possible you are right," he said. He made his face serious and concerned. "I think I know what's behind your decision to leave like this. And I think you should know why it happened. Your mother."

"My mother?" She repeated the words in a voice without intonation.

"Rather, all that your mother is, Elizabeth."

She believed him, as she had not believed William, for he spoke in words that she could understand and that were in her nature.

"Are you responsible for telling—anyone—about my mother's peculiarities, Timothy?"

"No. Nor my mother, either, nor Amanda. Elizabeth, what your mother is, is common knowledge. And what your grandfather was. Such people are not accepted among the British. I'm sorry. But you wanted to know the truth, didn't you?"

A manservant came for Elizabeth's bags, and the girl waited until he had gone before she spoke again. "Yes, I wanted the truth. My grandfather was a nobody and an adventurer, and my mother is a miser and perhaps worse. I've heard people say that she is mad." Elizabeth was very calm. Then she smiled slightly. "But she does have such a lot of money."

She regarded Timothy with curiosity. "You're ready for the break with my mother, aren't you? You'd not have told me all this if you weren't. By the way, it would be dangerous for you—for me—if you told her I had come here. You understand that?"

Timothy hated her now. He was not capable of seeing a tortured young girl who was suffering beyond any suffering he could imagine.

"'Break'? What do you mean? You asked me to tell you what I've told you; I didn't volunteer it, you'll remember. What my own opinion of your mother is, is my affair. I merely informed you of British opinion and what it would mean to—a man—who would marry a woman with a grandfather like John Ames and a mother like Caroline Sheldon. You practically forced me to tell you. When you first asked I told you I had nothing to say. Please remember that."

"I will," said Elizabeth. "I'll remember everything. You'll also have something to remember, later." She picked up her purse and passed him without another glance and went quietly down the stairway.

CHAPTER FIVE

John Sheldon visited his mother a few times a year, not out of affection, but to exhibit his well-being and success to her. To others, his own fortune and business would have seemed picayune compared with his mother's enormous estate and holdings, but he knew that to Caroline no money or fortune was small and that one dollar to her was as precious as a million. Moreover, as he was a naturally optimistic person, unlike his brother Ames, he was somewhat convinced that when his mother saw that he was really a "responsible" man she would come to change her will or at least modify it. He had increased his inheritance from his father with some wild but lucky investments. If nothing else, his mother was keenly interested in the market, and she would listen to the stock quotations as some women listen to sonnets.

"We shouldn't let everything go by default to that scheming sister of ours," John would say to Ames when he came up to Boston from New York.

"You haven't any proof that she's not the victim of a 'spendthrift' clause too," said Ames. "You know how suspicious Ma is; she's also convinced she's going to live forever."

While in Boston, John stayed with Ames. The two brothers were not natively congenial, but they had been almost exclusively thrown together as companions in early childhood and they had much in common, such as their hopes of inheriting a large part of their mother's money.

John knew that his sister was abroad, and so she would not be there with her icy and sneering face when he visited his mother today. When he arrived at the station he was pleased with the coolness that greeted him; Boston was usually a sweat box in the summer. He hired a hack and drove to his mother's house. Each time he arrived he thought that it appeared more abandoned and decrepit than ever, though it was little more than a quarter of a century old. Shingles curled and fell and were never replaced; the woodwork about the stone windows had not been painted in years; the doors were beginning to take on the ancient silvery appearance of neglected wood. The glass was filthy everywhere, the walks neglected, the grimy draperies like coarse ropes, the gardens overgrown and forgotten, so that the once beautiful grounds had reverted to wilderness. The whole scene had a wild and desolate air; mortar and fragments from the stone and brick littered the three walks that led to the house, and there was an immense silence about all things except for the silken hiss of the summer sea.

John rang the bell and heard it echoing through the house. He waited. He rang again. There was no answer. What the hell! Didn't the old lady keep a maid any longer? Where was she, herself? He tried the door facing landward, and it was locked firmly. He went to the side and found it ajar, so he entered. The musty smell of a closed house was all about him, and the acrid stench of dust and grease and neglect. He went through the rooms, calling for his mother, half hoping that he would find her dead in her bedroom. He was a lawyer; there were ways of getting around a will. "Nuisance" suits. But his mother was not in the house.

If she had been in the village he would have been told. However, she was never seen in the village any longer, though he had heard rumors that she haunted the graveyard on the hill, where both cemetery and church had been abandoned three years ago.

He looked in the kitchen, and the smells revolted him, and the heaps of unwashed dishes and the bulks of newspapers and financial journals piled against the walls. The wooden floor was dark with spilled oil. A skillet filled with half-melted fat stood on the black stove. The bedroom, untouched and the bed unmade, and these other evidences of recent occupancy told him that his mother was still alive. He grunted. But where the hell was she, the recluse who never left her house, who had not been seen in the village lately, who no longer went in to Boston to her office? The kitchen windows facing the sea were open, and John went to them and looked at the long mass of boulders which had once been the sea walk.

He heard voices now, for the first time, clear in the fetid silence. Both voices were familiar. One was his mother's and the other his pretty little Mimi's, whom he intended to marry when she was eighteen. He could not believe it. Carefully concealing himself at the side of the window, he bent his head and listened intently.

Caroline was absorbed in what Mimi was doing. They were sitting on low boulders, and Mimi was painting a shattered heap of them against the hot blue sky.

"The girl—the child—on them won't come true," Mimi was saying in a dissatisfied voice.

"No," Caroline reflected in her rusty voice. "She looks too expectant, doesn't she? But she should never have been expectant; there was nothing to expect."

There was a silence, increased by the sound of the sea. Then Caroline said, "Give me the brush, Mary. I'll darken the side of her face just a little. Umber, perhaps, mixed with a touch of black." Another silence, then a cry of delight from Mimi.

"Aunt Caroline! That's just what was needed! What a wonderful feeling you have!"

Good God, what is this? thought John, dumfounded.

"You are a better artist than I!" cried Mimi.

"Nonsense," Caroline grunted. But it was evident that she was excited. "I never learned to paint anything but dreary little water colors at Miss Stockington's. I'm glad you took up oils, Mary. They have much more depth."

"And much easier," said Mimi. "It was you, Aunt Caroline, who taught me how to use oils, even though you never worked in them yourself. What do you think? Should I brighten that red ribbon in the girl's hair? In spite of the sky, it all looks so somber."

There was silent consultation. Then Caroline said heavily, "Yes. It must be scarlet. It should imply hope, even though there was never any hope."

John leaned against the side of the window, incredulous. His mother—and Mimi. It wasn't possible. Then he began to smile with delight. How in the devil had these two come together—his mother, who hated everybody and never saw anyone except on business, and whose conversation was confined to her financial affairs; and bright little Mimi, who loved all things and whose hope was as ardent as sunlight on a butterfly's wings? The little imp! Why hadn't she told him of this in her letters?

The voices came closer. He peered around the window frame. His mother was standing against the sky in her stained black, as tall and massive as ever, and as formidable, her gray braids like a silvery crown on her head. But her dark face was flushed by sun and wind, and she was smiling. John had not seen her smile in many years. Her hand was timidly on Mimi's arm, and then it rose to smooth the girl's blown hair, and it lingered.

"I'll miss you, Mary," Caroline said.

"I'll miss you too, Aunt Caroline," said the girl, and she bend forward and kissed Caroline's cheek. Caroline stood rigid. When the girl shyly withdrew, Caroline put her hand to the kissed cheek, as if to hold something there.

"But you can't miss the opportunity to go to Paris for a few weeks to study painting and art," said Caroline with sudden firmness.

"If I do well, Mama has promised me I can stay for a year! Isn't that marvelous?" The girl laughed with joy. Her pink dress whipped away from her ankles in the sea wind, and then her whole body was outlined, free and airy and alive.

"A whole year," said Caroline. "Yes, you will be away a whole year."

John already knew of this plan, for Mimi had written him. This was one of the reasons he had come to Boston, to say good-by to Mimi and to laugh at her indulgently. He was much more interested now in his mother's expression of sorrow and loss, the sudden sagging of her heavy body. Then Caroline said briskly, "This is a wonderful opportunity. There has been no female artist of consequence before or since Rosa Bonheur. Why? Art is sexless, and so is pure intelligence. What has kept women from the sciences and the arts? Children? But I have children and they never stood in my way. Women must advance a better explanation of their failures as artists than children." Then she softened. "You are a naturally great artist, Mary; you can be as great as David Ames, for you have his style and power and eye for color and vitality. You must never let it go."

"Never," said the young Mimi.

Caroline looked at her long and silently, and she saw what she herself might have been. Then she said abruptly and with pain, "Good-by, Mary. Remember, you've promised to write to me."

"I'll write all the time!" cried Mary. "And don't worry about me. Mama's friend, Mrs. Wentworth, will take good care of me while Angela is at the

Sorbonne. But I'm afraid I'm not really so very good; I may be back within a few weeks after all."

"No," said Caroline, "you will not be back. They'll be astonished at you." Then she said again, with more abruptness, as if she could not linger with pain of parting, "Good-by, Mary."

She took a few steps toward the house, and Mimi was alone, lovely and alive against the blue shadow of the sea, watching her aunt with yearning and wonder. All at once she ran after Caroline, holding out the small canvas in her hands. "Aunt Caroline! I know this isn't very good, but do you want it? Will you take it? I'd like to know you have it!"

Caroline took the canvas and looked down at it. "You are giving it to me, Mary?"

"Yes," said the girl eagerly. "In some way it reminds me of you."

Caroline nodded, then turned away again and laboriously moved among the boulders toward the house, and Mimi watched her go. Caroline did not take her eyes from the painting. Once or twice she stumbled.

She mustn't find me here right now, thought John, and he rushed through the kitchen and let himself silently out through the side door. He hurried toward the public road beyond the house. He was a burly and strong young man, but by the time he reached the road his heart was racing and he was exultant. He hid behind a clump of pines and waited ten minutes by his watch. Then he went back to the house and vigorously rang the bell, as if he had just arrived.

It took his mother a long time to come to the door. First there were two shootings of bolts, then the rattle of a chain, a cautious wait. Then the door opened a crack. "Oh," said Caroline surlily, "it's you. I wasn't expecting you until tomorrow."

"I came a day earlier, Ma," said John easily. "Well, aren't you going to let me in?" There was a furtive and hesitant air about his mother. She opened the door, let him in, then walked away toward the dusty living room, and he tossed his hat, whistling, onto the gritty hall table and followed her. She was already sitting stiffly in a straight chair when John entered. He remembered this room as a child, sunlit and pleasant. Though the sun was still high outside and the sea bright, the room was cold, musty, and dark. No wonder, with those dirty windows and the shutters half over them, thought John with new disgust.

"Are you staying overnight?" asked Caroline sullenly. "I may as well tell you. I let the girl go when Elizabeth went to Europe with Timothy and his family. A worthless slut. So if you stay you can't expect any waiting on."

"You are doing everything yourself? And staying here all by yourself?"

"Yes. I have good doors. And bolts." She smiled grimly.

"But there are the windows," said John. "It's dangerous. You know what rumor is. Someone may get the notion that you keep a pile of gold in here."

"I also have a gun," said Caroline with a still grimmer smile. "And I know how to use it. You might let a rumor of it around in Lyme."

"You need a big dog," said John.

"No."

"Well, for God's sake, get another maid! You can't live in a rubbish heap like this!"

"My wants are few," said Caroline. "Groceries are delivered to me twice a week from the village. I use only my study, the kitchen, and the bedroom, and I'm not helpless, even at past fifty. If you think this is a rubbish heap you don't have to stay, you know."

"I intend to stay overnight," said John. He looked at her curiously. "Don't you ever need to speak to anyone?"

"No."

"You haven't seen anyone to speak to since Elizabeth left?"

"I talk with New York every day, and Boston. That's enough."

So the old lady was keeping her association with Mimi to herself.

"I'm having some stew for dinner," said Caroline. "I also have some fresh bread and milk and tea and a tin of pears. That's what you'll eat if you stay."

"You don't want me to stay?"

"Please yourself." She shrugged. Then her face changed darkly. "I know you visit that Bothwell woman before you come here. I don't like it."

"You never did," said John easily, but watching her. "I've even lost my curiosity."

"Don't go there any more," said Caroline shortly. She paused, "Or at least not this time."

John pondered this remark.

"What's the inducement?" he asked lightly.

"Inducement?"

"Never mind. I do intend to go there, however."

"Why?" She was sitting up and staring hard at him.

"I like Aunt Melinda," he said. "And I hear that kid Mimi is going abroad in a few days and I want to say good-by to her."

"Stay away from her!" exclaimed Caroline almost fiercely.

John pretended astonishment. "Why should I? That child? What does it matter? What do you know about Mimi, anyway? You've never even seen her."

"I don't want to," said Caroline. "I don't want you to either."

"That's unreasonable," said John. "My father liked the whole family. I like them too. I particularly like Nat, Mimi's twin brother. A fine boy."

"He can't be, if you like him," said Caroline with harsh rudeness.

"Thank you," said John. "Oh, come. I'm really a remarkable young man. I came to tell you the good news. I've had an increase in salary. Moreover, when I'm twenty-five I'm going to be a full partner in your dear old law concern."

Caroline was interested in spite of herself. But she scowled.

"Moreover, again, I've just made five thousand dollars in a very keen investment," said John. "Nothing you would touch. A new small concern making small arms. The stock was sold for ninety cents. It went up to two dollars in less than two weeks."

"Why?" Now Caroline did not hide her interest.

"I don't know. I sold out. At two dollars. Then a few days later it went down to one-fifty and I bought in again. Ten thousand shares. There's a dividend, too, a juicy one, in December."

He leaned back in his chair, enjoying this. "It went up to three-ten yesterday. Possibly because of the rumor that Bouchard is trying to buy them out."

Now Caroline was intensely interested. "They're the biggest munitions concern in the world, almost as large as Kronk in Germany. Why are the munitions stocks going up?"

"I don't know. Maybe we're going to try some new forays in Mexico."

Caroline shook her head. "No. It can't be that. I've never seen so much activity in munitions stocks and subsidiary concerns. Not even during the Spanish-American War. What's the name of your little company?"

"Enright Arms. They have a patent for an automatic pistol. Bouchard is definitely interested. If Bouchard buys, my stock will be worth a fortune, for Enright will sell out only to Bouchard." He scrutinized his mother. "You don't buy what you call fly-by-night stocks. But I definitely suggest you buy Enright. There's some stock still on the market; some people are buying like mad."

Caroline thought. Then she stood up and left the room without a word, and John heard her mounting up to her study, and he ran to the bottom of the stairs and listened. She was telephoning New York. He nodded happily. If the rumor got out that the old lady was buying all the available stock of Enright there would be a boom, indeed, and Bouchard would pay more. And the dividends would be much, much juicier. He went back to his chair. In a few minutes Caroline returned.

"I forgot," said John. "While I was waiting in the depot the stationmaster came out and said there was a cable for you from England. Probably Elizabeth. Here it is."

He gave her the yellow envelope, and she opened it abstractedly. Then she uttered an exclamation. "Elizabeth's on the way home! She'll arrive in seven days. I thought she was going to stay with Timothy for the rest of the time—four weeks."

"Is she sick?" asked John with hope.

"No. She says she's decided to come home. Why, I wonder? She was so anxious to go. She has something to tell me, she says."

"Maybe she's fallen in love with some blooming Englishman," said John.

"Nonsense. She's too sensible. She knows I need her here." Caroline frowned, looking at the cable.

Then Caroline said, as if speaking to herself, "It must be very important. Elizabeth has been visiting my English associates."

Without warning, Caroline suddenly remembered the night of her father's death. She could see the room in Switzerland; she could see all those faces, many of them dead now. She could hear the voices and what they said.

"What's the matter?" said John.

"Nothing." But Caroline felt both sick and excited. The girl she had been struggled with the woman she was now. The woman won, as usual. She looked at John. "If I were you I wouldn't speculate with the Enright stock. I'd hold it, not sell it for a quick profit."

"I'll hold it," said John.

John visited the Bothwells the next day. Mimi said never a word about his mother. He probed lightly, speaking of Caroline, but though Mimi flushed uneasily she was silent. Melinda, as usual, asked kindly about his mother, and he said, "She seems younger, somehow, and more alive. As if she had a new interest or something."

Mimi glanced at her mother unhappily.

"I'm very glad to hear that," said Melinda gently. "Poor Caroline, I wonder what interest it is. She never goes out."

John was more in love with young Mimi than ever. He had loved her for herself and had always intended to marry her. But now there was his mother's interest in this girl. He kissed Mimi for the very first time that night when they were alone, and when she clung to him he was not only excited and happy, but exultant.

"Don't stay away too long from me, dear," he said.

"Not too long," she said in return, and lifted her young face to his again. Aunt Caroline was wrong about John. He was the dearest thing in the world to her now, dearer even than her mother or her twin brother.

CHAPTER SIX

It was not possible for Caroline to know that she loved Mary Bothwell with an absolutely unflawed devotion. For her father she had had fear and shyness and uncertainty, mixed with her headlong love—and he had never treated her with overt affection. To Beth she had been "that poor child," and Beth had hated John Ames and had been a woman incapable of understanding that Caroline Ames, the woman, was not Carrie Ames, the child. Tom Sheldon, too, had seen Caroline as he wished to see her. He had obstinately insisted on his own conception, and when it failed to materialize he was alienated and wounded, feeling himself cast out and rejected. No one had accepted her for what she was.

Caroline's children were her tragedy, and the tragedy was no less terrible because she was the author of their indifference, their exigency, and their greed. She did not honestly believe that Elizabeth loved her; that first illusion had withered several years ago. Caroline had too penetrating an eye to be deceived by her daughter, though she clung to Elizabeth out of her desperate need for love, given or received.

But Mimi Bothwell loved her, did not find her peculiar, had no interest in her money, did not doubt or shrink from her, and accepted her with an ardent devotion. The affection between them was maternal and filial, sisterly, childlike, accepting, purely unselfish, and illuminated with their mutual passion for color and light. There was no demand between them, no false images, no distortions, no self-serving, no fear. For the first time in her life Caroline felt a love that was utterly free and unhampered and without awkwardness. When Mimi had told her that she was to leave for Paris almost immediately, Caroline was dismayed and sad, but at once she knew this was the best for the girl and had put aside her own dread of approaching loneliness and loss.

So deep was Caroline's love for the girl that she could feel something stir in herself at the thought of the girl's going abroad and studying, and she did not know that this was pleasure and a kind of youthful anticipation. The projection of herself into the future of Mimi brought her a sense of well-being and hope, things she had never known since childhood. So when Elizabeth arrived home she was momentarily astonished at the color in her mother's face, the confident ring in her voice, and the peculiar if abstracted gentleness. Elizabeth thought it was because she had returned. If the old hateful fool was really so dependent on her, so much the better. Now.

Caroline, Elizabeth now fully believed, was the cause of her rejection by William, and she had spent the days on the ship in fits of incoherent vengefulness. Her mother would pay for what she had done to her daughter, though how this would be accomplished Elizabeth had only a few vague ideas at the best. But two of them were Ames and Amy Winslow, and not only would Elizabeth be revenged on her mother through them, but she would be revenged on Timothy also.

She had overheard Timothy say to Amanda, "Thank God Amy never speaks of Ames Sheldon any longer since we came here. She's gotten over that foolishness." Elizabeth had been startled at this piece of news; she had not known that her secretive brother Ames and Amy, his cousin, had anything in common or even saw each other often. She had filed this news in her mind.

Caroline was so contented because of Mimi that she did not immediately notice Elizabeth's increased thinness, which had become almost emaciation, and the sharp brittleness in her young voice. There was a new maid in the house, who had attacked the hopeless grime of the years hopefully and then had given up. But she could cook to Caroline's austere taste and with frugality, and that was sufficient. The only room in the house which the maid had been able to clean well was Elizabeth's, for it had not been dirty at any time.

Elizabeth neatly unpacked in her room. When she came on the fine dresses she had bought with William in mind, she suddenly, and for the first time, broke down. She clung to them and wept silently. She no longer hated William for her humiliation and frightful suffering. She sat on her hard white bed and cradled the dresses in her arms as a mother cradles a child. One of the dresses still held a white rose he had plucked for her and pinned on her shoulder. It was dry and crushed now and fell into fragments in her hand. She held them to her lips. She put them in a small box, then returned to cradling the dresses, pressing them to her breast. Her grief was more than she could endure. There was a blue ribbon at the sleeve of the white Swiss dress; it had loosened one night, and William had gently tied it, then kissed it. She kissed it now, and the tears ran down her cheeks. The dresses crackled in her arms; she smoothed their folds with a gentle hand as a mother soothes a complaining child.

She had never loved before, and the emotion devastated her, exploded with agony in her. She had no philosophy for it, no strength or experience to bring to it. She would never be rid of the pain. All at once a convulsion stunned the side of her head and pulsed there like fire, and she put a hand to it. It took some time to subside, and when it did her flesh was prickled over with shivering moisture and she was dizzy and sick. She forced herself to put the dresses between sheets of tissue paper, then was struck by some strangeness. She looked about the room. Nothing was changed; the sunlight, reflecting from the sea, filled the room, glanced off the white walls. Yet something had changed, a faint distortion, perhaps, a shortening or lengthening of perspective, an ominous quality to the sun's light. A slight glaze appeared to have settled on the few pieces of furniture, and there was a sensation in her as though she looked at everything through a sheet of glass which stood between herself and the world. But now her grief was more diffused, more bearable.

She noticed that the gritty stairs appeared elongated as she went down them. Do I need spectacles? she thought, and then the thought was gone. She was conscious that she had a new strength and a new hardening. She had not slept all the way across the ocean; it was possible that sleeplessness was giving her a kind of hallucination. But she would sleep tonight. She had so much to do.

Tea had never been served in this house since Beth's death, and Elizabeth was coldly amused to find that her mother had prepared tea for them in the dank and moldering living room. The cups and saucers were of the original fine set Tom had bought, glowing Sèvres porcelain. They were all chipped, and there were stains in the larger crevices. Fresh from the fine mansion in Devon, Elizabeth looked at them with distaste, then she thought: Nothing matters. Only money. Only what money can do for you. Why waste it on trivialities? She sat down opposite Caroline, who, as always, was shy and uncertain even if massive and monumental. "There're cakes too," Caroline mumbled, pointing to a silver plate, very tarnished, on which stood some "store" cookies hard with sprinkled sugar.

"Can't Jenny bake?" said Elizabeth, pushing one away with the tip of a finger.

"She has a lot to do. Not only the house, but the laundry. There's no time for baking," said Caroline. She had never been able to look fully at anyone for long, not even her husband after the first year of their marriage. She peered under her thick black eyelashes at her daughter. Then she was apprehensive. What had happened to Elizabeth, sitting so rigidly opposite her, her blue eyes a little glassy and fixed, her body, in its white duck skirt and shirtwaist, so thin?

"What's wrong?" she asked bluntly as she poured tea for Elizabeth from

393

a silver pot so tarnished that it was black along the handle and spout and yellowish all over. "Europe didn't suit you?"

"Not particularly." The tea was weak and lukewarm and had a sickening taste to Elizabeth. She put down the cup. "But you're not interested in my travels, I'm sure."

"You haven't told me anything," said Caroline. She bit into a cookie with her strong white teeth and appeared to enjoy it. "Who did you see? What did they say? But first, why did you come back to America so soon? I thought you were going to stay another month."

"I changed my mind," said Elizabeth. The one sip of tea lingered with an odd taste on the back of her tongue, like some sweetened astringent.

"Why?"

"I was bored. You haven't any idea how boring Amanda and her children can be." Elizabeth laughed. Caroline quickened and glanced uneasily at her daughter. Elizabeth very seldom laughed, and even then it was more of a short light murmur. But now Elizabeth's laughter was loud and abrupt, without mirth, and it had a ring of uncontrol, as though she had been profoundly amused beyond her expectations. Caroline listened to the sound, and she felt a sensation as if a cold finger had been laid on the back of her broad thick neck. She, too, put down her cup, and she stared at her daughter. As abruptly as she had laughed, Elizabeth stopped and looked beyond her mother at the smeared windows and the bright shadow of the sun on them.

Even when she had believed Elizabeth understood her, even when she loved Elizabeth with the awful and helpless love she had felt for her father, Caroline had been diffident with the girl and oddly uneasy. Now she exclaimed with a dread that was without a name, "Elizabeth!"

The girl still looked at the windows, and Caroline could see the grayish shadow under the beautifully formed cheekbones, the colorless lips still half open after the last burst of laughter, the frozen blue eyes. It was the face of one in a trance, and Caroline half rose and cried again, "Elizabeth?"

"Very boring," said Elizabeth, as if she had not laughed at all and her mother had not spoken. "London, too, is dull; it was worse with my dear cousins. Amy is especially stupid." A flicker appeared in her eyes for an instant. "We toured constantly, except when I had to be away from them."

She took a cake and bit into it, then threw it from her. "Why, these are horrible! Sawdust and flour! How can you eat them?"

"You don't look well," Caroline said. "I thought Europe would do you good; it wasn't only a matter of business." Her throat had a weight in it.

"I am well enough," said Elizabeth. She looked at the windows again. It would be long dim twilight now in Devon. The family would be gathering for dinner. The scent of roses and the sea would be coming in the long french windows, and the firelight would be brightening the soft draperies. And beyond the window there were the dark gardens, the arbors, the hushed trees, voices coming across the grass, and joy in the windy air.

"I don't think you look well," Caroline persisted.

"There will be a war," said Elizabeth. "That is what they told me, and that is what I heard; there was a rumble about it in parliament."

Her voice had never been particularly resonant and had never had any sweetness or eloquent intonations except in England. Now it was a mechanical voice. It was also precise, controlled, and reasonable and revealed Elizabeth's great intelligence and awareness of what she was saying. If the eyes did not show any expression or the lips warm with any color, she appeared to have recovered from her trancelike condition.

This reassured Caroline. She listened, nodding occasionally.

"They talked of the Second Hague Peace Conference two years ago," said the girl, reporting steadily and with no inflection. "Your friends thought that was amusing; they also thought former President Roosevelt even more so for asking for the conference. But I don't think they were very much amused after all; there was too much venom in what they said about Mr. Roosevelt. They seemed to be afraid that he knew too much. They're much better pleased with our present President, Mr. Taft."

She ran a finger absently over the chipped handle of her rejected cup. "Mr. Taft, they thought, was a man without suspicions. They wondered why Mr. Roosevelt had had any. It was finally decided with well-bred British laughter that he was a dolt." She looked at her mother now, and Caroline had the impression that the girl really did not see her. "But of course Mr. Roosevelt isn't a dolt."

"When?" asked Caroline.

"When? Oh, the war. Soon, it is believed. I even heard the word 'inevitable.'" She smiled a little. "There was one old man, Mr. Purvey, who said he had known you when you were a girl, and he implied that you were much more 'conscious,' he said, of things than I am. They seemed to think I was a little young for consultations with them, and so I did not hear all that I should. Mr. Purvey merely sent you the message, to be prepared."

"Prepared?" Caroline pondered this. She remembered what her son had told her. She shifted her bulk on the frayed chair. "Yes, I see. Was it definitely decided it would be Germany?"

Elizabeth continued to speak. Not only did the English hate Germany for her "invasion" of British markets, they also hated America because of the passage of the Payne Tariff Bill. They also had contempt for America, especially since Mr. Roosevelt's "attempts" to get the red hat for Archbishop Ireland. They spoke of America's "racism" and said, "We can't afford that in the empire, you know." But it always came back to Mr. Roosevelt. One gentleman had remarked, "He's too previous. Or, rather, blundering. When we move, it will not be with his sort of 'public welfare.' It will have a design."

Caroline listened, and again she heard the voices in Switzerland so long ago. She shifted again on her chair and frowned. "A design," she repeated.

Then Elizabeth said, "I overheard—someone—call Timothy pusillanimous. And accuse him of wanting power."

The huge and terrible design was still shadowy, and it was even more shadowy to Elizabeth, who was merely reporting. It was not shadowy to Caroline. Little drops of sweat gathered on her dark forehead. Then she said, "Timothy? Pusillanimous? Wanting power? He has it, with his money."

"Apparently that isn't all he wants," said Elizabeth indifferently, "though I can't imagine what else it is."

"I can," said Caroline. She folded her big hands in her lap and looked down at them.

Elizabeth shrugged delicately. The furniture had not been polished in nearly a quarter of a century, but it all had a glassy surface to her vision. It hurt her eyes; she stood up suddenly and pulled the ragged draperies across the windows, and immediately the room was plunged into dusk and there was a smell of dust in the air. The girl sat down again. Caroline said, "Why did you do that?"

"The sun," said Elizabeth irritably. She was a pale blurred image in the darkened room. Caroline averted her head and thought again.

"Their recommendation," said Elizabeth, "is that you begin at once to invest heavily in Robson-Strong in England, Kronk in Germany, and the other munitions firms in Europe."

"And that is all they told you?"

"Yes." Caroline's associates had not found Elizabeth as alert and perceptive as Caroline had led them to believe in her letters. "Sad," they had murmured to each other later. "She has an intelligent look, but girls these days are not what their mothers were, particularly not what Caroline Ames is."

"I have some confidential reports for you," said Elizabeth. "They are sealed. I've put them on your study desk. Do you want to go up with me and look at them?"

"Not yet," said Caroline. The dusky room was full of ghosts. Shades were always pulled down firmly on the back of the house, which faced the distant public road. But on this side the windows were never covered. Caroline glanced at her daughter, and Elizabeth was no more substantial than the other silent ghosts here. Caroline was frightened, but she said, "Perhaps, as they are confidential, I'd better look at them alone."

"Please yourself," said Elizabeth. Then her eyes glowed in the semidarkness. "You'll have to do something about Timothy."

"Why?" asked Caroline, startled.

"He hates you," said the girl.

"That's nothing new," answered Caroline with a dark smile. "I've always known that. It doesn't matter."

"He's dangerous."

"I've never denied it." Caroline paused. She sat up straighter. "What is it, Elizabeth? Was he unpleasant to you?"

"No. Not at all. He was much pleasanter than Amanda and her children. Mother, he doesn't need you any longer. He'll try to injure you one of these days. Perhaps soon."

"How? I don't speculate wildly; I am safely invested in sound stocks.

There is nothing he can do against me. I have several times his money. Even more. He's not a fool; he knows there is no way."

"He'll find one." Now, for the first time, there was emotion in Elizabeth's voice; and, hearing it, Caroline was pleased and stirred. She believed her daughter was concerned for her. She reached out and awkwardly patted Elizabeth's stiff knee.

"Don't worry, child," she said. She regarded Elizabeth with diffident affection. "Have you been worried?"

"Yes," said the girl. "Mother, I hate him."

"So there was something," said Caroline slowly. "Why don't you tell me?"

"He despises you—me," said Elizabeth, and clenched her hands on her knee.

"Probably. Should that concern you?"

"I want you to—ruin—him, Mother."

There was silence in the room. Caroline's thick dark brows had drawn together. She had heard the high shrillness in her daughter's voice, the sudden gasping pause.

"I don't do things like that," said Caroline loudly. "What nonsense. 'Ruin' Timothy? Why? He's been of much help to me. We are quite friendly. Elizabeth! You aren't talking sanely."

Elizabeth did not answer. "How could I do such a thing even if I wanted to?" demanded Caroline, and again she was frightened.

"You can find a way." The girl spoke with a kind of dull and obstinate intensity. "You must."

Caroline nodded. She repeated, "There was something."

Again Elizabeth was silent. Caroline said, "If you won't tell me, I'll ask him."

Elizabeth said, "No. I tell you, there was nothing. I only think you should do to him what I honestly believe he will try to do to you."

"It must be very bad," said Caroline. She had not been so alerted and uneasy in years. "If you won't tell me, I am sure he won't." Then she was filled with outrage. What had Timothy done to this young girl, her daughter? If it had changed Elizabeth so drastically, then it must be very serious and unpardonable. She could not identify the sensation that rose violently in her now and made her teeth close together tightly. She thought of Timothy's mother and exclaimed, "That woman!"

"Who?" said Elizabeth.

"His mother! That old woman!"

"What has she to do with any of it?" asked Elizabeth, and she wet her dry lips. "I haven't seen her for years."

"She hates all of us! I know. She exploited my father, she made my childhood wretched, she laughed at us! She is an evil person. You refuse to admit that Timothy hurt you, but if he did, be sure his mother is behind it! Yes, be sure."

Elizabeth listened with fresh acuteness. Was it really possible that Cynthia had had something to do with this agony of hers? Elizabeth trembled,

397

and the stunning sensation in her head began again, but fiercer now, and her body collapsed weakly in the chair. The room swam, the walls tilted, and there was a sibilant rustling in the girl's ears.

"What is it?" cried Caroline, and she stood up quickly. "What's wrong?"

William, thought Elizabeth, and thought and hoped she was dying. She put her hands over her ears to deafen the shrill screaming in them. She rocked her head from side to side, trying to escape the torment and the noise. Something was pressing itself against her lips. She opened her eyes and dimly saw her mother and knew that a glass of water was in her mother's hand. She pushed it away.

"Oh," she murmured. "I don't want it. I just have a headache." She pulled herself up in her chair with a terrible effort. "Mother, I know you hate Aunt Cynthia and have reasons for it, but she never hurt me. I doubt she even remembers me."

"If Timothy has done something," said Caroline, "his mother is behind it." The water sloshed over her shaking hand.

"He's done nothing. I've tried to tell you. It's you I am afraid for," said Elizabeth. Like her grandfather, she had great powers of self-control. She brought them up now. She even smiled. She said, "Let us give a little thought to Timothy. Perhaps more than a little thought." She laughed that queer, mirthless laughter again, the senseless and echoing laughter, which ended as suddenly as it had started.

CHAPTER SEVEN

Nothing stirred, except on the surface, in the carefree world of the summer and autumn and early winter of 1909. Nothing stirred, except on the surface, in peaceful, jocular and buoyant America of 1910. Nothing, in fact, disturbed the millions of young men in America and Europe, the millions who were to die or to be made homeless or crippled or blind or desperate in only four short years. No one knew, except a few men everywhere, that the world was not only turning on its real axis but was preparing to turn implacably on an axis designed decades ago in a German city and, in turning, was to change forever the world of men, for greed and envy, for wars and death, for unending hatred and uneasiness, for violence and murder, for shattered cities and planned slavery, for fury and terror, for madness and agony.

Here and there some newspapers in America and in Europe caught stealthy whispers and reported them, but they were so vague, so "alarmist," so threatening to the nice and placid and expanding world of 1910, the brave and hopeful world of 1910, that they were laughed down.

Americans were more concerned with the danger of women's hatpins, long and sharp, in streetcars and in crowded places, than with faint murmurs in the press of some horror gathering. Women's skirts were scandalously revealing glimpses of ankles, and the churches were inflamed. Lillian Russell's hinted new amorous affairs delighted an innocently lecherous America. Jack Johnson, a Negro prize fighter, had won the world championship, and Americans seethed with a passionate desire for "A White Hope." "Suffragettes" were guilty of "outrageous conduct," according to indignant newspapers. Former President Roosevelt continued to delight his friends and enemies with his exploits. Leading journals of public opinion published solemn articles by distinguished physicians as to the effect women's corsets were having on future generations. Cries arose from clerics, duly published in the press, against Sunday baseball, and the controversy raged from coast to coast. An evangelist, a former baseball player, Billy Sunday, was just beginning to start his national "revival" meetings, and rumbles of his thunderous voice reached the farthest outposts and excited comment among a people who took their fundamentalist religion without question. Denunciations of moving pictures as "a prime force in the corruption of our youth" attracted audiences who were even more attracted to moving pictures. Elderly men and women, who were authorities on the subject, wrote to their senators and their pastors demanding that an amendment to the Constitution be passed prohibiting the sale and drinking of alcohol. Stories of foreign royalty, actresses and actors, murderers and impressive thieves were printed under portentous large headlines in the papers and could be certain of discussion among all classes of society. Condemnations of the wearing by women of false hair could excite conversation in the dullest of social gatherings. Mr. Taft sat stolidly in the White House and was somewhat ignored by the press, which preferred the antics of Mr. Roosevelt and his prophecies of vague doom, followed by ululations on the future of America. Chewing gum was blamed for the malaligned teeth of children.

The most trivial story, if headlined enough, was sufficient to alarm, delight, excite, enthuse, or terrify the innocent Americans of 1910, those ebullient, uninformed, childlike, unsophisticated, and rapidly walking people. Little foreign news appeared, except for implied scandals among royalty; Europe was light-years away, and England was not liked, and this dislike was vehemently reaffirmed every Fourth of July by speakers, after long and vociferous playing of brass bands in public parks, while children ran about among their elders waving small flags. The Revolution was reenacted over and over. When President Taft spoke of "dynamic humanitarianism" the majority of people vaguely connected this phrase with the recent visit of Booker T. Washington to the White House. Mr. Taft was accused of being pro-Negro, even by Republicans, and another controversy blew up on street corners and in the beery saloons. Aviation, of course, had no future. Airplanes were toys for those bent on suicide. But it was a mark of prestige to have an automobile, despite the fulminations of those who could not afford one.

The silly, happy, ingenuous, and eager world of America stood like an adolescent female Colossus on her continent and smiled and sang, became enraged over trifles and indignant over trivia, engrossed in petty scandals, and tossed her toys and smiled and smiled and smiled, and counted the golden coins in her pinafore pocket and jingled them joyously.

She was unaware of the convulsions beginning in the bowels of her kindergarten world, and the few who knew did not speak and did not sleep. While she sang the new ragtime, the men in New York, Washington, Paris, London, Berlin, St. Petersburg, Vienna, and Berne quietly exchanged cryptic messages, murmured to each other in passing, and prepared death for mankind and slavery and change and ruin—for their own profit and their own power. Among them was Timothy Winslow.

Elizabeth Sheldon dressed for her twice-weekly visit to her mother's office in Boston this blizzardly day in December 1910. All her clothing was now rigidly tailored and severe and, though expensive, gave no hint of money in a modern fashion that was all ruffles, long tight skirts, pleats and bows and ribbons. Even Caroline, amazingly, complained that Elizabeth's clothing was mannish, and this complaint was followed by a remark that as her daughter was approaching twenty-three a marriage should be considered.

"With whom?" Elizabeth would ask contemptuously.

"You meet worthwhile men in Boston," Caroline would then say.

"Where? In your board room?"

"You are still a member of the Assemblies," Caroline would offer.

Elizabeth would laugh that peculiar laugh of hers. "And where should I invite a young man who was interested? Here?" She would indicate the malodorous house in its increasing decay.

Caroline ignored this. "All men are interested in money," she said once. "You must consider heirs. I did."

Elizabeth had become silent. Then she had looked penetratingly at her mother and understood for the first time in her life. She and her brothers had been bred solely as heirs and not for love, not out of any longing of their mother's. She suddenly hated her mother more than ever before.

"Don't be surprised if I never marry," she said, and then regretted this. Caroline would not let her money come to a dead end in a spinster daughter who would have no other heirs but "spendthrift" brothers and their children. So she said immediately, "Give me time. I'm not as old as you were when you married." She smiled.

Her suit today was an old and bulky one of some dark tweed and with a mannish shirtwaist. The skirt swept her ankles in their buttoned boots. She put on a plain tweed topcoat, a felt hat, and then her gloves. She looked like a tall and rather emaciated seamstress or a schoolteacher or any other underpaid female. But she carried letters from her mother involving millions of dollars in her leather dispatch case. She looked at herself in the mirror and stared at her gaunt white image, her icy blue eyes, her pallid lips, and her straightly dressed light brown hair. The beautiful girl, charged with love and hope and innocence eighteen months ago, had existed only briefly.

Her mother was in her study. The morning newspaper was on a filthy littered table in the hall. Elizabeth picked it up and turned the pages list-lessly, for she had a little time until the station hack called for her. (There were no carriages or horses in the stable now.) Then her throat burned and her heart was struck.

"Mr. and Mrs. Timothy Andrew Winslow of Boston and New York an-nounce the marriage of their brother, William Lord Halnes, of London, Devon, Biarritz, and Nice, to Lady Rose Haven on December fifth, in London, at—"

Elizabeth carefully refolded the newspaper. Pages 10 and 12 had some-how gotten themselves intertwined with pages 22 and 23. "Really!" said Elizabeth, aloud. "People are so careless these days." She was extremely annoyed with the newspaper; she formulated a protest to the editor. "Dear Sir: One knows that in these days there is a very dowdy sense of responsi-bility . . . I discovered this morning . . ."

I discovered this morning. I discovered that I thought I had died but I was not quite dead after all. I discovered what pain is; I rediscovered what pain is. How can I live? I've waited. A footstep, a letter, a knock on the door? Really, I must have been mad.

Very priggishly she relaid the newspaper on the hall table and readjusted her hat. What cheap materials they made these days! This was felt, but it was weightless in her hands. Her body had a curiously flimsy sensation. She had only to lift her feet and she would float through the door. There. She had done it, without any motion at all. It was a matter of will power only. She began to laugh, and the gray snow-filled air rang with her laughter. She was so amused. People thought they needed to use muscles to open doors, to walk. It was the most foolish illusion. She bustled down the path, taking long wide steps, and floated into the hack. She was still laughing. When she could control herself she told the man, "The station, please. As usual." He was a tired man; he wondered why Miss Sheldon laughed so heartily in the back of his vehicle and why she doubled over in her ex-tremity of mirth. Finally he could not stand her laughter, and he huddled in his thick brown coat and was resentful. It was all right for the rich to laugh like that. What worries did they have, anyway? Here it was, close to Christmas, and all the things his wife expected of him for the children! When he was a boy a penny and a wizened orange was enough in a stock-ing. Now the kids wanted toys and candy and gum. It was all right for Miss Sheldon to laugh. She could go into any store and buy it out. He spat surlily. She was going to Boston to buy anything she wanted, for all her friends, and she wouldn't turn a hair at the price.

Dear God, said Elizabeth's spirit, and she had to press her gloved hands against her mouth to stop her laughter. Dear God. It was so very funny. She said to the driver in a suddenly serious voice, "Did you know there isn't any God?"

Now, that was atheism. Everybody knew about that rich old mother of hers and all that money. Only the poor folks knew about God. He was filled with virtue and expanded. "Well now, miss, I don't know about that. I never miss a Sunday at church." The driver's virtue increased, and he helped Elizabeth from the hack with a very superior manner. "Down you go. Watch that skirt, miss. You almost tripped on it. Two minutes to train time."

"Oh, I could float to Boston," said Elizabeth. "It doesn't mean anything at all. So foolish."

He stared at her. Miss Sheldon wasn't given to jokes, but there she stood, smiling and laughing. There was just the mitest thing queer about her eyes, though, come to think about it. They stared and didn't blink, and she smiled and smiled. Well, at least she was feeling friendly for a change. Perhaps she would remember him at Christmas.

Elizabeth had no memory of boarding the train or of the trip to Boston. She saw only long shadows and strange brilliant angles and jagged perspectives. Once or twice she put up her hand to feel the thick glass between herself and the world. She nodded with satisfaction. So long as the glass was there nobody could touch her or hurt her. She always kept it very clean and polished. It was her protection. She continued to press her hand against it in the train. She had not really believed in it when she saw it on her first day home after she had left England. She had originally thought it an illusion, as elongated stairways and narrowing walls were an illusion, as the screaming sounds in her ears were also an illusion. But not lately, not for more than a year. She settled contentedly in her seat, secure and protected. Everything was soundless.

She talked very calmly and clearly to the people in her mother's office. She discussed the papers she had brought. She held her head tilted seriously as she listened and nodded and made notes. She did not laugh at the suddenly pulled-down faces, the squashed sides of heads, the grotesque hands. That would be unpardonable. When the session was over she refused lunch at the Beverley and said that she was expected home. She went out into the snowstorm and stood there in the street, with the flakes battering her face and her hot forehead. Then she said aloud, "There's something wrong with me. It must be my eyes. Everything looks very strange."

People walked at a peculiar angle, as if the street were the side of a hill. The buildings opposite lay down the hill; she herself stood on a ledge. She began to walk, at first slowly, then very rapidly. Then she began to run very neatly, in a ladylike fashion. Part of her mind guided her. She reached a large wide building, high and full of many windows, the hospital of the Sisters of Charity. She pushed open the heavy doors with the finger of her left hand and was pleased to see how well cumbersome matter obeyed her will.

A figure floated to meet her, all black and white and excessively tall, with a wimple and clear brown eyes. It was too familiar, honestly, for the figure to embrace and hold her, and very stupid of her to cling to the figure. However, the floor did whirl under feet. Was this a way they had to confuse patients or intruders? Elizabeth smiled slyly. "I am Miss Jones," she said to the figure. "I think there is something wrong with my eyes. I don't seem to see very well. Now if you please——" She was very annoyed at this familiarity, this strong embrace. She settled her hat. "Now if you please," she repeated severely. "I have money to pay. No doubt you have an eye doctor here."

It was ridiculous, the way people could instantly change sex and appearance. The nun who had held her so tightly dissolved sheepishly into a man behind a desk in a large warm office. Elizabeth was surprised to find that she was sitting and not standing. The man had a kind face and a mustache. The mustache was gigantic and filled all his face. Elizabeth laughed, put her hands to her mouth, politely begged his pardon, then stared at him. He was watching her with a concerned expression. The nun who had brought her here stood quietly near the door.

"There is something wrong with your eyes, Miss—Jones?" he said. He looked at Elizabeth's old tweeds, at her long white hands, at her pure stark face. He knew Boston ladies. They were often discreet to the point of being ludicrous. But there was something about this young lady's eyes that disturbed him.

"Jones!" she exclaimed angrily.

"Yes. I have it here. Do you live in Boston?"

"Oh yes," said Elizabeth. She paused. She knew these doctors; they always wanted money. "I'm very poor, really," she said. The doctor looked at the dispatch case on the corner of his desk, and when Elizabeth saw the glance she snatched the case and held it tightly in her arms.

The doctor heard the careful intonations of her voice. Miss Stockington's, beyond any doubt. He had two daughters there. "It's odd, isn't it," said Elizabeth, "that there should be thunder at this time of the year? It hurts my ears."

"Very odd," the doctor agreed gravely. He looked at the silent snow flowing against his office windows. "Now, shall we look at your eyes, Miss Jones?"

He examined her eyes. She could not endure the glare of his light, but she struggled against her inclination to hide. It surprised her that he could pass through the glass. "Didn't you feel it?" she asked him when he sat down again. "How could you pass through it?"

"What?" he asked gently.

She made a wide, vague motion in the air. "Why, the glass. In front of me."

The nun at the door lifted her beads and held them in her hand, and the doctor stared down at his desk. He said, "I'd like a colleague to question and examine you."

It was like a fairy tale. He no sooner had said this than another man stood beside him, conjured out of the thin air. Elizabeth laughed like a child.

The two doctors sat side by side. Elizabeth was not afraid of them, for the glass was gleaming before her. The new doctor was an older man, and he looked at Elizabeth compassionately.

"Now, Miss Jones, you must answer some questions. Have you had a nervous breakdown recently or a shock?"

"Oh no, indeed." It was very necessary to be precise. "In fact, we have no family doctor at all. I've never been sick. I am very healthy."

"I see. I must ask you some questions."

The questions, thought Elizabeth indignantly, were very personal and embarrassing. In the midst of them she beckoned to the nun, who came to stand by her side. "Really," she would murmur to the nun before answering the questions, and would look for feminine reassurance. The Sister smiled and sighed and nodded.

"And there have been no—nervous—disorders in your family at all?"

"Certainly not! We are a very vigorous family."

The doctors exchanged glances. Then they looked at Elizabeth and studied her strained and haggard face, her staring eyes, her trembling mouth. "It is just my eyes," she said, and said it over and over.

They asked her repeatedly where she lived, and she always gave an address in Boston. She did not know it was Miss Stockington's school; she had forgotten. No, she said, she was an orphan. She had no father, no mother, no sisters, no brothers. She was all alone in the world and had to work hard for a living. The doctors looked at her smooth and elegant hands and listened to her well-bred voice.

Then the nun gave her a white pill and a glass of water. Elizabeth eyed them suspiciously. She swung to the doctors. "Am I in a hospital?" she demanded.

"Yes, the Sisters of Charity." They watched the girl whose mother was anonymously responsible for this fine new wing and the new facilities. Elizabeth swallowed the pill, drank the water, and thanked the Sister politely. As the Sister began to move away Elizabeth took a section of her habit and smiled. "I always knew it was only mist," she said, and smiled again, knowingly.

"And there have been no recent deaths in your family?" asked the new doctor in so kind a tone that tears came into Elizabeth's eyes. Then she was sobbing. She put her hands over her face and cried wildly. The tears ran through her fingers, down the front of her shirtwaist, her suit, and then onto her knees. Her cries filled the large warm room. The doctors did not try to restrain her. She finally fumbled in her purse and wiped her eyes, but her sobs continued.

"Who died?" asked the new doctor in a tone of pity and understanding.

"Who?" Elizabeth stared at him. "Why, you should know. Elizabeth Josephine Sheldon." The doctors looked up alertly. Elizabeth said, "She died a long time ago."

Timothy Winslow wrote to his brother William: "It will come as a shock to you, and a surprise, though it did not to me, to hear that Elizabeth lost her mind two weeks ago and is now confined in a private mental hospital near Boston for the insane. I had always suspected that there was some latent madness in that branch of the family. I have talked with Caroline about the unfortunate girl, and she admitted to me that Elizabeth had been 'strange' for at least a year before the climax, when she ran into a hospital in Boston complaining of her eyesight. I also visited Hillcrest Sanitarium, where Elizabeth is hospitalized, and they would not let me see her, merely telling me that she had gone into a mute state which is symptomatic of her disorder. The diagnosis is pessimistic; she will probably never recover. It is a blessing that Elizabeth's mental disturbance came on before marriage, for some man is spared the misery of this situation, at least."

William read this letter, and then he went into his young wife's sitting room. She was asleep before the fire, her rosy face contented, a little stupid, yet gentle. He had a quiet affection for her. He thought of Elizabeth. He was sick with grief and despair. He went to find his mother and gave her Timothy's letter. Her eyes filled with tears, and she looked at him without comment.

He spoke slowly and thoughtfully. "I am an ordained priest, but before God I say this: I hate Timothy with all my heart and soul, and I curse him with all the strength I have. I shall never write to him again, and you must never speak his name to me in this house."

He asked his bankers to write to Elizabeth's hospital, through their New York associates, and order white roses to be placed in the girl's room three times a week. But Elizabeth never saw them, never was conscious of their presence.

CHAPTER EIGHT

In the summer of 1913 Elizabeth spoke for the first time since her confinement. She spoke in a slow and halting voice, a few rational words. She wanted to know where she was. This so heartened her doctors that they decided she could go home over one weekend in the company of a nurse, and if she improved, the treatment would be extended. They had no illusions of a cure; they had seen this sad condition too often. But she was still young; perhaps familiar surroundings might bring back the world of reality to her, and eventually she might come into some contact with it.

Eventually she was allowed to go to Lyme every month for two days, and always with a nurse. She expressed neither pleasure at nor revulsion for the idea; she merely accepted it. On her return the doctors would always question her, but her answers, though rational, expressed no emotion. She lived in the half-world of the living dead. The doctors were well aware that this world was not sluggish or dreamlike or stagnant, but filled with nightmares of sufferings and terrors, and that her symptoms were not "objective" but were the faint echoes of the horror in which she lived. She was under drugs most of the time. She did not speak of her mother and appeared more relieved than anything else when she returned to the hospital.

The monthly visits went on for a year; now they had become two a month. Elizabeth's soft brown hair, so smooth, with the light deep wave over her forehead, had turned to the color and texture of flax, though she was only twenty-six. Her pale face was rigid and without expression; her eyes, fixed and without emotion, had faded. She was almost fleshless; her fine bones lay closely to her pallid skin. She walked and moved like an old woman. She was docile and obedient to the nurse and spoke hardly at all to her mother. It was as if she had difficulty each time in recognizing her. The nurses never knew what Caroline felt. They believed her to be very old because of her white hair, the stoop in her broad shoulders, the clefts in her big face, the awkward and fumbling motions of her hands, her slowness. They thought that Elizabeth must be the child of her middle age, and they conjectured whether such children were not often calamities to their parents.

A new young nurse, very intelligent, small but strong, dark and lively of face, brought Elizabeth home for her visit on Saturday June 27, 1914. She had been told of the wretched house to which she would bring her charge. The other nurses had said, "Take your own sheets and other linens! Everything is so grimy there, so dirty, so old and fallen apart. You'd wonder, with all her money, why Mrs. Sheldon lives like that, but you know all the stories about her in Boston. They call her a recluse. She could buy the White House, if it was for sale, and never even know it. Only one maid, too, who does everything in that big old filthy barn of a place. The grounds are just like a jungle; nothing's been done there for years and years. You'll hate it. But you just have to stand it a couple of days. Take some books with you, too, or you'll end up biting your own fingernails."

The nurse, Sally Crimmens, had indulgently thought her friends were exaggerating. But she found conditions to be much worse than the nurses had told her. She was a cheerful young soul, but she became despondent in three hours. She took Elizabeth for a walk along the beach and drew in great breaths of clean ocean air. The house stank, and it was a mercy that it was so close to the water. The June light lay wide and brilliant on the sea, and all the world was at peace.

As Miss Crimmens was more intelligent than the other nurses, she thought: If only that house had the feeling of God in it, and love, and sympathy, and kindness, and family! It would help poor Elizabeth so much, and it would give her some consolation and perhaps it would cure her eventually. But Miss Crimmens did not know that those blessed things had never been in that house and that it was because of this that Elizabeth had never acquired fortitude, had never known any consolations, had never been able to armor her soul with faith and resignation, had never been taught at all how to deal with life, and had never, at any time, had a confidante to whom she could express her agony and desolation. When faced with loss and tragedy she had had no resources to sustain her. Her spirit had died for lack of a voice or the help of a hand, or even the knowledge that somewhere there might be someone who would listen and help.

Miss Crimmens was sure, after a very sharp inspection, that Mrs. Sheldon loved her daughter and that she was stricken to the heart. This was evident in the very first glance she had given Elizabeth, the timid touch of her hand to the girl's shoulder, her first uncertain words. But more than anything else, by the look in her large hazel eyes, at once childlike, hoping, despairing. She had said, "Elizabeth? You are home, Elizabeth. Don't you know? Don't you remember?" But Elizabeth had not answered her, and Caroline's big shoulders drooped and she had turned away.

Later, when the three sat in an intolerable silence in the living room, after a dinner which had revolted Miss Crimmens because of the bad cooking and worse serving, the nurse saw Caroline watching her daughter grimly; her nostrils kept expanding and contracting, as if she were holding back some terrible expression of her thoughts, and it was as if she hated. This place is getting on my nerves, thought the young woman. I'm beginning to imagine things.

It had not been until five o'clock that night some years ago that the Sisters of Charity had called Caroline to tell her of Elizabeth's breakdown and to add that the girl was under restraint and drugs in the mental ward. The four o'clock train had come and gone, and the call from the hospital had arrived just when Caroline was beginning to feel acute anxiety. She listened to the gentle words of the Reverend Mother, and she could feel nothing and hardly understood anything. The Reverend Mother had had to repeat her message several times. The maid had entered Caroline's study with an emptied wastebasket, and Caroline, shaking her head over and over, gave the girl the telephone and muttered, "I can't understand that woman. Let her give you the message." But she finally understood. It was only that her mind refused to accept it.

The doctors had searched Elizabeth's purse for identity and had found it. They had exclaimed in astonishment, for this was the daughter of the immensely rich Caroline Ames. "Why, my sister went to school with Caroline!" said the first doctor. And then, thoughtfully, "She was always more than a little queer. I wonder . . ."

The maid avidly reported to Caroline that the hospital requested that Mrs. Sheldon not visit her daughter for a few days, "until she is more rested." The winter twilight came into the room, and the sound of the winter gale, and the little fire in the study could not warm the air. Caroline clumsily and heavily knelt down before it, trying to warm hands as cold as stone, and the maid watched her. Then Caroline said, "Bring me some hot coffee." When the coffee arrived Caroline was behind her desk again, and her eyes were great and glittering. "I want to talk to you," she said.

She did not know how to begin. She moistened her lips over and over. Then she could speak. "I didn't see Miss Sheldon before she left for town today. Tell me everything you can remember about this morning. Everything."

The maid was an uneducated country girl with a small vocabulary. Caroline's aspect frightened her. "Why, there wasn't nothing," she said.

"Think," said Caroline. "Was Miss Sheldon any different this morning than at any other time?"

The girl shook her head vigorously. "No, ma'am. Just ate a piece of toast and drank some coffee. I fixed her some eggs, but she didn't eat 'em. Then she got up and went out into the hall and put on her coat and hat and gloves, and the hack come up and she went."

"She said nothing, did nothing, but that?"

The girl, unused to thinking and interrogation, began to shake her head. Then she paused. "Why, it wasn't nothing," she said. "There was just the paper on the hall table. I'd just brung it in when the boy left it. Miss Sheldon picked it up and turned the pages and looked up and down 'em. And then she said, 'Really!' And made a big fuss about putting the paper together again. And shook out the pages." She paused, screwing up her eyes. "She said somethin' else, about people bein' so careless these days, or somethin'. And then I heard her laughin' outside, and she kind of ran to the hack, and she never runs. Least, I've never seen her do it before."

Caroline sipped her coffee. The power of her disciplined mind began to work. It scrutinized every word the girl had said. And it was remembering, also, the day eighteen months ago when Elizabeth had returned from England. Caroline was recalling Elizabeth's shrill remark that she hated Timothy, that Timothy was dangerous, and that her mother must "ruin" him. Elizabeth's face, as on that day, rose before Caroline, and she remembered the girl's collapse and then her almost terrified insistence that Timothy had "done nothing" to her. From that day on Elizabeth had not been quite the same. She had immense powers of self-discipline; she behaved normally, worked harder than ever, appeared to be more acute than usual. But something had been wrong.

Yes, Elizabeth had been sick when she returned from England. She had not improved after all. And she had seen something or heard something in the house this morning which had finally crashed down all her control, had sent her reeling into madness. Caroline's daughter, her child, her loved child who resembled John Ames—driven to madness. This morning. But there must have been some long-silent suffering before it; Elizabeth's mind had broken finally. Why?

"Bring me the morning's newspaper," said Caroline. "It's the top one in the kitchen." She sipped her coffee. She kept pain from her by an enormous effort of will. There was time enough for pain later. Now she must know.

The girl brought the newspaper, and Caroline dismissed her. Then inch by inch she searched the first page. Nothing. Then the second, the third, and on. Nothing. Only scandal and reports of murders and thefts and the mayor's demand for more money for the police. Next came the Society news. Very thoroughly, though without much hope now, Caroline examined it. "Mr. and Mrs. Timothy Andrew Winslow of Boston and New York announce the marriage of their brother, William Lord Halnes——"

Caroline folded her hands on the paper and thought. Cynthia's son, whom she had never seen. How old would he be now? As old as John. She examined every item Timothy had ever carelessly let drop about his brother, his resemblance to old Montague, his wealth, his title, his coming marriage to Lady Rose Haven. When had he first mentioned that engagement? Nearly two years ago. He had taken his time in marrying, the son of the Weasel! Nearly two years. What had delayed it? Caroline studied even the minutest thing with inexorable thoroughness.

Timothy had mentioned that he and Amanda and their children had gone to Devon to see his mother and brother. Again he had mentioned the coming marriage. But it had not taken place then, eighteen months ago.

And then, vividly—had Elizabeth gone to Devon with the family? No one had said a word of it to Caroline. Why? Elizabeth would have known her mother would be angry. Caroline looked at her telephone, then lifted the receiver and called Timothy, who was at present in Boston. When he answered, her throat was so dry that she could not speak for several moments. Moreover, she was not accustomed to dissimulations, for she had no training in being a liar, no training in the way of speaking lightly when one's whole life depended on the answer. It was only by a deliberate act of her will that she could finally say, "Timothy, you should have told me that Elizabeth went with you to Devon to see your mother."

There was a long pause. Her hand tightened on the receiver pressed to her ear. Then Timothy laughed quietly. "Oh? Did Elizabeth finally tell you? Don't be angry, Caroline. We didn't want her to go, but she insisted. We had even arranged for a chaperone for her in London, but she refused and continued to insist. You know what a strong-willed girl Elizabeth is."

"Yes," said Caroline, thinking of the strong will which had broken so tragically today. "I know."

"It was embarrassing for Amanda," said Timothy. "She was annoyed at Elizabeth's insistence; it seemed strange to her. Elizabeth had seen Mother and my brother William a few times when she was younger. Now, Caroline, you aren't going to be hard on the girl, are you?"

Caroline knew all about her cousin; he had never been able to deceive her, though he believed he had. She heard the change in his voice; she could hear uneasiness in it, for all its quiet geniality and pretended amusement.

"Why should I be hard on my daughter?" asked Caroline.

"Oh well." He was relieved; she could hear that. "Did Elizabeth finally tell you?"

"In a manner of speaking," said Caroline. She paused. "Good night, Timothy."

So Elizabeth had seen William and Cynthia when "she was younger," at school affairs, or perhaps in Timothy's house. The fact that she had not spoken of these meetings to her mother took on intense significance for Caroline.

Why had Elizabeth insisted on going to Devon, to the house where she could not be expected to be welcome? It was not like Elizabeth, the proud, the cold, the restrained. She had insisted in spite of first refusals on the part of Amanda, and Caroline knew Amanda's bluntness.

Caroline got to her feet and weightily climbed the stairs to Elizabeth's room. It was chill and neat, as always. Methodically, and still holding the hungry pain off, Caroline examined the girl's wardrobe. She came on the dresses folded tenderly in their tissue paper. They were like a bride's garments, cherished, put aside, remembered, not to be destroyed by wearing. Caroline's legs trembled and she sat down suddenly on the hard edge of Elizabeth's bed. Her hands made fists against her breast. Her face appeared carved of broad bone, without skin or flesh, in the dim light of the lamp. Elizabeth had gone to Devon for only one purpose. To see the son of the Weasel. He had rejected her. Now Elizabeth's avoidance of eligible young men in Boston was explained. She had loved this man, and when she had seen the announcement of his marriage she had lost her proud mind.

Caroline looked at Elizabeth's small plain dresser, and she got up and went to it. Here were all the plain, if expensive, underclothes which the girl had bought lately. Under them were "frivolities" of lace and ruffles, hardly worn. Caroline opened the top drawer and saw a box, and she lifted the lid. Inside were brown and withered petals of a once-white rose and a piece of narrow blue ribbon. And two pieces of paper. Caroline opened one and did not recognize the handwriting. It only said: "Tomorrow? In the garden after breakfast, as usual? All my love. W."

So. They had loved each other. What had kept them from marrying, Elizabeth and the rich, titled son of the Weasel? Surely not Elizabeth's fear of her mother, for in marrying William she would have a great fortune and a title. She would not mind parting forever from her mother, and Caroline knew that with sudden great clarity.

Caroline opened the next folded piece of paper and saw that it was in Elizabeth's handwriting and dated only last night.

"I know," she had written, "that it was all Timothy's plots and doing. He's always hated my mother. He hates me. I confronted him on the morning I left you, William. He was so happy, so pleased, so gloating. I could see it. He lied to you. But what does it matter now? Occasionally he mentions that you haven't as yet married that girl. Had you married her soon after I left I should have known that you had not really loved me. William, I love you. I don't think I can go on living without you. I told you about my mother. You didn't mind; it didn't mean anything to you, so I finally know that Timothy lied when he told me that no British man would marry me because of her. I've just begun to see it. How could I have been so blind as to believe Timothy? William, write me. I've tried for eighteen months to forget you. It gets worse every day; I can't forget. Sometimes I can't think because of the pain. Come to me. Or even ask me to come to you, and I'll be there on the next ship. William——"

Something had interrupted her. Caroline now remembered. She had called the girl into her study to give her the dispatch case and her instructions. She had intended to finish the letter later, the abject, the anguished, the humble letter, full of passion and suffering. She had thrust the letter hurriedly into this box when she had answered her mother's call. And then she had seen the newspaper this morning.

"Elizabeth!" cried Caroline in so loud a voice that it was almost a scream. She beat the bed in a frenzy of agony and despair, and now the pain was in her heart, worrying it like a wolf. She took Elizabeth's thin white pillow in her arms and held it against her breast. She had not cried since Tom had died; she wept now until the linen was soggy and the ticking showed through it. "Oh, my little girl," groaned Caroline. "My child. My poor, broken child. What would it have mattered?"

The story was not quite clear to her, except that Timothy had done this thing, with deliberate lying, with deliberate hatred not only for Caroline but for her daughter.

Caroline did not go to bed that night, nor the next. On the third night she slept in absolute exhaustion. When she awoke, it was with vengefulness. She would ruin Timothy. She would destroy him. She needed only a plan.

But he was invulnerable. He did not need her. He had not only his own money, which she had helped him gain, but the Bothwell fortune. He was established and powerful. But there must be something. For weeks and months, and then years, she searched and pondered while Elizabeth lay unseeing and unknowing at Hillcrest Sanitarium. When Timothy saw her she spoke to him in her usual fashion, and he believed she had forgiven him for taking Elizabeth to Devon. She saw that he watched her closely while inquiring about the girl. He had had no pity, no remorse for what he had done. There were three parts to her mind now—Elizabeth, her affairs, and Timothy.

One plan was for the future, concerning Timothy. She had worked it out. It would take time. But another plan was still closer. On May 31, 1913, appointment of senators by the legislatures had been changed to direct election by the people. Three days ago Timothy Winslow had announced that he would seek the office of senator in November. She had known for a long time that he intended to go into politics "when the time was ripe." It was ripe now.

So now, on June 27, 1914, as she sat and looked at her daughter, her shattered daughter, she thought of Timothy and what she would do to him in a few days. Miss Crimmens saw her face, shivered, then sturdily told herself that she was imagining things. This was only a poor old woman who had nothing but money and a daughter who would never really know her again and never again be alive.

On Monday morning, four hours before Elizabeth was to return to the sanitarium, Caroline received calls from her brokers. But she already knew. The morning paper, June 29, 1914, was spread before her. "Heir to Austria's throne is slain with his wife by a Bosnian youth to avenge seizure of his country."

So the Jacobins had finally moved, with silent power and surety. The Bosnian youth had been only the instrument, the commanded ignorant finger. Caroline listened to the congratulations of her brokers, because she had bought so much munitions stock lately. Then, in the midst of a freshet of more congratulations, she hung up the receiver of her telephone. Later she would think. But first came Elizabeth.

Miss Crimmens had informed Caroline at seven this morning that Elizabeth had not slept well. Caroline, too, had not slept. She had listened all night to Elizabeth's distressful cries, to her mutterings, to her groans of torment. The drugs had had no effect on her, as they had had before when she visited her home. She had made sounds of a soul in extremity, in the process of dissolution.

The nurse had exhausted herself in her attempts at quieting Elizabeth. She had failed. Caroline went up to her daughter's room. Elizabeth was running about, her blanched hair in wild disorder around her distorted face. Her arms flew in aimless gestures. When she saw Caroline she became fearfully excited.

"Why did you do this?" she screamed, clutching lengths of her hair. "What did I do to you? Why do you hate me? Why don't you let me alone?"

Miss Crimmens, like a small but active young bird, fluttered about her charge, murmuring. Suddenly Elizabeth became aware of her and with super-strength she flung the girl from her so that the nurse fell violently on the floor. Then Elizabeth advanced on her mother. Caroline waited, and when Elizabeth reached her she seized her hands and held them tightly.

"Elizabeth," she said.

Elizabeth stared at her, her faded blue eyes wide. She stopped struggling. She looked down at her mother's hands. "It's all right," she muttered. "I won't be late for the train to Boston. Where is the dispatch case?" She moved, as if in pain. But she was flaccid now. Caroline led her to the bed and made her sit down, and she looked at her. Great drops of water appeared on the girl's forehead, like tears.

"You don't understand," said Elizabeth with quiet seriousness. "I can explain it. It was all that money for William and me. It isn't wrong to want money, is it?" Her far eyes questioned her mother intensely. Caroline shook her head. Elizabeth leaned toward her. "You'll ask him to come, won't you?"

"Of course," said Caroline, out of her own agony. "This very minute."

Elizabeth shook her head vigorously and she laughed, that shrill meaningless laugh. "But it wasn't the money, really. It was Timothy all the time." Again she leaned toward Caroline and whispered confidentially, "Do you know what he said? That William couldn't marry me because of my dreadful mother and her father. They were so notorious! Everyone despised them. Timothy explained. Do you think he was right?" she asked anxiously.

"Did William, too, tell you that?" asked Caroline.

Again the pathetic hair flew as Elizabeth shook her head in emphatic denial. "Oh no! You remember that. You were there." She smiled slyly. The pulses were beating violently in her throat and temples, and her face was the color of death. "He just told me we couldn't be married. And I found out that Timothy had done it all. He'd lied to him. You will send for William, won't you?"

"Yes, Elizabeth." Caroline squeezed her eyes shut for a moment.

"I never loved anyone but William," said Elizabeth with the slow care and patience of one explaining to an obtuse woman. "I've loved him since I was a little girl, for, you see——" She paused and frowned and shook her head. "My father was stupid. He wanted us to love him, and it wasn't any use. A very silly man. Did you ever know him?" she asked her mother suddenly. Her wandering eyes stopped, clouded fretfully.

"Oh yes," said Caroline. The nurse had gotten up off the floor and was standing and looking at mother and daughter.

"I don't know why, but I think I feel sorry for him," said Elizabeth. "It's so foolish, isn't it? And my mother goes up to his grave and looks at it. I hate her, but she was more sensible than my father; she never wanted anyone to love her." Elizabeth sagged on the bed. Her color became more livid, and now the drops on her forehead trickled down her cheeks.

"Could we send for the man she calls William?" asked Miss Crimmens hopefully. "She called for him all night. Perhaps he could help her." She crept softly to Elizabeth, took her wrist and felt her pulse, and glanced worriedly at Caroline. Caroline shook her head.

"I don't know," said Miss Crimmens, paling. "Her heart—— There's something wrong. We must send for a doctor!"

"Go to my study upstairs. You will find his village number." But Caroline spoke dully. The nurse raced from the room, and Caroline took her daughter's hands.

"You must tell me, Elizabeth," she said with the utmost quietness. "It was Timothy, wasn't it? I must be sure, very sure."

"Oh yes," said Elizabeth with the earnestness of a child. "But you must excuse me. I have a letter to finish to William, and then he will come. For now he must know that Timothy is a liar and that he hated me and was trying to do something to my mother through me. Wasn't that very wrong?" Her eyes pleaded with her mother. Her lips had become leaden, and there were leaden patches about her eyes.

"It began a long time ago," said Caroline, holding her daughter.

"Oh, God," said Elizabeth with the awful weariness of the dying. "Do you think William will come, after all? It's a long way, and it's getting longer every minute. I can't stop thinking of Timothy. Where am I? Timothy hates all of us. He's afraid Amy will marry Ames. Just as he was afraid of William marrying me. Where am I?"

Caroline wanted to say "Home," but she could not. She could only say, "Here. With me." She could no longer look at the ravaged face, at the expiring and tormented eyes. She dropped her head on her chest. She heard Elizabeth breathing in short sounds as she leaned against her mother, broken with exhaustion. The girl muttered incoherently over and over.

"Longer and longer," she muttered. "Farther and farther. I'm getting farther away from William. I wish you'd stop the ship. The waves are very high and I think a storm is coming—— Did you see the lightning?"

"Oh, God. Please, God," said Caroline.

"Hush, you shouldn't say that," said Elizabeth with faint severity. "There isn't any God, you know. I wish I could sleep, but I'm afraid—all those awful things and colors and going into darkness. I'm always afraid I'll never come back and never find William again."

Her eyes closed. Caroline had to hold her upright, and strongly. Elizabeth suddenly slept. She weighed so little now. She was hardly a pressure in her mother's arms. A mysterious change spread over her face, peaceful, removed, young, and quiet. It became the face of the dead John Ames. She sighed once, deeply, then did not breathe again. A slight convulsion, as of intense cold, rippled over her body.

Caroline laid her dead daughter on the bed and stood over her, and when Miss Crimmens returned she found the mother gently smoothing the tangled hair. And then Caroline bent and kissed Elizabeth's cheek.

She walked out of the room then, and Miss Crimmens stepped back, feeling that the older woman did not see her at all.

CHAPTER NINE

The funeral was quiet and private. Only Timothy and his family and Elizabeth's brothers. At Caroline's request there were no flowers. But she had heard from Miss Crimmens of the mysterious white roses, fresh and pure, which had always been in Elizabeth's room at the sanitarium, a room Caroline had never entered. She had seen her daughter only in the reception room, when permitted.

It did not take much pondering on Caroline's part to know who had sent those roses through the years, though he was married now and had a son. So Elizabeth's coffin was surrounded by identical roses from Caroline, and there were white rosebuds on the satin pillow. They filled the parlor with a heavy sweet scent. Elizabeth slept in death, serene and at peace.

Her brothers had not loved her, but they were vaguely sorry. However, they could not help conjecturing about their mother's will now, since the contender was dead. The old girl was very composed, even when she looked at her daughter. Her voice was normal. Her sons often caught her glance at Timothy, who appeared definitely uneasy. Amanda cried and silently regretted that she had not liked poor Elizabeth. Her two fine boys, young men now, were very sober. Amy, very subdued, cried a little, even though she had hardly known Elizabeth. It seemed very sad to her, and she would look timidly at her second cousin, old Caroline, who was also Ames' mother, and she wanted to comfort her. It surprised the girl to find Caroline looking at her very often.

The service was short. Elizabeth was carried to the Sheldon lot on the hill and laid near her father. The white roses were piled high on her grave in the hot July sunlight. Caroline took one bud from them.

John and Ames had been in this decaying house for three days and could not leave fast enough. John, saying that he must get back to New York, left the day after the funeral, after some vague words of consolation to his mother. "It's all for the best, Ma," he said. "She wouldn't have gotten better."

"Leaving on the same train with me?" he asked his brother.

"No," said Ames. "I just go to Boston. Someone should stay a little longer with the old lady."

John was slightly suspicious, then shrugged, kissed his mother, and went away. He was having his own troubles these days with Mimi.

Caroline and Ames sat in the dank living room, which felt chill in spite of the heat and light outside. Ames waited for his mother to speak. But she only sat there in her black old-fashioned clothing, looking at the rosebud in her hands. Then Ames said, "You asked me privately to stay for a little talk with you, Mother."

"Yes," said Caroline. She lifted her eyes and regarded her son thoughtfully—the subtle triangular face, the fair hair, the delicate coloring, the hard slate-gray eyes. She said, "That girl Amy. Timothy's daughter. I've heard you want to marry her."

Well, this was bound to come sooner or later. He said, "Yes. She's a fine girl, a nice girl. I've wanted to marry her since she was eighteen."

"Yes? Why didn't you?"

"I'm not a favorite of dear old Timothy's." Ames paused. There had been an odd note in his mother's voice; he looked at her more closely now and was surprised that she did not appear angry, but only intent. "In fact, he as much as suggested that I shouldn't see as much of Amy as I was doing. That was a year ago. I should give her an opportunity to meet other men. Younger men. The devil! I'm only five years older than Amy. I think he heard," said Ames with a full, hard look at his mother, "in some way, of the arrangements in your will. I don't know how, but I suspect it. It would be just like old Timothy."

"Of course," said Caroline.

Ames was more surprised. "I wish you really knew Amy," he said cautiously.

"I think I do," said Caroline. "I'm not blind. The girl would make you an excellent wife. She has a sweet, good face. She might improve your character."

Ames could hardly believe what he was hearing. He sat up in his chair, and color came into his thin cheeks.

"Whether you'll improve hers is a moot question," said Caroline.

She spoke dispassionately. This was a damned strange conversation to have just after the funeral of Elizabeth, to whom Caroline was devoted, thought Ames. He was more than a trifle bewildered. But then, she was granite.

Caroline said, "What is Timothy's objection?"

Ames shrugged elegantly. "Since I was a very young child I knew there was no love lost between you and old Timothy. Then, as I've said, he's probably caught a rumor of your will. He was still in your law firm, you'll remember, when you made it, and lawyers have a way of finding out. However, I think it is a more personal objection. He's very cordial, of course, and is quite an actor. But I've caught him off guard a few times. Why he should hate me, I don't know; I'm a rich man. Amy could do worse." Ames regarded his mother blandly.

"What is Amy's attitude toward you?"

"The same as mine toward her. We want to be married."

"And so?"

"She happens to be devoted to her father. She wants more time to make him change his mind. He won't. He hardly spoke to me today. And Amanda shows her antagonism very clearly. So Amy and I are just wandering about at the present time, and it isn't making her very happy."

"You've been dilly-dallying," said Caroline. She looked again at the rosebud. "Haven't young men any enterprise these days? If you want the girl, tell her to make up her mind immediately. In fact, you can mention that you won't see her again unless she consents."

Ames had to control his sudden and powerful excitement. "And you wouldn't mind? I thought you hated her grandmother."

"I did. I still do. But that doesn't matter. I like the girl."

Ames lit a cigarette. He was, like his dead sister, a person of immense self-control. There was something he could not understand here, but he was not going to explore it.

"I suppose if Timothy heard I was changing my will a little, he would not object then?"

Ames' greed urged him to say "Yes!" But he was too involved with Amy for games. He shook his head. "No. It's more than that. I just recently had another talk with Amy. We meet now in the Boston Museum. She practically promised me that if her father was not reconciled to the marriage she would marry me when she is twenty-one."

"You think it is the lack of love between Timothy and me? I put him on his way, you know."

"Yes, I know." Ames paused. Then he said with unusual bluntness, "He told Amy something. He said he'd rather see her dead than married to me, your son."

Caroline smiled grimly. "That is what I suspected."

"But why, for God's sake?"

"He hated your grandfather too." Caroline smoothed the leaves of the rosebud with a slow hand.

"But my grandfather has been dead for ages. What does he have to do with it?"

"Timothy thought him ill bred. Besides," said Caroline calmly, "there was a personal hatred. His mother was my father's mistress for many years."

"Oh. The devil!" exclaimed Ames. "Honor of the family, eh?"

"Not in the way you mean. Besides, he hates me much more. It is envy. He is a very greedy and voracious man, in spite of his fine airs. But again, it is much more than that. He thinks we have bad blood, yet he is one of the most corrupt men I've ever known. But such men are very careful of their daughters. No doubt he believes you are quite corrupt, yourself."

Ames smiled. "It is possible I am. I feel quite respectable these days, however. I haven't turned out as frightful as even you thought I would."

"Quite right," said Caroline.

She held the rosebud with both hands now, almost clutching it. "Let me tell you this. On the day you marry Amy Winslow, I will give you three million dollars. As my wedding present to you. If that does not make you press the girl at once, nothing else will."

Ames was so stunned that he took the cigarette from his mouth, stared at it as if wondering what it was, then threw it into the littered, cold fireplace.

"You will put that in writing?"

"Yes. Before you leave. On one condition: that when you marry Amy you will show it to her parents."

"I see," said Ames. He narrowed his eyes at his mother.

"If it will convince you more, I will, within a few days, set that money aside for you, in your name, to be drawn only when you marry Amy."

"I see," repeated Ames.

But he did not really "see." He would let himself wonder and conjecture later. He was swept up in excitement.

"I am tired now," said Caroline. "I think I will go to my room and rest. But you must keep me informed. Moreover, you must not let your brother know."

She began to walk away, then stopped. "There must always be a time limit to everything. I suggest you marry Amy Winslow within one week after the elections this fall."

Ames considered this. "After Timothy is elected senator?" He smiled. "That will soften the blow."

"I said, after the elections," answered Caroline. She looked at the rose she held. "After the elections. Is that understood?"

Ames repeated, "Yes. I see." The dreary room was heavily weighted with the scent of roses.

Mr. Higsby Chalmers alighted stiffly and chubbily from the train at Lyme on August 16, 1914, the day the Germans captured Liége. It was very hot in Boston, and he was pleased to find the air so cool in Lyme. He had been reading his morning paper on the train with great concern, for he was one of the few men in America—except for those who had planned this war a long time ago and were now bustling like evil wasps behind their shut doors in New York and Washington—who realized what was about to happen to the world. His knowledge was not precise, for he was a good, sound, and conservative Bostonian, and he was extremely intelligent and state chairman of his political party. His awareness was more than a little intuitive, sharpened only to a degree by his favorite pastime of "reading between the lines" and political acumen.

What had alarmed him particularly this morning was a statement issued by President Wilson to the effect that "America is in no danger of being involved" in the holocaust in Europe. Americans were not as yet interested in a war they regarded with less concern than baseball; there were few, if any, editorials about the war in this country. In fact, many newspapers put the war on the back pages or second pages, to give headlines to the more engrossing news about the "White Slave Traffic," fulminations against the modern dance and ragtime, Mr. Elbert Hubbard's sparkling little publication called *The Philistine*, the belligerence of the Woman's Christian Temperance Union, the latest philanthropies of Andrew Carnegie, Mr. Henry Ford's "tin lizzie" and accompanying jokes, prospects for the coming football season, the new Freudian theories of sex, and, as always, Fundamentalist religion and "the crime against youth" contained in naïve motion pictures and popular magazines. The picture pages of the newspapers were filled with photographs of the building of Grand Central Station in New York, actresses, happy dogs, airplanes, fashion portraits, and ballroom dancers in the contortions of the Turkey Trot and Grizzly Bear.

So, thought Mr. Chalmers with increasing alarm, why did President Wilson "reassure" the country that it would not be involved in Europe's wars when the country was not asking "reassurance" about anything except the lifting of a mild depression and more and more popular entertainment and vulgar excitement? Was Mr. Wilson warning men who were as yet faceless to the people, or of whose existence the people did not even dream? Was he telling them, in effect, that so long as he was alive and President, America would not abandon George Washington's emphatic admonition to beware of foreign entanglements?

"An unknown source close to the Vatican," however, was more pointed than Mr. Wilson. That source was warning the world in a strong and steadfast voice that it must beware of the seeming in Europe and halt hostilities before it was too late, for the men behind an apparently simple war were men who were enemies of Germany and England alike. "Thunder from the Left," said the source urgently. But only those who already knew listened to Rome, and then with a derisive smile and with hateful words of contempt. Did Rome actually think, they asked each other, laughing, that the stupid and simple masses would stop their rush to suicide behind the Judas-goat the plotters had provided?

Mr. Wilson's reassurance appeared on page 5 of the newspaper, and the "source close to the Vatican" appeared over the obituaries. And that, thought Mr. Chalmers, was a terrible and ironic, if unconscious, bit of humor. He felt restless and vaguely frightened, and he thought of his young grandsons. Like all dignified Bostonians, he made few concessions to weather and wore his usual fine black broadcloth suit, with high stiff collar and tight knotted tie. He was a short man, and very stout, and wore gold cuff links, a gold watch chain, and a gold and diamond stickpin, and he had trouble mounting the high step of one of the station hacks. He said, "The Sheldon residence," and sat on the ragged leather seat, reread Mr. Wilson's statement and the warning of the "source close to the Vatican," and fanned himself agitatedly with his hat.

"What?" he said with some irritation when the driver asked him his destination. "I thought I told you the Sheldon residence, Mrs. Caroline Ames Sheldon's residence."

"Ayeah," grumbled the driver, applying his whip to his horse. "That's what I thought you said, mister, but there ain't hardly anyone ever going out there and I wanted to be sure." He looked over his shoulder at the very red stout face of Mr. Chalmers and stopped a snigger at Mr. Chalmers' old-fashioned gray-and-auburn little beard.

"Well, you are sure now," said Mr. Chalmers, rustling his paper pointedly. He sniffed. He preferred horses to automobiles, for he was sixty years old and very dignified, but this poor nag not only was covered with flies but had a very bad smell indeed. Still, it wasn't worse than gasoline fumes.

Then he was curious. As the hack rattled away from the dusty depot and took the rough public road lying a little distant from the ocean, he said, "I'm sorry to hear Mrs. Sheldon has so few visitors. She must be lonely."

The driver snorted. "Not her! With all that money! What more she need, anyways? Nobody ever sees her, except folks who go up to the old graveyard once in a while—right there over that first hill—and she never speaks to nobody. Keeps her girl's grave covered with white roses; they come twice a week from Boston, in big boxes. Nobody ever gets buried up there any more, but you should see that there Sheldon plot. Acshully pays a man to keep the grass nice and green, and urns planted! Crazy!"

Nobody, my man, thought Mr. Chalmers with a slight smile, is "crazy" who has been able to increase one hundred million dollars to nearly three hundred millions since 1884. When Caroline's curt note asking him to call upon her had arrived three days ago, his wife Clara had said, "No one has seen Caroline Ames for centuries, just centuries. I wonder what on earth she wants with you, Higsby?" Mr. Chalmers wondered too.

He had expected to find a rather neglected house, for rumors ran avidly in Boston, but he had not expected to find the large mansion in such incredible decay. The house had been built—1885?—not even thirty years ago. Yet it had the appearance of an old crumbling ruin in the sad countryside of poor Ireland or in some forgotten section of Wales. The great lean pines were almost strangled by vines and scrub; there was no garden; there were no lawns, but only stretches of sea grass, nettles, weeds, and boulders. Good God, thought Mr. Chalmers, paying off the hack driver, surely even Caroline should be aware of this jungle, this dreadful forlornness, this indecent neglect. Every window, he saw as he carefully picked his way over small rocks and gravel and fallen ancient leaves and small dropped branches, was covered with blown sand and dirt. The pines sighed in the sea wind, and Mr. Chalmers sighed also. He pulled the bell and heard it echo in the house, and he half expected no one to answer. But eventually the door was opened by a homely and slatternly maid who peered at him suspiciously. He gave her his card, and she examined it, turning it over and over in her dirty hands.

"You wait there," she said in a hoarse voice, "and I'll see if Miz Sheldon wants to see you." She closed the splintered door loudly in his face.

The whole house looks as though no one had ever lived here, thought Mr. Chalmers, suppressing his irritation. The door opened and the girl said, "Wal, come in. What you waitin' for?" And Mr. Chalmers entered a beautifully proportioned but filthy and littered hall and immediately sneezed in the dust. The maid led him to the drawing room, the most wretched room Mr. Chalmers had ever seen in his life, and abandoned him on the threshold. He saw the once-lovely furniture, now broken and smeared with old oil, the threadbare rug, the tattered draperies. It was cold and dark in here after the hot bright sun outside, and Mr. Chalmers, still sneezing, blew his nose.

"Come in, Higsby," said a well-bred but rusty voice from the interior of a room which he thought resembled a dirty and abandoned warehouse.

"Thank you, Caroline," he said, and walked into the room and found his hostess sitting massively and stiffly on a chair. She indicated an opposite chair and said curtly, "Tea?"

"No, thank you, Caroline," he said hurriedly, thinking of the maid's dirty hands and sore eyes.

"I have nothing else," said Caroline.

"It doesn't matter in the least," said Mr. Chalmers, sitting down carefully, and politely repressing his impulse to dust off his chair first.

He looked at Caroline, whom he had remembered as a tall, shy, but somewhat imposing girl in plain clothing. His mother had said, "If only someone would take that girl in hand—what on earth is Cynthia Winslow doing, anyway?—she could be quite handsome and very impressive." He understood that people changed with the years; he had once, himself, been a short but slender and graceful youth, and a fine dancer and sportsman, and beardless. Now he was sixty, solidly fat, with high blood pressure, bifocals, and a beard. But surely he had not changed so drastically as Caroline had changed. He would not have recognized this bulky great woman with her scanty white crown of braids, her dark yet pallid skin, her leaden mouth, hard and sullen, as the Caroline he had known as a girl. Poor soul, poor girl, he remarked to himself, and blew his nose again.

"How are you, Caroline?" he asked, feeling quite shocked.

"Well enough," she said shortly. "And you, Higsby?"

"Well enough," he repeated, and smiled. "Clara sends you her regards."

"Um," said Caroline. Her large hands were folded in her lap. She wore an old black dress which was of a fashion of many, many years ago, with leg-of-mutton sleeves and a tight bodice with a row of buttons down the front, and a full long skirt. The color was tinged here and there with a hint of green age. Then she stirred just a little. She did not actually smile, but Mr. Chalmers believed she did.

"Clara was in my form at Miss Stockington's," she said. "She always complained that her family name, Higsby, was so ugly that she would marry the first man who asked her—so she could change it. Yet she married you, a distant cousin with the very same name, only Christian—Higsby."

This was a long speech for Caroline, and Mr. Chalmers' fine acute ear caught it, and he understood. Caroline was trying to be pleasant, and it was a fearful effort for her. He said, "And one of my sons and one of my grandsons are named Higsby too." He laughed gently. His trained eye was studying Caroline without appearing to do so. He was remembering that she had lost her only daughter, a poor, beautiful, mad thing, only a short time ago after years at Hillcrest.

"I suppose," said Caroline, "that you are wondering why I sent for you."

"Frankly, I am," said Mr. Chalmers.

"It is a political matter," said Caroline.

Mr. Chalmers was startled. He was a lawyer, and a very successful one. He had believed that Caroline had sent for him because of a problem she preferred not to discuss with Tandy, Harkness and Swift.

"Political?" he echoed.

"You are state chairman of your party, are you not?"

"Yes, of course." He paused. Women could not vote, and he could not conceive of Caroline, the immured recluse, being a suffragette or interested in politics.

"And the candidate for senator of your party is Gideon Lowe, isn't he?"

Mr. Chalmers, feeling his way, coughed. Caroline's cousin, Timothy Winslow, was now of the opposite party and also a candidate.

"Yes. A splendid gentleman, Gideon. You knew his family in Boston, I believe."

Caroline said impatiently, "No matter. I am not interested in Gideon, except that I want him to be elected senator and defeat my cousin, Timothy Winslow."

"What!" exclaimed Mr. Chalmers, and took his handkerchief from his mouth. Caroline was silent; she merely waited. Mr. Chalmers stared at her. "Er—pardon me, Caroline, but am I mistaken in believing that Timothy is the only member of your family with whom you are on cordial terms? I've heard such a rumor."

Caroline's face appeared to retreat in the duskiness. "The rumor is correct," she said. "That has nothing to do with the fact that I wish him defeated, and very soundly."

Mr. Chalmers was quite stunned. "You do not—er—agree with his principles and politics?" he murmured.

Caroline grunted. "As a woman, I cannot vote and so am classified with idiots, criminals, and children," she said. "It is of no interest to me. You will remember that I wrote you that the matter I wished to discuss with you is most confidential?"

"Yes indeed."

"I know nothing of Timothy's principles or politics, at least not of his averred ones, which I believe are only for public consumption, as are all politicians' promises and opinions. I merely want him so defeated, so discredited, that never again will he offer himself for public office."

"Indeed," murmured Mr. Chalmers, who wondered if he was hearing correctly.

Caroline stirred again on her chair. "He wants political office and political power; he has only money. So it must be brought to his attention that he will never attain that office, that power. And that will take a great deal of money, will it not?"

Mr. Chalmers, who had been a politician since he was twenty-five and who thought he had encountered everything extraordinary in his career, was truly speechless now. He rubbed the moist palms of his hands on his handkerchief and could only look helplessly at Caroline.

"I am a very busy woman," said Caroline with new impatience. "Do you accept or not?"

"Accept what?" said the dazed Mr. Chalmers.

"Money! I thought it takes money to elect anyone."

"So it does," said Mr. Chalmers. He pulled himself together. He became grave. "I will be brief. I never liked your cousin. I was always suspicious of him, even when we were youths together." He lifted his plump palm. "Please, Caroline, let me finish. I have heard that your father called him 'pernicious.' So he is. I hardly expected him to become the candidate of a party which calls itself 'progressive' and is enthusiastic about Mr. Wilson's 'New Freedoms' and is really responsible for the passing of the Sixteenth Amendment—the Internal Revenue Act—of February 1913. After all, Timothy is a rich man. I won't even expound to you my well-grounded theory that that amendment was rushed through, not to gain revenue for the benefit of America, but to finance the present war in Europe and ultimately involve us in the catastrophe. That is my opinion; it is shared by many others. No matter. We are not discussing that now.

"Timothy is an unusually rich man, even for Boston. He has the Bothwell money in his control. I should have thought such a man would be emphatically against the 'New Freedoms,' whatever on earth they mean—are we not a free, strong nation as it is? Yet Timothy is the candidate of those people, for senator! That is what I do not understand."

"He is a Jacobin," said Caroline. "I have been reading his speeches lately. He is fervent about the workingman. Timothy despises what he calls 'the people.' Yet he is very eloquent now about the 'rights' of the poor worker. So he is a liar."

Mr. Chalmers, the astute politician, knew that something else lay under Caroline's sudden and curious air of violence. He kept his voice quiet, and he watched Caroline carefully. "A Jacobin. Very good. Very good, indeed. I suspected that."

"My father suspected and disliked Timothy," said Caroline.

But it is not that, thought Mr. Chalmers. He leaned toward her. "I will be brief, Caroline. It takes a great deal of money to get elected. A man cannot put too much of his own money into his campaign; there are laws against that. But he can have friends— Timothy has much influence in Boston and many influential friends who are indebted to him. Moreover, it is becoming quite fashionable, even among Bostonians, to be slightly 'progressive.' There are fashions in politics as well as in other things. There is something in the air— I do not say that all men who are concerned with the deplorable conditions of the workingman today are liars and potential oppressors. No. My great-grandfather was a bricklayer, himself. But, as a conservative, I believe in the balance of power. This country will fall when there is only a rich and powerful elite and subservient masses, no matter how many circuses and free food are furnished the latter, and how many flatteries. The plan, I am afraid, was laid long ago."

He sighed. "I have said that it is becoming somewhat fashionable, even in Boston, to be slightly 'progressive.' It gives silly, rich people a feeling of éclat, takes them out of their fat sluggishness and gives them a sensation of being part of a dynamic movement. It is only an illusion, of course, but I doubt they will awaken in time to the fact that not only has their own ruin been well plotted, but the destruction of their country as well.

"To be desperately candid about it, I think Timothy will be elected. Gideon has only honor, integrity, and justice to offer."

"I am not interested," said Caroline. "Are you aware that I own the mortgage of the Boston *Morning Enquirer*, which is supporting my cousin?"

"No!" cried Mr. Chalmers in consternation.

Caroline nodded. "Within a few days they will change their tune decisively. They will take 'second thought.' They will 'weigh the issues.' They will be very grave. They will support Gideon Lowe. With growing emphasis."

Mr. Chalmers stood up, put his hands under his coattails, and walked about the room on his short fat legs. Caroline watched him with her intent hazel eyes. Then he stopped before her. "Thank you, Caroline," he said. "You don't know what this means to me and Gideon."

"I am not interested," she said wearily. "Why can't you understand? I am only interested in defeating Timothy."

Mr. Chalmers stood very still, his hands under his coattails, and looked down at her. He did not know why he thought it, but he said to himself: The cost of revenge is very big. Often, it is too high. As a sensitive man, he could feel Caroline's enormous weariness in his very bones. He sat down heavily.

He said, "It will take a vast amount of money to defeat Timothy, Caroline. Perhaps more than you are willing to expend. The newspaper will be of great help. But money is necessary; I know, in some measure, how much is being expended, through force, flattery and threats, and friendship, on Timothy. Gideon, who is honest, intelligent, mild, and good, does not have that money and does not have Timothy's friends. How much are you willing to expend to defeat your cousin?"

"What is needed?" The August sun was moving to the west. Long fingers of gold and rose touched the decaying wall near Caroline.

"The Boston *Morning Enquirer* is the largest newspaper in Boston, Caroline. It also reaches all the suburbs and small towns in our vicinity. I suggest thousands of free copies be distributed everywhere. That is only the beginning. Then we must have eloquent speakers, who will demand a fee, and posters and advertising. We must buy expensive pages in other local newspapers. We must have workers. We are not a poor party, but we simply don't have the outlets our opponents have. We must bring the important issues to the people. As the state chairman of our party, I, too, am limited in what I can spend. We must flood the whole state with news of Gideon, not only Boston."

"What is needed?" repeated Caroline.

She reached over to a table and took a slim slip of paper in her hand. "I can trust you, Higsby," she said. "I am giving you this check. When you need more, you have only to call me."

Mr. Chalmers looked at the check, could not believe it, then readjusted his glasses.

"Not enough?" asked Caroline sardonically.

"Enough," said Mr. Chalmers in a subdued voice.

"As a beginning," said Caroline. "I will spend whatever you need to defeat him."

Mr. Chalmers held the check in his hand. He looked at Caroline. He was not an impulsive man, but he said, "Caroline, can I help you?"

She stood up. "No one can. I must leave you now, Higsby. The maid will order a hack for you. Your train to Boston will leave in half an hour."

She left him and went upstairs. He could hear the rustling of her dress, the sound of grit under her shoes. He heard a door open, then close.

Caroline lay down on Elizabeth's bed. "My darling," she whispered. "My darling."

There was a stunning blank feeling in her head. She had a strange dream about Elizabeth, who stood before her silently. She said to the shadow, "But I was betrayed long before you were born. Perhaps even before I was born."

Six days later the maid came to Caroline in her study. "Miz Timothy Winslow wants to speak to you, ma'am. She's downstairs. Should I send her away?"

Caroline reread a letter from her son Ames and smiled. "I will see Mrs. Winslow," she said. She went downstairs.

Amanda was waiting in the drawing room, sitting on the edge of the chair where Mr. Chalmers had sat. She did not speak when Caroline came into the room, nor even when Caroline sat opposite her in silence. The two women looked at each other, Amanda's candid brown eyes straight and steady, Caroline's indifferent. Amanda was dressed in a light tan suit, long and pleated, and she wore a large feathered hat, and her hands were gloved. Her round and pleasant face was grave and pale.

"A warm day," said Caroline at last.

"Oh, Caroline. You must know why I've come all the way from Newport to see you," said Amanda in a tired voice.

"Yes?" said Caroline. "But you and Timothy quite often come here, don't you? What is so unusual about your visit today?"

"Ames. Your son Ames," said Amanda.

"Ames?"

Amanda looked at her.

"Has something happened to Ames?" asked Caroline.

Amanda did not speak.

Caroline spoke irritably. "I'm afraid I'm not very good at guessing, Amanda. What has Ames got to do with you?"

"Then you know," said Amanda flatly.

"I know nothing and care about very little," said Caroline.

Amanda looked at her gloves and purse. She had never noticed it before, for her family had always been rich, but now she felt power in the room, and ruthlessness, and a force beyond money.

"You've always hated Timothy's mother," said Amanda. "I suppose you still hate her, though she died a year ago. And you hate Melinda, my sister-in-law."

"I don't follow you," said Caroline. "I thought you were speaking of my son Ames."

"You and Timothy have always been such friends," said Amanda. "I had hoped you and I could talk frankly today."

"Why don't you then?" asked Caroline with impatience.

Amanda wanted to cry. She swallowed her tears. "Very well. You know our daughter Amy."

"I have seen her a few times. A pretty young thing. But a little vacuous, isn't she?"

Amanda was shocked. "Caroline! Amy may be quiet, but she is a lovely girl."

"What has Ames got to do with Amy?" asked Caroline.

"Amy told us last night that she and Ames are going to marry after the elections," said Amanda.

"Indeed," said Caroline. "Well, isn't that their own business? Amy is of age, isn't she?"

"Not until November the first."

Caroline frowned with more impatience. "Ames and I are not very close," she said. "He has gone his way, and I have gone mine. Are you asking me for my approval, Amanda?"

"I'm asking you to disapprove, Caroline."

"Why should I?"

Amanda said, "Ames asked Amy to keep their decision to marry to themselves until after Timothy is elected senator. But Amy is devoted to her father; she felt she ought to tell him. Timothy is wild, Caroline."

"Why?" said Caroline brutally. "Is my son such a poor marriage prospect? Aren't you being a little insulting, Amanda?"

The harsh large face confronted her with derision. Amanda exclaimed, "You did know, Caroline! You knew all the time! You've always hated Timothy's mother, but you don't mind Ames marrying her granddaughter! Why, Caroline?"

"I make it a point not to interfere in anyone's affairs," said Caroline. "Don't be hysterical, Amanda."

"I, hysterical?" Amanda was outraged. "I've never been hysterical in my life! Oh, it is all too much! That Boston newspaper attacking Timothy all at once! The letters, the advertisements in the other newspapers! All the new posters! Editorials! Poor Timothy. He was so certain he would be elected, and now all this! It's too much for him to bear."

"You are incoherent," said Caroline coldly. Amanda had snapped open her purse and taken out her handkerchief and was wiping her eyes. Her plump shoulders shook. "What has this political matter got to do with Ames?" Caroline continued.

"I don't know!" cried Amanda. "You are muddling me. I am trying to say that Timothy has a great deal to bear just now, and then Amy tells us that she will marry Ames after the elections. And you sit there, Caroline, and it means nothing to you."

"What have you against Ames? You and Timothy?"

Amanda lost all caution in her extremity. "We don't want our little girl to marry Ames. He's only five or six years older, and as you say he is doing well and has many friends. But there's something else. We feel, in many ways, that he is too old for Amy, and it's not just his age. I'm sorry, Caroline, but we don't like him."

"That is unfortunate. But evidently your daughter does."

Amanda, who was never wild, became wild now. "He's corrupt! He isn't a *good* person, Caroline!"

"I still don't follow you," said Caroline.

Amanda stood up and looked about as if searching for an escape. Then she swung toward Caroline. "You corrupted him! He hasn't any real human feelings. You never treated him as a human being, as your son. And so he is callous. You destroyed your children, Caroline, because your father destroyed you. You didn't know any better."

Caroline's face swelled and became an ugly red. "Go on," she said.

"I never knew your father. Timothy hated him." She blushed under her tears.

"I never did care for family history," said Caroline calmly.

"Timothy doesn't want our daughter to marry the grandson of John Ames. There it is, Caroline, and I'm sorry if I've hurt you."

"Let me see," said Caroline. "You have just insulted my father, me, and my son. Yet you are 'sorry.'" She smiled tightly. "Is it that Timothy thinks Ames won't have enough money?"

"Oh, Caroline!" Amanda sat down again and looked at the other woman in despair. "We aren't talking about money. It's Ames. We don't want him to marry Amy! He will destroy her." She put her hands to her mouth.

"Timothy mentioned your husband, Tom Sheldon. I always liked Tom."

"What has Tom got to do with this?" Caroline began to tremble with sickness and wrath.

"You don't understand. How can I say it? We are afraid you—that you —that Ames will treat Amy as you treated Tom. Harshness and indifference would kill her."

"So you think I was harsh and indifferent to my husband."

"You were, Caroline, you were. Not that Timothy blamed you too much."

"You must not speak of Tom," said Caroline with great quietness. "I can't understand what you are talking about. What do you want me to do?"

"Stop Ames from marrying Amy!"

"What would you suggest?"

Amanda wrung her gloves in her hands. "You surely have some influence over Ames. Perhaps you could promise him some money if he didn't marry Amy."

"I certainly will not offer Ames money to prevent any marriage he wishes to make. Why should I, even if the girl he wants to marry is the daughter of Timothy Winslow?"

Caroline stood up, and Amanda stood up also, slowly, as if pushed to her feet. They confronted each other.

Then Amanda said in a hushed and fearful tone, "What do you mean, 'even if the girl he wants to marry is the daughter of Timothy Winslow'?"

"I am only returning insult for insult, Amanda. You are trying my patience."

"I don't think so," said Amanda. She shook her head. "You helped Timothy. Do you hate him, Caroline?"

"If I helped him so, why should I hate him?"

But Amanda said, as if she had not heard, "There was his mother's will. She left him two thousand dollars. That was all. Why?"

"I'm sure I don't know."

"And William never writes to Timothy; only to me. He never sends his regards to Timothy. When his last child was born Timothy sent his congratulations and a check. The check was returned," said Amanda faintly, her brown eyes dazed and clouded.

"How you do harp on money, Amanda," said Caroline. "Have you no other conversation?"

Amanda cried, "I was brought up in such a kind, good family! I don't understand all these overtones! I don't understand anything!" She sobbed. "And there was Elizabeth, who lost her mind. There must be something wrong in the family."

At the expression on Caroline's face she fell back. Caroline pulled the bell rope, and when the maid answered Caroline said, "Mrs. Winslow wishes a hack to the station. Please call for one."

She turned abruptly and left the room, and the maid smirked disdainfully at Amanda, the rudely abandoned.

CHAPTER TEN

The war in Europe blundered and rolled on, weltering voluptuously in hatred and blood and murder, in lies and countercharges of atrocities, in hysteria and rage. Now even bubbling, childlike America could ignore it no longer. But she did not know what to think in this morning of her confused awakening. Newspapers published accounts of crematoriums in Germany (*Life*) where the bodies of Allied and German soldiers (some only wounded, many of the accounts read) were thrown for their "lubricant oils, fats and fertilizers." An alleged American newspaperman declared that he had bluffed his way to the front and had seen German soldiers gaily carrying "bagfuls of ears." (Mark Sullivan's *Over Here*.) There was not an atrocity allegedly committed by the German troops which the German government, with photographs, did not declare had been committed by Allied troops. "Super-Dum-Dums inflict awful injuries on victims!" cried the New York *Herald* of October 1914 in an article execrating the German armies. With perfect photographs taken in German field hospitals, and with German meticulousness, the German government revealed that it was the Allies who were using these "soft" bullets. The Kaiser protested that German soldiers were not being taken prisoner; they were being murdered after their arms had been taken from them. The Kaiser vehemently denied any atrocities on civilian populations. He invited American newsmen to the areas now under his fist, so that they might inquire and see for themselves. The invitation was not accepted.

The fiendish charges and countercharges blazed at Americans from the headlines in their newspapers. At first. But by late October the newspapers no longer published the German charges; it was as if a signal had been given; the accounts now were all of "Hun inhumanity." When the German ambassador in Washington implored American tourists not to travel to England on British vessels, the newspapers were loud in their indignation. America was neutral; Americans "had a right" to travel when and how they wished. The German government published pleas to American tourists. They were laughed at or ignored.

A large Chicago daily declared, "There is a curious flavor to this war. It seems only a prelude to something that is still obscure to the whole world, something dangerous to all humanity, perhaps. It is well that President Wilson has assured us that Americans have no desire to embroil themselves in this mysterious conflict." A Buffalo, New York, daily said with facetious truth: "This European war suggests that maybe the white man's burden is the white man himself." An Indiana paper declared: "We never appreciated so keenly as now the foresight exercised by our forefathers in emigrating from Europe." The Chicago *Herald* said: "Peace-loving citizens of this country will now rise up and tender a hearty vote of thanks to Columbus for having discovered America." A New York newspaper wrote warningly:

"There is something in the European war which does not honestly meet the eye. There is a shadow over the guns belching in Belgium and France, and it isn't clear yet."

To Caroline Ames Sheldon the war meant nothing. She had more important things to think of, as the stable world she had known died hour by hour. She was becoming richer daily; the golden fortress rose higher about her. She waited and planned for the day when she would destroy Timothy Winslow utterly, completely. Her money and her vengeance were now her sole reasons for living. As summer merged into autumn, she did not go to the abandoned graveyard on the hill. She sat in her study and thought and plotted. Her voice, almost unused except when she called her Boston office or her bank or lawyers or brokers in New York, became as rusty as abandoned iron.

Her only truly human pleasure came when she received letters from Mimi Bothwell. Mimi had left Paris after a series of triumphs, because Paris had no time for art exhibits, even the most provocative, after the first weeks of the war. She had gone to London for several shows. But London, too, had begun to have more serious matters on its mind, such as the zeppelins showering death and fire upon the old city. So Mimi, on October 1, left England for America. She cabled both her mother and her aunt. The two women feared the submarines. One prayed. The other did not, for she had long ago forgotten how to pray. One thanked God when Mimi's ship arrived safely in New York after a long and tedious and dark voyage.

Two days before the elections, Timothy Winslow came to Lyme to see his cousin Caroline. They had not seen each other for some time. Not even their financial paths crossed now.

When the slatternly maid came to Caroline to tell her that Mr. Winslow had arrived and wished to speak to her, Caroline smiled darkly and briefly. She made Timothy wait for fifteen minutes. Then rustling in her ancient black silk, which was frayed at the hems and seams, she went down to the rotting drawing room. Timothy was standing near the cold fireplace. It was a day of gloom and chill, with a flaying wind from the sea. "Well?" said Caroline.

Timothy did not answer immediately. He looked about the room slowly. His shiver was not affected. He felt the gritty carpet under his feet; he was afraid to touch anything in the room, for he was meticulous and had a horror of dirt and soil. The house smelled of must and damp and grease and abandonment. He did not know why it was, but the very house convinced him that he had come here only to be defeated. Then he looked at his cousin with open hatred, and she stood at a distance from him and stared at him with eyes that were curiously fervent.

His appearance gave her satisfaction. Timothy was still tall and lean and upright and elegant. But he had completely faded. Exhaustion and desolation were painted in gray shadows on his gaunt face. His light eyes were sunken in wrinkled patches; his fine hair was colorless, as were his lips, and there was a wizened look to his aristocratic nose. There was no resemblance in him to his mother now. Her vitality and grace had been washed from his face and expression, leaving behind only a parchness and dryness and an emaciated angularity.

He studied his cousin in silence, and he thought that the old gray hag looked much older and much more battered than when he had last seen her. Then his satisfaction disappeared. For the first time he was impressed by her aspect of absolute power and relentlessness. His voice almost shook as he said formally, "How do you do, Caroline?"

She sat down without answering, and her brittle silk rattled like paper.

He stood before her and said, "I've been too busy for visits. The elections, you know."

She still did not speak. So he said, "Amanda told me only yesterday that she came to see you in the summer—about Amy. And your son. She should not have done that, Caroline."

Caroline said, "I agree."

"It was my place, not Amanda's, to come." It was cold, drafty, and dank here, but a light dampness broke out on Timothy's forehead and in the palms of his hands.

He continued: "I'd have come before this—but the elections. One can never trust the electorate—capricious. I thought it was all settled; I'm not so sure as of today." He paused. He knew he was rambling and even slightly incoherent, but he could not help himself.

"But you think you will be elected?" said Caroline with indifference.

He tried to smile. He remembered that he had rehearsed this scene with Caroline all the way to Lyme. He would be gravely jocular and reasonable. He had been deeply alarmed at Amanda's account of her clash with Caroline, but then Amanda was tactless. She had not approached Caroline in the right fashion; she had set her back up. Even Caroline Ames could be insulted, it seemed. He said, putting confidence in his light voice, "Certainly I'll be elected, Caroline."

Caroline looked down at her hands. They were big hands, and good, but they were dry and gnarled, and the knuckles suggested grime. Caroline said, "I have just read one of your recent speeches, Timothy. I never knew you were so eloquent." Her voice filled the room, and it was toneless and mechanical. "I also never knew that 'the plight of the working people' affected you so much. You were lyrical in places about 'the new future, the new world of justice.'"

"You think I'm insincere?" He watched her.

She studied him, and her hazel eyes, so deep now beneath her black brows, sparkled. "Of course you are insincere. But I am also sure that you are absolutely sincere about your aims—which you don't permit the people to know anything about."

He almost forgot Amy in his sudden alertness. "And what are my 'aims,' as you call them, Caroline?"

She shrugged her great shoulders. "I know them as well as you do, so why discuss them? But I can tell you that you won't succeed. Not in America."

Now he was really alarmed. But how could she know, this recluse who spent her life in this disgusting house, spinning her golden webs like a huge spider and knowing nothing of the world?

"I haven't the faintest idea what you mean," he said.

She shrugged again. "No matter."

But he thought suddenly of that morning, years ago, when his brother William had sat on his horse and had looked down at him and had known him, to his apprehension. He had thought William a little stupid, always. But William had not been stupid at all. Was he making the same mistake about Caroline?

Caroline said, "But why did you come to see me today? Amanda surely must have told you that I have no interest in my son's love affairs and that I refuse to interfere."

It was actually an effort to bring his thoughts back to Amy, because his perceptive mind had become engrossed with a sense of danger in this room.

"As your cousin, Caroline, and one of your very few relatives, I thought we could discuss this matter reasonably."

She smiled and did not speak.

"No one can know Ames better than you, Caroline," he said. "He is only a few years older than Amy but seems much more. She is a quiet, innocent child. I want her to be happy in marriage. Ames won't make her happy. I know you haven't anything against my child—how could you have? She's been particularly sheltered, for she has a frail character. She's too gentle and shy and unassuming. Ames—well, he's worldly, to say the least."

"He's very much like you," said Caroline abruptly.

Timothy could not speak. A liar, even in his spirit, he recognized the truth of what Caroline had said, and he had always hated truth.

"No doubt you feel I am insulting," said Caroline, smoothing one of her wrists with the fingers of her other hand.

Timothy, in his shock, decided to be honest. "You are quite right, Caroline. Ames would crush her." He paused. "If Ames thinks that by marrying Amy he'll come into a fortune, he's badly mistaken. I'll leave her nothing."

"That is your own affair," said Caroline.

"And I understand from Ames himself—and from others—that he will inherit little from you."

"He has his father's money," said Caroline in a tired voice. "And he's done very well for himself. He doesn't need your money."

"And you have no objection to Amy, considering her grandmother? You always hated my mother, Caroline."

"I am not in the least interested in what my sons do or whom they marry," said Caroline.

Then Timothy, really distracted, lost control of himself. Had his party chairman been more optimistic about his chances of becoming senator, he would have been more assured, more able to guard his speech, more confident. But the party chairman had told him only yesterday that if he won—if he won—it would be only by the smallest margin. Yet only a few months ago his election was practically sure. It was the damned newspapers. It was something else, much more stealthy and hidden. It was money somewhere, and pressure, which was threatening him.

"Your son will kill Amy!" he exclaimed with despairing hatred.

"Is she that weak?" said Caroline. "That feeble?"

"You've made Ames what he is!" said Timothy recklessly. "He's distorted, deformed, perverted. You know that. You did it to him."

His sunken and faded cheeks flared with furious color. He wanted to take Caroline by the throat and strangle her.

"What kind of a life did he have in this house?" said Timothy. "A stupid, illiterate father! A mother who had no interests beyond money, who lived in filth and never saw it." All his old envy and loathing for Caroline were thick in his throat, and all his disgust for her father, and all his aversion for his mother. "Did you ever care for your children, Caroline? Your son John has been invited to leave Tandy, Harkness and Swift because of his shady manipulations and practices. Your daughter died insane. Your father was a cheap nobody, a thief on a monumental scale, despised by everybody. That is the background your son Ames has, and he wants to marry my daughter! God! I'll do anything to prevent it. Anything!"

Caroline's face became remote and closed. When Timothy had stopped speaking she waited for him to finish mopping his haggard face and his sweating hands. Then she said, "What can you do?"

Timothy was actually groaning. He put away his handkerchief.

"You can do nothing," said Caroline calmly. "But I won't overlook your insults. And your errors. You speak of Ames' background. Let me enlighten you first about your own. You are proud that your mother was an Esmond. But who was your mother, really? The granddaughter of a kitchen slavey. A pretty slavey who entangled your great-grandfather. I understand she never learned to read and write and that even her daughter's father was in doubt. You see, Timothy, I have done some investigation. Over all these years. For my own reasons.

"Your father, Timothy? George Winslow? His father was a physician who was indicted for malpractice—in other words, illegal operations. It was very fitting, wasn't it, that your mother, with her spotted ancestry, should marry such a man? George Winslow's father was not only a criminal and a clever dullard, but he left little money. My father supported your mother, your father's widow, and she was his mistress. She bore my father an illegitimate daughter, your sister Melinda. Your sister Melinda, who is my sister also, has a much better ancestry, for she has mine."

Timothy stood in absolute silence, staring at this woman who was blasting away his pride, destroying the pedestal on which he had stood all his life. He could not disbelieve her. There was such surety in her voice and manner, and such cold gloating, and such absolute power. "But who cares for ancestry?" said Caroline in a peculiar voice. "Certainly not I. However, you may be interested to know mine, which is much different from your own murky family's.

"You've said that my father was a 'cheap nobody.' You are quite wrong. His father was the famous American painter, David Ames."

"I don't believe it!" cried Timothy.

"You are perfectly free not to believe it," said Caroline. "I have many of his paintings upstairs in my private gallery. And what was David Ames' ancestry? His father was the youngest son of a British peer. I have the full genealogy. And who was my grandmother? A Hollingshead of England, a family of poets, historians, teachers, philosophers, and nobility. One of her family is buried in Westminster Abbey. A very old family.

"If anyone should object to a marriage on the plea of ancestry, I should be the one."

She stood up. "If you insult me much more, Timothy, I will supply the press with your family history. How your friends in Boston will laugh."

Timothy, who had nothing now, not even patrician ancestry, said in a weak and shaken voice, "I don't care about ancestry either. But I do care about my daughter. I won't have her taken away from me!"

Caroline turned and looked at him fully, and he saw the great hate in her face.

"You took my daughter from me. You killed her. You drove her to death with your lies. Did you think I didn't know?"

An awful silence stood between them. It continued moment by moment.

Then Caroline said, "I am not finished with you, Timothy. You will see me everywhere because of Elizabeth. You will remember Elizabeth until the day you die."

Timothy could finally move, stiffly and painfully. He was full of dread and fear.

"You, too," he said, "will remember Elizabeth until you die. You had a part in killing her."

CHAPTER ELEVEN

The Boston *Morning Enquirer* published its editorial on the front page the day before the elections, and it filled half the columns. Its headline asked: "Shall Timothy Winslow Be Our First Senator?"

Inexorably, doggedly, it demolished Timothy's claims and aspirations, ruthlessly, one by one, "He declares himself the great champion of the 'working class and all those who are afflicted.' A careful examination of Mr. Winslow's charities, which this newspaper has undertaken over the past few weeks, shows that always he has given niggardly, even among a population that is prudent and careful of its gifts. It is true that he has allowed his family name to be used in the promotion of charities. Nevertheless, the sums given by him fall far below the gifts of family physicians of modest income, the managers of small factories, dentists, shopkeepers, independent businessmen, and struggling office superintendents. Yet Mr. Winslow is one of the richest men in Boston, in the Commonwealth, and his fortune is respected even among such men as Mr. J. P. Morgan and Commodore Vanderbilt. He has considerable control of the Bothwell money, into which he married.

"We have come into possession of documents from Harvard University. In his student speeches and themes, Mr. Winslow insistently repeated his dogma of 'Family Prestige and Name' as opposed to those he chose to call 'Vandals.' His diatribes against Irish Catholics—'the newcomers whose religion and race are alien to us,' to quote his own words—were extremely contemptuous and intolerant. One wonders how he brought himself to condescend to the great-granddaughter of an Irish Catholic immigrant and marry her. Yet now this gentleman cultivates our Irish Americans and recently accepted an invitation to speak before the Holy Name Society in fervent periods and affection, during which he frequently mentioned Mrs. Winslow's great-grandfather who had been a hod carrier.

" 'In the name of office every man is a liar,' said Scipio Africanus over two thousand years ago. That was true of Rome; it is also true of America, which uncomfortably resembles Rome just prior to her period of decline. But, we must ask, is it necessary? Is it not possible occasionally for Americans to elect an honorable man and a just one? Must we always have charlatans and hypocrites who are so lured by the power of office that they will speak piously, with their tongues in their cheeks? Are there no Americans of honor and uprightness who will not only ask for office but will receive it? American politics have been arousing the amusement and disgust of other nations for decades, and rightfully so. We have consistently elected liars and thieves and plunderers and rascals, until our political parties are notorious for their stenches and cannot be trusted either with their constituents' money or welfare.

"These are the days when men in office should not be plunderers and hypocrites and liars. The events in Europe, however we ignore them today, will shadow our future, for we no longer are an island complete in itself. We need patriots, not betrayers. We need prudent men, not profligates. We need politicians who will think first of their country before they vote in the Senate and Congress. We need legislators who will not cater to special segments of our society but will consider the welfare of all the people. 'Equal justice for all, special privilege for none,' said Thomas Jefferson. In inciting the basest instincts of humanity, such as greed and envy, lust and hate, any would-be politician is doing the most terrible disservice to his country.

"Mr. Winslow speaks movingly of 'the workers.' Let us call his attention to the fact that the greater part of the American people are workers, whether they are surgeons or sweepers, plumbers or planters, mechanics or merchants, bricklayers or businessmen, lawyers or layers of streets. Only those who have inherited fortunes—and they are few—cannot be considered 'workers.' And the politician who attempts to create classes in America, in the style of corrupt old European governments and societies, will help to destroy America.

"We have no distinct 'labor' in America. All who work with their hands or brains for their sustenance are 'labor.' No man is a 'common man.' We are mightily uncommon in America, and we must remain that way!"

It continued: "There is something sinister abroad in America today. It is our opinion that it has its roots in Europe and that the European war is the result of some malign philosophy. If we listen closely enough we can hear its whisper in our own land. That whisper will grow to a shout of death and destruction if men of the caliber of Timothy Winslow are elected."

The Boston *Enquirer* was a morning paper and had a high repute in Boston and was read in streetcars and in commuters' trains, in kitchens and factories, in offices and shops. Timothy Winslow read it and called his campaign manager in rage. The manager said, "I have some possibly good news for you, Tim. I've just found out that your cousin, Caroline Ames, has a large mortgage on that paper. It's very late, but can't you call her at once and tell her to have the *Enquirer* publish a retraction of that editorial? It could come out in special editions tomorrow morning, just before the voting starts. She's a recluse and probably doesn't know what that rag is up to. Tim? Tim?"

But Timothy had hung up. He sat for a long time, alone, staring at the vision of Caroline's face as he had seen it yesterday. "Probably doesn't know what the rag is up to!" She knew. She had done all this. His pale face whitened with hate and fear. But he finally assured himself he would win. The sheepheaded electorate would not understand half the words in that damning editorial; it did not have the intelligence to understand its implications. The American people were stupid dogs, and on that stupidity he would gamble, as so many others before him had gambled—and won.

Ames Sheldon loved Amy Winslow as much as it was possible for a young man whose emotions were superficial.

He had not been exactly candid with his mother. It was not Timothy's opposition alone, nor Amy's unwillingness to hurt her father, which had kept him from marrying the girl. He, too, had dallied, in spite of his shallow love for her. A penniless girl was quite another thing from a girl who would inherit a large part of the Winslow and Bothwell fortunes. He had waited, not because of Amy's sentimentality, but in the hope that Timothy would be reconciled to his daughter's marriage to him. His waiting had proved to him that Timothy would never openly consent to the marriage or welcome him. Until he had had that talk with his mother on the day of Elizabeth's funeral he had been more than reconsidering, if reluctantly.

He had greatly increased the fortune which had come from his father, though not as spectacularly as his brother John had done. He had more of the nature of his mother, prudent, calculating. His construction business was sound and prosperous; he now employed twelve architects, the best in the city, and paid them well. But he had no intention of marrying a poor girl without financial prospects. He had only to withdraw from the situation gracefully. He did not consider Amy's feelings or the fact that the girl loved him desperately.

Caroline's offer had made all the difference in the world. The three million dollars waiting for him in the bank, for the very hour of his marriage to Amy Winslow, was the most golden of lures. It even increased his affection for Amy; in a way, it was her dowry. He would smile at that. Then, of course, there would be children, and Caroline's money had to go somewhere. Certainly not to charities or foundations or funds!

A plotter, he had wondered why the Boston *Morning Enquirer* had changed its tune about Timothy Winslow only recently. There was a reason behind everything. It needed only money in the proper hands. He soon discovered that his mother owned the mortgage on the paper. He had no doubt this morning, as he read the devastating editorial, that Timothy would be defeated.

He had been almost sure a week ago, and that was why he had been pressing Amy to marry him before the elections. Had Timothy had a real chance to be elected, he would have waited, as his mother had originally suggested, until after the votes were in. But Timothy's defeat would be so disastrous to him that his daughter, in pity and love, would delay marrying Ames until her father's calamity had lost its full force. In that delay Ames might lose her. Worse, he would lose that three million dollars.

Though he had much work on his desk and it was only nine in the morning, he called Amy. He must see her at once; it was imperative. She demurred; Daddy seemed very upset about something. Had Ames seen that dreadful editorial in the *Enquirer?* How could a paper be so cruel? Mama was with him now, upstairs in the study. Couldn't Ames wait until the afternoon, perhaps, or the day after tomorrow, when it would be all settled?

Ames could not wait. Amy had never heard his voice so urgent and so cajoling and so sincerely ardent and pleading. She would meet him, then, in about two hours in the Boston Museum. The girl was intrigued and more than a little excited by Ames' voice. She loved him dearly. Her experience of real life was very little. She was certain that the world was mainly composed of gentle and affectionate people, good people, kind and honorable people, people who sheltered the weak and protected them, people who had extreme good will.

At two o'clock that afternoon, after hours of pleading, threats, expressions of love, renunciations, reconciliations, tendernesses, and assurances, Ames Sheldon and Amy Winslow were married in Brookline in an office of the justice of the peace. Amy was in a state of immense confusion before and during the marriage. Mama and Daddy would be very hurt. Mama, especially, would want a large wedding for her only daughter. "We can have the church wedding at any time, after the elections," said Ames.

"Then why not wait until after the elections?" asked Amy.

Ames repeated over and over: in the excitement and joy when her father was elected he would naturally not be too displeased at this clandestine marriage. Later, when he became accustomed to the idea that he was now a senator, he would have many second thoughts and again he would oppose it. He would take his family to Washington.

Amy, the trustful, the innocent, the loving, and the confused, could see no flaw in these arguments. She hated the little untidy office of the justice of the peace. She shrank from the two witnesses. But when Ames kissed her, she was filled with wild, shy joy and clung to him. At that moment he felt a deeper love for her, but more than love, he felt gratitude. The three million dollars was now his. He sent a telegram to his mother. Caroline could move very quickly on occasion. In less than an hour the bank welcomed Mr. Ames Sheldon and had him sign documents, while Amy, in Ames' carriage outside, sat and waited and wondered dimly why her bridegroom should bother about any bank at all.

After his bank visit Ames took Amy immediately to his tasteful flat on Beacon Street and saw to it that the marriage was consummated then and there. At five o'clock, disheveled and flushed and trembling, Amy called her mother and explained that she had met some friends while shopping but would be home very shortly. Then, in her innocent nakedness, she turned to Ames on the bed and embraced him with a sweet passion of which he had never considered her capable. He held her and felt the first true tenderness of his life. He kissed her hair, her throat and breast—her childish breast —and her hands and knees. I'll be good to you, sweet, he said to himself silently, and actually believed it then.

He sent his shaken and ecstatic bride home in a hired hack. Amy was to say nothing, not even to her mother, until tomorrow night. "I'll come in about nine," Ames said, kissing her over and over. "It'll be a welter, but think of the excitement!"

Amy could not even remember her mother's objections and warnings. She was too full now of the force of life and her own joy and fulfillment. There was no one in the world for her but Ames. While the hack waited outside, she kissed Ames with abject love and passion and mourned that she had to leave him. The black vapor of her hair blew about her face, and her child's face was radiant with delight and happiness. Twice she ran back up the stairs to hug him and cling to him, her brown eyes full of shining tears. Once she even humbly kissed his hand, and feeling that child's kiss on his flesh, Ames shrank, vaguely ashamed.

But within an hour, complacent and smiling, he was at his desk in his flat, with papers before him and a pen in his hand, calculating just exactly what he would do with that glorious three million dollars. He actually forgot his cousin, his bride, and the trusting kiss on his hand. He remembered her at midnight, after a gourmet dinner in his flat and a bottle of Chablis, and toasted her smilingly. Then, as usual, he made his accustomed round of his treasures in their various cabinets and sipped a little brandy and laughed a little to himself. There was a shop on Bond Street, in London, full of greater treasures. He saw himself examining them closely.

Timothy could not sleep. He was filled with forebodings. Amanda pretended to sleep beside him. She watched him later pacing the large bedroom and prayed for him and wondered, as she often did, if prayers were effective for such as Timothy Winslow.

Long before noon Timothy was at party headquarters. Telephones rang and shrilled about him. The first returns were very good. The Silk Stocking districts were voting for him solidly, though they were not usually of his party. (Nor was he.)

Then, at three o'clock, the votes of the working-class districts began to come in. They were three to one against Timothy Winslow. "Impossible!" cried Timothy, stunned and aghast. "I thought the bas— I thought they would be the ones who would solidly support me!" He remembered the almost empty union hall of the night before. He had been reassured by his campaign manager: "After all, they work twelve hours a day and are tired. So they just went home. But wait for tomorrow."

It was tomorrow. The returns came in faster now. The "working people" were not supporting Timothy Winslow. He was their self-declared champion, but they were not supporting him. They had unflawed instincts. They were voting for Gideon Lowe, who had not promised them a "rich, full life." He had promised them only prudent government, and they had believed him. He had spoken of a fair day's work for a fair day's pay. "This is a matter of morality, and morality has always been the prime mover of Americans. The immorality of great wealth and great poverty, side by side, has no place in our nation."

He had attended Groton with Timothy, and then Harvard, through the stinted generosity of an old aunt who was still alive and in her nineties. His family was truly "First Family," if impoverished. A gentleman, he had not replied to Timothy's elegantly phrased but vicious attacks in the newspapers. Shy and quiet, he had few rich and influential friends. He did not know who it had been, at the eleventh hour, who had come so lavishly to his assistance. He sat with Higsby Chalmers, who smoked cigars contentedly, and watched the returns being marked up on the big blackboard in party headquarters. By half-past three he was more than a little amazed. Higsby merely asked for more hot coffee and lit another cigar.

The polls were within an hour of closing when Timothy Winslow knew he had been defeated. Party workers, with dark faces, were already drifting out of the room.

Then Amanda called him. "I can't talk with Mrs. Winslow just yet," said Timothy, who looked sick and faint. (He knew what this dreadful and resounding debacle meant; he would never get the nomination again for any political office.)

"She says it is most terribly important," said the wife of the campaign manager, who was attending to the telephones. "She sounded very upset, Timothy."

So Timothy took the telephone. Even before she spoke, Timothy could hear her sobbing. "Oh, I didn't want to disturb you just now!" she cried. "Not just now! But the reporters——" Her voice broke.

"Send them away," said Timothy bitterly. "I'll make a statement later. About seven o'clock."

"No, Timothy! It isn't about the elections! It's about Amy." Amanda's voice broke again. "Timothy! She was married to Ames Sheldon yesterday in some justice of the peace's office, away out somewhere in Brookline. The reporters just found out about it, and they came here; that horrible justice must have called them this morning."

"What?" said Timothy softly. "Amy? Ames? Amanda!" His voice rose. "I don't believe it. Where is Amy now?"

"I don't know! She left at noon to shop, she said, and she isn't home. I've called Ames' office, and he isn't there, either! I've called his flat, and there's no answer. I'm sure it's true! I—I talked with the justice himself while the reporters were here. Oh, Timothy," she groaned. "Today, of all days. And our little girl and that awful, cruel Ames. Can't you get the election returns sooner than seven? I can't stand it, Timothy!"

"I'll be home at once," said Timothy. "Don't interrupt. I've already lost. Yes, I said Lost. I'm finished, Amanda."

"No, no! It can't be! It can't be!" exclaimed Amanda, appalled. But he had already hung up the receiver.

He left the office without a word, in spite of the weak questions and calls. He rolled home through the city, looking at the posters with his name upon them which had been nailed to telephone and electric poles. But he did not see them. There was a murmurous buzzing in his ears and a constriction about his temples. His coachman had to help him from the carriage and then had to half carry him into the house through the avid groups of reporters about the door and the flash of floodlight powder. He did not even see them.

He said to Amanda, looking at her blankly, "I never want to see her again." Then he collapsed at her feet in the hallway.

The newspapers hinted delicately the next day that it was possible that Mr. Timothy Winslow's stroke had been caused by more than his ghastly defeat at the polls. Under this they reproduced facsimiles of the records of the justice of the peace. They quoted the justice at length. "A lovely young couple," he said under a photograph of his beaming face, which was under a photograph of Amy making her debut and a photograph of Ames Sheldon taken on a tennis court last summer. "Happy young people. But it took me several hours to realize who they really were."

Timothy's friends were at a loss to know over which event they should be more shocked, the elections or "that child Amy's" vulgarity at being married in the office of a justice of the peace. The latter event finally engrossed their attention. Grim old ladies nodded portentous heads as they sat in their carriages on the way to visit Amanda and offer their condolences. Amy's brothers came home from school to be with their stricken mother and their sick father.

439

Amy and Ames came to the house three days later, after Amanda had refused to talk with her daughter on the telephone. But when she saw the crying girl she could only take her into her arms and weep also and make no complaints or accusations. She would not look at Ames or speak to him, though he sat near her in the small morning room. This coolly infuriated him. He was no leper; he was the son of one of the richest women in the world. He was a rich man in his own right, and successful. But Amanda's plump strong back was turned coldly upon him, as though he were a stable groom or a ribbon clerk who had seduced her daughter.

So, maliciously, he gave Amanda his mother's written promise to give him three million dollars on the day he married Amy Winslow. He had to thrust the paper into her hand, and he smiled into her glaring eyes. Amanda pulled her glasses from the clip on her dress and read. "What is it, Mama?" asked Amy timidly.

But Amanda returned the paper to Ames, and her blunt face was glazed over with stony silence.

Ames was satisfied. He had other satisfactions in the weeks that followed, and many congratulations, and quite a number of new orders. He was not surprised at all this; he understood his fellows very well, indeed. He did not even wonder how the news of his mother's "wedding gift" had reached the ears of his friends. Perhaps it was the manner in which he was greeted at banks. Just before Christmas, cautious invitations were extended to him and his young wife, who had less color these days than before her marriage and who was even quieter than ordinarily and much more timid. No one spoke to them of Timothy; everyone knew that he would not see his daughter. Here and there a voice rose, criticizing Timothy. After all, his girl had really made an excellent match, even if it had been done in an unapproved, shopgirlish fashion. These modern young people!

John wrote a short and very pungent letter to his brother, which highly amused Ames. He was even more highly amused at the after-wedding gifts which arrived not only from Amanda's and Amy's friends but from John himself. There was no church wedding after all. It was not reasonable to expect one, everyone said. While Timothy was regaining his speech rapidly and had already partly regained the use of his left leg, he was still quite unwell and was immured at home. No one knew of the sincerely kind letter Gideon Lowe had sent to the man he had so overwhelmingly defeated. Timothy put it in the fire; he was alone, and suddenly he was crying as he had not cried since he was eight years old.

CHAPTER TWELVE

Former President Theodore Roosevelt was at war with Germany and her allies. He execrated Democratic President Wilson, and part of his hatred for Germany lay in his detestation of the Chief Executive. By nature an ardent and active man, physically vibrant, he loathed quiet contemplative men, prudent men. He declared that Mr. Wilson was "the worst President by all odds since Buchanan, with the possible exception of Andrew Johnson." Had he been President, he confided to intimates, he would have declared war on Germany months ago. Hearing of this, President Wilson said mildly, "I believe that only Congress can declare war. Or has Mr. Roosevelt suddenly changed the Constitution?" He disliked Mr. Roosevelt intensely. He had only one strong wish: to keep the United States out of the European war.

When Congress and the people, angry over the British seizure of American seamen on neutral vessels carrying contraband to Europe, demanded war with England, Mr. Wilson exerted himself ceaselessly to prevent it. He did not sleep on the night of December 13, 1914, nor on the fourteenth, either, while Congress debated. Sometimes, as he lay sleepless, he dimly recalled his radical youth and the insidious voices of older men, and he was terribly alarmed. To harass him further, there appeared to be too many men in the Senate and the House who had what he designated as "wild schemes" which went far beyond his modest "New Freedoms." When war with England was averted on December 15, he earnestly implored the American people not to give their government too much power. "Centralized government eventually becomes centralized despotism," he warned the country.

A writer on military affairs, one Frederick Louis Huidekoper, returned to the United States after a tour of France, England, and Germany. He became active in founding his National Security League, a preparedness organization. "Adequate preparation for war has never yet in history been made after the beginning of hostilities without unnecessary slaughter, unjustifiable expense and national peril."

"We shall not go to war," said President Wilson.

The Regular Army consisted of some three thousand officers and seventy-seven thousand men, the organized militia some eight thousand officers and about one hundred nineteen thousand men. Mr. Roosevelt repeatedly brought this to the attention of the American people. They became confusedly alarmed. But Mr. Wilson said, "Why should we increase this strength? We are not at war; we do not intend to be at war. No one is threatening us." But in their quiet and hidden places the men who were determined that America should go to war quickened their activities. They supported, with large sums of money, the National Security League. Their long patience was becoming impatience. There could be no revolution of any kind, peaceful or bloody, in America without war. There could be no power for them. Editorials approving General Leonard Wood appeared mysteriously in newspapers all over the country, for the general had said from the beginning, "We shall be drawn in; we cannot avert it by good intentions nor protect ourselves by exhortation." The general was a good man and, like all soldiers, he was single-minded and greatly innocent. He did not know who was using him or why. He sincerely believed that England and her allies were "good" and that Germany and her allies were "evil."

In the meantime the holocaust of furious death screamed with increasing madness in Europe. In Russia the enemies of all men prepared to make their first savage blow against the world, and their counterparts in all other countries, at war or at peace, prepared also. There were, as Mr. Wilson said, "no quarrels in hell."

The munitions makers in America were now so organized, in December 1914, that they could at a moment's notice produce ordnance to satisfy even General Wood. In the meantime, with noble impartiality, they filled orders for military goods from both Great Britain and Germany. If vessels were sunk carrying these goods, it was a matter of indifference to them. They had already been paid, in gold. Their prosperity began to extend itself to the country at large and other industries, and the American people tried not to think of Europe in their relief at the lifting of the "depression."

Three days before Christmas, Caroline had an occasion to go to her office in Boston, which she rarely visited.

The streets in Boston were full of the sound of festivity and children's voices and the tinkle of bells and movement of carts, carriages, automobiles, and streetcars. The shopwindows sparkled. Salvation Army girls and Santa Clauses stood hopefully by their buckets. Church bells sounded through the snow; roofs whitened. The paths through Boston Gardens and the Common seethed with hurrying crowds carrying packages.

The noise and the bustle finally reached Caroline's immured consciousness. She had not been in Boston at this time for many years. All at once she remembered Fern and Son and Beth Knowles. She stopped in a doorway for shelter against the wind and snow, a massive huddled woman in worn black garments and an ancient black bonnet. It was twilight now, and Caroline looked dully at the lights and the laughing crowds. She was both frightened and affronted. What foolishness. What noise. How absurd it was. A group of schoolgirls ran past her, giggling with silly joy, their hair and their ribbons blown back from their wind-stung young faces. Miss Stockington's girls! Then all at once Caroline was a girl again, fearful but with some hope, shivering, but possessed of love. She clutched at her purse as the young Caroline had clutched her own purse. But this purse was full of gold bills, and the strap was wound tightly about her wrist.

A young policeman, pacing and smiling, became aware of her in her lonely doorway. He looked at her searchingly. Why, the poor old soul, in those old clothes like his grandmother used to wear! Worn out, too. And those woolen gloves—not even a muff—and those patched boots. A cleaning woman, very likely, tired out and taking refuge from the wind and snow before going home. What kind of a home did the poor soul have? A rat's nest, probably. And nobody there to give her a hot cup of tea.

"Everything all right, ma'am?" he asked.

She was not aware of him. She did not know that there were tears on her pale, seamed face. He came closer and saw the tears, the fixed, unseeing eyes, the big trembling lips. He touched her arm gently, and she started violently and looked at him.

"Everything all right?" he repeated.

"Yes. Yes," said Caroline.

"Can I help you to a streetcar?"

"No." She would have to hurry to the station, for her train would soon be leaving. Two girls flashed by, and one had the hair and face of Elizabeth in the lamplight. "You're cold," said the policeman, seeing the woman shiver. "A cup of tea or coffee against the cold, ma'am?"

"What did you say?" said Caroline, who had forgotten him and was straining to follow the girl with her eyes. He was like a fly buzzing in a room filled with agony. Then she gasped. A pain like a coiling serpent of fire clutched at her heart, and her mouth opened on a smothering and choking. The purse dropped from a suddenly paralyzed arm, and it burst open at the policeman's feet. A huge roll of gold certificates fell out. The policeman stared at it, stupefied. Thousands of dollars! Maybe! Still stupefied, he bent and picked up the roll; it was very heavy. He looked at Caroline, and she looked at him in her extremity of pain.

"Your money?" said the policeman, incredulous.

The pain was too great for her to speak. The street darkened all about her. Her shaken heart stammered, pounded, raced, and seemed to bulge in her throat.

"Where did you get all this money?" cried the policeman, wildly thinking of bank robberies or rifled safes. He took Caroline sternly by the arm. Then he saw her eyes, dim and flickering in her livid face, and her dry and speechless lips open and panting. It was not fear that stood there, for he recognized fear. It was desperate illness. Hastily thrusting the roll into the purse, which he snapped closed, he put his whistle to his mouth.

In the darkness that roared and seethed about her Caroline became faintly aware of supporting arms, of the helpless movement of her legs under her heavy woolen petticoats and worn skirts, of manly voices that encouraged, of faces that rushed in on the darkness, then receded—staring, curious faces. She forgot even her own identity and where she was. She was one huge and crushing anguish. Each choking breath came with more difficulty than the last. An awful weariness made her body as heavy as iron. She wanted only to lie down somewhere, but they made her move, and there were questioning voices and the ringing of bells.

Then she was sitting down. She was terribly cold, but she could feel warmth on her face and lights against her shut eyes. A glass was pressed against her lips; a pellet was on her tongue. She swallowed listlessly, uncurious, unresisting. She opened her eyes and saw a large quiet room and the figures of nuns about her, and beyond them two policemen looking at her intently. She could speak now, and with an ancient fear. "My purse? My purse!" The pain in her chest was receding like a dark tide.

"In your lap, my dear," said an old nun who had given her the pellet and the water. "Don't be afraid. You are very sick, aren't you?" As the young policeman had done, she looked at the worn clothing with pity.

Caroline was silent. Her face was all intensity as she waited for the tide to recede still more. Her body felt sheathed in ice. Her arms were numb. Then there was only the shadow of pain beyond her, and her heart was weakly pacing. Her fumbling fingers opened the bag, and she saw the roll there, safe and secure. She sighed. The nuns saw the money, and they were startled. Caroline covered the purse with her hands, as if to protect it.

"The doctor will be here at once. Just rest," said the old nun.

"The hospital?" Caroline said. "I am in the hospital?"

"Yes, dear. These kind boys brought you here; it was only a little way."

"I was only faint," said Caroline, trembling with her old dread of strangers. She was also ashamed; her shame made her ashen face flush with dull color. "I am perfectly well now. I must go home at once."

"In a moment," said the old nun, pressing her hand on Caroline's shoulder. "Ah, here is the doctor now."

The physician who entered was the very physician who had first examined Elizabeth when she had run here in her terror. He recognized Caroline at once. He was shocked. He exclaimed, "Mrs. Sheldon!" He came to her and tried to take her hand, but she held back, confused and mortified.

"I was only faint," she repeated. Her weariness rested on her shoulders like an intolerable weight. The nuns murmured to the doctor; the young policeman hurriedly told his story. The doctor, more shocked than ever, looked at Caroline.

"I must examine you, Mrs. Sheldon," he said. "You may have had a heart attack."

But Caroline pushed herself to her feet. "Nonsense," she said. "I was only cold. It was the wind. I'm not accustomed any longer to being out in bad weather." She had forced her voice to be steady and loud. No matter what happened, she had to leave this place of her humiliation and pain. She must hide herself again in her house and close her doors and pull down her shades. "I'll pay for—— How much is it?"

No one answered her. All the faces were concerned and anxious. She looked at the nuns, and she was in the room in Switzerland and they were speaking to her in mercy and gentleness. Her throat became full, and there were tears in her eyes. She opened her bag and threw the roll of money onto the table beside her. "Take it," she mumbled. "I have my ticket for the train." She looked at the young policeman. "Give a bill to him," she said. She tried to smile. "It's Christmas, isn't it?"

"We don't want your money," said the doctor, very moved. "We only want to help you."

"Then," said Caroline, "find me a hack to the station. And you must keep the money." How little it was, compared with what she was annually giving to this hospital! The thought made her smile again, and she felt power and returning strength.

"I think you are very sick," said the doctor, whose excellent salary she paid. He thought to himself that it was quite out of character for Caroline Ames to throw money from her indifferently, even in the name of charity.

"No, no," she said impatiently. "A hack, please, or I'll miss my train."

The doctor unwillingly took her in his fine chauffeur-driven automobile to the train, through the Christmas streets, through the crowds, through the snow and the voices of the bells. She did not speak to him, for she was again utterly spent. She knew now that she had looked at death. She had the irrational belief that once in her house, alone, she would be safe. The doctor watched her closely by the light of the street lamps and saw her dreadful color and the blueness of her mouth. "Promise me," he said, "that you will call your own doctor at once when you get home."

She was so eager to be rid of him and his solicitude—which was only because she was Caroline Ames, she thought—that she nodded. She had no intention of calling a doctor. Within her own walls, she would be safe from all her agonies. She would be blessedly alone. There would be no voices there, no confusions, no mortifications, no pain, no memory.

She slept heavily in the cold train, her hands clutched on her purse. The station hack was even colder. She could not stop her shivering. When she arrived home, she found feeble fires and a badly cooked dinner awaiting her. She could not eat. She went at once to bed and lay under frayed blankets, unable to warm herself. The moldering house was full of sounds, of distant footsteps, of half-caught voices. The snow fell against the windows, and the boulders outside became shapes of white, and the sea's harsh voice filled the room.

Caroline started from a sick sleep and sat up, her old flannel gown rough against her skin. "Tom?" she cried. "Tom, is that you?" The sea answered her.

CHAPTER THIRTEEN

Ames Sheldon had been married to Amy less than two months when he discovered that he was utterly bored by his young wife. And boredom was one condition for which he had no tolerance.

One of Amy's schoolgirl friends had once said, "Amy Winslow is so absolutely sweet that she sets your teeth on edge and makes your ears ring." Others, even more malicious, had remarked on Amy's lack of "character." She was called cloying, had "nothing to say for herself," was "too eager to please," "uninteresting," "a darling but just a little stupid." "Everything is sweetness and light to Amy—so dull." Still others said, "It's impossible to spend an interesting hour with her. She's well read and educated, but she has no opinions. If you speak sharply to her, out of sheer impatience with her shy gurglings and assents, she looks so wounded that you feel like a dog and even more impatient." An old lady remarked that Amy was a most sweet young girl, "but she will make the most devastatingly boring old woman. I do believe the child is a little simple."

Though there was some slight truth to these malicious or forthright remarks, Amy was, in fact, by nature and training, an anchronism in an age where women were demanding to be respected not only for their sex but for their intelligence and their enlightened opinions. Her father had had a very intelligent, lovely, but exigent mother, and he had hated her. His cousin Caroline was a woman of power in spite of her reserve and avoidance of strangers, and he had feared that power as well as envied it. But his sister Melinda had always been his dream of fair women, for she was gentle, kind, and truthful. So it was on the image of Melinda that he had tried to impress the soft and fragile wax of his daughter's spirit. The result had been not only an accentuation of her natural shyness and gentleness but a trustfulness that men were not only physically stronger than women but spiritually, too, and that their very faults had some implicit virtue.

It had never occurred to Timothy that Amy might marry a man with not only her father's own attributes but with even more of his exigence and cruelty. He had never known that some women unconsciously sought men resembling their fathers if they loved those fathers. But while Timothy had been charmed with his daughter's blushing simplicity and shyness, gentleness and submissiveness, Ames found himself, just before Christmas of 1914, so bored that he would wryly remark privately that he felt as if his mouth were constantly stuffed with spun sugar.

He had never had too much of Amy's company before he married her. He had loved her for her prettiness and sweetness and her ardent admiration of him. His first pity for her, on the day of their marriage, his first promise to himself that he would be good to her, and his first shame had disappeared with the first flush of passion. He liked women with spirit and some independence, women who could cajole naughtily, pout, be capricious, a little demanding, and who had some irrational but pretty temper.

Amy was not only "yes-saying" but adored him indiscriminately, was in a state of constant anxiety to please him—which led him to some cruelties of speech and action even beyond his usual ways—and had a way of sweetly chattering which made him think of a single, saccharine violin note constantly singing in his ears.

"What do you think of this war in Europe?" he would ask her.

She would look at him, eagerly smiling, damnably hopeful, trying to guess from his expression what she should say that would meet with his approval and not annoy him. After a few times such as this Ames would deliberately mask his smooth, pale face so that Amy could not get a clue from him. This confused her, set her adrift, and frightened her. Then she would say timidly, "What do you think, Ames?"

"I asked you, Amy."

The eager radiance, which was by now beginning to irritate him, would die from her pretty face. "Oh, I don't know," she would murmur distressfully. "It is so sad, isn't it? I really don't know what it is about——"

They had been married six weeks when Ames said with exquisite brutality, "You never know what anything is about, do you, darling? You never had a single thought in that dear little pinhead of yours, did you? And yet you are twenty-one!"

No one had ever spoken to poor Amy like this before, not even her brothers in their roughest adolescent state. She did not become indignant and retort sharply, as her mother would have done. She was merely crushed. She was not living up to dear Ames' expectations; she was failing him. And so she would cry.

At first Ames thought the crying a little touching. Now it bored him, as everything about Amy was beginning to bore him. He had been a man about town since he was eighteen and discovered that he could charm and fascinate and delude both men and women and use them and delight them by his use. He belonged to the best of clubs. He began to leave Amy alone more and more in his exquisitely furnished flat with his finely trained man-servant. From the first he had warned Amy not to consider any changes to suit herself. His flat was perfect; it needed, he said a little viciously, no feminine touch.

He was in actual flight from his young wife, and for this he deserved a little pity also. In these early weeks he would often leave her abruptly for fear that he would lash at her malignantly and thus destroy the picture of himself as a civilized and self-controlled gentleman. Once he thought: I could become a wife-beater. Easily! When he came home for dinner Amy would be prettily dressed in her schoolgirl fashion. Sometimes he would say, "For God's sake, Amy, you are a married woman now! Do buy some distinguished clothes. Something with sophistication." But Amy could not be sophisticated.

By the end of December, Amy was serving tea to her old friends and going out to tea. Everyone observed that though poor Amy had never had much wit or conversation she had always been like a rose in a room, silent but blooming and scented. She was no longer like a rose; her high fresh color was fading. Her large brown eyes had a constant expression of lostness and anxiety. She became visibly thinner. She would have her mother for tea—for Timothy was up and about now in the old house—and would merely look at Amanda as if imploring her mother to give her the secret of suc- cessful wifehood. Not only was Amanda beginning to hate Ames more strongly each time she saw her pathetic daughter, but she was also begin- ning to hate Timothy, who had made this girl what she was.

She tried to give Amy advice. "If Ames goes out too much, set your foot down, dear." But Amy did not know how to set her foot down. "If he says nasty things, Amy, speak up with dignity." But Amy did not know how to speak up, with dignity or otherwise. "If Ames is disgusting—and men are frequently that, dear—tell him so and demand that he do better." But Amy had been taught by her father that no man is disgusting, and she did not know how to demand.

"If he stays out late, don't be there when he gets home," said Amanda, suffering for her daughter. "Or be even later than he is and refuse to tell him where you've been." Amy looked at her with horror. "Oh, Mama, I couldn't do that to Ames! He's so good! I couldn't hurt him like that. Be- sides, isn't a woman always supposed to be there, greeting her husband when he comes home?"

"Not always," said Amanda dryly. "In fact, not regularly. It gives him something to think about." But this baffled Amy; she did not understand her mother. "When your father was particularly atrocious—and you have no idea how atrocious men can be," said Amanda, "I would give him the silent treatment. It's very effective. You see, they are born with the myth that women are always talking; it throws them terribly when a woman is silent and refuses to speak to them." But Amy believed that when Ames was inexplicably displeased it was her duty to chatter at him and try to discover how she had offended him. Though he was cruel by nature, she evoked depths of cruelty in him which would have remained latent had he been married to a woman of more independent character.

"Oh, Amy, for God's sake, shut up!" he exclaimed once.

Amy's tension and bafflement began to show in little fine lines about her innocent and tender mouth. She was a foolish and silly wife. She had wronged Ames by marrying him. She exerted herself more and more to please, and only infuriated Ames. She excited the compassion of his man-servant, Griffith, a middle-aged Englishman of impeccable manners and understanding. He thought that Mrs. Sheldon was exactly like the English schoolgirls he had known. She was increasingly lonely. He let her help him with the dusting and polishing and would talk to her gravely, and she would listen in gratitude. He consulted her about the dinner menus and what guests should be fed. She had taste and a timid graciousness, and he admired her extravagantly and would cause her to blush and become radiant again. Poor little soul, he would think, and then would say, "Certainly, madam. That is exactly right. Thank you for reminding me."

Without Griffith, Amy would have found life intolerable and desperate. Griffith took it upon himself to discuss the war with the poor girl and give her thoughts and ideas. He encouraged her to visit the Museum again and her old friends. But all her laughter in this house was only when she and Griffith were alone. At Christmas she gave him three hundred dollars in gold. She thought it was gratitude—poor Griffith!—when she saw tears in his shrewd black eyes.

What little spirit Amy had ever had was fast diminishing, as was her color. Sometimes Griffith found her crying. He would bring her a little whiskey or brandy in hot water, with lemon, and solicitously remark on her "cold." He meant no harm. He had no way of knowing that he was initiating disaster for Amy.

It was understood by her sons that Caroline never wanted to celebrate Christmas and did not care to be visited on that day. She had not seen Amy since Elizabeth's funeral. She had no curiosity. She had had no malevolence in planning the marriage between her son and Amy, except for the effect it would have on Timothy. Secluded, turned immovably inward, unaware of human emotions and human disasters and fears and hopes and tragedies, she never once wondered how that young marriage was progressing. Her life was in her fortune, the trust her father had left her.

She did know, however, from talks with Mimi Bothwell, that all was not well between Mimi and John Sheldon. This was comforting to Caroline, and reassuring. This lovely girl, this girl so like herself in her own girlhood, this gifted girl, this darling, would never be so stupid as to marry Caroline's son. Not only was Mimi celebrated in New York and other cities for her marvelous paintings and praised for being "the finest colorist since Tintoretto" and "one of the most explicit and imaginative of modern painters," but she had a mind and character. People were misled by her air of refinement and dignified restraint and sudden, vivid smiles. When it came to selling her paintings, however, Mimi had the instincts of an excellent trader.

She thought that her Aunt Caroline was unjust to her son. Who could help loving John, so amusing, so colorful, so sprightly, so masculine, so strong, so brilliant? Of course John was very tiresome in insisting that a wife should be a wife and that this "nonsense painting" was only a feminine whim. He was not in the least impressed by the notices she received, nor the money. He had his grandfather's obdurate attitude toward art. He saw no color in Mimi's work. He knew he was color-blind. He concealed this physical flaw in carping, indulgent criticism. What in the world was Mimi trying to "express," to use the ridiculous modern term? Of course it was all "play." But Mimi was twenty-one, and it was time to marry, and her mother, Aunt Melinda, was agreeable to the marriage.

"You'll forget about all this when we are married, sweet," he would say to Mimi.

"No," said Mimi, feeling tired. "This is my life."

"But a woman's life is in her husband. Didn't you know?"

"Certainly, silly Johnnie. But does a woman have to lose her soul in marriage? Does she have to become only an echo of her husband? Hasn't she a life, a spirit, a mind of her own? John, if and when we marry, I don't intend to give up my painting."

John was a darling, Mimi would think with a woman's tenderness. She did not know that John was afraid of her success. He often thought about his brother Ames. Ames had married Timothy's daughter and had received three million dollars from his mother. John never forgot what he had overheard and seen that day nearly five years ago and the evidences of his mother's love for Mimi. The old girl should be good for at least three million dollars when he married Mimi Bothwell. John was shrewd as well as intelligent. He had guessed that his mother's gift to Ames was a vengeance, though what had inspired that vengeance he did not know.

He himself was doing very well. He had his own law firm now, finally free from the stuffiness of Tandy, Harkness and Swift. He was a criminal lawyer. If more sober law firms execrated him, and if judges looked at him mistrustfully and without admiration, it did not matter to him. He almost always won his cases, for he had a beguiling way, a virility, a confiding attitude, an amusing manner, a man-to-man approach, which melted the most uncertain of juries. In some way he always managed to get timid and wife-dominated men on them. He was their picture of the masculine male, burly, unafraid, free, independent, unharassed by intransigent wives and demanding daughters. He was the powerful Man, before whom women were silent.

Mimi was his only problem. He truly loved and desired her. His hatred for her "art" rose from the fact that it appeared to be his contender, his rival. He wanted Mimi to devote herself to him, unlike his brother Ames, who wanted no devotion. He was willing that Mimi amuse herself with her painting, provided it did not interfere with her absorption in her husband. But he did not want Mimi to be publicly admired and acclaimed. That would draw her from him.

Mimi thought John's dislike of her art only a masculine jealousy, an almost lovable quirk. She could not understand his occasional and passionate outbursts against it. He felt his love menaced, as his father's love had been menaced, and destroyed. John's greatest need was for a docile and compliant wife who would adore him and would assure him that in all ways he was loved.

Caroline said to Mimi, "You must never marry John. Of course you know better. He will ruin you. He's really very stupid, you know. What does he know of your art? You have an obligation when you have a gift."

"To whom?" asked Mimi with sudden sharpness.

"To yourself," said Caroline. "To others who gave it to you."

Mimi smiled then. She had no intention of stopping painting. John would understand finally, dear strong, vigorous John, who was merely being pettish. He would understand that women in this era had a right to a life of their own. This was the twentieth century. John would learn that eventually. Her golden eyes would glow, thinking of John.

She had seen her cousin Amy only once or twice since Amy's marriage. Mimi had never liked Ames; he seemed far and desultory to her, an enigma. But she loved Amy, so tender and weak and yielding. She was baffled by Amy's babbling, however. What in heaven's name was the child talking about with this insistence that she had "failed" Ames and was not pleasing him? "If you please yourself, you please everybody," said Mimi, who was in her way as innocent as Amy. It was a nice aphorism, she complimented herself, and just what little Amy needed. Amy looked at her with stark pleading, and Mimi was exasperated.

Mimi had lost much of the artlessness of her girlhood, though not her honesty. She was less deluded than most young women her age, except in the case of her cousin John. She was reserved in showing her emotions and affections, but with John she was ardent. On Christmas Eve, fearless of the dark and the snow, she went to see her Aunt Caroline. She was never reconciled to the bleakness and grime and abandonment of the house, but she often reminded herself that every person had a right to his own way of life and should not be criticized for it unless it caused others pain or inconvenience. Caroline herself opened the door, for the maid had demanded and received the night off and the next day also.

"Mary," said Caroline, and put out her large hands and pulled the girl into the dank hall. Mimi could make her smile almost immediately, as one smiles at a fire or a flower. "But what are you doing here at night, and alone? Did you walk?"

"It's only a few miles," said Mimi. Her cheeks were bright, her beautiful hazel eyes shining. She kissed Caroline, then looked at her searchingly. "Are you sick?" she asked. "You don't look well, dear Aunt Caroline."

"I'm perfectly well," said her aunt. Mimi removed her black seal coat and round seal hat, threw her muff on a chair, and shook out the flounces of her red wool frock. Her vitality lit the hall like a lamp. She put her arm about Caroline, and they went into the dingy, dimly lit drawing room together, where the smallest of all possible fires lurked on the ash-strewn hearth.

Caroline was happy that the girl was here but was anxious about her return. "Oh, please don't worry," said Mimi. She looked at the fire and said, "My brother Nat is coming for me in our sleigh at ten."

"Your brother?" Caroline was not pleased. She had never seen Mimi's twin and did not wish to see him. Mimi smiled at her. "He looks just like me," she said. "And like you." She opened her purse. "But I have brought you a present."

"I don't want anyone in the house," said Caroline. "I never see anyone."

"He doesn't bite at all," said Mimi. "Honestly."

She put a small box in Caroline's unwilling hand. "Well, aren't you going to open it?" she asked.

"A present?" said Caroline. No one ever gave her gifts. She opened it reluctantly. It was a large golden locket on a chain, beautifully worked. Caroline snapped the locket open, and Mimi's smiling face, in miniature, looked up from her hands. "I painted it myself," said Mimi.

Caroline could not speak; her big fingers trembled as she held the trinket. "There," said Mimi, "let me put it around your neck." With loving fingers she pulled the chain about Caroline's throat and stood off to admire the effect. Then she gently kissed Caroline's cheek. "I'll be here with you always now," she said.

Caroline put up her hand and touched the fine black hair that fell over the girl's forehead. Here was truly her daughter, as Elizabeth had never been her daughter. She still could say nothing. Then she got heavily to her feet in silence and left the room. Mimi was not disturbed; her aunt often did unexpected things. So the girl sat down and waited; then, muttering, got up again and threw a scuttle of coal on the fading fire and wielded the poker vigorously. Caroline returned to the room, holding a small picture in her hand. It was the painting of the Capri rocks and the Bay of Naples which she had bought for Tom so many years ago, the painting which even Mimi had never seen.

"Here," said Caroline. "I'm not the only one who can get gifts."

Mimi exclaimed at the beauty, bent to the bustling fire, and examined the painting with her expert's eye. "Genotti!" she cried in disbelief and delight. "Yes, yes! It actually is!"

"I don't know," said Caroline, happy again at the girl's extreme pleasure.

"I don't know any paintings any longer, except—— Who is that painter?"

"Why, only the best Italian painter in the world!" said Mimi. She studied the picture again. "This is priceless! His early style, his 'yellow' period. Where did you get it, Aunt Caroline?"

"I bought it in Rome when I was very young," said Caroline. She sat down, as if suddenly sick. "Before I was married. Over thirty years ago." There was a tremor in her chest, a premonition, and she clenched her will against it. "For my husband." She passed her hands over her clammy face.

"I see," said Mimi, who did not see at all. She paused. "Do you really want me to have it, Aunt Caroline? Don't you think it belongs to Ames or to John?"

"No," said Caroline.

"Do you know it is worth thousands of dollars?"

"Is it?" said Caroline with interest. Their heads touched as they examined the painting. "I always thought it very beautiful, Mary."

"And that's why you gave it to me," said Mimi. She felt like crying.

"Your mother won't mind?" asked Caroline surlily.

"Mama? Certainly not. She will be so happy for me."

Never once in all the years she had known the girl had Caroline ever wondered what her childhood had been like, and her mother, and her early girlhood. Mimi, when she came to this house, came alone, without a background, without parents. Mimi was simply there. But now Caroline stared wonderingly at the girl. She moistened her lips. "Did—do—you love your mother, Mary?"

"Mama? I adore her," said Mimi, and her eyes sparkled. "You see, I was so young when Daddy died. She and Nat were all I had. And it was a lovely life, so peaceful and happy. We all had such good times together, boating, fishing, swimming, picnics. And endless walks, to church, to the village, through the woods, along the beach. And going in to Boston to visit friends and relatives. I can't recall a single bleak day in my childhood."

This was a new world to Caroline, one practically impossible to believe. It was a world that suddenly fascinated her but which she did not comprehend at all. Love and laughter, trust and faith, the calling of children, the family affection—she did not comprehend. A terrible hunger, a sense of deprivation, struck her savagely.

"I couldn't wait to get back home on weekends from school," said Mimi, her face soft with remembrance. "And very often, especially during the first year in Paris, I had to stop myself from running to the first ship home."

"Does your brother ever envy your talent, Mimi?" Caroline probed, trying to find a flaw in the background.

Mimi was astonished. "Nat!" she cried. "Why, he's my greatest admirer! He's my brother, Aunt Caroline. How could he envy me? It would be like envying himself."

"Brothers often envy sisters, and sisters envy brothers," said Caroline wryly. "You are so innocent, child. Haven't you ever heard of Cain and Abel? It isn't a rare story and never was."

"It is to me," said Mimi. Then she remembered that John and Ames disliked each other, perhaps even detested each other. Her face lost its light.

"You are thinking of something," said Caroline. "It wasn't always so well, was it?" She did not begrudge the girl her happiness, but something in her, deprived and wounded, wished for understanding.

"Oh, I wasn't thinking of Mama and Nat," said Mimi. She held the Genotti painting on her lap, and now she looked down at it. "Aunt Caroline, I must tell you. John and I are going to be married in March."

"No," said Caroline, and shook her head over and over. "No. That must never happen. Your mother, if she loves you, will never let it happen. Haven't I told you all about him? I have told you so many times. It must not happen."

Mimi sighed. "Mama is very fond of John. She's very pleased about the wedding, Aunt Caroline. I came tonight not only to give you my Christmas gift but to tell you." She looked up pleadingly, then started. "Aunt Caroline! Are you sick? What is the matter?"

Caroline held up her hand. "You must listen. How often must I tell you, Mary? I thought you had begun to listen. What more must I say to reach you? He is a bad man; he and his brother are both bad men. You——"

"You didn't mind Ames marrying Amy," said Mimi. "And Amy can't take half as good care of herself as I can——" She stopped abruptly. But her astute aunt had heard the change in the girl's voice, the sudden vague distress. She leaned toward Mimi.

"Why should you say that?" she asked. "Is there something wrong with Amy?"

"Of course not," said Mimi hurriedly. "But she's a very shy girl; she'd always been so sheltered. Imagine Amy living abroad for years, as I did! She doesn't know anything about people. They—bewilder her."

"I see," said Caroline, looking at the girl's face keenly. Was Ames making Amy wretched? She had not considered Amy at all, not as a human being, only as an object to aid her vengeance.

She cried, "Don't you see? Ames is a bad man, and John is his brother. John is even worse than Ames! I can see in your face that you are trying to conceal something from me about Amy."

"I didn't say that Ames was making Amy wretched," said Mimi. But she flushed guiltily. "Ames is very worldly, and Amy knows so little. But I'm sure he is teaching her; it's only a matter of adjustment. Aunt Caroline, I'm not like Amy, and John isn't like Ames. We are two different people." She held out her hand pleadingly. "You love me, don't you, Aunt Caroline? And I love John, and he loves me. We'll be very happy. You'll see."

But Caroline stood up, her face darkly colored. "No, you must not marry him. I tell you, and I know." She was smothering with her awful effort to communicate.

There was a brisk knock on the door. Caroline turned massively but swiftly, her fear of the stranger stark on her face. "It's only Nat," said Mimi. "Shall I let him in, Aunt Caroline?"

"No!" cried Caroline. "But wait, just a minute." She left the room, and Mimi could hear her heavily stumbling up the stairs, and then she heard a door open and close. And so it was that Caroline never saw her nephew Nathaniel, not once in his life.

CHAPTER FOURTEEN

The new village girl whom Caroline had employed was in a rage of importance as she directed a temporary assistant in the cleaning up of the blighted house. "You can't do nothing with a house like this," the assistant complained. "Years and years of just plain mean dirt. I'm doing the best I kin. Look at this pail of suds; I just washed this little bit of skirtin' board, and it's like I cleaned up a pig pen. What've you been doin', Maizie, all these weeks?"

"It was worse than this when I come," said Maizie. "A big house like this, you got to have more help. I cleaned this here window three times this week, but the dirt's ground in. Some folks don't care about dirt, like her."

The cold gilt of the February sun streamed through windows which no amount of scrubbing would ever make bright again, for salt and sand and soil had eroded the glass. However, there was a smell of suds and varnish in the house, and wax for the first time in decades. These only accentuated the ragged draperies, the worn rugs, the splintered wood. Caroline was preparing for a visitor this afternoon. She looked out at the fierce gray-dark ocean, the snow-robed boulders, the faintly blue sky. She had put on one of three dresses, an old black silk. Here and there it had split. The high neck was fastened with Tom's pin, which she had not worn for many years. She touched it; it was like a talisman to her. Her hair was quite white now; it had lost even its gray since her seizure at Christmas, two months ago.

She who had cared for her appearance only briefly, and once, in her life studied herself in her dulled mirror, the ashen shadow under her cheekbones, the purplish patches under her sunken eyes, the faint blue along the edges of her big mouth. She had always eaten very little, yet she was heavy, almost monolithic. She rubbed the pin at her throat; the pearl had darkened with age; the silver had dulled. She said to her image in the mirror, "Tom, you must help me. I never believed that anyone survived after death—but you must help me. Tom?" There was only silence about her, except for a clattering of cups and saucers. Maizie was trying to find enough unchipped china for the tea Caroline intended to serve that afternoon. Caroline, listening, winced. There had been no tea served in this house for years before Elizabeth's death, and the last had been served when Elizabeth had made her disastrous return from Europe. Caroline went into Elizabeth's room, still stark, austere, and very clean.

She smoothed the white cotton spread on the bed and sat down near it. She said, "Elizabeth? Where are you, my child? There is a girl we must help, Elizabeth. Will you help me?" The room was full of cold clear light; Caroline could see the ocean rising and falling through the window, and the snow. Had Elizabeth ever really slept in this room? Had she ever sat in this chair? Had she ever lived here at all? No, thought Caroline, my child never lived except when she was in England. I don't know why. I gave her all I had, all I could give. She never loved me; she never loved anyone but that man. How could you love one so weak, Elizabeth, who would listen to lies? Had he really cared for you, he would not have let you go. Does he ever think of you, Elizabeth? Elizabeth?

Small gilt clouds moved across the sky; the sea lifted its breast in a vast dark heave. Caroline heard a tinkle of sleigh bells, and she rose wearily and went down. She sat by the drawing-room fire; the tea table waited with its chipped, beautiful china. She saw that Maizie had polished the teapot and the other silver, but their crevices were still black and oily from neglect. The fire was high and warm, but Caroline felt as cold as death. She looked at the door, waiting. A tall and slender woman in her middle forties entered the room; Caroline saw ash-fair hair, a lovely calm face with smoky gray eyes and a gentle pink mouth. She wore a long brown beaver coat and a broad beaver hat to match, loaded with beige ostrich plumes.

"Caroline?" she said, and her voice was the voice of the dead Cynthia. It was still very bright outside, with the sun reflecting from the snow, but here it was dull and dim in spite of the fire. Caroline could not answer for a moment as the lady hesitated on the threshold. Then she grunted, "Here. Come in. Near the fire."

The lady came forward with her graceful and timid movements, loosening the coat which the untrained girl had not helped her remove. She removed her gloves. She reached Caroline, and the two women looked at each other in silence. But the lady was shocked; she hardly recognized this old woman. "Caroline?" she said uncertainly. "I—I'm glad you asked me to come. I've wanted to for so long."

She held out her hand hopefully. Caroline looked at that hand, and then she touched the palm with the tips of her fingers. The lady had the sensation that harsh stone had been pressed briefly against her flesh. She sat down and tried to keep the pity from her face. "Dear Caroline," she said.

"Don't say that," said Caroline suddenly, involuntarily. "First I must ask you one thing, for it is important, and the time for secrecy has passed. Do you know I am your sister?"

"Oh yes," said Melinda. "I've known for a long time." Her smile left her face. "Amanda told me—a long time ago."

"But not your mother," said Caroline brutally.

"Please," murmured Melinda in distress.

But Caroline hardly heard her; she was searching for any resemblance in Melinda to their mutual father. And then she saw it, in the molding of the cheek and chin, the strength about the mouth, the forehead. These had not been evident in the face of the child Melinda, but years had brought them out. Melinda sat like John Ames, upright, firm, and quiet. Caroline looked away. She said hoarsely, "No matter. You received my letter. I wrote you fully, so we wouldn't need too much conversation. I asked you here. You came. I don't invite people, except in extremity, and this is an extremity."

"I'm afraid you think it is," said Melinda apologetically. "And I'm afraid I don't. You wrote me that you've been seeing my daughter Mimi for years and that she's like a daughter to you." She smiled. "That made me very happy. But, you see, Mimi is not the sort of girl who can deceive for very long. She's told me all about it. Don't be offended. Daughters just can't keep things from their mothers, can they?"

Caroline thought of Elizabeth. Melinda thought of her, too, and remembered that the girl had not been dead a year. She said impulsively, "I shouldn't have spoken of daughters, Caroline. I was so grieved about Elizabeth. I often visit her grave. You see——" She stopped, coloring.

"So it was you who planted the white rose bushes on her grave," said Caroline.

"My brother asked me to," said Melinda. "I hope you don't mind."

Caroline could not help herself from speaking in a loud and bitter voice. "He always sent flowers to her when she couldn't see them or care about them! Why did he let her go? Why didn't he marry her, my daughter? Lies? So Elizabeth let me know; I found a letter she had begun to write him. That was before she lost her mind. If he had wanted her—after he had persuaded her he did—he wouldn't have let her go, Timothy's lies or no lies!" Her hands doubled on her lap. Her breath was fierce and uneven in the room. "What sort of man is it that would destroy a girl like that with the feeble excuse of 'lies'?"

Melinda was shaken. She was torn between her loyalty for Timothy and for William. But she saw the enormous agony on Caroline's face, the rage and the despair, and she herself was a mother and knew a mother's thoughts.

She exclaimed, "You and Elizabeth never understood, Caroline!" Tears blurred her eyes. "You are wrong about William. He wanted to marry Elizabeth; he loved her and he still loves her. If it had meant hurting only himself and ruining himself, he'd have married her. But there were others. My mother wrote me just before she died."

"What? What?" cried Caroline, leaning toward her like a toppling monument. "Tell me! I must know!"

Melinda shrank from that overpowering presence. "It was Timothy. I'm afraid—Caroline, I'm afraid he hated you. I never knew why. Perhaps he envied you and resented your money. I love him, but I don't understand him." Her tears hung on her lashes, then dropped. "I love him," she repeated, and her voice broke. "But he's very strange. You see, he was very fond of William—William has never written him since Elizabeth—became so ill. Not once. He never answers Timothy's letters."

"Tell me!" said Caroline.

Melinda was helpless before such huge imperiousness. "My mother said 'hat Timothy hated Elizabeth because she was your daughter. How can people hate so? Timothy had threatened—Caroline, if William had married Elizabeth, Timothy would have destroyed all of us, so that Elizabeth would be destroyed. Dreadful, dreadful. He would have ruined William; he would have let everyone know that—that I am illegitimate and that I am William's sister. I'd have been disgraced, and my children, and my mother, and William would have been disgraced, too, because of Mama. And even Elizabeth would have been laughed at. There'd have been such a scandal. William is a peer; we don't understand all the implications of all that in America. Caroline, William had to protect our mother, myself, my children, and even Elizabeth. It was a matter of Timothy's revenge."

Melinda's face glistened with tears. The room had steadily darkened; only the fire lit it now. The voice of the sea invaded the air with distant thunder.

"I think," murmured Melinda, unable to see Caroline clearly in the gloom, "that, above everyone else, Timothy hated our father. All the misery in the world starts with hatred."

"I see," said Caroline huskily after a long time. "And Elizabeth never knew about it, did she?"

"No. William couldn't tell her. How could he?"

"I see," Caroline repeated. A film of sweat spread over her face. Now she was filled with the power of complete vengeance, warming, exhilarating. She could never avenge her daughter enough now!

"And Elizabeth died thinking that your brother had refused her because of a few silly lies!" she said. "What trivial things can destroy a mind and a spirit. If only I'd have known. But we never know until it is too late."

"Never, until it's too late," said Melinda sadly. She felt drained and weak. Then she started. For Caroline had abruptly reached out and had touched her knee awkwardly.

"But I think Timothy's been punished enough now for the wrong and cruel things he did," said Melinda. "He lost the election. He was so sure he would win; he's so proud. And then he had that stroke and suffered so much. And I'm afraid he didn't want Ames to marry Amy; men are so strange about their daughters. Sometimes one is frightened of the justice of God."

Caroline smiled grimly. She nodded, a large figure of black and crimson in the firelight. "Yes indeed," she said. "The justice of God." She turned her head slowly and looked at the fire. "Perhaps justice is eternal."

"I hope not!" said Melinda. "I'm sure that God forgives, too. I'm sure He doesn't pursue His children through eternity, endlessly punishing them!"

Her voice, sweet and piercing, filled the room. Caroline said with hard insistence, "I hope He isn't merciful. If there is a God." She looked at the teapot as if it were a strange object. She lifted it and poured the lukewarm tea and said, "I should have poured it before. It isn't very warm now."

"It doesn't matter," said Melinda. Had Caroline really touched her? It seemed incredible now, that involuntary and human gesture, that desperate movement. "That girl," said Caroline. "She never thinks of turning on the lights." She made no movement herself to do so. It was apparent she preferred the safety of darkness. And now Melinda remembered the shy and bulky and awkward young Caroline, always in the background like an unwanted ghost, always overlooked, always rejected. Oh, Caroline! thought Melinda with passionate pity.

"Let us talk about Mary," said Caroline. "That is why I asked you to come here."

"Mary? Oh, you mean Mimi," said Melinda. "You don't want her to marry John. You think John will hurt her. I've known John since he was a little boy, Caroline. Albert and I were always very fond of him. He's so full of life. And humor, and strength. He adores Mimi." She could not understand Caroline's inflexible antagonism, for she had known love all her life.

A large piece of the soft coal suddenly blazed, lighting up the women in a yellow glare. Caroline saw Melinda's face, earnest and gentle, and she was full of bitterness. What did women like Melinda know of others? They judged by externals; they took pleasant manners literally; they were deceived by pleasing voices. They urgently preferred to think of the world as a lovely place, full of kindness and simplicity. Of what were they afraid? The truth? Yes, the truth would demolish these fragile creatures.

In the end, these butterflies, these criers of happiness, these implorers who wished to be reassured that they were safe from living, were consumed like so many pretty snowflakes. They talked of love, and love had its victims as well as hatred. On the tough battlefield of life their tinsel spears broke into a thousand heatless sparks, and they were stricken. And they never understood even when fierce steel pierced their hearts and killed them. Fools, fools!

"Can't I reach you?" Caroline said roughly. "I've seen the world. Why do you suppose I live like this? Because I know people. I also know my sons. I know my son John. I know that if my son marries Mary he will destroy her. You must take my word for it. I know."

Melinda was horrified and repulsed. How was it possible for a mother to speak so of her child? She thought of her son Nathaniel. She measured all young men by her son. She had measured John Sheldon by him. Lively, burly, athletic, fun-loving John. A dear boy.

She was mournfully sorry for Caroline, the recluse, the hidden, who had no real contact with the world. She said, "Oh, Caroline. I'm afraid you don't really know John. Not at all. I've seen a great deal of him. I know how much he loves Mimi. They've loved each other for years. You wrote me that he'd stop Mimi from painting. I don't think so! She is to have a New York show in about a year, and he's so interested. Truly."

"No," said Caroline in a dull voice. "He isn't. How do I know? I know John. I know Mary." Her voice rose. "Don't let Mary marry him. If you do, it will end in calamity."

Melinda was sure of herself, sure of the love she had always known, and the comfort and protection, and the tenderness of mankind. She murmured,

"I'm afraid you are too disillusioned, Caroline. One must have hope and trust. How else can we survive?"

"By knowing the truth," said Caroline hopelessly. "Why don't you look at it?"

"I do. I have," said Melinda gently. "I love living, and so do my children. There's nothing to fear in life, nothing at all."

Caroline stood up. "I have nothing more to say to you. I thought you might be intelligent, that I could make you think, if only a little. Very stupid of me."

Melinda looked at her mutely. Caroline cried, "Have you thought about this war? Do you think it is just a quarrel between what you'd call 'good' and 'evil'? I've known since I was a girl that it was coming, and I know the real reason for it! Don't stare at me. Your children will know, and their children's children, but you won't! Good night!"

PART FIVE

My help cometh from the Lord,
which made heaven and earth.

PSALMS 121

CHAPTER ONE

Ames Sheldon, this warm late-summer Saturday afternoon, was carefully examining some fine late-sixteenth-century Italian enamels under his magnifying glass. Excellent! The Boston Museum had made a bid of twenty-five thousand dollars for them, but the dealer with whom Ames always dealt had confided that Ames could have them for three thousand dollars less, out of "old" friendship. But twenty-two thousand dollars, thought Ames, frowning. That would be his entire net profit for a year, excluding, of course, the income from his wisely invested three million dollars which his mother had given him. (He reinvested the income, for it was sacred and not to be used even for treasures.) For a moment he considered using that income for the purchase, but with a revulsion which would have pleased his mother he put the thought aside. He considered his bank account. It held nearly fifty thousand dollars. He sighed. A loan? He shuddered from that thought also. There was nothing to do, of course, but to use half his bank account.

He suddenly felt poverty-stricken and degraded. And, so feeling, he was both frightened and humiliated. No money had been forthcoming from either Timothy or Amanda. Of course, on Amanda's death, there would be a certain portion of the estate in behalf of her daughter, but Amanda appeared in fine health. Timothy had made it quite clear that he would leave Amy only one thousand dollars; the word had come from his wife. He had never forgiven his daughter for her marriage. So he, Ames, had literally a penniless girl on his hands who had brought him nothing. He discounted the three million dollars his mother had given him; that was a separate department entirely.

Not only was Amy penniless, but she was a fool. Ames concentrated on Amy's "foolishness" and on an even worse crime she had recently committed. He reached out to his desk and restudied a physician's report, only another report to add to the unbearable six other reports he had received over the past five months. I've been had, thought Ames with sudden bitterness, indignation, and disgust.

Everything was lost. That damned John's wife, Mimi Bothwell, was already doing her duty, John had happily written his brother from New York. (Ames overlooked the fact that his mother had not only violently opposed the marriage but had again vindictively informed John that he would not receive a penny from her, now or after her death.) Yes, thought Ames, I've been had. Saddled with a fool for a whole lifetime, a penniless fool. He felt so alarmed and so poor that he could think of Amy with quick hatred. He thought of her "silly" face, with the dark eyes growing so wit-lessly large and enormous over these months, the lost color in her cheeks and lips, her thin young body that could no longer entice him. Prattler! Stupid! Not even a whole woman! He would look at her with disgust when she was in her pretty, girlish night dresses and turn from her, revolted.

John could afford to be triumphant. There was that enormous Bothwell estate which Mimi would partly inherit! No wonder John was as smug as a tomcat who had drunk deeply of cream. Then John would have children, and they would inherit Caroline's vast fortune. Leaning back in his chair, Ames tapped his teeth with a pencil. He could divorce Amy, who infuriated him with her foolish adoration and clinging. What then? Ames considered his mother. How would she look upon a divorce? Why, thought Ames with a sudden surge of hope, she might even approve of it! That would be more revenge on Timothy—a rejected and despised daughter again on his hands. He must consult a lawyer at once. He pulled a sheet of thick ivory paper toward him and wrote a rapid letter to his mother.

"I am enclosing a final report . . . Under the circumstances, I am con-sidering divorcing Amy." He paused, glanced at his enamels. The sunlight streaming through a window in his elegant flat struck them, evoking blue, crimson, scarlet, green, and golden fire. Those old monks and artists knew how to do these things with infinite artistry and genius and taste. No one any longer took the patience to work like this, and in this tumultuous twentieth-century world no one even cared to learn. The enamels would grow increasingly priceless with time. Ames touched them with real love and reverence. He glanced at his cabinets. He had already prepared a shelf for his new treasures. When he had finished gloating and admiring he would draw tight curtains over his cabinets. He would not share their glory with others, and his cabinets were always in his library, and the library was al-ways locked and he carried the key with him. He himself cleaned the li-brary and the cabinets and the treasures, as Caroline cared for her secret hoard of paintings.

He looked at the letter he was writing to his mother. Then a restless im-patience came to him. Why write? He could go to her. His impatience increased. Go to that decaying huge hovel again? He had been there only three months ago and had felt a smothering. He remembered how that house had been during his early childhood, pleasant, sunlit, warm, polished. But his father had been alive then. Yet the house had begun to decay and sift even before Tom's death. How many rooms did the old hag use now? Two bedrooms, one for herself and one for the maid from the village, and the kitchen, her gallery, and what used to be the "breakfast room," and her locked study. That was all. The rest of the rooms, all fourteen of them, including the "help's" rooms, were never entered, never cleaned. They were as molded as tombs and as earth now. They loomed over the old hag like a towering and powdering and moss-grown mausoleum, and she huddled in the depths beneath. Toad, thought Ames.

Yet, she still had power. Houses were streaming up from Lyme and from other directions, smallish and cheap little houses crowded with laughing children and inquisitive adults who possessed the repulsive American spirit of neighborliness and friendly curiosity. Ames chuckled. The old hag had handled the matter deftly. She had actually spent money to wall in her property, high stone walls with splintered glass on their tops, the walls extended to the very shore. The walled property was like a moated castle in the midst of a teeming town of barbarians, its massive iron gates always locked. There was a bell on the gates; one yanked it and Caroline came to admit a visitor—rare, indeed—or a tradesman. Sometimes the sullen maid strolled out, glowering, her hands wet and grimy.

But it protected Caroline, and that was all that mattered. There was one way to reach her which the walls could not stop, and that was the telephone. Ames went into the beautiful hall, stopped to admire his genuine Cézanne for a moment, and lifted the receiver of his telephone from its hook. He called his mother. While waiting he studied his cool pale reflection in the very fine Florentine mirror which had cost him five hundred dollars and which reflected the Cézanne. The hard slate-colored eyes stared back at him, unrelenting. There was not pity in him for the girl whom he had married less than nine months ago and who was growing quieter, more timid, and thinner each day.

"Mother?" he said in his light and charming voice.

"Well?" Caroline grunted. "What is it now?"

He raised his eyebrows humorously at himself in the mirror. "Now, Mother, you know that this is almost the first time I've ever called you. This is serious——"

"Make it short," said Caroline impatiently. "I thought you were the important call I am expecting from New York."

"Investments again?" asked Ames, as though there had ever been anything else but investments. "Anything worthwhile?"

"Bethlehem Steel," said Caroline with slightly less impatience. "It's high, but I expect it to go much higher very shortly. Well? What is it?"

"Bethlehem Steel," Ames repeated, remembering that he was invested quite heavily in that stock. "You'd advise me to buy more?"

"Did you call me to talk stocks?" his mother demanded. "Don't you have a broker in Boston?"

"None as perspicacious as you, dear Mama," said Ames.

Caroline said nothing, but he could hear her rasping breath clearly. "I am really calling for some advice," he said, looking at the fingernails of his right hand. "I am thinking of divorcing Amy."

He could not see Caroline's sudden violence of expression. He could not know that she was again standing at her dying husband's bedside and that Tom was speaking of divorcing her, almost with his final breath. She was feeling once more the awful, incredulous despair, the bitter anguish, the tearing sorrow, the sense of complete abandonment and loss.

"No! No!" she shouted at her son, and he had to pull the receiver from his ear. "How dare you say such a thing! It's all wrong— No! No!"

He was deeply shocked, almost frightened. It was as if Caroline's monumental personality had surged into this small but beautiful hall with its sacred Cézanne, its Florentine mirror, its gleaming Kirman rug, its chartreuse-colored damask walls. He actually glanced over his shoulder, more than half expecting to see his mother rushing at him.

"Divorce?" she cried. "No, never, never, never!"

"I've been thinking of it for a considerable time," he said, trying to ride over that furious voice. "I didn't know you objected to divorce. Of course First Families don't indulge in it often," and now his own voice turned vicious. "But I wasn't aware we were First Family. That was Timothy's main objection to me, you know." He tried to laugh.

But the furious voice thundered at him again. "He isn't First Family! He's nothing but gutter blood!"

"Oh?" said Ames, standing up very straight and beginning to smile. "Tell me. I'm curious."

But Caroline had fallen silent. "Hello, hello?" said Ames, and jiggled the telephone hook eagerly.

Then Caroline spoke derisively. "It won't do you any good," she said. "Don't you remember that I'm supposed to be an Esmond too? His mother and mine were twin sisters."

He looked at his smooth long face, so like Timothy's except for the sharp triangular chin with its deep if narrow cleft. His grandfather and his father had been "nobodies." He had entry in Boston because of his "Esmond blood." A nervous and infuriated itch began between his lean shoulder blades. "I hope I'm no fool," he said, trying to keep his tone reasonable. "But I'm married to a fool and I've reached the end of my endurance."

"But not the end of my three million dollars," said his mother brutally. "What's wrong?"

The itch subsided a little. "I'd stand even a fool if she could give me children," said Ames. "But Amy can't." He winked at himself in the mirror as he said, "I want children, deeply. Deeply." He put a note of baritone sincerity in his voice.

"Oh, you do, eh?" said Caroline. "Why? You'd make a dreadful father; you were a dreadful little boy, and I have no doubt but that you are a dreadful man." She paused, then said abruptly, "You haven't been married a year yet. Give the girl time."

He wanted to say, "I can't bear sleeping in the same room with her; the very air becomes sticky with sweetness when she breathes it. I detest her." But he held the words back and said instead, "You will remember that I wrote you last March that Amy had been seriously ill with pneumonia. We had the best men caring for her. She recovered her strength very slowly, and then they gave her a most complete physical examination. She'd become lifeless——"

"I shouldn't wonder, with you as her husband," said Caroline. "Well? Go on."

"Is it necessary to go into painful and intimate details?" asked Ames, who knew his mother to be excessively prudish. He could not see her dark flush, but he had no doubt that it was there. "Since the first verdict that she'd never be able to have any children, we've had several consultations with other specialists. We even went to New York, to the best. Amy will never have any children."

"Um," said Caroline. She considered. She said, "I think I understand. You aren't thinking of children, you're thinking of natural and legal issue to inherit the Ames money. Don't bother to try to deceive me with sentimentalities." She paused. "I won't bother to deceive you, either. You were born for the very same reason."

"I gathered that. Over all the years," said Ames. He fumbled for one of his delicate Turkish cigarettes. "Pardon me a moment." He let the receiver swing as he lit the cigarette. He looked, a little startled, at his fingers. They were trembling. He wondered why. It was a very warm day; he had a slight headache suddenly. "Yes," he said, speaking again to his mother, "I think I first knew when I was about four years old. I heard my father accusing you of that very thing. Elizabeth wasn't the only one who listened at doors, you know."

He could not see his mother at her desk in her study; he could not see her shut her eyes as if she had been struck by a powerful pain which was almost unendurable. She had known so much tormented and abysmal sorrow. But this was quite different, and she could not recognize it as grief and the instantaneous black flowering of remorse. The pain did not ebb quickly. It retreated but remained as a vast dark haunting in her mind, only a shadow waiting for features and form.

"—all the time," Ames was saying lightly.

"What did you say?" asked Caroline in a voice so dull and empty that Ames became alert again. He repeated patiently, "We all knew it, even John, who had the least brains in the family, the least perceptiveness. Why, Elizabeth was only ten, and I was younger, when we discussed it. We thought it great fun to be born as cattle are born, for a definite purpose."

"Elizabeth?" said Caroline so faintly that he could hardly hear her.

"Why, certainly. She was a girl. And so she was more sensitive than we boys. That's what made her a bloodless fiend. Probably."

The vast shadow sharpened in Caroline's mind. Ames smoked rapidly; he felt a trifle breathless, as if he were suddenly running. He regarded the thought with surprise. He recalled that when he had heard his father's accusation he had had this sensation, this quickening to flight. He became suddenly reckless. He said kindly, "It's much harder on a girl, you see. She had no—what do they call it now?—yes, resources. I don't know why she went out of her head; she was always peculiar, though, I remember. A girl likes to think she means something important to her mother besides her actual existence. So when whatever it was that came up, she hadn't any strength to fight it. I wonder what it was."

His mother was silent. Ames smiled to himself. He rubbed his forehead with the back of his hand. He smoked again, rapidly. Then Caroline said in that same faint voice, "Don't pity yourself, Ames. Your father loved you and wanted you, and you all repaid him with contempt. Is that the return a parent can expect from children? You at least respected me. Or my money. That's better than contempt."

"You taught us to despise our father," said Ames. He no longer, at this moment, cared for his mother's money. He would care later, he knew, but not now. "Yes, we respected you and your money. We also hated you, all of us."

He felt vaguely nauseated. This damned heat! "What did you say, Mother?" he asked gently.

He could not see the enormous effort Caroline was making to speak through the huge pain.

"Don't divorce Amy, Ames," she said, and he was astonished to hear the pleading in her voice.

He said, "I want a woman who can give me 'natural and legal heirs,' Mother. Just as you wanted them. I thought I explained."

"You mustn't divorce Amy. She's a good little girl. I've not seen much of her, but she's good. And she—cares—about you. You can't throw that away."

"Is my staying married to her worth a little money, Mother?"

He waited. "How much?" said Caroline, and she was defending herself and not only Amy.

"Well, seeing that I'll never have the managing of the Ames estate because there'll be no children, I should say a few million dollars."

He knew his mother was flinching and cringing, as she always did at the mention of large sums of money. He let her suffer, and winked and smiled at himself in the mirror.

"Twenty-five thousand dollars a year, from this year on, as long as you remain married to Amy," said Caroline. Her voice had become stronger and firmer. "Even after I'm dead. I'll call my lawyers now."

"That's not a fraction of what John will get through Mimi's share of the Bothwell estate," said Ames, affecting dissatisfaction. "Or what he'll get from the estate you'll leave his children."

"You don't know," said Caroline. She added, "Thirty thousand dollars a year. That is all I am going to offer you."

Ames was exultant. Not the endless millions of the Ames money which should come rightfully to him, but quite a sum. And what was that cryptic remark of his mother's?

"Done!" he said. "I suppose I can expect the first installment almost immediately?" He thought of the enamels.

"Yes." There was a click in his ear. Ames hung up. He began to hum and went back to his locked library. He sat down and pondered. Was it possible the old girl was sweet on Amy, that little prattling and apprehensive fool? In that case, there was hope of much more than his mother had offered. "You don't know," she had said. Ames laughed aloud. Perhaps old Johnnie was due for a shock on his mother's death.

Griffith looked up from the board on which he was carefully slicing carrots for the julienne soup. "Yes, madam?" he said to Amy. Then he ran to the white-faced girl and caught her in his strong arms and helped her to a chair. "Madam!" he exclaimed. The girl sprawled in the chair like a broken doll, her gloves and purse spilling to the floor, her head dropping. Her eyes were closed; her mouth sagged. Griffith held her, for she would have fallen without his support. He wondered whether to shout for the master, whom he had heard talking in the hall for a considerable time.

Griffith looked down with deep pity and concern at the fainting girl half in his arms, half on the chair. She appeared to be dying. The soft dark hair spilled from under her wide gray silk hat; her thin throat palpitated feebly. Then she opened her eyes and looked at Griffith blankly, in a state of extreme shock.

"I heard," she whispered slowly. "I—was looking for my key, in my purse. I'm always losing it. Ames——" She swallowed and shivered.

"You should have rung, madam," said Griffith. "I'd have come."

But the blank, blind eyes only stared at him. "He—was in the hall. His mother." The whispering voice was almost too low to be heard, so Griffith bent closer. "He was talking to his mother. Then he told his mother—— He wants to divorce me. I—I didn't hear much after that, I don't think." She shook her head feebly. "But there was something about money if he'd—if he'd—keep me."

Griffith's face darkened. He should not be listening to this, he told himself sternly. He was only a servant. Young Mrs. Sheldon would regret this later. He said, "It's very hard to hear correctly through a stout wooden door, madam. Everything is blurred, distorted. Do you think I could leave you for a moment to get you a little refreshing brandy?"

But Amy seized his arms in her little white hands. "Griffith! I heard. He hates me." The pathetic face lifted to his with the dying expression in the eyes. "I—I thought he loved me, Griffith." She began to shake her head over and over, and her loosened hair fell in soft clouds over her shoulders. "I found the key. I even had the door a little open—I think I was stunned. He said it, Griffith, he said it. He hates me. I can't have any children, you see." And the eyes implored him.

"Oh no, no, indeed," said Griffith, overcome with his compassionate distraction. "You heard wrong, madam. Why, the master——"

"Hates me," she said. She was like a shattered child clinging to him. "He is all I have, Griffith. My father won't see me. I can't go to the house, you see. Papa found out I was visiting Mama, and he told her not to let me come any more. And my brothers—I hardly ever see them, Griffith. Mama comes here twice a month. The last time——" She could not go on.

"You were not in, madam," said Griffith. Like a father, he smoothed the hair on one of Amy's shoulders. "You were ill. You didn't want to worry your mother."

"Yes, Griffith. I wasn't in," she said. "I was in bed. I was drunk, Griffith."

"No, no, madam."

She sighed, almost moaning. "Yes, Griffith. And one day—I was shopping

—I could hardly walk. Old Mrs. Spencer—she was with her daughters. They had to help me—to a room—I lay down. I don't know. When I could open my eyes again I was in our automobile and Peters was looking straight ahead, driving. That was the day after Ames moved to the other bedroom. You remember?" she asked earnestly, as if it was most important that he remember.

He shook his head. "Madam, I will get you a little brandy. You are not yourself." He slowly and carefully released his arms. Then he ran into the dining room and returned with a glass of brandy. Amy was still sitting, sprawled, in the chair, staring blankly at a wall. "Thank you," she said in a little girl's voice, and took the glass and put it to her lips. She drank the liquid down in one gulp and did not even cough. Amy gave him the glass politely.

"I don't like brandy much," she said. "Whiskey is much better. Peters buys it for me now. I just ran a few minutes ago into my room and took a big drink, and then I had to talk to you."

Griffith wondered distractedly if he should tell Mr. Sheldon. No, that would never do. He must talk to Peters, the chauffeur. No, the least said, the sooner mended. Peters was young and surly. He would not listen to threats. But what could he, Griffith, do to help this poor little lady? A young lady, still hardly more than a girl, and whiskey. More horrifying was the thought of the talk which must inevitably be going about Boston even now through that old Mrs. Spencer and her daughters. Or would they, being First Family, murmur about a member of another First Family? Certainly, thought the despairing Griffith with anger. A lady who used a plush-seated water closet was no better when it came to gossip than a farm maid and her odorous outside privy.

"I'm so lonely," Amy was saying. One tear after another was dropping off her thin cheeks onto her immature breast. The gray silk was becoming rapidly spotted.

"Yes, madam," he murmured. "It will be well again, madam."

"Oh no," she said, and she shook her head once more, over and over. "Never again. How could it, Griffith? He'll let me stay, for the money his mother will give him. Not love, not children, not being happy together. Just money." The slurred voice was almost unintelligible now and weaker. "Ames doesn't love me. That's why I have to drink, to stop thinking about it, Griffith."

"May I help you to your room, madam?" said Griffith, more and more despairing.

"Yes, please get me some more brandy," said Amy. "Then I'll be strong enough to walk." Griffith did not move. "Please!" said Amy. Griffith took the glass away, refilled it, and returned. Amy swallowed the brandy as neatly as she had done before. He had seen drunkards in his time, and they had drunk as Amy drank, swiftly, as if seeking an anodyne. But surely this delicate shy child was not a drunkard. Dear God, thought Griffith, thinking of the whiskey hidden in some drawer or closet in Amy's room. Should he tell the master? Griffith shook his head. There was violence under Ames' sleek exterior, but also a kind of wickedness which might find Amy's awful condition highly amusing. Rage or amusement in this case would be equally disastrous to the girl.

"It's because I'm so stupid," the childish voice was continuing. "It's not Ames' fault. It's all mine. Poor Ames." Then she cried out, "But how can I live without him! He's all I have! I can talk to him better when I have my whiskey. You see, you see? I'm not afraid of him then; I can make myself feel he loves me, though he doesn't. It's awful to be lonely, isn't it, Griffith?"

She had talked rapidly, almost incoherently. She tried to get up, staggered, and Griffith caught her. She clung to him and began to laugh wildly. With consternation Griffith looked at the closed kitchen doors.

"I can't sleep unless I drink," Amy said after her laughter had abruptly stopped. "I can't live, knowing—it's always the knowing—isn't it, Griffith?"

"Yes. That is it. The knowing," he said with aching pity. Then he lifted her in his arms, swung open the kitchen door, crossed the hall on tiptoe to Amy's room. He laid her down on the bed, removed her crumpled hat and her little gray slippers. He opened the windows. The girl was already deep in alcoholic slumber, her flushed face, like a child's, turned into the pillow, her hair streaming about her. Griffith shut the door. He had come to a stern and desperate decision.

The butler went back to the kitchen. In about an hour he would take strong coffee to that child. He thought of what she had said. The "knowing." Yes, it was always that, the knowing that one was without love, and lonely, and abandoned. A drunkard did not have "loved ones," as the foolish said. He was always alone, and the starved spirit reached instinctively for a little death.

Henry Bothwell Winslow came into the Boston house of his parents sweating heavily on this hot August day. He removed the stiff straw sailor from his head, laid down his smart white cane, and unfastened the broad red, white, and blue ribbon which spread from his waist and over his right shoulder in the manner of the British Order of the Garter. He had been marching for three hours in a Preparedness Parade through the main streets of Boston, and he was hot, foot-blistered, and weary. He was just twenty-three years old; he thought President Wilson a cautious old fuddy-duddy; he was afire with patriotism; he hated Wilhelm, Emperor of Germany, and was absolutely convinced that should the Kaiser be victorious in Europe he would immediately order the whole German fleet and every foot soldier and every howitzer and "big Bertha" to set themselves on the United States of America.

"Preparedness," he would tell his mother firmly, "is the only way to prevent war with Germany."

"It seems to me that the Kaiser has enough to do with Europe," Amanda would reply. "Why should he bother with us?"

"Because he wants to conquer the whole world," Henry said with unusual irritability.

"Who says so?" his mother inquired.

"Why, everybody. Don't you read the papers?"

"Certainly." Amanda thought of Timothy, her husband. "Do you believe every excited opinion you read, child?"

"I am not a child," said Henry with exasperated patience.

"There is something going on in the world much more dreadful than this war; I'd had a glimpse of it years ago when we were all in London. This war was for a reason, and it isn't an ambitious war on Germany's part, though we are being led to think so. Does it ever occur to you, my child, that President Wilson, who isn't of our party, might have some very sound reasons why he doesn't want us to get involved in the European war? Reasons so terrible but so hidden that he doesn't speak of them because everyone but the men responsible for this war would laugh at him?"

Henry frowned. "I don't follow you, Mother."

"Do you actually believe that all of Europe would have been embroiled in this war merely because a crazed Bosnian boy killed the Archduke of Austria and his wife? There have been many assassinations in Europe over the past one hundred years, and no war resulted from them. But this war was planned."

"By whom?" Henry asked incredulously.

"By people I hope you will never meet," said Amanda. "From some of the opinions I've heard you airing recently, I am even more afraid that you've already met them." She looked at the handsome, kind face of her son, so ingenuous and so honest, and shook her head. "I've heard you talk very kindly about Eugene Debs, for instance. Where did you first hear of him?"

Henry looked bewildered. "Why, at the university, of course. Mother——"

"There's been a Communist organization in this country since 1872," said Amanda. "Didn't you know?"

Henry considered this. "But socialism isn't communism, dear."

"No? Of course it is. Despotism is only socialism in a hurry, I've recently heard."

"But what has all this to do with us being prepared for any actuality, such as war?"

"Everything." Amanda looked at her son with terror. "You and Harper! You are just the right age. Oh dear God! Deliver us from this evil!"

The old lady was really getting old, Henry had thought with concerned affection. She was almost forty-five; at that age one could get the most outlandish ideas. What had socialism and communism to do with that insane Kaiser's war "against humanity"? Oh, there were profs at Harvard who were as cautious and as conservative, as far as this war was concerned, as was President Wilson, and who hinted there were "other matters" hidden behind it, but they were never explicit. Henry considered, baffled. But other profs were vehement about America not only being prepared but actually engaging in the European imbroglio. They were great admirers of Eugene Debs; they spoke of the "class struggle" and "oppressed workers and criminals of great wealth." They gave young men such as Henry Winslow, now in the law school, twinges of guilt and embarrassment and then fired them with the vague passion to do something about "social inequities."

"I'm not sure I know exactly what is under all this," said Amanda, her round face red with urgency, "but I heard hints about it in London years and years ago. Oh, dear me! I just wish I'd found out a little more when I had the opportunity!"

"Dad thinks we should be prepared and then get into the struggle against the Kaiser, Mother."

"Yes, I know." Amanda's voice was bitter.

"Well, what stake would he have in it?"

"A great deal, I am afraid," said Amanda. "Your Uncle William in England told me when we were there that there would be a war, but not for the reasons we'd be given. Much more terrible ones."

"What?" asked Henry indulgently, thinking of his clerical uncle.

Amanda spoke hesitatingly, trying to find words. "William did say that there would be a series of wars in this century for the sole purpose of driving free government and liberty from the face of the earth—for the benefit of wicked men who wanted to rule all of us like the ancient despots. I believe he mentioned Karl Marx once."

"Oh, Mother! What in God's name has an old dead Socialist got to do with this mess in Europe, and an insane Kaiser, and the threat of war against us too?"

"You never heard any of your profs mentioning Karl Marx, Henry?"

"Well, yes, I did. But, Mother— Why, this is fantastic! Of course socialism, at least some of its ideas, aren't bad at all. Even Dad says so."

"Yes, he would say that," said Amanda with greater bitterness.

Henry had marched in the Preparedness Parade behind very martial drums and trumpets and felt very patriotic and high-hearted and stirred. The only way to avoid war was to be prepared to fight it. There was only one thing which had puzzled him: while marching he had passed a large body of shabby men who had shouted their approval at the young and old marchers and who had yelled, "Down with all kings and emperors and despots!" Well, that was ridiculous, Henry had thought, striding manfully. All of Europe, except Switzerland, was ruled by monarchs, very good ones except the Kaiser. Well, those shabby men were just hysterical and excited and carried away by the music. What else had they shouted? Oh yes: "Workers of the world, Unite!"

A maid came to him and said that his mother wished to see him in the morning room. Henry, walking with a long military stride, went to the morning room. The doors were almost never shut, but they were shut now. Henry sighed, knocked, then opened the double doors.

His mother, her round face blotched with tears, her eyes filled with them, was sitting there with a lean, middle-aged man. The man looked faintly familiar; it was not until he stood up respectfully that Henry recognized him as Ames' butler, cook, and houseman, Griffith. Henry immediately thought of his sister, whom he visited occasionally, perhaps every six weeks or so. He didn't like to be disloyal to his father and was always uncomfortable with Amy, whom he deeply loved. (Why did she have to do this to Dad, on the very day he had been so shockingly defeated and had had his stroke?)

"Is something wrong with Amy?" Henry asked in an unusually sharp tone, out of his affection for his sister.

"Terribly wrong, dear," said Amanda. "Sit down. Listen carefully, Henry. Griffith has been telling me the whole story. Amy—well, it seems Ames hates her and has been abusing her in subtle ways almost since the day they were married. He—never cared for her, Henry, not truly. I never told you. But his mother gave him three million dollars to marry Amy. Don't look so damned incredulous!" cried poor Amanda wildly. "You've got to accept some things as facts without everything being in black and white—that comes from your damned law training! I tell you, these things are true! Caroline Ames wanted to revenge herself on your father——"

"But why?" asked Henry. "She put him on his way, didn't she?"

"Never mind!" Amanda said in a muffled scream. "I know things you don't, you young careful-minded idiot! Oh, God, shut that door; I hope your father hasn't already heard me screeching! Tight; shut it tight. Sit down; don't hover like a big damned befuddled bumblebee, Henry! Henry, you must just *listen!*

"He wouldn't have married her without that money, Henry. Of course he was always after her, and perhaps he did care a little about her, but he had to have that money. Now he thinks Amy's a fool. He's always calling her half-witted. I didn't know! I knew she was unhappy about something, the silly, timid little thing, but she'd never tell me much. And now he's driven her to drink."

"Nonsense," said Henry, paling. "I—I've never seen her—— What is all this? It sounds pretty ridiculous to me." He turned to Griffith and said sternly, his kind young face tight, "What are these wild stories you've brought my—— Mrs. Winslow?"

"Oh, Henry!" said Amanda, weeping again. "Just listen. Griffith is like a father to Amy. He wants us to help her. A few nights ago Amy heard Ames telling Caroline that he was going to divorce Amy, and then apparently Caroline offered him money not to. She just wants him to keep on torturing your little sister! She hates all of us so!"

"Divorce? Torture? Mother, you haven't swallowed all this?" He again turned to Griffith. "Are you trying to get even with Mr. Sheldon? Has he fired you or something?"

"No, sir, he has not. I am still in his employ, and he pays me a large salary. But Mrs. Winslow is merely condensing what I have been telling her for over an hour." Griffith spoke with dignity. Then his long slash of a mouth shook. "I'm afraid I am partly to blame, perhaps a great deal to blame. When young Mrs. Sheldon would be most distressed I would bring her a glass of brandy, to calm her. She spent much time with me in the kitchen. She was so lonely, you see; she had no one to talk with, to confide in, except me. She could hardly tell her mother that so early in her marriage she was being derided and abused and tormented by a—by a young man who is strangely—shall we say—corrupt? Perhaps it is not his fault.

"Mrs. Sheldon would come crying into the kitchen at all hours, very badly shocked and shaken, sir. And I would give her brandy. I only thought to soothe her, to calm her. Had I thought that it would lead to—this—this —I'd have cut my right hand off first, sir, and you must believe me."

Henry bent his curly dark head and considered this for some long moments. Like his mother, he had a bright color. It was all gone when he finally lifted his head.

"But, accepting all these things tentatively, why should Ames want to divorce Amy? They haven't been married a year yet."

Griffith hesitated, coughed. Amanda said, "I didn't know until today, when Griffith told me. Amy will never be able to have children. Don't ask me for details! Just listen! And so Ames really hates her now. He wanted children who would inherit his mother's money."

"A drunkard? Amy?" said Henry after a moment's contemplation. "I just can't believe it." Then he clenched his big hands. "I'll beat Ames—I'll kill him."

"Don't be hysterical," said his mother with some malice as she remembered that Henry had called her that when she had protested some of his ideas. Then the malice was gone in fresh tears. "We've got to get Amy away from him! We must! She's drunk almost the whole time now, Griffith tells me. Oh, my God! I've heard rumors all over Boston that Amy 'doesn't seem herself.' And sly smiles at me. People know, Henry; we are the only ones who didn't. We must get Amy away before she dies, poor, darling, little baby."

"He hates her because she can't have children?" said Henry, who was methodical and orderly in his thoughts. "Oh yes, you've said the money. He married her because his mother bribed him to. I've never heard anything like this before; it sounds——"

"You've been a shielded infant all your life!" cried Amanda. "A downy infant! Loved, protected, pampered, secure! What a horrible thing to do to children! Then when they come face to face with reality they are lost and wandering and look empty, just as you're doing, Henry. Damn it, boy, grow up this very minute! I need your help. And forgive me for keeping you a child until you were this age!"

Devastated, she thought of Amy, who had suffered the most from her childish belief that mankind was good and kind and decent, inclined to virtue rather than evil, to justice rather than cruelty, to honor rather than theft, to life rather than death.

"Oh, dear, dear God," wailed Amanda as her son paced up and down the small but handsome room with its view of a walled garden. "What a family that is, the Sheldons! And the Winslows, coming down to that. And in the center of all this misery—Caroline Ames. How can any woman be as horrible as this?"

Griffith coughed again. "Perhaps she is not, madam," he offered. "I have seen these matriarchs in London, in the counties, in New York and Boston. You will remember, if you'll pardon me, that the Recording Angels will not take as an excuse for your wickedness that the world of men has abused you, or parents, or children or brothers or sisters, or friends or neighbors, or even enemies. Each man molds his own soul. If Mr. Ames is what he is, he as well as his mother is guilty."

Henry stopped abruptly in front of him. His young face was hard and still. "We aren't blaming you for Amy's—her bad habits. You did your best. Indeed, we should thank you for your concern, Griffith, and that you came to us to ask help for my sister."

He looked at his mother. "I know law, Mother. You can't just abduct Amy or persuade her to leave her husband against her real will. Apparently she likes that swine, or she'd have come to us for help herself. Moreover, if you do bring her here and prevent her from seeing Ames, he could sue you and Dad for alienating his wife's affections and influencing her against him. He's just the sort. Wouldn't you agree?" he asked Griffith.

"Yes indeed, sir. I have thought of that very thing myself. But the young lady will die if she remains with her husband." He paused. He looked at Amanda. "There is something else, Mrs. Winslow. I have protected Mrs. Sheldon from her husband; he did not discover that she had a—a weakness —until three days ago. You see, they occupy separate bedrooms." He looked down at his hands modestly. "But three days ago, on a morning, he went into her bedroom and found her already drunk, with the very bottle beside her."

"Well?" said Henry after Griffith had paused for some time. The older man lifted his eyes wretchedly.

"This will make you very unhappy, sir. But Mr. Ames expressed himself as outraged. At any rate, I heard the young lady scream and ran to her assistance, to discover her husband——"

He could not go on. But Henry looked down at him and moment by moment the young man grew older and he was no longer a boy.

"So," said Henry, "you discovered him slapping her and probably calling her filthy names."

"Yes, that is it, sir."

"Amy, beaten?" said Amanda faintly. "Amy, cursed? Our little Amy? Why, no one even smacked her, not once in her whole life, not even I! No one even raised a voice to her! Amy!"

Henry did not speak like a boy now; he did not repeat, "I'll kill him." He just stood and thought and he seemed to grow taller and wider. He said to Griffith, "You will testify to this, if necessary, in court?"

"Yes. I came to suggest that myself."

Henry smiled at him briefly, while his mother cried and mopped at her face and swollen eyes. "Good," he said.

"However," said Griffith, "as I have met ladies like Mrs. Sheldon, Mr.

Ames' mother, I suggest that you permit me to see her myself and explain the situation and ask her assistance."

"Caroline!" shrieked Amanda. "Are you mad? Caroline Ames!"

"Hush, Mother," said Henry severely, still looking at Griffith. "When are you thinking of going?"

"I believe there is a train to Lyme within a half hour," said Griffith, taking out a large old gold watch and studying it.

"You aren't serious!" exclaimed Amanda. "She's the most hateful and detestable creature in the world! Have you forgotten that she bribed her son to elope with my little girl so that Timothy would be injured and hurt? This news about my child will only make her happier."

Griffith shook his head. "I've never met Mrs. Sheldon, but the family history has interested me and I have studied it. She has a reputation for high integrity and strictness of character. Perhaps she was, indeed, looking for revenge on Mr. Winslow for something we do not know, but she is, after all, a mother, and I cannot feel that she bears little Mrs. Sheldon any malice. There are imponderables that I know."

"Well, then," said Henry, "arm yourself with those imponderables, Griffith. I'll drive you to the station myself. But I'd advise you to telephone Caroline first. She's walled herself in, I hear."

He led Griffith out to the hall to telephone, then ran lightly upstairs to listen at his father's door. There was only silence behind it, so he leaned over the stairway and nodded to Griffith. Griffith asked the operator to connect him with Mrs. Thomas Sheldon of Lyme and waited. The only sound in the great pleasant house was the muffled sobbing of Amanda in the morning room nearby.

"Are you there?" asked Griffith politely. "Ah, yes. Will you please inform Mrs. Sheldon that a gentleman wishes to call upon her within the hour on a matter of the gravest importance—concerning Mr. Ames Sheldon and three million dollars?" Henry smiled down at him grimly, leaning his elbows on the balustrade. The two waited. Then Griffith said, "No, I cannot give my name. I hope you impressed Mrs. Sheldon with the importance—— Yes, I will wait."

Griffith stood thinly poised in his respectable black broadcloth suit and stiff white collar, leaning courteously toward the telephone. Then he said, "Yes? Thank you. No, I will not give my name over the telephone, as I have mentioned before. Very sorry, indeed."

They waited again. Griffith murmured, "Most extraordinarily incompetent young woman, that, sir. She does not sound her consonants." Then he bowed to the telephone and said, "Thank you. I shall be there shortly."

He hung up the receiver and nodded to Henry. "I think," he said thoughtfully, "that I have aroused Mrs. Sheldon's curiosity. Ladies are very similar, I have discovered."

As Henry drove Griffith to the station he found himself thinking of the servant not as a menial but as a friend in whom one could confide. He said, driving rapidly through the warm and golden streets of summer Boston,

"There's my father, you know. He's almost an invalid now since his stroke. He can walk with difficulty, with a cane, but his left leg drags and his left arm is weak, and sometimes he can't express himself clearly. He's become an old man since last November. Two very bad blows in one day, you see, the election and then my sister. He won't let us even mention her in our house; he'd be infuriated if he knew my brother and I visit her sometimes. If we can get this thing straight and my sister away from Ames, what shall we do?"

"I am sure that when you bring her home she will be welcomed by her father," said Griffith.

Henry nodded. He said, "My mother hates herself for Amy's being as she is now. But it was my father's doing, you know. He never let Amy become a woman. He thought women should be dependent and clinging and soft and sweet; he thought they should never have an opinion of their own or any intelligence, really. Their whole lives, he thinks, should revolve about the men in their families."

"No doubt there were ladies of very independent character in his life," said Griffith after a moment's thought. "His mother, perhaps. And——"

"Oh, Mother," said Henry. "My mother is filled to the brim with common sense, and I've noticed that most men resent common sense. And then, of course, there was old Caroline, who is sort of like a monument in the family. Dad hated her. We men are always telling women to be sensible, but when they are we resent it. We are weak characters, aren't we?"

"No," said Griffith soberly. "Merely, I should say, romantics. It is strange, is it not, that there are very few innocent ladies of any consequence in history? Could it be that what we demand in women is not what we honestly wish?"

CHAPTER TWO

"I am a busy woman, Higsby," said Caroline with irritation, that morning. "You said you had something important to ask me today and that is why I let you come. Now you ask me for money."

Then she said sourly, "I've told you before. This war was planned long ago; I heard of it when I was a young girl. So do you think Wilson can keep us out? No."

"No," said Higsby. "I quite agree, however, that this war and the others which will follow it have a purpose beyond the knowledge of most people. But at least we can disseminate information so that even if America is embroiled there will be a large body of the population which will be informed, and in turn they will inform their children and their grandchildren, and America will know the real enemy, the old ancient reactionary enemy which is as old as man himself. Despotism. All-powerful centralized government. Rule by men and not by law. Did you think America is, and will be, immune from the efforts of evil men to establish a despotism here?"

"No. We're no more immune than any other nation," said Caroline with contempt. "We'll fall, just as Rome fell and other despotisms. So why should I waste my money on a lost cause to 'inform the people'? Besides, even despots respect money and power. I'll have no difficulty." And she gave Higsby a dark, cold smile.

"You don't care what happens to your country, Caroline?"

"Not particularly. Why should I? When a nation starts declining it never stops and returns. But money is money everywhere."

"And so are human lives and souls, Caroline." It was dank in this decaying and sifting room, though the hot late-summer sun simmered outside. Mr. Chalmers leaned toward Caroline pleadingly. "Is your money more important, Caroline, than the lives and freedom of millions of innocent people?"

"Certainly," said Caroline. "Don't be a fool, Higsby. You're entirely too moral for me, I'm afraid. Don't you remember what Macaulay said about his own countrymen? 'We know no spectacle so ridiculous as the public in one of its periodic fits of morality.' "

"And I," said Mr. Chalmers, "know no spectacle so tragic as any nation which does not have 'periodic fits of morality.' That nation is already dead." He paused. "Your fellow Americans——"

"I've told you, they're nothing to me!" exclaimed Caroline. "Why should they be?"

"If you don't know by instinct and by emotion and affection, then I can't convince you," said Higsby, and he pulled his fat thighs over the torn fabric of his chair and stood up. Caroline immediately jerked the bell rope, and when her slatternly maid sullenly appeared at the doorway Caroline ordered her to call a hack for Mr. Chalmers.

Higsby said, "When you see the despair, bankruptcy and ruin and slavery in this country, Caroline, you'll regret you didn't help us."

"I doubt it," said Caroline, and left the room with her lumbering stride. She did not hear Mr. Chalmers go; she had forgotten him by the time she opened her study door. She made her usual late-morning calls to her brokers in New York, called her New York bank and her Boston office. Then suddenly she was aware of the intense silence about her. For the first time it was an intrusion, not a protection. She looked about her uneasily. She glanced through the large uncurtained window at the blue and shimmering ocean. There was no hint of a storm. Nevertheless, she had the impression that something calamitous was brewing. "Nonsense," she said aloud, "it's just that foolish Higsby and his silly prophecies. What or who can harm me, with my money and my power?"

She ponderously leaned back in her chair and contemplated her money and power. She would be safe. But the uneasiness persisted. Exasperated, she threw down her pen and went to her gallery, where there was always peace and understanding for her, and quiet.

She had hung Mimi Bothwell's little painting of the girl on the boulder, with the bright red ribbon in her hair, in a conspicuous spot. But she avoided looking at it now. She could not remove it, and still she would not look at it since the day her son John had married Mimi. She had offered John money not to marry the girl and had been confused by his refusal. "You don't seem to understand that I want Mimi," he had said smilingly.

"You mean," said Caroline, "the Bothwell money, don't you?"

She had been surprised when John did not answer immediately. He had finally said, "Partly, but not completely. I should have wanted to marry Mimi without the money."

Caroline had not believed that. "Again, I warn you that if you marry her there'll be nothing for you. And nothing for your children."

That had caused John intense anger and dismay. "What the hell will you do with your money? Leave it to Ames' and Amy's brats entirely?"

"Perhaps." She thought she had reached him. Certainly he was staring at her murderously. But he stood up at last and said, "Well, so that's it. I am still going to marry Mimi."

Caroline had received a wedding invitation from Melinda and had thrown it into the fire. She sent no gift. She had not seen either John or Mimi since that cold bright day in March when they had been married in the Bothwell house in Boston. The girl, Caroline said to herself, deserved John, apparently. But she had never recovered from the grief of the marriage. It was as if Mimi, too, were buried on the hill with Elizabeth. There had even been one frightening occasion when Caroline, visiting Elizabeth's grave, had actually looked for Mimi's. The stunning realization that she had been so looking had upset Caroline for days and had given her another fear, this time for herself. In consequence she had visited a physician in Boston. What had the fool said? "It is your heart, Mrs. Sheldon. It is badly over-strained; I don't want to be too technical. There are indications of stresses. At your age——"

"Nonsense," said Caroline. "I have no physical stresses and never have had. What are you going to charge me for this concoction of yours?" And she looked distastefully at the bottle of digitalis in her hand. "Doctors always overcharge those they think are rich."

The young doctor had smiled wryly. "Suppose you give a donation to the Sisters of Charity Hospital in the city," he said.

The digitalis had helped her very much. Therefore, she considered herself cured of whatever had ailed her. She had not feared for her heart; she had feared for her mind. She could feel a new anger now. Mimi had betrayed her and her love. "Everyone is alike at the last," she would say to the self-portrait of her grandfather. "I thought Mimi was different. But I was wrong."

So she did not look at Mimi's little painting which so resembled her young self and she could not take it down. She merely avoided glancing at it. Mimi was no part of her life any longer; where the girl had lived in Caroline there was now a huge sick place. Cynthia, Melinda, Mimi: they had all injured her to a most terrible extent. She would never forgive any of them. As for John, she had removed him neatly from her consciousness as if he had never existed; it had been no trouble at all for her.

She talked to her grandfather. "I don't know why I feel calamity in the air," she said to him. "Of course, at my age, it is expected that I be nervous at times. Occasionally melancholy. But not morbid, I trust! Was it peaceful when you were alive? Of course not.

"My father, your son, used to say that men were devils. So there was no peace, ever, in this world. Was there?"

The portrait looked into her eyes, and the gentle smile appeared alive. "Except," said Caroline astonishingly, "in some people's souls."

She considered her own remark, and a vague and enormous distress came to her. She said, "Now that was a foolish remark, wasn't it?"

She looked into her grandfather's eyes. "Were you at peace?" she demanded. The calm and tender face smiled at her. She stepped back and rubbed her right cheek. She muttered, "Yes. Yes, you were. In spite of everything."

She was so overcome that she had to sit down in the one chair in the gallery. Her whole body felt heavy and old and overpoweringly tired. Had she forgotten to take her last dose of medicine? No, she had taken it at ten o'clock. But she could feel a dull loud thumping in her chest. "I've said everything to you that I possibly could," she said. "I've told you everything. You know all about me. But now there seems to be so much that I haven't told you, though I don't know what it is. Do you know?"

It was absurd, of course, to believe that someone living was in the gallery with her and that his face was reflected in the portrait. "What?" muttered Caroline. She pushed herself to her feet, then caught the back of the chair. A doomful atmosphere filled the sunny room in spite of the fresh sea wind that gushed through the window. Caroline swung her white head slowly and ponderously from side to side, trying to breathe through a sensation of smothering. "I'm all alone," she muttered. "I always wanted to be alone, except for Beth and my father. And Tom."

She looked at the portrait. "Where are they?" she said. "Where are you? And— Oh, God! Where am I?" She forced herself, wavering step by step, to her grandfather's paintings. She looked at the tower, at the church and the fearful sky. And finally she looked at the painting of the blindfolded man wandering among the gigantic boulders against the apocalyptic mountains. She leaned toward it, pressing her hands against her big breast. Who was that man? Surely she recognized the half-hidden face! What was his name? His groping hands, his staggering blind step, his shrouded eyes— they were all familiar. Where had she seen him? He had walked like that, fumbling in self-willed darkness. Looking, searching. For what?

"I knew you!" Caroline shouted. "You're as familiar to me as myself! Why didn't I see that before?" She appealed to her grandfather's portrait. "You knew him too! Tell me! You see, I must know. It's terribly important for me to know, and I don't know why."

The vague distress became terrible now. She had only to listen to it. "No, no!" she cried, retreating. "Don't tell me! I mustn't know! If I do—if I do——"

She put her hands over her face. "I'll die if I know," she said through her fingers. "You must never tell me. All my reason for living will be gone then."

Heavily but rapidly she ran to the door. Then she stopped and looked back over her shoulder, and her eyes struck on Mimi's painting of the hopeful young girl on the boulder looking eagerly to her left, waiting. "No," said Caroline. "There was never anything to wait for. It was all a lie." She thought of her children, and they were like cardboard lithographs to her, even Elizabeth. "A lie," she repeated; a great pain struck her heart and she gasped under it. But she pulled open the door, stepped into the hall, and locked the door behind her. She did not know that tears were pouring down her cheeks; the slatternly maid, suddenly materializing in the dusk of the dusty hall, saw them and stared curiously.

"What do you want?" said Caroline.

The girl peered at the evidences of unconscious weeping. She licked her lips. "Why, there's a big red autermobil at the gate. Mrs. John Sheldon, and she's got to see you."

"Send her away," said Caroline with immediate harshness. The girl nodded. Then Caroline put up her hand. "Wait." She had to lean against the wall. She was so weak suddenly, so prostrated. Her head fell on her chest. No, she thought, I don't want to see her. I told her never to come here again. It will just make everything far worse for me. "Mary!" she said aloud. She moved away from the wall and went downstairs. She could not move fast enough; her hand slipped on the greasy balustrade; her feet fumbled on each step; her black old skirts rustled behind her. She was in flight from the terror she had experienced in her gallery. "I must run, run," she said, and the girl following her was tantalized with more curiosity. The old lady was crazy, but she paid good because she couldn't get nobody to stay with her unless the pay was good. The folks in the village said a person's life wasn't safe in this house, but they didn't know about the money. The girl saw Caroline run across the hall, and she said, "Ma'am, want me to go to the gates?"

Caroline did not answer. As she had run to Tom so long ago, so she ran now to Mimi Bothwell sitting in the big red automobile on the other side of the gates, the chauffeur standing at the door stiffly and watching Caroline's lumbering rush toward them. There was only a mere hint of a gravel path through the sun-struck wilderness of wild and dying trees and shrubs and high grass between the walls; the decaying house loomed behind Caroline with an ominous glowering, its brick walls covered with a weed-like vine.

Mimi watched Caroline's passage, and then she said, "I'll get out now, please," and the chauffeur opened the door and Mimi ran to the gate and clung to the rusting bars like a child. She called, "Aunt Caroline! Don't run, don't run. I'll wait." For there was something in Caroline's running movements which frightened the girl. She was like a terrified old woman running, her black thick skirts fluttering about her, her face half blind in expression. "Oh, Aunt Caroline," said Mimi, and wanted to cry. Then Caroline stood within touching distance, and the two looked at each other. Oh, my God, thought Mimi, she's dying. She put her hand through the gate and held it out mutely to her aunt.

Caroline, panting, looked at the extended hand as if she did not know what it was. The sun lay on the strong white fingers, the smooth palm. The whole hand had a posture of love and strength and consolation. Caroline's hand rose unsteadily; then, like a child, she took Mimi's and held it, and the girl could feel the roughness and dryness of the hand so like her own. She felt the desperate clinging, the loneliness, the abandonment. "Dear Aunt Caroline," said Mimi, and swallowed so that she would not burst into tears.

Caroline clung to the hand and blinked her eyes in the sunlight, old sunken yellowish eyes. She said, "The lock. It's the lock." She looked at Mimi's pretty and sorrowful face, at the red lips that tried to smile and could only tremble, at the golden eyes shining with tears. "It's the lock," said Caroline in a far dull voice, as if explaining.

"Yes, dear," said Mimi. The sea wind moved her cloud of dark hair.

"I must open the lock," said Caroline.

"Of course," said Mimi.

"So you can come in," said Caroline in that anxious voice of explanation. She needed both hands to open the lock, and the key was on a ring in the pocket of her frayed black dress. But she would not release Mimi's hand. She held to life, to youth, to beauty, to herself, to the young Caroline Ames.

Mimi understood, in her sad and perceptive young mind. She held her aunt's hand firmly. Then, to her relief, she saw the maid hovering avidly at the end of the path. "Come here, please," she called. The girl came running, eager to see this extraordinary thing so she could gossip about it in the village. She stared at Mimi when she reached the gate; she stared at the clasped hands. Why, that was the funniest thing! She wanted to laugh out loud, the old woman clamping onto the hand of this young woman.

"Do you know where the key is?" Mimi said sharply.

"Why, sure, ma'am," said the girl, inclining her head with sly derision at the silent and clutching Caroline, and speaking as if Caroline were not present. "She keeps the key on a big ring in her pocket. Right there."

"Well, take it out and open the gate," said Mimi in a voice that flogged the girl angrily. "What are you waiting for? Stop staring. Can't you see my aunt is sick? Open the gate!"

The cold command in Mimi's voice startled the girl into fast action. She thrust her hand into Caroline's pocket and pulled out the clattering ring of keys. Gulls cried in the shining silence; the wild and dying brush rustled. Caroline still looked blindly at Mimi's face. Then the maid snapped the lock open and stepped back. "You just got to push it now," she said sullenly. Who did this girl, no older than herself, think she was, anyways, yelling at people like they were dogs or something? She, Maizie, was as good as anybody else, and she wasn't going to take this ordering around like she was nobody at all. That's what everybody said nowadays; you didn't take orders if you'd a mind not to, not even from a rich somebody in a big shiny red autermobil with a fella in a silly uniform like a policeman.

"You may go now," said Mimi, seeing the malice on the girl's face.

Oh, was that so? But Maizie scuttled away reluctantly.

Mimi said gently to her aunt, "Dear, the lock's open. May I come in?"

Caroline started. She blinked again, rapidly. Then she retreated in silence, and Mimi pushed the creaking gate open and stood beside her aunt. Caroline's face changed from an expression of far lostness and despair to one of immediate attention. She was herself again.

"Why did you come here?" she demanded. "What do you want?"

Mimi was dismayed. "I wanted to talk to you, dear Aunt Caroline."

"What for?" The voice was no longer wandering and vague, but loud and bitter.

"Aren't you going to invite me into the house?" asked Mimi.

Caroline was silent. She studied the girl acutely. She said in anger, "I see you're going to have a baby. What stupidity."

Mimi reached out to take the big arm in its fraying old bombazine, but Caroline moved back repudiatingly. "I told you not to come again," she said. "But you are here. Very well. Come into the house." She turned about and marched slowly but steadily away. Mimi sighed. Very carefully she picked her way over the lumpy gravel and followed her aunt. When she reached the steps of the house Caroline was not in sight. Mimi stopped for a moment to survey the rank jungle growth within the walls, the dead and tattered leaves mingling with fierce green ones, the waving grass, the weed-covered mounds which once were flower beds. Sticks of an old arbor pointed sharply against the blue sky. There was a stench of mold and death in this place. The walls resembled the walls of a prison.

The girl, sighing, tested each splintered step before resting her weight upon it and entered the house. There were windows, but there was no sun in this silent dark place. Mimi could smell the rotting furniture and rugs and woodwork; she had glimpses of rags of old draperies. It was much worse than her memory of only a few months ago. The bleared windows shut out air and light. But the silence was the worst. Mimi went into the parlor and found her aunt sitting tall and stiff in a chair, her back to her visitor. So Mimi walked into the room, found a chair facing her aunt.

"What do you want?" Caroline demanded. "I'm a busy person, so you must speak briefly."

She would not look at Mimi. Her eyes were fixed on the floor.

"I came for two reasons," said Mimi in a soft voice. "I've always wanted to come, but you never answered my letters or my telephone calls. You didn't remember that you loved me one time, Aunt Caroline. And that I love you."

Caroline's gray lips moved contemptuously. "Did you?" she said. She still would not look at the girl. "I told you not to marry my son John. You wouldn't listen. You thought you knew more about him than I do. I suppose you are happy."

"Yes," said Mimi. "I am. Aunt Caroline, don't you wear the locket I gave you?"

"No," said Caroline. "Why should I? I'm not sentimental. Well?"

"All right," said Mimi sadly. "Now I'll tell you my second reason for coming. Please listen to me. My cousin Amy, who's married to your son Ames. I saw her yesterday in Boston. I went in to shop, for I've been visiting Mama the last two weeks. John thought I'd feel a little better at the seashore, and I did want to spend some time talking to Mama. Nathaniel can come home only on the weekends, you know, and so she is lonely, I'm afraid. She doesn't go to Newport any more." Mimi's expression saddened. "Didn't you know, Aunt Caroline? Mama had a heart attack two months ago."

"Heart?" said Caroline suddenly.

"Yes."

Caroline said nothing. Her father; his daughters. But she would not look at Mimi. After a little she said, "What is this about Ames? What are you talking about?"

"I was talking about Amy," said Mimi, and her young voice hardened. "I didn't know. I hope no one else knows! Ames' man wouldn't let me in at first to see her, but I insisted. Aunt Caroline, little Amy was in bed. Drunk."

"Drunk? What are you talking about?"

"She was drunk, Aunt Caroline. Ames abuses her. His man, Griffith, brought her coffee and I made her drink it. Then she told me. Ames hates her. I always disliked him; there's something wrong with him; perhaps you know."

Then Caroline looked up. Mimi expected to see indifference and coldness again, but Caroline's eyes were suddenly alive. While Mimi looked into those eyes, expecting her aunt to speak harshly and furiously, Caroline shrank. She seemed to dwindle in her chair, to become old and feeble. Mimi paused, bewildered. Caroline averted her head; her profile became flabby, unreadable, not with inscrutability, but with blankness. Her skin was gray and had a peculiar shine.

"Aunt Caroline!"

"Go on," said Caroline. Her ancient dress appeared too large for her.

"I didn't mean to hurt your feelings," said Mimi, distracted. "I just wanted to ask your help. For Amy. She overheard—something. Perhaps she was mistaken. But she thought she heard Ames talking to you and that he wanted to divorce her; she said you must have offered Ames money to stay with her."

"I did! I did!" cried Caroline. "I wanted to protect myself!"

She began to wring her grimy hands together, folding her big fingers over and over each other in desperate gestures.

"Yourself?" said Mimi. "From what, Aunt Caroline?"

The young voice, suddenly loud, startled, and afraid, aroused Caroline from her old agony. She pulled herself up in her chair. Mimi was on her feet now, her face very pale. Mama had been right; she ought not to have come here. The very smell of the house was evil and deathly. When Caroline reached out her hand, pushing it forward, Mimi stumbled back and fell against her chair, her white face glimmering in the semidarkness.

"I was talking about something else," said Caroline, and her words came rapidly. "It happened a long time ago." She began to stammer, and her hands groped blindly, as if feeling for something. "It doesn't have anything to do with Ames and Amy. I—I was thinking of something else."

Mimi regarded her with fear.

"Tell me about Amy!" shouted Caroline.

"I've told you, Aunt Caroline." The girl clumsily felt for the chair and sat on its edge, still frightened and also wary now. "Ames doesn't want Amy. I don't know why he ever married the poor little thing; she's as gentle as a kitten and knows just as much about the world as a kitten. Then you——" She stopped.

"It's so stupid. You are all stupid," said Caroline abruptly, and she swung her head on her short neck as if to scatter buzzing insects. "Your Amy can't have children. Ames wanted to divorce her, possibly so he could later on marry a woman who could have children." She gave Mimi her surly and bitter smile. "To inherit my money. But—I thought about the girl. Washed out, no character, one of those puny little creatures, soft as butter. I can't imagine why, but she wants my son. So I protected her. If any of you had thought of it for a moment you could see that I meant her no wrong. I protected her!"

"I see," said Mimi. She smoothed her gloves over and over. Again she wanted to cry.

"And now the girl doesn't want him. Is that it?" said Caroline accusingly.

Mimi looked at the bleared windows through which little light could penetrate.

"She still wants him, Aunt Caroline. He'll stay with her for the money you gave him. But he hates her. He found out that she is drinking. You know how fastidious he is, like Uncle Timothy. He abused her." Now Mimi could not prevent herself from crying.

"What!" cried Caroline, and felt the bruises on her own flesh. "My son did that? No one ever hit him in all his life except a nursemaid, perhaps. Are you certain?"

"Yes." Mimi opened her purse, took out her handkerchief, and wiped her eyes.

"Why does she drink? Drink!" said Caroline.

"I thought I made it clear. Because she knows that Ames can't stand her any longer. He very seldom speaks to her, she told me. She isn't the Amy he married less than a year ago. She looks so small, so broken, so pale. She always had the nicest color; now she hasn't any. Poor little Amy. Why, no one ever lifted a voice to her, not even Aunt Amanda. She's like a little ghost. That's what Ames did to her."

But Caroline was suddenly not hearing her. She was listening to what Ames had said to her a few days ago: "You were a fine model, dear Mama." She said aloud, "Oh, dear God."

At that broken and wretched murmur Mimi became eager. "So I thought I'd tell you about it and ask you to help Amy. She'll die, one way or another, if she stays with Ames. If you tell Ames that you won't withdraw the money"—and her young face became a dark younger replica of her aunt's—"and that you want him to let Amy go home again, then there's a chance that she'll recover in time. And forget Ames."

Caroline regarded her niece, and Mimi looked back at her sternly. Caroline put up her hand and muttered, "What if the girl won't leave him?"

Mimi smiled with brilliant hope. "Amy hasn't any will left. Aunt Amanda and the boys will take Amy home."

"Her father? Ames told me she never sees her father."

"No," said Mimi, and she was stern again. "Amy adored him. I often wonder if Uncle Timothy ever cared about the child at all. A father doesn't abandon his daughter; he doesn't go away and leave her lonely and afraid. Forgive me, I shouldn't——"

"He didn't!" Caroline was trembling. "He had to go away when he did! It was all a lie that he didn't care about me! He was the only one who ever did."

Mimi paled again. She could see Caroline's trembling face and blindly motioning hands. "I don't know what you mean," said Mimi. "You are talking about Uncle Timothy?"

Caroline pressed her hands over her eyes and did not reply. Mimi looked at her helplessly and then with loving compassion. She put her hand gently on Caroline's knee, and Caroline started violently. She dropped her hands. Her eyes were vague and dim.

"I was thinking of something else," she said in that muttering voice of hers. "I wasn't talking about Timothy." She looked about her. "Would you get me that bottle on the table? I feel tired, I think. The spoon and glass are beside it."

Mimi went to the table; her heel caught in the ragged carpet and she almost fell. She clutched the table in alarm, thinking of her child.

"What is it? What is it?" exclaimed Caroline.

"Nothing," said Mimi soothingly. She looked at the table, at its oily and dirty top, at the smeared lamp. She picked up a bottle of brown fluid. It was stoppered with a medicine dropper, and there was a warning on the label: "To be taken only as directed, three times a day, and once at night if in pain." Now Mimi was alarmed for her aunt. She made her hand steady, counted out the meager drops into the glass which was half filled with water. She took the glass to Caroline. The gray shine was on Caroline's face again. She drank the fluid slowly, as if it were difficult for her to swallow. Now Mimi was conscious of the gray-white hair. The hand, holding the empty glass, fell limply on the broad lap.

Mimi took the glass and put it on the mantel. "Aunt Caroline, what is that medicine?"

"A tonic," said Caroline impatiently. She lay back in her chair, and her big breast rose and fell as if struggling. She closed her eyes. An expression of grim exhaustion and suffering ravaged her face. Mimi waited. Then Caroline said, so faintly that the girl could hardly hear, "It was all a lie. I've known it all my life. He didn't want me at all."

Who? thought Mimi with intense pity.

"All my life," Caroline repeated. "But I hid away from it. It was just now that I knew it." She opened her eyes. "I wonder how I came to know just now?"

"I don't know," said Mimi, speaking softly. "I wish I knew what to do for you, Aunt Caroline."

But Caroline was staring beyond the girl. Her eyes were empty, and her face.

"I think I began to know when I recognized him in the painting," said Caroline. "I ran away from it. All these years—and I refused to recognize who he was. But my grandfather knew from the very first; he wasn't a coward. As I am."

"Aunt Caroline!" said Mimi with sharp fear. She pushed herself to her feet and went to Caroline and rested both her pretty hands on the old woman's shoulders. "Please don't hurt yourself so, dear! Please. I can't bear it!" Mimi cried again, without understanding and knowing only that Caroline was suffering.

Caroline's hands rose slowly and then closed on the young hands on her shoulders. But she shook her head over and over. "I mustn't think about it all at once," she said. "I must go over it very slowly, so I'll know it all—all the years.

"But what shall I do now, now that I know?" she pleaded. "What shall I do with my life and all the thoughts that will come?"

She pressed Mimi's hands fiercely into her flesh. She implored the girl with her eyes. "Tell me what I shall do with my life after that waste, after all those years?"

"Let me help you to bed, dear Aunt Caroline," said Mimi.

"No, no," said Caroline. "It doesn't matter. Nothing ever matters, not truly. Except if someone loves you. No one ever did." She coughed deeply, rackingly, but held to Mimi tighter than before, and the palms of her hands were cold and wet.

"I did! I do! I love you, Aunt Caroline!" Mimi bent her head and pressed her cheek to Caroline's, and then Caroline was still, and her furrowed cheek moved a little against Mimi's as a tormented child's would move.

"I'm sorry I came," said Mimi, crying. "Forgive me. I've upset you."

"No," said Caroline. "It was waiting for me, all of it. It isn't your fault. No, it was my fault, lying to myself ever since I can remember. Lying. A lying coward."

Then she said in a faint, wondering voice, "So was my father. We were cowards together. And I know now why he hated me. I look like his father. He couldn't stand the truth that was my grandfather." She paused. "He could never stand the truth. He ran away from it, always. He made me run too."

She raised one of her hands and lovingly placed it against Mimi's wet cheek. "Don't cry, love," she said in a voice she had never used to anyone before, for now it was strong and gentle and not timid. "Don't cry, little Mary. It isn't any good at all."

With a strong gentleness like her voice she put Mimi away from her so that the girl could sit down. She smiled. Her haggard face became bright for an instant, and reassuring. She who had never consoled anyone before in her crippled life spoke consolingly. "You mustn't cry. It's very bad for you. And the baby. There'll be plenty enough time to cry in the future when you are old and alone." Her eyes became as warm and golden as Mimi's and full of compassion. "But now you mustn't let yourself be sad because an old woman was remembering too many things all at once. You have your mother and your brother." She paused. "And you have your husband."

"Yes, I'm so happy, Aunt Caroline. John and I—we love each other so much. That's why he's so foolishly jealous of my painting. He says he wants all of me, everything I can give him, because——" She bit her lip.

"Because he didn't have love here," said Caroline. "Yes, I can see that." Her eyes were blank and empty again. "I didn't know how to love anyone except my father, I think. And even that wasn't real love; it was just need. I couldn't love my husband as he needed to be loved; I didn't love my children at all. There is Elizabeth, all alone on the hill. But she isn't more alone now than when she was in this house where she was born."

She folded her hands together and looked down at them, and Mimi could see the thin white crown of her head. "I believe it all began when I talked to Ames the other day about his wife. It was something he said. Yes, it began then."

She smiled at Mimi tenderly, and she herself had the sudden majesty and beauty of a worn statue.

"I'll tell Ames that he must let Amy go and that he'll have the money I promised just the same. It is a kind of debt; yes, a debt."

She reached out and took Mimi's hand like a mother. "I'll talk to Amy's father. He won't dare send her away—as he sent my own daughter. Not after I've talked with him."

She considered that. "Yes, I'd have done it. Yes, I've waited a long time. But for Elizabeth, I'll help Amy."

The maid came into the room surlily. "Your telephone was ringin', Miz Sheldon. In the study. The door wasn't locked, like usual, so I went in. It's a man saying that he wants to talk to you about Mr. Ames Sheldon. And three million dollars!" The pale eyes rounded, and the pale mouth. "He wants to come out to see you."

Caroline walked to the gate with Mimi, her hand on the girl's arm. She unlocked the gate. Then she said, "There's nothing I can do for John. It's too late. Perhaps you can do something, Mary. I don't know."

"If you'd just see him," Mimi pleaded.

But Caroline shook her head. "We have nothing to say to each other that would be kind. It could only be true. Truth is the most frightful thing in the world. There, love, you mustn't cry again. No wonder we run away from truth; who can stand it? Your painting, Mary? You won't abandon that? You mustn't let John take everything from you just because his mother was no mother at all."

Mimi smiled, her eyes still wet. "I won't let him," she said. "I'm not going to hide in a corner with him when he comes home to our house in New York, though he'd like that. He doesn't even want Nathaniel to come too often. I tell John that I'm afraid he's going to eat me alive!" She laughed shakily. "That makes him so angry."

But Caroline was grave. "I don't know why it is, but every one of us, I suspect, tried to eat others alive, in more ways than one. The human race is very terrible."

She kissed Mimi, not with the shyness of a whole lifetime, but with deep love and strength. The girl clung to her. Caroline patted the young shoulders, the soft fine hair, the tinted cheek. "There, there, love," she murmured.

"Promise me you'll wear my locket," said Mimi. "With my miniature in it."

"I promise. I'll put it on at once." Caroline shivered and looked about her vaguely. "I put it away very carefully in Elizabeth's box with a blue ribbon."

She turned then and went slowly up the path to her house, to meet Griffith, who would arrive very soon. Then she looked back; she did not even remember that she had not locked the gate. Mimi was standing there, watching her. When Mimi saw Caroline turn she kissed her hand and blew the kiss to her aunt. Caroline had never made the gesture before, not once in her life. Awkwardly she put her own fingers to her lips and returned the kiss.

The shadow in her mind had a face and form now. Her father's. She looked at it and said very gently in her mind, "Yes, Papa, I know. Let us help each other. I don't know how, but let us help. It's probably too late for both of us, but we can try."

Her hand could hardly lift the latch on the door, yet she felt strength in her like a fortress. It would not last, no. But for this minute she could be strong.

CHAPTER THREE

While Amanda shuddered at the thought of the impression that would be created on Griffith by Caroline and wondered if Caroline would demolish "that poor man" immediately, Griffith himself, sitting in the crumbling parlor of the house in Lyme, was not in the least intimidated or dismayed.

While he thought the decay of the house shocking, in view of its fine proportions and possibilities, he had seen worse in the Counties where indifference, morbidity, or lack of finances had been the cause. Elderly widows, he recalled, often let their houses deteriorate like this when there were no direct heirs to take over entailed estates and fortunes. He rather suspected that, in a way, this was the case with Caroline Ames Sheldon, among other reasons.

He was impressed, not alarmed, by Caroline herself. How well she would be understood, if occasionally censured, in England! (However, the censure would include a sort of esteem.) In England, now, she would be surrounded by ostensibly adoring nieces and nephews and grandchildren and cousins and children, and more distant relatives, over whom her command would be supreme, her advice lavishly admired and often taken, her power reverenced, her lawyers always in attendance, her neighbors discreetly solicitous, officials deferential, the community always conscious of her presence and invariably respectful of her desire for privacy and seclusion. It would all come to her by a natural and organic process, through her power and her personality. The old were honored in Europe, especially if they had money and influence, no matter how bad-tempered they were or irascible or eccentric, or how possessed of the most deplorable character, or how heinous their acts, or how abominable their tongues. In fact, these things only added to their importance in the eyes of hordes of relatives; no family was complete without a formidable and potent old uncle, aunt, or grandmother of whom tales would be told long after their deaths, until they became affectionate legends.

But unfortunately it was quite different in America, where the old were expected to heap adulation on the young—and the younger the better—and where hard wisdom was derided and dullness was deified. Eccentricity in America was never regarded as the height of individualism and character, and treasured. It was attacked with a vicious, if playful, public and private yowling and with malice and resentment. Walls and hedges about one's property, as well as about one's soul, were considered an affront. All must be open to monkey fingers, to monkey curiosity, to monkey flea-searching. No wonder America had produced no awesome devils in the historical tradition, or mighty saint, or any blaze of grandeur.

Never once in her life, not even by the two who had loved her most—Beth and Tom—had Caroline been given open approval for herself, as an individual entitled to her way of life and her opinions. Looking at her as she sat grimly opposite him, Griffith could see that she had suffered deeply from many profound and obscure things, some of them possibly quite terrible. He regarded her with serious respect and deference.

She had known who he was immediately when she had admitted him, though she had never seen him before. Ames had talked of him frequently. She was prepared for some curious story, or even a blackmailing one. Griffith's attitude toward her first caused her astonishment, then suspicion.

Then when she saw his acceptance and respect, something had dimly eased in her. She was astonished again.

She had listened in silence to his measured recital of her son and Amy, and she was vaguely pleased by his lack of hysteria and absence of emotionalism. Then when he had concluded she sat and looked at him, not with her usual evasive glance when with strangers, but directly, and a young woman, not an old, stirred in her clouded hazel eyes.

She said abruptly, "Will you have tea?"

Griffith bowed in his chair. "It will be delightful, madam."

Caroline looked at the bell rope and hesitated. Griffith rose. "Perhaps the young person in the kitchen is not very efficient?" he murmured. "This is quite common these days, due to the war factories draining off the more trained. May I assist?"

Caroline said, "Certainly." (That was exactly what a great lady would say, thought Griffith with satisfaction as he found his way to the kitchen. Great ladies accepted miserable situations and embarrassments and contretemps calmly, with a rationality that conceded that the world was quite mad, frequently disgusting, and not to be regarded with too much excitement and consternation.)

Caroline waited for Griffith's return, yet it was not really a waiting. She continued to sit stiffly, and now she looked at nothing. There was a great hiatus in her, an awesome abeyance, in which silent but urgent tongues were waiting for her will to speak. She would have to listen to them eventually: she would have to realize what they told her. She said to herself, as she had said earlier this day: But for this minute I can be strong. Courage, she thought, must often consist of facing only the immediate. To face it all at once would be total destruction. The busy mind which had never been still for many decades was now still. She was exhausted; a sinking sensation lay in the middle of her body; the very act of blinking or swallowing was almost more than she could do automatically; she did it only by an actual act of will. Then she pushed herself to her feet and went to the table and gave herself another dose of her digitalis. She turned very feebly and slowly and saw the sea and the yellow-bright air and the mountainous boulders heaped one upon another on what once had been Tom's proud sea walk. Had it changed from monotony, all this; had it quickened and taken on another aspect? She closed her eyes briefly; she wanted no change, no strangeness—not yet.

She did not hear Maizie's angry and then sullenly complying voice in the kitchen, nor the brisk movements of Griffith. But all at once she felt that in this house was someone who neither judged, derided, feared, envied, cajoled, nor hated her, nor found her peculiar or her house revolting. He had actually seemed to find her perfectly normal and familiar. The lonely woman smiled a little and realized that in the true sense she had never had a friend before. This thought was so unique, yet so soothing, that she lay back in her chair and fell into a light sleep, which, in her mental and physical condition, resembled a state under anesthesia.

She started awake at a discreet clatter. Griffith was placing a tea tray on the table before her. The sun was lower, and long blurred rays struck through the grimy windows; some time must have passed, thought Caroline. The silver was clean and bright, though the crevices would never be anything but black because of long neglect. There was a little plate of smoking tea biscuits and jam. "I took the liberty, madam," said Griffith, "of making the biscuits. Fortunately there was a fire in the stove—simple enough, these."

He sat down, his head inclined. Caroline stared at the tray. "It's been a long time," she said. "I always associated teatime with my aunt, whom I disliked, and her friends, whom I also disliked."

"I do not believe," said Griffith, "that there is anything in the American Constitution which gives us the right to dislike, or even hate. But it is implicit in freedom. I have disliked more people in my life than I have liked. What man of spirit and perception can live in this world and then diffuse a warming-pan affection over all humanity? Children are much more astute, even in the nursery. They fear and dislike practically everyone but the immediate family, and they reserve judgment even for these."

"Yes," said Caroline. "Do you prefer your tea weak or strong?"

Her hand trembled as she held the heavy silver teapot. Griffith said, "Strong, please." The poor lady. He glanced discreetly about the room and through the windows and sighed. He glanced at Caroline's massive profile, at the straight and monumental set of her body, and sighed again. The neglect that surrounded her testified to the neglect of her whole life and the lovelessness of her condition. He took the cup Caroline extended to him and let her serve him sugar and weak milk. Caroline had watched people sharply all her life. She felt no such necessity to watch Griffith. She poured tea for herself, then took a tea biscuit, put it absently into her mouth. She smiled like a young girl at him, shyly.

"No wonder my son Ames considers you a treasure," she said.

"I do my best, madam," he said with polite severity. "But the best is no longer admired. I have read and reread your Elbert Hubbard's *Message to Garcia* many times. He was quite correct in his contempt for what he called 'dowdy work' and lack of responsibility."

Caroline ate another biscuit. She considered. Then she spoke without fear. "I have always done my best. Contrary to sentimental opinion, the best is rarely successful. Quite often it results in tragedy for everyone. It did so for me and my family. Do have one of your very excellent biscuits, Mr. Griffith."

A little flush had come over her livid cheekbones. "It is a very long story," she said. "Have you heard of the great American artist, David Ames?"

"Yes, madam."

"I will take you to my private gallery upstairs where I have several of his paintings. When I was a young girl I wanted to be an artist; I loved color and form." Her eyes, brilliant now, were the eyes of youth.

Griffith expertly concealed his surprise. Caroline was smiling with a freedom she had never known before, not even with Mimi. "My father thought all life ridiculous and evil. For that reason"—she paused a moment—"he was a blind man. My grandfather painted him, even when he was still only a boy, showing him blindfolded and stumbling about on an ominous landscape. I've come to the conclusion that blindness of the mind evokes terror; I'm afraid I'm not making myself clear, am I?"

"Indeed you are, madam."

"I didn't know until this morning that the young man in the painting was my father; he stood, symbolically, for men like him all over the world. I loved him with all my heart and soul."

Their eyes met, and Griffith saw the sorrow and all the tragic years in Caroline's face.

"It is true," said Caroline, "that environment and character shape men. But where one man of similar environment and character will become great and noble, his brother will become a——" She stopped, looked down at the cup in her hands. She murmured, "A disaster to himself, and all about him." She put the cup on the table and breathed painfully and loudly. "But that is something I must not think about yet. You've told me about Ames and little Amy. I had already decided what to do about them both. Your visit was not necessary."

She smiled at him again, and he thought in astonishment: She must have been beautiful as a girl!

"But I am glad you came," said Caroline. "I am very glad you came."

She took him upstairs to her gallery, where the low and level sun still shone. Slowly he went from one painting to another, studying each carefully. He paused before Mimi's painting of the girl on the boulder. "You, madam, of course," he said.

"Of course," said Caroline. She looked at the painting. "The girl will wait for nothing, forever."

Caroline, dressed in her rusty black and her ancient bonnet, went to the depot the next morning. She walked with a slow but stately step to the train for Boston, now oblivious of the fawning and slyly derisive folk on the wooden platform. Twenty minutes later she arrived in Boston and took a cab to her son's apartment. It was still late August and there was a golden haze in the warm air. The streets were full of people. Caroline, for almost the first time in her life, became conscious of individuals in the masses; she felt an odd excitement as she picked out a mournful or tragic or youthful face. She even wondered who these people were, where they lived, how they lived.

Griffith let her into the apartment. "Mr. Ames left for New York this morning," he said. "Mrs. Sheldon is all alone." He paused. "She is—sleeping. I have just made some strong coffee for her. Would you like to come into her bedroom, madam, while I fetch the coffee?"

But Caroline looked at the long living room with its high ivory ceilings, its fine furniture, its paintings, its mirrors. She said almost gently, "Ames, I see, likes exquisiteness and beauty. Once I'd have called all this a 'bou-

tique.' Who am I to talk of blindness? I've been blind most of my life."
She went to Amy's bedroom. The draperies, of pale gray silk, were still
drawn, and the furniture and bed were only shapes in the dimness. But the
air was filled with the rank odor of sour whiskey and drunkenness.

Caroline sat down in a tufted chair near the bed and let her eyes become
accustomed to the dimness. While she waited she said to herself: It is my
fault. It was my father's fault before me. He gave his whole life to his work,
and it meant nothing but calamity for me, for my children. For this poor
child in her drunken sleep on her bed. It meant calamity for Melinda. The
children who will come—will the calamity stretch out to them also? Where
did the evil begin, and in whom? In what generation? My father's mother—
why hadn't she had the honest courage to return to her parents with her
son and tell them that she could not understand an artist and that she must
leave him? Love? But one must forgo love when it is necessary to save someone else: it's a luxury we sometimes can't permit ourselves.

She shook her head and thought: Who knows where the weakness began,
or the evil, which is only another word for weakness? Why doesn't the
world realize that the weak are not pitiable, but a threat to all the generations? They spread their helpless wickedness over the unborn and destroy
them when they themselves are dead.

But love was necessary for life. It should be strong love. To whom could
one give love, and from that one receive it, without damage to others? Whose
was the love that did not destroy?

Her mind hovered, shrinking, on the edge of a tremendous revelation.
She lifted her hand against it, protecting herself. Not yet! she cried in herself.

Amy stirred, moaning feebly. Griffith entered the room on tiptoe, placed
a tray of coffee near the girl, and drew back the draperies. The hot morning
sunshine gushed into the pretty room. Caroline looked at Amy and saw the
haggard young face, the sunken eyes, the fallen mouth, the thin throat and
sticklike arms, the snarled, disheveled dark hair. Caroline sat, while Griffith,
murmuring, spoke like a soothing father to Amy, fluffed her pillows, and
urged coffee on her. She wailed, as a child wails, peevishly, fretfully. But
she drank the coffee obediently. She had been taught obedience in her cradle
by her father, who was a weakling and therefore evil. She blinked in the sunlight, wailed for darkness. Then her glazed eyes saw Caroline.

"Cousin Caroline," she muttered stupidly.

"Do drink the coffee," said Griffith. "It will make you feel much better."

Still staring at Caroline, Amy pushed back her long dark curls. She moistened her cracked lips. She still stared at Caroline. There was a vague whimpering in her throat. The only sound in the room other than that was the
painful swallowing. But the explosive uproar and honking of automobiles
outside invaded this dolorous misery, and the rattle of wheels. Now a flickering ray of sun touched Amy's right cheek, rimmed it with gold, revealed
the sickly color, the smear of tears, the spittle in the corners of her gray
mouth. Caroline forced herself to look, remembering the young girl of little

more than a year ago, blooming, her flesh dewy, her eyes bright. She had stood and looked with childish compassion at Caroline on the day Elizabeth had been buried. Like Elizabeth, she too had been struck down by forces set into movement long before she had been born. Like Elizabeth, she would die unless she was rescued. But this girl had resources, unlike Elizabeth; she had the love of a mother and brothers, if not the love of a father.

Griffith made Amy drink another cup of coffee. Then he lifted her on her pillows. Her head fell back on them. Slowly, drop by drop, tears began to run down her cheeks.

Her eyes were stark with mute suffering. "I think," said Caroline to Griffith, "that we can be alone now."

"Cousin Caroline?" said the frail voice. "It is Cousin Caroline?"

"Who else?" said Caroline. "It isn't my ghost."

Amy sat up suddenly, the white silk falling partially from her shoulders and showing their boniness and hardly lifting over the childish breast. A film of sweat appeared on her forehead.

"Ames!" she cried. "You've come to take Ames away from me!"

"No," said Caroline. "I've come to take you away from Ames."

She rose clumsily and went to the girl. She lifted a corner of the sheet and wiped away the sweat. Her movements were awkward, for no one ever before in her life had inspired maternal tenderness in her. The girl submitted, her eyes pleading cravenly. "I can't live without Ames," she sobbed.

"You can," said Caroline firmly, sitting down again. "There is no such thing as not 'living' without anyone, unless you are old and tired. You are young and you aren't tired. A year from now, or at the most two, you'll have forgotten this. You will have hope. And you'll probably want to marry someone who will understand, who has some kindness."

"Oh no!" cried Amy wildly. "I never loved anyone but Ames; I never will!"

"Nonsense," said Caroline. "What does a child like you know of life? Be quiet! You must listen to me. Be quiet!"

"How can you be so cruel?" the girl wept. "But Ames always said you were."

"Ames," said Caroline calmly, "is a liar. I may have been stupid, but I was never deliberately cruel. However, it may be the same thing."

"Why did you come here?" The girl was becoming very agitated. "To laugh at me, to take Ames away?" She still could not believe this was really Cousin Caroline, Cousin Caroline who never went anywhere.

"I came to save your life," said Caroline.

"You bribed him to stay with me!"

"Yes. Stupid, wasn't it? I should have bribed him to let you go. For your sake. Stop crying. You are almost twenty-two, and not an infant. I want to talk to you as one woman to another, as a mother to a child."

Her voice was strong and dominant, and Amy subsided to a whimpering again. She dropped back against her pillows. She was dreaming: Cousin Caroline was not really here. This was only one of her sick nightmares.

"I came," Caroline repeated, "to save your life. How long do you think you will live if you go on like this? Are you trying to kill yourself? To revenge yourself on Ames? I can tell you this: It won't matter in the least to him if you die. In fact, he'll be relieved. You see, he never loved you at all, never."

"Oh no," said the girl. "Oh, you are wrong." The tears poured.

"You mustn't be a fool," said Caroline. "Look at me. I'm the reason Ames married you, the only reason. I gave him three million dollars to marry you."

Amy's trembling mouth fell open, and the swollen eyes widened.

"Ask your mother," said Caroline. "Ask your father. They will tell you."

Amy pressed the back of her right hand dazedly against her forehead. "But why, Cousin Caroline?"

"Because I hate your father. It is a long and bitter story. We always hated each other. Don't you understand hate, you child?"

"But why?" whispered the girl again.

"Because of what your father is and I am. I am old, Amy, and so is your father. The story is old. It began perhaps with my grandmother, or her grandparents before her, or other ancestors we've never even heard of. We should have stopped it in ourselves when it began in us. We did not. That's our crime against our children and our children's children, and probably against generations not even born and who won't be born even in your lifetime. That, I believe, is what is meant by the sins of the fathers."

"Ames wouldn't have married me without your money?" The girl pushed her thin hands frantically through her hair. She pressed her cheek against her knee, hard, trying through pain to reach some reality. She closed her eyes. In a moment she would open them and Cousin Caroline would not be there looming blackly like a monument, telling her wicked things, battering her with her voice. It was only another nightmare.

She opened her eyes, and Caroline was still sitting, watching her. Amy groaned. It was not a dream at all, nothing from which she would wake up, sweating in weak relief that she had escaped. She murmured, "I can't believe it. Ames wanted to marry me long before he really did. It didn't matter about money then. You didn't even know about us."

"True," said Caroline. "But he thought that your father wouldn't really disinherit you or cut you off if you married him. When he finally realized that your father would, he wanted to—get away from you. I know; he told me later." She stopped; she stared at the girl, willing her to know the truth out of her own despair. "He only married you because I bribed him to do it. I think I'd give my life now not to have been responsible. But, you see, I was also stupid. I thought he had the capacity to care about you, child."

Amy became very still and rigid. A change began to come over her face; the slack bone structure tightened, the mouth firmed a little. Now her eyes focused themselves between their bloated red lids. She looked at a point near Caroline. Was it possible, thought Caroline, that from somewhere in all that artlessness and immaturity there was a latent strength which was now beginning to push itself through the flowery softness of her nature? Was there some pride there under the weakness and innocence?

Caroline said, "I now know so much about you, child. You remind me of myself when I was your age. Unworldly, adoring a father. Neither of them," said Caroline, "deserved the love of a decent dog."

Amy looked at her with sudden intensity.

"Look at me," said Caroline when she could breathe again without pain. "An old ruin which can never be rebuilt. You see, I am facing my own truth for the first time, as you must face your own truth. You know what I am; you've heard in Boston and from your mother, and no doubt from my son. It is quite true. Do you want to be like me? Do you want to lie to yourself that Ames really wants you, as I lied to myself that my father loved me?"

Amy's small hands clenched on her knees. She was silent. The gentle young mouth was pale and set.

Caroline said, "Look at me. My father crippled me. I could have escaped him several times when I was young. But I was a liar to myself. My aunt, your grandmother, tried to enlighten me and save me, and I hated her for it. I ran away from the truth she tried to tell me over and over. Are you hating me for telling you the truth too?"

"Yes," said Amy. She turned her face again to Caroline and looked at her with bitterness. "But I'm also believing you."

Caroline smiled, and the smile was kind. "You're an honest little girl, Amy. I'd never have admitted the truth when I was your age. Even if an angel from heaven had tried to tell me, I'd have refused to listen. It was very necessary for me to believe a lie because I was weak."

A white furrow appeared between Amy's dark brows, and small firm indentations about her pale mouth. "You've implied that Ames isn't capable of loving anyone, Cousin Caroline. What do you mean by that?"

"I made him incapable. I never loved him when he was a child or at any other time. Ames' father gave him love; I robbed Ames of the capacity to return it, for I had let him know when he was still only a baby that I despised his father. I despised and feared everybody all my life. Children absorb attitudes from their parents. Ames never knew the reason for my fear of people, but he adopted my attitude toward the world without my own reasons, real or imagined. He'll never be free from it. You will break your life on that fact if you stay with him."

The furrow between Amy's eyes deepened, and the firmness of her mouth.

"Then Ames is a cripple in his feelings?"

"Yes," said Caroline, surprised and encouraged. "Just as I was. And am."

"There can be help. There's always God," said Amy. She bowed her head. "I'm ashamed. I'd forgotten about Him. It's been very terrible, but I'd forgotten."

Caroline turned away. "My husband loved me," she said, as if she hadn't heard Amy. "I threw it away. He wasn't patient enough; he didn't understand. Amy, you mustn't expect from any human being more than he is capable of giving."

Amy again pressed her cheek against her knees, but she did not close her eyes. She was quiet for a considerable time, and when she lifted her head her cheek was red, as if it had been struck fiercely. She looked older and resolute.

"Don't blame yourself too much, Cousin Caroline," she said in a very quiet voice. "Don't take all the blame on yourself. That's as bad as taking no blame at all. I'm not going to blame everything on Ames; I was a little fool myself. I was old enough to know that things aren't as simple as I thought. I could blame my father for that. Mama tried to teach me differently. I didn't listen. Yet it was all there.

"I could forgive Ames and even try to make him love me, in spite of what you've told me, if he hadn't taken your bribe. I could be sorry for him, if it weren't for the money. It was the money he married. Once he liked me; I'm sure of that; he was even a little fond of me. A woman can't be deceived about those things. Then I poured all that sticky, unthinking love on him; he must have felt he was drowning in syrup." The girl actually smiled a little. "Neither you nor I, Cousin Caroline, will ever really know if he can love, honestly love. But he certainly won't ever love me! Because I don't love him either now. I'm a different person, and that person couldn't love Ames Sheldon under any circumstances." She paused and then said almost briskly, "I think I'll go home now."

Caroline looked at her. Why, the little thing had courage and character after all. She said gently, "I'm proud of you, Amy."

"Don't be, please," said Amy, looking about her room with self-contempt. "I don't deserve it. I've been drinking like a dirty sot, whining because I felt inadequate and not good enough for Ames. I should have had more sense."

"We all have our breaking points," said Caroline. She stood up. "I'll take you home. That's why I came. To take you home."

Amy began to slip out of bed, and Caroline saw the girl's childish legs sliding from under the white silk, the immature figure, the girlish breast. Amy tried to stand up quickly and tottered, and Caroline caught her. She was alarmed by the slightness of the girl's body, but Amy laughed, and a sour reek struck the older woman in the face. Caroline hardly noticed; when Amy had laughed she had uttered the amusement of a woman and not a child.

Caroline had never bathed any of her own children or helped to dress them, but she assisted Amy in the pretty bathroom with its long pier mirror. Amy anxiously studied her thin white face as Caroline dried it. "It will take months for me to look right," she said. "What a damned fool I have been!"

"Doubtless," said Caroline. Her mouth was both wry and sad. Amy would marry again and be a serene wife and perhaps an affectionate mother. But she would never love as Caroline had loved or as Elizabeth had loved. Out of adversity, starvation, and spiritual agony, love often rose like a giant. It rarely came, it seemed, out of gentle beds, solicitude and shelter, and from the environment of tea tables and the muted laughter of cherished women. Amy would lick her hurts now firmly; she had been "wounded but not slain."

498

There were other things in her life besides rejected love and the misery she had suffered, and these would give her strength to face her life and plan for a calm future. But what of those who had no other resources, like Caroline and Elizabeth? Love was their destroyer. Who would want such love, having nothing else besides?

Caroline brushed Amy's long hair. The girl seemed abstracted while using hairpins. Once a look of anger and deep disgust flashed in her eyes. She said, "I am just beginning to realize, Cousin Caroline, what it meant to you to come here for me and say and do what you've done. I can't thank you enough."

"Don't," said Caroline. She left Amy and went to see Griffith. "I will take the girl home," she said to him. "Will you bring her baggage later?"

"Yes, madam," said Griffith. He hesitated. "How is Mrs. Sheldon?"

"You need not be anxious about her," said Caroline dryly. "So you mustn't be sentimental. She's become quite mature."

She pressed her ungloved hands together and looked away from him.

"My father—no matter what anyone did or could have said about him, it wouldn't have mattered to me. I had to have my fantasy because I had nothing else. It is quite different with Amy. Is that good or bad?"

"I don't know, madam," said Griffith. Again he hesitated. "I am only your son's servant. May I ask a favor of you? I should like to remember that I shook the hand of a great lady, if only once in my life."

"What nonsense," said Caroline, but she stuck her hand out to him, and when he took it she smiled.

When she was in the hired car with Amy they were both silent, though Amy watched the streets and the people eagerly, as if she had been delivered from a dark prison. Her young face took on color; her eyes sparkled. She had put almost a year of her life from her and was not looking back. Youth? Resilience? Caroline asked herself these questions. But once she had been young, too, and had had considerable resilience. They had not helped her in the least.

Caroline saw that there was no doubt in the girl's mind that she would be accepted by her parents and her brothers. But Caroline doubted. Timothy would not accept his daughter into his house without pressure and threats. She was certain of that. In Caroline's mind Timothy and John Ames had begun to merge.

When the cab halted before the Bothwell house Amy jumped out joyfully. She was a little impatient at Caroline's slow descent. The warm sun shone rosily on the brick walls. Amy ran to the white door with its fanlight and rang the bell. The door was opened by a new maid, who stared without recognition.

"Please tell Mrs. Winslow her daughter has come home, with Mrs. Sheldon," said Amy in a newly peremptory voice. She assisted Caroline into the quiet and massive hall. When the maid went away Amy sighed with delight. "It's good to be home," she said. Caroline did not reply. She stood in the cool dusk like a large statue of black marble.

Amanda, though stout and not young any longer, came running into the hall. Mother and daughter rushed into each other's arms, Amy crying happily, Amanda sobbing. What emotion, thought Caroline. For just an instant she remembered how she had once rushed into Beth's arms, and she put her cold damp palm behind her to steady herself against the wall. What if she had listened to Beth all those years ago? Her flesh seemed to drag her down, to be more that she could support. Then she saw that Amanda, over Amy's shoulder, was staring at her incredulously. Amanda held her daughter tightly in her stout arms, but she was looking only at Caroline.

"I've brought your daughter home to you," said Caroline. "To stay. She's left Ames. The rest is your affair."

"I must see Daddy," said Amy.

Amanda's face changed. Caroline thought she was frightened, but Amanda was only resentful. "Don't be afraid," said Caroline quickly. "I'll manage Timothy."

"What?" said Amanda. She was still incredulous that it was Caroline who was standing there, leaning against the wall, and was overwhelmed with warm gratitude for Griffith.

"I said," Caroline repeated, "that I will manage Timothy."

Amanda, stroking her daughter's wet face, thought: Why, she thinks she has to browbeat Timothy into accepting his ewe lamb! This is ridiculous. She opened her mouth to tell Caroline that, as Amy had left Ames, Timothy would be more than happy to take back his daughter. Then, shrewdly, she closed her mouth. "Timothy," she said carefully, "is upstairs. This is the time for his afternoon nap, since his illness."

"Then have someone wake him up," said Caroline. "Where may I wait for him?"

"The library," murmured Amanda. She could hardly speak for joy and excitement. Caroline had brought Amy home. Caroline was in this house for the first time in her life. Caroline with the large gray face. And the innocent eyes. The innocent eyes, Amanda repeated to herself. She had never pitied Caroline before, but now she was sick with her pity. Compassion did not come easily to Amanda Winslow, who had known nothing but love, strength, assurance, and money all her life, and everlasting protection since birth. She had detested and feared Caroline and all Caroline's children. Now she was ashamed. She felt tears in her eyes again. True compassion could be devastating, she thought. Strange that I never really felt it before. Why should I have? I was always loved.

"I'd like to talk with you for a moment in the library before you send for Timothy," said Caroline.

"Dear God, how can I thank you?" Amanda asked Caroline. But Caroline did not hear her. The old worrying pain was in her chest again. It was very stuffy in the hall, she thought. Why was Amanda staring at her like this? But women like Amanda were slow-witted. "Where shall we go?" asked Caroline.

Holding Amy's hand, Amanda led Caroline to the library with its large windows and cool and leathery chairs and walls of books. Caroline said, "I thought Timothy cared for the girl. It appears he never did, or he wouldn't have forbidden her his house or refused to see her."

Amy was startled. She could not understand her mother's quick frown, the pressure of her hand. Caroline said with her old grimness, "You must let me manage this. I'm quite capable."

She went into the library and settled herself in a brown leather chair, and Amanda sat near her on a brown couch, firmly holding her daughter's hand and keeping the bewildered girl quiet by the pressure of her fingers. Caroline was having some difficulty in breathing. Chill water began to run from under her arms, down her back, her chin, over her forehead. She opened her large sound purse and wiped her face. She took a sheaf of papers from the purse, glanced through them quickly, and nodded. Then she looked at Amanda.

"Tell me," she said abruptly, "are your sons like their father?"

Amanda did not answer for a moment. She looked into Caroline's suffering eyes, and she understood.

"No," she said. "Not at all. Not in the least, Caroline. They are like me."

"And what are you like?" said Caroline bluntly. "What do you know of what is going on in the world today? What do you care about anything?"

Amanda was not shocked or angered. She understood exactly what Caroline meant. She said very slowly, "I am like my father. I think you knew him a little, Caroline, when you were a girl. My father had very few illusions about the world. Before he died he was worried about—things. And then I was in England some years before this war. With Elizabeth," she added, not taking her eyes from Caroline's.

"Yes," said Caroline. She looked at the papers in her hand. "What did you think of England, Amanda?"

"I knew something was happening, though Timothy laughed when I tried to explain. Something terrible. No one listened to me. Henry doesn't listen now, not too much. But my younger son, Harper, does. Is that what you want to know, Caroline?"

"Yes. That is what I wanted to know." Caroline stared at her. "You were right, of course. You are still right. Timothy knows too. That's why I wanted to know about your sons. Now everything is clear to me." She glanced away. "I don't want to see your sons; I just wanted to be sure they aren't like their father."

"They aren't," said Amanda earnestly, leaning toward Caroline. "Believe me, they aren't."

Amy sat up indignantly. But her mother's hand tightened on hers.

"I believe you," said Caroline. "You were never a liar, like Timothy. Now, would you please take Amy away and send for Timothy? I want to see him alone."

CHAPTER FOUR

Amanda took Amy to her old bedroom and closed the door behind her. The girl looked at her furniture, at the serene warm sunlight filtering through the silk curtains, at her girlhood bed, and she began to cry in relief and happiness. Amanda watched her with a grimness very much like Caroline's and waited as Amy ran from chair to chair and opened one closet door after another and touched the draperies lovingly.

"Everything is just the same!" she exclaimed.

"No," said Amanda. "Nothing is ever the same. I hope you've grown up now, Amy. I hope you've learned a little." Amy was standing here in her room before a wardrobe and inspecting an old pink dress she had worn nearly two years ago, and her expression was full of remembrance.

"Yes, Mama," said Amy, lifting the rustling lengths in her hand. "I've learned. I'm not quite as stupid as I was." She let the dress drift from her hand but continued to look at it. "You think I left Ames too easily, don't you? It wasn't easy, Mama. When Cousin Caroline came today she didn't know that I'd begun to leave Ames in my mind several days ago. Or perhaps several weeks, or even months. Today was the final leaving." She stroked the dress. "I know what the doctors have said, that I'll never have any children. I don't believe it, Mama. I think I will have, later. Much later."

Amanda was touched. Her daughter continued, "I think I'd have left Ames much earlier and wouldn't have taken to drinking"—and she turned and looked at her mother fully—"if Daddy hadn't refused to see me. I thought there was no one. You and I didn't meet very often; I rarely saw my brothers. But Daddy's refusing to see me, to have me in my old home, that was the worst. I love him. But not as I did before. Do you think he will let me stay?"

"You know he will," said Amanda, and came to her daughter, and they kissed as women who understand each other. Amanda said, "One of the sternest lessons we have to learn is that we should never be too dependent on anyone for love or consolation. We live alone, really, and die alone."

Amanda went to Timothy's room. He was already sitting up in his bed and fumbling for his slippers. "What was all that talking?" he asked irritably. "Who is here? What is the matter?"

His wife was sorry for him, for his weakness and his isolation. She closed the door behind her and said without preliminaries, "Amy has come home. To stay."

He dropped the slipper in his hand. "What? What! What are you talking about? Amy here? To stay? Has she left that scoundrel?" He glared at her disbelievingly. "And if so, why?"

"She couldn't stand him any longer. Timothy, I'll let someone else tell you about it. Your cousin Caroline. She brought Amy home."

His face became blank with amazement. "Caroline Ames? Here? Have you lost your mind? What are you telling me? She'd never come here. What has she to do with Amy?"

"I told you, she's brought Amy home. She's here, Timothy. You mustn't excite yourself. I just want to tell you something, and it's very important. You must let Caroline talk, and you mustn't disillusion her. You see, she thinks that you don't want Amy. She thinks you're like her father. She's going to battle you for Amy's sake."

"Are you mad?" cried Timothy. He tried to punish his wife with his voice, with his coldly furious eyes. "I still don't believe it! I don't believe that old hag is here! Are you trying to drive me out of my mind with your stupidities? You were always a stupid woman, Amanda."

"Yes," said Amanda. "Several people thought I was very stupid to marry you, Timothy. They couldn't understand how a girl in her right mind could have loved a man like you, and frankly, I don't understand, either."

He tried to beat her down with his look, but she was not intimidated. Then he began to smile slightly, a crooked smile which was distorted by his stroke. But immediately his mind, which had not been in the least affected, enveloped the whole astonishing situation.

"Let me understand, get matters straight," he said, stroking his feeble hand with the strong fingers of the other hand. "You say Caroline Ames has brought my daughter home. The question is why? I know her only too well; she's a schemer and a liar——"

"No," said Amanda. "She never was. You are."

Her words, her quiet voice reached Timothy. He twisted his head on his thin neck to glance at her.

"I've told you," said Amanda. "She thinks she will have to browbeat and threaten you to get you to accept Amy again and let her stay home. She isn't throwing Amy at you, taking her from Ames. She brought Amy home, knowing that our child would probably die if she remained with that wretch."

"I don't believe it," said Timothy. "You're all demented. She took Amy from me in revenge. She thinks it was because of——" He paused.

"She knows you had more than a little to do with Elizabeth's death," said Amanda. "You thought I didn't know, didn't you? But I do. Melinda told me. Timothy, you are a very wicked man. I love you, I think, but I know you're wicked." Amanda wanted to cry suddenly. She knew that Timothy must not be upset, for fear of another stroke. But she could not help herself, could not keep from speaking, even though he appeared newly sunken and white. "I don't know if Caroline's forgiven you. But she won't take revenge on Amy. She never wanted that. When she found out how Ames was treating our child she went to rescue her, she who hasn't left her house for years. Can't you understand that?"

"How has Ames been treating Amy?" asked Timothy, and he sat up very straight.

"We never told you, because you were so ill. He has been abusing her.

When Caroline found out she went to Amy at once. She took Amy away."
Amanda found it too hard to speak any longer. She merely held out her
strong arms to help Timothy get to his feet. She helped him down the stairs
in silence. She could feel him trembling. She took him to the closed door
of the library. Then she could whisper, "You must listen. You must let her
believe what she wants. It's little enough to do for her, poor Caroline." She
opened the door quickly and left her husband on the threshold.

Caroline looked up. Her black eyebrows drew together in surprise. Was
this tall bent man with the thin white hair and ghastly face actually Timothy Winslow, this man who leaned on a cane, who shuffled in slippered feet,
this old man who was still only in his fifties, this emaciated, narrow-featured
man with the slack arm and leg? Caroline would hardly have recognized
him except for the gray eyes, undiminished in their steady malice and coldness. Only his virulence remained, as powerful as ever.

"Well, Caroline," he said, and the old contempt was there and the hatred.
These, she thought, would never die because they were part of his spirit, and
he had been born with them. She had a sudden startled thought; was it
possible that at the very moment of conception a man's character was
completely formed? Who was the poet who had said: "So must thou be.
Thou canst not self escape. So erst the sybils, so the prophet told. Nor time,
nor any power, can mar the shape impressed—that living must itself unfold"?
Was "free will" only the ability, if used, to heighten or depress the innate
personality? Caroline, thinking, did not speak while Timothy made his way
slowly and carefully to a chair behind his vast library table. He took the
position of authority, while she sat before it like one being interviewed by
the grand seigneur. He thought he was diminishing her, she told herself,
even in his decay. But he had, all through his life and hers, tried to diminish
her, with a gesture, a smile, or a look, and he had never succeeded.

Their last interview had been violent in impact and words, but Timothy,
Caroline reflected with some humor, was always the Boston gentleman. He
actually bowed toward her in his chair.

"What brings you here, dear Caroline?" he asked. "This is such an honor,
you know."

"Don't waste my time with lies," said Caroline in a loud voice. "I'm not
here to visit you or exchange casual conversation. I've brought your daughter
home, from her husband who doesn't want her."

Timothy looked at her, blinking. He had carefully folded his good hand
over his weak.

"If you had cared for that child, she'd never have married my son, in
spite of the money I offered him," said Caroline. "This affects me personally,
but that is no matter. There must be no argument; we must speak from
premises we both know."

The old stupid witch, thought Timothy. She is out of her mind. But
his caution and wariness kept him silent, made him keep his face impassive.

He had always listened in his life; one learned a great deal by listening, and nothing much by talking.

"For some reason," said Caroline, "that poor silly girl loves you and thinks you love her. I'd advise you to keep up the illusion. I'd also advise you to let her stay here where she thinks she is wanted. By you."

She averted her large and livid face. She was remembering the houses in Lyme and in Lyndon where she had lived as a child and a young girl, cherishing the delusion that her father loved her. The very memory was anguish almost beyond bearing. It was the young Caroline who said now, "Is it so necessary for you to lie to your daughter? Is there nothing about her that you can love? Is she so ugly, deformed, hateful? Have you ever really looked at her?"

Why, she's absolutely insane! thought Timothy, his strong fingers tightening over his feeble ones.

"Had you cared anything about her," Caroline continued, her voice rising, "she'd never have come to this condition, to loneliness and drunkenness."

Timothy stirred abruptly. "What are you talking about?"

"Your daughter. My son didn't care enough about her; he really only wanted my money. He thought she'd have children to inherit my money. But it seems she is incapable of having children, so he doesn't want her."

Now Timothy moved violently in his chair. He looked at Caroline with fury.

"You're insane!" he cried. "Drunkenness! Amy! Children—what do you mean? What's wrong with Amy?"

Caroline was glad she had reached him in his impervious coldness. It was her father again who sat across from her.

"It wasn't Ames' neglect entirely that almost killed Amy through drinking. It was yours. Because you hated the child. Why? Because she believed you and loved you? Were you revenging yourself on Amy because of your mother, whom you hated?"

(She was utterly mad!) Timothy struck the table with the flat of his hand. His eyes glared with angry fear at Caroline. "Will you stop blabbering? Will you tell me what is wrong with my daughter?" How he hated her sitting there, a huge grimy mound of stinking flesh, as ugly as the devil, as powerful as the devil, this monstrous woman who had ruined him!

"I told you," said Caroline. "Amy began to drink when she found out that Ames despised her. No matter how I discovered these things. But I went for her today and brought her home. To safety and to her mother, at least."

(But I never had a mother, thought Caroline. I had no one to go to who would care for me just for myself, who would accept me as I was.)

"Amy? Drinking?" Timothy's voice was becoming shrill. He could not believe this; it was all part of this nightmare gibberish he was hearing from a demented woman.

"Yes. Can't you understand anything? I thought I spoke clearly enough."

"And Amy's here?"

"Yes. With her mother. Do you intend to drive the child away?"

The shrewd hard wisdom of many years prevented Timothy from speaking. But he watched Caroline now with intense alertness, silently listening, his thoughts shut away in himself, but rapid and conjecturing.

Then as Caroline appeared to be waiting, he said slowly and cautiously, "But it was you, as you've admitted, who caused this disastrous marriage." (Drunkenness!) "You probably thought you had valid reasons. Now you want this marriage to end. I'm not a young man; I've been very sick and am still sick. Would you mind enlightening me why you've changed your mind about this marriage—if you have?" (He had it! She had taken his daughter, degraded her, and then was throwing her back at him, revenging herself for Elizabeth.)

"I thought I explained," said Caroline, and now her voice was as truculent and heavy as he remembered it. "Ames doesn't want her. I saved her for her mother because she is only a child, and I'm sorry. I didn't know the marriage would end this way; Ames had persuaded me he wanted the girl and that she wanted him. It was calamitous for both of them. I don't know which of them should be more pitied." She paused.

Timothy's twisted mouth jerked involuntarily.

"Are you trying to say that you're sorry, remorseful, for what you did to my daughter through your money?"

He could not believe it when Caroline said, "Yes. You deserved to have it done to you. I had, and have, no pity for you. But I regret that Amy was so hurt; she is a nice, good child. She is happy to be home. Are you going to reject her again?" She leaned toward him, and he saw her threatening face.

"Do not think," said Caroline, "that I've changed my mind about you only because of Amy. I changed it also because of your sons and because you are powerless now, or I'll make you powerless."

She's only my age, thought Timothy, but she's senile. My sons. "Powerless." I must humor her. He imagined that Caroline had brought into this room not only the dark and dusty horror of her ruined house but the very essence of the ruin which was herself.

"Certainly, Amy may remain here," he said, making his slowed voice good-humored. "Does that satisfy you, Caroline?"

"Not entirely. I'm here for another reason, and to give you warning."

"About what, may I ask?" He was beginning to enjoy himself a little. He watched with some curiosity while Caroline opened her purse and brought out a thick sheaf of papers. She perched glasses on her big nose and studied the documents. She began to speak carefully, dispassionately.

"A long time ago, when I was only a young girl, my father took me among his associates. They had a great plan, which was really an old plan, a very ancient plan. It had been revived periodically in Europe. It was revived disastrously during the French Commune, following the Robespierre violence."

A cold stillness settled over Timothy.

Caroline's eyes became full of hazel light as she studied him. Then she returned to her papers. "There's nothing simple in living or in any of our motives," she said. "As we are human we are naturally evil, and so we have a dozen motives for anything we do, being devious. So my plan to destroy you, once and for all, didn't arise only because of what you did to my daughter Elizabeth. Eventually I'd have come to this very moment, in this room, remembering my father, who couldn't betray his country when it came down to that. But it would have taken a little longer, perhaps a lot longer, when it was too late. Your treatment of my daughter precipitated, in short, what I should have eventually been compelled to do to you, Timothy."

She's insane, Timothy tried to tell himself, to stop the sudden clamoring of his fear. But he strained toward his cousin. "I haven't the slightest idea," he murmured.

"Oh yes, you have. Don't interrupt me, Timothy. Let me tell you what I've done and what can happen to you if you make one single move after today.

"You mustn't ask me where I've received much of my information about you, because I don't intend to tell you. From our earliest childhood you hated me. I understand why. You envied me because I was the heiress to my father's fortune; you always wanted money more than anything else, even when you were a child. It's strange," said Caroline thoughtfully, "that money should have obsessed you even when you were in knickerbockers, and living quite comfortably, even luxuriously, with your mother. It didn't obsess me until many years later, and I had lived in absolute penury as a child. No matter," she said abruptly. "There are things which one just has to accept as facts, even if there is no explanation for them.

"You know by now that I prevented you from being elected senator last November."

She looked up at him from her papers. His face told her nothing. He sat like a thin gray image across the desk from her, his paralyzed lip twitching involuntarily.

"That was revenge for Elizabeth. Since then other motives have entered the picture, partly, as I've said, because of Elizabeth, and partly because of what you are. In 1914, last year, Timothy, you had reached the point in your affairs when you felt secure enough to begin to speculate in the market. However, when the European war began in August 1914, the Stock Exchange in New York closed, and there was no market for stocks, especially for large blocks, which could not be negotiated privately. I'll come back to that shortly. Prior to the war you wanted to amass a fortune as large as mine; nothing else would satisfy you. The Bothwell estate was sensibly divided into irrevocable trusts by Amanda very recently, so you could do nothing with it. Did Amanda know you so well?"

Timothy's paralyzed arm moved spasmodically, without his volition. His pale nostrils widened; he stared speechlessly at Caroline, who nodded, satisfied.

"So you had only the money you had saved from the large salaries you had earned through my generosity, and the money you had inherited from your mother. But you knew something only a few knew: a war was impending. You'd known it for several years, a long time, before it broke out. I know the names of all your associates in America and in Europe, Timothy, because I know them all myself and have always known them. They recognized you for what you are, and they knew you were one of them, even if you had comparatively very little money of your own. Devils always help each other. So on their advice you began buying stocks in steel, munitions, railroads, and chemicals, and then you pledged these stocks as security and borrowed money from affable banks on this collateral. You bought the last stocks in July 1914 with this borrowed money."

How did she know? Who told her? Who violated confidences? thought Timothy with hate and fear. A fine prickle of sweat appeared all over his face; a dull sickening pain began in his head.

The dispassionate voice went on, filled with indifference: "You bought those stocks at high prices with that borrowed money, and you gave your banks, at their insistence, in spite of their affability, the power to sell them in an emergency, which you thought would never come. You signed the certificates to make them negotiable.

"In the meantime, the Stock Exchange closed in August 1914. You hadn't known that would happen, had you? Your friends in Europe and in New York and Washington neglected to tell you it would happen." Caroline smiled a little. "But I knew. I wonder why your friends didn't tell you."

She's laughing at me, thought Timothy, trembling. His whole body trembled; he felt the shaking of every nerve and bone. It was her money, he thought, and her threats. Even "they" had to listen to her.

"Then," said Caroline, "you ran for office. Your state chairman told you that he'd have to have $250,000 for the campaign. You had no large store of cash. You did have considerable real estate in Boston and a small amount of liquid assets, but not the cash you needed. So you placed mortgages on all your real estate—the Bothwell house belongs to Amanda, and she wouldn't let you touch that—renewable every three months. But you were confident; the market would reopen soon, and your pledged stocks would boom, and you would be a senator. You'd be able to redeem your stock when the market opened, and you'd renew your speculations and pay off your indebtedness on your real estate."

Caroline folded her big ungloved hands quietly on her papers and looked at her silent cousin thoughtfully. "It would all have happened as you had planned—if it hadn't been for what you did to Elizabeth. But you helped to kill my young daughter with your hate and lies."

Timothy could not speak. The pain in his head was sharpening disastrously. He glanced at the paperweight on his desk, heavy, glassy. He was not and had never been a man inclined to physical violence; all his violence had been of the mind and intellect. But if he could have moved now, in this nightmare, he would have taken up the paperweight and thrown it murderously at his cousin, wanting to kill her. He would have stood up, screaming without control.

"You lost the election, Timothy," said Caroline in the voice of a disinterested schoolmistress. "You were heavily in debt. Your daughter married my son. You had a stroke. You were very sick for weeks. And—I waited."

He could only look at her, mute, trembling, vaguely conscious of his pain, but powerfully conscious of his hatred and his desire to kill.

"Last December," said Caroline, "the market did open again, but it went down from the Dow Jones average of eighty in July to about fifty-three, and it kept on falling every day thereafter. The banks to whom you owed money and who had your stock as collateral were frightened. They did not want to sell your pledged stock, as it wouldn't be sufficient to cover the loans. They knew you were sick, and they knew that Amanda couldn't raise the money, all that money, to cover the loans, because of the irrevocable trusts. Moreover, your mortgages came due, and the banks didn't want to foreclose on them. After all, you have friends in those banks, don't you, who are men like you?

"So, Timothy, they came to me, those bankers. I was your cousin; your daughter had married my son. Who else would be willing to help you but your first cousin, the mother of Ames Sheldon? I have huge deposits in many banks, including my own in New York; the money was available to me at any time. The closing of the market didn't affect me, and I owed nothing to anyone. I have never had to borrow money."

She turned her head and looked at the sunlit library windows. "I never dissembled in my life; I never knew how to do it and I never wanted to learn. Perhaps it was because I didn't need to dissemble at any time, so I can't count my honesty as a virtue. But now I did dissemble, for the first time, when your frightened bankers came to me. I paid the amounts you owed and took over your stock and also your mortgages. I made only one condition; I said that you were very sick and shouldn't be exposed to another shock. You must not be informed by your attorneys that I had your stock and your mortgages. I, I said, would in due time tell you myself, when you were better able to face your calamities, and I would let you repay me and would return to you all your property. You would over a period of time, I said, be able to repay me at the price I had paid for your stock and your mortgages. Everyone was relieved; they congratulated me on my family feeling. But until you could face it all you weren't to be told. Some of the bankers were even able to bring tears to their eyes as they thought of my family affection for you. In the meantime, not to alarm you, you received rents from your mortgaged property."

I am finished, done, thought Timothy. I'm beggared. A glassy haze, mingled with a pink tint, began to float before his eyes, and he had the sensation of dropping rapidly through space. He brought up his unaffected arm, placed the elbow on his desk, and leaned his withered cheek in the palm of his hand.

"No," said Caroline, "I haven't ruined you. Not yet. I am willing to return your stocks to you, and your mortgages. You may buy back the stocks at the price I paid for them, though the stocks are worth double that price now. You may take all the time you wish. On two conditions."

I'm dying, thought Timothy. He hardly heard what Caroline was saying. Then her words came back to him like a far but enormous echo, slow and ponderous. The lids of his eyes were heavy, and he had to make the most dreadful effort to lift them and look at his cousin.

"What?" he murmured.

"You've paid for Elizabeth," said Caroline. "The debt is settled. But there are two things you must do. You must take back your daughter willingly. More even than that, you must, from this time on, dissociate yourself from your friends in Washington, New York, and Europe."

Timothy could feel the hysterical laughter gathering in him, the sick, deathly laughter. But his face did not change.

"I have ways of knowing," said Caroline. "It will take many years for you to repay me, and during that time I can refuse to let you repay me for your stocks and mortgages at the prices I paid for them. I can, at any time, sell your mortgages. I can insist on current market prices for the stock. Until the last cent is repaid, you can do nothing, Timothy."

Timothy thought of his "friends," who insistently wrote him almost daily, in spite of his physical condition. They did not know that he was financially impotent now; if they knew they would abandon him at once. At this stage they needed men with money and power and influence. He had none of these. It was this which had made the hysterical laughter bubble in him.

"Well?" said Caroline abruptly.

He opened his mouth, but he could not speak. So he gravely nodded his painful head.

"You've already said that you'd take Amy back," said Caroline. "And I assume you are meeting my second condition?"

He could suddenly speak. "Yes," he said. "But I haven't the faintest notion, Caroline——"

"Yes," said Caroline wearily. "You do, indeed."

She put the papers into her purse. Her hands shook. "You are only one man of your kind among tens of thousands, but your friends need every one of you, even you, struck down as you are. They need your money. They must never get another cent, Timothy, from you. That is my warning."

She stood up. "Your sons," she said. "If they were like you I'd not have been here in this room with you. Not even for Amy. But they are good young men; they'd never betray their country; your friends will never reach them. I satisfied myself about that. They are like their mother."

She went out of the room and closed the door behind her. Timothy watched the door closing. The pain in his head was frightful now, unendurable. He let it drop on the desk. He would rest a little. And then he would think. He would find a way; his friends would help him, in spite of Caroline, in spite of all her money. Her accursed money! His eyes were closed against the pain, but he saw the heap of her money, a golden mountain, and he said to himself: I can't climb it. But I must. I must. There must be some way to destroy her.

Amanda met Caroline in the hall. "It's very well now," said Caroline in the stately tones of Miss Stockington's School. "He's accepted Amy."

Amanda smiled at her gently. "Dear Caroline," she said.

"No," said Caroline. "Don't say that to me. There are often things you must do for many reasons, but they don't give pleasure. Would you call a cab for me?"

"No," said Amanda. "I will call our car to take you to the station. Caroline, how can I tell you——"

"Don't," said Caroline shortly. "I only want to go home."

"Tea, first," Amanda pleaded, seeing Caroline's gray and exhausted color.

"No. There is a train in half an hour." Then Caroline raised her voice, almost in despair. "Please let me go!"

When Caroline was driven away Amanda went quickly to the library. She cried out when she saw her husband half lying over his desk, his head dropped upon it. "Timothy!" she exclaimed, going to him quickly and full of dread. But he had not died. He could lift his head a little; however, he could only gibber, and Amanda ran at once for her sons, and her cries filled the big house with tumultuous and terrified noises.

I must get home, thought Caroline in the large automobile which belonged to Amanda. She looked listlessly at the smart back of the uniformed chauffeur and at the plate of glass which shut him off from her. Once Elizabeth, in her delirium, had mentioned the glass wall which protected her from the world. I've lived behind it all my life, too, Caroline thought, and there was a sensation of prostration just below her heart. She had forgotten her medicine. I must get home, she repeated to herself. Home, where there was nothing, where there never had been anything.

The handsome and formal people on the street did not interest her. She had never been part of them, of their teas and dances and charity balls and long, dull dinners. Why do they bother to live? she thought. For what end?

As the car approached the station the streets became a welter of hurrying people, shops, warehouses, streetcars, wagons, carriages and automobiles and bicycles, and noise and hot sunlight. The topaz haze which always seemed part of Boston hung over the streets, clouded the distant vistas in strong golden light. The chauffeur brought the car to a stop to allow a billowing crowd of people to cross the street, and Caroline languidly looked through the window. There was a church on the corner, and pacing slowly on the sidewalk was a priest with bent head, a tall, middle-aged priest who looked both tired and stern, gentle and remote. That is the church I visited, thought Caroline. And that must be the priest who wanted to help me—to help me —so long ago.

She had rarely moved impulsively, but now she tapped on the glass, and the chauffeur slid it aside and turned to her. "Wait for me on the next street," she said. "I have something to do. I will come back in fifteen minutes."

The chauffeur was confused, and hesitated. This frowzy and bustling street was no place for Mrs. Caroline Ames Sheldon; surely she did not want to shop in those stores nearby! But he had heard about Caroline's eccentricities, so he formally left his seat and opened the door for her, bowing. She waved him on impatiently and stood there, dusty and black-clothed, in her ancient hat and carrying her big purse, until he reluctantly turned the corner. The priest was returning along the sidewalk. Caroline looked at him, beginning to tremble as she always did when about to speak to a stranger. When he was almost upon her she lifted her head and she saw his thin, pale face, his calm deep eyes, his quiet expression, and in his turn he saw a woman he considered elderly, evidently poor, dressed in an old fashion, stocky, and gray and solid. She stood directly in his path, and he had to stop, inclining his head questioningly and smiling a little.

"I want to talk to you," said Caroline in her brusque way.

"Of course," said the priest. "Are you one of my—"

"No," she said impatiently. "But a long time ago, years ago, you wanted to help me. I've never forgotten."

He had helped thousands like this "poor old soul" over all the years. They had become one face to him, one face of anguish and despair and bewilderment. "I'm Father Bellamy," he said. "I'll be glad to help you. Will you come into the rectory?" And he glanced at the shabby clapboard house next to the church.

He waited to hear her name, but she did not give it. She marched ahead of him up the walk to the house, then stopped on the wooden porch with its neat chairs and its struggling wistaria vine. She had an air, he was surprised to see, of compact decisiveness in spite of her evident misery, and there was nothing cringing about her. He opened the door of the house for her, and she stepped into a long dark hall, glimmering with cleanliness and wax, and very quiet. "You people," said Caroline, "always keep things so clean, don't you, so uncluttered?"

Now the priest became aware of her voice. He had heard those intonations before, sharp and firm and trimmed, when he had gone with considerable shyness and trepidation to the homes of fine Boston ladies to ask for some donation, however small, for the endless needs of the clergy and their churches and their schools and the convents and the missions. He felt some bewilderment; this "poor old soul" spoke with the authority and accents of the great ladies of Boston in spite of her wretched clothing and appearance of dilapidated poverty.

"Uncluttered? Clean?" he murmured. He opened a door in the hall, and Caroline entered a small dark parlor with wooden walls and spare furniture and brilliantly polished linoleum floor. "I never did like clutter," said Caroline. "This is how I'd have liked a house if anyone had ever consulted me." She looked at the great crucifix on the far wall, then walked firmly to it and looked up at it with intense concentration. After a moment she sat down on the edge of a stiff chair the priest indicated, and he sat down in a wooden armchair. He waited. He spent a great part of his life waiting for people to speak, to cry out to him, to weep, to ask him stammering questions.

Caroline looked at the calm face, the quietly folded hands. "I never had anything I really wanted," she said. She thought of her grandfather's paintings. "Except, perhaps, for a very few things. And now it's too late to want anything—for me." She stared at the crucifix.

"It's not possible to get everything we want in this world," said the priest tentatively. "Mrs.——"

But Caroline ignored the question. "Too late," she repeated.

"Poverty isn't the worst state in the world," said Father Bellamy.

Caroline was silent, looking at him. Then she smiled her dark, grim smile. "I'm not poor," she said.

Ah, thought the priest, the honest pride of the very poor! How pathetic it was, but how noble! He knew it very well; he had been born into it and still lived in it. He glanced at her hands, expecting to see the coarseness and broken nails of hard labor. But Caroline's hands were well shaped, if large and broad, and now the priest understood that she was not poor and shelterless and afraid. Vaguely, then, he remembered the shining automobile which had stopped at the corner; someone had alighted from it—this woman?

"But you want my help?" he said in his confusion. "That is why I'm a priest—to help you."

"I don't know why I stopped you," said Caroline after a frowning moment. "I don't know why I'm here, not in the least. It was just an impulse, and I'm not an impulsive woman. It was perhaps because you stayed to speak to me one winter afternoon when I was in your church. You wanted to help me; you didn't ask anything of me in return, understanding or money or response of any kind. I never forgot that. You were the only one."

She stared at him. "I'm not a Roman Catholic," she said. "I belong to no church. I was never taught any religion, except very briefly, by our housekeeper. I didn't come to you now to hear about religion."

She had large intelligent eyes, he saw, commanding yet very reserved, and once, no doubt, they had been extremely beautiful. Even now, as a thin thread of sunlight touched them, they became strongly hazel, touched with gold. She had, thought the priest, the immense dignity of a column, the immovable power of it.

"But you wanted help," he said gently.

Caroline looked aside. "Yes. But I don't know what the help could possibly be."

He had heard this so many times in his life as a priest, but not with this cold puzzlement. He waited.

"I want to know, with all honesty, if you really believe that there is a God," said Caroline.

"Would I be here if I didn't have faith?" asked Father Bellamy.

She shook her head. "I don't know. Habit, custom, helpless fixation in a certain sphere—they imprison us. I'm wretched where I am, but there is nothing I can do about it. How do I know that you, too, aren't helpless where you are, and unable to free yourself?"

"I could free myself, as you call it, madam, by simply taking off these clerical clothes of mine, putting on others, and walking through that door. I'm not held by anything, except God and my faith."

Caroline again shook her head. "When you were young, as I was, perhaps you were pushed into this mold, so it seems the only one acceptable to you, even if it may be a prison."

"No," said the priest. "My parents were against it; I was their only son. I should say that God chose me, and I did not choose Him. The 'compulsion,' if there was any, came from Him, but there is no 'compulsion,' because we have free will."

"And you think that I 'chose' what I am?" said Caroline with some derision. "You think I did it deliberately, against other choices?"

"I don't know, madam. Only God knows."

"I did not choose it. I was lied into it, led into it."

The priest smiled sadly. "That is one plea which is not acceptable to God. No matter the circumstance, we all can, by an act of free will, choose what to accept or what to reject, even if it is only in the silence of our hearts."

Caroline was silent for a long time, her head bent. Then she looked up. "Certainly," she said, "you are quite right. I think I always knew it. I'm sorry you told me the truth. However, there were other circumstances. I was only a young girl—a child, really—and my father lied to me and gave me a picture of the world that was only in his frightened and terrible mind. I loved him and I believed him. Can you understand?"

"But there must have been others," said the priest.

"There were. But I didn't believe them. I adored my father. Why should I have doubted him?"

"You became a woman. And," repeated the priest, "there must have been others."

"No one who really loved me," said Caroline. There was a dull flush on her cheeks and over her forehead. What am I doing here, she asked herself, and saying what I am saying to a stranger who cannot possibly understand? She was ashamed of herself. She tightened her hold on her purse and started to rise.

"No one?" said the priest.

"I beg your pardon? Oh yes, our old housekeeper, a simple woman who thought that even I, and all I was and had, should fit into her simple conceptions of life." Dear God, thought Caroline, what a fool I am! I must be going into my dotage.

"I had a grandmother like that," said the priest, and Caroline paused in the very motion of rising. "A good old soul. She thought the highest calling in our village was to be a shoemaker, and I was rising above myself, she said, when I told her I wanted to be a priest." He smiled at Caroline, and his worn face became tender and boyish. "Do I understand that your old—

housekeeper?—thought you should be less than you were? That isn't very peculiar, because none of us thinks of himself as a humble person; we all believe that what we are is the best possible state. Many of us couldn't go on living if we didn't think that."

Now his human curiosity was aroused. "All I was and had," this shabby and unprepossessing woman had said. He did not consider her mad; he knew that she was not only a lady but an extremely intelligent and honest one. Then he was concerned again with her look of distraction and despair. "There wasn't anyone else but your old housekeeper?"

"My husband," said Caroline. The pain became like a dark cobweb over her face. "He has been dead for many years. He, too, thought I should fit into some comfortable conception of his about me. When I didn't, when I could not, it broke his heart. He wanted to divorce me. He told me so the night before he died." She looked at the floor. "My daughter is dead too; she died a year ago. It was my fault, for I'd made her what she was, or I should say that as I had never had any resources of my own I was unable to give her resources to help her."

"But you survived," said the priest with pity. "You had no resources, as your daughter had none, yet you survived. Why didn't she, then?"

Caroline did not move; she continued to look at the floor.

"You suffered as much, perhaps?" continued the priest in his gentle voice. "You lost your parents, your husband, your daughter, but you didn't die. Are you reproaching yourself too much? It is very good to feel guilt and repent and do penance, but you can't take the blame for everything on yourself, can you? Your daughter had a father also; perhaps he was to blame too."

She lifted her head, and her eyes were large and searching and anxious. "That is possible?"

"Yes. But then, I don't know all the circumstances. Only your own conscience can tell you if what I've said applies to you."

"I must think about it," said Caroline. "I have a great deal to think about, and I don't, I think, have much more time. You see, I have nowhere to go, and that is why I asked you if you really believe there is a God."

"I know there is God," said the priest with emphasis. "Even when I feel absolutely dry, I still know it. One of the greatest saints of the Church, St. Thérèse of Avila, wrote that she spent many years in 'dryness' and sometimes doubted heaven, but she did not doubt God. You have no pastor you can speak to?"

"No." Caroline was coloring again. "I wish you to know that this isn't like me at all. I've always shrunk from strangers all my life. I live the life of a recluse; I have no friends. I have two sons——"

Looking at her intently, Father Bellamy had a sensation of familiarity. He had seen this lady somewhere. He said, "Two sons?"

"Two sons," she repeated. "But they aren't more than that to me, possibly because I was never really a mother to them. That is something else I must think about. One lives in Boston; I see him four or five times a year. The other lives in New York; we are estranged."

Her large and lead-colored lips set themselves firmly, and he knew that she would not discuss her sons with him. The sense of familiarity became stronger.

"I wish," said Caroline, "that I could believe there is a God. For, you see, I have nowhere to go; I think most of us are like that. It's the human tragedy." She stood up. "I destroyed a man today," she said, and looked him sternly in the eye. "I began to destroy him a year ago, and today I finished it. You would not be able to understand it, but he was more your enemy than he was mine, though I've never had so terrible an enemy as he is in all my life. You will not be able to understand this, either, but someday you will, unfortunately."

She waited for a look of incredulity to appear on his face, but it did not. He had heard too many strange things in his life to be incredulous of anything. He went to the door with her, and he said, "You've asked me about God. Faith is a grace which comes from Him; we cannot truly will it for ourselves. But if we ask for it in hope and longing, He will give it to us. Ask Him for that grace." He stood on the doorstep with her and felt deep compassion. "And when you pray, pray that that dreadful war in Europe will end soon."

"There is no use praying for that," said Caroline. She frowned at Amanda's chauffeur, who had driven the automobile fretfully around the block several times, looking for her. Seeing her, he stopped the vehicle at the curb and got out and stood at attention respectfully. The priest regarded him thoughtfully, then looked at Caroline.

She said, "It was planned a long time ago. I first heard of it in Geneva with my father when I was a very young woman. I listened to his associates. The war will go on, and America will enter it; it was planned. And this is only the beginning."

"Surely not," murmured Father Bellamy.

There had been very few times in Caroline's life when she had noticed that others were suffering or were afraid or poor. All at once, in the strong summer sunshine, she saw the priest's tired and wasted face, his shabbiness. She remembered the shining poverty of his house, the worn linoleum.

"Would you mind if I gave you some money?" she asked abruptly. "It's all I ever had—money."

The priest was astounded. "All I ever had," said Caroline. "I'd like to give you what I have in my purse. I beg you to take it; it would give me some pleasure." She turned her back to the street and opened her big purse and brought out a thick roll of yellow bills held together by a rubber band. She pushed it into the priest's hand.

"I can't," began the priest, but she almost rudely pushed by him and went down the steps. He followed her helplessly. She stopped at the sidewalk and looked at him earnestly. "It's all I ever had to give," she said. "You mustn't refuse it; you'd be refusing my life."

She walked with quick if lumbering steps to the car, and the chauffeur said, "Mrs. Sheldon, I'm afraid you've missed your train."

"No matter," said Caroline impatiently. "There will be another in less than an hour." The man closed the door briskly after her with deep respect, and then the automobile moved on, leaving the dumfounded priest still standing on the steps of his house.

"Mrs. Sheldon." Then the amazed priest knew. His visitor had been Caroline Ames Sheldon, the famous tight-fisted recluse. He went slowly into his house. He put the roll of bills on his desk and counted them. Then he went to the telephone in the hall and called Dr. Clarendon of Sisters of Charity Hospital, his friend, and told him.

"Well, well," said Dr. Clarendon, marveling. "Old Caroline, eh? She was in the hospital for a few minutes around last Christmas; a heart seizure of some kind. But an indomitable woman, isn't she? And she gave you—two thousand dollars? Congratulations, Francis. I'll wager that was her first charitable donation in all her life. Now you can have those new bells you've wanted, or your organ, and then there are all your charities. Old Caroline! I must tell everybody. No one will believe it! And calling on you! What reason did she give? I must tell——"

"No, please," said the priest. "You don't understand, I'm afraid. I only called you to verify that she was indeed Mrs. Sheldon and that I could keep the money. Your description of her was exact. But you mustn't tell anyone, please. I never saw such despair. I think I know why she came, poor woman. She's desperate."

The doctor chuckled. "I'd like to have her three or four hundred million dollars, or it's probably a lot more than that, and I'd take the despair along with it. Old Hag Caroline Ames! Did she leave a smell of brimstone behind? Better start sprinkling the holy water."

The priest went into his church and he prayed for Caroline, remembering her face. She reminded him of his aunt, who had been blinded. He had seen Caroline before; he could remember now. He had not only seen her photograph; he had, as she had said, seen her in this church a long time ago. He prayed for her passionately and with all the strength of his soul.

CHAPTER FIVE

While Caroline waited for her son Ames, she picked her way through the great boulders covering the sea walk and reached the shingle. It was seldom hot near the sea, but now a steaming giant's mouth seemed to be pressing over land and water, gaseous and fuming. It concealed the sun; it was the color of wet smoke. The long waves, rushing toward the land in uneasy thunder, were dark gray, ridged with breaking foam and splashes of turquoise, and the horizon was tumultuous. Here and there in the sky lavender clouds were forming in tormented patterns, and now, as Caroline watched, they were veined with branching lightning, and immediately steely paths flashed over the water in answer. But there was no wind; the air suffocated one's lungs.

Caroline looked to the right and left; her high walls shut off any view of new neighbors, of any view at all but the sea. I should feel, she thought, now that I am released from an old evil lie, a sudden desire to see others besides myself. But that is romanticism. Sudden convulsions of feeling can occur only in the very young. I've grown old in my spirit; I'm only a speck of unwilling life still throbbing faintly deep inside the calcified, serrated, and thickened shell I have built about myself for many years, perhaps from the moment I was born. I am blinded by it, deafened by it, imprisoned by it, held immovable by it. I could not change if I wanted to, and I do not want to. What other life could there be for me but the one I know? It's all such a weariness. If the shell were cracked open I should die in a different environment from the only one I've ever known. And I'm not ready to die—not yet —though there is no reason why I should live.

Her father had not really left her a "trust." Yet she must continue as if her old fantasy were still with her. It was still a wall, all that money, which protected her from what could only destroy her.

She went back through the boulders, slowly, heavily, around the side of the dying house and into what had once been Tom's cherished gardens. The brush and the wild trees and the knee-high grass murmured apprehensively, though there was still no wind. It was a gray-and-green jungle of struggling life, inhibited by its very profusion. The birds, usually so noisy, were silent. There was not even a bee or a wasp or a butterfly visible. They had all hidden themselves; they had all gone to shelter before the coming storm. But we, thought Caroline, have no shelter, we have no home, none of us. We are open to everything, like exiles pushed from safety. Even I, with all my money. We build our strong cities and they don't shelter us. We formulate philosophies which do not comfort us. We make all the world clamorous, and nothing listens to us, and everything that is innocent avoids us as though we were death itself. I wonder why?

We have nowhere to go—humanity.

The crowding and monolithic trees whitened with the lightning, and the darkness increased. Now a heavy wind struck the earth, and the trees and the shrubbery roared in green rage, and the voice of the sea echoed the voice of thunder. Caroline still stood and looked at the savage growth within her walls. She stood under a great and twisted tree, and so when the first hard drops of rain came she did not feel them.

Where shall I go? she thought. Where is there any shelter for me, any quietness? Any peace? Nowhere, of course. There is nowhere for everyone else, either. We were given the capacity to think and reflect on that—that we have nowhere to go. No creature receives a faculty that is of no use to it; nature is economical. We received the faculty to be aware that there is —nothing—and I wonder why? Of what use is it to us, except to make us kill ourselves, one way or another?

We all kill ourselves, one way or another. We are the race of suicides.

We don't resemble any other creature, in this. What drives man to murder himself, through hate, ambition, work, striving, hope, despair, struggle, building, destroying, and war? Does he hate himself so much? Caroline looked at the sky; the lavender patterns of clouds had become a deep and furious purple, and the lightning that veined through them was too brilliant. What had someone once written? "We are born so that we should know God. That is the only reason. When we refuse to know, then we die in many ways."

Caroline shook her head, over and over. It was too simple and yet too impossible. How did one "know" God—if there was a God? It was beyond an act of will. It had to come from without oneself. What had the priest said? "Grace." Faith was a grace given to man. Why was it withheld from almost every human being, then? Did God hate man too?

Her eyes fixed on the lightning-torn purple clouds, Caroline said aloud with bitter lips, "Give me Your grace. I can't will it for myself. If You exist, give it to me."

After a little she stepped from under the tree and did not feel the rain on her face. She stopped in the shelter of her doorway and said again with increasing bitterness, "Give me Your grace. Perhaps then I'll understand why I was born, and to such a father, and in such circumstances, and why I never had happiness, but only pain and fear, and why I have always hated living."

Thunder exploded in the sky. Meaningless noise. I have lost what meaning I had for living, even if it was false, thought Caroline. Does the knowledge that there is no meaning make man murder himself? Had nature given him that awareness so he would destroy himself and his fellow man? Was man so hateful, then, to the very source of his existence? If so, why had nature produced him at all?

Caroline went into her expiring house. Every dank room was full of purple shadows, slashed with lightning, and silent except for thunder. Maizie, she thought, was hiding in some closet; she was terrified of storms. Didn't the poor girl realize that there was no place to hide? Man was open to calamity, and there was no shelter. Animals died, without any knowledge of death. Man had that knowledge. Why? If, thought Caroline, You had any mercy, You would never have created man—if You exist. Life is too terrible for us. We didn't deserve this blind punishment.

She paused, and was struck, and then shaken. For the first time she felt a huge and swelling compassion for all humanity, a sense of sharing in universal disaster, a sense of pain and companionship and sadness. And as she felt this she lost, for the first time in her life, her terror of mankind. It was gone, in the storm of her pity, and she knew that it would never return again. So, she thought vaguely, dimly, that is the first step. The very first step. She leaned her cheek in the palm of her hand. Tears dripped over her fingers. What had she said to herself? The first step. What was the next, and to where? She lifted her head, her eyes dazzled by the lightning that shot vividly into the dusky room. She must wait. She only knew that she had a sensation of something releasing her.

She suddenly thought of all those whom she had hated and feared in her life. The Alecks. The Ferns. She could not feel the usual throb of fear which only yesterday she would have felt. She examined this curiously. They, too, had lived in a context of their own, as she had lived, and who was to say which was the more terrible? Had they sensed, as she had, the anarchy which lived just beyond the flicker of man's sight, just beyond the detection of his ear? If it was Order and not anarchy, it was nonetheless affrighting, for man could not understand it, could not relate it to himself. Who could blame the Alecks and the Ferns for trying to create a distorted and frantic order of their own?

Caroline thought of Cynthia, and all at once she was smiling and was astonished that she was smiling. There was nothing in herself which would ever understand the Cynthias of the world, but one had to grant that they were graceful and never willingly harmed anyone. I have done more harm in my life innocently, thought Caroline, than my aunt ever did in her life uninnocently. I have never committed adultery; I have never borne an illegitimate child; I have never contrived, gaily betrayed, been frivolous and artful and exigent. Yet I suppose I am a more wicked woman than was my aunt, for I was blind and I lied to myself when the truth was wholly visible to me.

She stood up wearily in the glitter and dusk of the room and went to her bottle of medicine and measured out a dose, for her heart was pounding with pain and was erratic in its struggle. She drank the bitter dose and looked about her musingly, seeing her surroundings clearly for the first time. "This is what I did," she said aloud. "No one else did it; only I."

Forgetting the storm, Caroline climbed laboriously to her study and called Higsby Chalmers in Boston. While she waited a tree was struck in the far part of Tom's ruined garden, and the telephone receiver tingled in her hand. She saw the sudden flare of flame; the house trembled. Now a roar of rain slammed against the old windows and drowned them. "Higsby?" said Caroline in her rough voice.

"Caroline?" said Mr. Chalmers.

"Yes. I've read your letter, though I've not answered it. And now I understand. Will you come to see me tomorrow here in Lyme?"

Mr. Chalmers was moved and elated. "Certainly, dear Caroline! I will bring you some new information also." He paused. "Is that the storm I hear over the telephone? It is here in Boston too."

"Something was just struck near the house," said Caroline.

"Really?" said Mr. Chalmers. "Isn't it dangerous, then, to be using the telephone, Caroline? Is there a fire?"

"I suppose so," said Caroline. "Thank you, Higsby."

The rain drowned the struck tree; Caroline could see, very faintly through the rain, the stream of smoke. Poor creature, thought Caroline, you lived and burned as meaninglessly as we do, and your death is as meaningless as ours. She went into Elizabeth's room, so like a nun's cell. She looked about her and said aloud, "My child, where are you? Pray for me, if you can hear me. We were both victims of ourselves as well as others."

She smoothed the narrow white bed, and then a most extraordinary thing occurred. She felt the actual presence of Elizabeth, tentative and understanding. She looked about her eagerly. The lightning strode into the room, and the sound of the thunder, and yet it all seemed so silent, so alive, so filled with peace. "I'm glad," said Caroline. "I'm glad that you're not here any longer, Elizabeth. You are safe——"

Tears gushed down her cheeks, yet she was smiling when she left Elizabeth's room, and she was still smiling when she closed the door gently behind herself. "Safe," she whispered to herself in the dark hall. But she could not quite understand what she had said. She went into Tom's room. She said, "Tom?" She waited, but there was no answering presence. She said, "I am sorry, Tom. Will you wait for me?" There was no answer. Sighing, she left the room.

She went to the rooms formerly occupied by her sons. Ames' room had a cool, barren air, rejecting. John's room was still pervaded by an air of confusion and helplessness. Now, she thought, that is strange. I always thought of John as a very strong and potent and self-sufficient young man. She stood in John's room and then was struck with pity and fear. She went back into her dark study and called John's office in New York. While she waited the storm became more fierce and even closer.

"John?" she said at last.

"Yes?" His voice was sullen and weary.

"I'd like to see you, John," she said.

He was silent. She could feel his astonishment. "Why?" he said at last.

"I want to see you."

"Wouldn't you rather see Mimi?" His tone was hard and sarcastic.

"No. You, John."

He paused. She could sense his astounded and conjecturing thoughts. "All right," he said. "When?"

"A week today?"

"Very well."

She did not know why she felt so defeated when she went slowly down the gritty stairs and why there was such a weight on her chest. The outside door opened and Ames ran into the house, his hat pulled down to protect his face from the rain, his shoulders stained with large dark spots. He threw his hat from him and shrugged as if the rain had, in some way, violated him. He looked at his mother. "Well," he said. She sat down in her usual chair, silently, and he stood at a little distance from her and lighted a cigarette with neat, controlled gestures. The glimmering lightning touched his pale hair, his smooth face with its lack of expression.

"You asked me to come," he said. "I received your message in my office."

"Yes. You know that Amy has left you."

"Thanks to you," said Ames. His voice was light but venomous. "You do like to play cat and mouse, don't you? You persuade me to keep my wife, then when I'm in New York you abduct her. It's no loss to me to have her gone; I wanted that myself. I'm thinking of another loss to me, much more important."

Caroline did not speak for a moment or two. The lightning revealed her son's face sharply, then the following darkness obscured it. She leaned her head back against the chair.

"You have no loss," she said. "I will keep my part of the bargain. You will receive what I agreed to allow you."

"Well!" he said again, but with quick pleasure and gratification. He sat down opposite his mother. He began to speak again, but his voice was lost in the thunder. He glanced at the windows, and Caroline suddenly remembered that he had been afraid of storms when he was a child and that Tom had always held him in his arms during them. She could see them so clearly, the young and tender father, the screaming little boy with his hands over his ears. She looked at Ames now and waited for the long rolling to subside. I've never really seen him before, she thought. My son. My son.

"I never thought of you as being capricious," said Ames. He smoked rapidly, and his slate-gray eyes kept darting at the windows, which glared repeatedly.

"I am not," said Caroline.

Ames paused. "I appreciate all this, Mother. But, just to satisfy my curiosity, will you tell me why you shifted from one opinion to the direct opposite? Not," he added hastily, "that I'm not grateful."

"It would be very hard to explain," said Caroline. "There are things beyond explanation. One just has to accept them. I suppose you are willing for Amy to divorce you?"

"The sooner the better," he said. He was very nervous in this storm. He had never seen a worse one, and he was exasperated at himself. "I smell smoke," he said.

"Of course. A tree was hit in the garden."

"That close?" he said, alarmed.

"Ames," said Caroline, ignoring the question, "I must ask you something. Did you never care about Amy at all?"

"Certainly," he answered. Was the old hag becoming sentimental in her old age? "But that was before I found out how stupid she was. Surely you knew that?"

"I know a great many things. Now," said Caroline. A red flare of lightning lit the room and was followed instantaneously by a deafening explosion of thunder. The house shuddered. Ames jumped to his feet, and his tall and slender body appeared to cringe. He looked at his mother and saw her eyes in the lightning, strange and large and inscrutable. He laughed a little.

"I never liked to be in a house when there's a storm about," he said. "I prefer large office buildings or railroad stations."

"You don't like to be exposed," said Caroline. "Or threatened. Yes, I understand that. I hated storms myself when I was a child and when I was your age. I hated them until today. I hated them for the very reasons you hate them."

Her voice, to him, sounded far and weak. As he had never heard her speak gently before, he did not recognize the gentleness now. "I'm sorry, but I don't understand you," he said politely. "Exposed? Threatened? I'm not a child, Mother. I do know, however, that storms aren't to be laughed at by anyone. Do you know that about a thousand people a year are killed in this country alone by lightning?"

"No, I didn't know. But the fact that you found that item interesting is very revealing," said Caroline.

Ames' fine fair eyebrows drew together, and his eyes became a little mocking. "Are you analyzing me, Mother?" he said. "And if so, why?" The thunder, after that annihilating crash, was suddenly retreating, though the wind and the rain and the lightning continued. But Ames was still nervous; he was, to his disgust, trembling slightly, like a cat. He took his eyes from the windows and turned to his mother and was startled. What a peculiar expression she had!

"You will marry again, I suppose," said Caroline.

"No doubt," he said carefully, watching Caroline. "But not immediately. After all, I've not had a very happy experience."

Caroline nodded. Her hands were like gray stone as they lay in her broad lap. "You will be able to marry again, and not for money," she said.

"One can always use that," said Ames, smiling, and relaxing now that the thunder was only growling in the distance. A wan light began to fill the room as the hidden sun brightened behind the thinning clouds. And in that light he saw his mother's eyes again, quiet and probing.

"It is stupid," said Caroline, "to wish anyone happiness in this world, for happiness doesn't exist. It's a word for children. But I hope you will be better satisfied the next time you marry. I hope your wife will bring you——"

"Children," he said, watching his mother again.

"As my ultimate heirs?" Caroline smiled drearily. "No, that isn't what I meant. I hope your wife will bring"—she turned her head abruptly from him—"some contentment, some meaning, into your life."

The suddenly quiet room was filled only with the sound of wind and rain and distant thunder. His cigarette fell from his fingers, and he bent and picked it up, and then to his own amazement he was throwing it violently into the cold and ash-filled fireplace. His chest felt tight, constricted, his face hot and stiff, and there were quivers of something closely resembling pain about his mouth. He had experienced it all before as a very young child. Several times. Even as the sensations increased helplessly in their intensity, he could remember the helplessness, the sensation of abandonment and rage and hysteria. He tried to steady himself, but he was suddenly on his feet and breathing hard and he could not stop.

"Why should you care about any contentment or peace I might have?" he said, and he was shocked at the uncontrolled sound of his own voice.

Caroline did not answer him because she could not. The enormous defeat was on her again, the vast spiritual sickness.

I must control myself, thought Ames, and heard himself say, "You never did before. Not once in my life! Why now?"

Caroline closed her eyes. "I've learned a great deal. Lately. I told you I couldn't explain, Ames, for I don't have the words. You must let it remain at that."

He swung from her and went to one of the windows. The rain poured against it in long livid paths. He traced a mark in the dust on the inside of the glass. He watched the shaking of his finger, and he was enraged at himself and he hated his mother. The very salt of hatred was in his mouth. The quivering hysteria thrilled all about his lips. He forced himself to stand there, to stifle his disgusting emotions, the mindless fury that surged all through him like the storm. He began to talk inwardly. I never could stand lightning and thunder. The air's charged with it. It would make anyone else, but one like her, as nervous as all hell. I'm a sensitive man, not a clod.

Caroline saw his thin back, his lean shoulders, his bent head. She could see part of his profile, thin and very pale. "Ames," she said.

"Yes?" He did not turn to her. He was humiliated; he did not want her to see his face yet. "What have you learned, Mother?"

"Things I'm afraid you'll never learn, Ames."

The tracing finger halted on the glass. What a stupid remark, he thought. She's out of her mind at last; there must be a taint in the family. Elizabeth. My grandfather—I've heard that he was not quite sane himself.

"I'd like to show you something," said Caroline. She forced herself wearily to her feet. "In my gallery."

His loathing for her was a force that helped him to self-control. His trembling stopped, the hysteria disappeared at once, the fury died down. He could turn now and could smile. "Ah, your paintings," he said. "I've been very curious."

He followed her up the stairs. The crunching of grit under his feet, the darkness, the closed and musty smells, the airlessness so revolted him that the last rage left him entirely, and he could smile slightly in contempt, seeing the broad black figure rising painfully above him. He followed his mother down the hall; the carpet was in shreds and stank of old dust and decay. He glanced at the door of his room, at the door of John's room. Had he ever lived in this shut horror, this aged grime? His mother was unlocking the door of her gallery, and when she pushed it open the emerging sun shot long beams of warm yellow light into the room, and it was like walking into goldness.

He was surprised. Here all was neatness and quiet and serenity, with only one chair standing before a lined wall of paintings, and the floor was polished, the windows clear. He raised his eyebrows. His eyes involuntarily met his mother's. She pointed mutely at the pictures. He went to them eagerly, alertly, the connoisseur once more, not knowing what to expect. It had been his opinion that his mother, who was without taste or sensitivity or perception, had bought ridiculous paintings for her private enjoyment. He stopped before one and was astonished. He bent and peered at it acutely. He went to the next, and to the next.

"David Ames!" he cried incredulously.

"Your great-grandfather," said Caroline.

"Originals!" exclaimed Ames in awe. "Originals!" He stopped. Then he turned very slowly. "What did you say?" he said, astounded. "My great-grandfather?"

"Yes," Caroline said. She was unknowingly wringing her hands. "They will tell you what I can't, Ames."

"My great-grandfather!" he said again, staring at her and then at the paintings. "Good God! Are you sure?"

She pointed to David Ames' self-portrait, and he went to it and stood for a long time before it, remembering his young mother and seeing the absolute resemblance. Then his next sensation was exultation. He had no more need now to think of his grandfather with disdain, the "buccaneer nobody." He did not need now to focus his family pride on the Esmonds. He was the great-grandson of David Ames! It was with something like profound gratitude that he swung about to his mother.

"Why didn't you let me know before?" he demanded.

"Why should I have? Is it so important to you?" asked Caroline with that new and dreadful pity of hers, and understanding.

"Good God, yes! David Ames! I've seen only one original, or perhaps two. All the rest have been copies or prints." He was elated, smiling. He walked from painting to painting, with deepening excitement and awe. He filled his eyes with color and form as a drunkard fills his mouth and belly with his one delight and one consolation.

Why, he isn't thinking of their worth in money, thought Caroline, and her eyes filled with tears. He isn't now even thinking of the honor of having David Ames as his great-grandfather. Elizabeth deceived me, but Ames is not deceiving me. She saw him touch a line of vivid red paint. He was moving rapidly from one painting to another, over and over, his footsteps clicking fastidiously on the polished floor. He was murmuring joyfully, lustfully, to himself and nodding his head. Then he stopped before the tower and was still. "Where—where did you get them?" he murmured, marveling. Then the tower held him once more, and he could not have enough of looking.

"Does it mean anything to you, that painting?" asked Caroline.

He did not answer for a long time. Then he said, "I've never seen such marvelous work. I've seen prints of this; they were like black-and-whites. Copies never have caught the depth, the splendor, the form, the line, the perspectives, the glow."

"The tower," said Caroline. "Does it mean something to you, anything at all?"

"A ruin," said Ames, staring at it greedily and with immense pleasure. "A bleak ruin. Lost. Abandoned. Eerie. The light of another world."

Caroline sighed. "You feel that?" she asked, and she did not know if the pain she was enduring was physical or spiritual.

"Yes. Of course. But each viewer finds something in any painting which relates to himself," said Ames, and did not know what he was saying.

"Yes," said Caroline, heartbroken. But Ames did not hear her. He was moving again, overcome with his powerful excitement. Caroline stood still, her hands clasped hard together, and watched his rapid movements. Then he stopped before the little painting of Mimi's, the picture of a young girl waiting on a boulder, her profile turned ardently and with hope to the viewer, the red ribbon in her hair streaming in the wind, and the ocean before her. "This," said Ames, frowning. "I don't know whose this is. Childish, in many ways, but showing true strength and artistic feeling. What is it doing here?"

"A friend gave it to me," said Caroline. "Long ago."

"Who? Has he done much lately? What is his name?"

"It doesn't matter," said Caroline listlessly. She pointed to the painting of the blinded man stumbling among great stones, with the purple mountains behind him and the ominous sky above him. "Do you understand that?" she asked.

Ames gave the painting all his attention. Caroline had never seen that powerful concentration of his before, that giving of himself to beauty and the terror of beauty, and her hope came again.

"A man incapable of seeing," said Ames.

"Seeing what?"

Ames was irritated at what he considered a most foolish question.

"Form. Order. Style. It's the picture of the perpetual fool, without taste or comprehension. The universal fool. The common man. The dolt who should never have been born. You see him on every street, everywhere you go. The blind."

"The man who will not see?" asked Caroline.

His irritation became anger. How dare a woman like his mother have these tremendous things, these glorious things! She had bought them, of course, as one of her damned investments. Well, she had done excellently; that is all that interested her.

"The man," said Ames, "who was born incapable of seeing, a man without discernment or sensitivity. The common man. The color-blind animal."

"No," said Caroline, shaking her head heavily from side to side. But Ames did not hear her. He was again studying another painting.

Then Caroline's new huge compassion took her again, and this time for her father, who had destroyed her and who had destroyed his grandchildren. She could only pity, and the pity devastated her. She sat down abruptly in the chair, and her head fell on her breast. Dear God, she thought, have mercy on Your children. Have mercy. Forgive us; we never know what we do, because we never try to understand. Ames was laughing delightedly.

"He must have been in Mexico," he said. "This girl—what power, what color, what subtlety!"

He went again to the painting of the church and the apocalyptic sky and the small vivid cross soaring valiantly against the furious and threatening color, in defiance, in promise, in a strength that not even the shaking of all the earth and the heavens could move from its place, could throw down.

Ames was nodding. "Wonderful," he murmured. "How he's portrayed the uselessness, the vulnerability, the littleness of human superstition. The stupidity of religion. The utter defenselessness of it in the face of a crashing reality."

Caroline was silent. Ames came to stand beside her. "What are you——" And then he stopped.

"What am I going to do with them?" said Caroline feebly. "I intend to give them to the Boston Museum, in my will. But you may make three choices, and I will arrange for you to have them when I am dead."

Ames was aghast. "The Boston Museum!" he cried, pushing his hands deeply into his pockets. "For every dog to look at, for every blind eye to see?"

"For everyone to see," said Caroline.

"But that's blasphemy!"

"If you had them all, you'd lock them away? As I did, as I do? Just for yourself?"

"I tell you, it's blasphemy," said Ames. "Yes, I'd lock them away for myself."

"As I did."

Ames paused. But you only bought them as an investment, he said to himself. They have no meaning for you.

He tried to speak reasonably. "Mother, it's true that they are worth a fabulous fortune now. They're beyond price. You aren't serious when you say you'll give them—give them!—away?"

"I am perfectly serious," said Caroline. She stood up. "Shall we go now?"

He hated her. She was mad, of course. "Don't you know how I feel about them myself?" he said, still controlling his voice. "My great-grandfather's paintings? Don't you know how I'd treasure them? You know what I am."

"Yes," said Caroline. "I know. Please make your three choices, Ames."

He did, but his sickness grew during the difficulty of choosing. "You aren't leaving any of them to John?"

"No."

"He's your son too."

You mean, thought Caroline, that if John has a few you'll buy them from him.

"I don't think," said Caroline, "that John would care for any of them."

"He cares for anything that's valuable," said Ames. "Did you know, by the way, that he's color-blind?"

"Is he?" said Caroline. "No, I didn't know." So her son John was married to an artist, and he would never know what she was doing; he would never see the coloring, the light, the shade of hue, the exquisite and subtle tint.

Ames had chosen the tower, the picture of the little church against the mad and insensate fury of destruction, the girl in the exotic garden. Caroline, watching him as he made his choices, saw that the painting of the blind man made him vaguely uneasy.

They went downstairs together. The maid had opened a few windows, and the ragged draperies were blowing in a fresh wind. Everything outside dripped and sparkled, even the lost garden. The sea spoke in its great voice. Ames listened. "It is the only thing I miss," he said. "The sound of the sea."

But nothing else, thought his mother. There was nothing else for you to remember, my son.

She watched him run lightly down the broken path to the cab he had brought. He did not look back. There was nothing to draw his eye to his mother in a last kindness, in a farewell. He had forgotten her. As I forgot him, always, when he was a child, she said to herself, desolated.

Higsby Chalmers was extremely shocked at Caroline's appearance. She appeared to him to be dying steadily with her house, to be pacing with it in its decline into wreckage. He murmured, "My dear Caroline," when he took her hand, and could helplessly say no more for a while. When Caroline offered him tea he accepted, though he wished to decline. He had need to recover from his human consternation and his pity. Then he became aware that there was some subtle change in her, for she was looking at him not with her old expression of withdrawal and indifference but intensely, as if weighing and considering.

The teacups were sticky, the tea itself foul, the little cakes uneatable. But Higsby, usually fussy about such matters, was not aware of them now. He was conscious only of Caroline. There was a change in her; it was as if she had come up a cobwebbed companionway from the dark bowels of some ruin of a ship, and her eyes were looking, for the first time, on the running sea and comprehending its existence.

Caroline always came to the point, unlike other people, and Higsby was not surprised when she said, "I read your letter fully and then put it aside. It did not concern me. But lately it has. Why isn't of importance. Tell me more."

Higsby put down his teacup, leaned forward toward her, clasping his plump hands between his knees. "As I've written you, Caroline, the thing that is in the world now, the war, is the opening of the grand design against mankind. You told me last year that you had known of it since you were less than twenty-four. President Wilson is dimly coming to understand too; you will remember that only lately he warned America again never to permit a strong centralized government in Washington."

Mr. Chalmers stood up and walked slowly and distressfully up and down the gritty floor. He stopped and stared through a smudged window at the wild garden, and he thought: That is the way it will all be soon unless we can stop it.

"Can we stop it?" asked Caroline in her low, rough voice. "I don't think so, Higsby. We have too many idealists and simple men like Mr. Roosevelt in Washington. I've known all you've been telling me since I was a young girl. We can't stop it, Higsby."

"Perhaps not," said Higsby with sadness. "We have the enemy here, too, in full force. Eugene Debs, who was indicted for conspiracy to kill. The Socialist movement. Now new, in America, as it is not new in Europe. Like you, Caroline, I feel that these creatures will force us into a war with Germany to prevent a quick, negotiated peace between Germany and England. And to give impetus to revolution, beginning in Russia."

"I know, I know," said Caroline. "I've known, perhaps, for much longer than you have, Higsby. But you must have some plan or you'd not be here."

He sat down and wiped his cherubic face. "I have. Education of the people. A foundation, such as the Carnegie Foundation which established free libraries. I even have a name for it," and he smiled sadly. "The American Foundation for Constitutional Freedom. The Constitution stands in the way of the tyrants. It will be destroyed unless we begin to enlighten the people. I have the idea of a large, permanent building somewhere, perhaps in New England. We will staff it with informed intellectuals, experts on the Constitution, teachers, professors, historians, people aware of what is truly happening in the world. They will write pamphlets, sheets, bulletins, perhaps a newspaper. All this will be disseminated profusely over every section of the country. Free. To schools, to clubs, to organizations, to newspapers, to universities and colleges, to the professional and business people. Without charge. We must alert writers and newspapermen, everyone who has access to the public means of communication."

Caroline shook her head. "You won't win, Higsby. It's impossible. The American people will be offered everything in exchange for their liberty. You must remember ancient Rome. A country never greedily took the path to tyranny, in all the world's history, and turned back. Not once, anywhere."

Higsby said stoutly, "There was never a Constitution like ours, Caroline, in the history of the world. You see, miracles do happen. Perhaps America will turn back—one day. Who knows? But shall we let her go without one protest, by default? Shall we hopelessly, by our silence, accede to her destruction? For our souls' sake, we cannot!"

"How much?" said Caroline. Higsby sat down and talked quietly and steadily. Then Caroline, when he had finished, went to her study and wrote out a check. She brought it downstairs again and gave it to Higsby. He caught his breath.

"That is only the beginning," said Caroline. "There will be more. And I will establish a trust for your hopeless, your surely hopeless, foundation." She smiled grimly. "But we'll have tried, won't we?"

She folded her hands together and looked beyond him. "I've never taken any interest in my country until now. I never took any interest in anything until now. When it is too late, perhaps."

CHAPTER SIX

Before calling on his mother, John Sheldon first went to see his mother-in-law, Melinda Bothwell, who had a great affection for him. He did not deliberately take advantage of that affection, but he reached for it greedily. He everlastingly wanted to be liked, to be regarded fondly. It was like a protection which he urgently needed. Melinda always spoke to him kindly and tenderly, knowing his desperate need, and he basked in whatever she said and in her accepting presence. She knew how weak he was now; she only prayed that that weakness would not injure her daughter.

He laughed when she told him that her son Nathaniel had enlisted for an officers' training school. "He was always quixotic, wasn't he, Mother Bothwell?" said John. He resented Nathaniel's existence; he would inherit half of the Bothwell fortune, and Nathaniel did not particularly care about his brother-in-law.

Melinda looked at John gravely, her beautiful calm face showing no annoyance. "Quixotic? Perhaps. Both my children always had passions of devotion to something or other. It is their nature. Nathaniel is sure we'll be in this war; he wants to do his duty, he says. It is not that he's convinced this is a just war, but he wants to help his country if she needs him."

John shrugged and laughed again. For one instant he hoped that, in the event of a war, Nathaniel would be— He hurried away from the thought in his mind. Mimi would be brokenhearted. Then, as always, he was jealous. Mimi should have no other loves but himself.

"How is Mimi?" Melinda asked, understanding everything, and full of pity. John was so vital, so full of physical strength, so ruddy and imposing, and in many ways so intelligent. He did not have the intellect of his brother Ames, nor his appreciation for beauty. There was much of his mother in him.

"Splendid, splendid," said John. And then his hazel eyes hardened. "She is almost six months expecting, Mother Bothwell. Yet she is working all day and part of the night in preparation for her one-woman show in New York—just about the time the baby is due! I wish you'd speak to her; write to her."

"Why?" asked Melinda mildly. "That is a great part of her life, John. She is an authentic genius, though you don't seem to know it. Those two gold medals she's already received weren't given her because she is a Bothwell or because she is pretty!"

John covered his anger with an engaging, coaxing smile. "Oh, I know that. I'm not entirely a fool." But he thought: Mother Bothwell is an idiot, and though she is a very feminine woman she doesn't seem to understand that a woman should devote all her life to her husband and have nothing else in all the world but him. Even her children should be nothing in comparison. There were moments when he tightly resented, even disliked, his coming child. He only endured the thought of it, sure that his mother, in spite of everything, would make the child her heir.

"Her work is noted for its marvelous color, in particular," said Melinda. "You know what they say: power, depth, fervor, as well as drawing. No other living artist, some critics say, is able to get so intense a red, so living and so vital a yellow, so furious a blue."

"Well," said John. He sat with Melinda in the beautiful room overlooking the sea. It was particularly brilliant today, a passionate aquamarine. He had long known his defect and had hidden it, he thought, from everyone. It was only that damned Ames who knew. Like all those who had secret defects, he had made it wholly his own and had even come to regard it as valuable, or at least distinctive.

"Don't you think so?" Melinda said.

"I'm no art critic," said John with a beguiling expression and a carefully cultivated gesture of self-deprecation which always disarmed a potential critic or enemy.

"Of course not," said Melinda, whom he had, as usual, disarmed. "Do have some more tea, John."

He wanted a good sound whiskey before he saw his mother, but he never offended, even slightly, if he could help it. He accepted more tea, which he loathed, and with an air of gratitude that she could be so kind. "You know that Amy has left Ames?" he said.

"Yes."

John laughed. He knew Melinda's fondness for Amy and Amy's brothers and Amanda. "She should never have married him," he said. "That nice little girl." He did not think Amy "nice" at all. He thought her a stupid, vacuous little fool whose only virtue was her father's money.

"I agree that the marriage shouldn't have taken place," said Melinda. "It was disastrous for both of them. Ames is entirely too intellectual and too— finished—for Amy."

John was not sure that he liked this statement. He thought his brother a poseur, with all those "treasures" of his and his malicious insistence that John observe the delicate colorings of enamels or porcelain when he knew all the time—

Melinda looked at the watch on her breast. "Dear me, it's almost time for you to go to see your mother," she said. "Don't call for a cab. My own car is here, and Gregory will drive you to your mother's and then to the station."

"I don't know why she wants to see me," said John. "We haven't seen each other since Mimi and I were married. And she tried to prevent the marriage, at that."

"Perhaps she wants to talk about Mimi's show," said Melinda.

"I hardly think so," said John. "They haven't seen each other for ages."

Melinda smiled. When the car came for John she gave the young man her hand affectionately, but her large gray eyes were full of concern. She did not know why she said out of impulse, "Be kind to my child, John.

She is a dedicated artist; she had no choice in the matter. Do try to understand a little, won't you?"

John patted her hand. He always knew what to say, and now he said generously, looking into Melinda's eyes, "I try. I don't always succeed. I hope it's enough."

John had been greatly disturbed over the separation of Ames and Amy. His brother had blandly told him, smiling that subtle smile of his, "Now I'll soon be free to marry a healthy woman who'll give me children. Not that I like the little swine, but there is all Mama's money, you know."

Ames had seemed very complacent, like a white and slender cat of aristocratic breeding. He had looked at his brother with one of those infernal mysterious expressions of his.

"I thought the old lady had bribed you to marry Amy. I heard some rumors."

"You must never," said Ames, "credit rumors."

"But you seemed very damned prosperous after the marriage! In fact, the old lady as much as admitted to me that she bribed you to marry Amy. Everybody knew."

"I am not one to make public announcements," said Ames. He said with a glint in his cold slate-gray eyes, "I hope when I marry that I have a dozen children. I intend to marry a good breeder. With the exception of Mama, the family doesn't run to breeding. Even she had only three of us."

So Ames would soon be free again to marry—and have children who would inherit the great Ames fortune—Ames, whom John had thought would be eliminated.

As John was driven to his mother's house he began to have some sanguine thoughts, as he was a naturally optimistic young man. Had the old white hag repented? Was she going to announce a softening of her decision? What else could be the reason? She had done her worst to John. Anything else she could do would be for the better. He remembered her voice on the telephone, strange, faint, hesitating, almost questioning. His always buoyant spirits rose higher as he rang the bell at his mother's gates. When he saw her approach down the broken path, he noticed how old she had become, how slow and ponderous in movement, how laboring. Her head was bent. He had never seen it bent that way before, as if she were mortally tired. He wished she would look up to see his broad white smile. She did. He smiled wider, took off his hat, made his brightly colored face affectionate. "Mother!" he called to her.

Caroline paused on the path. She saw John through the gates, confident, smiling, appearing to be delighted to see her. It isn't the money, she thought; please God, it isn't the money. She knew the thought was foolish. When had it ever not been the money? But a starving man, seizing food given to him by an enemy for the enemy's own evil reasons, does not question. Let it be that I can reach him, she prayed.

Her lips moved. Was she actually smiling? thought John in astonishment. His thoughts ran quickly, plotting, arranging themselves, conjecturing.

Something was "up." He became a little confused, and he sweated under the August sun and was excited. He told himself to be careful, to watch her before speaking, to turn every word over before it was uttered. He remembered that his mother was no fool; it was almost impossible to deceive her. She couldn't have added so enormously to her father's fortune if she had been a fool. Yet, he thought, even people like his mother became senile, soft, open to cajolery, to false affirmations of concern. Look at old Brundage, a hard-fisted old Wall Streeter at eighty, hating his children, hating his wife, hating everyone. But one of his daughters, who had made a bad marriage, had, within a month of his death, so diddled him, so lavished hypocritical affection on him, so hovered about him, that he had made her his major heir. He had refused to see her for fifteen long years before that.

John thought: Maybe Mama wasn't as complacent about Amy's desertion of Ames as he had pretended. It's possible that she's up in the air and he was lying to me.

"I'm awfully glad to see you, Mother," he said with just the right amount of awkward sincerity in his voice as she unlocked the gates. He put on an embarrassed expression and looked aside. His mother's hand paused on the key. He knew that she was examining him, listening. Waiting. So that's it, he thought exultantly. But what "it" was, he did not quite know.

"Why are you glad to see me?" asked Caroline abruptly.

Under the same circumstances Ames would have said, "You sent for me, didn't you? You must have had a reason. It may even be a good reason!" Caroline would have understood that sourly. But John said with an impulsive flow of words, "After all, you're my mother, aren't you? I've missed you." Caroline knew it was a lie. Slowly she turned the key and in silence admitted her son.

He followed her up the path to the house, and he maintained a jocular and boyish air. He said to his mother's back, "A man likes to think he has some family. I wondered when you'd ask me to come."

"Did you?" said Caroline without turning.

He sat opposite his mother in the deathly living room. He had not been here for many months. It's like an abandoned cemetery, he thought. He remembered it as it had once been, full of firelight and lamplight and sun. For almost the first time since Tom's death he thought of his father. Poor devil. Poor ignorant devil.

"Mimi sends you her love, Mother," he said.

Caroline felt the hidden miniature which Mimi had given her warm against her heart, for now she wore it inside her clothing. "I suppose so," she murmured. Then she could not help herself: "Is she happy?" Caroline's voice rose. "You are not making her miserable?"

John looked at his mother and frowned. "Certainly she's happy, Mother. I wish you'd see her or let her come here to see you."

Caroline said, "She came here. Just recently. Didn't she tell you?"

"No." John smiled over his anger. So Mimi wasn't as open as he thought. Why hadn't she told him? "She likes her little secrets, like all women."

"And," said Caroline reluctantly, for she had not intended to ask this at all, "the baby. It will be born in December?"

"Yes." John brightened. "If it's a girl, would you like her named after you?"

"No," said Caroline.

John's brightness dimmed. His mother's tone had been harsh and firm. He could not know that the very thought of a child being named after her frightened her with something that was very like superstition. John said, "Mimi wants to call her Christina."

"Christina," said Caroline. The syllables seemed to cling to her heart as a child's fingers cling to one's hand. She smiled faintly. "A very nice name. And if it's a boy?"

"Thomas," said John promptly, thinking of that only at that very moment.

Caroline was silent. John was sure that he knew the way now; it was through Mimi. He was no longer angry with his wife. Why, the little devil was smart and cunning! She, too, had a nose for money.

"Her painting?" said Caroline.

John considered his mother. He shrugged and said lightly, "She still plays around with her paints. Even now. She wants to have a show just before the baby is born. It's true that I don't know very much about art"—and he watched his mother warily—"but it's also true that Mimi isn't a real artist—that is, of any importance—though she's received some recognition and even some money. If she were an important artist she'd be wallowing in gold bills."

Caroline's broad face was closed. She thought of her grandfather, David Ames. And then she studied her son sharply. Did he value everything only in terms of money? But, she said to herself, I have always been that way, always, except for my grandfather's paintings. Why should I expect something different from my sons? Her eyes left John and stared desolately at a distant window.

How can I reach him, she asked herself, if there is anything there to reach? What words can I say to him to ask his forgiveness, to beg for some affection, to explain that all my life was a victimization and I crave his pity for what I am and for what I did to my children? How does one say this to one's children in one's old age, especially if one never knew how to use words?

"I think," said Caroline, "that Mary is a true artist and that someday she'll be famous."

John sat up, smiling brilliantly. "If you say so, then it must be so, Mother."

"Why do you say that?" she asked with disconcerting sharpness.

"Well. You have your gallery; you've had it for years."

Caroline paused. She tested him. "Would you like to see it?"

She hoped that he would say, "If you want to show it to me, but I know nothing about it. You see, I can't distinguish color at all; I'm color-blind."

If he had that honesty, some of her anguish would leave; she would then have a way to reach him.

But John shone like the sun. "I'd love it! I've always wanted to see it! Ames told me of the—the color, the vitality, the meaning."

It's no use, thought Caroline. What a fool I am.

Desolation, like death, filled every portion of her sick body. In other years she would have said to John, "You are lying. You could not see the colors in those paintings." But now she was full of compassion. She said almost gently, "I'm sorry. But I'm afraid I'm too tired today to climb the stairs. By the way, did Ames tell you that my paintings were done by David Ames, who was your great-grandfather?"

"Yes," said John. He was glum. At least, thought Caroline, he is being unconsciously honest now. Ames has told him of the Boston Museum, and he is resenting it. She began to lean toward him when John forced a large white smile. "I'm glad about the Museum, Mother. Of course you are quite right in leaving those paintings to it."

Caroline was not angry. She said wryly, "I'm glad you think so. They are extremely valuable now. You know that Mimi has seen them? I am leaving two to her, the ones she admired most." And one, thought Caroline, is of your and her grandfather, the blind man who would not remove his blindness, because he was a coward and he was afraid.

She made one last effort. "Do you remember your father very often, John?"

John studied her. The old white hag had hated her husband, had despised him, had made her children despise him also. He said with an air of great candor, "Frankly, not often. He wasn't a man of much character, was he? Ineffectual, simple. Of course I'm grateful that he left me half his money."

Caroline held back her pain. "He used to pamper you," she said.

John suddenly remembered something. He must have been only four then. He had been wandering about the garden, which had form in those days, and order. For him, however, the greens and reds had not existed, nor the yellows and blues. He had been a restless and vital child and was always wandering. And then he had come on a large snake, a harmless one, but it had terrified him. He had screamed. Tom, sitting in an arbor, smoking, had come to him at once, in great bounds. Tom had caught him up in his arms, had talked to him soothingly and laughingly. The snake would not harm him; it was a poor innocent creature. Besides, his father was here, wasn't he? Nothing could hurt him while his father was here. Tom's arms were strong and warm; his bare brown throat had been strong and warm too. His kisses were full of reassurance and tenderness. The little boy had huddled in his father's arms, safe and protected, and he had loved Tom then.

Tom had carried him into the house. Caroline was there, in the living room, reading one of her financial reports. Tom had affectionately told her the story. She had dropped the report in her large lap and had looked at Tom with resigned impatience. "Oh, Tom," she had said, and John, after all these years, could hear the young and disgusted voice, "don't treat him like a baby. He's a big boy now, too old for kisses and slaverings. Do put him down; I'll ring for Beth. He should be having his supper now."

Tom had instantly put John down. John had helplessly, and in terror, resented it. He had stared at his father. Tom looked crushed, beaten. Caroline was smiling darkly. A strong, contemptuous smile. Then John had despised his father for the first time. But more than all else, the little boy had felt betrayed, naked, bewildered, vengeful, unloved. John now remembered that he had begun to scream and that when old Beth had carried him up the stairs he was still screaming. He remembered the devastating sensation of desertion, of fear. Even now he did not know why.

He jumped to his feet and went away from his mother. He went to one of the smudged windows where Ames had stood only a week ago. He looked out at the ruined garden, the bursting and struggling trees, the wild vegetation. His heart was thumping furiously. He thought of Mimi, and he was enraged. Her damned art! A shocking rage came to him, blinding him.

Why was John standing there at the window, staring out? Caroline asked herself. She had only mentioned that Tom had pampered his older son. Yet he was standing there, rigid, as Ames had stood, and his profile, much larger and heavier than Ames', had Ames' sudden whiteness and intensity. Always sensitive to fear, Caroline could feel John's fear.

Then she knew something else. Her older son, so bulky, so apparently puissant and strong, was innately weak, vulnerable, helpless, confused. He was a man; in character, he was a child. Somewhere in his soul he had stopped growing. He had kept his childishness, his dangerous childishness.

"John!" she exclaimed.

She has abandoned me, John thought, my wife has abandoned me, her husband. I need her, but she's rejected me. She's let me go so easily. I thought she was strong and sure and could help me. He felt exposed again, vulnerable, frightened, vaguely terrified. And vengeful. Above all, vengeful, for being deserted.

"He was no good," said John. "He would never stand up against anything."

"What are you talking about?" asked Caroline, feeling her son's confusion, his darkness of mind. "Do you mean your father? He was the best man I've ever known, the kindest——"

John laughed vaguely. "I'm sorry. I was thinking of something. It isn't important." He went back to his chair. "Don't be upset. You don't look well. Have you been to a doctor recently?"

"I didn't ask you to come to discuss my health, John," said Caroline. No? said John inwardly. What then?

"I thought we might have a talk," said Caroline, knowing it was no use at all.

"Certainly," said John, as if he understood.

"I'm not young any longer," said Caroline.

John remembered old Brundage and was elated. "Of course you're not," he said in his rich and soothing voice. "This house, for instance, is too much for you. Your business is in New York. There is a house for sale next to ours, a gem of a house——"

"No," said Caroline.

John went on with an assumption of great eagerness: "Mimi would be there, and I know now how fond you are of each other. And there will be the baby."

Yes, thought Caroline, Mary would want me, but she has always had love. My son has not had love, not from his mother, his brother and sister. John would like to have me in New York, where he believes that he could influence me for his own good.

"I've lived here too long," said Caroline. "People my age don't move so easily. A change of environment can be distressful."

What did the old hag want of him? John asked himself. It couldn't be that she wanted some demonstration of affection in her old age, as he, John, had hoped. She had said no to everything he had suggested; she was still like iron, immovable, dull. He was depressed and restless. He wanted to leave this hideous place. Why was she looking at him so hard, so piercingly?

"I'd like to know that you and Mary——" said Caroline, and stopped.

John was eager again. "We're splendid," he said. "Why don't you visit us and see for yourself?"

I'd like to know that Mary truly loves you, my son, thought Caroline, and accepts what you are without resentment or misunderstanding.

"Let me know when the baby is born," she said. She was so very tired.

John took hope from that. She was interested, actually interested, in his coming child. Her first grandchild. Who knew? The thought elated him again. He could even, without taking much thought beforehand and with an air of boyish affection, take his mother's arm and lead her out to the gate. Caroline could feel the warmth of his flesh through his sleeve and hers, and his flesh was hers, but it was the flesh of an absolute stranger separated from her forever.

He waved to her gaily from the automobile, and she saw the false gesture and the hearty false smile. And the disappointed eyes. I promised him nothing; I gave him nothing, thought Caroline, I've done that for him today, at least.

She was no longer afraid for Mimi; she was only afraid for John. There was strength in the young wife; there was no real strength or fortitude in the husband. "Be kind, Mary, to my son, in your youth and strength. Be kind to him, for I have never been kind."

Caroline went into her house, and it was silent and filled with the smell of dissolution. "Oh, God!" she groaned to the silence and the emptiness. "Oh my God, have mercy on me!"

Caroline, the next morning, early, was called to the telephone. Ames said to her in a light and bantering voice, "Have you read your newspaper this morning?"

"I was about to do so," said Caroline, "when you interrupted me. Is there something that might be of interest?"

Ames laughed. "Yes indeed. Dear Cousin Timothy died late last night." He chuckled. He could hear his mother's sharp breathing. "Do you want me to send flowers in both our names, Mama?"

"No," said Caroline. "Not in mine."

"Pathetic, isn't it?" said Ames. "You'll find a very distinguished photograph of my father-in-law on the first page, with a magnificent eulogy. 'Of the famous Esmond family, distinguished not only in Boston but in the capitals of Europe. Distinguished this, distinguished that. First Families. The funeral is on Friday. You won't be attending, of course."

"Don't be a fool," said Caroline. She thought: So one enemy is less in the world; one of the terrible has died. "Of what did he die, if you know?"

"Oh, I know. I was respectful enough to call at the house, though I didn't see Amanda or Amy. Just Henry. He was doing the honors and he looked at me as though I had personally murdered his dear father. News travels in Boston. Though it was so early, the whole damn street was full of automobiles and the carriages of the old pussies. The old pussies shied at the sight of me and lifted their circa 1880 bombazine and black silks as if I was manufacturing mud."

"Why did you go?" asked Caroline.

"Darling Mama, have you forgotten, and you a Miss Stockington girl? Don't you remember Boston? If I hadn't made a properly grave appearance today I'd have had to move out of the city soon. I'm a scoundrel, they all think, but they can stomach scoundrels who make money and are of good family. But they can't stomach anyone who flouts one of their mossy conventionalities. Amy's deserted me, and as her mother was a Bothwell, Amy cannot possibly have been even slightly in the wrong or culpable. Amy's on the market again, or will be in the near future, and so will I. Young love—and money—you know."

"You haven't told me what caused Timothy to die. He looked well enough when I saw him, though he had had that stroke."

Ames' chuckle was louder. "Oh, he had another stroke." He paused. "Immediately after you left his house. It's all over the city that you'd been there; possibly servants have been gabbling. So you are the villainess, Mama. You killed Timothy."

"What nonsense," said Caroline.

"Why, Mama. Don't you know people now, at your age? Certainly they are crediting it. You see dear Cousin Timothy; he has an immediate stroke; he dies of it last night. Very simple. Everyone's quite excited. I haven't seen so much excitement in Boston since old Henry Fromage hanged himself three years ago. Aren't you upset?"

"Not in the least," said Caroline. "I would advise you not to go to the funeral. That would be hypocrisy."

"It would be flouting convention again. Certainly I will go to the funeral."

He laughed with delight. He was still laughing when Caroline put the receiver back on its hook. Yes, she thought, I am glad. As long as he lived he was a threat. She considered Amanda and Amy and the good sons. She had never written a real note of condolence in her life, but now she did.

CHAPTER SEVEN

Late in September, as she was working in her study, Caroline, without any warning of previous depression or any increase in her slowly growing tiredness, suddenly felt a sudden and overwhelming loathing for living, for existence, for being, for merely being present on the earth. It appeared to come from outside herself rather than from her own spirit. She put down her pen slowly; it fell from her fingers and rolled, smearing, over her neat ledger.

She was battered as by waves of some dark horror, some profound list-lessness, some mighty aversion and turning away from life, from everything that meant life. She studied it objectively while her mouth and lips dried and her heart, as if aroused from some secure cave, felt the presence of an enemy. She was, all at once, interested in nothing at all—the day, the hour, her money, her ledgers, herself, her pains, the world fast rolling into convulsions. She pushed aside her financial magazines and newspapers; she closed her ledgers. Then she stood up and went to the window and looked at the calm and smiling ocean.

Living, she thought, has never brought me any joy or satisfaction. But this is quite different. This is a repudiation of life. All men share it with me at different times; millions, perhaps, are now sharing it with me at this very moment. How can we, at these times, bear to go on living? "He who hates his life in this world . . ." Where had she heard that, a long time ago? She pondered. Beth, of course, who had read those very words of Christ's to her in the Bible almost half a century ago. Something else, however, was missing—the last of the sentence. There was no Bible in this house; suddenly she wanted to know it all, and what it meant.

A feeling of awful, black confusion came to her, and terror. "You haven't given me Your grace," she said aloud, and bitterly. "I asked You, but it never came." She thought of the priest in Boston. Half stumbling, she went to her telephone and called his rectory, and she did not even pause for a moment to consider how extraordinary this was for Caroline Ames. When the priest answered she said with abruptness and urgency, "You may remember me. I was in your study some weeks ago. I didn't tell you my name, but I came to you for some kind of help and you spoke about the grace of God. But I'm not calling about that now. I've just remembered something from childhood, about hating one's life—I don't know. Can you tell me?"

"Yes, Mrs. Sheldon," said the priest. "Hello? Yes, I knew your name. I overheard the chauffeur mention it. Will you wait a moment? I want to read it to you in its entirety."

He didn't sound surprised; he didn't sound confused; he just accepted it, thought Caroline with gratitude.

The quiet and accepting voice sounded in her ear again. "St. John, Chapter 12:24: 'Amen, amen, I say to you, unless the grain of wheat falls into the ground and dies it remains alone. But if it dies, it brings forth much fruit. He who loves his life, loses it; and he who hates his life in this world keeps it unto life everlasting . . . Now my soul is troubled. And what shall I say? Father, save me from this hour! No, this is why I came to this hour. Father, glorify Thy Name!'"

The priest paused. "Do you want me to explain the words of Our Lord?"

Caroline said, "No. Repeat it to me again, please."

He did so. Then the priest said, "You are very troubled, aren't you? You are experiencing what all of us experience, sometimes only once in our lives, sometimes very often. But you are not alone."

Caroline said, "I must think about it." She hesitated. "I've asked for that—grace—but it didn't come."

"I think it's come to you now," said the priest.

"Thank you," said Caroline brusquely. "Good day."

She sat at her desk and stared blankly before her, and the awfulness of what she had experienced began to retreat. She thought of what the priest had read to her; somewhere, hidden in her brain or perhaps her spirit, something had been planted, something still in its hard husk but something alive and waiting. It was as if her first overpowering emotions had been a crude spade which had dug into earth for the thing that had been planted a little later.

It was not calmness that came to her, but a quietude. I'll have to wait, she thought. The time came for her digitalis, and she forgot it. She sat and looked before her. At last, sighing, she returned to her ledgers and then her newspapers. Then she was blank again. They meant nothing at all to her just now. Her telephone rang and she answered it with impatience.

"Madam?" said a man's voice. "This is Griffith."

There had been so few times during which she had felt warmth and response in all her life. But she said quickly, "Griffith. Of course. Is there anything wrong?"

"I'm afraid so, madam." The devoted man hesitated. "I don't like to disturb you; I know how busy you are."

"No," said Caroline. "I'm not busy. I don't think I ever was really."

I sound mad, she thought immediately. But like that priest, Griffith accepted her extraordinary words with simplicity. "Tell me," she said.

"It began, I think, last spring. That was the first time Mr. Sheldon spoke of it, and he was irritated. After all, he's only a young man still, too young for spectacles. His eyes were blurring, he said. I made him an old mixture, of boric acid with just a little salt in water, and he washed his eyes with it.

I believe it helped him a little. But not his headaches. He bought a bottle of that new drug, aspirin. That was last spring. He took only a few tablets occasionally, but now he buys a bottle every few days."

He stopped, for his voice had become distressed. Caroline's instincts, always ready for flight and fear, rushed in on her. "Yes, yes!" she exclaimed. "Go on."

"He is never ill, madam. An extraordinary constitution; not even a chill occasionally. I suggested a doctor a week ago for his headaches. He thought it very amusing. But he went to one this morning. He must have been suffering. He returned this afternoon. He sat in his *objets d'art* room for a long time. When he came out—madam, I say this without exaggeration—he seemed desperate. He left the house; he did not even speak to me when I asked him what he wished for dinner. He appeared to be—running—madam. I'm not a man given to exaggeration——"

"The doctor's name?" said Caroline sharply.

"An eye physician, madam. Dr. Irving Shapiro. I overheard the conversation on the telephone when he made the appointment."

"I will call him at once. Thank you," said Caroline, and hung up the receiver.

She reached for the telephone book, then her hand was paralyzed with terror. Ames. Her most unlovable son; her son who was incapable of love. He had nowhere to go for the love he needed. She, his mother, had never told him of love and that it was in the world somewhere. "He appeared to be—running—desperate." She forced herself to find the doctor's number, and all her flesh was shaking, rippling, with a horrible cold. Ames was not an emotional man; he did not "run." He was self-assurance itself. "Is he?" said Caroline aloud as she waited for the doctor to answer. "Is anyone?"

She said at once to Dr. Shapiro: "I am the mother of Ames Sheldon. I am Mrs. Caroline Ames Sheldon. Let us not waste time, Doctor. There is something the matter with my son's eyes. I must know."

Dr. Shapiro said in a professional voice: "I can't divulge—Mrs. Sheldon." He paused, then remembered that this woman was Caroline Ames, the incredibly wealthy recluse, and not some frightened, obscure mother. She could command senators, bankers, the whole world, with her money. But still, he was a young man full of integrity and professional ethics. "I suggest you ask Mr. Sheldon himself."

"Let us not be stupid, Doctor," said Caroline, raising her voice. "My son and I rarely see each other. But I am his mother; he has no one else. If he needs help, I am the one who can give it. Who else? Haven't you a mother yourself? Wouldn't she want to know about you?"

As Dr. Shapiro had a very tender mother he forgot all about professional ethics and the sacred right of patients to privacy. He even forgot that he was speaking to the formidable Caroline Ames. His cool voice warmed. "I confess," he said, trying to retain some formality, "that I was a little anxious about his reaction. Of course shock is natural, in these cases, for everyone. But Mr. Sheldon, in a way, reacted differently. It was as if——"

He stopped. "As if he had suddenly made up his mind"—the doctor coughed —"to die."

Caroline was silent; her throat became like stone.

"I tried to help him," said Dr. Shapiro. "I told him to get another opinion, perhaps in Rochester, perhaps in New York. This is too serious for one opinion alone, though I am positive——"

"What is wrong with my son?" Caroline said in a dwindled voice.

"I am afraid, Mrs. Sheldon, that he has a brain tumor. He will soon be blind. I told him. We don't often operate on the brain, you know. One of the forbidden chambers still, like the heart. Someday, perhaps—— Of course there have been some rare operations. The Egyptians—but still we don't know if the patients survived."

Ames. Blind. Ames, who saw all beauty through his eyes; his treasures, the rare paintings he bought, his rugs, furniture. Blind. "Oh, God," Caroline said.

"I told him," said the young doctor with compassion, "that perhaps he should see his clergyman. He laughed at me."

"Of course," said Caroline in a voice like a groan. "How long——"

"The tumor will grow. There's no way of finding out if it's benign or malignant unless the skull is opened. In any event, it will——"

"Kill him," Caroline broke in. "How long will that take?"

"If benign, perhaps many months after he is blind. If malignant, only a short time."

"There's no surgeon who can help him?"

"Mrs. Sheldon, I think there is one, the best I know. I've read reports of his operations. Amazing. If the tumor is benign, of course. But he is interned in Canada; he's a German, and there's the war in Europe. He's in Toronto."

"His name?" asked Caroline.

"Dr. Moritz Manz. He had his own clinic in Berlin and came to Canada before the war to demonstrate to colleagues. But——"

"Thank you," said Caroline, and replaced the telephone receiver. She called Griffith and said, "When my son returns—and I don't care what time it is, for I won't go to bed—you must tell him to call me at once. At once."

Then she called Higsby Chalmers. "Higsby," she said without a salutation, "my son Ames has a tumor of the brain. There is a man who can help him, a Dr. Moritz Manz, a German interned now in Canada. Toronto. I want him here to operate on my son."

"Caroline!" exclaimed Higsby, much perturbed. "Oh, I'm sorry to hear this about Ames! But a German, and interned. I don't think it's possible. I can't see how——"

"My son," said Caroline. She wiped sweat from her forehead with the back of her hand. Ames! "Oh, God," she said. "Higsby, I want that surgeon here; I want him in Boston. I don't know how you can arrange it, but arrange it you must. That senator I helped elect, what is his name? Never mind telling me! Let him go to the White House. The President has invited me many times. I don't care how it is done! Ames—he will go blind and die. Unless I can get that Dr. Manz."

"Caroline, there is Dr. Cushing——"

"I want Dr. Manz!" shouted Caroline. "Get him, Higsby! Call your politicians. Move anything, anyone. My son will die, do you hear me?"

"I will do what I can," said Higsby in distress.

"You will do it," said Caroline harshly. "You must do it. I want no excuses. I want no pleas about a war. There is that matter of a $500,000,000 loan between the British and French governments and American bankers; it will come up soon, and it is to be signed in the offices of J. P. Morgan. I know Mr. Morgan well; he is the only American in favor of that loan. All others are against it." She paused. "I am too."

Higsby was silent in the face of that huge implied threat. A Caroline Ames could do even more: she could wreck the frightened stock market. She had many associates in America and Europe. There was a great deal she could do.

"We are a neutral country, aren't we?" said Caroline with an almost violent rage. "Let us not waste time. I want Dr. Manz in America as fast as possible. How or with whom you can arrange it, I don't know. I don't care. But he must come."

"I will try," said Higsby. "That is all I can promise, Caroline."

"Do not try," said Caroline. "Do not promise. The man must come. Good day, Higsby."

"Caroline, please listen," said Higsby. There was no answer. He put the receiver down, troubled and anxious. Then he picked it up again.

Caroline walked down the broken sea walk in the cool, bright September sunlight, in the great silence of the land, in the murmurous voice of the ocean. She stopped on the shingle and looked about her, and suddenly she saw the brilliant glory of the blue water and the vivid burning of the deep blue sky. They came to her like a shock, like a discovery. She had not seen them for many years. She had never really seen them at all since she was a child.

To be blind. Not to see. To grope in darkness. Not to see this little gray and marvelous shell at her feet; not to see the way the incoming tide threw long and bubbling foam on the sand, the color of breaking silver. Not to know the way the watery horizon tumbled in and upon itself in turquoise, streaked with rose, veined in white, vaporous with azure. Not to watch the manner in which the radiant clouds formed vast images of men and castles and unearthly caverns and mountainous gods and racing horses and walls of light. She bent and lifted a handful of sand and watched the endless tiny colors rush between her fingers, scarlet, gray, rose, pale blue, green, gold. A little stone—smooth and full of a thousand hues. A piece of driftwood, pale and carved by water into the shape of a sleek crouching cat. The sea grass, gray and green. The pines, gray and green also, valorous against the wide luminescence, the majestic loneliness of earth and heaven. Not to see the simplest thing—and it, itself, the very core of wonder and mystery.

Then, without warning, something spoke in Caroline. "But you, too, have been blind. You haven't seen or looked for many years. You have been like your father in your grandfather's painting; you have willfully blinded yourself with fear. There are many kinds of blindness, but yours has been the worst."

Yes, thought Caroline, that has been the worst. There was everything for me to see, but I refused to see it. Because I was afraid. Because I preferred to see darkness. I walled myself against the sight of a tree or a stone, a face or a blade of grass, a cloud or a leaf. I was afraid of the emotion they might bring, and the understanding. I had to have my blindness because I was afraid. Shall I blame my father because he cut off my sight? No. That priest was right. God will not accept a plea that others sinned against us. We sin against ourselves, deliberately. And against Him. We refuse to see Him, the Lord our God. Yet He is all about us, visible, if only we look and know.

She looked at the sky and said, "Dear God, have mercy on us, Your deliberately blind, and show us the light. Have mercy on us. Lord, have mercy. Christ, have mercy."

She waited. God had not given her His grace. Not yet. She looked about her and saw His grace and felt it within her. "He who hates his life in this world . . ." His stupid, foolish, tragic, blundering, wicked, blind life. She knew now. She had only to ask to be given.

She went back to her deathly house. She would find a way for Ames, her son, her crippled son. He was calling for her when she came into the living room, and she went upstairs to her study.

"What is it, Mother?" he asked lightly. "There seems to be some emergency, according to Griffith."

"You," said Caroline, and told him.

"You will do this for me?" he asked.

"I will do anything for you. My son," said Caroline.

There was no answer. Then Caroline heard his breath, fast and shallow. "For me?" he said.

"For you."

Another silence. "May I ask," said Ames, "where all this maternal solicitude has come from so suddenly?"

"I deserve that," said Caroline. She spoke in a louder voice. "But you also deserve a lot that has happened to you. You aren't a victim, Ames. You have had plenty of opportunities to be different from what you are. I am not going to take the sole responsibility. No more, now, than I blame my father for everything that I am. I had had opportunities too."

Still another silence, longer than the others. Ames finally said, "I won't be blind. I will kill myself first."

"Let us wait," said Caroline. "A man can always die. It is the living that requires stamina. Are you entirely without courage?"

"No," said Ames. "I think not. And then I think so. But I'll wait."

"You must," said Caroline, making her voice hard and brusque. "We all have to do that. Only cowards don't wait."

"I'll wait," said Ames.

CHAPTER EIGHT

On October 15 Dr. Moritz Manz crossed the border at Buffalo and went at once to Boston, to Sisters of Charity Hospital, where Ames Sheldon was waiting for him, and Caroline also.

The new tests were all ready for him, and the X rays and the blood tests. He was a little fat man with a tiny goatee on his round and rosy face. He had shining blue eyes behind his glasses and an air of brisk competence. His small nose was as pink as a rose, and his big skull was completely bald. He spent several hours examining his patient, who occupied a large suite of luxurious rooms. He had a lordly air and was autocratic to all the nurses and Sisters, who seemed larger than himself. These big American women! But then, all woman always seemed larger than his small self. He was very fastidious. He called for many things and many instruments. He tested, then tested again. His patient, he observed, this son of a famous mother, appeared to find him a little ludicrous, and this was strange, considering the misery in his gray eyes. The smiling and the faint laughter were all about the lips only. Dr. Manz made large gestures to compensate for his size, and he had a larger voice which filled all the corridors. The doctor felt defensive for several hours, until he discovered that the Sisters and the staff and the nurses had only kindness and respect for him, and no disgust or aversion for him as a "murderous" German.

He lost considerable of his pomposity. Finally, as this was a very warm October day, he took off his coat, which hung to his knees, and he was a physician face to face with a desperate emergency. He had found that many of the Sisters had been born in Germany, and he conversed with them. He had been told that Americans were completely barbarous, but he found the medical staff very competent and serious. They did not speak of the war, not even once. Dr. Manz expanded. He was a Jew and not always liked, even if always reverenced, and he basked in this atmosphere of goodness and acceptance, this eagerness to help, this anxiety over a patient. It was so—personal. One did not usually encounter this, and it warmed him.

He said to the Reverend Mother, who was also a surgeon and had been born in Germany, "These X rays, Mother. I do not find them superior. I should like more."

"Of a certainty, *Herr Doktor*. At once. Will you preside?" She added, "This is a great honor to us, for you to be here, *Herr Doktor*."

He smiled, and he looked like a gentle gnome. "I do not know how it was done, but it was done. I was very astonished. Ah, one does not know what goes on in the world, does one?"

"Very occasionally," said the Reverend Mother. "But only occasionally."

"One must trust in God," said Dr. Manz.

Ames, listening, and thinking this was all like a formal minuet, said in precise German, "I am not merely a specimen, *Herr Doktor*. I am concerned in this also."

The Reverend Mother and Dr. Manz looked at him with kind severity. "Have we forgotten?" asked Dr. Manz. "Are we not here for you, Herr Sheldon? What else? We were speaking of God. At the last, we must bow before the Great Physician and await His verdict."

"Of a certainty," said the Reverend Mother.

"Amen," said Ames. "I only hope He has not turned His thumb down." They ignored this remark.

"I came," said Dr. Manz, "incognito. I have never before been in America, Reverend Mother, and I have colleagues here with whom I have corresponded. I wished to meet them. It is now impossible. Those were the conditions. I do not understand many things, but I was given an order to come. I am a medical officer; I hold the rank of colonel. Hundreds of poor young men with torn heads need me; it is to break the heart to see them when they are brought to me for operation. They look at me—their eyes. I do not say, 'Are you a Frenchman or an Englishman or a German?' I, who am a bachelor, say to them, 'Do not fear, my son. God is close at hand, and He will help me, for you are His child also.' This war! One does not understand it. One is never told."

He sighed, and as he was a sentimental man, he wiped his eyes with a flourish, but there was a sternness about his mouth.

"So we shall operate as soon as I have seen the new X rays which we shall take." He smiled at Ames, who was lying tautly in his narrow bed. "You must not be afraid, young Herr Sheldon. You must have faith."

Ames began to smile; his face was very pale. Then he said, "If anyone can help me, it is you, *Herr Doktor*." He seemed surprised at his own words. He continued, "I ask only one thing: if it is malignant and I must go blind, do not let me become conscious again. Let me die."

The Reverend Mother caught her breath. Dr. Manz said, "I am a doctor, not an executioner." He pointed to the crucifix on the wall. "Contemplate that. He was a man not much older than you. He could have willed not to hang there, but He chose it, it is said. For you. Contemplate it."

The new X rays were taken, and only the awe of the staff kept them from expressing human exasperation, for Dr. Manz was meticulous and excessively thorough. "This angle, ah. And that. Just a little, two millimeters; careful. And now it must be this. Lift. Drop." He did not wait for the plates to dry; he held them, dripping, up to a strong light and studied them, and the staff exchanged glances. Then he said briskly, "Prepare the patient for operation. Immediately. It is a tumor."

It was as if a death sentence had been given. A deep silence stood over the staff while Ames was being wheeled from the room. Then one of the doctors raised his voice and started to speak slowly and carefully. "I speak the English also," said Dr. Manz with a noble gesture. "I am no illiterate.

You were saying? Ah. Is there a possibility the patient will survive?" He touched the left side of his head, near his ear. "It is there, too close to the centers of speech. Another week, another month—— No, I do not know if it is benign or malignant, but I have studied the blood. The potassium is not above normal, so there is a good possibility that it is benign, that ugly tumor. I have done much research on this. The optic nerves are in great difficulty, but the patient is young. Of a certainty, if it is benign and there has not been too much injury to the delicate tissues, the patient will survive and he will not be blind."

"The whole staff of surgeons and neurologists will be present, *Herr Doktor*," said the Reverend Mother. "Do not be alarmed; we will be discreet, though they all know you are here."

"How was it possible to see the tumor, Doctor?" asked a surgeon.

"It is a matter of instinct, of recognizing the faintest of shadows. I cannot explain it," said Dr. Manz with large simplicity. "But I am not wrong often. I am in the process of preparing a dye to be injected in the carotid artery and have done interesting experimentation on animals. If it had not been for this war, when one must do gross work! There is a matter, too, of a certain gas with which I am experimenting. The dye and the gas will outline a tumor so it can be seen clearly on the plates. Until I have them, I must move by instinct. I must consider objective symptoms, few though they are, from the history, from the eye examinations."

He went into the large and sunlit living room of the suite where Caroline was waiting for him. He had met her briefly on his arrival. He took her hands in his own little fat ones and pressed them warmly, bending over her. He thought her magnificent; there were older ladies at Court like this, stern and still and plain. One could always recognize aristocracy. He bent over her and said, "Dear lady, this is an occasion of courage for you. I have decided to operate as soon as your son is prepared."

"He has the tumor?" Caroline spoke quietly in her impeccable German.

"Unfortunately, yes. A little longer and he should have been blind, or he should have had a stroke from the squeezing of the blood vessels. I can promise you I shall do my best. More, I cannot promise."

"Is it malignant, do you think?"

He admired her great calm, but he saw how alive and brilliant her eyes were, so purely hazel streaked with gold. What young eyes, what a soul!

"Ah, dear lady, that I do not know until I have opened the skull and see with my two eyes."

"But, so young, if it is cancer." Caroline bent her head a little.

"Frau Sheldon, it is not something which others care to face. Cancer is no respecter of persons or age. Many children have that evil thing, but the people do not want to know it. At this time, one person in thirty-five will have it and possibly die of it. Twenty years ago it was one in fifty or less. It is increasing. One day, I am afraid, the ratio will increase. We conquer one destroyer to see the rise of another, perhaps more deadly. Why this is so is inscrutable. Nature, too, is no respecter of persons. We can only struggle with her for our survival, which at the end is not in her hands but in God's. I have always considered that we live in a vortex of mysteries."

"If it is cancer?"

"Then he will not only be blinded but will be paralyzed, and he will die. Mercifully, it does not take long. On the other hand, if it is benign he will be perfect again after removal. He is being prepared; before he subsides under drugs, you will wish to see him."

Caroline stood up, and the doctor ceremoniously offered her his arm. But she shook her head. "I must see him alone."

Nurses were already shaving Ames' pale fine hair when his mother entered his room. He hardly seemed aware of them; he was looking straight before him, and his white face had a dwindled appearance, tight and small and hard. Caroline said, "I should like to see my son alone for a few moments, if you please." Ames did not look up or turn to her even when the nurses had left the room.

Caroline stood beside his bed. She said, "All that can be done shall be done, Ames. The rest——"

"I know," he said in a cramped and vicious tone, "is in the hands of God."

Very slowly he turned his suffering head on his long thin neck and looked at her, and he smiled his cold and mocking smile. "Really, Mama! Is this really you?"

"Yes. It is I."

"Astonishing," he said. "I'd not have believed it."

"Believe it," said his mother.

"But why this simple piety? If I remember correctly, you used to sneer at my father's unsophistication, as you called it. You would not permit him to take us to church."

"I was a fool, and I was stupid," said Caroline. "I don't expect to be forgiven for it, not by God, and not by you. I can only confess it."

Ames narrowed his lilting eyes at her, and then he stopped smiling.

"Mama, you've changed. I don't know what it is, but you're not the same. Astonishing. Have you been 'born again,' as old Beth used to call it?"

"I don't know," said Caroline heavily. "Laugh at me if it amuses you. I deserve it."

Ames pursed his lips judiciously and looked solemn, and Caroline sighed. What had she hoped for: that she might reach him? He was laughing inwardly at her, and she knew it. He rubbed his tortured left temple reflectively.

"Is this sermon supposed to give me 'courage'?" He leaned back on his pillows. His senses began to float as the drugs acted upon him.

"I was a fool to think it might. But I do want you to know this: The blindness that threatened you opened my own eyes. I was blind; I am beginning to see again."

"Because of—this?"

"Yes. Because of many other things too."

"It couldn't just be approaching old age, could it?"

"I think not," said Caroline wearily. Ames yawned. The drugs were be-musing him, but his inner mirth still chuckled silently. Caroline said, "I'd like to kiss you, Ames."

"Kiss me?" He began to laugh a little. "Why?"

"Because," said Caroline, "I love you. I didn't love you before, but I do now."

The slate-gray eyes fixed themselves in real surprise on her. "Could it be detestable pity?"

"No. I don't know. I think it is just—love."

"An interesting emotion, I've heard. Well, if you'd like, kiss me then."

Caroline bent stiffly. Her dry lips touched his forehead; it was cold with sweat, and she knew how afraid he was, and all at once she was stabbed with pain. She took his face in her hands and she kissed his cheek. "It will be all right!" she cried, and her eyes were wet. "Believe it. It will be all right! I'm here, Ames."

He started to say something, and then he stared at her. She could not understand that narrowed and thoughtful look. He said, really gently, "I hope so. I think you hope so too."

"I'd give you my life if I could," said his mother, and left the room. The waiting nurses returned. She looked at them helplessly. When she went back to the sitting room Dr. Manz was not there. And now she must wait. She had such a fortune, and she could do nothing but wait in this pleasant room where all the furniture had taken on the distorted shapes and shad-ows of anguish. She heard them wheel Ames out; she heard his voice, hu-morous and light. A nurse answered with respectful laughter.

Caroline had called John that morning. He had pretended great concern and solicitude. She knew he felt neither. He said he would come up that night or the next day. But Ames might be dead by then, she had thought. She could only wait in loneliness and torment, as she had waited all her life. All that waiting, in barrenness and emptiness, and without a point. At least she had a reason now. How did one pray? How did one ask God for mercy, for intimate compassion? What were the words, the always difficult words? She could only say in herself: Please let it be well. Please. I don't even know how to ask You to be kind to my son, when I was never kind to him and never told him anything at all of importance.

There was no one in all the world who would come to her, who would comfort her. She was absolutely alone. There was none she could call who would care about this, not one. She had no friends anywhere in the world. Nor, she thought, had Ames. Word about the children of Caroline Ames, or anything in connection with Caroline Ames, automatically flew about the world. But no one had called; no one had cared about Ames Sheldon or his mother.

Caroline sat upright, thinking. But what of all Ames' "friends" in Boston, the members of his club, the First Families who knew him, and their sons and daughters? He was part of the "gay" set, as they called themselves, and went "everywhere." Yet none had called, none had cared. I can understand about myself, thought Caroline, for I have never pretended to be other than what I was; I was always indifferent to the thoughts or feelings or lives of others. Yet my son Ames, so popular everywhere—and now I see what an enormous effort he must have made!—is no more cherished than I. Who, then, has friends? Is that part of our tragedy, knowing that in reality no one really cares about us and that the hubbub of friendship is only a pathetic make-believe? A fantasy out of our eternal loneliness, a busy hurrah! In the eternal emptiness? There were magnificent stories told of undying friendships. Were this a common phenomenon, there would be no such tales, for legends are not made of the commonplace but only of the rare and unique, the very extraordinary.

I have come to this place, thought Caroline, where I am alone and my son is alone. No doubt all men come to this place eventually. There was no one and nothing to wait for. That, Caroline said to herself, is everyone's final epitaph, no matter the number of his "friends." This is the end of all the watching and the hoping and the working and the fearing and the crying in the darkness: there is nothing to wait for. We can share nothing with anyone else, for no one will wait with us.

She heard a rustle near her and started. The Reverend Mother was seating herself beside Caroline. She looked into Caroline's eyes and smiled gently. "I thought I'd come and wait with you," she said.

Caroline did not reply. She looked at her hands clenched over her purse. The Reverend Mother followed her glance, and she was full of pity. "Forgive me," she said, "but I must tell you something. When you came here last Christmas, Mrs. Sheldon, you would not let us help you. However, you suddenly opened your purse and poured out all you had at that time for us. Then it was like a revelation to me: your gesture, the way you looked at us. I don't know how I knew or why, but all at once I knew you were our unknown benefactor who has done so much for us over all these years. I thought of your young daughter, who had run to us instinctively when she was taken so ill. She was in charge of all your affairs to a great extent. Did she know, that poor child, even if you hadn't told her? And then Father Bellamy told us about your gift to him."

Caroline lifted her eyes and looked dumbly at the Reverend Mother.

"We knew you didn't want your identity known, so we never made any inquiries. But all through those years I prayed that somehow I'd know, so that if you needed me I could go to you and comfort you. Or wait with you in an extremity."

She put her long white fingers over Caroline's cold hand. "You aren't alone," she said. "God is with you." Caroline shook her head over and over.

She said, "It is easy for you to say that, for you are young, but I've lived longer than you have." She looked at the Reverend Mother's calm alabaster face, as smooth as marble and as unwrinkled, at the quiet forehead without furrows, at the full young eyes, clearly brown and serene, at the beautiful and faintly colored mouth.

"I am old enough," said the Reverend Mother, "to be your own mother. I am seventy-six."

Caroline stared at her incredulously, and in her mind's eye she could see herself, prematurely old, haggard, gray of face and white of hair, flesh plowed with living, body heavy and weary, clothing dusty and wrinkled, hands withered.

"I have been a nun for fifty-six years," said the Reverend Mother. "I have worked very hard in God's service, and I am grateful. In return, He has given me His peace and His joy. I am in the world, but not of it."

"I have always been in the world, but I was never of it," said Caroline, able to speak now. "So we are the same, it seems."

The hand on hers remained, firm and comforting.

"My son," Caroline said. "I'm afraid for my son, and it's not only about whether or not he'll live. I can't explain about Ames. It's all the years——"

"Would you like to go into the chapel and pray with me for your son?"

"No," said Caroline. "I feel I must stay here. I feel I must just sit here and wait." She became agitated. "I feel that if I leave here something will happen."

"I will wait with you," said the Reverend Mother. She took her rosary in her hands. Caroline watched the tranquil face; this praying woman was indeed old enough to be her mother, and yet it was hard to believe. What gave her this eternal youthfulness and vitality? Peace, said Caroline to herself. Peace and faith. Then she saw that the Reverend Mother's face was full of quiet shadows which could have come only from suffering in the past but which had been overcome steadfastly.

Caroline looked at the door. She said, "You believe, don't you?"

"I know," said the Reverend Mother. She hesitated. "I hope I haven't offended you by guessing you are our benefactor. Would you like to tell me why?"

She spoke with the gentle authority of a mother. Caroline said, "It happened a long time ago in Switzerland, when I was twenty-three years old." She paused. "Do you think my son will live?" And she turned her eyes to the door again.

"It's in God's hands," said the Reverend Mother. "You've done all you could for him, as his mother."

"No," said Caroline, "I've done nothing for Ames, for any of my children."

"It's much easier for God to forgive us than for us to forgive ourselves, Mrs. Sheldon. We repent and are forgiven. But we hug our guilt to our breasts, forgetting that we alone are not the only guilty."

A nurse came in with a lunch tray. Caroline shook her head. "We'll have tea together," said the Reverend Mother with her authoritative calm. "I've often thought that those who can drink tea and eat a little in a crisis must have great faith."

Caroline filled the cups; her big hand trembled. The October sunshine lay on the polished floor and furniture. Then Caroline, who had never had a confidante, began to speak, her voice uncertain and sometimes incoherent, rusty and faltering. It was as if some abscess had opened and was draining in her. The Reverend Mother listened to the broken words; she heard the torment and the agony in the wavering sentences, the loneliness and pain, the bewilderment and despair. She saw Caroline's face, shattered and gray and helpless, and the shaking lips. The nurse came and removed the tray; the sunlight slanted lower in the room. A great bell rang somewhere. Feet hurried in the corridor; there was a cry, a soft laugh, the sound of rubber wheels, the opening and shutting of doors, a quick murmur of voices. The sunlight became more and more level.

"You see," said Caroline finally, "there isn't much to be told, after all. Nothing has happened to me that hasn't happened to everyone else at my age."

The Reverend Mother gazed at her earnestly, and her face was full of compassion.

"There was never anything to wait for," said Caroline, staring at the door.

"There is an end to waiting," said the Reverend Mother. "I think you have come to that end, my child."

The door opened and Dr. Manz, still in his white coat and cap, came into the room, his face exhausted and drained. Caroline stood up speechlessly, her mouth dropping open. He went to her and took her hands and held them tightly. He looked up into her eyes and said firmly, "It was benign. It is removed. Your son will live. He will not be blind, thanks be to God."

Caroline became aware that someone was holding her strongly and that her head had fallen on a womanly shoulder, and she wept like a child.

And I am waiting again, thought Caroline as she sat in her son's suite. The door between the living room and his bedroom stood open now, as it always did. She slept in another room, for three days had gone by and Ames was still unconscious. She would not leave him. The whole world had stopped for her. John had come to Lyme. He came to the hospital every afternoon and evening. He spoke to his mother, but she hardly answered him. At least every ten minutes or so she would go into Ames' room, where he lay as if dead, his nurses beside him. Caroline would look at him without speaking, and then at the nurses, who always smiled at her encouragingly. She would touch the thick white bandages on Ames' head; somewhere deep in that hurt skull he lived and had his being, though the white sheet on his chest barely lifted with his shallow breath. Sometimes he groaned, but his face never changed; it lay ashen on his pillows, the eyes bruised and shut. Don't go away, my son, Caroline would speak to him in her mind. Sometimes she would take his hand, thin and flaccid and as gray as his face, and very chill. What was he suffering, crouched in the shell of his skull, the frail cave that held his life? Did he dream? Was he frightened?

Dr. Manz had promised to wait until his patient recovered consciousness. He was almost always there, gently examining, sitting and watching. "When will he wake up?" Caroline asked. "It's three days."

"Sometimes, dear lady, it is longer. We must wait."

"We are always waiting," Caroline would say, and would return to her chair in the living room, where John, uneasy about his young wife, who was now with her mother, and uneasy about his affairs in New York, would attempt to show proper gravity and solicitude. On the third day Caroline said wearily, "Don't pretend any longer, John. You don't care very much about your brother. I am not condemning you; I'm merely stating fact. It will be easier for us both if you don't pretend."

His florid face flushed a deeper red. His mother looked at him sadly. "I know," she said. "You'd honestly like to feel more about Ames. I think it's upsetting you because you can't. Mary has taught you what a lack there has always been in your life, and I'm glad that you know. If you hadn't come to know that, I'd be afraid that there would never be any hope for you."

He looked away from her, his full mouth sullen yet uncertain. He almost jumped when his mother leaned toward him and put her hand on his arm. He turned to her in astonishment, and he saw that she was smiling a little.

"You'll soon be a father," Caroline said. "I hope you'll love your son or daughter very much. I won't ask you to try to make the child happy, for happiness is something that doesn't really exist, except for a flash of it occasionally. But if you love your child he will remember it all his life, and life won't ever be too hard to endure when he remembers."

She folded her hands on her knee and looked at them. "When no one has really cared about you when you were a child and accepted you as you were and given you strength and self-respect through love, then life becomes progressively intolerable as the years pass. You are—unarmed. Anything can reach you and shatter you. You haven't any resources. Each day just brings a new despair and new betrayals and losses."

He had never heard his mother talk like this before, quietly and steadily and freely. Why, the old girl seemed to be actually human! He wondered how he should respond to this. Gravely? Understandingly? Earnestly? Or with an expression of sober humility?

Caroline said, "You still don't know what to say, do you, John? You're so afraid of people, as I was, but in another way. You think you must always cajole and placate and please them. It may help you to remember that in their own way they are just as frightened as you are, no matter how they bluster or pretend."

John's face felt hot. "I don't think Mimi is afraid of anything," he muttered.

"Yes. She is. She's afraid that you won't ever understand how much she loves you, and that you won't realize you'll always be first in her life. She's afraid of your fear."

John lit a cigarette. "If she thought that, she'd forget her damned art."

"You are wrong. Her painting is as much a part of her as her eyes. Perhaps you won't ever understand it or what it means to her. That doesn't matter to Mary. You are only distressing her by not understanding that you are first, before everything."

"How do you know?" asked John suddenly.

"She hasn't told me, so don't suspect you are being betrayed again, John. But she's very like I was, for a year or two, perhaps, and she is as I'd have been if——"

"Was anyone ever first with you?" asked John with sincere curiosity.

"Yes. My father."

John nodded. "But not my father?"

Caroline hesitated. "I don't know how to answer that. Yes, I think he was. But I didn't trust him." She looked into John's bold hazel eyes, and all at once they shifted away from her. She said, "I didn't trust his love for me. I thought he was capable of betraying me, not for his own gain, but because of his attitude toward life. No, I didn't trust him, though I loved him." She paused.

John was silent.

"I finally believed he didn't love me at all," said Caroline. "I made his life so terrible that he stopped loving me. That is the worst faithlessness: to make someone stop loving you when once he had. Don't make Mary stop loving you, John."

John smoked in silence. She saw his burly profile, and it was vulnerable now.

"Mary didn't marry you for anything but yourself, as your father married me for myself. What had either of us to give them? Except ourselves? I didn't give myself, because I was so frightened of living. Don't be afraid, John. That's the greatest crime we can commit, not only against ourselves, but against others. We destroy each other in our fear. You want Mary to give herself completely to you, as you've done to her, and she has, and you haven't believed it. But you must, or one day you'll be sitting alone as I'm sitting, and it will be too late."

John had never asked himself before: Why is my mother so concerned about Ames? Does he actually mean something to her? Do I?

"Yes," said Caroline, "it's too late. I didn't love any of you when you were children. I suppose you all knew it. I was concerned about you because of my money. I needed heirs. Otherwise Melinda would have inherited it. And so my three children grew to maturity without ever having had any love in their lives, except from their father, and I made them despise him, made them incapable of accepting his affection. You don't love what you despise."

John cleared his throat. Some remark was called for, but he did not know what to say. Caroline said, "But I want you to know this, John: I now love my sons because I know how I've injured them. It's too late for Elizabeth."

It came to John that he must say something, and he felt elated. So the old girl was softening, was she? Like Old Brundage? Senility, perhaps?

"You can't possibly love me," said Caroline. "I'll never ask you even to try, for it would be impossible. How could you love me? But perhaps some-day when you sit waiting for someone to live or die, like this, you'll remember that I did come to love you and to understand, and it might comfort you."

John had a sudden vision of Mimi lying in a room like that one in which his brother lay, and he was sick with fear and helplessness.

"I know," said Caroline, watching him, "that you are thinking of Mary. Just remember that perhaps she often thinks that of you too. There's so little love in the world that we must try to hold it to us, for there is nothing else, John. Nothing else at all."

She stood up and went into Ames' room again, and John was alone. He felt confused, and he was still afraid. He lifted the telephone and called Melinda's house, for he wanted, more than anything else, to speak to his young wife.

"Of course I'm all right, dear," she said laughingly. "But how is Aunt Caroline?" Her voice dropped. "And—Ames?"

He felt his old familiar anger that she should be concerned with anyone but himself. But at the very moment of anger it vanished, and he felt the first shame of his life. He stopped to consider it. Then he said, "Mother is —I don't know, darling. But she's changed in some way. I'll tell you about it later. I'm coming back early tonight."

"No," said Mimi. "You must stay with your mother until the last train home. She needs you."

John paused. Then he said, and more than half meant it: "You're right. She's pleased with your flowers too. And you and your mother may come just as soon as visitors are permitted."

He went to the door of Ames' room and saw his mother stooping over the bed. Funny about Ames, he thought. They'd never had anything in common; Ames had always been able to find the weak spots in anyone, then press on them. It amused him. There was something hellish about Ames, thought John, something laughingly cruel and disgusting. He had had a marriage that hadn't been a marriage—that silly little girl. But perhaps he never could care about anyone, not even someone like Mimi. Now that, he said to himself, is a kind of deformity or a crippling.

John turned. A young woman had entered the living room, dressed in black, carrying her slender body proudly, even nobly. Her black hat was far down on her forehead, and its wide shadow almost hid her face, which was further concealed by a black veil. But her dark eyes gleamed through the mesh, and she was smiling a little at him.

"Amy!" he exclaimed. Was it possible that this girl, so calm and poised, was actually the terrified and cringing child he had last seen only a few months ago?

"I had to come," said Amy, giving him her hand. "I didn't know until this morning. We were all away in North Carolina and just arrived home a few hours ago. No one told us by letter. I suppose they thought the situation was awkward, or something just as ridiculous. One of the housemaids told us this morning; she'd seen something about Ames in the newspaper, and where he was." Amy removed her hand. "Ames, you know, is still my husband."

She looked at the open door anxiously. "How is he? I called Griffith and he only told me that Cousin Caroline had informed him today that Ames was still unconscious."

"No change," said John, drawing a chair forward for her. "It takes time, I hear. At least it wasn't cancer."

Amy seated herself with grace and composure. "I know. Griffith told me." Her pretty face saddened. She lifted her mourning veil. She looked at John with straight clear eyes, no longer shy or afraid. "How is Cousin Caroline?"

"Bearing up. You know Mother."

"Yes," said Amy thoughtfully. "I do know your mother. My brothers blame her for everything that happened to Daddy. Mama thinks they are ridiculous, and so do I." She waited a moment, then said, "I love Cousin Caroline dearly. She saved my life. I never knew anything before."

The soft and hesitating voice was gone. Amy spoke like a woman, a beautiful and assured woman, with the strength of maturity. It was too bad, thought John with sincere regret—which surprised him—that Ames had never known this woman and never would now.

"Oh, Cousin Caroline!" said Amy in a soft voice, and rising. Caroline came into the room, and Amy was shocked at the visible aging, the deathliness, of the other woman. But she went at once to Caroline and put her arms about her neck and kissed her cheek. She wanted to cry, not for Ames, but for Caroline, so broken and slow and old.

"Well, Amy," said Caroline, and patted the girl's back.

"I didn't know until this morning. We were away. As soon as I could, I came," said Amy. "Do sit down; you look so exhausted. How is Ames?"

Caroline let the girl lead her to a chair. She sat down and closed her eyes, and Amy saw the dry and wrinkled lids, the purplish lips. "He hasn't recovered consciousness yet," said Caroline. "I suppose we must just wait. It was very serious."

"Can't we have some tea or something for Cousin Caroline?" asked Amy in such a peremptory and rebuking voice that John was startled and ran to the bell like a chastened boy and rang for a nurse.

"And something to eat. Sandwiches and little cakes," said Amy sternly. "It's far past noon. I suppose you never thought about it, John."

Caroline made a dismissing motion. "I don't want anything, Amy. They asked, but I refused."

"I'm sure John had an excellent lunch," said Amy with scorn.

"Now, look here," said John, coloring.

"At his club. Before he came," said Amy remorselessly. "Men are very unfeeling and inconsiderate. "Well, *did* you have your lunch?"

"What of it?" said John. But again, for the second time, he was ashamed.

"You should have taken care of your mother. You're all she has just now to depend on."

When the nurse came in Amy said, "A hot, nourishing soup for Mrs.

556

Sheldon, please. And a hot sandwich. And tea. And some cakes. Perhaps you'd better bring three cups, nurse, please, for all of us."

"I couldn't possibly," said Caroline. But she smiled a little. She patted Amy's hand.

"For me," said Amy firmly. "You'll do it for me. You will?"

"Very well," said Caroline.

"May I see Ames?" asked Amy.

"They don't want anyone in the room except his closest——"

Amy looked at the distant door. "It seems to me that I'm his 'closest,' too, even if he never knew it. I won't disturb anyone. I just want to look at him." She moved to the door, walking smoothly and with her new assurance, and Caroline and John watched her. She went into the room. "Well!" said Caroline, and her deathly color was less, and her usual grim smile was gentler. "There has been a change in the child, hasn't there?" She seemed amused.

"She's damned arrogant now if you want my honest opinion," grumbled John. What had the damned girl said? "You're all she has just now to depend on." He looked at his mother coldly. "I should have insisted when you refused your lunch. From now on I think I'll start to manage things."

"Do," said Caroline. But she gave him a sharp glance, conjecturing.

"You probably haven't eaten for these three days," said John. "That's ridiculous. I'll have my lunch here with you after this."

His voice was no longer cajoling or pleasing. It was actually and honestly annoyed. "I don't like snips telling me what to do," he added, "but I suppose it's all my fault. But a man sometimes lets women manage him just for the sake of peace." He squared his shoulders in displeasure and looked his mother in the eye.

It's too much to hope for, thought Caroline.

Amy came back. She was pale and moved. "Are you sure he is doing well?" she asked of her cousin. "He looks so—emaciated. So still."

"He is doing well," said Caroline. "At least his doctor says so. We can expect him to become conscious at any time now. His blood pressure is rising, and his heart is stronger."

Amy sat down and did not speak. Once her mouth trembled. "Poor Ames," she said as the nurse entered the room with a lunch cart. "And now, Cousin Caroline, you must start with this good beef broth. John and I"—and she looked at John with a hard expression—"will have to take care of you."

"You are just like your grandmother Cynthia," said Caroline, and almost meekly lifted her spoon. "She would take over everything."

But John, forgetting his dislike, thought she resembled Mimi, who would stand no nonsense, and smiling, he sat down beside his mother. He felt warm and protective, and he decided that women were not too obnoxious after all. He gave Caroline a surreptitious glance, and suddenly she was not formidable any longer, but only a prematurely old woman who needed an adequate, manly protection.

CHAPTER NINE

Caroline, in her bedroom near her son, was dreaming. She was talking to a little girl who appeared to be hardly five years old, with her own young eyes, her cheeks rosy, her small mouth serious and listening, her dark curls a vapor on her childish shoulders. Caroline, in her dream, showed the little one a roll of yellow bills. "What is it?" asked the child.

"It is money, Christina," said Caroline. "A lot of money, darling, a lot of money. Look at it. There are lives in it and all kinds of stupid dreams, and lies, and death and thousands of hopes, and envies and hatreds. There's war in it, too, but very little peace. The philosophers say it is nothing, but they reach for it. The good say it has no value, but they'd sell their souls for it if the price is high enough. The idealists say it is worthless in itself and can buy nothing, but they are the first to envy the possessors and to hate all those who have it. Look at it. It is only paper. But it can buy a world, and the world is all we know."

Caroline and the child were in a gray twilight and, it appeared, in a cold open space on a hill. Below them village lights glittered, and there was a hissing sound among old, dead trees. The child reached curiously for the money in Caroline's hand, took it, examined it. Then she laughed and threw the bills into the air, and suddenly it was summer and the money had turned itself into golden fruit on leafy boughs. "Why, of course," said Caroline.

Someone was shaking her gently, and she tried to throw off the hand which would lead her from this shining place. She could hear Christina's laughter; then the child ran to her and kissed her warmly on the cheek. The hand became more insistent and Caroline woke up. A nurse was beside her, and her bed light was lit.

"The doctor is here," the nurse whispered. "We sent for him. Mr. Sheldon is waking up, the doctor thinks."

Caroline looked about the pleasant lamplit room and could not move for a moment. She could see her little granddaughter's face in every corner of the room, the laughing golden eyes, the fluttering of dark hair—her granddaughter who was not yet born. Caroline brought herself heavily from the bed. She pulled on her old brown robe and thrust her feet into slippers and, with her white braids on her shoulders, she went into Ames' room. Dr. Manz was sitting at the bedside, watching, and a nurse and an intern stood at the foot of the bed.

Ames was moving restlessly and muttering. He lifted his hands aimlessly, then dropped them. Once he touched his bandaged head and groaned. His legs shifted under the covers. Dr. Manz said in a low voice, "There is no paralysis, thanks be to God." He took one of Ames' uneasy hands and felt the pulse and nodded with satisfaction. He saw Caroline and stood up. "It is well," he said cautiously. "But we shall see."

Caroline stood at the bedside. Ames' bruised eyelids were quivering; his muttering grew louder. There was distress in it, and impatience, and anger. Once his words were coherent. "I said, don't touch it! It's my own; I don't want other hands on anything that's mine."

All the hospital was silent around them, for it was only three o'clock in the morning. Dr. Manz tenderly wiped Ames' lips with a cloth dipped in water, and he murmured soothingly. He spoke in careful English and quite loudly: "Ames. Ames Sheldon. Wake up, please. Ames!"

But Ames subsided and began his distressful muttering again, and the doctor frowned. He felt the pulse again, and his face took on alarm. Caroline saw this. Her heart was beating with strong, fast, and physical pain. She reached for her son's hand and held it tightly. "Ames!" she called. "Ames, come home. It's Mama, Ames."

She bent and kissed his wet forehead, his twitching cheek. He lay suddenly still. Then, very quietly, with no sound at all, he opened his eyes and looked directly up into his mother's face. She smiled at him and pressed his hand firmly.

"Why," he murmured. "Mama, of course."

"Certainly," said Caroline briskly. "Now you are all right." She still held his hand tightly, and he did not try to remove it. His eyes slowly wandered about the room; he saw the doctors and the nurse, and then he frowned.

"Have I had the operation?" he asked in his weak voice.

"Yes," said Caroline. "And it is all right. It was benign, and you are not going to be blind, and you will be all well in a few weeks."

His eyes came back to her, and they gleamed a little, as if with amusement. "Mama, you never lied in your life, did you? So I believe you."

"That's a compliment," said Caroline. "But I'm not the only one in the world who tells the truth."

"Too bad," said Ames with mock sympathy. "Must be damned uncomfortable."

But Caroline felt a pressure in her hand; her son was actually pressing it, as if in affection and understanding.

"Now," said Dr. Manz, "we must sleep. We must sleep very much for several days."

"Good old boy," said Ames. He fell asleep suddenly, and the gray face became cool and smooth again.

Dr. Manz took Caroline into the living room. She saw his tiredness and his satisfaction and pride. "Now I can go home, gracious lady," he said. "I can do no more." He regarded Caroline with kindness. "It was your love which brought him back; he responded to it."

"I don't know," said Caroline. "I have always thought him incapable of love."

"No," said the doctor. "No man is, not even the lost or the mad."

Melinda came, and Mimi and John. Melinda looked ill and worn, but her sweet gravity lit up her gray eyes when she embraced Caroline and kissed her cheek.

"How terrible it must have been for you, dear Caroline," she said. "I'd have come before, but I've had a little cold, I'm afraid. And how is Ames?"

"He woke up three days ago, as John probably told you. He sleeps almost all the time, but each time he wakes up he is stronger and can speak better."

John, who always held his young wife's hand when he was in her company, said, "He's becoming his old, disagreeable self again. He followed my last case in court in the newspapers, and he asked me how much I had to pay in bribes." John smiled. "Yes indeed, the Young Master is himself again. You'd think, after all he's gone through, that there'd be a change for the better."

"People don't change very much," said Caroline. "That's for fairy tales. But," she said, looking directly at John, "we can discipline ourselves to be less obnoxious than we are naturally, and eventually being sensible and decent may become a habit."

"Touché," said John. He gently released Mimi's hand, and she smiled at him. Her young body was swollen with her child, and Caroline thought of the Christina who had not yet been born. "It will be a girl—Christina," said Caroline with her old abruptness.

"We've practically decided on the sex," said John, smiling, and he spoke easily and without his old jealousy. "And the name will be Christina."

Melinda had sat down, and Caroline could see her pallor and weakness. Now she resembled their father, and Caroline felt pain and deep sorrow. Melinda smiled at her. "I think it's a lovely name," she said.

"You must take care of yourself," said Caroline.

Melinda was startled. "I beg your pardon, Caroline? Oh, myself. I've just had a little cold, and now I have a cough. The children are leaving tomorrow, but I am here, you know. I will call you at least once a day and will come when I can."

Caroline looked at Mimi, and the girl was looking at her mother. She knows, thought Caroline. But she is strong; she is already accepting whatever there will be to accept. Caroline said, "I've always thought of Mary as my daughter."

Amy came, as she did every day, but she had not yet seen Ames. She sat with Caroline, talking gently and peacefully. She said, "Mama will come when Ames can have regular visitors. She wants to see you more than anyone else, though, Cousin Caroline."

"Your mother," said Caroline, "is a very sensible woman. I hope her children appreciate it."

Amy smiled. "Mama manages everything now, since—— Even the boys are afraid of her."

"Love can be as crippling, many times, as hate," said Caroline with her old brusqueness. "Unless it is judicious as well as accepting and doesn't demand everything. And doesn't keep its hands pressed blindly over its eyes. Love, too, has its victims."

She added with authority, "I wish everyone understood that."

Amy reflected on this. "You know," she said at last, "I was a damned fool. I ought to have known better. I may see Ames now if he's awake?"

"He's awake," said Caroline, and the old grim smile lifted the corners of her mouth. "In fact, he's probably listening to us. Go to see him, Amy."

Amy walked into Ames' room. He was indeed awake. "Well, child wife," he said, "how nice of you to visit your husband."

"Don't be an idiot," said Amy calmly. She sat down near his bed. "I really don't know how you survived all this. You didn't deserve it. But only the good die young, I've heard."

"Well, well," said Ames from his high pillows. He scrutinized her. "Is this really Amy, this gracious young lady with all that damned serenity and poise and Old Boston restraint?"

"It certainly is," said Amy. "I'm so restrained and dignified that I don't need corsets to keep me rigid." She cocked her pretty head at him humorously. "I wonder what I ever saw in you, darling Ames," she said. "You are really despicable, you know. Like a mean little boy. And I wonder why I was ever afraid of you. By the way," she said, "I went to the apartment. Griffith informed me that you had thoughtfully taken the key to your treasure house with you, and I thought everything would be very dusty. So I called in a locksmith and he made me a set of keys, and I spent two evenings washing up all those little knickknacks of yours so they'd be quite splendid and shining when you went home."

Ames frowned at her with his old coldness. "You had the audacity?"

"Oh, I have plenty of audacity these days," said Amy. "I'm audacious all over the place. My beaus just love it, though, of course, since Daddy's death we go out very seldom. But that will all end by next summer, and in the meantime I'm taking inventory. Our divorce will come through in December, you know. We plan a quiet celebration at home. With a birthday cake and candles."

Ames flushed. "Do drink a glass of your damned cheap sherry for me, won't you? Your father thought he was a connoisseur, but he wasn't, you know." His voice was gently vicious. "In fact, he was all plebe, in spite of his airs."

"Was he?" asked Amy with smiling indifference. "I didn't notice."

Ames was annoyed. Amy was out of the reach of his little barbs and delicate insults. "I suppose," he said, "that just as soon as possible you'll be marrying again?"

"I wouldn't for the life of me remain single," said Amy with a smirk that goaded him. "And by the way, I've just visited a specialist in New York. They have discovered a way to cure me, and it's very successful in most cases. I intend to have at least six children when I marry again, and I'll love them and beat them regularly, as you should have been beaten when you were a child."

"Why did you wash up my collections? And I hope to God your clumsy hands didn't chip any!" He sat up a little higher on his pillows, and there was fire in his eyes.

Amy considered. She put a gloved finger to her lips and looked both

561

arch and serious, and Ames wanted to slap her. She said, "I suppose it was all my solid-gold good heart. I knew how you slavered over them——"

"Slavered!" Ames shouted.

"A vulgar word, but the only one that fits," said Amy. "No, I didn't chip any. They're really exquisite, and I love them. You never knew that, did you? I belong to the Tuesday Club, and I gave serious thought to inviting the ladies to view your collections, at so much a lady, the proceeds to go to charity."

"Go to hell," said Ames.

"I think not," said Amy. Her eyes were dancing. "I think I'm going to have a very nice and pleasant life from this time on. When I have my own home again I'm going to be mistress in it. I am going to choose the rugs and the draperies and the furniture. It won't be much different from your apartment, dear boy, because you really have excellent and impeccable taste."

"I suppose," said Ames, "that you have already picked out your victim?"

"Come to think of it, I have," Amy said.

"I hope he'll find you more interesting that I did," he said.

"Indeed. I'm a much more interesting person day by day, dear boy. There were too many oppressive men in my life, Daddy and you."

"Too bad I didn't die," said Ames. "Then you'd be a merry widow instead of a tarnished divorcee."

"There's no tarnish on me at all," said Amy. "I never took money to marry anyone; I'll not consider money when I marry."

Ames grunted. He scrutinized her again. She seemed older, and more mature, and a grand lady, and not the cringing little Amy he had known who had exasperated him. She was a woman who would never again piteously demand kisses and love but would casually accept them if they came. If both were temperate, that would please her just as well.

"I find you a little interesting now, but not very much," said Ames. "I think you've become conceited, and I always hated conceited women."

"Does it matter what you think about me?" asked Amy reasonably. "As acquaintances and relatives, if not friends, and soon to be not even husband and wife, don't you think you should be more polite? Not that I care, knowing how venomous your politeness always is."

"Have you been back to finishing school to learn how to be a woman instead of an infant?"

"Indeed, yes. Your mother was my first teacher. I'm so grateful to dear Caroline. And then my mother became my teacher; she's so sensible, you know. But I really think I did my own teaching. I developed self-respect. I also inherited a lot of money from poor Daddy. He had indicated in his will that I would inherit that money only if I had left you at the time of his death. Otherwise, not a penny. Dear Daddy. He did know all about you, didn't he, darling boy?"

"Blood will tell," said Ames. "I suppose you count your bankbooks daily."

"There is nothing so interesting," said Amy, "as bankbooks. I recommend them for everybody. But I am doing a lot of investing too. The stock market is really fascinating."

"Blood will tell," Ames repeated.

"I do hope so," said Amy piously. "Well, I have stayed long enough, haven't I? Do get well soon. Do you like those yellow roses I sent you?"

"Yes," said Ames sullenly. "You remembered at least one thing about me, didn't you? That I like yellow roses."

"I remember so many things about you, unfortunately, that it sometimes depresses me. But I am learning to control even that." Amy stood up and smiled down at him. "I must leave you now. So good-by. You need not, you know, even appear in court."

Ames looked up at her. How pretty she was, really beautiful. He had never noticed before the loveliness of her serene eyes, the firm curve of her pink lips. She had spirit and grace. She was a woman, too, and she was tender and not maudlin. She had the power of self-assurance and self-control and kindly warmth.

Ames said suddenly, "Oh, I'll be in court, all right! To contest the divorce."

Amy stood very still. Then she said quietly, "But why? You never really wanted me, Ames."

"I do now." He darted out his hand and took one of hers.

"My dear," she said, watching him and holding back her tears, "you'll never see one cent of my money. Not one cent."

"I don't want it," said Ames.

"Good heavens. What's come over you?"

"You," said Ames.

Amy let him hold her hand. "I must think about all this. I'm not sure I care a thing about you. The girl who loved you has gone. I am a different person entirely, a stranger."

"Let's get acquainted, then," said Ames gravely. "Permit me, madam, to introduce myself. Your husband. May I have the next dance?"

"You may, sir," said Amy. "But only that one dance. My program is all filled up."

"I'll manage that," said Ames.

They looked at each other, then they began to laugh together, and Amy bent down and gave him a chaste kiss. But his arm went about her neck and he kissed her thoroughly, until her hat fell from her head.

"You're not the only one who's been a damned fool," said Ames. "But as former damned fools, and therefore dangerous, let's take each other out of circulation. Who else could stand us?"

When Amy, adjusting her hat, came into the living room, Caroline was waiting for her in cold and somber silence. Amy sat down near her, and then Caroline said, "When I took you home you told me that you could not love my son, for you had become entirely different."

"Yes," said Amy. "I did. I am. But I think, too, that Ames has become a little different too. We'll see."

"I don't believe in happy endings," said Caroline.

Amy shook her head. "I don't either, Cousin Caroline. I don't believe in endings at all."

Caroline studied her, then her hard expression softened. "I never saw it before, but you resemble your mother more than a little. What do you mean by not believing in endings?"

"Every day is different, and in some way we change with every day," said Amy. "I must think about all this."

Caroline walked into her son's room. His bandaged head was turned to Amy's yellow roses. Caroline said at once, "I hope you fully understand what you and Amy are doing."

He half turned his head and slanted his eyes at her. "Does anyone?" he replied. "Did you always know?"

Caroline considered this. Then she said, "I don't think, really, that I ever knew."

He looked at the ceiling. "It's very funny," said Ames, "but I felt I was sliding down a long black slope and couldn't stop. Then I heard you call me, and I began to be rushed back. When I woke up, you were here."

"Did you want to come back, Ames?"

He thought about it. "Frankly, I don't know. I never had that lust for life that I hear about. That teeming exuberance for living, like John's. I wasn't afraid of dying; I was only afraid of going blind, before the operation. But when I heard you calling me, I came back, and I can't tell you if it was willingly or not."

"Did life always seem immaterial to you, Ames?"

He thought to himself: What a strange conversation to be having with the poor old girl! He said, "I think so. I can't ever remember being all worked up about living, now even when I was a kid. I can stand it fairly well if things don't become too involved and emotional, for life's just not worth all that trouble. That was a great part of the difficulty between Amy and me. But now I think she'll never be that way again." And he smiled.

"And you?"

"I? Well, dear Mama, for the first time in my life I think there may be something to this life-loving hullabaloo. I'll explore the matter. Gingerly."

Caroline said as she turned to leave, "I told you before that I love you, Ames. I love John also. It doesn't matter in the least whether you care about that or not."

No, thought Caroline, there are no happy endings for anyone in the world. But when we repent and try to make amends, there is hope, not for a happy ending, but for peace. And some small understanding.

CHAPTER TEN

The gray wind and the gray sea shouted at Caroline's back on this cold, early November day as she climbed up the steep and forgotten road to the cemetery. Her head, in its knit cap, lifted to the top of the slope where the ancient and abandoned gravestones stood at desolate angles or had fallen on their faces, names obliterated, memory vanished, love forsaken. The black spire of the empty church raised its point against the bitter and turbulent sky. It was almost dusk; it was hard to see the slipping earth and knotted roots that covered the path. Tall and empty trees lined the forgotten road, but here and there some small maple or elm had clutched at its handful of red or yellow leaves tenaciously, as if to deny the coming darkness and the coming death of winter. But the wind tore them away, and the leaves rattled and scurried along the path, alive in their deadness, their dry voices scrabbling. An owl cried. The air was filled with the threat of sleet, and a low and melancholy thunder invaded it as the sea raised its voice.

Though the graveyard was forgotten, even by all those in the village below, there was an area, wide and groomed, surrounded by a low iron fence. In the center of it stood a great tall shaft, white and glimmering in the dull light of the day's ending. Here lay Tom's father and his mother, and Tom and Elizabeth and Beth, under the large lettering: "Sheldon." Even Beth, who had never had that name. There was much space for more graves, and here, thought Caroline, I'll lie, myself, and perhaps it won't be too long to wait. There were urns here, filled with ivy, and cypresses, and flower beds, blasted now. In the summer it was beautiful and had become somewhat of a local spectacle. Caroline opened the low gate, which was surrounded by all those many forgotten headstones, and stepped inside the private area she had bought.

Something, or someone, moved suddenly in the dull light, and Caroline found herself confronted by a stranger in the black garments of a priest. He was not very tall, but he was plump and had a very peaceful and serious face, and his bared head was somewhat bald, with fine flying hair sparsely fluttering over the empty places. He smiled at Caroline's sudden halt and look of alarm, and when he smiled his face was instantly charming and radiant. Caroline stared at him with shock, remembering. She put her hand, gloved in rough wool, to the breast of her old brown coat.

"You are Caroline Sheldon, aren't you?" he asked, and his voice was strong yet gentle. "And I——"

"I know," said Caroline. "You look like your father. I called him the Weasel."

"So I understand." He was kindly amused. "I'm also Melinda's brother."

He could see Caroline's gray and sorrowful face and the fear-filled gleam of her eyes. "I came to see my sister," he said. "She is very ill, I am afraid."

"I know," said Caroline, breathing with loud difficulty against the wind. "I call her house every day. I promised Mary."

"She would like you to come sometime," he said. "It's very lonely for her, with Nathaniel at Plattsburg—that is the name of the place?—and Mimi in New York."

"How could she be lonely?" said Caroline. She stumbled as she went to a stone bench and sat down. "She had everyone to love her all her life. And

Amanda and her children visit her often, and all her many friends in Boston. Melinda and I—what can we speak about together? Nothing."

She panted on the bench, and William came to her and sat down beside her.

"But what are you doing here?" she demanded shortly.

"I came to see Melinda. And to say good-by." He paused. "My wife died a year ago. I suppose you didn't know."

"Yes. My son John told me." The dusk had taken on a peculiar steely transparency, and Caroline looked at the face so close to hers, the face Elizabeth had loved, and had died in the loving. Her whole body felt encased in pain.

"But I'm not going back to England," said William. He pointed to his garments. "I'm a simple parish priest now, as you can see."

"Your father is probably turning in his grave," said Caroline sourly, trying to breathe against her torment.

He laughed a little. "Probably." He was silent for a few moments, then said, "I am going to the battlefields in France. My children are provided for and surrounded by all Rose's large family, and so I can go, as I now am, with no regrets or worries."

Caroline's eyes slowly roved over her private graveyard. "Why are you here?" she asked.

"To see Elizabeth's grave. To think of her and pray for her soul."

Caroline bent her cheek on her folded hand. "I had nothing to give her and no way to help her, and so she is lying here now, and she'd be only twenty-six if she had lived. That is too young to be dead."

"There are younger, every day, dying," said William. "Is life so glorious that we should regret to leave it?"

He got to his feet and went to Elizabeth's grave and looked at the white shaft that towered over it and then at the small flat white stone with her name upon it.

He said from his little distance, "It is the living for whom we should feel pity. And the unborn, who shall be born, to face the world they must face. Elizabeth is safe." His plain features expressed his pain and sadness. He came back to the bench.

"I want you to know," he said, "that I loved Elizabeth more than anyone else, more than my parents and my sister, and far more than my poor young wife, who would not even be Elizabeth's age if she had lived. I never forgot Elizabeth. And it wasn't until only recently that I stopped hating the man who was responsible for so much of my misery and hers." He hesitated. "Perhaps sometime I can even pray for his soul."

"No," said Caroline. "Never for Timothy. It was not only Elizabeth; it was something else, besides. It was what he was."

"I know what he was," said William soberly. "A thoroughly evil man, a dangerous man. You look surprised, Mrs. Sheldon. Don't be. I knew, as you probably knew. But I pray sometimes that perhaps there was something else, too, which will serve as his first step to heaven."

"There never was," said Caroline in a loud and breaking voice. "The world is full of such men now. No one knows or can guess how many. They will destroy all of us if they can, and it's very likely that they can and will."

"Nothing can happen that God will not permit to happen," said William, and he put his hand on her arm. "If these men do get their power it will be because of the sins of the rest of us, our apathy, our own faithlessness, our own greed and stupidity." He folded his hands on his knee and looked at Elizabeth's grave and then over all the graveyard. "Our own lack of manliness and resolution. Our godlessness. Attila the Hun, Genghis Khan, Napoleon—they were all the scourges of God, the whips of God, punishing mankind for its sloth and its forgetfulness and complacency and sin. Its pride and selfishness. Its boasts and its own ugly lusts. Who knows what face the next scourge will wear, and what his name is, and where he lives at this very moment? We can only know that he does live and is watching and waiting."

The first drops of sleet stung their faces. William rose and offered his arm to Caroline, and they went together to Elizabeth's grave. William blessed himself and murmured his prayers, and Caroline looked at the stone mutely. When they turned away she said, "I came today. I don't know why today. It's ridiculous, but it was as if I knew I'd never come again. Except for the last time."

She leaned on William's arm as they crept down the forsaken path, and there were tears on her cheeks. William's arm was like the arm of a son, and she turned her fingers and clung to the cloth that covered it.

And again, thought Caroline, as she sat before her sparse fire and looked at the small red coals, I am waiting. Our life is nothing but a waiting, and I'm not sure, even now, that there is anything to wait for, except for a little quiet and a little peace.

There was such silence about her now, as if she had been totally forgotten. But I've never been remembered, she said to herself. She thought of Amy and Ames, together again, and of the pleasant bulletins she received from Griffith at least once a week. "The young mistress," he stated, "is managing very well, indeed. Sometimes the master is even subdued. Young Mrs. Sheldon is very determined, and I think, in a way, that he likes the new regime. There is no weeping, but only occasional sharp words, and the mistress's are always the sharpest," he reported happily. "Quite often the master will come into the kitchen for a drink with me and a few pungent remarks about women. All is well."

All was "well" with John and Mimi too. John, wrote Mimi, was helping her to prepare for her show in early December, which would be about two weeks before her child was to be born. He had disliked some of the frames; he had ordered others, and Mimi laughingly confessed that John had been right. He talked of the coming baby with enthusiasm, she wrote. There was such a change in dear John. He no longer called her several times a day to be reassured that she was thinking of him. He knew, said Mimi.

I have undone a little, thought Caroline. At the very last moment, I have undone a little. The rest lies with my sons and their wives. It isn't much, but it is something, some recompense. My sons will never love me; that would be impossible. But in some way I have learned to love them, and that is more than enough. It is only this waiting, this endless waiting.

She went up to her gallery and looked at the paintings of her grandfather. She saw more in them these days than ever before. Often she forgot to be in her study at the usual hours. She had a tremendous fortune to manage, which would belong to her grandchildren, and in another way it had become a trust again. But what would they do with it, these unborn? Would they be frightened, or would they love? Would they hoard, or would they live? She tried to imagine their faces, but they eluded her except for Christina's; she saw their forms and their movements, but not their faces and their eyes. Sometimes she would pray awkwardly for these children. What would their world be like, this frightfully turbulent world on the eve of much more turbulence and terror? Would their world die, and them with it?

"It is in the hands of God," William had said to her when they had parted. But who knew what fearful designs were in the heart of God? He was a God of Justice and wrath, as well as tenderness and mercy. He did not consult men; He warned them, if they would listen, in their hearts. But who listened to Him? Occasionally astronomers saw a nova, "a new bright star," which disappeared shortly afterward, in days or weeks. Were they worlds which had brought God's anger on them, and so their own destuction? The endless whirling nebulas were the hot vortexes, too, of new creation. But why, when it was all such a great weariness and an endless repetition? Or was God waiting for something too?

Ames and Amy would come about twice a month to see her, and now John and Mimi came to see Melinda and always spent a few hours with Caroline. She would look at them with secret tenderness, but she would also feel an enormous fatigue, so that when the door closed upon them she would climb upstairs to her bed and be forced to lie down. It was as if she had mysteriously moved far from them and they were no longer even a small part of her life, and it exhausted her to shout over the tremendous distance to them. Their very voices, young and vibrant, took strength from her. They belonged to a world she had already left. But in leaving, she still had nowhere to go. She could only wait, her face turned to darkness. Did something move in that darkness? Was something developing there? She did not know. Day by day another tendril of her life attaching her to the world raveled and broke, another distant door closed.

This is what it means to grow old, she thought. But her Aunt Cynthia, had lived to a much older age and had enjoyed every moment of it, and no doubt had regretted to leave. There were old, old dowagers in Boston, immediate and always aware, and engaged in life, and dominating it. Some were in their eighties and even their nineties. Their zest had not diminished. They would consider Caroline Ames young, compared with themselves. But I am old, thought Caroline. I was never young. Except for just a little while with Tom, who, at the end, had not wanted me and had wished to leave me forever.

Sometimes she would lie down in Elizabeth's room, but now Elizabeth's face did not come to her, not even as a shadow. Elizabeth had not lived here; why should she return even for one instant? Sometimes Caroline would lie down in Tom's room and sleep, but she never dreamed of him. She never felt his presence.

It is this which is the worst, she would say to herself, the knowing that even the dead have left you, finally and for all time.

She went to New York and remade her will. Higsby's organization would not fail for lack of money, but only from lack of resolution. There was a larger perpetual fund for Sisters of Charity Hospital. There was a large sum for Griffith and Father Bellamy. There were trusts for medical research on cancer and heart disease. There was a fund for the everlasting care of the Sheldon graves. Then there were the new trusts for her sons and for her grandchildren whom she would never see.

"Certainly you'll see them, dear Caroline," said another Mr. Tandy in a courageous voice. "Why, you are in the prime of life."

"Nonsense," said Caroline. "I never was."

He looked at her dying face and agreed silently. Her body, always so stocky and wide, was dwindling rapidly; her face was old and sunken. Only her eyes, as if new life had been born in them, were young and clear.

She shook hands with Mr. Tandy on leaving. "I don't suppose I'll ever see you again," she said. All that money, he thought with more than a stab of envy. All that miraculous money! Yet she had disposed of it indifferently, as if it no longer belonged to her, as if it meant nothing to her at all. One could only think of that money in connection with joy and luxury and comfort and security and power, but it was evident that Caroline did not think so.

She said at the door, "I suppose you think I am quite mad." Then she smiled, and he was astonished at the sudden shining of her eyes. "But I'm not, really. You remember the phrase: 'In sound mind and in sound body.' You put it there yourself."

He thought about Caroline for a long time after she had gone. She had given all her life for her money; she had tripled the fortune her father had left her. She had devoted herself to it, as everyone knew. It had been her life. Now it was nothing to her. "Incredible, incredible," said Mr. Tandy to himself.

Then during one week in early December, Caroline stopped reading her business and financial magazines and journals. They gathered in her study, still in their wrappers. When her Boston office called, or her New York bank, she did not answer. She walked in the first early snows of December, along the black and shining shingle, looking at the gray and splashing ocean and at the gray and uneasy sky. She was taking stock of her life, for all at once that seemed to be the most important thing in the world. But when she attempted to sort it out so that it presented an orderly pattern or had some significance that she could discern she could see only confusion and lack of significance, and pain and misery. It was as if all her existence were a mass of many-colored ropes, slippery and twisting, tangled together, in which she was bound and beyond escape. Yet, escape she must, if she was to live, or even die in a measure of peace. As she struggled for order in her mind she was repeatedly overcome by an awful spiritual weariness, a repugnance, that was really despair. The soul's night of darkness was on her.

She had sent Maizie to the village for a Bible, though up in the attic, somewhere, forgotten by her, was Beth's Bible, rotting away. "Yes," said Maizie in the general store, "the old lady wants a Bible! Gettin' scared in her old age." The people in the store laughed heartily and with viciousness. Only thing in the world the old lady ever cared about was that cemetery plot up on the hill and her money. Never gave a cent to anybody; that was her. Now the growing village needed another school; kids were getting born much more than they used to. And the "new" church needed lots of work, and there was old folks needin' help, and their sons and daughters got too much to do with their own kids to care about the old folks any longer. If the old lady down there behind her walls wanted to do something with her money—and why shouldn't she?—there was lots to do in the village and roundabout. People were smartenin' up these days; they knew they had a right to be helped by folks who had the money, though they hadn't earned it theirselves. Come to think of it, everybody in the world had a right to everything everybody else had, hadn't they? They was born, weren't they?

Why was I born? thought Caroline. That priest had told her she had been born to know God, to serve Him in this life, and to join Him in eternity. But if God was omniscient, as He was, then He knew very well, when He created each soul, just what its destiny was and how few there were who would ever know Him or serve Him or join Him. Free will. Yet everywhere, it seemed, the cruel old doctrine of predestination challenged the doctrine of free will. There was some tremendous mystery here which perhaps only a few could interpret and understand. Why blame a man for his life, when it was determined and known from the instant of conception?

The cheap Bible felt strange in Caroline's hand as she opened it in the December darkness in Tom's room. It fell open on the Psalms. "In my distress I cried unto the Lord and He heard me . . ." "I will say of the Lord, He is my refuge and my fortress; my God, in Him will I trust . . . thou shalt not be afraid for the terror by night, nor for the arrow that flieth by day . . ."

The dusk became heavier and colder. The wind threw itself violently on the windows of the rotted house. Large handfuls of snow gushed down from the sky, spotted the windows in clumps, and clung. The house cowered like a ruin in the storm.

" 'The arrow that flieth by day,' " said Caroline. Oh, the endless hail of arrows that assaulted every soul that came into the world, the barbs, the spears, the swords. Under all that nice and rosy cotton batting man desperately and eagerly strewed over his fearful world, crying out desperately and eagerly that all was well in this best of all possible worlds, lay the bottomless deeps of despair, the anguish, the loneliness, the terror and the ugliness, the horror and the hating, the perverted and the degraded, the blasphemous and the lost, the voices that cursed and the voices that never answered, the dark streets without an ending, the deformed and skulking shadows, the threat and the stinking and the death, the betrayals and the multitudes of murders and sins of the true world which man denied until dust stopped his mouth and he could lie no more.

"Remember now thy Creator in the days of thy youth, while the evil days come not, nor the years draw nigh . . ."

Caroline struggled to her feet, gasping. "Beth! Beth?" she cried. "Is that you, Beth? I heard you. Beth!"

She lumbered into the hall, which was black; only the small window at the end cast a little crepuscular gray below it. Caroline looked about wildly. "Beth! Is that you, Beth?" A door opened on the floor above, and Maizie's stumbling footsteps descended the narrow steps. "Ma'am? You call me?" she whined.

Caroline had to lean against the wall, for her heart was leaping with agony, and she could not breathe. A necklace of burning thorns tightened about her throat. Maizie, seeing only that shadow in the dimness, turned up the hall light, weak and bluish, and stared at Caroline. "I thought you called," she said, and peered at the woman before her, whose panting was loud above the roar of the wind. She could see Caroline's eyes, great and wild and golden in her pallid face, held still, listening, fixed.

"Ma'am!" said Maizie, frightened, pushing back her pale and disheveled hair, for she had been sleeping in the cold and silent afternoon. "You sick or something?"

Slowly the unseeing eyes saw the thin and slatternly girl, saw her not as her servant, sly and treacherous and pilfering, but as a stranger, someone she did not know, someone who suffered and was afraid, whose young hands were already worn with work, whose young lips already drooped plaintively, whose attitude was already wary. The pain began to recede from Caroline's breast and throat. She wanted to weep. She murmured hoarsely, "I thought—I thought I heard someone call me from your room. The room where an old friend—"

"What?" said Maizie eagerly. (She was already relating, in her mind, this incident in the large general store in the village, where customers loved to hear tales of the "old lady" with all the money, and who would whoop in ugly and delighted laughter when the tale was done.)

"I was asleep," said Caroline, "and dreaming." Why did the girl look at her with such a gleam in her eye, the gleam that shines in a dog's eyes the moment it begins to lick its lips?

"Oh," said Maizie, disappointed. (But she could tell how the old lady had screamed and yelled and come running out of her room like Old Scratch was after her.)

"It's late," Caroline mumbled. "The fire must be out downstairs. Put more coal on it. I'll have my supper there." She began to slide along the wall, for her legs were trembling and bending, and her body felt so weighty that she could hardly move it. She found the banister and went down into the darkness, and Maizie followed, muttering. Why, it wasn't more than four, and the old lady didn't eat until seven or later. Well, an early supper and the dishes would be over, and she could go back to her room and sleep again, early. It was wonderful to sleep.

The house groaned and creaked like a ship in a great storm, and the gale roared about it like an enormous beast looking for an entry. It was very cold downstairs, the fire almost out. Shivering, Maizie knelt on the hearth and shoveled more coal onto the embers. Her dress, once a bit of cheap finery the color of cherries, glistened sleazily in the light of the one lamp she had lit, and it was dark with spots and dusty with grime. Her long hair, the color of bleached straw, was frizzed and bunched untidily all over her head; it resembled nothing more than a heap of lint. She had thin shoulders and a gaunt neck, though she was only in her mid-twenties, a large and crooked nose, a little dip of a chin, and big, watery blue eyes. Caroline, in her usual chair near the fire, saw all this, the big elbows, the slack and shapeless body, the line of thin thighs under the crude fabric of the imitation-silk dress, the ankles in black and mended stockings, the patched button boots, the chest without the soft curves of young woman- hood, the fleshless waist.

Caroline forgot herself, the memory of Beth's voice, loud and clear and loving in Tom's room, her own pain and her awareness of coming dissolu- tion. She saw Maizie (and what was her surname?) and she saw her with a suffering clarity. The dirty hands—had they ever fondled anyone? Had that sullen profile ever smiled with innocent pleasure or joy? Had those petulant thin lips ever kissed? Did the girl know how piteous she was, how the very sight of her tormented her mistress and filled her with sorrow?

"Maizie," said Caroline, and her voice was still dwindled and feeble. "Have you ever thought of marrying?"

Maizie gaped up at her from the hearth. The old lady had never, not once, ever spoken to her unnecessarily, had never indicated that she was alive, had never seemed to think "that a person got tired in this big old house with all the rooms and the dirt."

The girl, after that long gaping, turned back to the fire. "Well, yes," she said sullenly in her whining voice. "But how, Miz Sheldon? A girl's got to have a little money, don't she? Especially when she got to give some of her wages to Ma, with the three kids still not grown, and everything costin' so much all of a sudden, with that war. Wasn't fair."

"Nothing is," said Caroline. "For anyone. Didn't you know that, Maizie?"

Maizie peeped at her slyly. Oho. Easy for *her* to say, with all that money! The rich folks was always talking that way. Like the minister. "All the best things in life are free." You bet they wasn't! How was a girl going to get married if she didn't have the money to buy sheets and pillowcases and blankets and tablecloths and some "silver" and a "tressoh"? Fellers didn't get married these days if a girl didn't have a few dollars in the bank, especially not around here in this godforsaken Lyme. They went and looked for Boston girls who had good jobs in the stores or way off in the textile mills, and they left Lyme and got theirselves jobs, too, and they never came back. Never.

"What would you do if you had some money?" asked Caroline in that faint and difficult voice.

The gleam came back into Maizie's eyes, and she sat on her heels, and a wistful glow of daydreaming made her plain and colorless face almost pretty.

"Why, Miz Sheldon, I'd give Ma half of it, and then I'd buy myself some nice things in Boston and then I'd stay in Boston and get a good job!"

Caroline was silent. The gale became enormously imminent; it screamed in all the chimneys of the house. The windows were only gray blotches. Then Caroline said, "You could have gone to Boston before this, Maizie, and found some good work if you had wanted to do it; you had the choice, the free will."

Maizie stared, the glow going quickly from her sullen face.

"Yes," said Caroline, as if to herself, "you were born here, it is true. But you could have left; you could have made your life quite different. You had only to will it and then act on your will. It isn't your circumstances, which you could not have helped, but what you did with your circumstances— your choice."

Is that so? Maizie said angrily in herself. *You* try bein' born in a broken-down old house with a god-awful dad who didn't give a damn about you, and wearin' old clothes all the time and never havin' a cent, and eatin' cheap food and never goin' anywhere, and nobody wantin' you! *You* try it! You don't know what it's like, never havin' a chance.

So, thought Caroline, I have answered myself, too, and now I understand without any doubt at all. I was no better than this weak girl here, who is enraged at me and clattering coals on my fire. Then she was filled with pity again, and she did not know if she was pitying her young self or Maizie.

"What you want for supper?" Maizie said. "All we got is some of that tapioca puddin' from last night and some cold boiled meat and potatoes and cabbage and some bread and a little butter."

"I think I'll just have some toast and a cup of tea," said Caroline listlessly. She leaned back in the chair and listened to the wind and the crying in the chimneys and the mysterious sounds in the house. The coals caught, and a thin blaze of scarlet light touched Caroline's face, and it appeared already dead, but very composed and stern.

"Remember thy Creator in the days of your youth." Yes, Beth had read that once to her and, remembering, Caroline had also recalled Beth's voice. (But how clear and strong and loving it had been in that recalling!) I had the opportunity to remember my Creator in the days of my own youth, thought Caroline, and Beth tried to help me, but I turned away in my self-willed ignorance, my dark stupidity, my fear. I repudiated it all, and it was my own choice and not another's. And so I have come to these bereft days, searching in the darkness for what had been so purely bright in my youth and so greatly offered. If we do not accept it when we are young, with our young simplicity and trust, then we must look for it in the wilderness when we are old, and perhaps not find it then at all.

She ate a mouthful of the burned toast Maizie brought her and drank a little of the tepid tea, and suddenly she was nauseated. She put the tray aside and crept heavily and wearily to Tom's room again. She lit a lamp. It was utterly cold in here and lonely. Shuddering in the icy air, she took up the Bible again, looking in her own wilderness for the lost light.

It evaded her. There was an ominous sensation in her chest, and she shifted restlessly. She remembered Maizie. She pushed herself to her feet and went into her study and wrote out a check for the girl. For five thousand dollars. Her surname? She had never paid the girl by check. Caroline closed her eyes in her weakness, leaning back in her chair in the orderly study which was gathering dust; her desk was heaped with mail and journals and magazines which she had not touched for days. Yes, it was, of course, Smith, so ordinary a name that it was hard to remember. Caroline added the surname, dated the check as of a week ago, and put it in an envelope. She placed the envelope in the middle of her desk, all alone. Then she said to herself: Why have I done this? Do I intend to give that girl this check tomorrow? Why have I done this? Am I losing my mind?

But all at once her mind blurred. Her flesh was as cold as the air in the study, for no fire had been built in here for days. She crept back to Tom's room and took up the Bible, and it opened on the 121st Psalm:

"I will lift up mine eyes unto the hills, from whence cometh my help. My help cometh from the Lord, which made heaven and earth. . . . The Lord is thy Keeper; the Lord is thy shade upon thy right hand. . . . The Lord shall preserve thee from all evil; He shall preserve thy soul. The Lord shall preserve thy going out, and thy coming in, from this time forth, and even for evermore!"

"Oh, God!" Caroline's voice was a great cry in the room, of mingled anguish and joy and revelation and heart-shaking gratitude. She fell back upon the cold pillows of Tom's bed and wept and sobbed and clutched the pillows to her breast.

When she could cry no more she lay very still. The mighty and comforting and sonorous words were repeated in her mind in letters as bright as the sun. They grew larger, illuminating all the dark places, outshining them, revealing all things. Caroline fell asleep, smiling. Her breath went in and out, slowly, weakly. And then, finally, there was not even the sound of breathing in the room, but only the voice of sea and wind.

Caroline was sitting on the boulder in the deep blue twilight of dawn, feeling and seeing the peace of the ocean. Sea grass whispered and rustled. The sea gulls cried. The wet shingle glimmered. She could smell the sea

pines and the grass, and the water sang like a great organ. Something fluttered against her cheek, and she caught it. It was a slender scarlet ribbon,
satin and vibrant, hanging from her hair.

Then Tom was coming toward her along the gleaming shingle, with the
wind lifting his crisp black hair and moving his shirt and blowing the smoke
from the pipe in his mouth. Caroline could see his strong face, smiling. He
lifted his hands to her, beckoning, and she jumped from the boulder and
ran to him, and she was in his arms, crying and holding him and kissing
his mouth.

"I dreamed you were dead!" she cried. "Oh, Tom, I dreamed you were
dead!"

"Of course I wasn't, darling Carrie," he said, and she listened to his voice.

"I had a most terrible dream!" she sobbed. "An awful dream. About us,
about the whole world!"

"Yes," said Tom. "I know. It was very bad, wasn't it? But it's over for
you now, Carrie. There's nothing for you to be afraid of any more."

He took her hand and they walked together along the beach, just as the
sun came up.